YOU AND ME AND THE SPACE IN BETWEEN

BOOKS BY PHYLLIS REYNOLDS NAYLOR

Shiloh Books
Shiloh
Shiloh Season
Saving Shiloh

The Alice Books
Starting with Alice
Alice in Blunderland
Lovingly Alice
The Agony of Alice
Alice in Rapture, Sort Of
Reluctantly Alice
All But Alice
Alice in April
Alice In-Between
Alice the Brave
Alice in Lace
Outrageously Alice
Achingly Alice
Alice on the Outside
The Grooming of Alice
Alice Alone
Simply Alice
Patiently Alice
Including Alice
Alice on Her Way
Alice in the Know
Dangerously Alice
Almost Alice
Intensely Alice
Alice in Charge
Incredibly Alice
Alice on Board
Always Alice

Alice Collections
I Like Him, He Likes Her
It's Not Like I Planned It This Way
Please Don't Be True
You and Me and the Space In Between

The Bernie Magruder Books
Bernie Magruder and the Case of the Big Stink
Bernie Magruder and the Disappearing Bodies
Bernie Magruder and the Haunted Hotel
Bernie Magruder and the Drive-thru Funeral Parlor
Bernie Magruder and the Bus Station Blowup
Bernie Magruder and the Pirate's Treasure
Bernie Magruder and the Parachute Peril
Bernie Magruder and the Bats in the Belfry

The Cat Pack Books
The Grand Escape
The Healing of Texas Jake
Carlotta's Kittens
Polo's Mother

The York Trilogy
Shadows on the Wall
Faces in the Water
Footprints at the Window

The Witch Books
Witch's Sister
Witch Water
The Witch Herself
The Witch's Eye
Witch Weed
The Witch Returns

Picture Books
King of the Playground
The Boy with the Helium Head
Old Sadie and the Christmas Bear
Keeping a Christmas Secret
Ducks Disappearing
I Can't Take You Anywhere
Sweet Strawberries
Please DO Feed the Bears

Books for Young Readers
Josie's Troubles
How Lazy Can You Get?
All Because I'm Older
Maudie in the Middle
One of the Third-Grade Thonkers
Roxie and the Hooligans

Books for Middle Readers
Walking Through the Dark
How I Came to Be a Writer
Eddie, Incorporated
The Solomon System
Night Cry
The Keeper
Beetles, Lightly Toasted
The Fear Place
Being Danny's Dog
Danny's Desert Rats
Walker's Crossing

Books for Older Readers
A String of Chances
The Dark of the Tunnel
The Year of the Gopher
Send No Blessings
Ice
Sang Spell
Jade Green
Blizzard's Wake
Cricket Man

YOU AND ME AND THE SPACE IN BETWEEN

Alice in Charge

Incredibly Alice

Alice on Board

PHYLLIS REYNOLDS NAYLOR

Atheneum Books for Young Readers
NEW YORK LONDON TORONTO SYDNEY NEW DELHI

ATHENEUM BOOKS FOR YOUNG READERS
An imprint of Simon & Schuster Children's Publishing Division
1230 Avenue of the Americas, New York, New York 10020

For information about special discounts for bulk purchases, please contact Simon & Schuster Special Sales at 1-866-506-1949 or business@simonandschuster.com.
The Simon & Schuster Speakers Bureau can bring authors to your live event. For more information or to book an event, contact the Simon & Schuster Speakers Bureau at 1-866-248-3049 or visit our website at www.simonspeakers.com.
Also available in an Atheneum Books for Young Readers hardcover edition
The text for this book is set in Berkeley Oldstyle Book.
Manufactured in the United States of America
2 4 6 8 10 9 7 5 3 1

The Library of Congress has cataloged the hardcover edition as follows:

Naylor, Phyllis Reynolds.
Alice in charge / Phyllis Reynolds Naylor. —1st ed.
p. cm.
Summary: Along with the usual concerns of senior year in high school, Alice faces some very difficult situations, including vandalism by a group of neo-Nazis and a friend's confession that a teacher has been taking advantage of her.
ISBN 978-1-4169-7552-6 (hc)
[1. High schools—Fiction. 2. Schools—Fiction. 3. Neo-nazism—Fiction. 4. Race relations—Fiction. 5. College choice—Fiction. 6. Family life—Maryland—Fiction. 7. Maryland—Fiction.] I. Title.
PZ7.N24Akdm 2010
[Fic]—dc22 2010000798

Naylor, Phyllis Reynolds.
Incredibly Alice / Phyllis Reynolds Naylor. — 1st ed.
p. cm. — (Alice)
Summary: Maryland teenager Alice McKinley spends her last semester of high school performing in the school play, working on the student paper, worrying about being away from her boyfriend, who will be studying in Spain, and anticipating her future in college.
ISBN 978-1-4169-7553-3 (hc)
[1. High schools—Fiction. 2. Schools—Fiction. 3. Theater—Fiction. 4. Dating (Social customs)—Fiction. 5. Family life—Maryland—Fiction. 6. Maryland—Fiction.] I. Title.
PZ7.N24Io 2011
[Fic]—dc22 2010036982

Naylor, Phyllis Reynolds.
Alice on board / Phyllis Reynolds Naylor. — 1st ed.
p. cm.
Summary: Seeking one last adventure before going off to college, Alice and her friends find summer employment on a Chesapeake Bay cruise ship.
ISBN 978-1-4424-4588-8 (hc)
[1. Friendship—Fiction. 2. Cruise ships—Fiction. 3. Summer employment—Fiction. 4. Chesapeake Bay (Md. and Va.)—Fiction.] I. Title.
PZ7.N24Alb 2012
[Fic]—dc23 2012010641

ISBN 978-1-4424-8664-5 (pbk)
These titles were previously published individually.

Alice in Charge

To Victoria

Contents

1
STARTING OVER

It was impossible to start school without remembering him.

Some kids, of course, had been on vacation when it happened and hadn't seen the news in the paper. Some hadn't even known Mark Stedmeister.

But we'd known him. We'd laughed with him, danced with him, argued with him, swum with him, and then . . . said our good-byes to him when he was buried.

There was the usual safety assembly the first day of school. But the principal opened it with announcements of the two deaths over the summer: a girl who drowned at a family picnic, and Mark, killed in a traffic accident. Mr. Beck asked for two minutes of silence to remember them, and then a guy from band played "Amazing Grace" on the trumpet.

Gwen and Pam and Liz and I held hands during the playing, marveling that we had any tears left after the last awful weeks and the day Liz had phoned me, crying, "He was just sitting there, Alice! He wasn't doing *anything*! And a truck ran into him from behind."

It helps to have friends. When you can spread the sadness around, there's a little less, somehow, for each person to bear. As we left the auditorium later, teachers handed out plastic bracelets we could wear for the day—blue for Mark, yellow for the freshman who had drowned—and as we went from class to class, we'd look for the blue bracelets and lock eyes for a moment.

"So how did it go today?" Sylvia asked when she got home that afternoon. And without waiting for an answer, she gave me a long hug.

"Different," I said, when we disentangled. "It will always seem different without Mark around."

"I know," she said. "But life does have a way of filling that empty space, whether you want it to or not."

She was right about that. Lester's twenty-fifth birthday, for one. I'd bought him a tie from the Melody Inn. The pattern was little brown figures against a bright yellow background, and if you studied them closely, you saw they were tiny eighth notes forming a grid. I could tell by Lester's expression that he liked it.

"Good choice, Al!" he said, obviously surprised at my excellent taste. "So how's it going? First day of your last year of high school, huh?"

"No, Les, you're supposed to say, 'This is the first day of the rest of your life,'" I told him.

"Oh. Well then, this is the first minute of the first hour of the first day of the rest of your life. Even more exciting."

We did the usual birthday thing: Lester's favorite meal—steak and potatoes—the cake, the candles, the ice cream. After Dad asked him how his master's thesis was coming and they had a long discussion, Les asked if I had any ideas for feature articles I'd be doing for *The Edge*.

"Maybe 'The Secret Lives of Brothers'?" I suggested.

"Boring. Eat, sleep, study. Definitely boring," he said.

From her end of the table, Sylvia paused a moment as she gathered up the dessert plates. "Weren't you working on a special tribute to Mark?" she asked. Now that I was features editor of our school paper, everyone had suggestions.

"I am, but it just hasn't jelled yet," I said. "I want it to be special. Right now I've got other stuff to do, and I haven't even started my college applications."

"First priority," Dad said.

"Yeah, right," I told him. "Do you realize that every teacher seems to think *his* subject comes first? It's the truth! 'Could anything be more important than learning to express yourselves?' our English teacher says. 'Hold in those stomach muscles, girls,' says the gym teacher. 'If you take only one thing with you when you leave high school, it's the importance of posture.' And Miss

Ames says she doesn't care what else is on our plate, the articles for *The Edge* positively have to be in on time. Yada yada yada."

"Wait till college, kiddo. Wait till grad school," said Lester.

"I don't want to hear it!" I wailed. "Each day I think, 'If I can just make it through this one . . .' Whoever said you could slide through your senior year was insane."

Lester looked at Sylvia. "Aren't you glad you're not teaching high school?" he asked. "All this moaning and groaning?"

Sylvia laughed. "Give the girl a break, Les. Feature articles are the most interesting part of a newspaper. She's got a big job this year."

"Hmmm," said Lester. "Maybe she *should* do an article on brothers. 'My Bro, the Stud.' 'Life with a Philosophy Major: The Secret Genius of Les McKinley.'"

"You wish," I said.

In addition to thinking about articles for *The Edge* and all my other assignments, I was thinking about Patrick. About the phone conversation we'd had the night before. Patrick's at the University of Chicago now, and with both of us still raw after Mark's funeral, we've been checking in with each other more often. He wants to know how I'm doing, how our friends are handling things, and I ask how he's coping, away from everyone back home.

"Mostly by keeping busy," Patrick had said. "And thinking about you."

"I miss you, Patrick," I'd told him.

"I miss *you*. Lots," he'd answered. "But remember, this is

your senior year. Don't give up anything just because I'm not there."

"What does that mean?" I'd asked.

I'd known what he was saying, though. We'd had that conversation before. Going out with other people, he meant, and I knew he was right—Patrick is so reasonable, so practical, so . . . *Patrick.* I didn't want *him* to be lonely either. But I didn't feel very reasonable inside, and it was hard imagining Patrick with someone else.

"We both know how we feel about each other," he'd said.

Did we? I don't think either of us had said the words *I love you.* We'd never said we were dating exclusively. With nearly seven hundred miles between us now, some choices, we knew, had already been made. What we did know was that we were special to each other.

I thought of my visit to his campus over the summer. I thought of the bench by Botany Pond. Patrick's kisses, his arms, his hands. . . . It was hard imagining myself with someone else too, but—as he'd said—it was my senior year.

"I know," I'd told him, and we'd said our long good nights.

In my group of best girlfriends—Pamela, Liz, and Gwen—I was the closest to having a steady boyfriend. Dark-haired Liz had been going out with Keeno a lot, but nothing definite. Gwen was seeing a guy we'd met over the summer when we'd volunteered for a week at a soup kitchen, and Pamela wasn't going out with anyone at present. "Breathing fresh air" was the way she put it.

There was a lot to think about. With our parents worrying

over banks and mortgages and retirement funds, college seemed like a bigger hurdle than it had before. And some colleges were more concerned with grades than with SAT scores, so seniors couldn't just slide through their last year, especially the first semester.

"Where are you going to apply?" I asked Liz. "Gwen's already made up her mind. She's going to sail right through the University of Maryland and enter their medical school. I think it's some sort of scholarship worked out with the National Institutes of Health."

"She *should* get a scholarship—all these summers she's been interning at the NIH," said Liz. "I don't know—I think I want a really small liberal arts college, like Bennington up in Vermont."

We were sitting around Elizabeth's porch watching her little brother blow soap bubbles at us. Nathan was perched on the railing, giggling each time we reached out to grab one.

"Sure you want a small college?" asked Pamela, absently examining her toes, feet propped on the wicker coffee table. Her nails were perfectly trimmed, polished in shell white. "It *sounds* nice and cozy, but everyone knows your business, and you've got all these little cliques to deal with."

"Where are you going to apply?" Liz asked her.

"It's gotta be New York, that much I know. One of their theater arts schools, maybe. Somebody told me about City College, and someone else recommended the American Academy of Dramatic Arts. I doubt I could get into Cornell, but they've got a good drama department. Where are you going to apply, Alice?"

I shrugged. "Mrs. Bailey recommends Maryland because

they've got a good graduate program in counseling, and that's where she got her degree. But a couple of guys from church really like the University of North Carolina at Chapel Hill. . . ."

"That's a good school," said Liz.

". . . And I've heard good things about William and Mary."

"Virginia?" asked Liz.

"Yes. Williamsburg. I was thinking I could visit both on the same trip."

"You could always go to Bennington with me," said Liz.

"Clear up in Vermont? Where it *really* snows?"

"It's not Colorado."

Just then a soap bubble came drifting past my face, and I snapped at it like a dog. Nathan screeched with laughter.

What I didn't tell my friends was that lately I'd been getting a sort of panicky, homesick, lonely feeling whenever I thought about leaving for college—coming "home" at night to a dorm room. To a roommate I may not even like. A roommate the complete opposite of me, perhaps. I don't know when I first started feeling this way—Mark's funeral? Dad's worries about investments and the store? But at college there would be no stepmom to talk with across the table, no Dad to give me a bear hug, no brother to stop by with an account of his latest adventure.

It was crazy! Hadn't I always looked forward to being on my own? Didn't I want that no-curfew life? I'd been away before—the school trip to New York, for example. I'd been a counselor at summer camp. And yet . . . All my friends had been there, and my friends were like family. At college I'd be with strangers.

I'd be a stranger to them. And no matter how I tried to reason myself out of it, the homesickness was there in my chest, and it thumped painfully whenever college came to mind, which was often. I didn't want to chicken out and choose Bennington just to be with Liz or Maryland just to room with Gwen. Still . . .

Nathan tumbled off the railing at that point and skinned his knee. The soap solution spilled all over the porch, he was howling, and we got up to help. That put an end to the conversation for the time being, and time was what I needed to work things through.

The school newspaper, though, kept me busy. Our staff had to stay on top of everything. We were the first to know how we'd be celebrating Spirit Week, because we had to publish it. We had to know when dances would be held, when games were scheduled, which faculty member had retired and which teachers were new. We were supposed to announce new clubs, student trips, projects, protests. . . . We were the school's barometer, and in our staff meetings we tried to get a sense of things before they happened.

We were also trying something different this semester. Because of our newspaper's growing reputation and the number of students who'd signed up to work on *The Edge*, we'd been given a larger room on the main floor, instead of the small one we'd been using for years. Here we had two long tables for layout instead of one. Four computers instead of two. And on the suggestion of Phil Adler—our news editor/editor in chief—we were going to try publishing an eight-page newspaper every week instead of a sixteen-page biweekly edition.

We wanted to be even more timely. And because the printer's schedule sometimes held up our paper for a day, we were going to aim for Thursday publication. Then, if there was a snafu, students would still get their copies by Friday and know what was going on over the weekend.

"I've got reservations about this, but it's worth a try," Miss Ames, our faculty sponsor, told us. "I know you've doubled your number of reporters, and you've got an A team and a B team so that not everyone works on each issue. But you four editors are going to have to work *every* week. That means most Mondays, Tuesdays, and Wednesdays after school. Can you can swing it?"

We said we could. Phil and I and Tim Moss, the new sports editor (and Pamela's old boyfriend), and Sam Mayer, the photography editor (and one of my old boyfriends), all wagged our woolly heads and said, yes, of course, no problem, we're on it. All completely insane, of course.

It will keep me from thinking so much about missing Patrick, I thought. But each day that passed brought me that much closer to D-day—decision time—and what I was going to do about college.

It was through *The Edge* that I found out about Student Jury. Modeled after some counties where student juries meet in city hall, ours would be a lot simpler, according to Mr. Beck. He decided that if more decisions and penalties were handed down by students themselves—overseen, of course, by a faculty member—maybe Mr. Gephardt, our vice principal, could have more time for his other responsibilities, and maybe the offenders would feel that the penalties were more fair. Students guilty of some minor infraction would be referred to the jury and would be sentenced by their peers.

The Edge agreed to run a front-page story on it, and I found out that I'd been recommended by the faculty to serve on the jury.

"No way!" I told Gwen. I had assignments to do. Articles to write. If anyone should serve on it, she should.

"So what have you got so far on your résumé?" was her answer.

"For what? College?"

"Well, not the Marines!" We were undressing for gym, and she pulled a pair of wrinkled gym shorts over her cotton underwear. "Extracurricular stuff, school activities, community service. You've got features editor of the paper, Drama Club, the Gay/Straight Alliance, some volunteer hours, camp counselor . . . What else?"

"I need more?"

"It can't hurt. You've got heavy competition." Gwen slid a gray T-shirt down over her brown arms and dropped her shoes in the locker. "Student Jury—dealing with kids with problems—might look pretty impressive, especially if you're going into counseling."

I gave a small whimper. "I told you the paper's coming out weekly, didn't I? I'm still working for Dad on Saturdays. I've got—"

"And William and Mary is going to care?"

Gwen's impossibly practical. "You and Patrick would make a good couple," I told her.

"Yeah, but I've got Austin," she said, and gave me a smug smile.

Later I whimpered some more to Liz and Pamela, but they were on Gwen's side.

"I've heard you need to put anything you can think of on your résumé," said Pamela. "I'm so glad you guys talked me into trying out for *Guys and Dolls* last spring. If I was sure I could get a part in the next production, I'd even jump the gun and include that."

They won. I told Mr. Gephardt I'd serve on Student Jury for at least one semester.

"Glad to have you on board," he said, as though we were sailing out to sea.

Maybe, like Patrick, I was trying to "stay busy" too. Maybe it made a good defense against going out with other guys. But I *did* keep busy, and whenever I felt my mind drifting to Mark, out of sadness, or to Patrick, out of longing, or to college, out of panic, I wondered if I could somehow use my own musings as a springboard for a feature article: "When Life Dumps a Load," "Long Distance Dating: Does It Work?" "Facing College: The Panic and the Pleasure"—something like that.

Amy Sheldon had been transferred from special ed in our sophomore year and had struggled to go mainstream ever since. I'm not sure what grade she was in. I think she was repeating her junior year.

It's hard to describe Amy, because we've never quite decided what's different about her. She walks with a slight tilt forward and is undersized for her age. Her facial features are nonsymmetrical, but it's mostly her directness that stands out—a childlike stare when she talks with you about the first thing on her mind . . . and the way she speaks in non sequiturs, as though she's never really a part of the conversation, and I suppose in some ways she never is. Somehow she has always managed to attach herself to me, and there have been times when I felt as though I had a puppy following along at my heels.

The same day I said yes to Student Jury, Amy caught up with me after school. I had taken a couple of things from my locker, ready to go to the newsroom, when Amy appeared at my elbow.

"I've got to wait till Mom comes for me at four because she had a dentist appointment and then I'm getting a new bra," she said.

"Hey! Big time!" I said. "What color are you going to get?"

She smiled in anticipation. "I wanted red or black, but Mom said 'I don't think so.' She said I could have white or blue or pink."

"Well, those are pretty too," I told her. I realized I'd closed my locker without taking out my jacket and opened it again.

"I went from a thirty-two A to a thirty-two B, and a year ago I didn't wear any bra at all. I hate panty hose. Do you ever wear panty hose?"

"Not if I can help it," I said.

"I wouldn't want to wear a rubber bath mat around me," Amy said.

I blinked. *"What?"*

"Grandma Roth—she's my mother's mother—used to wear a Playtex girdle when she was my age. She said it was like wrapping a rubber bath mat around her. She even had to wear it when it was hot. I hate summer, do you? Am I asking too many questions?"

I tried to dismiss her comment with a quick smile but saw how eagerly she waited for an answer. "Well, sometimes you do ask a lot."

"My dad says if you don't ask questions, how do you learn anything? You know why I like to ask questions?"

"Um . . . why?" It seemed she was going to follow me all the way down the hall.

"Because people talk to me then. Most of the time, anyway. Most people don't come up to me and start a conversation, so I have to start one, and Dad says the best way to start a conversation is to ask a question. And you know what?"

If I felt lonely just thinking about college, I imagined how it must feel to be Amy, to be lonely most of the time. "What?" I asked, slowing a little to give her my full concentration.

"If somebody just answers and walks away, or doesn't answer at all, you know what I say? 'Have a nice day!'"

I could barely look at her. "That's the perfect response, Amy," I said. "You just keep asking all the questions you want."

I was deep in thought, my eyes on the window, as Phil went over our next issue. We could give free copies to all the stores surrounding the school, he said, just to be part of the community and maybe help persuade them to buy ads; the art department had suggested we use sketches occasionally, drawn by our art students, to illustrate some of our articles; and we still needed one more roving reporter in order to have an equal number for each class. A few reporters from last year had graduated, and some had dropped out for another activity.

I suddenly came to life. "I'd like to suggest Amy Sheldon," I said, and the sound of it surprised even me.

There was total silence, except for one girl's shocked *"Amy?"* Then, embarrassed, she said, "Are you sure she can handle it?"

"I don't know," I said honestly. "But I'd like to give her a try. She's good at asking questions."

There was a low murmur of laughter. "Boy, *is* she! Remember when she went around asking other girls if they'd started their periods?" someone said.

"Now, *there's* a good opener," said Tim. More laughter.

"Everybody likes to be asked questions about themselves, and if she bombs, we don't have to print it."

Silence. Then Phil said, "Can you offer her a temporary assignment—so she won't get her hopes up?"

"Sure, I could do that." I waited. The lack of enthusiasm was overwhelming.

I watched Phil. I'd met him last year when I joined the Gay/Straight Alliance in support of my friends Lori and Leslie. He'd been a tall, gangly roving reporter before, but now that we were seniors, he was head honcho and looked the part. It was weird, in a way, that all the people who had run the paper before us were in college, and now we were the ones making the decisions.

"Okay," Phil said at last. "We'll give it a try. But have a practice session with her first, huh?"

"Of course," I said, and realized I'd added still one more thing to my to-do list.

"In the same spirit," Miss Ames said, "I'd like to suggest an article now and then by Daniel Bul Dau." When a lot of us looked blank, she added, "He's here from Sudan—you may have seen him around school. He's eighteen, and his family is being sponsored by a local charity. I think he could write some short pieces—or longer ones, if he likes—on how he's adapting to American life, his take on American culture, what you have to overcome in being a refugee . . . whatever he wants to write about. He's quite fluent in English."

We were all okay with that. More than okay.

"Feature article, right?" Phil said, looking at me, meaning this was my contact to make.

"Give me his name and homeroom, and I'll take care of it," I offered, and wondered if there would be any time left in my schedule for sleep.

Daniel Bul Dau had skin as dark as a chestnut, wide-spaced eyes that were full of either wonder or amusement or both, and a tall, slim build with unusually long legs. On Tuesday he smiled all the while I was talking with him about the newspaper and the article we wanted him to write.

"What am I to say?" he asked.

"Anything you want. I think kids would be especially interested in what you like about the United States and what you don't. Your experiences, frustrations. Tell us about life in Sudan and what you miss. Whatever you'd like us to know. I'll give you my cell phone number if you have any questions."

"I will write it for you," he said, and his wide smile never changed.

Gwen and Pam and Liz and I were talking about teachers over lunch. Specifically male teachers. Who was hot, who was not, who was married, who was not. We were trying to figure out Dennis Granger, who was subbing for an English teacher on maternity leave.

"Married," Pamela guessed. "I wouldn't say he's hot, but he's sort of handsome."

"Not as good-looking as Stedman in physics," said Gwen.

"I caught him looking at my breasts last week," said Liz.

"Stedman?"

"No, Granger."

"Kincaid looks at butts," said Pamela.

"Kincaid? He's as nearsighted as a person can be!" I said.

"That's why he has to really study you from every angle," said Pamela just as Dennis Granger approached our table and looked at us quizzically as we tried to hide our smiles. I think he deduced we were talking about guys and jokingly ambled around our table as though trying to eavesdrop on the conversation. He leaned way over us, pretending to mooch a chip or a pickle from somebody's tray, his arm sliding across one of our shoulders. We broke into laughter the moment he was gone.

"The best teacher I ever had was Mr. Everett in eighth grade," Liz said when we recovered. "I wish there were more like him."

Pamela gave her a look. "Yeah, you were in love with him, remember?"

"Crushing, maybe," said Liz.

"One of the best teachers I ever had was Sylvia," I told them.

"And then your dad goes and marries her," said Liz.

"Well, she couldn't be my teacher forever. I liked Mr. Everett, too. But I totally loved Mrs. Plotkin. Remember sixth grade? I was so awful to her at first and did everything I could to be expelled from her class. She just really cared about her students."

"That's why I want to be a teacher," said Liz.

"You'll make a great one," I told her.

"And you'll make a great counselor," said Liz.

Pamela rolled her eyes. "While you two are saving the world, I'll be working for a top ad agency in New York, and you can come up on weekends."

"With or without boyfriends?" asked Liz.

"Depends on the boyfriends," said Pamela.

"I thought you were going to a theater arts school," said Gwen.

Pamela gave an anguished sigh. "I just don't know what to do. I used to think I'd like fashion designing, but I've pretty much given that up. So it's between theater and advertising. I'm thinking maybe I'll try a theater arts school for a year to see if they think I have talent. If I don't measure up, I'll leave and go for a business degree somewhere. Of course, then I'd be a year behind everyone else."

"Pamela, in college that doesn't matter," said Gwen. "Go for it."

Liz looked wistfully around the group. "You'll be off doing medical research, of course," she said to Gwen. "Remember how we used to think we'd all go to the same college, sleep in the same dorm, get married the same summer, maybe? Help raise each other's kids?"

"I'm not having kids," said Pamela.

Gwen chuckled. "Hold that thought," she said. "We'll check in with each other five years from now and see what's happening."

2

MARSHALING THE TROOPS

I caught up with Amy after seventh period when I recognized her somewhat lopsided walk at the end of the hall. I sped up. From outside, I could hear the buses arriving.

"Amy?"

She looked around, then stopped and turned. Her face lit up like a Pepsi sign. "Alice!"

"Your hair looks nice," I told her, and it did. "How are things going?"

"I curl my hair on Tuesdays and Thursdays. Oh, and on Sundays," she said.

"Are you taking a bus home?"

"Yeah."

"Well, I have a favor to ask, and I could drive you. We can talk about it in the car," I said.

She stared at me in delight, like a kid being offered a marshmallow cookie. "Sure! Anytime! You just name it and I'll do it! Except sometimes I'm slow on account of I'm slow, but that doesn't mean I can't do something. I have to stop by my locker."

"Okay. Why don't I meet you at the statue in about five minutes," I suggested.

"If I'm not there in five minutes, I'll be there in six minutes, maybe, on account of I'm slow," she said.

"I'll wait, don't worry."

"Because if you don't wait for me and I miss the bus, I can't get home. Then I have to call my dad, and he has to leave an important meeting or something to come get me and he says, 'Amy, I am not pleased.'"

"I'll be there, Amy. The statue near the entrance."

"Yeah. The man on the toilet."

I laughed. "That's *The Thinker*, Amy. By Rodin."

She laughed too. "I knew that, but he still looks like he's on the toilet."

Amy's a small girl with a nice figure. Tiny waist. She sat in the passenger seat with her knees together, shoulders straight, a bit like a soldier at attention.

"Is this your own car?" she asked as I turned the key in the ignition.

"No, it's Dad's. Sometimes I drive him to work, and Sylvia picks him up and brings him home."

"If you ever asked me to drive this car, I couldn't," Amy said.

I smiled. "I wasn't going to ask you that. I wanted to talk to you about—"

". . . because I'd get the brake and the gas pedals mixed up, Dad says."

"Don't worry. I can't let anyone else—"

". . . Or maybe the windshield wipers and the lights."

This is a huge mistake, I thought, but I took the plunge. "I have a question to ask you."

She grew quiet.

"You read *The Edge*, don't you?"

"Of course! I'm up to seventh level now, and Mrs. Bailey says I'm doing great."

"Good! So here's the thing. We're missing a roving reporter for the issue after next and wondered if you'd like to try out."

Amy turned sideways and stared at me. Then she faced forward again. "No," she said.

"Really?" I glanced over. "Why not?"

"Tryouts make people laugh," she answered. No non sequiturs there.

"What I meant was, we'll give you a question to ask, and then you ask it to maybe five or six people and write down their answers. We'll choose the best ones and help edit them. And if we use yours in the newspaper, we'll print your name, as reporter."

Amy shook her head. "I don't have a car. I can't drive anywhere, and when I'm twenty-one, I probably still won't have a car."

"You don't need one, Amy." I turned off East-West Highway and looked for her street. "You just ask kids at school. You can choose anyone you like, and you won't have to leave the building."

"And you'll help me?"

"Absolutely. I won't go around with you to ask the question, though. You'll have to do that on your own, but we'll need to practice first. We could do it before or after school."

Amy sat motionless for a few seconds when I stopped at her house. Then she opened the door. "Maybe," she said. "I'll talk to Dad."

She called me that night, excited to the point of giddy. I almost told her the deal was off, but I couldn't back out now.

"Dad will drive me in tomorrow, Alice, and I'll be there at seven o'clock and you just tell me where, because if I don't write it down, I'll probably forget. . . ."

She was waiting for me when I got to the newsroom the next morning at six fifty-five.

"I'm here, Alice!" she said, her notebook and pen at the ready.

"Great!"

We sat down across from each other at one of the long tables.

"We're going to do a feature article on sleep," I told her. "One of our senior reporters is going to write the main story about how students don't get all the sleep they need. We want you to ask five students how many hours of sleep they get at night. Write down exactly what they say and be sure to get their names—spell them correctly too—and what class they're in: freshman, sophomore, junior, or senior."

I could tell by Amy's expression that these were too many instructions, all coming at her at once.

"Let's practice," I said. "Pretend you're sitting across from me in the cafeteria. What are you going to say?"

Amy shook her head. "Nobody sits across from me. Not usually."

"Okay. Let's say you came up to me in the hall. What are you going to ask?"

"How much sleep do you get at night?"

"That's it, but first you need to explain why you're asking. Something like, 'Hi, I'm a reporter for our school paper, and I'd like to ask you a question.'"

"But I'm really not."

"Not . . . a reporter?"

She nodded.

"Well, for this one week, you are. Let's try it."

Amy took a deep breath and stared at me unblinking. "Hi, I'm a reporter, and I'm going to ask you a question."

"Very good, but you need to mention our paper and then *ask* if you might ask them a question."

"That's too many questions."

I felt both my confidence in her and my patience waning. "It's the polite thing to do, though, because maybe this isn't a good time for them to be stopped and questioned. Maybe they're in a hurry. Try it again and mention *The Edge*."

Amy's eyes drifted to the wall, and her voice sounded like the automated message you get on an answering machine: "Hi, I'm a reporter for *The Edge*, and . . . do you care if I ask you a question?"

"That's pretty good, Amy."

"Now what?"

"Ask the question."

"Oh. Do you sleep at night?"

"How *much* sleep do you get at night? And it would probably be better if you said, 'On average, how much sleep, or how many hours of sleep, do you get at night?' Can you remember all that?"

Amy gave a big sigh and bent over her notebook, laboriously writing down the whole sentence, then reading it aloud: "Hi. I'm a reporter for *The Edge*, and could I ask you a question?"

"Excellent!" I said.

"On the average, how much sleep do you get at night?"

"Well, I guess I average about five and a half hours. Maybe six," I told her.

Amy stared at me. "I go to bed at nine thirty. I get eight and a half hours."

"No, Amy, you're supposed to be writing down my answer. You don't need to tell people how much sleep *you* get. *You're* the one asking the question."

She bent over her notebook again. When she had finished, I said, "Wanna try it once more?"

Another deep breath, and she faced me again: "I'm a reporter for *The Edge*, and could I ask you a question?"

I nodded and smiled to let her know we were rehearsing: "I guess so," I said. "What's the question?"

She paused and glanced down at her notebook. "On average, how much sleep do you get at night?"

"I suppose about five and a half hours. Maybe six."

She bent over her notebook and wrote it down. "Okay, thanks," she said.

"Don't walk away yet, Amy," I said. "Ask my name and what class I'm in."

"I already know that," she said. "You're a senior."

"Reporters always have to double-check. Ask even if you know."

"What's your name and what class are you in?" Amy asked.

"Alice McKinley, senior," I said.

She beamed.

"Don't forget to thank them, Amy," I instructed.

"Thank you, Alice. I'm a reporter now!" she said delightedly.

I only wished I felt that confident.

There was a short assembly on Friday to talk up Spirit Week, the last week of September. Gwen, as a member of the Student Council, brought down the house by coming onstage in a wet suit and flippers. Her left foot kept stepping on her right flipper, almost tripping her, and we screamed with laughter.

When she took the microphone, Gwen told us she was getting in the mood for Beach Day, the first day of Spirit Week. The other days would be announced in *The Edge*.

Then she turned the program over to Mr. Gephardt, who told us what great sports teams we had this year and that they'd be introduced at the pep rally at the end of Spirit Week.

Then he spent the rest of the time talking about the Student Jury system we were now ready to inaugurate at our school, explaining in detail how certain kinds of misconduct would be handled as usual by him and Mr. Beck, but some students might find themselves facing a jury of their peers. The judgments made by the jury would be respected by the faculty, and the penalties it imposed would be enforced. It was time, he said, for students to participate not only in the victories and celebrations of our school, but in reinforcing the values and conduct in keeping with our reputation and traditions.

I'll admit that the main thing I brought away from that assembly was the memory of Gwen in those flippers, but her hair was remarkable too. Her friend Yolanda had given it an elaborate cornrow design in four large triangles, two braids on either side sweeping around her head and joined in back.

"Seriously," I asked her later, "how long did it take her to do your hair? It's amazing."

"Six and a half hours," Gwen confessed. "But I did my history assignment while I was sitting there."

I don't know how Gwen does it. The school year had only begun, and already I was questioning how much I could handle. Saturdays I worked for Dad at the Melody Inn. The only morning I could sleep in was Sunday, and sometimes I wanted to hang out with the high school discussion group at church.

"I wish I could clone myself," I said one evening after dinner. "I could take on Mondays, Wednesdays, and Fridays, and my clone could do Tuesdays, Thursdays, and Saturdays."

"I'm glad you're the one who brought this up, because Sylvia and I have been worried about you," said Dad. "Sometimes your light's still on at one in the morning. I hate to see you studying so late."

"Ha! I'd like to know what time *Gwen* turns out her light," I said. "I don't do half the stuff she does."

"You've got to apply to colleges, Al. The only one you've visited so far is the University of Chicago."

"I've got a list," I said. *A mental list, anyway*.

"You do?"

"You don't have to worry. Les is taking me around," I lied.

Now both Dad and Sylvia looked surprised. "When? Which colleges?" Dad asked.

You know how in the movies the phone rings at exactly the right moment to further the plot? I'm not kidding, the phone rang right then, and I almost fell out of my chair getting up. I reached for it on the wall. Les usually calls about this time when he calls at all, and yes, right on cue, it was Les. Am I lucky or am I lucky?

"Hey, Al!" he said. "Dad there?"

"Yeah. It sure is, Les!" I said brightly. "Let me get the list."

"Huh?" said Lester.

"Are you at the apartment?" I asked.

"Yes. What's going on? I just want to ask Dad a question."

"I'll call you right back," I said, and hung up.

"It was Les. We're making plans," I told Dad and Sylvia, and zipped upstairs for my cell phone.

I was still breathless when I punched in his number.

"What the heck?" he said when he answered.

"Les, you've got to help me!" I pleaded. "I need this huge favor. What are you doing the third weekend in October?"

"Al, I don't even know what I'm doing *this* weekend," he said.

"Well, that Friday is an in-service day for teachers, so I've got the whole weekend to visit colleges."

"Now, listen . . ."

"It's making me crazy, and I don't have enough time—enough brain cells—to do all I'm supposed to be doing. I have to get my applications out, and Dad thinks I should look at some colleges first, and—"

"*What* colleges? Why can't Dad or Sylvia take you?"

"Les, you *know* how they are! They'll ask me to talk to financial advisers and find out the number of books in the libraries and—"

"So?"

"How many colleges did *you* visit, Lester?"

"I'm not your role model."

"Les, just take me around to a couple, okay? I told them we had it all planned."

"Alice!"

"*Please!* I already know the University of Maryland, and I just want to see a few more."

"What colleges are you talking about? Southern California, I suppose?"

"Of course not. I was thinking about the University of North Carolina—"

"Chapel Hill? That's the whole weekend right there!"

"But we can do it, Les. I looked at a map. After that, William and Mary and George Mason."

"William and Mary is in Williamsburg, Al. It's not just across the Potomac River."

"Listen, Les. Do you remember how I traded that fur bikini last Christmas for the granny gown you gave a girlfriend by mistake? Do you remember when Liz and Pamela and I bailed you out of jail?"

I heard a deep sigh. "Can we do this in two days, Al, and be home by Sunday afternoon so I can watch the Redskins with my buddies?"

"I promise!" I said gratefully. "We can start out at four in the morning if you want."

"But *you've* got to do all the preliminary stuff—set up the appointments, arrange for tours, bring a list of questions. I'm just the driver, understand?"

"You're worse than Dad."

"I mean it, Al."

"Okay. I'll even help drive."

"No, thanks."

"Promise you'll put it on your calendar?"

He sighed again. "It's on. I'm writing it now in big black letters. Underlined. Exclamation point. Now tell Dad I've got a tax question."

"Thank you, Les," I said. "You're the best!"

And I rushed downstairs to tell Dad and Sylvia that—like I said—it was all arranged. Sometimes life *is* just like the movies.

3
STUDENT JURY

I was one of five jury members, all juniors and seniors, who'd been selected by the faculty. My friend, Lori Haynes, a member of the Gay/Straight Alliance, was on it; so was Darien Schweitzer, a guy from the debate team; Kirk Manning, a friend of Patrick's from band; and Murray Hardesty, the junior class treasurer.

We'd been through an orientation session with Mr. Gephardt. We weren't pretending to be lawyers, he'd told us. We weren't police officers or judges. Our job was to listen to a complaint brought in against a student, get his take on it, and decide on the solution or the penalty. We selected Darien as jury foreman for these sessions that would take place about once or twice a month on Wednesdays after school. One of our teachers, on a rotating basis, would be present each time as faculty adviser.

Our first "offender of the month," as Darien put it, was led into the faculty conference room by the school secretary, Betty Free, followed by one of the custodians. We five jurors were seated around the long polished table, notepads and pens in front of us, unsmiling.

But this didn't prompt the sophomore coming through the door to adjust his cocky walk or wipe the smirk from his face. I was thinking how hard it is to keep from making first impressions, because the smirk and the careless way he walked made me want to say, *Nail him. Case closed.*

Mr. Gephardt and two teachers observed our first session.

"Would you give the jury your name?" Darien asked him.

The kid cast him a somewhat disgusted glance and mumbled, "You already got my name."

"For the record," Mrs. Free said, seating herself at the end of the table with her laptop.

"Kenny Johnson," the defendant said.

"You've been called before the Student Jury for making a mess—several of them—in the cafeteria, despite warnings from Mr. Garcia to stop," Darien read.

"Hey, there were other guys. It wasn't just me," said Kenny.

"Please remain silent until the charge is read," Mr. Gephardt instructed from the side of the room.

Kenny shrugged and slowly faced forward again. Darien went on reading the charge: "On two occasions last week and one the week before, you were seen dumping food on the table, throwing food, smearing mustard on someone's T-shirt . . ."

Kenny grinned a little. We didn't respond.

"Mr. Garcia, do you want to add anything?" Mr. Gephardt asked the angry custodian.

"I tell him to stop, he laughs. I make him clean up the table once, and then I see he greased all the chairs," Mr. Garcia complained.

Kenny suppressed a chuckle.

"I got no time for this! I got whole cafeteria to clean by three o'clock." Mr. Garcia turned and stared hard at Kenny, who only lowered his head, grinning at the floor.

"Okay, Kenny. Your turn," said Darien.

"Aw, it's only in fun, man. I didn't hurt anyone. The other kids were laughing, and it was Joe's idea to butter the chairs. So I cleaned them up! What's the big deal?" Kenny said.

"Big deal for me!" Mr. Garcia said heatedly. "You got time, maybe, but I don't have time to watch you all day, see what you do next."

Mr. Gephardt broke in, not allowing Kenny more time than he deserved. "Any questions from the jury?"

"How old are you?" Lori asked Kenny.

"Fifteen," Kenny answered.

"You bring your lunch or buy it?" asked Kirk.

"Buy it, mostly."

"Your money or your parents'?" Kirk wanted to know.

Kenny had to think about that a few seconds. "My dad's, I guess."

We nodded to each other that we'd heard enough, and the secretary escorted Kenny back to the library across the hall while we discussed it. The custodian was excused. Mr. Gephardt and the teachers let us debate it among ourselves.

"What do you think?" asked Darien. He's a round-faced, somewhat pudgy guy, with a radio announcer's voice, who could run for any office on his smile alone. But he wasn't smiling now.

"Ten years, maximum security," Murray quipped. "It's obvious he thinks he's funny."

"Mr. Garcia has the whole cafeteria to do single-handed, with community groups using it some evenings," Lori said. "All he needs is a joker like Kenny."

"What about the other kids who he said were in on it too?" I asked.

"Mr. Garcia says it's always Kenny who starts it, from what he's observed," Mr. Gephardt said.

"And I've seen one instance of it myself," a teacher put in. "I was there the day he was 'buttering the chairs,' as he put it."

We deliberated for about five minutes, then Darien went across the hall to tell Mrs. Free we were ready. She led Kenny back in.

His shoulders were a little less relaxed, we noticed, as he stood at one end of our table, his smile a little less fixed.

Darien read the verdict: "The jury has decided that Kenny Johnson's problem seems to be that he's forgotten how old he is and thinks he's still five. So we've decided he needs the job of a man for a week to keep his focus on being fifteen. We recommend five days' detention in the cafeteria during the lunch hour. He'll be responsible for seeing that all garbage is removed from the trays, all trash bags are tied up and hauled out to the Dumpster. He'll wash down the tables, wipe off the chairs, mop the floor, or do any other job assigned to him by Mr. Garcia. If he doesn't do his work well or does it discourteously, he'll repeat his detention the following week." He looked at Kenny. "Any questions?"

This time the defendant wasn't smiling. "Yeah, when do I eat?"

"That's your problem," said Darien. "Excused."

After Kenny left, Mr. Gephardt nodded his approval. "I'll tell security to keep an eye on him, make sure he gets there every day," he said.

The only problem with bimonthly jury duty was that our newspaper deadline is also on Wednesdays. I got back to the newsroom in time to do a short write-up and get it on the computer in the space Phil had allowed. We decided we'd report each Student Jury case so students would be aware of how the panel worked, describing the incident and the penalty assigned, but we wouldn't name the defendant. Enough for Kenny to be embarrassed doing cleanup in front of his friends, and they'd guess soon enough.

It was a mistake to send Amy around asking questions. The feature story would focus on how much homework teachers assign and how much sleep, or how little, we get because of it. Amy came by the newsroom over lunch on Thursday, and I could tell she was down.

"Nobody makes any sense," she said, looking at her notebook. "And they won't even give me their names."

I hadn't expected this much trouble. Usually kids are eager to get their names in *The Edge*. "You asked how much sleep they got at night?"

She nodded and read off the five replies: "'Who wants to know?' 'You're a *reporter* now?' 'Yeah, right.' 'Don't bother me.' 'Later, maybe.'"

I felt anger rising inside me as I imagined her humiliation. But it was largely my fault. "You know what, Amy? You just need an official badge," I said, my mind racing. I opened the drawer where we keep plastic holders for name tags when we send reporters to a board of education hearing. I printed out a badge in Times New Roman bold typeface and slid it in the holder. But I realized when I pinned it on her that even this might not be enough. Did I really want her to fail twice?

"Listen, Amy," I said. "I just want you to ask five teachers the same question. We'll include them in the article so kids will realize they're not the only ones up late at night."

She did it. By the close of school on Friday, Amy had five quotes from teachers, and after I'd typed them into the computer, I showed her the printout of what the article would look like. The teachers, of course, had answered Amy's question politely, and Miss Ames was pleased with the way the whole thing was coming together. Following the feature article, "Who Stays Up Late and Why?" with a byline from a senior reporter, were the two questionnaires:

HOW MUCH SLEEP DO YOU GET A NIGHT?
(STUDENTS)
—Josh Logan, roving reporter, senior

Courtney Brookings: "Six, usually. Five, if there's an exam."

Sherry Hines: "You've got to be kidding. Four to five hours, if I'm lucky."

Todd Gambi: "Depends who I'm sleeping with."

Emma Herringer: "Last night I was up until two."

Lei Song: "Five hours. Weekends, I sleep all day."

HOW MUCH SLEEP DO YOU GET A NIGHT? (TEACHERS)
—Amy Sheldon, roving reporter, junior

Oscar Evans (history): "The eleven o'clock news is my cutoff time."

Luis Cardello (Spanish): "Four to five hours, don't ask me how."

Dennis Granger (sub): "I never go to bed till I've watched *The Tonight Show*."

Jennifer Smythe (biology): "From midnight on."

Roy Peters (phys ed): "Sleep? What's that?"

"Amy, you did a great job!" I told her. "How did you get such short answers?"

"I told them there wasn't a lot of space," Amy said, obviously thrilled at seeing her name on copy. "I remembered how it looked before."

Now that she'd been seen around school wearing a badge, saw that her name was in the paper, she'd be more accepted, I told myself.

"Should we tell her she can keep the job?" I asked Phil.

"Try her a few more times—see how it goes," he said.

Gwen, Pamela, Liz, and I sat in Starbucks Sunday afternoon discussing life, or "getting a life," as Pamela put it.

"I've never had so much homework!" she complained. "I thought senior year was supposed to be a breeze. If I go to a theater arts school, what does any of this matter? Grades, I mean."

"They show you can think—that you can complete an assignment, you're not a quitter," said Gwen.

"What if you got a part in a historical play and didn't know anything about England? Or about how it was during the Depression?" asked Liz.

"Ugh," said Pamela, skimming the whipped cream off her latte and eating it with a spoon. "That's not exactly what I had in mind."

"What *did* you have in mind?" I asked.

"I don't know. TV. Sitcoms. I haven't decided yet. I still think about design sometimes. Or advertising. I'm all over the map."

"So be a travel agent!" Liz joked. "You'll travel the world and see exotic places. *Meanwhile*, who's going to the Homecoming Dance? Why don't we all go together?"

"Aren't you inviting Keeno?" asked Gwen. "I'm bringing Austin."

"I did, and he said he could get his mom's SUV for the evening if he pays for the gas. Can pack in eight people."

"Make it seven," I said. "I'm not going with anyone."

"Make it six," said Pamela. "I'm not either."

Gwen looked us over. "What's wrong with you guys?"

"I just want it to be fun and easy," said Pamela. "If I meet someone at the dance, fine, but I'm not looking right now."

Gwen turned to me.

"Ditto," I said. "Patrick told me not to give up dances and stuff just because he's not here. Fine. I'm not giving up the Homecoming Dance. I'm just not inviting another guy, that's all."

"And we're wearing . . . ?" asked Gwen.

"The tightest jeans we've got," said Pamela.

4

AN UNEXPECTED INVITATION

Monday: Beach Day; Tuesday: Twin Day; Wednesday: Garage Band Day; Thursday: Tacky Day; Friday: Time-Warp Day.

Our school did it up big this year. Each class was assigned a hallway to decorate for Spirit Week with some particular theme: Between the four classes, we chose Arabian Nights, Disney World, Chicago Mobsters, and the Cosmos. It felt sort of schizoid to walk past Mickey Mouse at one corner and then find yourself on Mars.

I liked Tacky Day best—liked going to the Gay/Straight Alliance meeting after school in an old green polyester sweater with pill balls all over it and a red, white, and blue scarf around my neck. Waist down, I wore baggy brown sweatpants and some gold ballerina slippers with pink butterfly buckles.

The guy I sat next to just had his shirt on inside out.

"That's *tacky*?" I teased, but he looked a little embarrassed, and I was sorry because he was new to the group. A junior, I think.

"I'm Alice McKinley," I said. "I only look this bad part of the time."

He gave me a little smile. "Curtis Butler," he said. And then, glancing around the group, "How many members?"

"It varies," I said. "A dozen. Sometimes more."

"Just wanted to see what it's all about," he said.

"Tolerance and acceptance—that whatever you are, you're welcome here," I told him.

Lori and Leslie arrived in camouflage-type jackets, plaid pants, and purple socks rolled down around their ankles. Each person who came in seemed to look more tacky than the one before, and we especially cheered and clapped when Mr. Morrison, our faculty sponsor, showed up in striped pants that rode up as far as his rib cage and a sweater vest over a yellowed nylon shirt.

Some of the members rehearsed the crazy skit they'd be doing at the pep assembly the next day, and we laughed and applauded as three guys, dressed as girls in hockey uniforms, and three girls, wearing football uniforms, came face-to-face on a practice field and didn't know what to make of each other. After circling uncertainly, the football girls tackled the hockey boys, who swung at them with their sticks, and they all ended up in a heap on the floor, where everybody disentangled, hugged, and sang a syrupy rendition of "People" to hoots of laughter.

I'm not sure what kind of impression we made on Curtis, except that we have a good time at our meetings.

The fall sports pep rally was probably the best ever, and I was glad that Phil was going to do the write-up on it because I just wanted to enjoy it without taking notes. It's mostly run by students. The junior and senior class presidents acted as hosts, introducing the various sports and dance teams, and the clubs on campus that performed the skits. The senior girls did their traditional dance, and I did okay, even though I'd missed a few of the six a.m. rehearsals. But the skit by the GSA got a huge laugh and loud applause, and I felt even better about that.

For the first time the principal didn't come onstage to announce our annual blood drive. Instead, the Health Occupations Students of America Club performed a mock operation with an IV full of bright red "blood," to remind people of the current shortage, and told the audience how we could go about giving blood on a scheduled day.

The rally ended with bleacher mania, led by the cheerleaders—a competition to see which class cheered the loudest. Liz and I had put coins and rice in plastic bottles for noisemakers, and Pamela brought a whistle. Justin Collier brought a cowbell. Our ears were ringing when we left the gym, but every person was smiling.

The game that night was something to celebrate because it was the first time in three years that we won our first home game. The bleachers went nuts. None of my best friends had gone out for cheerleading—Pamela thought about it once—but we knew the cheers and started a few of our own when we got the chance.

The best part, though, was the old senior tradition of streakers at half time. All week long the school had buzzed with speculation about which guys were going to do it, and just after the marching band had strutted its stuff, two seniors dropped their clothes and went racing across the field as we shrieked and cheered them on.

But it was the next day that really got to me. Dad let me have the afternoon off at the Melody Inn so I could watch the homecoming parade. It was the music, I guess, that reminded me of how much I was missing Patrick. It was nothing we shared—I can't even sing. But each year when there was a band concert or a game, Patrick was there, playing the drums. When the school put on its spring musical, Patrick was there in the orchestra, doing percussion.

The way he held his back so straight. The way his feet moved, absolutely in step. The way he held the sticks. The way the chin strap on his hat creased his jaw. The little smile he'd give me as he marched past, letting me know he saw me, even though his eyes didn't move left or right.

Now, watching the band go by, there were parts in the marches where the drummer played solo for a couple of measures, and I wanted it to be Patrick playing those parts, not the short guy out there in the street, and I could feel tears welling up momentarily.

Justin and Jill—surprise! surprise!—had been elected homecoming king and queen, and they rode the float along with the full homecoming court. It was a gorgeous October day. Everyone in Maryland, it seemed, was outside in the red-orange of this autumn afternoon, taking photos as the band passed, including Sam, our *Edge* photographer. I knew I'd treasure the next issue of the newspaper because this would be my last homecoming parade in Silver Spring. My last Homecoming Dance. Senior year: the last of everything.

"Wow!" Sylvia said, rolling her eyes as I ate a little supper at the kitchen counter. "Can you sit down in those pants?"

I laughed and swallowed a last bite of cheese. "They're brand-new, but I should have them broken in by the end of the evening. You like?"

"They're terrific! Too bad that Patrick—" She stopped suddenly, but I picked up where she'd left off.

". . . isn't here to take me to the dance, right? I know. But a lot of kids are going solo. Having a carful helps."

Keeno phoned to say he was running late—his mom just got home with the SUV—so as soon as I heard him pull up in front, I grabbed my jacket and ran out.

Music was playing inside the car, and I slid in beside Gwen and Austin, the guy with the dreadlocks and the linebacker shoulders. Liz was up front with Keeno, and Pamela was in the very back. The inside of the car smelled great—Pantene shampoo and Abecrombie's Fierce. I was glad to see Gwen in heels, because I wasn't sure of the footwear.

The people who weren't at the dance were as obvious as the ones who were. Mark. Patrick . . . Patrick on an October night in Chicago. Roaming the campus alone? Sitting on a bench by Botany Pond, thinking of me?

I have to say we seniors looked great. Hot. *Finally* our faces were almost blemish-free. Maybe a spot or two on the forehead or a makeup-covered zit on the chin. But looking around at all the other girls in their slim pants and sparkly tees, we looked rather magnificent. We all had breasts; we all had waists. Had learned to wear eyeliner expertly, abandoning the old raccoon look.

And the guys! How had they grown so tall in just one summer? The guy who used to be called Mr. Zits now had beard shadow all over his face, like some movie star. We were top of the heap, king of the hill. This was our time, and we immediately began to dance.

The sophomore Student Council members had decorated the gym with streamers intertwined to form a canopy over the dance floor, and there were balloons everywhere. One of the football team's blockers served as DJ. I was glad to see Amy Sheldon happily tagging along with two other girls, and she waved to me as they circled the gym.

"Best turnout yet!" said Phil as he came over to dance with me. "Sam says he's got some great photos. We'll try to get them in the next issue."

"We're going to be working our butts off to get a paper out every week, Phil," I said, thinking of Sam and all he had to do.

"Well, we'll see how it goes," he said. "Ames is really pleased at the reviews we got last year. Some of the graduates even want their parents to send the paper to them at college."

I danced with Darien, too, and then I ran into Pamela and Gwen, who were teaching Daniel Bul Dau to dance.

It was a riot, the way he towered over them, but he seemed to be enjoying himself, taking his mistakes with good humor.

"To dance by myself, I do very fine. When I dance with you, we have four feet to get in the way of each other," he explained, laughing, when Pamela tried to teach him the basics of slow dancing.

He held her so far away from his body that I could have walked between them. But Daniel so wanted to fit in. By the end of the evening he'd perfected the box step and had managed to dance with three of us. His smile made him look as though he'd conquered the world.

"What kind of dances do you do in Sudan?" Austin asked him when we gathered at the refreshment table.

Daniel laughed again. "Not very much like this one. And not with girls."

"Really?" said Pamela. "Who do you dance with?"

"All of the men dance together, but they are not touching like this. They dance, and the women watch them."

"Aha!" said Gwen.

"But I never danced because I was too young. My brother is twenty-three, and he did not dance either. We were small when we had to leave our village."

"Well, you're doing great," Pamela told him. "We'll even give your brother a lesson if he wants one."

For me, it was a sort of bittersweet evening—the first year of school since we'd moved to Silver Spring that I wasn't in a class with either Patrick or Mark. Like life was going to go on same as before—it was interesting and happy—except that there was a big hole in it, and a lot of the time I felt I was just watching other people live their lives. Every so often I'd feel that rush of loneliness—sort of a panicky, sinking feeling—and wondered if Amy Sheldon felt this way a lot. It wasn't that I was here without a boyfriend necessarily; I had fun with my female friends. It was just that somebody important in my life was missing. This was my senior year! I wanted Patrick now, I wanted him here, and I felt envious of Jill and Justin.

"What in the world are you thinking about?" Liz asked when she found me standing in a doorway holding a cup of Sprite. "You look like the Girl Without a Country."

"A violin without a string," I said. "A pebble without a beach. A nest without an egg. A—"

"Omigod," said Liz. "A pity party if I ever heard one."

And then it was over, and I felt better.

I went to church with Dad and Sylvia the next morning. The senior high group meets over in Chalice House during the second service, and it's usually like a discussion group, focusing on some general problem in society or with ourselves. If anyone's home from college, he knows this is a place to catch up with friends and trade news and gossip, and sometimes we head for the Tastee Diner afterward for waffles.

I didn't see any of the kids who had left for college, but I did recognize one of the girls from "Our Whole Lives"—a series of classes Dad signed me up for in my sophomore year. I'd met Emily at the first awkward session of that group, and she was the one who had suggested we might just crawl out the window and escape.

"Hey, how are you?" Emily asked. "Haven't seen you for a long time."

"Just catching up on life," I said. She goes to a different school, and we compared teachers and classes.

Bert Soams, one of the instructors of "Our Whole Lives," was leading senior discussions now, and he'd written a single sentence on the board. Eventually the conversation drifted to that:

> *At the moment of your conception, four hundred million spermatozoa were racing for the egg, but only one of them fertilized it, and that one became you.*

It was pretty awesome when you thought about it, and it didn't take long to start a discussion. If any one of those other sperm had got there first, we'd all have been different people. Maybe the opposite sex. I mean, think of the odds. What a gamble! What a coincidence! What a miracle! All of us sitting in that room were miracles.

I told Dad and Sylvia afterward that I was going to the diner and that someone else would drive me home. And then six of us squeezed into a booth and ordered a communal platter of waffles, sausage, and eggs.

A tall guy in a Redskins cap held up a bite of scrambled egg and studied it. "The hen who laid the egg was a miracle," he said in mock reverence.

It didn't lessen the miraculous feeling that just being alive at all was so hugely special.

I was *so* not caught up with homework. Printouts of college campuses, along with notes and phone numbers, were in a heap on one side of my desk. I had to spend the rest of Sunday afternoon and most of the evening on a physics assignment I didn't understand and an essay for English on the twentieth-century novel. Sylvia said they were going to have a tray supper in the family room watching *60 Minutes*—did I want to eat with them? I opted for dinner in my room, knowing I couldn't afford the distraction. I promised myself that I could call Patrick at ten, but only if I finished both assignments.

It was about nine when my cell phone rang, and I reached for it eagerly.

There was nothing in my promise that said I couldn't talk with Patrick if he called first. But it wasn't a number I recognized.

"Hello?" I said.

"Good evening," said a voice.

"Hello?" I said again, questioning.

"I am calling to speak with Alice," came the voice, and then I recognized Daniel Bul Dau. "Am I speaking with Alice?"

"Daniel! Hi!" I said. "How *are* you? It was great to see you at the Homecoming Dance."

"It was a good evening," he said, each word enunciated with perfection. "I am telling my brother about the game and the dance, and he is doing same thing at the George Washington."

"Excuse me?" I said.

"The university," he explained. "Geri is a student there at the George Washington's University. That is how we get to America with my mother. We are all of us refugees, but he is also a scholarship there. We are very, very lucky."

"Well, we're lucky to have you at our school," I told him. "And I'm really looking forward to the article you're going to write for *The Edge*. You have a lot to tell us."

"I will tell you whatever you want to know," said Daniel. "And I have something else to tell."

"What's that?"

"I am calling to take you big Snow Ball."

"What?"

"I am hearing about another dance, a Snow Ball dance. I am inviting you to be my guest."

The invitation, or the statement, seemed to hang in the air in front of me, the letters dancing up and down. Was he serious? Daniel had only been in this country a few months. He had only been in our school since September. He had learned to dance only the night before. But what other answer could there be?

"Sure," I said.

Was he ready for this? Was I?

5

THE MEANING OF EIGHT

I didn't call Patrick, I called Gwen.

"What am I going to *do*?" I said in a panic.

"What do you mean? You're going to the dance with him. We taught him to dance, remember?"

"But . . . what about all the other stuff? The tickets, the flowers, where we eat before the dance? He probably doesn't have a clue. He doesn't have a car. He doesn't drive. Gwen, he's a refugee! He doesn't have anything!"

Gwen sure put me down in a hurry. "Then I guess you should have said, 'No, Daniel. You're a refugee. You don't have anything.'"

I could feel the flush in my cheeks. Gwen had never said something like that to me before.

"You're not being fair," I snapped. "Who's going to clue him in about what he should wear and what's expected of him?"

She was more patient now, but I still wasn't home free. "Well, what *should* we expect of a refugee? Why can't he wear whatever he likes and celebrate his originality? Does he *have* to come in a black-and-white penguin suit? Does he have to have big bucks in his pockets? Is there a rule that says *you* couldn't drive to the dance?"

I don't know what it was—shame, perhaps—but she was so politically correct that I just said, "Thanks, Gwen," and hung up. I'd never done that before either. I sat on the edge of my bed, cell phone in my lap, hugging myself.

Just fifteen minutes ago I had been eating a bowl of chili, writing an essay for English, feeling like I had a grip on my life, and now I was going down a sinkhole.

The phone rang again. *Not Patrick! Please, not Patrick!* I picked it up. It was Gwen.

"Relax," she said. "You can double with Austin and me. We'll think of something."

The school was still in high spirits on Monday. Balloons confiscated from the dance were tied to locker doors, and streamers flew from car antennas in the parking lot. Kids were already talking about the next game and the next.

I was heading to the staff room after school to go over the layout of the paper when Daniel caught up with me, his smile taking up the whole of his face.

"I am pleased you will go to the Snow Ball with me," he said.

"Thanks for inviting me," I said. "I think it will be loads of fun."

"It will be a . . . a number one for me. A first," he said. "I asked my brother about it, but he doesn't know anything about snowballs."

"We'll work out the details later," I told him. "It's not until the first week of December, so we don't have to do anything right now."

"So many customs," Daniel said, walking along beside me. Then he stopped and pulled something out of his notebook, handing it to me, his smile a bit more bashful.

"I find this in my locker this morning. It is . . . drawn by the hand? I am thinking it is maybe from you? It means a girl says thank you?"

I studied the index card in my hand. There were no words, just a circle. And inside the circle, two figure eights, side by side.

"It's not from me," I said, puzzled. "I really don't know what it means. Maybe someone on the newspaper staff would know. Want me to take it and ask around?"

"Okay," said Daniel. And then, "Perhaps another girl is wanting me to take her to the dance?"

I had to laugh at his cocky self-assuredness. "Hey, Daniel, if you change your mind, go for it," I teased.

"No, I did not mean that! But I don't understand all your customs."

"I don't either," I said. "But when I find out about this one, I'll let you know."

In the newsroom everyone was gathered around Sam's photos from homecoming weekend, spread out on one of our long tables. We each had our own opinion about which six photos we should use and whether to save some for the following issue.

"Wish we got one of the streakers," I said, grinning.

"So does the faculty," said Phil.

We decided on a shot of Pam and Gwen teaching Daniel to dance, for starters. And of course we had to use an image of the float carrying the homecoming king and queen. The one of the winning touchdown . . . a close-up of the crowd . . .

The roving reporters checked in with their quotes and left, and it was finally down to Phil, Tim, Sam, Miss Ames, and me to make the final decisions. When we'd about wrapped things up, I remembered the index card in my bag and pulled it out.

"Hey, Phil," I said. "Any idea what this is? Daniel Bul Dau found it in his locker this morning. He asked what it meant. I haven't a clue."

Phil stared at it a minute, then at me. "You've never seen one of these before?"

"No. What is it? Please don't say it's porn."

"You might call it that," Phil murmured, and showed it to Tim. "The two eights are shorthand for the eighth letter of the alphabet, 'H.' Using two in a row stands for 'Heil Hitler.'"

"I don't believe this!" I gasped.

"It's a Nazi symbol. Believe it," said Phil.

We sat around the conference table looking at the two eights. Nobody wanted to touch it, like maybe it should be dusted for fingerprints or something.

"Nice welcome to our school, isn't it?" said Sam. "Hey, I'm Jewish. Where's mine? Who's next?"

Phil looked at Miss Ames. "Should I do an editorial on it?"

Miss Ames is a thin woman with an oval face and small features, straight brown shoulder-length hair. Now she studied the card with her hands locked beneath her chin, fingers covering her mouth. Finally she said, "I think that, for now, we should just sit on it. What white supremacy groups want more than anything else is publicity. For us to come on full force, in full battle regalia, just because somebody drops this pitiful little card in a locker, would be giving them more attention than they deserve."

I wasn't sure about keeping it under our hat, though. I thought of something we'd discussed at church—that the greatest wrong is not that evil exists in the world, but that good people sit by and do nothing. Something like that. Weren't newspapers supposed to find out what was going on beneath the surface and inform the public?

"Maybe we do more harm just by opting out," I said. "Maybe there's more than one person behind this."

"There's that possibility too. I'll show the card to Mr. Beck. But my guess is that this is a single act by a coward and that no acknowledgment at all would be the best response."

"And if there *is* more than one person involved, maybe they'll do something else to get attention, and then it might be easier to flush them out," said Phil.

We mulled that over awhile.

"Except that things might already be going on that we don't know anything about," said Sam, absently turning his Coke can around and around on the table. "Isn't there a new club here—SSC—Student Safety Council, I think? What's that about? Maybe they've got wind of stuff like this on campus."

"We sent one of our freshman reporters to check out the new clubs, and he visited that one last week. Said it was a small group—five or six. Talked with somebody named Butler, who said they focus on the dangers of drugs and alcohol, dealing with thugs, things like that," Phil said. "But that could mean that one of them has been attacked or something."

"Curtis Butler. I met him," I told the others. "He attended our last GSA meeting, Phil. Remember? Do you think there are gay students being harassed who never report it?"

"*The Edge* serves as the eyes and ears of the school," Miss Ames said. "Let us know of anything you find out. In the meantime, I'll give this card to Mr. Beck."

I wondered if we were right in not responding to this. As far as we knew, Daniel—because of his . . . what? race? nationality?—was the only one to get this card. But what about the other African-American students in our school? What about Curtis, if he was gay, or Lori and Leslie? What about socially challenged students like Amy Sheldon?

Sometimes the most difficult assignment of all is waiting to see what happens.

I was hoping that Daniel wouldn't ask me again about the double eights, but he asked the very next day. He absurdly stuck to his hope that it was a note of some kind from a girl. No bashfulness there.

"I'm afraid it wasn't," I said, looking up at him. "I asked around at our staff meeting, and it seems it's a Nazi symbol—just some jerk showing off his prejudice." I'd already told Miss Ames that I would tell Daniel the truth. I saw the puzzlement on his face. "We don't know who it's from, Daniel—some cowardly person—but please don't take this too seriously. I think you know that most of the students are glad to have you here."

You never forget the way a smile disappears.

"They told us before we left Sudan . . . that there are those like that in America," he said dispiritedly.

"Yeah. Unfortunately. And not just in America, as you know. Miss Ames turned the card over to our principal. *We're* the ones in charge, though, not the person who drew that thing."

"That is good to remember," Daniel said. And his smile came back, not quite what it was before.

I helped Sylvia with dinner that night and told her about the double eights. She teaches in middle schools, and was pondering the way they might have handled it if the card had been deposited there.

"We probably wouldn't do anything either if it were a single incident—a note, a scribble. You want to pick your battles and not bring too much attention to something stupid," she said. "But it's a shame it happened to Daniel."

"This is going to be the busiest semester of my life," I told her, letting out my breath. "You solve one problem and something else pops up. I wish we had a mid-semester vacation."

"Patrick coming home for Thanksgiving?"

"I'm not sure. His family's been spending a lot of time at his uncle's in Wisconsin, but I think he said he was coming home." I gave Sylvia a wistful smile. "Hope so, anyway."

Marilyn Rawley Roberts was wearing real maternity clothes now. For the first four months of her pregnancy, she'd gotten by with denim jumpers and big shirts. Now when I went to the Melody Inn on Saturdays, I found her in the "official uniform," as she calls it—stretch pants and smock tops. Customers smiled and asked the due date (the end of February) and whether it was a boy or girl (Marilyn and Jack wanted to be surprised).

"Wow, Marilyn!" I said that Saturday when we were rearranging the CDs on a new rack. "I feel like I've known you since . . ."

"Forever," she said. "Since I was Lester's supposedly number one girlfriend." She laughed when she said it, without a trace of resentment or regret, which meant we could discuss it.

"Unfortunately, that's what several girls thought, I guess," I said, accepting the handful of CDs she gave me and putting them in alphabetical order on the rack. "You always seemed like . . . like Nature Girl or something to me."

"*Nature* Girl?" Her eyes widened for a second, then crinkled in laughter.

"In fact," I went on, "your wedding was exactly as I'd imagined it would be—in a meadow with wildflowers. Except . . . you'd be barefoot and the groom would be Lester."

"Yeah, well, sometimes life knows what's best for us, and I can't imagine being married to anyone else but Jack. I love him to pieces. How *is* Les, by the way? Did he ever finish his thesis?"

"Almost done. He graduates in December."

"Wonderful! Then what?"

"I don't know. He has a full-time job in the personnel department at the U. Maybe he'll stay there awhile, which means I could see him every day if I'm accepted."

"You're applying to Maryland?"

"And a few others. They have a good program in counseling." When she didn't respond, I asked, "Where did you think I would go?"

"I hadn't thought much about it, Alice. It's so entirely your business."

"Well, if *you* were graduating from high school this spring, and if Jack weren't in the picture, where would *you* have liked to go?" I asked.

"If money wasn't a consideration, you mean? Oh . . . Berkeley . . . USC; University of Seattle, maybe. Love that campus. Or some little college up in Maine."

I felt a prick of anxiety and a weight that settled in. "You wouldn't want to be closer to home? Friends and family?"

"I'd expect to make new friends. But when I settled down, like I am now, I'd want to be near my folks if I could, especially if I was planning a family. But college is our chance to explore a little."

"I just think . . . I mean, with the economy the way it is . . . and we're not exactly rich . . ."

"The University of Maryland is an excellent school, Alice,

and will save your dad a heap of money," Marilyn said quickly. "You always were a considerate person. You'll do fine."

Our new clerk came back from lunch just then. At first Dad had considered hiring two new people when David Reilly left, as Marilyn would be going on maternity leave in February. But with sales down and some of the stores around us closing, Dad settled for one more full-time employee. Kay Yen was a college student, as David had been. She'd earned her bachelor's degree and wanted to take a year or two off and work to save some money before she started graduate school.

She and Marilyn got along famously from the start. They were both on the short side, and both had brown eyes. Marilyn had shoulder-length brown hair, however, while Kay's was short and black, turned under at the edges. Marilyn wore dangly gypsy-type earrings, while Kay wore tiny pearls in her earlobes. But when you heard them laughing together in the next room, you couldn't tell them apart.

"What did you major in?" I asked Kay, my mind still on college.

"Chemistry," she said as she cut open the next box and began stacking CDs on the counter. "I have a minor in music and was trained as a singer, but I'm really not good enough to do concert work, and I'm not sure I'd be happy teaching. So I guess I'll go into chemistry, my second love."

"You sound like the guy you replaced," I said. "He couldn't decide between marrying or entering the priesthood. He chose the priesthood."

"Well, I'm sort of letting my profession find me," said Kay.

"My parents want me to marry and give them a grandchild. It's hard to think about having a child when you feel so much like one yourself."

That sure resonated with me. Maybe it's normal to feel so unsettled. Maybe there are more Lesters and Davids and Kays than I'd thought, and it's the unusual person who knows from day one just what she wants to do and where to go to school. "Brothers and sisters?" I asked Kay.

"I'm an only child. The one-child policy in China, you know," she said.

I thought about the card Daniel had found in his locker. "Do you feel welcome in America?" I asked her.

"Of course!" Kay replied. "I've lived in this country since I was six. But then, we've always lived in college towns. You can get complacent in a college atmosphere and feel that everyone in America accepts you. And that's not always the case."

6

ROAD TO CHAPEL HILL

The Gay/Straight Alliance was celebrating National Coming Out Day on October 11, a day set aside to encourage gay, lesbian, bisexual, and transgender people to be themselves, to support them if they decide to "come out" to their friends and families. Just as *quarterback* defines only one part of who a student might be, Mr. Morrison likes to say, so does *gay* or *straight* represent only a part. "We are the sum of all our parts," we say at our meetings.

Some people call it International Awareness Day, so we had posters using both names. The GSA had been working on a huge paper rainbow, and some of us got to school early that Monday morning to attach it to the arch just inside the main entrance.

We had rainbow armbands available on a little table outside the auditorium for students to wear to show support for everyone's sexual orientation.

Daniel Bul Dau was clearly shocked when he saw two guys greet each other at the table with a kiss.

"In my country," he told us, "we would be put to death. There is no such homosexuality in Sudan."

"Really?" asked Phil. "Then who do they put to death?"

Daniel seemed confused. "If there is homosexuality, I have never heard one speak of it. And not with rainbows. But I will ask my brother about it."

A lot of kids paused to look the table over and pick up a brochure. Curtis Butler was one of them. Others stopped to ask questions, and a few accepted an armband.

Gwen and Pam, Liz and I sat out under a tree at lunchtime along with Lori and Leslie. Leslie was telling how she came out to her mom a couple of years before, when she and Lori started hanging out a lot.

"Mom was trying to get me interested in a guy down the street—his mom was in her book club—and I decided I just had to tell her or else she'd go on pressuring me all through high school," she said.

Lori listened sympathetically, though she must have heard this story a dozen times.

"Finally, when I'd run out of excuses," Leslie continued, "I said, 'Mom, I really don't want to go out with guys. I'm a lesbian.'"

"My mom would freak out," Pamela interrupted. "She really

would. To her, that would be worse than . . . worse than me getting pregnant. And she'd blame herself."

"Well, it was a relief, mostly," Leslie said. "I never worried she'd kick me out or anything. I guess I wasn't sure *how* she'd handle the news. She just stared at me for a minute; then she laughed and said, 'You are *not*! Don't be ridiculous.' It took me an hour or more to convince her. She just sat there shaking her head. Sometimes I think that she still doesn't believe it and that if I could ever just meet the right guy . . ."

"That's the way it was with my parents," said Lori. "It wasn't till I reached way back and told them how I'd felt when I was five and six that they began to understand. How I'd always hated dresses, loved my truck collection, cried when I got a Barbie doll instead of a G.I. Joe. They began to see that this wasn't just a temporary phase because some guy rejected me or something. Our parents can't seem to imagine *us* ever rejecting *guys*."

We smiled at the thought—Lori, tall and brunette; Leslie, a natural blonde, shorter, sturdy . . . both of them pretty.

Liz picked up her egg salad sandwich. "What I *can* imagine," she said, "is feeling entirely out of step with everyone else—feeling that what I wanted was natural to me but seemed unnatural to other people. And what *they* wanted for *me* seemed disgusting."

"And the more they try to 'fix it,' the more unnatural it feels," said Leslie.

"Daniel told me that homosexuals in his country would be killed for it," I said.

"Well, people in this country have been killed for it too," said Gwen.

That afternoon, as the buses were pulling up at the main entrance, I saw a small crowd gathering inside.

"What's going on?" I asked a girl who was walking away, shaking her head.

"Go look," she said.

I did. The large paper rainbow we had constructed was still hanging overhead, but there was a little pile of rainbow armbands on the floor beneath it, bent and crumpled, like trash. And on top of the little heap, a hand-lettered sign in Magic Marker: FAG DROPPINGS.

The administration had debated how they should handle this, Miss Ames told the newspaper staff. There were pros and cons about giving these incidents any publicity—treating them as anything more than scribbles on a restroom wall. One of the GSA guys had cleaned up the pile of armbands quickly before too many kids had even seen it. We'd heard no rumors, picked up no gossip, and Miss Ames said that the next step might be to send out our roving reporters on an investigative mission, armed with the right question. Perhaps that would give us some clues.

But choosing the right question itself caused a debate among the staff. We first proposed *What do you fear most about your safety here at school?* but decided that was too suggestive. The question *Is there anyone or any group here at school that makes you feel intimidated?* sounded as though we were pointing the finger at someone. We finally decided on *What, if anything, makes you fear for your safety here at school?*

The B-team reporters promised to go to work on it and would turn in some replies by the following Monday.

With the teachers' in-service training day coming up, and therefore our three-day weekend, I called Les that night and left a message on his cell phone.

"Remember, Les? This is the weekend you promised! UNC on Friday, William and Mary on Saturday, George Mason on Sunday. And you can be home in time to watch the Redskins play at four. I already checked their schedule. How early do you want to come on Friday? Call me."

Then I sat down at my computer, went to Yahoo for directions, and printed out a map of the whole trip—drive south to Chapel Hill, northeast to Williamsburg, then back up to Fairfax before heading home. The map planner gave me the routes, the travel times, and local attractions. I checked my notes. I was pretty sure I had a dorm room assignment for Friday night—I was supposed to call someone at Welch Hall; I was waiting for a callback about Saturday. I'd received a brochure from George Mason, a packet from Maryland, another from Chapel Hill. . . .

The phone rang Wednesday night. "*This* weekend?" Les bellowed.

"Yes!" I said. "Lester, I already *told* you! You *promised*!"

A huge sigh followed by silence.

"It's my only three-day weekend this fall! I've got to see

some colleges before I apply, and you have to admit you owe me one, because—"

"Okay, okay, let me think, will you? It's . . . what? Three hundred miles to Chapel Hill?"

"Two hundred ninety-three."

"Al, have you got *everything* planned?"

"Yes. I told you! I've got the maps and the mileage and—"

"Where am I staying?"

"What do you mean?"

"You're staying overnight on campus, right? Where am *I* staying? Have you checked out motels?"

Omigod! Lester! "Right. Um . . . I've got the numbers right here. I'll have it all down for you in black and white."

"When's your first appointment on Friday?"

"Two o'clock," I said.

"We need to allow five hours, minimum. Six, if we stop to eat."

"I'll call you about the details," I said. "Dad said he'll pay all expenses."

"Okay. I'll fill my tank."

"Thanks, Les!" I said cheerfully. "We'll have a ball!"

"Right," said Les.

A few minutes after I'd talked with Lester, Patrick called.

"How are things?" he asked.

"Crazy," I told him. "We're seeing three schools this weekend. Lester's driving me to UNC, William and Mary, and George Mason."

"All in one weekend?" he asked.

I sucked in my breath and let it out again as I plopped down on the edge of my bed. "Yes, Patrick. Three schools in three days. Is that so unusual?"

This time I could hear the amusement in his voice. "What are you going to do? Sample the food in the dining hall, check out the student union, and move on?"

"I'm going to get a feel for each place. I think I can at least rule some of them out after I've been there. This doesn't mean I can't visit one again if I really like it."

"How did you rope Les into this?" he wanted to know.

"Brownie points," I said. "He owes me big-time for a lot of things."

"Wow! You're keeping score. So what else is happening?"

"Well . . ." I smoothed out my bedspread with one hand. "I guess I'm going to the Snow Ball."

"Oh!" Now I really had his attention. "Who's the lucky guy?"

"Daniel Bul Dau."

"Who? Do I know him?"

"No. He's from Sudan."

"So . . . what's he like?"

"Tall, dark, and handsome," I teased. "Even taller than you are."

"Should I be jealous?"

"Wouldn't hurt," I said. "Actually, he's very nice. Polite."

"You invited him?"

"No. He invited me. And I didn't know what to say, Patrick. Gwen got on my case because I wondered if he was up to it, but he doesn't really know much about our culture. I think he's a little overconfident because we taught him a few steps at the Homecoming Dance."

"Well, someone will clue him in," said Patrick. "Lucky Daniel."

"What have *you* been doing?" I asked.

"Catching up on Bollywood movies," he said. "I've missed most of them, but we're having an Indian film festival, so I walk over to Ida Noyes when I can."

I took a chance. "By yourself?"

"And whoever else wants to go. You met John and Adam and Fran, I think."

"Yes . . ."

"They go sometimes. I even sat beside one of my professors last week. He was there with his girlfriend."

"You're getting up in the world, Patrick," I joked.

"Yeah, before you know it, I'll have a graduate assistantship, teaching nerds like me." We laughed, but he didn't exactly answer what I wanted to know.

We talked for another twenty minutes, and then I said, "You're coming home for Thanksgiving, aren't you?"

"Well, actually . . ."

I couldn't breathe.

"My folks want to have Thanksgiving at my uncle's house in Wisconsin."

"Oh, Patrick! I haven't seen you since—"

"I know. Mark's funeral. I'm disappointed too."

"They were just *in* Wisconsin! I mean—" I stopped. What right did I have to decide where Mr. and Mrs. Long should spend the holiday?

"But I'll definitely be home for Christmas," Patrick said.

"That's a long way off."

"Two months, is all."

"Ten weeks."

"You miss me?"

"More than you can imagine. I thought of you all during the homecoming parade. . . ."

By the time we'd finished talking it was nine thirty and I went back to the website I'd bookmarked to confirm that I was signed up for the Friday tour at two. Then I found the website for William and Mary and clicked on TOURS to sign up for Saturday. *Two p.m. filled*, it read. Next available tour: three weeks.

By Thursday it seemed as though every teacher had assigned a little more homework, just to fill up our three-day weekend. One teacher did say that those who were planning to visit colleges over the weekend would have three extra days to get their assignments in.

I hadn't even thought about what I'd be taking with me to visit schools. Hadn't checked to see if I had any clean pajamas. Hadn't made motel reservations yet for Les. For a girl who might be leaving home in less than a year, I was pitifully unprepared. Somehow I'd thought that signing up for a tour was no big deal. Colleges were always happy to show students around, right? How could William and Mary be filled? I called George Mason directly and asked about tours, but they didn't have a tour that Sunday.

The lonesome, homesick, panicky feeling returned as I

pulled a duffel bag out from under my bed and opened it, trying to organize my thoughts: jeans, top, T-shirts, sweater, sneakers, tampons, makeup kit. . . .

Next I looked up hotel chains in the Yellow Pages, called some toll-free numbers and asked if they had any locations near the UNC campus. The closest I could find was a motel called Sleepy Inn, and I made a reservation for Les for Friday night. Then I did the same thing for Williamsburg and got a Ramada.

Les called around seven."You find a place for me in Chapel Hill?"

"Yep, and my tour's at two," I said.

"I think we should leave at eight, then. Make it seven thirty if you want to stop and eat somewhere."

"I'll bring sandwiches," I said.

He must have sensed the tension in my voice. "And, Al," he said, "hang loose."

Dad and Sylvia were falsely impressed with my arrangements. Dad was absolutely gleeful, I think, that he didn't have to drive. "Any expenses within reason," he said, handing me his credit card.

"Hope all goes well!" said Sylvia.

My hair was filthy, so I set my alarm for six thirty, and hoped to be asleep by eleven. But I realized I still hadn't received a callback about my request for a place to sleep at William and Mary. I tried the number I'd called before, but no one answered. Then I called the number I had for Welch Hall, to confirm my room at Chapel Hill, and got voice mail.

I left a message that I was arriving Friday and would drop off my bag there.

By the time I did get to bed, I was wakeful and didn't drift off till after midnight. I dreamed I was in a room that kept getting smaller, and I couldn't tell if the walls were moving closer together or the ceiling was coming down or what. When the alarm went off, I sprang out of bed as though it were on fire, glad to be out of the dream, I guess.

Later, when I opened the fridge, I found a lunch Sylvia had already packed for us, but this just proved how dependent I'd become, always having someone there to look out for me, remind me, encourage me, pick up the tab. I thought about Patrick at the University of Chicago, getting right to work, fitting in, doing assignments, learning his way around. . . .

I was sitting on the steps when Les pulled up a couple minutes past eight, and I could tell he saw this as a mission of mercy, not a pleasure trip.

"Good morning!" I chirped as I got in, dropping my bag in back.

"Morning," he said. He reached for his Starbucks cup and took a long drink.

We were two blocks away when I realized I'd left my folder with all the necessary addresses and brochures in it, and we had to go back. While I was in the house, I remembered I'd also left the lunch Sylvia had prepared, so I got that, too.

"Better now than later," I said as I climbed back in the car, and at last we were headed for the beltway.

I took out my map and directions and began to read aloud: "Take ramp onto I-495 West toward Beltway/Northern Virginia. Go 6.7 miles. Continue on I-495 South for 17.5 miles."

"What's the exit we're looking for?" asked Les.

"Uh, 57A/Richmond," I told him.

He took out one CD and put in another, lifted the Starbucks cup again, then rested his arm on the open window.

It was a beautiful October morning, and it was sort of exciting going somewhere with Lester, our bags in the backseat. I rolled down my window too and pretended we were in a convertible. A beautiful girl on her way to college. I smiled at a couple of guys who passed us in a truck, and they waved.

Les gave me a look. "Watch it," he said, and grinned.

There's not a lot to see from a beltway except cars, and even less after the exit. But I-95 South was worst of all, and we had to go 118 miles on it.

We stopped for a bathroom break, but Les wanted to eat as he drove to make sure I made my two o'clock campus tour.

"You're not going with me, are you?" I asked.

"No. I'm going to drop you off and pick you up in the morning. You have the address of my hotel?"

"Yes. It's called Sleepy Inn. And I'll give you Dad's credit card too. Boy, this is the life, isn't it, Les?" My hair was blowing around my face, and the warm breeze rustled the map in my hands.

"Pretty sweet," he said.

I'd noticed Les had brought some books and papers along with him and would probably be working on his thesis while I was visiting schools. I thought about how many years he'd been in school and how he was finally almost finished. I tried to imagine Christmas and a college graduation both in the same month.

"Sometimes I wish I could just press a button and be through school and starting my real life," I told him.

"This *is* your real life, Al," he said. "Don't start living in the future. That's like gulping down a piece of fudge cake and then asking yourself, 'Where'd it go?' You're missing the moment."

"Ah! The philosopher is back," I said. "I know how to enjoy a moment, Les. I'm enjoying this, aren't I?"

"You'd better."

"Frankly," I told him, "I don't think about the future enough. Sometimes I can't even see what's coming right at me, and I get blindsided."

"Yeah? Anything in particular?"

"Our student from Sudan asked me to the Snow Ball, and it caught me off guard. I said yes."

"And?"

"I don't know what to expect."

"Well, neither does he. Obviously, though, he feels comfortable with you."

I sighed and rolled up my window halfway because my hair kept blowing in my mouth when I tried to talk.

Les glanced over at me. "How does Patrick feel about you going with someone else?"

"I *hope* he's a little bit jealous, but he says he's comfortable with it. *Too* comfortable, maybe."

"Well . . ." Les drove for a while without speaking. Then he said, "He's hundreds of miles away, Al. He's there, you're here, life goes on. But nobody's written the last chapter."

"Meaning?"

"Just that what happens today or next week or next year isn't necessarily the way things are always going to be. As soon as you settle into a routine, life throws you a curveball. Sometimes you hit it, sometimes you don't."

"It sure threw a curveball when Mark died."

"Yeah. It sure did." He was quiet for a moment. "Getting back to Patrick, though . . ."

"He wants me to live it up my senior year, even though he's not here to share it with me."

"Smart boy."

"Which means that he plans to live it up his first year of college even though I'm not there to share it with *him*."

"Ditto."

"Which means that's why he doesn't mind that I'm going to the Snow Ball with somebody else, because that means that the equal opportunity rule is alive and well in Chicago." I turned to Lester. "You're not even thinking of marriage yet, are you?"

"Not really. Are *you*?"

"Of course not. But I'm curious: How many women do you think you will have dated before you find the right one? I mean, honestly, Les, not to get personal or anything, but how many girls have you been out with in your whole life up until now?"

"To the nearest hundred?"

"Seriously! There was Claire last year, Tracy, Lauren, Eva, Joy, Crystal, Marilyn . . . Any others?"

"Lord, yes. Gloria, Mickey, Maxie, Amy, Lisa, Josephine, Caroline . . ."

"Omigod, Les, did that say Exit 51/Durham/Atlanta? That's the one we were supposed to take!"

"Al, you're supposed to be navigating!"

"Turn around! Turn around!" I cried.

"Are you insane? This is a freeway. We have to go to the next exit."

Les was cussing, I was hyperventilating, and then we saw we hadn't missed it after all:

EXIT 51/DURHAM/ATLANTA, NEXT RIGHT.

Saved. Now all I had to do was pretend I knew what I was doing when we got to Chapel Hill.

7

CALL GIRL

Lester stopped in the driveway of an official-looking building. It was already past two, but I told Les I'd catch up with the tour.

"This where it starts?" he asked.

I was digging through my folder of papers and couldn't find where I'd written the starting place for the Chapel Hill tour. "I think so," I said. And then, when Les frowned, I leaned forward and took a quick look at the name of the building.

"Yep! This is it!" I said, and reached in back for my bag.

"What residence hall are you staying in?" he asked.

"Welch," I said.

"Okay. We've got a four-hour drive to Williamsburg, so we

need to leave here at eight tomorrow morning. Nine at the latest. You okay with that?"

"Let's make it eight thirty. I'll be waiting right here on the steps," I answered, leaning forward again to memorize the name of the building, Jackson Hall. I pulled my bag out after me. "Thanks loads, Lester!"

"Have fun! Ask questions! Check out everything!" he said.

"What are *you* going to be doing?" I asked.

"Walk a little. Eat a bite. I brought some work with me," he said, nodding toward his old briefcase in back, stuffed with his thesis.

The car pulled away, and I took a few steps forward to show I was at least in motion, duffel bag over my shoulder, a folder of papers in my hand. But my inability to find the notes I'd made on Chapel Hill made my mouth dry. I had the catalog of undergraduate studies, the admission form, tuition chart. . . . Even if I *had* known where the tour was starting out, I would have missed the first fifteen minutes by now.

I was walking over to the steps to sit down and look for my campus map when I saw a small group of people walking by. There were fifteen or so, both teens and adults, following a female guide who was walking backward and talking to them. The campus tour!

I waited for them to pass, and then slowly, nonchalantly, I sauntered after them, a short distance behind. I couldn't hear everything the guide was saying, but I could at least see whatever she was pointing out.

If I were in a movie playing the part of a spy, everybody in the audience would have guessed it was me. *Which person in this picture does not belong?* The girl with the duffel bag, pretending to study the trees.

"Perhaps some of you aren't aware of our rich two-hundred-year history," the cheerful guide was saying as I transferred the bag to my other shoulder. "We'll talk about that next. . . ."

There were times I got a little too close to the group and some of them looked at me warily, as though I might have a bomb in my bag. And once, when I was standing on tiptoe, trying to see what the guide was pointing out, she stopped a moment and said, "Excuse me, can I help you?"

I had no name tag like the others. I had not started out with the group. I wasn't even sure this was the right tour. I murmured that I was looking for the admissions office. Then everyone turned and stared at me as the guide replied, "Well . . . that's where the tour started: Jackson Hall."

My face aflame, I walked into the first building I came to and found a café. I ordered an iced tea and a doughnut and collapsed on a chair.

Why hadn't I come right out and said who I was and how I was late for a tour, and whoever they were, did they mind if I tagged along? Why hadn't I at least asked the guide to direct me to Welch Hall? If I couldn't speak up about something as minor as this, did I belong in college at all? Everyone else on campus seemed to know what they were doing and where they were going. Everyone else had a plan.

By the time I'd finished the doughnut, though, I was feeling a little better. I decided I'd find the residence hall first, drop my bag, and explore the campus on my own.

The campus was huge—*huge*—but I had a map, and I spread it out on the table. Then, with my duffel bag hoisted over my shoulder once more, I set out to find Welch, the University Plaza (aka "the Brickyard"), the Memorial Bell Tower, the Free Expression Tunnel underneath the railroad tracks, where anyone could paint graffiti. . . . There was a lot to see.

I tramped all around, but not only could I not find any of these places, I couldn't even find the right streets. I asked a student where I'd find the University Plaza, and he said he didn't know.

Even though I kept transferring my bag from one shoulder to the other, both shoulders were sore. Finally I sat down on a bench and took out my cell phone. I looked through my notes again and this time found the number for Welch Hall, punched in the number, and waited. Someone answered—a student, probably.

"Hi, I'm Alice McKinley, here for a student visit, and I can't find Welch Hall," I said.

"It's a huge campus, I know," the girl said comfortingly. "Can you tell me where you are now? Maybe I can direct you."

I looked around. "I'm sitting on a bench facing the Memorial Building."

"The Memorial Tower?"

"I . . . guess so. I don't see a tower."

"Are you anywhere near the Brickyard? I could probably direct you from there," she said.

"I can't find that, either. I've even picked up a copy of the *Daily Tar Heel*, but—"

"*The Tar Heel*?" came the voice. "Are you sure you're at North Carolina State?"

I felt as though I were on an elevator and was plummeting toward the basement. "I'm right here at Chapel Hill," I told her.

"We're in *Raleigh*," the girl said. "Who were you supposed to see at Welch Hall?"

It was like one of those dreams where you suddenly discover it's the day of your midterm exam and you haven't studied for it. Not only haven't you studied, but you haven't opened the book. Not only have you not opened the book, you haven't attended class since school started, and you don't even know where the class is.

"My God!" I gasped. I wondered if I was going to pass out. I felt light-headed and dizzy. "I'm just checking out colleges. I thought someone said I could stay there tonight."

"Wow," the girl said. "Even if you wanted Raleigh, Welch doesn't have any room for visitors. We're full up."

"I—I wanted Chapel Hill. But I—I must have brought the wrong map. S-Sorry to have bothered you," I said quickly, and hung up.

I sat there breathing in and out, in and out, one hand on my chest. Maybe I was having a heart attack. Finally, when the throbbing noise in my ears began to fade, I decided that the only thing left to do was find my way back to Jackson Hall and throw myself on the mercy of the admissions staff. But I was exhausted and stopped at the student union for the special of the day, glad to drop my bag at a table by the window.

I got my chicken à la king on toast and began shuffling through my papers again in a state of disbelief. Somehow I had printed out information on both North Carolina State at Raleigh and the University of North Carolina at Chapel Hill, and most of what I'd brought along, including the campus map, was for North Carolina State.

But they're both in North Carolina, right? I asked myself. Both schools had the words *North* and *Carolina* in them. I quickly thumbed through every paper I had and found only a page or two about Chapel Hill. I yanked the duffel bag from the floor to my lap and thrust the papers back inside.

"You hitchhiking cross-country?" a guy asked.

He'd taken the empty seat across from me, and his feet had collided with mine. I took it as a joke and laughed a little. "No, I'm checking out colleges this weekend and have to carry this with me until I find a place to crash," I said.

He took an analytical approach: "You could always try the gym," he said. "We heard of a guy who hung out there for three days before maintenance threw him out. Used the showers, a locker—slept on an exercise mat. Probably find one of those in the women's locker room." He was serious!

"Thanks," I said. "I'll look into it."

"I hiked the Appalachian Trail one summer," he said, and pushed his glasses back up the bridge of his nose. The stems were too long, though, because the glasses slid right down again. "Not all of it. Got through South Carolina and part of Georgia, and then I got dysentery and had to quit."

"Bummer," I said, and got up to return my tray.

I went straight back to Jackson Hall, but the admissions office was closed.

What was this, a death wish? I grabbed my cell phone again and called the number I had for William and Mary, where I had originally left a message about needing a place to stay. All I got was the same automated voice asking me to leave a message. I ended the call and sat watching students walking by in little groups of three or four. Classes were over for the week, and people were calling out to each other, making plans for some Friday-night fun.

Okay, I told myself. *If all that is left for me is a Friday night at Chapel Hill, I'll at least sample that.*

There was a movie that evening on campus. I'd read the postings on a bulletin board. It was an Italian film revival, and one of Fellini's films was playing. You could get in for a dollar, so I went. I sat in the middle of a row so people could exit on either side of me, and used the duffel bag as a footrest.

There were no subtitles, though; the whole film was spoken in Italian, and I realized after a while that most of the audience understood it. This might even have been an assignment, because sometimes somebody translated a line aloud. I fell asleep toward the end, and when I woke, the lights had come on and people were leaving. I dragged my duffel bag into a restroom and used the toilet, then hauled it again to my shoulder and went outside.

It was raining—a light but steady rain that was more than a passing shower, I could tell. The sidewalk was slick with pine needles, and I hadn't brought an umbrella.

I followed a group of students to a chili dog shop, but all the tables were full, so I ate mine standing at a little counter by the window, one foot on my bag, listening to a group of guys argue about the Tar Heels' chances against the Terrapins.

The chili dog didn't agree with me and I needed a restroom again, so I found one of the libraries and used theirs. When I came back out and walked by the large reading room, it looked as though some students came to study all night. Several had stacks of books and papers scattered around them on the table, and I didn't see any sign indicating library hours. Hadn't I heard Les talk sometimes of "pulling an all-nighter" at the library?

I went in, dropped my duffel bag on a chair, got out my pen and notebook, laid my head on my arms, and drifted off.

I must have been more tired than I thought, because I woke finally to a series of thumps against my chair. I opened my eyes and had to lift my head slowly because there was a crick in my neck.

The custodian had bumped the legs of my chair with his vacuum and apologized in Spanish. Only a couple of students were still in the library, and the clerk at the desk was looking at me without smiling. I sat up and rubbed my neck. The clerk came over.

"Excuse me," he said. "May I see your ID card?"

"Uh . . . I'm just visiting the campus," I said.

"The library's for university students and faculty only," he told me, and glanced down at my duffel bag. "Sorry."

"That's okay. I didn't mean to fall asleep." My mouth felt crummy. "Is there any place on campus I could stay overnight?"

He shook his head and glanced up at the wall clock. Two minutes past eleven. "Have you tried the YMCA?" he said.

I went back outside. It was still raining. Still steady. I wondered whether the gym was open and couldn't remember where I'd passed it on campus. I really needed a shower. Really needed to wash my feet. I stuffed my purse and my cell phone into the duffel bag to keep them dry and started to walk.

There were lights on in a hamburger shop and a bookstore, but I knew they'd be closing soon. The streetlights would be on all night, but they didn't do me much good. Beyond the streetlights, I could see the outline of a department store and office buildings against the night sky. And beyond them, the glow of a neon sign, a huge eye—now open, now closed—and the words SLEEPY INN: VACANCY.

I shifted my duffel bag, turned up the collar of my jacket, and with my sneakers sloshing and squeaking through the puddles, I headed up the street.

A light in still another store went out, then another across the street. I knew I shouldn't be out alone at this hour in a neighborhood I didn't know—even a university neighborhood—and I kept my eyes on the Sleepy Inn sign in the distance.

The rain was pelting down even harder as I approached the motel, and I hurried my steps as I went up the sidewalk. The small lobby was empty, and when I pulled on the door handle, I found that the door was locked. I couldn't believe this. The lights were on, but no one was at the desk.

Then a man came in from a back room and spread a

newspaper out on the desk. I rattled the door handle. He looked up, pressed a buzzer, and the door unlocked. I went inside, my wet sneakers leaving footprints on the tile.

"Help you?" the clerk asked in monotone. He had a long, thin face with deep creases on either side of his mouth. He made no effort to hide the newspaper, probably sensing I wasn't a serious customer.

"Yes. My brother's staying here, and I wondered if you could tell me his room number," I said, realizing that my jacket was dripping water too.

The man studied me. My wet hair. My duffel bag.

"Your brother?" he asked, cocking his head to one side, a trace of sarcasm in his voice.

"Yes. Lester McKinley. He checked in this afternoon."

I saw the outline of the man's tongue in his cheek. He slowly put the newspaper aside and checked his computer. I could see only half the screen. Then he looked at me again. "You live around here?"

"No. I'm . . . sort of checking out the university," I told him.

"Your name?"

"Alice. He *knows* me!" I said impatiently.

"I'll phone his room and tell him you're here," he said.

The last thing Les needed to hear was that his dripping, drippy sister was standing in the lobby soaking wet, with no place to go. I had to handle this myself.

"Can't you just tell me his room number?" I begged.

"No. Sorry." He pressed a three-digit number, listened for a moment. "Busy," he said, and hung up.

"Well, I'll wait," I said, and tried to shake some water out of my hair. The clerk frowned as some of it hit his desk. "Sorry," I said quickly, and patiently stood aside. The clerk went back to reading his newspaper.

A minute went by. Two. Three. Les could be on the phone with a girlfriend, if he had a girlfriend. Or maybe he'd just taken the phone off the hook. After another minute of waiting, I said, "Could you try again, please?"

The look again. The tongue in the cheek. But this time I studied closely as he pressed the three-digit number: 2 . . . 1 . . . 7. I'd bet that was his room number.

"Busy," the man said again, and hung up.

"I guess I'll just have to wait," I said.

I dragged my wet bag over to the vinyl couch and sat down. The clerk folded up one section of the paper and opened another. Two more minutes went by. Three.

I knew the desk clerk wouldn't try the phone again until I begged. He enjoyed making me plead. I thought of digging out my cell phone and calling Les on that, but I had a better idea.

"Excuse me, could I use the restroom?" I asked. And when he looked up without answering, I said, "It's urgent."

He gave me a disgusted look, then nodded toward a doorway behind him. "Back there," he said, and added, "Keep it neat."

I walked to one side of his desk and through the doorway with my bag. It led to a side hall. There was a restroom marked EMPLOYEES ONLY on the left and, just down the hall, an elevator.

It took only a second to decide. I opened the door of the restroom and let it close again without going inside. Then, when the clerk turned a page of his paper and leaned over it again, I edged my way down the hall to the elevator. I pressed the button and the door slid open. I got on and pressed 2.

8

NIGHT IN CHAPEL HILL

Oh, man! I wondered how long it would take Mr. Sarcastic down at the desk to go to the door of the bathroom to check if I was still in there. How long before he simply barged in? Would he figure out what I'd done? Probably.

The elevator door didn't open immediately when it reached the second floor. I panicked at the thought of the elevator getting stuck, how I'd have to push the alarm button and scream. And how the clerk, guessing it was me, would take his time calling 911.

Then the elevator door groaned and slowly slid open. I sprang out, checked the numbers on the doors, and made a left to room 217.

There was no sound from inside. I knocked lightly.

Still no sound. What if the room number wasn't the same as the phone number? What if I woke up a stranger? I knocked again, a little more desperately, and heard a toilet flush. Then the door opened, and there stood Les in his boxer shorts and a tee.

"Al! What the heck?" he said.

I darted inside and closed the door after me. One of the beds was strewn with books and papers, pillows piled up against the headboard. Lester's cell phone was charging on the second bed.

"What *happened*?" Les asked, still standing by the door as though he expected me to leave momentarily.

"It was getting late, and I didn't know the neighborhood," I told him. "Please let me stay, Les. I screwed up."

"What do you mean? They couldn't find a place for you to sleep?"

I took off my wet jacket and put it in his bathtub, then came out and slumped down in the one chair. "Well . . . yeah, that too," I said in a small voice. "But . . . I got the wrong school."

He stared at me. "You . . . *what*?"

I curled into a fetal position. "I got things mixed up and brought the map and notes for Raleigh. North Carolina State."

Les just kept staring at me. "We're supposed to be at *Raleigh*?"

"No, we're supposed to be here, but . . . Oh, Les, I just really goofed up. I'd Googled a lot of schools and printed stuff out before I chose the ones I did, and I brought the wrong map along."

"But you said you had a room in a residence hall."

"It was in Raleigh, and I didn't know it. I *thought* I had a room, anyway, but when I called they said they were full, so even if we'd gone there . . ."

"*Damn*, Al! You didn't plan for Chapel Hill at all? We drove all the way down here just to hang out at the Sleepy Inn?"

"Don't yell at me, Les," I mewed. "I checked out the campus. The library. I ate somewhere on campus—I forget where."

"Great. You checked out the pizza." Les still hadn't moved. He stood with his arms crossed and glared at me.

"Les, I don't even know if I belong at Chapel Hill! If I could even get accepted. Everybody's weird and smart."

"How can you tell? You hardly even talked to anybody. Why did we come here at all?"

"Because I have to check out some schools. Dad would freak out if I didn't look at some. You know that." Then, trying to change the subject, I asked, "Who were you talking to on the room phone? The guy at the desk tried to call you a couple times, but the line was busy."

Les refused to be distracted. He leaned against the door, arms still folded, and said, "I was talking to Paul about a gift for George's wedding. As for you—"

At that moment someone knocked, and Les jumped. He turned around and peered through the peephole.

"Jeez!" he said. He gave me a look and opened the door.

A man stood there in a security uniform. "Excuse me," he said. "This room registered to one person? You Lester McKinley?"

"That's right," said Les. "And my sister just arrived. Seems she's spending the night."

Yes! I silently cheered.

"Your registration lists only one occupant," the security guy said.

"That's what I thought at the time," Les said.

It wasn't fair to make Lester take the rap for me, and I knew it. "I was supposed to spend the night somewhere else, and it didn't work out," I told the man.

I could tell I was making things worse.

"Identification?" he asked.

I reached for my bag on the floor and rummaged around till I found my wallet. I showed the guard my driver's license.

"You need to go down to the registration desk and sign in," he said. And to Les, "There's an additional charge for her."

"Okay," said Les. "Let me put on some pants."

The security guard put one hand against the wall outside and waited, to show he meant business.

Les let the door close and yanked on a pair of jeans.

"Les, I'm so sorry!" I kept saying. "I really didn't mean to cause trouble."

Silently, he got his sneakers from under the bed and thrust his feet inside them.

"Let's go," he said finally. I followed him out the door and down the hall, the security guard at my heels.

At the desk the clerk glowered at me, then at Les. In slow motion he reached for his pen and asked for my driver's license. He copied everything down—ID number, age, weight, address. Then he turned to the computer and slowly entered all the stuff he'd written by hand.

Les got the picture pretty quick. "Anything else?" he asked. "You want her passport? Birth certificate? Vaccination records?"

Mr. Sarcastic didn't even answer. Just printed out a new page, shoved it toward Les, and said, "Sign."

The elevator didn't seem to be working. Les kept pressing the buttons, but the door wouldn't close. We could hear mechanical grinding and groaning. The door started to close, then slid open again.

"What *else* can go wrong?" Les muttered. "Let's take the stairs."

We didn't know where they were, however. Les turned left, so I followed. We were halfway down the hall when a man called out, "Where you folks going?" We turned to see the security guy, hands on hips.

"Elevator's broken. We're looking for the stairs," Les said.

"This end," the guard told us, turning to lead the way, but he stopped when he came to the elevator. He reached inside and pressed a button. The doors slid closed but opened again when he pressed the button on the outside. He cocked his head to show his impatience with us.

Les shrugged and we got on. He pressed 2. The door slid closed and the elevator moved. But when we got to the second floor, the door wouldn't open.

"Dammit!" Les exclaimed. He pressed OPEN. Nothing happened. He pressed 1. Nothing.

"*Blast* it!" Les cried, and pressed the alarm button. Somewhere a loud bell sounded. There was no phone or intercom that we could see.

I sat down in one corner. I'd worried about being stuck in

the elevator by myself but hadn't figured it would happen to me and Les.

Les looked dumbfounded. "Can you *believe* this? Could anything top this?"

"Yes," I said. "One of us could need a bathroom."

I saw Lester's face crinkle into a smile, and then we were both laughing. Les leaned against the wall, and his arm hit the alarm button again. It rang a second time, and this really set us off.

Now the security guard was on our case for good. I guess he was standing outside the elevator on the second floor and could hear us laughing. He banged on the door.

"*Excuse* me!" he yelled. He said something about waiting for emergency maintenance and how if that didn't work, he'd call the fire department. And please don't ring the alarm again—he knew where we were.

Les sat down beside me, our feet straight out in front of us.

"This place is a dump, isn't it?" I said. "Sorry. The price was right. I was trying to save Dad some money. Probably bedbugs too."

"And no hot water after midnight," Les joked.

"Was there even soap in the bathroom? Or is that extra?" I said.

"After they rescue us, they'll add 'rescue' to the bill," said Les.

We laughed some more, then grew quiet, listening to the sounds of mechanical tinkering coming from the elevator shaft.

Les sighed. "Okay. Give it to me straight," he said. "You don't have a place to stay tomorrow in Williamsburg either, right?"

"Yeah, but I'll find one, I promise."

He covered his eyes. "I don't *believe* this. And if you don't find one?"

"Well . . ." I searched desperately for a silver lining. "Did we ever do Williamsburg, Les? I mean, did Dad ever bring us? Once we're there, with its history and all . . ."

Les stared at me incredulously. "You're serious?"

"I don't mean that we should see Williamsburg in place of William and Mary," I said hastily. "I could look around the college first, and then we could do the sights in the afternoon."

He was shaking his head. "You really think we're going to get up in the morning, drive two hundred miles, visit a whole campus—the buildings, the library, the residence halls—and do Williamsburg in the afternoon? Are you insane?"

I could feel my face heating up, and I swallowed. Les turned away and sighed again. He was disgusted with me, I knew.

At that moment the elevator jerked slightly and the door slid open.

We scrambled to our feet and bounded out the door before it could close again. When we got to our room, Les put up the DO NOT DISTURB sign so we wouldn't have to face the security guard again.

He looked tired, and he nodded toward the second bed. "We've got to get an early start, so why don't you turn in," he said, removing his cell phone and unplugging it.

I picked up my bag, dug around for my pajamas, and took them into the bathroom.

Les had good reason for being disgusted with me, I told myself, staring into the mirror. This whole trip was a waste of time, a waste of gas. He had carted all his thesis stuff along, trying to use his time efficiently, and I had really goofed up.

When I came out and crawled in bed, Les said, "Ready?" and turned out the lamp. The room was black except for some light from the parking lot that came through the venetian blinds.

"I'm not ready for college, Les," I said into the darkness, my voice shaky.

"I'm not buying," he answered.

"I'm just stating facts. I'm not even sure I want to go."

"Cut it out, Al."

"Really! I used to dream about Liz and Pam and Gwen and me all going to college together, sharing a dorm room. . . . It's not going to happen, Lester. We're all going off in different directions, and Pamela may go to a design school or something. I'll have to make friends all over again with a huge bunch of new people. . . ."

"Not all at once. You'll make friends just like you made them in Silver Spring—one at a time."

"I just feel like . . . if I don't . . . if I can't make friends . . . the right friends . . . if I screw that up, I'll ruin my whole four years. I'll be homesick and lonely and my grades will suck and—"

"What if I promise you that will never happen?"

"You can't promise that, so I wouldn't believe you."

"What if I promise that if you don't put a lid on it, we're going straight home tomorrow, and you can tell Dad the trip was a bust?"

"I believe you," I said, and after a long time I fell asleep.

I felt better in the morning. My clothes were dry, anyway, and Les let me have the bathroom first. I got ready as fast as I could and decided I was going to treat him to a good breakfast before we got on our way. There was a new person at the desk.

"Room 217 checking out," Les said, handing in his key card.

"I'll have your bill printed out in a moment," the young woman said cheerfully, checking the computer.

"Is there a place nearby where we could get breakfast?" I asked.

"There certainly is," she answered, pulling a paper out of the printer and handing it to me. "There's a pancake house just around the corner, Mrs. McKinley. Enjoy!"

Lester's jaw dropped. He turned his head slowly and looked at me.

I howled when we got outside. "Must be my hair," I said. I'd piled it on top of my head that morning because I hadn't washed it, and I'd fixed it in place with a comb.

But Les was laughing too. "Get in," he said, slinging my bag in the back of his car and putting his briefcase beside it. "Man oh man, life with you is like living in a monkey house."

Over chocolate chip pancakes I asked him about George, the roommate who was getting married the following weekend. "Are you and Paul in the wedding?"

"Yeah, if it ever comes off. It was already delayed a month due to some scheduling problem," he said. "We're still trying to figure out what stuff is ours and what belongs to George."

I tried to imagine a bachelor pad with only two guys in it instead of three. "You've got three bedrooms," I said. "You going to get somebody else?"

"I don't know. We'll see what happens."

I thought about the four years of college ahead of me before I could graduate, and at least another year after that to get a master's before I could be a school counselor. Where would I live after I left home? By myself, or sharing an apartment?

"I'm glad you're going through all this first, so you can fill me in when it's my turn," I told him.

But Lester's disappointment in me really hurt. I knew myself that I'd prepared school assignments more carefully than I'd prepared for this trip, and I wanted Les to know that I was now serious. After our pancake breakfast and coffee, I paid the bill myself, and when we were on the road again, I paid attention:

"We're going to turn left on South Fordham Boulevard and go four miles," I instructed.

"I need route numbers," Les said.

"U.S. 15 North," I told him, map in my hand.

"And then?"

"Go 7.2 miles, then merge onto I-85 North."

"Got it," he said.

It took three and a half hours, and we were hungry again when we got to Williamsburg. Because I didn't have a scheduled tour, we took time to get some hoagies at Ye Olde Sandwich Shoppe and enjoyed the costumed actors who passed by on the brick sidewalk occasionally, carrying on conversations with tourists as though it were back in the 1700s.

"All right," Les said when we'd finished eating. "You know where I'm staying, but let's not have a repeat of last night."

"We won't," I said. "First thing on my list is to find a place to crash."

"On *campus*," Les emphasized. "That's important."

I really did do better at William and Mary. Les let me off in front of the administration office, and I told the woman there that I didn't have a reservation for a tour but would like a map for a self-guided walk around campus. She was glad to help and told me to check one of the residence halls to see if any of the women would show me what the rooms were like. I heard her tell someone else that there was no place for visiting students to stay overnight, so I didn't ask, but I'd already made up my mind that I would pay for a motel myself if I couldn't sleep on campus, regardless of what Les had said.

I started off, duffel bag over one shoulder. *Welcome to William and Mary*, the brochure read, *one of America's oldest and best universities, which claims both Thomas Jefferson and Jon Stewart as alumni.* I "walked the brick pathways where Thomas Jefferson ran when he was late to class" and asked questions whenever I could, even when I knew the answer, just to sample the conversation.

The campus was smaller and more manageable than the one at Chapel Hill, more my style. *Next September this could be me*, I thought as I breezed along, my bag thumping against me. I could see myself as a student here on a fall morning, and when a guy smiled at me and said hi as he passed, I smiled back and thought, *Not bad!* I walked to the library, the sports center, the stadium—all the usual places, and was glad to put my duffel bag down at the bookstore and just browse and have an iced tea.

But I got really lucky in the caf, as they call their cafeteria, when a girl put her tray across from me on the table and, seeing the Moroccan chicken on my plate, said, "Oh, you love it too."

"It's great," I said.

"It's all I ever eat," she told me, and began shoveling food in her mouth. "I'm on a fifteen-minute break. Feed the dishwasher on Saturdays."

"Well, I'm visiting colleges this weekend," I told her. "My first time here."

"Yeah? Where you from?"

"Maryland. Silver Spring. I'm Alice."

"Judith," she said. She had short, dark, curly hair that seemed to bounce with every word. Dark, intense eyes, but friendly. "How do you like the school so far?"

"Nice," I said, "but I didn't make arrangements in advance, and my brother's sort of pissed. He drove me down and wants me to find a place to stay overnight on campus."

And just like that, Judith said, "You can stay with us. We're in a suite, and one of our roomies went home for the weekend. You could have her bed."

"Really?" I said. "How do you know she'd let me?"

"Because she loaned out my bed two weeks ago," Judith said. "Just don't leave makeup on her pillow. She hates that."

As she chewed the last bite of chicken, she scribbled the address of her residence hall on a paper napkin. "I'll meet you right here between five and five thirty," she said. "You can drop your bag off at the dorm."

"This is terrific," I said. "Thanks."

"Gotta run," she told me, and in one quick sweep, she slid her tray off the table and disappeared through the metal door leading to the kitchen.

9

DECISIONS

This was way too easy. I'd toured the campus myself—well, some of it, anyway—and I already had a place to sleep. I'd agreed to meet Les at nine o'clock in the morning right where he'd let me off, and he wasn't going to get a kid sister knocking on his motel door at midnight.

I spent the next couple of hours at the bookstore so that I didn't have to carry my bag and listened to the conversations going on around me to get a feel for the student life:

". . . I absolutely have to take another semester of Spanish or I can't graduate . . ."

". . . the best cookies! But if you want a fantastic fruit salad . . ."

". . . His face said it all. I mean, Rob's perfect for the part of Aaron, but I know Nick feels he should get the part . . ."

". . . the problem with the Drake equation is that he's only taken *this* galaxy into account, and when you consider the thousands of millions of galaxies . . ."

Judith got off work about five fifteen, and I walked with her back to her residence hall. It was a relief to be rid of the bag for the evening, even though it was more cumbersome than heavy. I had a crease in my shoulder from the strap, and I gratefully deposited the duffel bag on the floor beside an unmade bed in Judith's suite. The room wasn't much bigger than a large bathroom. There was barely enough room for two beds, two desks, and two dressers.

"I'll leave a note on the door for Mack that the bed's occupied," Judith said as she pulled off her sweater and headed to the second bedroom to change.

I did a double take. "Mack?"

"Yeah. Neat guy," she said over her shoulder. "I've known him for two years. He can fix any problem at all with a computer."

I tried not to appear shocked. It was like I was back at the University of Chicago. But after a night on Patrick's couch there, and after sharing a room with Les last night, I was ready for anything.

When Judith came into the common area of the suite again—the "living room"—she was wearing skintight jeans, ankle boots, and a low-cut jersey top. Her curly hair was hard to contain, and it didn't look as though she'd really tried. She ducked into the bathroom to put on mascara.

I wasn't even sure she knew my last name. How did she know that I wasn't a psycho with razor blades in my pocket or that I wouldn't sneak off during the night with all her stuff? I guess that with someone named Mack sleeping across from me, it was safe to conclude I wouldn't try.

"I'm going out with my guy tonight," Judith told me. "Make yourself at home—turn on the TV, whatever you want. If you go out, just leave the door unlocked. My own roomie's still out, and so is Mack. If you leave and can't get in the front entrance when you come back, ring the bell and I'll let my resident manager know to let you in. Bye."

I was tired from tramping around all afternoon with a bag over my shoulder. But it was a beautiful night, so I went for a walk around campus, careful to stay near people and not wander off in the shadows alone. I called Les on my cell and told him I had a place to crash. Then I got some ice cream, listened to a couple of guys playing guitars, and pretended I was a resident student like everyone else. As Les said, everyone would be strangers at first when I went to a new place. And then, little by little, a face would become a friend.

I got to bed about eleven thirty, tossed around a bit, and was just drifting off when I heard a door slam—the door to the living area. I heard a guy cough. Mack. Had to be.

I kept my eyes shut. I heard the knob turn on the door to our bedroom. Then a pause. He was reading Judith's note.

The handle turned more slowly. A rectangle of light fell on the floor, then his shadow as he came in and shut the door behind him. The tune to "Mack the Knife" played in my head.

Footsteps. I didn't even know these people. I didn't know whose bed I was staying in. Didn't know Judith, and I was sure I didn't know Mack.

I cleared my throat to let him know I was awake.

"How ya doin'?" said a male voice.

"Okay," I said. "How about you?"

"Great."

He kicked off his shoes. Left the room and went to the bathroom. I turned over to face the wall and pulled the covers up to my cheek. If a guy can find a stranger in his room and say, "How ya doin'?" he couldn't be so bad.

Next thing I knew, I woke once during the night. It was past four. Loud, steady breathing from Mack. The smell of his sneakers. When I woke again, it was going on eight. I got up, dressed, put my stuff together, and left a thank-you note for Judith. Les pulled up at our meeting place at a quarter past nine, and we were on our way.

"So where did you find a place to sleep?" Les asked me.

I casually leaned my elbow on the armrest. "Well, believe it or not, I lucked out and spent the night with a guy," I said.

I think Les lifted his foot off the gas because the car suddenly lost power, but then it picked up again, much more slowly.

"This . . . somebody you know?" he asked, and he sounded strange.

"I never saw him before," I said, trying to keep a straight face. "And I still don't know what he looked like. He just came in the room in the dark and . . ."

"And?"

I laughed. "Relax," I said. "He was my roommate. Separate beds. Somebody loaned me a bed for the night. The girl had gone home for the weekend. I guess you could say it's coed."

I could tell he felt better. "So how did you like the college?"

"It's okay. Fine, really. Two down, one to go."

It was a two-and-a-half-hour trip to George Mason, and by the time we got to Fairfax, I'd memorized the names of the football teams, the student newspapers, the famous former alumni, and the histories of all three colleges I was inspecting.

At this point Lester was more interested in getting back for the four o'clock Redskins game than he was in making sure I got a full dose of what George Mason was all about, so he gave me a whirlwind tour of the campus himself by car.

We did the Patriot Circle, following the map I'd printed out on the Internet. Then Les turned onto George Mason Boulevard and drove slowly around campus, all the little lanes between buildings.

From what I could tell from my printouts and from posters nailed about, Johnson Center was where all the action was on campus, and it was right in the middle, maybe the largest building next to the Field House. There were posters advertising jazz concerts in the JC Bistro, comedy shows, movies at the JC Cinema. . . .

But there's not a lot going on at a college campus at noon on a Sunday. A lone student here or there heading for a coffee shop; a faculty wife, maybe, pushing a stroller; a couple having an intense conversation near the George Mason statue.

Les waited while I checked out Fenwick Library, the student

union, and the performing arts building. Then I got back in the car and said, "Let's go. Finished. Done!"

"Sure?" he asked.

"I'm saturated. I couldn't soak up another thing," I told him. "I've got a ton of homework waiting for me, and George Mason is close enough that I could drive over here for a second look by myself."

Les turned on the radio, and we headed back to the beltway toward Maryland. Les sang along with the music.

It wasn't really the way a college visit should go. I knew that. I knew that people like Gwen kept long lists of the pros and cons of various schools—scholarships, clubs, size, cost, dorms—while I had a manila folder and a couple of envelopes stuffed with whatever I got off the Internet, that and a few brochures.

But I liked William and Mary best, and it tied for first place with Maryland, which I'd visited several times with Les.

I liked the thought of going to the school that Jefferson had attended, but I also liked the thought of graduating from the same college as my brother and being closer to home. Maybe it was growing up without a mother that made me feel this way—like I needed an umbilical cord to *some*body.

I thanked Les when I got out of the car, pulled my duffel bag from the backseat and would swear I heard a relieved sigh as I closed the door and Les sped away.

I wondered if Dad and Sylvia had enjoyed having the house to themselves for the three-day weekend. No loud music coming from my bedroom; no bleary-eyed senior to look at over the breakfast table; no jacket on the back of a chair; no saucer left on an end table.

I walked through the living room and followed the sound of voices beyond the dining room and out to the high-ceilinged family room at the back of the house, where you could see the light yellow of the box elder's leaves through the windows.

The conversation seemed to stop in mid-sentence.

"Oh!" Sylvia said.

"Didn't think you'd be back until this evening," Dad said.

I realized by Sylvia's "Oh," by the redness of her eyes, and by the way they were sitting, Dad's arm around her, that she'd been crying. I didn't know what to do.

"We finished up early so Les could watch the game with his buddies," I said. "Am I interrupting something?"

"Not really," Sylvia said. She's no better at lying than I am.

"So how did things go?" Dad asked, extracting his arm from around Sylvia's shoulder and laying his hand on her knee instead.

"Okay. I got a good look at all three campuses, talked to some people," I said, wondering how to make a quick exit.

"Any of the three appeal?" Dad asked.

"I liked William and Mary the best," I said. "Anyway, I've got a ton of homework to do and some calls to make. . . ." I turned sideways to let them know I was leaving.

"There's some ham in the fridge," Sylvia said, and her nose sounded a bit clogged. "Some good cantaloupe, too."

"Thanks! I'll manage," I said.

I carried my duffel bag up to my room and dumped it on

the bed. What was wrong? It hadn't looked like an argument. Not with Dad's hand on her knee. Sylvia didn't sound mad, she sounded sad.

Could Sylvia's sister in New Mexico be sick again? Her brother in Seattle? Was the Melody Inn going bankrupt and were we in danger of losing our house? My imagination had kidnapped my brain and was running away with it.

I spread my notebook and papers out on the bed and had just started my physics assignment when Sylvia tapped on the door and peeped inside.

"Got a minute?" she said.

"Sure." I put down my book and waited as she came in, hugging her bare arms in her short-sleeved sweater. It didn't seem that cold to me. She gave me an apologetic smile.

"I'm glad you had a good weekend, because mine was sort of crummy, and I just wanted you to know what Ben and I were talking about when you came in," she began.

Here it comes, I told myself. *Get prepared.*

"Remember the doctor's appointment I had last week?"

"I think so."

"Well, I had a routine mammogram, but I got a recall on it so I had to take it over. They've found something they want to check on a little further, and I have a biopsy coming up. I was feeling scared, that's all. Most biopsies turn out to be negative, but this is my first, so I was having a little cry, that's all."

That's all? I thought. Sylvia could have breast cancer and be operated on and she could die and Dad would go into this deep depression and wouldn't be able to work and he'd lose his job and I'd already lost one mother and . . . By the time Sylvia spoke again, I'd had us moved back to Chicago to live with Aunt Sally.

"Chances are that it's nothing, Alice, but I just hate waiting," she said. "I like to get things over with."

"Who doesn't?" I said. "When's the biopsy?"

"Week after next."

"And . . . when will you know? What it is?"

"I'm not sure. They have to send it to a lab and everything. I may be hard to live with until then, but it has nothing to do with you, and I just wanted you to know that. Ben's been wonderful. Other women go through a lot worse than this."

"Well, you can bitch all you like and I'll forgive you," I said, getting up and giving her a hug. "Thanks for letting me in on it. I hate not knowing what's going on."

"That makes two of us," she said. "Listen, I'm going to do some stir-fry later. Ben wants to watch the game, so we'll eat it in front of the TV at the half. With chopsticks!"

I smiled and she smiled, and I heard her footsteps going back downstairs.

For a moment or two I sat staring at the door of my room. My homework was there on the bed, the college stuff on my dresser, my duffel bag on the floor.

I got up and went over to my desk. I opened a drawer and took out my early admission form for the University of Maryland.

10

THE FACE OF AMERICA

I ate dinner with Dad and Sylvia at the half—the Redskins were losing—but went back upstairs to finish the first part of the priority application and to tackle my homework.

The application didn't take long, actually. I didn't have to send in my transcripts, personal essay, and teacher recommendations till later—just a check for fifty-five dollars, the answers to four pages of questions, and Dad's signature.

During one of the commercial breaks, in the last quarter of the game when the Redskins had pulled ahead by three, I picked up the page where Dad had to sign, went back downstairs, got the checkbook from his desk, and took it to him.

"What's this?" he asked, putting down his coffee mug.

"I'm getting an early start on college applications," I said casually. "Just need your signature and a check for fifty-five dollars."

"Good for you," Dad said, taking the pen I handed him. "Which school?"

"U of Maryland," I said as the game came on again.

"Oh." He adjusted his glasses and took the checkbook, started to ask another question, but paused to watch the next play. "Watch that *de*fense!" he told the screen. Then he opened the checkbook. "I'll write the amount and sign it," he said. "You fill in the rest." He signed the application, too, where it said *Parent's Signature* and handed them both back to me. "There're only two minutes left of the fourth quarter, Al. You may want to watch," he said.

"Definitely," I told him. I took the big chair on the other side of the sofa. Sylvia sat curled up on the opposite chair, legs tucked under her. She wasn't looking so much at the screen as she was looking through it. Maybe all this was worse than she'd told me.

I made up my mind. I wasn't even going to apply to William and Mary. I wasn't going to apply to the University of North Carolina or George Mason. I would either commute back and forth to the University of Maryland, living at home where it was cheaper and where I could help Dad and Sylvia, however it turned out, or I wasn't going to college at all. I'd take a year off, work at the Melody Inn, and see them through this.

I hadn't told Dad a lie when I said I was starting to send out my college applications. I *was* starting out. I just wasn't finishing the rest, that's all.

* * *

We sent out two of our roving reporters to ask this question:

WHAT, IF ANYTHING, MAKES YOU FEAR FOR YOUR SAFETY HERE AT SCHOOL?

Mr. Samuels, if I don't find the keys to the chemistry cabinet.

—Rod Ferguson, senior

I feel pretty safe here. Especially with the security guards at the entrance and at games.

—Steph Bates, sophomore

Having to park a long way from school when there's a program at night.

—Elissa Collins, senior

Just the guys in the trench coats carrying the AK-47s.

—Bud Batista, senior

My gym teacher.

—Charlie Ingram, freshman

This was Amy's second assignment as an *Edge* reporter, and one of the replies she brought in made us blink:

> Besides the blacks and queers and Latinos who are polluting our schools and neighborhoods, you mean?
>
> —Bob White, senior

"Omigod!" I said. "Pay dirt!"

The others looked up.

"Did I do it wrong?" Amy asked anxiously, hanging around to see if what she'd done was okay.

"You did well, Amy," I told her, and looked at the others. "Who's Bob White?"

Everyone else looked as blank as I did. I checked Amy's handwritten notes again. "He's a senior. Are you sure he said 'senior'?" I asked her.

She nodded. "I wrote it down just like he said it."

"What did he look like?" Phil wanted to know.

That's asking a lot of Amy. Facts she can handle; faces she can't. "Just a boy," she said.

"Was he tall?" someone asked her.

Amy looked up, then down, as though measuring something on the wall. She hunched her shoulders.

"Dark hair? Blond? Can you remember that?" Tim asked.

She swallowed.

"It's okay," I said. "We can look his picture up in the office. You did fine, Amy." And then, to Miss Ames, "But we can't print this, can we?"

Miss Ames turned toward the rest of us. "What do you think? There's nothing that says we have to print all the replies we get. . . ."

"I say we print it," said Phil. "My guess is that some kids are being targeted and aren't telling. There wouldn't be a Student Safety Council if there weren't. There wouldn't have been that incident in the hallway, or the double eights in Daniel's locker. If the victims aren't going to 'out' the group, maybe the newspaper can."

"I'll head for the office and look at student photos," said Sam.

Fifteen minutes later he was back to report that there was no student picture of Bob White because there was no Bob White registered in the school. We decided to print the reply along with all the others in the "Question of the Week" column, and Phil said he was going to write a special editorial to accompany it.

"And maybe we should start a letters-to-the-editor feature—like a sounding-off column—for people to express an opinion about it," I suggested. "That or anything else."

"Then let's call it that: 'Sound Off,'" said Phil.

"Except that some people don't know when to stop. It could take up the whole paper," said Tim.

"We'll reserve the right to edit letters as needed," Miss Ames said. "Full speed ahead."

The next morning Phil showed me a draft of his editorial:

IS THIS OUR FACE OF AMERICA?

We are a school of 1,600 in the shadow of the nation's capital. Our student body is

> somewhat transient, because many of our parents work for the government, and every two years the population shifts.
>
> We are African American, Caucasian, Latino, Asian, and Native American. We are high school students, supposedly past the juvenile pranks of third and fourth grades and the thoughtless remarks of middle school. Yet in the past few weeks a student from Sudan has found a Nazi symbol in his locker and some armbands from the Gay/Straight Alliance were trashed. Someone using the pseudonym "Bob White" expresses racist views in our "Question of the Week" column. We published it because it was one answer to our question—and because it exposes a possible undercurrent of hate and intolerance on this campus. For a school that prides itself on our football team, our debate team, our band, our drama club and choir, is this *our* Face of America? Is this the best we can do?
>
> —Phil Adler, Editor in Chief

Immediately following Phil's editorial was the headline SOUND OFF and this paragraph:

> In future issues we will be devoting half a page to your letters to this paper. So that we may print as many letters as possible each issue, we ask

> that you keep them fairly short, no longer than 100 words. This is your chance to "sound off." You may write about school, politics, religion, life in general, but we hope your comments will be honest reflections of how you feel. All letters must be signed. You can e-mail submissions to *The Edge*; you can slip them under the door of room 227; you could put them in our box in the office; you can even put a stamp on them and let the U.S. mail do the delivery. But whatever you have to say, we want to hear it. To start things off, we welcome your comments on Phil's editorial.
>
> —Alice McKinley, Features Editor

A lot of possible replies to "Bob White's" racist comment were running through my head, but I had a lot to deal with at home. Sylvia was distracted and anxious over her scheduled biopsy . . . and angry at herself because she was.

"Every other woman I know has been through this, and it was nothing," I heard her say to Dad. "Why am I so upset by it?"

"Because it's happening to you and not some 'other woman,'" he said gently.

I heard her sigh. "I guess that's why I'm so sure that for me, it will be different. The results will be positive and I'll have to decide between a lumpectomy or chemo and I'll lose my hair and—"

"Good grief, you sound like Alice," said Dad, and there was a touch of impatience this time in his voice. He'd brought home some sales figures from the store, and they were lower than he'd expected for October. "Sylvia, do you have to borrow trouble? Can't we just deal with the problems we've got and not take on any more until we have to?"

I was silently placing dirty dishes from my room on the kitchen counter, but Sylvia was standing in the doorway between the living and dining rooms, and Dad was computing figures on the dining room table, so it was impossible for me not to hear.

"Two of my aunts had breast cancer, and one of my grandmothers died of it," she said. "I'm just plain scared."

Dad relented. I heard his chair squeak, then Sylvia's footsteps as she must have moved toward him.

"That's what makes you a good teacher." Dad's voice. "You look ahead, plan ahead, take all outcomes into account. I just try to keep my head above water. If it's cancer, we'll deal with it. Together. If it's not, then you're wasting some glorious autumn days worrying about it."

"What would I do without you?" Sylvia murmured, and I figured I needed to get back upstairs as noiselessly as I'd come.

We're not a rich family. Not even close. We aren't poor, either. We have a pretty nice house, now that we've remodeled, which Dad will be paying for for a long time. We have two cars, neither of them new. Les would graduate with his master's degree in December. But my tuition next year would take a huge chunk of our savings, I knew. Dad and Sylvia earned about the same, but they were both doing work they loved. The economy was down, however, and everyone knew it. I didn't understand the Dow Jones average in the newspaper, but I understood that there were a few more empty storefronts along Georgia Avenue.

Every time a store closed near the Melody Inn, it meant that those customers wouldn't be passing *our* store any longer. That there would be fewer people in *our* neighborhood. Maybe the owner of the Melody Inn chain would close Dad's store. Maybe Les would come back home to live. Maybe Sylvia would be too sick to teach and she'd lie in an upstairs bedroom and I'd have to give up dances and new clothes and my cell phone and . . .

I whacked myself on the cheek to bring me back to reality. *Think like Dad*, I told myself. *Don't expect trouble.* Except that there were signs of trouble brewing right there at school, and we didn't know where it was coming from or what would happen next.

I was on jury duty again that Wednesday. The accused was a girl who had been caught shoplifting—one of our sophomores. It would be her first offense, and the police, finding out that we had a Student Jury in our school, referred her to us to be disciplined.

She had already confessed and was both repentant and scared.

Darien asked her how her family had reacted to the news that she had shoplifted. Tearfully, she replied that her dad was furious with her, her mom had cried, and "my little brother doesn't look up to me anymore." Her voice trembled as she spoke.

"I'm really not like this," she said, seemingly shocked by her own behavior. "It was just . . . an impulsive thing. It's really not me."

We didn't have to discuss her case very long. We assigned her thirty hours of community service and sentenced her to write an essay about how the Student Jury experience would help her move toward her goal in life, which, she told us, was to be a wildlife photographer and a respected member of the community, not a criminal.

It was a beautiful October night with a full moon, and I went out back to sit on our screened porch after dinner. The scent of dry leaves made me think of hayrides and Halloween and the party back in junior high when Patrick French-kissed me in a broom closet.

I sat on the glider, a lap robe over my bare feet, a sweater around my shoulders, watching the moon rise higher and higher in the dark sky. On impulse I called Patrick on my cell.

"Heeey!" he said. "How *are* you? I was just thinking about you."

"Were you really?" I asked. "I was thinking about you too. In a broom closet."

"What?" There was laughter in his voice. "What's this about a closet?"

"Don't you remember? The French kiss?"

"You weren't supposed to know it was me! That's how I got up the nerve. It was dark!"

"Tell one friend, and you might as well broadcast it," I said. "Four different people told me it was you. What are *you* doing this evening?"

"Looking at the moon," he answered.

"You are? Right now?"

"I was. Coming back from dinner at the Medici. I found the initials you carved on the table."

I was delighted. "And the moon's full there, too?"

"Of *course* it's full here. You never passed second-grade science?"

I laughed. "Okay, go to the window right now and look at the moon so I'll know we're both seeing it at the same time," I instructed.

His voice moved in and out, and I knew he was walking around. "Okay," he said. "I have to move my roommate's plant first."

"What kind of plant is it?"

"I don't know. His sister gave it to him to take to college. Looks sort of like a cornstalk, but shorter. Marijuana, maybe."

I laughed.

"I don't know what it is. He forgets to water it and the leaves are turning brown. Okay, I'm pulling up the blind . . . Oops. The cord's got a knot in it. Wait a minute . . ." Then he said, "It's gone."

"What's gone?"

"The moon. It's on the other side of the building."

"Go outside, Patrick! I want us both looking at the moon at the same time."

"Hold on." There was a five-second pause. "I'm going down the hall . . . I'm passing the room on the left . . . passing my roommate who's coming back from a movie. Hey, Jonah, water that freakin' cornstalk, would ya? . . . Okay, I'm turning a corner . . . going out the door . . . there are a lot of trees in the way. I've got to go out to the sidewalk . . . Ah! There it is! The moon! Now what?"

"Sit down somewhere and look at it, Patrick. Just think—we're both looking at the very same moon at the very same time. Like our eyes are almost meeting."

"Well, not quite, because you're seeing the east side of the moon there in Maryland and I'm seeing it from a Midwestern perspective."

"What?"

"If you measured the telescopic distance of the perimeter of the istobulus . . ."

"Patrick!"

"Okay. The moon is beautiful, and if I could see you, you are too. Where are you sitting? What are you wearing?"

"I'm on the back porch on the glider, wearing jeans and a red tee, with a lap robe over my bare feet."

"Then I'm kissing your toes," Patrick said.

I giggled.

"Want me to move up a little? Ankles? Knees?"

"Uh . . . I think Dad's on his way out here. I heard him pouring some coffee, and he usually brings it out here on the porch," I told him.

"That's okay. He can't see us. I'm kissing your knees now. That tender area just behind the knee—"

"He really *is* coming out here, Patrick! What am I going to say?"

"He can't see *me*."

"But he'll hear . . ." I laughed again as I heard Dad's footsteps cross the kitchen floor, the family room, and then the creak of the doorstep as he entered the porch.

"Now, I'm between your thighs . . . ," said Patrick.

"Oh! I didn't know you were out here," said Dad, sitting down in the wicker chair in one corner. Then, seeing my cell phone, he said, "Don't let me interrupt," and pointed to his iPod and earbuds. He leaned back with a satisfying sigh and lifted the cup to his lips, listening to the music and smiling up at the moon.

"Go on," I whispered to Patrick.

11

LETTING OFF STEAM

We were beginning to get responses to Phil's editorial. Most had been stuck in the newspaper's box at the office:

> I think those things you mentioned happening were just jokes. Lighten up. I wouldn't know a Nazi if I saw one.
>
> —Mark Hurley, junior

> It's really disturbing to me that this happened at our school. I want Daniel Bul Dau to know how glad I am to have him here.
>
> —Gretchen Squire, freshman

> The only thing I can say for Bob White is that he's honest. God help us.
>
> —Craig Robinski, senior

But another letter was slipped under the door of the newsroom three days later:

> What people don't realize is that this country is becoming a third world ghetto. We have a special club for homos. We make a black feel like a king just because he's from Africa; and the clerks in half the stores around school speak only Spanish. Pretty soon the whole United States will be a nation of mongrels. Don't say you weren't warned.
>
> —Bob White, senior

"Oh . . . my . . . God!" said one of our junior reporters, one hand over her mouth.

"He's baaaaack!" said Phil.

"Who the heck *is* he?" said Sam. "It's driving me nuts!"

Phil looked over at me. "What do you think we should do with *this*?"

"Print it," I said. "I don't think too many people took the first one seriously."

We looked at Miss Ames. She nodded. "Print it—just like it's written. But we're going to add an editorial note that says from now on, every letter has to be signed by a registered student. I'm hoping that sooner or later we'll smoke him out."

"But can you *believe* this?" said one of our sophomore reporters.

"I'd love to know this guy's story," Tim mused.

"Or not," said Sam.

I hated to have "Bob White's" comments resting uneasily on everyone's minds, though. If he found other kids who felt the same way he did—and he undoubtedly could—wouldn't this just encourage him?

Fortunately for us, Daniel handed me his feature article on life in Sudan the very next day. It fit in so perfectly with Phil's editorial of the week before that we redid the layout and cropped a couple photos to get it in:

> *Salaam 'alaykum.* I am writing Sudanese way of saying hello—"peace be upon you." Thank you for invitation to tell you about my life as Sudanese national.
>
> I am from Sudan with my mother and older brother. Geri is student at George Washington's University, and we are having much gratitude to be in your country and give thanks to university for bringing my brother here to study. Also thanks to church for bringing my mother and myself, for how long, we are not sure. Here our mother helps cook in a restaurant her special Sudanese foods.
>
> Things are very bad in my country right

now. We have many tribes and many conflicts. There used to be music and dancing, but now in the place where we lived, women cannot dance with men even at weddings, and only religious music can be played for us on the radio. Many people have been killed, and when our village was burned, we ran all day and all night to get away.

Geri studies to be a lawyer so he can go back to Africa and change the government and help the people. I will study hard too, but it will not be easy to leave the United States of America if we are sent back. It is clean here and smells good, but I was a little much afraid before we came.

"You will get lost there," my friends said. "Don't get lost in America." I am careful not to lose myself. In refugee camp where we lived before we came, there was a school and I learned English. I can read your books and your street signs. In the U.S. of America there are so many streets that they are given letters and numbers. There is a First Street and a Fourteenth Street. There is an M and an R Street. Whoever saw so many streets?

You will understand that I had never been on an airplane. It crosses the ocean, and then it crosses the Potomac River. I ask my brother if there are crocodiles in the Potomac River. He doesn't know. The man beside him laughs. "No crocodiles," he says.

When I go back to Africa, I will tell my friends about the streets with numbers. About air-conditioning and machines that wash your clothes for you and microwave ovens that cook without fire. They will not believe me. And they will laugh when I tell them that in America, when it is warm, people seem to move about the streets in their underwear.

I will be glad to see my friends again if we go back to refugee camp. I miss hearing them laugh. I miss our games. But my brother does not think of these things. He loves America. He loves the rule of law, the elections, the jury system, and the hospitals with their clean floors.

Perhaps I will learn to love the U.S. of America as much as Geri does. Already I am liking the football here and the milk shakes and the chicken tenders that do not look like chickens. And I like that my mother sings.

—Daniel Bul Dau, senior

With all the budget cuts that had happened during the year, food banks and area shelters were really hurting. So at Halloween our school, along with the teen center and some of the neighborhood churches, announced that high school students would be trick-or-treating for donations—canned food or monetary donations—in place of candy. We had to register first, of course, and get an official collection can, but we loved any excuse to put on crazy outfits.

Four of us decided to dress up as food product emblems, which took a lot more time and glue than we'd imagined. Gwen had found a peanut costume at a secondhand store and, with a top hat, became Planters' Mr. Peanut. Pamela turned herself into the Jolly Green Giant. Liz was either Betty Crocker or Sara Lee, she couldn't decide which. And I dressed up like the Quaker Oats man—with a broad-brimmed black hat, a ruffled shirt under my chin, and holding a Quaker Oats box with the contribution can inside it.

"*Look* at you!" I squealed as Pamela arrived with green tinted skin and a sort of leaf-stitched tunic around her. It was Gwen who was funniest, though—the top half of her encased in a papier-mâché peanut shell, arms sticking out holes in the sides, and her legs in beige-colored tights. We had a great time going house to house, trolling for contributions, bringing whole families to the door to admire us.

It had been warm during the afternoon but grew colder after the sun went down. We'd got a late start, and though we often collided with groups of little kids at the start of the evening, we'd forgotten that porch lights usually went off around nine, signaling that the owners were shutting down.

We kept at it for another half hour and were about to head back to my place, where Gwen had parked, when Keeno drove up with a friend from St. John's.

"I don't believe this!" he called when he recognized Liz. "I thought it was a party you were going to. You're doing all this for *candy*?"

Liz and I raised our containers and rattled the money.

"Oh, man," said his friend. "Streetwalkers!" We laughed.

Keeno introduced us to the heavyset guy in the red St. John's sweatshirt. "Louie Withers," he said. "Soccer player."

We stood under a streetlight talking, and the guys tried to guess our costumes. They got Mr. Peanut, the Quaker Oats guy, and the Jolly Green Giant, but they had a little trouble with Elizabeth's outfit.

"Little Miss Muffet?" Keeno guessed.

"Bo Peep?" asked Louie.

"You flunk," said Liz. "No brownies for you."

We said we'd tell them if they would drive us to the Italian sandwich shop on University Boulevard, so that's where we ended up.

"So who *are* you?" Louie asked Liz when we got to the shop.

"Betty Crocker," she told them as we squeezed into the largest booth and Gwen removed her peanut top, revealing a T-shirt beneath.

"Huh? The woman who sewed the flag?" asked Louie, and we shrieked.

"That was Betsy Ross, moron," said Keeno. "Jeez, turn your sweatshirt inside out, will you? The headmaster would have a heart attack."

It turned out that the guys had been supervising a neighborhood Halloween party where Keeno had played his guitar with a funky band. We were all pretty ravenous and ate the freshly-made calzones, washed down with Sprite and Pepsi.

"I'm sweltering," I said, removing the black velvet jacket I'd borrowed from Sylvia.

"I'm freezing," said Pamela, her green shoulders bare. "Let me wear that."

"Not if you get green color on it," I warned. "It's Sylvia's."

"I know where you could get cool and Pamela could get warm, and it's free," said Keeno.

"Don't listen to any of his ideas," I warned the others. "Remember Tombstone Tag?"

"Cemetery Tag," Liz corrected.

"What the heck is that?" asked Louie.

"A way to get the cops on you," said Pamela.

"No, I'm serious. This'll be fun," said Keeno.

What's that old adage? *Fool me once, shame on you; fool me twice . . .*

Like lemmings, we got up, paid our bill, and followed Keeno out to his car. It was already after eleven, but we were up for anything.

"How far is it? Another state?" asked Liz.

"Nope," said Keeno. "Couple more blocks, in fact. The only thing you have to remember is that nobody talks or laughs out loud."

"Uh-oh," said Gwen.

The car slowed. Keeno turned onto a side street and parked next to an alley. "Keeno . . . ," I said, giggling.

"We're not hurting anything," he assured us, getting out. "Trust me."

"Right," said Pamela. "Where have we heard that before?"

Still, we followed him into the alley, sticking close to the high fence that separated the backyard from the garbage cans, our bodies bent at the waist like cops closing in on a suspect.

When we came to the first driveway, Keeno stopped. "Now you don't have to take your clothes off unless you want to—"

"*What?*" said Gwen.

"Shhhh," Keeno cautioned. "I've been here before. Just remember to whisper."

Despite our better judgment, we moved up the driveway, setting each foot down carefully. A thin veil of clouds moved across the moon, making it difficult, but not impossible, to see in the darkness. Straight ahead, on the back of the house, we could just make out a sign reading GUEST PARKING ONLY.

"Keeno, what *is* this?" I whispered, grabbing his arm.

And then I saw the second sign: PINEVIEW BED-AND-BREAKFAST.

"Omigod!" Liz whispered.

"I'm freezing!" Pamela whimpered.

The breeze had picked up. In a half hour or so it would be November, and I had mailed the first part of my application to the U of Maryland that morning. Maybe I deserved a little celebrating.

One finger to his lips, Keeno led us across the yard and into the shelter of a couple trees—evergreens, of course—and pointed to something attached to the back porch. A hot tub.

"Oh, no!" I heard Gwen whisper.

"You've got to be kidding," said Liz.

"What's wrong?" he whispered back. "It's wonderful! You should try it."

"You're out of your mind," said Gwen. "How do you know it's hot? How do you even know there's water in it?"

"Because they keep it hot year-round. It's in their advertisement," Keeno said. "Trust me. I've used it in the middle of February."

"They'll catch us!" said Liz.

"Not if we're quiet, they won't. Look." He pointed up to the dark windows. "No guests. The parking lot's empty and the lights are off."

"So who goes first?" asked Pamela, hugging herself.

"We'll go," said Keeno. "Just don't take long and don't make a sound."

We pretended not to look as the guys took off their shoes and slipped out of their jeans and jackets. But we stared wide-eyed, hands over our mouths to suppress the laughter, as we watched two naked bottoms go streaking across the short stretch of lawn to the porch steps, ascend in the darkness, then disappear at the other end.

"I can't believe we're doing this," said Liz. "Can't we undress on the porch?"

"With the guys watching us from the water?" said Pamela. "C'mon. Strip. My arms are like ice." She slipped out of her Jolly Green Giant costume, and the rest of us started undressing. Leaving our clothes in a little heap under the trees, we carefully made our way across the yard in our bare feet, then hurried silently up the steps, and across the darkened porch. One at a time, with the guys offering outstretched hands to help us down, we slid into the hot water and sank down to chin level, savoring the warmth. There we were, six floating heads in the darkness, with just enough moonlight to make out each other's faces.

"Keeno, this is your best idea yet!" I whispered as my toes touched someone in the middle of the large tub.

"I wish we could turn the motor on," Pamela whispered.

"Yeah, but they'd hear it, and the controls are inside," said Keeno.

The water was so deep that I was only half sitting. My bottom kept lifting off the seat and my legs floated effortlessly, tangled up now and then with other legs, our heads resting on the indentations around the rim, knees touching, side to side."We could do a water ballet," Liz whispered.

"What would we call ourselves? The Naked Six?" asked Louie.

We muffled our laughter and watched the clouds pass over the face of the moon. It was a little weird being in a hot tub without the hum of the motor, the swish of the water, the force of the jets. Like being in a bathroom together with no background music.

"Down!" Keeno hissed suddenly as a car turned into the alley, its headlights sweeping the back of the house and moving rapidly toward us. Instantly, all six of us submerged and rose up only when we ran out of air. The car had moved on and turned in someone else's driveway farther on. We wiped the water from our eyes and settled back again.

"Whose knee keeps poking mine from across the tub?" asked Pamela. "Keeno's, I'll bet. I swear, guys' knees are like ice picks. All angles and points."

"And girls' knees," said Keeno, one hand on Liz's knee, "are like soft, velvety, uh . . ." His hand was obviously kneading her flesh and moving slightly up the thigh. Liz laughed and pushed his hand away, and we unanimously cautioned her to be quiet.

We played footsies under the water and took turns being It—another of Keeno's ideas, obviously. With all of our feet together on the bottom, the "it" person would choose one foot in particular and, by examining it with his own two feet, try to guess whose foot it was.

I was It. I chose a foot and clasped it between my own. It could have been either a large girl's or a small guy's foot. High arch, I could tell that much.

"Somebody needs to cut his toenails," I whispered, and soft giggles traveled around the group. I pushed the foot up on its heel and ran the big toe of my other foot along its bottom. The foot immediately twitched and pulled back. "Ah! Ticklish, are we?" I whispered, and tickled some more. I saw Liz give her leg a jerk and immediately chose her. We laughed.

"Hey, hey! Keep it down!" Keeno whispered. "Shhhh." We submerged again up to our lips, looking in all directions, but no lights came on, no door opened on the porch.

"What time is it?" Pamela wanted to know.

"I don't know. Left my watch in my jeans," said Louie.

"What's this?" asked Gwen. She held up a flip-flop. "Did somebody wear flip-flops in here?"

"I did," said Pamela. "I forgot to take them off."

"Maybe we'd better head out pretty soon," whispered Keeno. "I don't want to press our luck."

"Where's my other flip-flop?" asked Pamela.

"Find it before we leave, or we're toast," said Louie.

We all felt around to see if it was caught behind us or floating under our legs. My hand touched something, but it sure wasn't a flip-flop, and Louie looked at me in surprise. "Sorry," I said, and felt heat rising in my face.

Pamela found the flip-flop on the bench behind her, and we agreed to get going.

Keeno rose up and looked all around. When there were no stirrings from indoors that we could see, no lights coming on or off, he whispered to Louie, "Let's go." They got out, backsides showing up white in the darkness, quickly climbing the steps out of the tub and onto the porch, then down the stairs on the other side, where they darted across the lawn and into the shelter of the trees.

"Omigod, you know what I grabbed?" I told the others as soon as the guys were gone. "I was looking for Pamela's flip-flop and took hold of Louie's . . ." We covered our mouths and submerged for a second to stifle our laughter.

"This was wild!" said Liz. "Leave it to Keeno."

"We've gotta go," said Pamela. "It's going to feel like forty when we get out."

"Gotta do it," said Gwen. "No squealing. Ready? One . . . two . . . three."

One by one we followed her up the steps to the porch, our feet making contact with the wood planks. It occurred to us only then that there were no fluffy towels waiting to envelop us, no towels at all. And at that exact moment, another car came toward us on the side street and slowed at the entrance to the alley.

We stopped dead still. Gwen put out her arms to keep us from going any farther as the car turned and its headlights moved across the back of the house. We might as well have been onstage because the spotlight shone on each one of us in turn.

Worse yet, the minute the headlights had reached the last cowering girl, the car suddenly braked, then started backing up. With little shrieks, we went racing down the steps. The headlights swept over the back porch again, but this time we were gone. Finally the car went on down the alley and pulled in somewhere else.

I don't know whose jeans I yanked on there in the cluster of trees. The guys kept handing us pieces of clothing, and we pulled them on as fast as we could. Gwen had worn tights under her peanut costume, but her legs were too wet to pull them on. She pulled on her underwear and a guy's sweater, and as soon as we could, we were running down the alley to Keeno's car.

"My jacket!" I cried. "Has anybody got my jacket?"

"Hurry up!" Louie was saying, holding the car door open.

No one had the jacket.

"I've got to go back!" I said. "It's Sylvia's!"

"Cripes, Alice!" said Keeno.

I was only half dressed—my jeans and bra. Somebody else had my shirt. I raced back up the driveway and into the cluster of trees, my eyes searching for a heap of black velvet.

My heart was pounding as I moved around the base of the trees, around the parking lot, scanning the ground. I exhaled in relief when I found the jacket against the trunk of a tree, and I swooped it up and ran back across the parking lot.

"Hey!" came a man's voice, and suddenly the porch light came on. Not only the porch light, but a floodlight illuminating the whole guest parking area.

"Hey!" the man yelled again. "You're trespassing, you know. Who the hell are you?"

"I'm sorry," I called timidly over my shoulder, but I didn't stop.

Liz was waiting for me in the alley. She grabbed my arm, and we ran as though dogs were after us. Keeno had the engine running when we reached the car, and we tumbled inside, shrieking.

I expected to hear footsteps coming after us. The wail of sirens, even.

But Keeno turned at the next corner, then again at the light, and we screeched and laughed as we melted into the traffic and cruised innocently along the street. Our hair was dripping water all over the place, and we used someone's fleece jacket to dry our heads, passing it from one to the other.

"Omigod, my heart's still thumping," I said, panting. "I was sure the owner would catch me."

"I'll bet the neighbors called him," said Louie. "Bet that last driver in the alley told him that some kids were goofing around in his hot tub."

"Relax, already!" said Keeno. "We didn't hurt anything."

"Yeah, but we can't go back there again. He's onto us," said Louie.

"Funny you never invited *us* here before," said Liz.

"Never knew you wanted to get naked before," said Keeno, and we all broke into laughter.

"Man, though, he almost nailed you," Louie said, turning around and looking at me.

"Yeah, he could have had a camera and taken your picture for evidence," said Keeno. "There it would be on the Metro page of the *Post*: 'Senior Arrested for Trespassing'!"

"Well, the *Gazette*, maybe," said Gwen.

"How about 'Features Editor of High School Newspaper Caught Nude'?" said Pamela.

"No, I've got it," said Liz. "'Member of Student Jury to Be Tried by Her Peers.' How's that for the next headline in *The Edge*?"

Nothing could ruin this evening, though. A perfect way to start November.

12

INCIDENT NUMBER THREE

The same day *The Edge* published "Bob White's" mongrelization comment and Daniel's essay, the local news reported four separate incidents of tire slashing in Latino neighborhoods, and on all the rims, the letters *HH* had been chalked. None of the incidents took place near our school, but on Friday, Mr. Beck's voice came over the sound system:

"Good morning, students. It's not customary for me to intrude on your news and announcements, but I have something important to say. Yesterday there were several instances of tire slashing in our community, and most of you are aware of a couple of hate-inspired incidents in our school as well. Two recent comments in *The Edge*, by a student using a pseudonym, serve as another example of the kind of prejudice that provokes vandalism or worse. I was glad to read that in the future no letters will be published unless the author can be identified.

"I am not suggesting that anyone in this school is responsible for the tire slashing. And I know by your letters to *The Edge* that most of you do not hold similar views as those of the anonymous student.

"We are proud of our ethnic diversity. The fact that there are at least thirty-one different countries represented in our school provides us with a cultural richness that enhances your education, not diminishes it. This school will always stand for the free expression of ideas and concerns, but we will not tolerate bullying, vandalism, violence, or racial slurs.

"To students of every race, nationality, religion, or sexual orientation, we promise that we will do our utmost to protect you and your rights in this country. To those who would like to express a difference of opinion, no matter how unpopular it may be, we invite you to engage in respectful dialogue. We do not prosecute students just because they might have different views on politics or social issues. But we do expect responsible behavior of high school students. Demand this of yourselves and of your friends, and make this school proud."

We noticed that another security guard was added to the two regulars, and Mr. Gephardt was very visible as he talked with students one-on-one in the hallways.

Earlier in the week Miss Ames had asked me to check out the Student Safety Council to see if we could get any leads on who else might be feeling intimidated here at school. Maybe do a write-up of how the council got started. Were students worried about what had happened at Columbine and Virginia Tech? Were they being harassed out in the parking lot or on the buses? Surely this wasn't just a look-both-ways-before-crossing-the-street kind of club. So I'd checked the activities calendar and saw that the SSC met on Fridays at 3:15 in G-108. That was forty-five minutes after classes were officially over.

That very day after school I did a little reading, listening to the hustle and shouts outside growing dimmer and dimmer as the buses rolled away. Gradually the parking lot emptied too, until finally there were only occasional footsteps in the hall, the close of a book, or the scooting of a chair to interrupt the quiet. At 3:05, I put my stuff in my bag, took out a small notebook, and headed down the main hall to the stairs.

There was band practice at the far end of the building. I could barely hear it as I descended the stairs, and by the time I reached the ground level, it had faded entirely.

I checked the number of one of the classrooms. Wrong hallway. Taking the first cross corridor, I passed the furnace room, the boiler, the custodian's office, then listened for conversation as I reached the second hallway. The science labs and photo studio, with their chemical smells, sat side by side along this corridor. Mine were the only footsteps on the tiled floor.

I found G-108, and it was empty. I went inside and turned on the light. I was still five minutes early. From all appearances, it seemed to be a freshman earth science room. A bulletin board had photos of a recent volcanic eruption in various stages, and a plastic model of the earth's layers sat on a side table.

I sat down in a chair near the back and surveyed a large maple tree outside the window. It had shed half its leaves, and with each gust of wind, a few more peach-colored leaves let go and swirled, forsaken, to the ground.

When another five minutes had gone by and no one came, I wondered if they had been scared off. It occurred to me that I hadn't seen Curtis Butler at our last GSA meeting either. Who else besides Daniel had gotten a warning logo? Who else might have had their cars vandalized and were afraid to report it?

Down the hall, the huge furnace cut on and off with clicks and swooshes. The hallway outside the room suddenly grew darker as the after-hours lighting went into effect. Outside, the sun emerged from behind some clouds, then receded. The wind blew, then calmed, then gusted again, as though the weather couldn't commit. The room seemed colder.

"You waiting for somebody?"

I jumped as a figure appeared in the doorway. One of the custodians poked his head inside.

"I thought the Student Safety Council was meeting today," I told him.

"Don't look like nobody's coming. I got to do this floor," he said.

"Come on in, I'm leaving," I said. "Maybe I've got the time mixed up."

He waited, swish broom ready, as I gathered my things and headed back to the stairs.

The office was open till four, so I went back and asked one of the administrative assistants,"Safety Council? No one was there."

"That's what I've got," she said, checking her calendar. "Fridays, three fifteen to four fifteen, G-108. Mr. Bloom is faculty adviser."

"Civics teacher?"

"Yes. Gordon Bloom. He was just in here a minute ago. I'll bet he's on the way to his car."

I used the faculty door, and sure enough, he was about twenty feet ahead of me, unlocking his station wagon.

"Mr. Bloom?" I called, and he paused as I ran over. "I'm doing an article for *The Edge* and wanted to mention the Safety Council, but no one was at the meeting."

"Oh, sorry about that," he said. "It's been scratched. I'll tell Betty to take it off the calendar."

"Why? Not enough members or what?" I asked. "Was there some particular problem they were concerned about?"

"To tell the truth, it was hard to put your finger on it," he said, smiling genially. "And I didn't make every meeting." He put his briefcase on the backseat, then rested his arms on the roof of the wagon. "There didn't appear to be any one issue exactly . . . just . . . a general uneasiness, I'd call it. Not a big group . . . five guys and two girls. But it seemed their focus was going to be on martial arts—protecting themselves, I guess—and I had to disband it."

"Why?"

"It was kids teaching kids. We're not insured for that. I told them they'd have to get their training somewhere else by a professional. Maybe talk with a P.E. instructor about starting a class." He smiled again. "Sorry, but I have to pick up a daughter from a dance class. Gotta scoot."

"Thanks," I told him, and headed for Sylvia's car over in student parking.

General unease. Self-protection. Martial arts. What did those students know that the rest of us didn't? *Who* was intimidating them? Could the majority of the student body be so out of touch that we didn't even know what was going on in our own school? Never an idea of what was going on until it happened?

Gwen and Pam and Liz and I took in a movie that night—anything to get away from the grind at school. I found that the easiest way I could use either Dad's or Sylvia's car was to offer to fill the tank and wash the windshield. They let me use their credit cards, of course, but hated the chore of having to stop at a station.

I picked up my friends early so I could get gas on the way. After I'd inserted the credit card in the slot, I was surprised when Liz got out of the car and asked if I could show her how to pump gas. Her dad usually filled their tank himself.

"In case I ever run low and have to do it," she said.

"You want to take over?" I asked, unscrewing the gas cap. She warily studied the hose and nodded.

"Okay," I told her. "After you take back your credit card, follow the instructions on the screen."

Lift handle, it read.

Gingerly, Liz grasped the handle with both hands.

Lift latch.

"Where?" she asked, looking around. I pointed.

She flipped up the latch.

"Now put the nozzle in the opening."

Suddenly gasoline started squirting out the nozzle, all over the pavement.

"It's coming!" Liz shrieked, jumping backward.

"Don't squeeze, Liz!" I yelled. "Stop squeezing!"

Gwen and Pamela piled out of the car, screaming with laughter as Elizabeth dropped the hose on the ground like a hot potato, and the flow stopped.

"You have to wait till you get it in," Gwen hooted as customers turned to look.

"I'm terrified of that thing," Liz said.

"Don't squeeze till you get the nozzle inside," I told her. "Pick it up and push it all the way in, but *don't* squeeze yet!"

Liz bent down and picked up the hose, holding it as far away from her as possible. She moved over to the gas tank and thrust the nozzle down inside.

"Now," I said, "squeeze the handle."

Liz's fingers clamped down hard. "Nothing's happening," she said. I looked up at the pump window. No figures moving across the screen.

"Are you squeezing?" asked Pamela, barely able to get the words out, she was laughing so hard. Liz's anxious concentration made it all the funnier.

"As hard as I can," said Liz.

"Let up and squeeze slowly this time," I said.

"Awk! It's coming! Take it, Alice!" she said.

"What?" I grabbed the nozzle before she could pull it out, and Liz jumped back.

"What's wrong?"

She backed up against the pump. "It's too embarrassing!"

"Embarrassing?" I asked.

"So . . . so *phallic*!" she cried. *"Put it in. Squeeze! Don't squeeze. Squeeze harder! Squeeze slower!"*

We exploded with laughter. When a young attendant came over and asked if he could help, we could only shake our heads and wave him on.

When Gwen finally caught her breath, she said, "Only one thing to do, girl. It comes natural to guys. Get Keeno to show you how."

My AP English teacher was sick for three days, and Dennis Granger filled in for her. There was sort of this unspoken feeling of . . . I don't know. Uneasiness? Excitement, even? Cautiousness? Like I couldn't be entirely comfortable around him. I wasn't the only one either, and he wasn't the first or only teacher who had made me feel this way. It was just that among girls, when we said his name, it was our tone of voice, the accent on *Granger*, that signaled to each other, *Oh,* that *guy! Watch it!*

He was always finding a reason, it seemed, to reach over us or around us. If his arm brushed against my breast, I'd think, *Did I just imagine that because he's so handsome?* If I thought his hand grazed my butt as I passed his desk and I turned to look, his attention was somewhere else, and I'd think, *That didn't happen.*

Yet it was the kind of thing you didn't talk about seriously with your friends for fear they'd say, or think, *You wish!* We didn't cluster around him, though, like we did with some of our favorite teachers. We each made sure we weren't the last girl out of the classroom. And what could we report, even? *He might have brushed my breast*? *He possibly touched my butt*? *He was undressing me with his eyes, I think*? Right.

It was a day after gym class that I got the vibes. We'd played a hard game of volleyball, and there was a line at the water cooler before we went to the showers. I decided to wait. But later, as I left the gym, I realized I still hadn't had a drink, so I headed to the fountain in the west corridor. Someone was ahead of me, and I waited until she was through, then eagerly bent over the machine, filling my mouth with the ice-cold stream, then swallowing it down, filling up again, my throat welcoming gulp after gulp.

I felt someone waiting behind me, and then I felt something else. Pressure, hardness, just for a moment. And when I straightened up and turned, Dennis Granger smiled and said, "Excuse me," and leaned over the fountain as I quickly moved aside.

That was no accident, I told myself as I walked on to my next class. I felt I was blushing, but there was no one to see. He didn't follow, didn't call out to me, but just knowing that I turned him on, that he . . . what? . . . must have found me attractive, made me feel . . . confused. Ashamed, sort of, I don't know why. Even excited. I hugged myself and felt a shiver. *The three Cs*, I told myself. *When you're not Comfortable with it, it's not a Compliment, it's Creepy*. Yet how do you walk into the office and say, *I want to report a teacher who stood too close to me at the fountain*? You don't. I didn't, anyway.

Just stay five feet away from him at all times, I thought, and was glad my English teacher was coming back the following day.

Christmas comes practically the day after Halloween—for merchants, anyway. As soon as the witches and black cats come down, the angels and Santas move in, and Thanksgiving gets lost in the middle. Step in any store the first of November and you'll be surrounded by twinkly lights and "I wonder as I wander . . ." over the sound system.

We're always late making the switchover at the Melody Inn. Because we have so many schoolkids trooping in for music lessons in the upstairs soundproof booths, we do Halloween up big, with fake cobwebs over the grand piano, black cats with arched backs protecting the sale table, and a life-size witch doll sitting on a stool by the front door.

In years past Dad declared that November should be dedicated to Thanksgiving. But this year, with sales down and stores closing on Georgia Avenue, we went right to Christmas. I spent one Sunday morning arranging a Christmas window display while Dad and Marilyn, in coats and scarves, stood out on the sidewalk and indicated whether I was to move the Christmas tree to the right or left and where to put the puppy.

It had taken three men to roll the piano up a ramp and into the display window. The scene we were trying to create—one of several that came from corporate headquarters—was of a happy family opening gifts from the Melody Inn on Christmas morning. The mom mannequin we'd rented was seated on the piano bench, wrapped in a blue silk shawl on which a score from the "Moonlight" Sonata was reproduced. The dad wore a sweatshirt with a profile of Beethoven on the front.

My job was to maneuver myself around this display in my stocking feet, trying to fit a teenage mannequin in place, holding a music box with a dancing fox on her lap, surrounded by more Melody Inn gift boxes, as well as a baby, sucking on a pacifier, crawling about in his little Santa Claus pj's. There wasn't a lot of space, and it seemed that every time I'd get one thing right, it accidentally threw something else off balance. The baby pajamas that came with the rented set were a size too small, however, and I struggled to make them fit. But Marilyn's nose was pink with cold and her coat wouldn't button all the way over her growing belly, so Dad sent her back inside and finally, when I was down to the small details, he came back in too.

We're usually closed on Sundays, but for the Christmas season we were now open from eleven to five, and I hurried to get things set up for my regular stint in the Gift Shoppe. When I returned to the main showroom at last, Dad turned on the twinkly lights that rimmed the display window and put in a CD of madrigal music.

"Hope it sells loads of pianos, Mr. M.," Marilyn said.

Kay came in a few minutes later, and when Dad unlocked the door at eleven, there were already four people waiting.

We were busy from the get-go. A father came in to buy a guitar for his son; someone wanted to mail an accordion to Kansas. I was gift wrapping a coffee mug for a customer when

Kay noticed some people standing outside the window laughing. More people stopped. They laughed too.

"Now what?" said Dad. "Al, check the display window, would you?"

I walked to the front of the store and saw nothing unusual so I went outside. The tightly stretched pajama bottom of the baby had slipped down his plaster body, and there he was, mooning the shoppers out on their holiday errands.

Things were getting more complicated at home. My decision to go to the University of Maryland so I could be here for Dad and Sylvia was being severely tested. Sylvia, in fact, had good news. She had just received the results of her biopsy of the week before and the test was negative, she announced to Dad and me when we got home on Monday. Her smile was one hundred percent genuine. On Sylvia, you can tell.

Dad gave her a bear hug and rocked her back and forth. "*Wonderful* news, sweetheart," he said into her ear.

"The radiologist wants me back in six months for a sonogram, just to check, but she said everything looks perfectly normal."

"Dinner out?" I said hopefully.

"I don't know why not!" said Sylvia, and out we went.

Well then, maybe I should *apply to the other colleges*, I thought. I needed a "safe" school, and that would be Maryland. Once again the thought of a whole new place, a new roommate, difficult courses, and possibly unsupportive professors—all happening to me at the same time—brought back some of that panicky feeling. But I thought of myself at William and Mary, walking to class with someone like Judith, walking on a brick sidewalk thinking of Jefferson and eating Moroccan chicken in the caf. I could do that.

So when we got back, I fished two more applications from the heap and began.

13

CALL TO AUNT SALLY

November is one of the dreariest months. It hits you on the day you realize that all the leaves have fallen and everything is gray—the trees, the sky, the ground. Even people look gray. Which is why the seventh-period assembly the following week was so much fun.

There's an organization that sponsors amateur actors—teens and college age—who emphasize responsible sexual behavior. They put on awareness-based shows at high schools, focusing on issues like abstinence, birth control, HIV, prenatal development. . . . Each show has a number of skits, and they're just goofy enough to keep our attention.

The skit I liked best had a guy with a long curvy tail playing the part of a sperm, and a girl, sitting in a large cardboard oval, playing the egg. Emphasizing that it takes both to make a baby, the sperm darts carefree about the stage, chanting, "Sperm alone, no baby," while the girl files her nails and chants, "Egg alone, no baby." But when the sperm finds himself drawn into her orb, she wraps them both up in her blanket, and they emerge holding a doll between them.

Then, to show that both are responsible for bringing up this child if they make a baby, they do a frantic pantomime where he's feeding the baby while she's changing its diaper, then he does the diapering and she feeds the baby, at fast speed. A voice announces that condoms are free from Planned Parenthood, and the skit ends with the couple singing a parody of "Don't Worry, Be Happy," renamed "Don't Hurry, Use Condoms." I guess you'd have to be there.

We've had assemblies like this before, and like this one, the actors are kids our own age, and the group's purpose—"to inform, entertain, and educate"—is easy to swallow.

Some of the other skits were about eating disorders, body image, sexual abuse, suicide, rape, teen pregnancy—any personal thing that affects our lives.

Okay, so maybe most of us already knew the facts about this stuff—it wasn't old hat. But Jill, sitting behind me with Justin, got on my nerves.

One of the actresses was stating the reasons she'd decided to be celibate until she married. Jill, in particular, was whispering and giggling, mimicking the girl. The actress wasn't being preachy or anything—just saying that for her, abstinence seemed best. Jill obviously found it hilarious. It was especially annoying because I was trying to take notes so I could write up the program for the newspaper, and I missed some of the lines.

"Hey, Jill, knock it off, would you?" I whispered over my shoulder.

There were a few seconds of silence, then sputtering laughter from Jill.

"Quiet, everybody. Alice is learning something here," she responded in a stage whisper, and got a few, but only a few, titters in response.

Later, when Jill began laughing again, I heard Justin say, "Shhhh," and I wondered, for maybe the hundredth time, what—other than her absolutely gorgeous body—he saw in her.

Amy Sheldon liked the show, though. She must have been sitting near Jill too because afterward she said to me, "I don't know why some people didn't like it. It was just facts. You shouldn't be afraid of facts, my dad says."

"And he's absolutely right," I told her.

"Except sometimes people use facts to fool you," she went on. "Some people call me a retard, and that isn't true. You can be good in some things and slow in other things, and I'm very good at memorizing lists. My mom says I'm the best memorizer she's ever seen. So does my tutor."

"You have a tutor? What subject?"

"Literature. I'm good at memorizing the characters' names and everything, but I don't always understand the story. The theme, I'm not so good with at all. But I like facts."

It was good to see Amy broadening herself, connecting more with other people. And I noticed she wore her *Edge* reporter badge even when she wasn't doing an assignment. *Whatever works*, I thought.

It was also good to see the number of letters coming in for the "Sound Off" section of our paper, and we included the few that responded to "Bob White's" latest comment:

> I'll bet B.W. doesn't even go to our school. I've never heard anyone else talk like that.
>
> —Caroline Eggers, sophomore

> How does he think *he* got to this country? Does he know where *his* ancestors came from? Every one of us came from somewhere else.
>
> —Mary Lorenzo, senior

> I thought Hitler died in 1945. Let's *not* resurrect him here.
>
> —Cindy Morella, senior

> This is America, "Bob White." Get over it.
>
> —Peter Oslinger, senior

Mostly, I think, his letter was ignored. There were dozens of other items to interest the reader. The newspaper staff couldn't ignore him, though. We kept mulling it over at staff meetings.

"Who the heck do you think he is—one of the jocks?" someone wondered.

"Or *she* is. Or *they*!" I said.

"Whoever they are, they evidently scared the Safety Council right out of the school," said Phil.

"Into the martial arts, anyway," I said.

"I'll bet it's one of the Goths," said a sophomore roving reporter. "Nobody wants to take on the Goths."

Amy Sheldon came in just then, flustered because she was late but wanting to fit into the conversation. "Some boys on the bus say bad things," she said.

"Like what?" asked Phil.

"Like calling people names."

"Do you know who they are?" he asked.

Amy shook her head.

"What kinds of things do they say?" asked Sam.

"One of them said, 'What do you get if you mix a retard with a Latrino?' And the answer was 'A clogged toilet.' I don't understand it, but I told it to Dad, and he said it wasn't even funny."

"And stupid besides," I told her.

Miss Ames pulled last year's yearbook from a shelf and turned to the student pictures of each class. She handed the volume to Amy and said, "Do you think if you looked over the photos, you could recognize any of the boys who were talking like that? We can skip the seniors, because they're gone."

"And this year's freshmen aren't even in that yearbook," said Phil.

I knew this would be too hard for Amy. But she dutifully

scanned picture after picture of juniors, sophomores, and freshmen, shaking her head, page after page. "That's okay," Miss Ames said, and closed the book. We were quiet for a while and sat doodling in our notebooks.

"What I hate is the thought that we're just waiting for something else to happen," I said.

"Well, at least we're giving them a place to sound off. We published this faction's letter. Maybe they'll write again, give us some clues. Maybe that will be enough," Miss Ames said. "We're all waiting. The principal is taking this very seriously."

Things were piling up on me. I had a difficult paper to write for my AP English class on how Ernest Hemingway's style relates to the main character's detachment in the novel we just read. I had to go over a catalog at the Melody Inn and help select Christmas items to sell in the Gift Shoppe. I needed to help Sylvia get the house ready for Thanksgiving. I still had not written the feature article I'd promised myself I would do back in September in memory of Mark Stedmeister. And I had to finish Part II of the application to the U of Maryland, not to mention full applications to the University of North Carolina at Chapel Hill and William and Mary. Just the list of stuff I had to enclose for Maryland was nerve-wracking: SAT scores; a 500-word essay; a response to each of the questions on page 11 of the application, each response five to seven sentences long; a résumé listing all of my experiences, interests, and extracurricular activities; a description of one activity most enjoyed by me and why. . . .

I scanned the list of questions: *If you could invent one useful thing for humankind, what would it be? Does multidisciplinary teamwork with a faculty mentor, lasting throughout your undergraduate years and dealing with the social implications of science and technology, appeal to you?* Huh? *How has your life experience and background shaped you into an individual who will enrich the University of Maryland community?*

Usually Dad took a cup of coffee with him into the family room and turned on the news after dinner if it wasn't his night to clean up the kitchen. But lately he'd been doing neither. He'd bring a folder of sales figures home from the store and go over his inventory, salaries, bills, rent. . . . Melody Inn headquarters had announced the closing of three stores on the East Coast. Ours wasn't one of them, but what if there were more?

In the past I would have curled up beside him on the couch and gone over some of the questions on the application—testing my answers out on him, how they might affect my admission. But now, more than ever, I realized I was supposed to be figuring all this out on my own. Even if I chose Maryland and lived at home to save Dad the cost of room and board, I would be expected to do the work myself. What if I gave up my chance to go to another school, another state, only to find that I wouldn't have the reassurance and support I'd wanted here at home?

From my chair at the dining room table, where I was drafting my responses to the application, I watched Sylvia sitting across from Dad, her chin in one hand, brows furrowed.

"It doesn't seem possible," I heard Dad say. "Last year at this time, sales were up thirteen percent."

"Maybe people haven't started Christmas shopping in

earnest," Sylvia said. "Things will probably pick up once Thanksgiving's over."

Dad took off his glasses and rubbed his eyes. "The shoe store down the street went out of business today."

"Lawfords? Really?"

"Yeah."

Sylvia sighed. "That's not good, is it? But the restaurant beside you is doing okay. That's always a draw for customers."

"It'll be tight this year, Sylvia. Really tight."

"I know."

"No trips to New York, I'm afraid. No New England tour in the fall. . . ."

"We can make it, Ben. I can live without a weekend of theater-hopping. And those trees in Vermont will still be there next year and the next."

I returned to my application to U of Maryland.

There were other things to concentrate on, though: Thanksgiving, the Snow Ball, Patrick, Christmas. . . .

Gwen had an idea for the Snow Ball, one of the two formal dances at our school. I could tell by her expression that it was going to be something different.

"Let's all trade dresses."

The four of us had gone to the mall Thursday night to hunt for dresses. Shop after shop, we looked the merchandise over and said, "Blah." Nothing looked that great—great enough to spend a hundred and fifty bucks on, anyway. We were standing outside of Macy's and turned to stare at her.

"You're serious?" I said.

"Yeah. It's crazy to buy new dresses right now, and when are we going to wear formal gowns once we get to college? From then on, it'll be bridesmaid dresses, right? No bride is going to want her attendants in leftover Snow Ball dresses."

"But we're not all the same size!" said Liz.

"Pamela and I are about the same, and so are you and Alice."

Smiles traveled from one of us to the other, and then they turned into grins.

"Let's do it!" said Liz, and we all high-fived each other and began chattering at once—colors, shoes, straps or strapless. . . .

And then I added a P.S. to Gwen's suggestion: We would announce it in advance. In fact, I'd get Sam to take a picture of all four of us and put it on the front page of *The Edge*—the very next issue, if we could get our act together in time. LATEST FASHION: DRESS EXCHANGE, could be the heading, and we'd lead off the story with, *Senior girls start new trend. . . .*

I'm sure we sounded like a bunch of chickens as we rode down the escalator and took over one of the tables by the ice-cream shop.

"Okay," said Liz. "What have we got?"

"Last year I wore that slinky black halter-top," I said.

"I loved that dress!" said Liz. "Oh, I can't wait." Then she hesitated. "I've just got that rose-colored crepe. . . ."

We both winced. Not with my strawberry blond hair, and not crepe.

"What did you wear last to the Jack of Hearts dance, Gwen?" Liz asked.

"The Kelly green number with the tiny black polka dots, remember? I'll bet you could wear it, Alice, because it was little big for me."

"With the wide black sash at the waist?" I asked. "That was cute."

"That's the one," said Gwen. "And *I* want to wear Pamela's salmon satin gown with the spaghetti straps."

"You've got it," said Pamela. "But then what will I wear?"

"Remember that midnight blue dress with the iridescent stripes in the skirt that I wore for the Jack of Hearts dance? Sylvia could alter it for you, I'll bet," I told her.

"I'm up for anything," said Pamela. "Bring on the photographer!"

The following day Les had good news.

"Signed, sealed, and delivered!" he announced when he stopped by for dinner. "My thesis has been accepted, and I graduate December eighteenth, free and clear!"

"Hey, bro!" I said.

"Congratulations, Les!" said Dad, giving him a hug with a couple of back pats thrown in. "What a relief, huh?"

"You're telling me! Had my first good sleep in months."

"Can I help send out the invitations?" asked Sylvia.

"Oh, wow. Invitations! Hadn't even thought about it. Sure!" said Les. "I might even get around to polishing a pair of shoes for the occasion."

Dad said we owed it to Aunt Sally and Uncle Milt to call them, so we sat around the dining room table after we'd enjoyed

Sylvia's impromptu dinner of shrimp scampi and a frozen Sara Lee cake, and made the call.

We all knew the routine and were smiling even before the conversation began: Uncle Milt usually answered the phone. We could fill in his part of the conversation just by listening to Les:

"Hi, Milt. How are things? . . . Well, that's why I'm calling. Wanted you and Aunt Sally to be the first to know that my thesis has been accepted and I'm cleared for takeoff." Les was grinning. "Me too. . . . Yeah, it's been a long road, that's for sure. . . . Roger that. . . . Uh-huh. Seems like I've been in school forever. . . ."

At some point, we knew, the phone would be handed over to Aunt Sally.

"Sure," Les was saying, "put her on. . . . Hi, Sal! Yes. . . . Yes. . . . Well, thank you. I appreciate it. . . . Yeah, I wish Mom were here too. . . . I understand. . . . Of course. . . ."

They were so proud. . . . Mom would be so proud of him. . . . They might not be able to make the ceremony. . . .

And then Les said, "Certainly! I'll put her on," and handed the phone to me. "Aunt Sally wants a word with Alice," he said, sotto voce to Dad and Sylvia, his eyes filled with amusement.

Me? I mouthed, shaking my head. When Aunt Sally, bless her bones, wants to talk to me, it's always an admonition of some kind. It fell to her to help raise us after Mom died, and she's still trying to do her best.

I rolled my eyes and took the phone while the others smiled and settled back, picking at the last crumbs of chocolate cake.

"Hi, Aunt Sally," I said. "It's wonderful news, isn't it?"

"It certainly is" came my aunt's voice, and either my hearing is so acute or her voice is so loud that I always have to hold the phone an inch away from my ear. "With everything going on in the world, it's nice to know that somebody's got it right. Oh, Alice, Marie would be so thrilled. Whoever thought that *Lester* . . . ?" She paused, and I saw Lester's eyes open wide in amusement.

"You never thought he'd make it?" I asked, making a face at Les.

"I just . . . wasn't sure. He always seemed to march to a different drummer, that boy! That band he had once? You know, the Naked Savages—"

"Nomads," I said. "Naked Nomads."

"And all those girlfriends?"

Sylvia had her head on her arms, and her shoulders were shaking with laughter. I had to struggle to keep from laughing too.

"Well, I just don't know," Aunt Sally went on. "But I remember saying to Milt somewhere along the line, 'It's a good thing they left Chicago when they did and moved to Maryland, because if they'd stayed here, Lester might have ended up in that mansion with all those rabbits.'"

Dad and Lester stared at each other, and then they broke out in silent laughter, but I didn't know what they were talking about.

"Rabbits?"

Aunt Sally cleared her throat. "You know . . . that Hefner man . . . and his little playmates."

I looked helplessly at Dad and Lester.

"Hugh Hefner and his Playboy bunnies," Dad whispered. "The Playboy Mansion."

"Oh!" I said to Aunt Sally. "Hugh Hefner and the Playboy Mansion. Why, Aunt Sally, if I'd known it was in Chicago, I'd have toured it while I was there for Carol's wedding."

Aunt Sally gasped.

"Joke! Joke!" I said, trying to remember that we were sharing good news here.

"But this is what I wanted to say to you, Alice," Aunt Sally continued, lowering her voice, conscious, perhaps, that the others could hear. "The newspapers are full of stories about young men who get to the pinnacle of their success and suddenly they self-destruct."

"They do?" I said.

"They do! You read about it all the time. A football player dies of an overdose; a politician gets drunk and kills someone with his car; a movie star leaves his wife and children. . . ."

"I don't know, Aunt Sally," I said. "Les isn't married, he's not running for office, and he doesn't play football."

The family stared at me, then covered their mouths and laughed some more.

"I just want you to keep an eye on him for me," Aunt Sally said. "With the economy the way it is and people losing their jobs, I didn't want to worry Ben or Sylvia, but do give Lester special attention right now, will you? Make sure he eats well and gets plenty of sleep and doesn't get so full of himself that he thinks he's above the law."

"I'll watch him every spare minute I get," I told her. "He just wanted you to know the good news. Pass it along to Carol and Larry for us. How are things with them?"

"Well, they haven't given me a grandchild yet."

"They just got married in July!" I spluttered.

This time Aunt Sally laughed at her own joke. "Of course. And they're happy."

We were too when the conversation ended at last.

"Okay, spill it," said Les when I'd hung up and we erupted in laughter. "What's she worried about now?"

"That you'll self-destruct," I told him. "You'll drive too fast, eat too much, sleep too little, and end up in the Playboy Mansion with all those bunnies."

Dad was laughing so hard, he had to pull out his handkerchief and wipe his eyes. "What would we ever do without old Sal?" he said. "Every family should have one, I guess, but ours is the genuine article."

14
RELATIONSHIPS

Big news flash. For our crowd, anyway. Something gossipy and trite in the general scheme of things, but a fact we could chew on awhile to forget the Nazi stuff at school and all the anxiety over college: Jill and Justin broke up.

Pamela and I were trying to figure out just how long they'd been a couple.

"I know they started going out the summer before tenth grade," Pamela said, passing around the bag of Fritos Gwen had brought. Pam had invited the three of us to sleep over on Saturday. Mr. Jones and Meredith, his fiancée, had gone to a movie.

"I think it might even have been before then. By that summer they were sleeping with each other," Liz said, and added comically, "I was shocked, I tell you! *Shocked!*"

We laughed.

"They probably had one of the longest relationships of any couple in school," said Gwen. "I'll give them that. But Justin—I think he deserves better than Jill, if you want my opinion."

"I think he deserves just what he got," I put in, remembering that he used to like Liz, and I'd hoped maybe those two would click. "Still, guys don't think a whole lot about relationships when they're freshmen. Sophomores, even."

"And who really knows what goes on between two people?" said Gwen.

"We do," said Pamela, grinning. "Jill loved to tell us every little detail. She'd tell you exactly what went on between the sheets if you asked her. And the answer was 'Plenty.'"

"So which of them called it off?" asked Liz.

"Jill," said Pamela. "I got it straight from Karen, and if Karen doesn't know, nobody does. Jill's furious at the way the Colliers have tried to break them up. She and Justin's mom in particular hate each other, and I guess she gave Justin an ultimatum: Stand up to your mom or else."

We groaned.

"Ohhh, bad call!" I said. "What did she expect him to do? Pack up his bags and say, 'Well, Mom, I'm outta here?' Is Jill nuts? Where would he go? Who foots the bill for college next year?"

"Jill's used to getting her way, that's all," said Pamela. "But his parents think she's after their money."

"And isn't she?" asked Liz.

"I don't know. But I think that when a couple's been together as long as they have, there's got to be a little something more," Pamela answered. "Jill's gorgeous—you've got to hand her that. There are a dozen guys who would love to go out with her."

We ambled out to the kitchen to see what Meredith had left for our dinner, and Pamela slung plates onto the table like she was dealing cards.

"How did the Colliers get so rich?" I asked. "I thought his dad was in the navy. You don't get rich in the navy."

"Was," said Pamela. "Career officer, but he retired and became a partner in his dad's real estate firm. You know, Collier and Sons? You see their signs everywhere. It was his grandfather, I think, who really had the dough."

"So how is Justin taking the breakup?" asked Gwen.

"Awful, according to Karen. Keeps calling Jill's number and she won't answer."

"Time for Mommy and Daddy to whisk him off to the Bahamas again," I said. "Remember how they did that on spring break last year, just to get him away from Jill, and Justin sent her money for a plane ticket and put her up in the hotel next door?"

We all whooped at the memory as we waited for the meat loaf and potatoes to heat up in the microwave. Gwen passed the silverware around.

"Speaking of couples," said Liz, "when are your dad and Meredith going to tie the knot, Pam?"

"Who knows?" said Pamela.

I wondered if I could ask the question the rest of us were

thinking. "Is it possible he's still . . . well . . . that your mom's still on his radar?"

"Veto that," said Pamela. "She's dating someone from Nordstrom, and they're hitting it off. A nice man, let me add—a manager from another store. No, my guess is that Dad and Meredith are waiting for me to graduate and go off to school somewhere so they can start married life in the house all to themselves. I can't blame them for that."

Sitting across from her, I slowly sipped my glass of iced tea, wondering if Dad and Sylvia have been waiting for *me* to clear out so that at last *they* can have the place to themselves.

At school even Daniel had heard about the "breakup of the year."

"How do you do a breakup?" he asked me as we sat in the library during lunch when I'd volunteered to help him with an assignment.

"It's not anything formal," I explained. "Either the girl or the guy tells the other it's over."

"Nothing is broken? Smashed?"

"No. There's no ritual. It just means the relationship is through. That they can each start going out with other people."

Daniel leaned back in his chair, deep in thought, skinny arms folded over his chest, chin tucked down. "That is hard to do in America for my brother. He would like some day to find a bride, but your ways and the Dinka ways are different."

"Your culture? What would be the Dinka way for a man to find a wife?" I asked.

"I remember once, before we left our village, when the

young men would gather. They would stand and sing for the girls and laugh. And the girls would smile at them. And they danced. I was only a small boy, but I liked to see the dancing."

"And that's where a man would meet his bride?"

"Perhaps a man and a girl would make plans to meet again. A man would go a long way off to visit a girl from another village. Even if the weather was very bad, a man would go. The more bad the weather, the more—how do you say?—more impress the woman would be. But . . ."

He sighed and slid down a little farther in his chair. "A man wanting a bride would have cattle. And that would be the dowry. In a refugee camp no man had cattle. All he had for a dowry was a promise."

"Is your brother looking for a bride here?" I asked.

Daniel shook his head. "Geri looks only at his books. He says first he goes to school. Then he finds a bride. I think he will find a bride in Africa, but he is like all men. He will want a wife."

Daniel looked at me then and laughed, a somewhat silly laugh. I could never quite tell if he found something amusing or if he was merely feeling self-conscious.

"What is your family doing for Thanksgiving?" I asked him. The week before, he had been asking Phil about American holidays, and Phil had given him a calendar with the days marked.

"Our mother will be cooking in the restaurant where she helps out. She will go in very early and come home very late," he said.

"Then why don't you and your brother come to our house for dinner?" I asked, sure it would be all right with Dad and Sylvia.

"We will come!" Daniel said enthusiastically. "We will bring a roasted pig."

"What?"

This time Daniel broke into full laughter, getting the attention of students at the other tables. He ducked down again, still grinning. "No pig," he said.

I got Sam to come over on Monday night with his camera and take a picture of Gwen, Pamela, Liz, and me in our traded dresses. We didn't do our hair or makeup.

"If everybody knows in advance what we'll be wearing, we've at least got to keep *something* a surprise," said Pamela.

It was a riot. Gwen's green and black polka dot dress was too tight for me, so I left the zipper open in back beneath the wide sash. My midnight blue dress was way too big in the torso for Pamela, so for the picture—the four of us lined up with our arms around each other—Gwen and I had a hand in back and each of us tightly clasped a big hunk of material to make Pamela's dress look, from the front, like it fit. Gwen was really hot in Pamela's salmon-colored dress with the spaghetti straps, and Liz looked seductive in my black halter dress.

"Say cheese," said Sam. "Woops. No, wait a minute. Gwen, that neckline is really dipping on the left."

We glanced over and saw half a breast visible—she needed a strapless bra and hadn't brought one, so she wasn't wearing any.

We howled as Sylvia moved in with a box of pins and pulled the strap down some in back.

Sam said he got at least three good pictures, and we could come by the newspaper office the following day when he'd have them at full size, so we could choose the one we liked best.

After he left, Pamela said, "Now all we need for the Snow Ball are dates. You going with Keeno, Liz?"

"Yeah, I mentioned it to him," Liz said.

"*Mentioned* it? Are you guys in a relationship or not?"

"We don't label it. We're just really close."

"Alice is going with Daniel, I'm going with Austin, Liz is going with Keeno, what about you, Pamela?" Gwen asked.

"Why don't you ask Louie and we'll double," said Liz.

"Keeno's friend from St. John's?" said Pamela. "I hardly even know him."

"So what? You've seen each other naked—how much more do you have to know?" Gwen joked.

"Shhhh," I said as Sylvia gave us a wary smile and raised one eyebrow. "Erase, erase. Why don't we all go together? Invite Louie, Pamela, and we'll make it eight."

"Okay," said Pamela. "Dress? Check. Date? Check. This'll be the easiest dance I ever attended. I'll worry about shoes later."

Sylvia went over our dresses while we were still wearing them, pinning up sides here and there and marking what needed to be let out.

"I'm not a fancy seamstress, girls, but I don't think anyone will notice my alterations," she promised. "There's just one problem," she added with a twinkle in her eye. "The dresses self-destruct if you try to take them off."

The photo looked great on the front page of the school newspaper, and Phil liked my idea and headline. *Four senior girls*, the article began, *have caught the wave of a new trend for school dances: exchanging dresses with each other.* This, of course, made it seem as though it must be happening all over the country, but so much the better.

Though we had one of the other reporters write this particular story, it was a thrill to see my byline under a growing number of feature articles—one on our new football coach and his family and, in this issue, one on relationships.

I hadn't even imagined that Jill and Justin were going to break up when I wrote the relationship piece; it was a follow-up to a question the roving reporters had asked in a recent survey:

HOW DO YOU DEFINE A "RELATIONSHIP"?

I'd say exclusive dating a few months or more.

—Marcella Bogdan, senior

Why do you have to call it anything? Why can't it just be "guy likes girl," "girl likes guy"?

—Chris Weil, junior

You've got to at least know her last name.

—Jim Donovitch, senior

I'd picked up on that second comment for my article—that from what I'd gathered, listening to people talk, girls were usually the ones who wanted it defined:

> The big question for girls is "Are we going together or not?" And if the guy agrees that "Yeah, we're going out," the girl wants a name for it. "Are we a couple? Is this a relationship or just a hookup?"

Amy had heard a lot of talk about Jill and Justin too, and when I told her that it was sort of awkward, my feature article coming out practically the very week the breakup had happened, Amy wanted to know who broke it off, Jill or Justin.

"I heard it was Jill," I said.

She was mystified. "If I had a boyfriend, I'd keep him," she said.

"Well, some time you will, Amy," I told her. "By the way, you've been looking great these days."

She really was looking better, dressing more carefully, choosing more figure-fitting clothes.

"I did my nails," she said proudly, and held out her hands. The nails were bright pink, with a little rose stenciled on the ring finger of both hands.

"They look fantastic, and you've been doing a super job as a roving reporter," I said.

"I like asking questions," she said. "It used to be when kids saw me coming, they'd whisper and turn away. Now you know what a boy said?"

"What?"

"He said, 'You want to ask me a question, Amy?' And I said, 'Yes. How do you define a relationship?' and he said, 'The first time a girl asks me out, I'll call it a relationship.' And then he said, 'No, don't put that in the newspaper. I was just kidding.' And I said I wouldn't. But he was nice."

"That was a good decision," I said. "If a person asks for a remark to be off the record, you have to respect that."

"Off the record," Amy said, and she fumbled around with her notebook and wrote it down.

It did seem to me that Amy was happier, but she also seemed a little more excitable and flustered than usual. There was just a certain charm about her in the brave and hungry way she approached life, and I figured if I accomplished nothing more my senior year, I'd at least done well by helping her become a roving reporter. The truth was I loved my job as features editor. I felt needed, appreciated, and capable when I was in the newsroom, and I even wondered now and then if I should major in journalism instead of counseling when I got to college.

We hadn't heard the last of Bob White. Hadn't expected to, actually. This time, though, the note was typed on a computer, and it was even more hateful than the one before. It was also unsigned:

> The only way to save this country is to take back our streets and our schools and kick ass. If we let the Jews, the beaners, and the black vermin

take over, who's going to carry the torch for the white race?

We silently passed the note around the conference table.

"This doesn't even sound like the same person," said Phil. "I don't think it is."

Tim nodded. "We're dealing with more than one. They know we're not going to print this, though, so what's the point?"

"To let us know they haven't backed off. That they're still out there," said Phil.

And that was the chilling part. *They're out there.*

15

DINNER GUESTS

Sylvia and I set a beautiful table on Thanksgiving. Some of the decorations she had brought along after she married Dad were two little log cabins, the kind the Pilgrims might have built, that were also candleholders. We put them at each end of the table, with a low bouquet of carnations in fall colors in between.

I'd baked two pies the night before—pumpkin and pecan—and Dad was doing the turkey. Sylvia took over the mashed potatoes and veggies; Les and Paul, his roommate, were bringing wine; and Kay, whom Dad had invited at the last minute because her parents were out of the country, was bringing a salad. We hadn't expected anything of Daniel and his brother, of course. I figured it would be culture shock enough just eating at a table with Lester.

Daniel and Geri arrived first. "We are on time!" Daniel announced proudly.

"We Sudanese are notoriously late for appointments in our own country, but in the United States of America we do as Americans do," said his brother. "I am Geri."

"Welcome!" Sylvia said. "Some of us are notoriously late for appointments too. Please come in. I'm Sylvia."

Geri was just as thin as his brother, cheekbones prominent like Daniel's, his skin even darker, but he was taller by four inches. Both of them wore lighter jackets than seemed practical for November.

Geri handed Sylvia a baking pan covered with foil. "This is a gift from our mother for your table. It is a special dish that we enjoy very much in Sudan."

"Well, we're glad to have you. Oh, it smells delicious! Thank you so much," Sylvia said, and introduced Dad, who came in from the kitchen.

"Come on back to the next room," Dad coaxed. "We've got a good fire going." They seemed reluctant to let go of their jackets so Dad let them keep them on. But they had barely sat down before the doorbell rang again, and this time it was Kay, with a large salad bowl in her arms, a bottle of dressing in one hand.

"Did you know it's snowing?" she asked. "Hi, Mr. M. Hi, Sylvia." Dad took her coat, but at the word *snow*, both Daniel and his brother went hurrying to the windows in the family room.

We had to look hard to see the flakes, but they were in the air, melting the minute they hit the ground. Daniel was entranced, though not enough to go back out in the cold.

"When do you make the men?" he asked.

"The *snow*men?" I guessed. "It has to come down a lot harder than this." I introduced Kay to them just as we heard Les and Paul arriving, and suddenly the house was filled with voices and introductions and exclamations about the possibility for a white Christmas.

There were the usual murmurs of praise as each person was asked to pass the platter closest to him. Geri asked about each dish and its relationship to Thanksgiving, and Sylvia gave a brief synopsis of the first somewhat mythical Thanksgiving Day.

Les, knowing he had a captive audience, couldn't help adding his own version: "With only two drumsticks per turkey, of course, the early colonists were already figuring out how they could trade each drumstick for a river valley, while the wily Indians offered a few steaming ears of corn for all the pies on the table."

"Les!" I said. "It's going to take me a week to untangle all that for Daniel. Why don't you say something useful?"

Lester pondered that a moment. "Hmm. Useful," he said. "Okay. How's this?" He held out his plate for Daniel and Geri to see, pointing to the turkey and mashed potatoes. "The bland and the bland," he said. He added a scoopful of dressing to the plate. "The *pièce de résistance*," he intoned, and then, lifting the ladle from the gravy boat, "and this is the gold that binds it all together." He poured the gravy over the meat, potatoes, and dressing, and in a final flourish, he added a little spoonful of cranberry sauce atop the heap.

Daniel and Geri, glad for the demonstration, prepared their own plates in the same manner, interrupted now and then with the arrival of hot rolls and sweet potatoes and green bean casserole.

"Whatever this is, it's delicious!" Kay said, savoring a mouthful of the dish Geri and Daniel had brought. She dissected another spoonful on her plate. "Spinach . . . peanuts? . . . some kind of wonderful spice . . ."

"It's my favorite," said Daniel. "Our mother cooks this for the restaurant where she works, in exchange for our apartment."

"How does that work?" Kay asked him.

"I am here because of a scholarship to George Washington University," Geri explained. "A church sponsored our mother and Daniel, and we live in an apartment owned by a man in the church who also owns a restaurant. That's where our mother is today—cooking."

"My parents are on a cruise, or I'd be at their place," said Paul.

"Mine are visiting family in China, or I would be eating with them," said Kay. "This is so wonderful, Mr. M—inviting me here."

"Then you, too, are a long way from home," Geri told her.

"Not really," said Kay, pushing back the shiny lock of hair that kept falling over one eye. "I was born in China, but this has always seemed like home to me. We've been back twice, both times before I was ten, but I don't remember a lot. I didn't want to go with them this time because I need to work; I'm saving for grad school."

"I would like to go back to Sudan as a lawyer," Geri told us. "I will be going back whether I work in law or not—that is the agreement. But I hope to be able to help my people make a better government."

I noticed that Daniel was paying close attention to how we ate—what we ate with our fingers and when we used a fork or knife. By the time the platters were passed around the second time, however, he didn't seem to care. He and his brother loved the meat, and they had second and third helpings.

When there was a pause in the conversation, I asked Les how George and Joan's wedding had gone.

"I didn't tell you?" Les said. Then he filled in the rest of the table: "George Palamas was our former roommate, and it was almost the wedding-that-wasn't."

"He tried to back out?" I asked.

"No. Sprained an ankle. The morning of the wedding, he was running up our side steps with his tux and tripped over the bottom of the dry-cleaning bag. We got an Ace bandage and bound him up as best we could, gave him a couple ibuprofen, and he held out long enough to dance with his bride at the reception. Then they were off to Greece for the honeymoon, and I haven't heard from him since."

"That's awful, spraining his ankle!" Sylvia said.

"Yeah. I was the best man," said Paul. "I could see sweat on his brow. I slipped him another pill when I gave him the ring, and I think he swallowed it without water just before they came back up the aisle."

"Well, better his ankle than getting cold feet," I said.

Daniel looked from Paul to me. "A man with cold feet cannot marry?"

We all broke into laughter.

"It's an expression, Daniel," I said. "It means he's having second thoughts." And when I still wasn't making myself clear, I said, "When a man or woman doesn't want to marry after all."

Geri shook his head. "That would not be good."

"What are weddings like in your country?" Dad asked.

"There were no big weddings in the refugee camp, and we were there since I was nine," Geri said. "But I remember some when we were still in the south. Those were great times and would last for several days. The bridal dance would go on almost till morning, with much singing. Now the wedding party must end before sunset prayers and be supervised by sheiks and the police. It is not a happy time for Sudan."

"Are the marriages arranged?" asked Kay, who was helping Sylvia pass slices of pie around the table, followed by a bowl of whipped cream.

"It is the joining of two families, and all are concerned with the arrangements, but there must be approval by the spouses," Geri explained.

"My parents had an arranged marriage, and it seems to have worked for them," Kay told us. "They're modern in some ways but old country in others. They want me to meet a son of their Chinese friends. I know that's why they wanted me to come with them this time."

"Maybe you'd end up liking the guy," I suggested.

Kay gave me an anguished look. "I already have a boyfriend,

and he's not Asian. I met him my senior year at Georgetown, and I don't know how to tell my parents. They don't even know I'm seeing anyone. They think I only go out with girlfriends. I would be with my boyfriend today, but he's a part-time waiter at the Hyatt and had to work."

"Perhaps your parents would like him if they met him," Sylvia suggested.

Kay shook her head. "No, I'm afraid not. They didn't let me date all through high school. 'Concentrate on your studies,' they would say. 'A boyfriend will not help you get to college.' Well, I got through college, and you'd think I could make some decisions myself, but they say, 'Trust us, we know best.' When you're an only child, so much is expected of you. They sacrifice so you can go to school, so you can go to college, have the best tutors, the music lessons, the chess, the challenges. . . . And then, when you disappoint them . . ."

"This all must be very hard on you," Sylvia sympathized.

"It's hard in one way, easy in another. When you have your life all laid out for you—what school to attend, what courses to study, how long you study, where you live, whom you marry—you don't have to worry about choices," Kay said. "You don't have to decide between this or that. It's all arranged for you. But it's hard because I might find—when I'm forty—that it's someone else's life I'm living . . . my parents', not my own."

There were a few seconds of silence while we thought that one over. Then Les raised his wineglass and said genially, "To life, everybody, confusing as it is!"

"To life!" we said, clinking our glasses, and I know we were all thinking about how lucky—or unlucky—we were.

On Saturday we had a girls' night out. Molly Brennan was home for the weekend from the U of Maryland, still leukemia-free, and Gwen brought her friend Yolanda. We went to a chick flick, and Yolanda said we could celebrate the loss of her V card. Gwen said maybe we should just celebrate Thanksgiving break.

The guys would have hated the movie—all about weddings and mix-ups and breakups and makeups, and so Hollywood that you could almost predict exactly where the car chase would take place and about when Mr. Right would enter the picture. It was afterward that we had the best time—at a little Greek restaurant where you could spend a couple hours just drinking strong coffee and eating appetizers. I told them about Kay's American boyfriend.

"I can't believe her parents are still so controlling when she's out of college!" I said. "I mean, I understand we're from different cultures, but why do they assume she'd be happier with an Asian boyfriend? She hardly even remembers China. She lives here now."

"Birds of a feather . . . ," said Pamela.

"Like that kook's letters in *The Edge* about keeping the races separate and pure," said Liz.

Gwen reached across the table and helped herself to the pita bread I'd left on my plate. "I don't know. Whether we like to admit it or not, we *do* like to be with 'our own kind' sometimes."

"Never thought you'd say that," Pamela said. "I'd think

you'd be sick to death of people saying they're happier 'with their own kind.'"

"It's the 'sometimes' that's important," put in Yolanda, caressing one of her dangly earrings. Her nails, half an inch long, were painted a bright canary yellow.

"Let's face it," Gwen went on, "there are things African Americans share that you just don't, that's all. Like, my grandmother can tell you about driving through the South and going straight through certain towns, no matter how hungry you were, because it just wasn't safe to stop. And when you did finally find a place to eat—even a take-out joint—you had to go around to the back door and pay for your supper there. Eat it back by the trash cans or in your car."

We had no answer for that.

"Yeah, and sometimes when I get together with my cousins," added Yolanda, "especially with Aunt Josie, we get to laughing and talking black English, and you wouldn't understand a word we were saying. Just something fun to do. We can talk about straightening hair, we can sway when we sing in church—stuff that may not have any meaning to you. Maybe Kay's parents feel the same about wanting her to marry an Asian."

"But . . . if you carry this out to its logical conclusion . . . ," I protested.

"No, you don't carry it out to any conclusion. You don't make it more than it is," said Molly, siding with Gwen. "Just because we're having a girls' night out, does it mean we don't want to get together with guys?"

"No!" we all chorused.

Molly was looking especially good in a cobalt blue sweater that made her wide blue eyes all the brighter, and she had a new haircut—loose curls about the face. It had grown out now a couple inches. "And by the way," she added, "I've got a boyfriend."

We pounded the table and cheered. Molly, one of our favorite people, who once told us she'd never been kissed. "Tell! Tell!" we begged.

"Well, he's Indian. Pakistani, anyway. And my folks love him."

We hugged Molly and gushed some more.

"And is he a good kisser?" Pamela asked her.

"You'd better believe it," said Molly mischievously. "I'm making up for lost time."

16

AMY

Because we'd had only three days of school the week before Thanksgiving, we'd delayed the printing of *The Edge* until this week. We still had a couple of things to add. One of the roving reporters had done a short piece on consignment shops catering to teens, where girls could get long dresses and heels and beaded clutch bags at fantastic prices. I had to edit it a little, but we wanted to make sure the story got in this issue, with only one full weekend left before the Snow Ball. And because Amy had done some of the calling to the consignment shops to get their contact info, her name was included in the byline. She was thrilled.

I stayed after school on Monday to research white supremacy groups, but all I really had to do was Google the term *hate groups* and I was in. So many different names! So many disguises! I'd read that what you first see on the Internet is fairly benign: *Our goal is simple—to show white youth a better way of life and teach them a sense of racial awareness and pride.*

Then you dig a little deeper and you get, *Bring our troops home and put them on the Mexican border* or, *Money given to a church may end up going to help irresponsible people who live just like parasites on the goodwill of society.* I even found a site promoting some kind of racial test. It said, *If the results show that you have a moderate or extreme bias in favor of whites, you are okay. If you get any other result, you could be at greater risk of being cheated, robbed, raped, or even murdered. . . .* Implying, of course, that if you choose mostly white, Protestant Anglo-Saxons as friends, you can live a relatively safe life. But if you start hanging around with Jews, you're at risk of being cheated; with Hispanics, of being robbed; with African Americans, of being raped or murdered.

There were promotions for musical and rap groups spewing out hate; preachers, black and white, predicting war between the races. Looking forward to it, actually. Our library received a magazine called *Intelligence Report* that kept tabs on hate groups, their leaders and methods, all over the United States. When Phil joined me at a table, we leafed through back issues, studying the ways the groups operate: racist disc jockeys with a new brand of neo-Nazi music; Holocaust deniers claiming that the German concentration camps during World War II were really filled with criminals or typhus victims; Klu Klux Klan supporters advocating death to the president.

Phil showed me a photo of a young woman wearing an American flag as a sarong, her face contorted with contempt, holding up a sign reading GOD HATES FAGS. Another of young children giving the Heil Hitler salute. "It just keeps coming," I said. "All the hate."

"So . . . we'll keep writing about it," he said. "We'll come at it from different angles. Think we should devote a whole issue to it?"

I thought about it a moment. "Let me see how much of this stuff I can stomach at one time," I told him.

Pamela called me that night. "About this dress exchange . . . ," she said.

"Yeah?"

"Can we exchange guys, too?"

"You want to swap *dates*?"

"I called Louie to invite him, and he said okay . . . and then he *belched*."

"Whoa!" I said. "You mean that was part of the response?"

"I don't know. He excused himself, of course. He said he'd just had dinner, but still. . . ."

"Was the burp a part of the 'okay,' or was it 'okay' and then a silence and *then* a burp?" I asked her. I saw Dad staring at me from across the room.

"Sort of part of the 'okay,' I guess," said Pamela.

"Was that the whole conversation?"

"No. He asked about flowers and who we were going with and the color of my dress and everything, but I think . . . I *thought* . . . I heard another belch toward the end. I mean, I was going to ask him what he'd had for dinner, but then I figured I wasn't supposed to have heard it. But if we're dancing and he's belching—"

"Pamela, this is the first guy you've gone out with since you and Tim broke up. Right?"

"Yeah."

"And Tim never belched the whole time you were with him?"

"I can't say that."

"He never grunted or scratched or blew his nose or picked his teeth? Never?"

"He probably did, but not on our first date."

"Pamela, chill," I told her. "You are going to the dance with Louie. Now cut him a little slack, huh? For all you know, your stomach is going to growl during a slow number."

"Now I have something new to worry about."

"Good. If your stomach growls, it cancels out his burp. Period," I said.

When I hung up, Dad was still staring at me. I started to explain, but he said, "I don't even want to know," and he settled down again with the paper.

After school on Tuesday, I stayed late again to check in with our counselor, Mrs. Bailey, about my college applications. By the time I left her office, it was twenty of five. I was walking down the hall toward my locker when I saw Dennis Granger come out of his classroom farther on, pulling on his jacket and heading toward the south exit. I automatically slowed, not wanting to let him hear my footsteps and be in an empty corridor with the man after school hours.

I wondered about the teacher he was subbing for this year—if she had had her baby yet and whether she was even coming back. How you manage motherhood and a career. Wondered if I should do a feature article on substitute teachers and what it's like to suddenly take on a class for a semester when you don't know the students, possibly not even the subject, and have nothing to go on except the teacher's class notes for the course.

No, I decided. It could undermine substitute teachers' influence on a class to find out just how unprepared, and possibly nervous, some of them were. And I sure wasn't about to interview Dennis Granger. I waited until I saw him disappear down the steps at the end of the hall, and then I walked on.

I was just passing the door of the darkened classroom when I heard someone crying—soft little sobs, like whispered speech. I stopped, listened, and tried to see through the glass. Finally I opened the door.

At first I didn't see anything, as the shades had been drawn against the afternoon sun. Then I noticed a girl leaning against the wall in one corner, hands over her face, her shoulders shaking.

"Amy!" I said, and went quickly over to her. "What happened? Are you okay?" But the sight of her disheveled clothes made me sick to my stomach, and the dark stillness of the room gave it an aura of evil.

Amy's face was turned to one side, as though she couldn't

look at me, and she covered the front of her khaki skirt with both hands.

My heart was pounding furiously. I didn't know whether to go screaming after Dennis Granger or stay with her.

"Amy," I said again, gently clasping her arms and looking her over. "You're *not* okay, are you?"

She shook her head, but tried to stop her sobs. "Hi . . . A-A-Alice," she said jerkily, tugging her clothes back in place.

"I saw Mr. Granger leaving," I said. "What happened in here?"

She wouldn't look at me. "He . . . helps . . . me with English," she said finally.

I backed off and stared at her. "*Granger's* your tutor? You've been coming to *him*?" *Oh, God!* "But something else happened, didn't it?" I asked, looking her over carefully. I gently removed the hands that were trying to hide a wet spot on the front of her crumpled skirt. "Amy, tell me. . . ." And now my own voice was trembling. "Did Mr. Granger rape you?"

"No!" she said explosively.

"Did you have your underwear off?"

"No, Alice. I don't take my underwear off for guys, even when they ask," she said.

"Did . . . did he ask?"

She wouldn't answer.

I felt we had both been violated somehow. That we had both been molested, one way or another, here at school. I wanted to get out of that room, but Amy wasn't ready yet, still crying.

"Please tell me what happened," I begged.

She sniffled some more but began shaking her head again. "I'm not going to come back to Mr. Granger anymore. I can do my English myself," she said, and her hand went back to the front of her skirt.

I eased her down in one of the chairs and took the one next to her. "Listen, Amy, this is molestation. If Dennis Granger put his hands under your clothes or pressed against you or anything like that, you need to report it. He pressed against me too."

She glanced at me quickly, then dropped her eyes again. "Did . . . did you report it?"

"Not yet, but I'm going to."

Amy scrunched up her face so tightly that her eyes closed. She shook her head. "I didn't get raped," she repeated.

"Maybe not, but he took advantage of you—of me—and that's never right for a teacher. For *any* guy. Let's go to the office. I'll go with you."

"*No*, Alice!" she said. "My mom's picking me up at five."

"Then we'll tell your mom."

Amy began crying again. "No! She'll say I did it."

"Did what? No matter what you did, Amy, he's the teacher." I studied her. "Has this happened before?"

"Just . . . well, last week . . . no, the week before . . . when the tutoring was over, I kissed him."

"You . . . kissed him?" It was as though we were suddenly little five-year-old girls searching our way through a forest. Turn here? Turn there? Do this? Do that? At what point was it okay to yell?

"I got a good grade on my English paper, and it was

because he helped me with that part, and I kissed him on the cheek for a thank-you. I've kissed him . . . well, maybe four times when tutoring was over, and . . . well, after the first time he said he liked it so I did it again. My mom would be really mad."

That sick feeling came over me again, and I swallowed. I tried to think of a way to get through to her, but she continued:

"Then . . . last week . . . when I bent over to kiss him, he asked if he could kiss me back, and I said I guessed so, and he got up and put his hands here . . . and here . . . and then he touched me here." She motioned toward her breasts.

"And what happened today, Amy? *I* won't get mad, no matter what." *How skillfully we are manipulated*, I was thinking. *How easy it is not to tell.*

"Well, I didn't kiss him when tutoring was over, because I didn't know if I should. But when we were done, he asked if I was going to kiss him, and I said maybe. He got up and moved me into a corner and kissed me, and this time . . ." She pointed to her breasts again. "He put his hand under my shirt and under my b-b-bra."

Her face was flaming, and she was on the verge of tears again, I could tell. She stopped to take a deep breath. "*Please* don't tell anyone, Alice."

"Amy, whether you kissed him or not, what he did was very wrong, and he knows it. If you don't report this, I will. The principal has to be told."

"No, Alice! Don't! I'll tell . . . I'll tell my dad."

"This is important, Amy! It's serious. Nobody's going to

punish you because Mr. Granger knows better. Promise me you'll tell your parents."

She wiped her face and took more deep breaths. "I'll tell," she said, and looked at the clock. "I have to go. Mom will be waiting, and if I'm not there, she says, 'Dawdle, dawdle dilly, that's you.' I hate dawdle dilly."

Amy picked up her book bag and started for the door. I got up too, put my arm around her, and walked along beside her. If I had reported Granger earlier, would this have happened to Amy? But then again, the old doubt: What exactly had he done to me? Who would ever believe it? He'd say that somebody going by had bumped into him, which made him bump into me. Perfectly possible.

"Why are you coming with me?" Amy asked, her voice still a bit breathy.

"Because I know how upset you are. I'm your friend, after all."

"That means you like me, and I like you too," she said.

As we approached the south entrance, I saw a silver Volvo waiting at the curb. When we got to the door, Amy put out one elbow to block me and said, "I can do this myself."

I hesitated. I had fully intended to walk her to the car, to be there for moral support. But then I realized that I was treating her as though she weren't capable of handling this herself.

"Okay, Amy," I said. "I'll see you tomorrow."

I watched her walk toward the car with her little lopsided gait, drop her bag on the backseat, and climb in the passenger side. I could see a woman's face turned toward Amy, see that something was being asked, something answered, and then . . . in far too short a time, the car moved forward again.

She hadn't told. If she had not told her parents by the time she got to school tomorrow, I would report the incident myself. I wondered if I should go back to Mrs. Bailey and tell her about it right then. But when I got to her office, she had gone.

I worried about Amy all evening. For one thing, if she told her parents what had happened, she would probably mention that she'd talked about it to me, and they might call me to verify her account. In any case, no one called.

But it was equally possible that they would not want to discuss it with anyone other than the principal, or possibly the police, and they could very well show up tomorrow at school. The more I thought about it, though, the more I doubted Amy would tell them. And if she didn't, who should I tell? Her parents? Mrs. Bailey? Mr. Beck?

Twice I was on the verge of talking to Sylvia about it. But the thought of going to her made me feel even more like a child. I'd already lost that assurance of safety and trust you're supposed to get in school. The only way I could see to feel seventeen again was to prove I could handle this myself.

Just thinking about Dennis Granger made me seethe. How did he dare? I didn't have to ask myself what attracted him to Amy. Her vulnerability, her need, her trust. It infuriated me that people like him could masquerade as responsible and caring, all the while trolling for girls like Amy.

I woke twice in the night, wondering if it was time to get up, and finally I rose at five thirty, showered, and was glad when Dad said I could have his car for the day, knowing I had Student Jury after school.

As soon as I got there, I looked for Amy, but I had to turn in some copy at the newsroom and still hadn't seen her when the first bell rang. I began to think she may have stayed home. When I caught sight of Dennis Granger over the lunch hour, chatting it up with students, I knew immediately that he was still on board.

I'll give Amy till two o'clock, I told myself. And then, *I'll give her a half hour more.*

Then I saw her going in a restroom after the last class and followed her in. Another girl was just leaving, and we were alone.

"Amy," I said, "did you tell your parents?"

She didn't answer. She was washing some ink off her hands.

I leaned over so she had to look at me. "Amy, this is too big a thing to keep secret. Not what you did, but what he did. To both of us."

Her lips quivered.

"If we don't report it, he'll go on doing this and embarrassing other girls. He may do more than kissing and touching, and that's not being a good teacher."

"I . . . I know," she said in a small voice.

"Do you want to be a good friend to other girls?"

She looked up at me and nodded seriously.

"Then you'll report this so it won't happen to anyone else. I'll go with you, okay? I'll tell Mr. Beck how Dennis Granger pressed up against me at the drinking fountain, and then it happened to you."

"Okay," she said. "But I wasn't getting a drink of water."

"I know."

Student Jury would be starting soon, but I didn't care. Like soldiers, we marched to the school office and asked for Mr. Beck.

Mrs. Free, his personal secretary, was at Student Jury, so we talked to another woman.

"Mr. Beck's in a meeting right now," she said. "He'll be at least forty minutes."

"It's important!" I said.

"Well, so is this meeting," the secretary said, smiling sympathetically, and added, "School board members."

I tried to think. "Is Mr. Gephardt available?"

"I'm afraid not. He had to leave early."

This cannot be happening! Not after I had to beg and plead to get Amy here.

"Could we make an appointment, then, for Mr. Beck at three thirty? We can't leave until we've seen him," I said. "It's urgent."

I could tell she took me seriously now.

"I'll put you down and ask him not to leave until he's met with you," she said, and took our names.

I looked at the clock. A quarter of three. Student Jury rarely took more than a half hour. Amy and I went out in the hall. She seemed more perky now, more confident. We had an appointment, and I was going with her. Our names were in the book.

"Look, Amy," I said. "I'm going to Student Jury. Why don't you come down to the library. I'll be just across the hall, and as soon as it's over, I'll come and get you. Do you mind waiting in the library?"

"I like to look at *National Geographic*," she said. "Except that I would never take off my clothes for a picture. Mom says they didn't have any clothes on in the first place. I wouldn't want to live in a place you didn't wear clothes."

"How were you going to get home today?" I asked. "I've got Dad's car, so I can drive you. Should you call your mom and tell her you'll be late?"

She pulled her cell phone out of her bag, and we stopped in the hallway to make the call. Amy carefully pressed her index finger on each number, concentrating hard.

"Mom?" she said. "It's Amy. Alice is going to drive me home because we have a meeting." She listened, then looked at me. "What time will we be home?"

"We might be as late as five," I told her. "If we're going to be later than that, we'll call."

"Five o'clock, Mom. And Alice is driving because I wouldn't know the brake from the clutch." Another long pause. "Okay. Love you too. And Dad and God. Bye."

I waited until Amy was settled in the magazine area just inside the library door. I pointed out the conference room across the hall.

"I'll be right over there, Amy. And if Student Jury isn't over by three thirty, I'll leave anyway and we'll go to the office."

"Right," Amy said. "And you're going to tell on him too."

"We're in this together," I promised.

17

ALICE IN CHARGE

I felt blood throbbing in my temples as I made my way to the conference room. And I almost stopped breathing when I walked in, because there was Dennis Granger.

I knew that teachers took turns as faculty adviser, but I felt sick as I listened to him tell Darien that he was substituting this time for the chemistry teacher. I could barely stand to look at him.

"You'll have to tell me how this works," he said cheerfully, glancing around the room. "Everybody's presumed innocent until declared guilty, right? And that's where you guys come in?"

I didn't even acknowledge him. Just settled myself in my chair and opened my bag, looking for a pen.

"Not exactly," I heard someone reply. "The offenders have

already admitted to whatever it was they did; we simply decide the sentence. You know—the solution."

Mr. Granger sat down and pulled his chair up to the table. So far the faculty advisers had always sat off to one side, more observers than participants. Sleazebag looked as though he were here to take over.

He must have caught me studying him covertly because his eyes fastened on mine for a moment before I chickened out and looked away.

The case this time was a freshman who had been trashing one of the boys' restrooms. He'd been caught twice tossing wads of wet toilet paper at the ceiling where they stuck and dried, and the ceiling looked like the beginning of a hornet's nest. The kid was small for his age and wiry. He stood with his arms straight down at his sides, like he was about to be executed and deserved whatever he got.

"Is this new behavior for you, or did you do this kind of stuff in middle school?" Darien asked.

"I did it some," the boy answered.

"Ever get caught back in middle school?"

The boy shook his head.

"Do you do this in front of other guys, or when no one else is looking?" I asked.

"Mostly by myself," he said. "Sometimes with other kids . . . if they dare me." His voice was barely audible. This was probably the least serious case we'd had to deal with, and I was glad that we would be able to settle it quickly.

Dennis Granger leaned forward and rested his arms on the

conference table. "Sometimes," he began, in a paternalistic tone, "people do destructive things simply because they know they can, and others do it for attention." I glared at him even though he wasn't looking at me.

"So which would you say it was?" Granger continued. "To see if you could get away with it or to get attention?"

The boy's face reddened a little, and he shrugged. "I don't know," he murmured.

Darien interrupted. "Excuse me, Mr. Granger, but this is Student Jury. We're supposed to ask the questions and impose the penalty."

Mr. Granger looked annoyed for a minute, then smiled and waved one hand as though to excuse himself and pulled back away from the table. "I guess I'm just here for decoration," he joked.

When the school secretary escorted the boy out of the room to await our verdict, it took us only a few minutes to talk it over.

"This seems pretty cut-and-dried to me," said Darien. "An 'experience-the-consequences' sort of thing. He did the damage, he undoes it."

"Does the school want him up on a ladder unsticking those wads of paper, though?" Kirk asked. "Is there an insurance factor here?"

"The school would be liable if he fell," Murray said. We looked at Mr. Granger.

"I can check that out for you," he said.

"Nix the ladder," said Lori. "Give him a long pole with a sponge on the end. He needs a workout."

"Why not tell the custodian to get the materials together and the boy does the job?" said Murray.

We all agreed. As the boy was brought in again—Betty Free came first and held the door open for him—I caught sight of Amy in the background. She was standing in the doorway of the library, waiting for me to come out, and in the five seconds or so that the door was open—the boy was taking his time—she saw Dennis Granger sitting there at the table. I saw the surprise on her face, the way she stared at him, at me. And then the door closed.

I gathered up my stuff. What if she thought I had talked to Granger about what she'd told me? What if she left the building?

Darien read the penalty, and when the kid agreed that it was fair, I pushed back from the table, slinging the strap of my bag over my shoulder. Darien set a date, and Mrs. Free told the boy he could leave. He skedaddled like a frightened mouse, and I stood up, ready to go. But when the boy opened the door to go out, I was astonished to see Amy Sheldon walk in.

Her cheeks were flaming red. She stood at one end of the long table and, in her high-pitched voice, announced too loudly, "I want to make a complaint."

Everyone turned.

"A complaint goes to the principal or vice principal first—," Darien began.

"No, I have to make it now, because what if nothing happens?" Amy said. She didn't look to the right or left, just straight at Darien.

"What's the problem, Amy?" someone asked.

I stood riveted to the floor as I heard Amy answer, "Yesterday when Mr. Granger was tutoring me, I got molested."

The school secretary stared at her, speechless.

"Now, Amy, what in the world . . . ?" Mr. Granger started, an incredulous look on his face.

She refused to even glance his way. Just stood there, tilting slightly to one side as though facing a hurricane gale, struggling not to blow over. If ever I admired anyone, I admired Amy Sheldon at that moment.

"That's what happened," she said. "I said he could kiss me, but I didn't want to take my clothes off."

"What?" said Mr. Granger.

The school secretary hastily got to her feet. "Amy, this is something we need to talk about with Mr. Beck," she said, putting one arm around her shoulder. "Let's go back to the office."

"We all know that she's disturbed," Mr. Granger said softly as he rose from his chair, but I was furious.

"What she's disturbed about is what happened to her in that room, Mr. Granger," I said. "And she deserves to be heard." The other kids turned toward me, openmouthed. "I'm going with her. We have an appointment with Mr. Beck at three thirty."

Mrs. Free looked at me in astonishment.

Dennis Granger continued to shake his head. "She has these fantasies," he said.

Mrs. Free guided Amy toward the hall. "I think I've got some apple cider in our little fridge," she said. "We'll have a cup while you wait."

Amy twisted around to look at me. "Did I do okay, Alice?"

she asked, as though I had put her up to this. "Am I a good friend?"

Now everyone was staring.

"Absolutely," I told her. "I'm right behind you."

Mr. Granger had exited the conference room through another door by this time, but as Amy walked out with Mrs. Free, Darien turned to me. "What the hell was *that* about? Do you think she's serious?"

"Dead serious," I told him, and followed Amy down the hall.

Mr. Beck was still in his meeting when we reached the office, but Mrs. Free invited us back to a little rest area near the copy machine and poured us each a cup of cider. My stomach felt jumpy so I took only a sip, but Amy gulped hers down and even drank another cup. As long as I was with her, she seemed to be relaxed, but I wasn't at all sure they'd take us seriously.

When Mr. Beck's door opened at last, I heard one of the clerks tell him that I had asked for an appointment.

"Now?" he said, and I saw him glance at the clock. "What about?"

She shrugged.

Mrs. Free stepped into his line of sight then. "Alice McKinley and Amy Sheldon are waiting back here," she told him. "I'll bring them in."

Mr. Beck was holding the door open for us as we walked into his office.

"What can I do for you girls?" he asked, closing the door behind us and motioning for us to sit down. But instead of taking his office chair, he sat on the edge of his desk, as though we all agreed that this wouldn't take long.

Amy looked at me.

"We're here to report that we were both molested by Dennis Granger," I said, a slight tremor in my voice.

Mr. Beck's face changed from casual friendliness to surprise, and his eyes grew intent, serious. "This . . . happened today? To both of you?" he asked.

"No. It happened to Amy yesterday. But just recently I was getting a drink at a water fountain and Mr. Granger came up behind me. He . . . pressed up against me . . . in an inappropriate way."

Mr. Beck nodded slowly, and this time he stood up, went around his desk, and sat down, pulling a pen out of his jacket pocket. "Do you remember the day and the time?"

"I could figure it out by looking at a calendar and let you know. But it was right after gym. And there were other times I wasn't sure . . . when he brushed his hand against my breast . . . It didn't seem definite enough to report. But this last time I was sure."

Mr. Beck nodded again. "I'm glad you girls came to me. This was the right thing to do." He turned toward Amy and waited.

She was a little less confident when she told her story, and I saw Mr. Beck wince when she said she had kissed Mr. Granger. I tried to help fill in the gaps where I could—things she had told me but was leaving out now—and the principal asked me not to comment on anything I hadn't seen directly. Somehow—without the convulsive sobbing I had witnessed and Amy hiding her face and the front of her skirt—it came off as less offensive somehow, less of an assault, and I wondered if Mr. Beck was taking her seriously. But I needn't have worried because he listened patiently, and when she was through, he said, "Amy, this is a serious matter and your parents need to be in on the discussion. Would anyone be home now if I called?"

Amy looked apprehensive. "Dad will say, 'Amy, I am not pleased,' if he is in an important meeting."

"Well, this is important too," Mr. Beck said gently. "What about your mom?"

"She's home."

"I'm sure they'll want to know that we are doing our best to protect you while you're at school, and they'll want to know what happened," he said. "Let's see if we can reach your mother."

When he did, once Mrs. Sheldon said she'd drive right over, Mr. Beck turned to me. "Alice, I appreciate you coming in and telling your version of the situation. I think it would be better if Amy told her parents the story in her own words, so you may go. But I want you to know we take this very seriously."

I wasn't sure of anything. Would Amy's story fizzle out when her parents were there to hear it? Would they think I had put her up to it—exaggerated it somehow? And where was Sleazebag Granger while we were there in Beck's office? He certainly wasn't sticking around. Suddenly I realized that *The Edge* was going to press tonight, at our usual five o'clock deadline.

I walked swiftly to the newsroom. It was my job to do a brief write-up of each Student Jury meeting—describing each case and the jury's recommendation—without naming names.

Today the staff had held off on finalizing the paper until I could insert this last item.

I was the only one in the newsroom. Phil had left a note:

> Alice,
> Got an appointment with the dermatologist, so you're in charge. Ames is at a conference. Wrap it up and send to printer.

Phil and Sam would drive to the printer's early the next morning to pick up the printed papers and bring them to the newsroom, then I'd help divide them up and distribute the bundles around school.

I sat down at the computer, where the unfinished page was already open. Phil had left very little room, but under the Student Jury headline, I typed:

> The jury heard the case against a freshman student for vandalizing a boys' restroom. He was assigned the job of removing the paper wads he'd thrown at the ceiling. . . .

My heart beat faster, an almost painful thumping. There was space left for two or three more lines. My fingers moved again:

> Jury was approached by an unscheduled student who reported molestation . . .

I took several deep breaths to allow myself to continue:

> . . . in room 208 after school hours. Complaint was referred to Mr. Beck.
>
> —Alice McKinley, Student Jury

I felt perspiration trickle down my sides, my brain sending off sparks in my head. I went over the rules again about reporting jury activities. I hadn't named names. I hadn't used dates. But . . .

I had one finger on the DELETE key. I thought of Amy's reddened face. I thought of Dennis Granger's smug smile. I thought of the wet spot on the front of Amy's skirt. . . . Taking my finger off the DELETE key, I pressed SAVE instead. Then I typed *Final Copy* in the subject line of the e-mail and sent the file off to the printer.

At home I went around all evening in a little protective cocoon, telling myself, *You did the right thing*. But the fact that I didn't tell Dad or Sylvia about it meant I wasn't sure. I didn't have any particular reason for believing that the principal might not believe Amy's side of the story, but I felt rage toward Dennis Granger. Not just about what he had done to Amy—her confusion and embarrassment—but that he had walked out on her so quickly afterward and left her to deal with her feelings herself. I can imagine he said something like, *I just can't help myself, Amy—you're so sexy*. And I can imagine she didn't start crying until after he'd left. But he *did* leave her there alone, so eager was he to get out, and I wanted to smack him down. I wanted him to suffer.

I worked on a physics problem after dinner and read another chapter in history. Didn't call anyone, but I checked my e-mail a couple times, looked up a few friends on Facebook without posting anything, then put on my pajamas.

Phil called around nine thirty. "Paper put to bed okay?" he asked.

"Yeah. I sent it in."

"Did I leave you enough room for the Student Jury update?" he asked. "You didn't have to cut anything?"

"It was enough," I said. "I probably wrote too much, I don't know."

"If you didn't move anything around, you're okay. See you tomorrow. I'll try to get some other staffers to help distribute," he said.

"See you," I said.

When I realized I was reluctant to tell even Phil what had happened, I knew I may have made a mistake. But then I thought of Amy, and said, *It's done.*

I woke Thursday with a headache. Dad drove me to school. When I got to the newsroom, Phil and Sam were back from the printer's and were already dividing the newspapers into bundles. I took off my jacket to help. We left one copy on Miss Ames's desk, then set off in different directions to leave papers at each school exit, the auditorium, the office—anywhere they were visible and students could pick them up.

We met Miss Ames as we were making the rounds."Right on time!" she said when she saw us. "How did things go yesterday?"

"No problem," said Phil. "Alice did the wrap-up, and the papers were waiting at the printer's."

"Wonderful," Miss Ames said. "Did you leave some for the office?"

I nodded.

Phil and I went down to ground level and left newspapers at both entrances to the gym and at the science labs. When we went back up to the first floor, the halls were already filling with students, and the noise and laughter grew louder as we reached the top of the stairs. Most of the papers by the auditorium had already been taken, so we left another pile. We were in the east corridor, about halfway to the band room, when we heard the click of heels on the floor behind us.

"Alice?" Miss Ames called. "Phil?"

We turned and I felt my throat constrict.

Her face was stiff. No, furious. There was a tremor in her voice, she was so angry. "Who okayed that story about Student Jury?" she demanded.

"Student Jury?" Phil hadn't even read it yet.

"I . . . did," I said.

She stared at me with a look I'd never seen before. "What . . . in . . . the . . . world . . . were . . . you . . . *thinking*?" she demanded.

Phil stared at me, nonplussed.

My mouth was suddenly so dry that my tongue stuck to my teeth. "I thought . . . I was supposed to report everything that happened. I didn't . . . use names."

"You reported a matter that wasn't even supposed to be handled by Student Jury! I just talked to Betty Free, and she had no idea you were going to write that up."

Phil was scrambling to open one of the papers and find it.

Miss Ames waited coldly as he scanned the paragraph. He blinked and read it again. *"Ouch!"* he said, and gave me a sympathetic but pained look. "That's . . . uh . . . Granger's classroom, isn't it?"

"We're waiting for Mr. Beck to come in. He's meeting this morning with Amy Sheldon's father." She turned on me. "This was so *totally* uncalled for, Alice. So completely unnecessary."

I tried to defend myself. "Miss Ames, I didn't use Granger's name."

"You used the room number, Alice."

"But . . . it could have been someone else—a student even."

"The inference is there, regardless."

The bell for first period rang, and the halls began to empty.

"Should we go back and try to pick up all the papers we left around?" Phil asked.

Miss Ames shook her head. "Too late for that." She stopped and looked at me again. "Alice, I am so, *so* disappointed in you."

18
CHANGE

I would rather have been slapped than to hear those words from our adviser.

I'd worked so hard for *The Edge*, moving up from roving reporter to features editor over the last four years. I so loved my job. And now . . . I remembered the sayings we had posted around the journalism room—Jefferson's statement that if he were asked to choose between "a government without newspapers or newspapers without a government, I should not hesitate a moment to prefer the latter"; Emerson's comment that it's not what lies behind us or ahead of us that counts as much as what lies within us; and the saying, "When in doubt, leave it out." I had been so full of doubt when I typed up that story that it was practically bleeding all over the keyboard. Somehow I'd known I was going too far, and yet . . .

Miss Ames walked away, and Phil turned to me. "Jeez, tell me what happened!" he said.

I told him how Amy had been waiting for me in the library and had seen Dennis Granger there with the jury. How she had come into the room and announced that he had molested her.

"Oh, man!" said Phil. "And you think it really happened?"

"I'm sure of it," I told him, and explained what I'd seen when I found Amy crying in Granger's classroom.

As the morning went on, though, I began to feel even more defensive. It *had* happened. Since when did I have to get permission from the office to report facts? Maybe this was something the students *should* find out about. Maybe this was a case where the faculty would try to protect one of their own. Maybe Jefferson would have said that if he had to choose between the faculty or *The Edge*, he'd choose our newspaper! I felt a little better.

I was called to the office around noon, and two policemen were there. Mr. Beck told me that Amy had given her side of the story to her parents and to the officers; would I now tell them what, if anything, I had observed of the incident? I repeated exactly what I had seen and what Amy had told me, as accurately as I could.

"And neither of you reported it to anyone on Tuesday?" one of the officers asked.

"I begged her to go to Mr. Beck or to tell her parents, and I'd made up my mind that if she didn't do it by today, I would. She agreed to wait for me in the library yesterday so we could go to the office together. Then . . . she saw Mr. Granger in the conference room—he was subbing for the chemistry teacher on Student Jury—and decided to report it there, I guess."

"You didn't expect that? You hadn't suggested it?"

"No!" I said emphatically. "She surprised us all. I didn't even know Mr. Granger would be there."

An officer was taking notes as I talked. "And you've reported inappropriate behavior toward yourself by Dennis Granger?"

"Yes," I said, and described again what had happened at the drinking fountain.

"You didn't report it then?"

"No. Things had happened before sort of like that—I wasn't sure. The way he brushes up against girls. That kind of thing."

"Thank you, Alice," Mr. Beck said when the questions were over. "You've been very helpful. This has been difficult, I know, but I do hope you'll keep this conversation confidential. It's unfortunate that other members of the Student Jury heard the charge and that it was mentioned in *The Edge*, but I assure you that we will follow through on this. You do understand that we want to make sure of our facts before we put a teacher's job and reputation in jeopardy? I trust we can count on your maturity as a senior not to discuss it further with anyone until the matter's resolved."

"Yes," I told him. "You can."

Kids did ask about it, of course, and everyone speculated, rightly, that it was probably Dennis Granger who did it. When asked, I simply said that I didn't know the outcome and that it would probably be in the county paper at some point. What was obvious was that Mr. Granger didn't come to school on Friday or the following week, either.

What I was most afraid of, since there were no witnesses to the act itself, was that Sleazebag would somehow convince the authorities that none of this had happened, that Amy was good at inventing stories, and so forth. That I, as her friend, had got caught up in the drama too.

But in the days that followed, Amy seemed more sure of herself, more confident. When kids gave her knowing, mocking smiles as they passed in the hallway, she interpreted them as a show of support, even though they weren't supposed to know that she was involved.

"You know what?" Amy told me. "Mom and Dad believe me one hundred and fifty percent. And some other people, too."

"You have more friends than you think," I told her.

"Do you remember when Jill accused Mr. Everett of coming on to her?" Pamela asked me at lunch as we sat on the floor outside the cafeteria, the seniors' favorite spot for lunch when the weather's bad and we have to eat inside.

"That was so scary," said Liz. "Everybody's favorite teacher, and we didn't know whether he'd be back or not."

"If Dennis Granger never comes back, I don't think anyone would miss him," said Pamela.

They looked at me, but they knew by now that I could tell them nothing.

Miss Ames was tight-lipped and all-business around me.

She didn't fire me and she didn't mention the matter again. But you could tell there was a pall over the newsroom, that Phil and I had lost some of her respect and confidence—me, for writing up the incident in the first place, and Phil, for not reading the final proof. Whether Granger was found guilty or innocent, I had overstepped the boundary of good journalism.

"Oh, it'll blow over," Phil said comfortingly. "I wish you'd have run it by me, though, before it went to press. I called you, remember, and you didn't even mention it."

"Would you have worded it differently?" I asked. "If I hadn't included the room number, everyone would have asked."

"Maybe this is hindsight, but I think I would have told you not to include any of it. Like Miss Ames said, it wasn't a case for Student Jury. It was irrelevant."

He was right. The point was that I was furious with Dennis Granger and had included that room number *wanting* to hurt him.

A promise was a promise, though, and I didn't even tell Dad or Sylvia about it. Sylvia might accidentally mention it at her school, and it would travel like lightning. I'd wait till it all came out in the newspapers. More difficult yet, I didn't tell Patrick.

When he called, he seemed surprised I was home. "After I punched in your number, I told myself you'd still be at school, wrapping up the paper, or working for your dad, you've been so busy lately. How's it going?"

"Just a weary week. All sorts of hassles at the newspaper and the usual rush at the store," I told him. "What's happening at the Hog Butcher for the World?" (Taking my cue from Carl Sandburg.)

"Haven't butchered any hogs lately," Patrick said. "It's too cold here even for hogs."

"That cold already?" I asked.

"This is Chicago. You walk along the lake, you almost get blown over. I hate to think what it will be like in February."

"All I can think about is how wonderful it was in July," I told him. "The beach was beautiful."

"Yeah, well, now there are whitecaps on the water."

"I wish I was there to keep you warm," I told him.

"That would help," said Patrick.

He asked if there was anything new. I told him Jill and Justin broke up, and he was as surprised as the rest of us.

"Any idea why?"

"His mom, Jill says. It's a 'your mom or me' kind of thing."

"I guess if you're still sleeping at home and eating home cooking, you've got to choose Mom," Patrick said. And then, "This is going to sound like an awkward transition, Alice, but I've got some bad news. Well, sort of, I guess."

I didn't move. Didn't breathe. Something about his mother? Something about breaking up?

"I just couldn't bring myself to tell you earlier. . . ."

"Patrick, what *is* it?" I said, almost angrily, I was so anxious. I didn't need any more problems in my life.

"Mom and Dad have decided to move to Wisconsin to be close to his brother. They found a house when we were there at Thanksgiving."

My brain just couldn't seem to compute this. I knew Patrick had an uncle. Knew that Mr. and Mrs. Long often vacationed at his home in Wisconsin. If Patrick was going to college out of state anyway, did it really matter that—?

His *home*! His home would be in Wisconsin. He wouldn't be coming back here.

"W . . . when?" I asked in such a small, pitiable voice that I didn't recognize it as mine.

"Over Christmas. They want me to help sort through stuff when I come home for the holidays. The movers come on December twenty-eighth."

I was crying into the telephone. I felt the tears on my fingers.

"Alice?" Patrick said gently.

"Oh, Patrick!" I wept.

"I know," he said. "I felt the same way when they told me. But . . . I'm in college now. I wouldn't be home a lot anyway, and Dad's not as strong as he used to be. I can understand he'd want to be near family."

"And . . . and your mom?"

"She says she'd be happy wherever Dad wants to go."

We talked some more—the reasons, the details—but most of it slid by me. All I could think about was Patrick's empty house. Of Patrick going to Wisconsin now on spring and summer breaks.

"I . . . won't ever see you!" I cried.

I could tell he was smiling when he answered, "Well, you could always invite me to your prom."

"Of course! You know you're invited!"

"Well, I'll see you then. And I'll be back for Christmas in just a few weeks. We'll squeeze in every spare moment."

We each lingered over our conversation until we were tired out.

"Good night, Alice," he said.

"Good night, Patrick." I slowly pressed END on my cell phone and lay facedown on my bed. I felt as though the world were whirling on ahead of me and I'd been left far behind.

In the locker room after gym the next day, I told my friends.

"The Longs are moving to Wisconsin," I said.

All chatter stopped.

"*What?*" said Pamela. "When?"

"A few days after Christmas. Patrick's coming home to help them pack. Mr. Long wants to be near his brother."

"Oh, Alice!" said Liz, sitting down with a shoe in one hand.

"And Patrick's going with them?" Pamela asked.

"Duh!" said Gwen.

"I mean, he's at the University of Chicago and—" Even Pamela realized how dumb her question seemed. "Yeah. Where would he stay if he came back here on spring break?" Then she brightened mischievously. "You've got a big house now, Alice. What about Lester's old room?"

"Don't even think it," I said. "Dad would be patrolling the hall all night."

"He wasn't so strict with Les, from what I heard—all the girlfriends," said Pamela. "How many dozen were there?"

"Not in our house, there weren't. Well, with a few exceptions," I told them.

Liz looked about as sad as I felt. "If he comes home at

Christmas to help them pack . . . and they move . . . you may never see Patrick again!"

"Liz!" the others chorused together, giving her signals with their eyebrows.

"Where there's love, there's a way," Pamela declared, and slowly the conversation drifted to Jill and Justin, how long they'd been battling his parents in order to stay together—Jill had, anyway. What reassurance was there in that? I wondered. Look how that turned out!

19

CONFERENCE

Toward the end of that week, almost everyone in school knew what had happened in room 208. The names leaked out from the other jury members, a substitute was hired in Dennis Granger's place, and when someone actually walked up to Amy in the hall and asked, "Was it you?" Amy answered, "I only said he could kiss me."

A letter went out to parents that the administration had zero tolerance for this—that an adult, and especially an adult in a position of authority, is always the person responsible.

But if there were any doubts about Amy's side of the story, they disappeared when a second girl came forward to report that Mr. Granger had groped her in a hallway after a late-afternoon band rehearsal, and in checking out her story, it was discovered that part of it had been caught on a security camera a month ago.

Amy became a sort of cult heroine. Even kids who joked about her social awkwardness were recounting her story, heard secondhand, of course, of how she had simply walked into the Student Jury room and announced that a teacher had molested her—in front of the very teacher. Her candidness, her ingenuousness, became her virtue. Kids high-fived her in the hallways. Told her she was brave, which she was. Honest, which she was. "Way to go, Amy!" they said to her with a smile, and she thrived on all the attention.

"You know what?" she said to me. "Mom and Dad were going to put me in another school, but I said no, I'm a roving reporter, and they said I could stay. Isn't that good, Alice?"

"It's terrific," I told her.

"And now that another girl had almost the same thing happen to her, it's not just a crazy story by a crazy person, is it?"

"Definitely not, and you were never crazy, Amy," I said.

I had thought that with a second girl coming forward with her story, and a police investigation begun, I would be exonerated somehow. I had been raked over the coals for including it in my write-up; Phil had been reprimanded for not reading my final copy; and Miss Ames was in the hot seat with Mr. Beck for allowing *The Edge* to go to press without her okay on everything in it. Didn't Granger's suspension prove I'd been right to do it? Shouldn't I be, like, *congratulated* for breaking the story?

Miss Ames called a conference of the four editors of the paper—Phil, Sam, Tim, and me. "We need to think about what happened last week," she said. "We need to clear the air, go over our policies, and make sure we're all on the same page. I think it might help if we begin where it started and explore exactly what Alice was thinking when she did the write-up. I'm not talking blame here. Let's just try to examine this critically and see where we could have made a different choice." She stopped and turned toward me, waiting.

What more could I say? "Well," I began, "one of my jobs, since I'm a member of the Student Jury, is to write up what goes on at each session, without using names. I guess I thought that's what I was doing."

"Okay. Fair enough. Let's start there." Miss Ames turned toward the others. "If some parent had arrived for a parent-teacher conference during your session and said they thought they were supposed to meet in the room you were using and one of you directed them to the office, would you have felt it necessary to include that in your write-up?"

I thought that over. "No."

"Wasn't Amy coming in to report something that should have gone to the principal the same thing?"

"Well, not exactly. She was reporting an offense that happened in our school, and as far as she was concerned, the jury deals with offenses," I said.

"Even though Betty Free immediately told her that the matter should go to the principal?"

I didn't answer, but Sam took my point of view. "Alice might have had the feeling that even if the complaint went to the office, there would be a cover-up."

"That's a pretty negative way to look at our school." Miss Ames seemed surprised. "Why would you think it might be covered up?"

We were all quiet for a few moments, and Miss Ames let us take our time. Finally I said, "I don't think the administration's been moving very fast on some of the stuff that's been happening with Bob White and Company, whoever they are—the white supremacy stuff."

Miss Ames didn't answer, just listened. "Okay," she said finally. "Point taken. But let me ask this: In the write-ups you've done about other people who were brought before the jury, did you include their locker numbers? Their homerooms?"

I could tell where this was going. "No," I said.

"Yet you reported the room number where the incident took place, and most people know that this is the room Dennis Granger uses."

"Yes," I said.

"Alice, looking at this with absolute honesty, did you have any hesitation at all in reporting the story the way you did?"

I wanted, of course, to deny it. But as the others waited, I remembered my nervousness as I'd hesitated over the DELETE key. Remembered the pounding of my heart when I'd pressed SEND.

"Yes," I said. "Not about reporting what happened, exactly, but about including the room number."

"Yet you put it in. Why?"

"Because I . . . I was just so mad at Granger. Amy was so vulnerable. And she was so humiliated, as though she were the one at fault."

"But why *didn't* you run it by me first?" Phil asked. "You could have called."

"You were at the doctor's."

"You've got my cell number."

"Or you could have called me," said Miss Ames.

"Phil said you were at a conference."

"I was home by then, but if not, you could have left a message."

"We're supposed to have the final copy at the printer's no later than five, so they can start running it before the day crew leaves," I said weakly, knowing full well that once in a while we don't make the deadline, but the printer usually still has our copies ready by noon the next day.

"You could have at least told me when I called you that night to check that the paper was all put to bed, Alice. You said everything was okay," Phil said.

Miss Ames leaned her arms on the table, her shoulders hunched. She looked tired. Even the scarf at her neck looked droopy. "The final responsibility for this paper rests with me because I'm faculty adviser," she said, "and I allowed the paper to go to press without my final okay, just as Phil did. I'm guilty as well. I trusted that Phil would do it for me, Phil trusted Alice, and Alice dropped the ball. This is a chance for all of us to look more seriously at our own responsibilities here at the paper."

"But . . . but doesn't the fact that the security camera caught

Dennis Granger with that second girl . . . I mean, if anything, shouldn't the administration be grateful to *The Edge* that we smoked him out? If Amy hadn't reported him, and if I hadn't written about it—" I halted for a moment. "Isn't the responsibility of a newspaper to follow through on reports and rumors and see if there's a story behind them? Isn't that what reporters are supposed to do?"

"Yeah, but what if it turned out that Amy made the whole thing up?" put in Tim, playing devil's advocate now. "At the time you wrote it, you had every reason to suspect Granger did it. But a guy's still innocent until he's been proven guilty."

"So looking back," Miss Ames said, winding it up, "would you say that we were biased in our reporting? That deep down, we assumed Dennis Granger was guilty even before we'd got the full story? Before the other girl came forward with an accusation?"

"I think we could assume that. But now that he's confessed . . . ," said Phil.

"So the end justifies the means?" asked Sam.

We thought about that, too.

"I guess that's what it sounds like," I said. Then, turning to the others, "I want to apologize to the staff. I know that the rest of you are taking the blame along with me. And I know that I felt—even at the time—I was going too far. And I didn't call anyone because I didn't want anyone to overrule me. I was afraid that if I didn't out him, Granger would get off scot-free, that the administration would believe him, not Amy. But . . . if that had happened . . . then we'd have to decide what to do next. It wasn't my job to predict."

I would have liked Miss Ames better if we could have just ended the meeting there, but she got sort of sappy and had us all link arms around the conference table while she told us that even great newspapers make mistakes, but we were still a team, a good one, that we'd move on, and she knew we'd produce articles and reports that we could be proud of for the rest of the school year.

I decided I should probably stick with counseling, not journalism, when I got to college.

It's amazing, with all that was going on, I even remembered the Snow Ball. But when I awoke on Friday, with the newspaper stuff behind me, I threw my whole psyche into the evening ahead, and Sylvia came home early to do my hair. We piled it high on my head, with some fake green daisies with black centers. Sylvia had let out the side seams in the dress as far as they'd go and told me if I was still uncomfortable in it, she'd put in another zipper. But I'd lost a couple pounds in my worry over Amy, so the dress was still tight, but okay.

And so I went to the Snow Ball.

Not all the guys wore tuxes; a lot of them were in suits and ties, and Daniel wore his brother's sport coat, with sleeves that reached his knuckles. But there he stood when I opened the door, and handed me a bouquet he'd picked up at the Giant. He was embarrassed because he'd found out too late the flowers were supposed to be in a corsage. I told him I'd appreciate them even more because they'd last longer this way, and he grinned.

Keeno and Liz were waiting out in the SUV with Pamela and Louie, and we went to pick up Gwen and Austin.

Daniel wasn't quite as spontaneous and extroverted as he'd been at the Homecoming Dance—awed, I guess, by all the formality, as well as by the large snowflakes that hung from a starry sky in the school gym. Astonished at the fake snowdrifts heaped along the walls and the rotating sparkles, like snowflakes themselves, that a strobe light cast on the dance floor.

"In America," he said as we danced the two-step, "there is real snow on the outside and imagination snow on the inside. It is amazing."

I laughed at his pleasure in the light dusting of snow we'd had the evening before. "You haven't seen anything yet," I told him. "Wait until there's enough to make a snowball. That's when it really gets interesting."

The big surprise of the evening was that Jill and Justin were together again, and when they made their grand entrance, they were the center of attention for the rest of the evening. They danced so close together, we felt the dance patrol would be after them to break it up—Jill's leg entwined around Justin's, he with one knee between her thighs. Pamela guessed that maybe the breakup itself had been a hoax, but Jill looked ravishing in a white dress with a low back—a very low back—and I had to smile when I sensed that Daniel was afraid to let his eyes linger at all in that direction.

"I do not know how to tell my brothers back in Africa how it is in the United States of America," he said when we gathered at the refreshment table. "Everything is so different here, they would not even imagine it. 'No, it cannot be,' they would say. Snowflakes from a light in the ceiling? What are snowflakes? What are corsages? What are the things you eat from boxes—the cereal? So many things from boxes. All are very strange to me. And salads!" he went on, getting warmed up. "In Sudan we cook our vegetables. We do not eat them raw like goats. 'Here they eat grass!' I will tell my brothers!"

We laughed.

"You've got to put that in your next story for *The Edge*," I told him.

"But what about us?" Liz asked him. "I've never seen a live camel. I've never seen a date tree. It works both ways."

"And I don't know a foreign language," I said. "I can't speak both English and Dinka."

Daniel grinned. "So we should trade for a year—your school with a refugee camp. I am sometimes feeling bad that I am here in America and my friends are still in a camp."

All the girls in our group managed to dance with Daniel during the evening, and toward the end he loosened up a little and tried some of the fast numbers first with me, then Pamela.

Just like at proms, a lot of girls came in groups by themselves, and some of the guys did the same, mixing or not as the evening wore on and things grew less formal. Girls took their shoes off and danced in bare feet, and the guys shed their jackets.

The eight of us left the dance an hour early and went to a Mexican restaurant for a midnight supper. Daniel loved the spicy food, and we all chipped in on the bill.

"What's the story with Jill and Justin?" Liz asked. "Anyone know anything?"

"I talked to Jill in the ladies' room and asked if the breakup had been just a trial separation," Pamela told us. "She said a trial, maybe, but that they'd started talking about getting back together sometime over Thanksgiving weekend, and now they're even closer than before."

"Maybe Justin inherits some of his grandfather's money when he's eighteen and they're going to elope," said Gwen.

"Maybe he'll leave home and move in with Jill and her parents," said Liz.

"Who's Jill? Who's Justin?" asked Louie.

"A couple who's been going together since Adam and Eve," Pamela answered. "We're taking bets on how it's all going to come out."

When Daniel walked me to the porch after Keeno dropped me off, the others undoubtedly watching from the car, he very courteously shook my hand and thanked me for accepting his invitation to the dance.

"I had a wonderful time. Thanks for inviting me," I said.

He asked again how long the flowers he had given me would keep.

"For several days, I'm sure of it," I said.

"If they begin to wilt . . . if you do not want them any longer then," he said uncertainly, "I will give them to my mother."

"Tell you what," I said. "I'll keep them till Monday, and then I'll give them back and she'll have a chance to enjoy them too."

Daniel beamed at his own cleverness.

* * *

Patrick called me on Sunday to see how the dance had gone.

"It was fun," I told him. "A bunch of us traded dresses."

"And . . . Daniel?"

"He didn't wear a dress."

Patrick laughed. "He put the moves on you?"

"A perfect gentleman from the beginning of the evening to the end. Oh, Patrick, I can't bear the thought of you moving."

"Then let's don't think about it, Alice. Let's think about my coming home at Christmas."

"I spend ninety percent of my time thinking about that already," I told him.

Sam had taken some good photos at the dance, and he printed out a half dozen to display in the showcase outside the auditorium on Monday. There were Jill and Justin, glued together, eyes closed; Keeno and Liz, their feet blurred in a fast dance; Daniel and me, dancing demurely, smiling at each other; Phil and his date; a couple of freshmen. . . .

Little crowds stopped at the showcase throughout the day, wondering which shots would appear in the next issue of the paper and how many more had been taken.

I helped out at the Melody Inn that evening. Now that the Snow Ball was over and I was on friendly terms with Miss Ames again, I discovered that the rock in the pit of my stomach still hadn't gone away. Each time I thought of Patrick moving to Wisconsin, my mind went into overdrive, thinking up all the reasons I could give him for this not to happen.

His parents had been living in Silver Spring for . . . seven . . . eight years? Didn't they have a lot of friends here they'd leave behind? Didn't they belong to a church? Did they really want to experience Midwest winters while we usually had mild winters here in Maryland? And what about tornadoes?

What about their house? I'll bet they wouldn't be able to sell their house in this market! How could they buy another in Wisconsin if they couldn't sell this one? And how could they ever pack in time?

A woman was standing at the counter with three CDs she wanted to buy and I hadn't even noticed. "I'm sorry," I said quickly, taking her credit card. "Too much on my mind."

"It's that time of year," she said generously. "Have a good Christmas."

Kay's boyfriend came to pick her up when we closed at nine.

"Where are you spending Christmas? Will your parents still be away?" I asked her.

She put one arm around the red-haired guy, who reminded me of Patrick. "Kenny's parents invited me over," she said.

"Lucky!" I told her.

Les called just as I was going to bed that night, to say that he had tickets to his graduation for all three of us.

Yikes! I thought. I'd forgotten all about it. Maybe one of the most important days in Lester's life, and it was getting lost in all the tribulations of my own.

"We'll be there, Les," I said. "How many people are graduating?"

"Two thousand seven hundred and fourteen," he said.

I sank down on my bed and tried to figure out how long it would take twenty-seven hundred people to cross a stage, one at a time, and listen to a graduation speech to boot.

"I can't wait," I said.

"Hey, I'll have to sit through yours, too," said Les.

I got to school early Tuesday to turn in a paper that was already overdue—the teacher had said she'd accept it if I got it in her box by seven o'clock. I made it, glad to check one more thing off my to-do list, and turned down the hallway to my locker.

My eye caught something dangling from the handle. As I got closer, I saw that it was a little ceramic bride and groom, the kind that appear on top of a wedding cake. The groom's face had been smeared with black ink, and the couple had been suspended from the locker handle by a thin piece of brown string, braided into a miniature noose. The loop was bound tightly around the neck of the bride.

20

CONFRONTATION

I was afraid to even touch them. Terrified, I looked around to see if anyone was watching, anyone who might have done this, but the corridor was empty. A girl and a guy appeared at the far end of the hall, their arms around each other. They paused to kiss. No one else was near.

Saliva gathered at the back of my throat, but I didn't swallow. I got the message, all right—the photo in the showcase from the Snow Ball. I stared at the figures of the bride and groom. If anyone was watching, I didn't want to appear scared.

I jerked hard at the string, but it didn't break. I reached inside my bag and took out my nail file, then sawed away at the cord and jerked it again. This time the string broke. The couple fell to the floor, chipping a piece off the groom's foot. Picking the pieces up, I dropped them into my bag and walked quickly to the library just to have a place to go, my breath coming fast. I wanted to be near people. I didn't know what to do with the bride and groom or whom to tell. Was this just a joke or a threat? I wondered if I should have touched them. Perhaps there were fingerprints. I sat at a table and pretended I was doing homework.

Don't act afraid, I told myself. *Treat it as a silly prank.* But another voice said, *Tell security*. Yeah, right. I had already stirred up one hornet's nest. There would be another "word from the principal" over the sound system. Perhaps another letter from the editor in our paper. Just like Amy's incident with Dennis Granger, the story would be all over school, and the one thing I didn't want *anyone* to think was that I was afraid, even though I was shaking.

Who was doing this? How could I go day after day wondering if I was passing that person in the hall, sitting beside that person in class? Waiting in line in the cafeteria in front of the person who had put a symbolic rope around my neck? How many people were in on it? Maybe a lot more than I thought.

It was cold, with an icy rain that pinged against the windows during morning classes. *Nobody wants to go Christmas shopping in this*, I thought, recalling that Dad had checked the forecast at breakfast that morning, wanting cold days to remind people it was December already; clear days, to draw them outdoors; and a little dusting of snow, perfect for putting them in a Christmasy mood. Instead, the ping of sleet played only a single tune: *Stay home*.

Maybe I was thinking about Christmas right then because I knew Patrick would be helping his parents pack up for their move when he came home. Maybe I was thinking about Patrick because if he hadn't graduated a year early—if he were still in school—he'd protect me. I could show him the wedding cake decoration at the bottom of my bag, and he'd drive me to and from school each day, wait for me at the end of last period, be with me in the halls. . . .

By mid-afternoon the sleet had stopped and the ceramic bride and groom were still in my bag. I tried to focus on some long-neglected schoolwork. I spent all of my free period back in the library researching the Marshall Plan after World War II. I'd found some material on the Internet, but the teacher also assigned one of two books to read about it, and I was scanning the history section to see if either book was in.

Daniel was hunched over a stack of books in a study kiosk near the back. Phil was there too, at one of the computers, and several other people were hard at work. The library had a new policy regarding noise and conversation. You could meet friends and chat before or after school, but it had adopted Amtrak's "Quiet Car" policy during school hours. Most of the time I appreciated this, but when I noticed Curtis Butler searching for a book a few feet away from me, I wished I could have a conversation with him. Just sit in the soft chairs near the back and ask why he didn't come to GSA meetings anymore. What happened to the Safety Council? Who, if anyone, was threatening him here on campus?

If he remembered me, he gave no sign of it. He took one book from a high shelf and sat down with it for a few minutes to search its pages. I was still standing at the shelves when he got up again to put it back.

I glanced up as he stretched to slip the book onto the highest shelf, and as the cuff of his jacket pulled back slightly on his arm, I saw a barbed-wire tattoo forming a bracelet around his wrist. And just below the bracelet, a dark double eight tattoo.

Curtis picked up his bag from the floor, slung it over his shoulder, and left the library.

Was it possible?

I sank down in the same chair where he had been sitting and waited for my breathing to slow. Of course! He came to a few GSA meetings because he was scoping us out, wanting to see how many came, who the "homos" were. And the "Safety" Council? Disbanded because they wanted to practice martial arts. And hadn't I remembered Curtis and some other guys at the Homecoming Dance, watching from the sidelines when the girls were laughing it up, teaching Daniel some steps? As for the Snow Ball, no one had to attend to know that I was Daniel's date for the evening, not after Sam put up that photo in the showcase. My mind kept leapfrogging over what I knew for sure and what I only conjectured.

I stood up and scanned the high shelf for the book Curtis had been reading, hoping I could easily spot it. It rested at an angle against the one next to it, and by standing on tiptoe, using another book as a tool, I was able to edge it forward and catch it when it fell: *The Rise and Fall of the Third Reich.*

* * *

When Phil left the library, I followed him into the hall and breathlessly told him about the bride and groom ornament, my suspicions about Curtis.

"Alice, I think it's time to do something," he said.

"What? Tell Beck?"

"I don't know, but you ought to report it. He could at least get security to keep an eye on the guy. And maybe on you."

"We have sixteen hundred students, Phil, and three security guards."

"Well, what do *you* propose? You're leading with your chin again, this time by keeping this to yourself."

"I'm telling you about it, aren't I?" I leaned against the wall and stared down the long row of lockers. "It's just . . . what if I'm wrong? I mean, I talked to the guy when he first showed up at GSA. He was friendly enough. I've seen him around, and he didn't seem violent or anything. Maybe he was tattooed by the gang. Maybe he was reading that book to try to find out what makes racists tick. Maybe he's scared to talk to me. I don't know. . . ."

The bell rang.

"Look, I've got to get to class," Phil said. "You busy after school?"

"Not right away. I'm going to work for my dad at six . . . or whenever I get there."

"You know that doughnut shop in the little strip mall across from the Giant? Can you meet me there after school to talk about this? I've got to return a form to the band room, but I'll be there around three," Phil said.

I said that I would, and made my way to gym. I found myself looking at arms, necks, even the legs of the girls in their gym shorts, looking for double eight tattoos. The fact that there might be girls in the group made it all the scarier somehow. Maybe they were just groupies. Girls who would do anything to get chummy with the guys. Or maybe they were true believers, who knew?

We volleyed the ball back and forth over the net, dipping and dodging to keep it in the air. No double eights on the court that I could see.

Daniel was at the drinking fountain after I'd showered and left the gym. He said the water was too cold. He always held it in his cheeks for a second or two before swallowing.

"You're like a camel," I told him. "All that water."

"Why do they put it in machines that ice it?" he wondered. "It does not even have taste when it's that cold. My teeth hurt from your water."

"Maybe we ought to buy you a canteen," I joked.

He walked with me to the next corridor. "When the weather gets very, very cold here—when the snows come—does the cold kill?"

"Only if you're out in the snow and get lost or something. If you can't take shelter and you're not dressed for it. We won't let it happen to you, Daniel," I promised. "By the way, is everything all right? No more notes or stuff in your locker?"

"No," he said. "People are kind to me. If they do not speak or smile, that's all right. There are very many people in this school. It is like a city. Not everyone speaks or smiles at you in a city."

* * *

I had nothing to do at school after the last bell rang at two thirty, but I remembered there was a dollar store over near the doughnut shop. I could use some notebook paper and eyeliner.

There was no sidewalk leading out from the east side of the school, and though the rain and sleet had stopped, the wind whipped at the scarf around my neck. I decided to take a shortcut and started across the football field. My feet made crunching sounds as I stepped on frozen grass.

Buses were pulling away from the front entrance, heading out in the other direction. I could hear cars starting up in the student parking lot, everyone leaving at the same time, the noise getting dimmer the farther I walked.

Off in the distance traffic whizzed by the strip mall. The football field was empty except for a couple of guys sitting on the second row of the bleachers, smoking, hoods turned up on their jackets. The shriek of a crow flying overhead brought answering heckles from the woods off to one side.

I wished I'd worn gloves, and I alternated hands, one keeping my scarf from blowing away, the other warming in my jacket pocket.

One of the boys noticed me and lowered his cigarette—forbidden on campus.

Don't worry, I thought, *I'm not about to report you*, and I plowed on, bucking the wind. Was that doughnut shop where I thought it would be, or was I thinking of another strip mall? I wondered. Phil had said it was across from the Giant, but wasn't there an Exxon station on that corner?

The second guy stood up. He was looking in my direction, but I couldn't see his face. For ten or fifteen seconds he seemed to be watching me approach, then he stepped over the bleacher in front of him and started forward. The other followed. They walked steadily in my direction, their pace deliberate, shoulders hunched. Too late, I recognized the face of Curtis Butler.

Fight or flight? I could feel the pounding inside my chest, the throbbing in my temples. Every nerve came alive, every muscle tensed. My legs, cold as they were, trembled slightly and my mouth was as dry as chalk.

There was no one else here. No road with steady traffic. No sidewalk with passing students. I could never outrun both of them, even if I turned and headed back. I was probably everything the racists were against: I supported gay rights, mingled with lesbians, dated a black guy. . . .

I remembered some of the things I'd read about—stories of what some white supremacists would do to "make an example of" someone. A storm trooper kicking a Hispanic woman in the face, a gay beaten to death, a homeless alcoholic stomped with steel-toed boots . . . all in a crazed expression of "keeping America pure."

As they neared, in a desperate effort to deflect them, I heard my own voice call out, "Hey, Curtis! I've been looking for you." My chest hurt with the pounding of my heart.

He slowed, paused, then stopped as I came up to him.

"Yeah?" he said coldly, hands in his pockets. "What about?"

I struggled to keep my voice from shaking. "I'd like to ask a favor."

The large boy beside him glanced at Curtis, then back at me. The hood had slipped partly down his head, and I could see that he had blond hair, a somewhat bent nose, deep-set gray eyes.

Curtis's eyes narrowed. "What kind of favor?"

"Thought you might do an article for us about your group."

There was an edgy silence. Curtis picked a piece of tobacco off his tongue, then spit. "What group you talking about?"

"The double eight, or whatever you call yourselves. I know there's a lot you want to say, so I'm offering you a front-page spot instead of the notes and stuff you've been leaving around."

Curtis shifted his weight to his other foot and studied me, eyes staring unblinking into mine. "Why you talking to me about this?"

I shrugged to hide the shivering. "Who *should* I be talking to?" He didn't answer.

"This the girl who goes for black guys?" asked his friend.

Curtis ignored him. "Who put you up to this?" he asked me.

"No one. C'mon, I get original ideas once in a while."

"What's the catch?"

"Only that other kids can respond, and we'll print their replies in the next issue, pro or con. But that shouldn't bother you. This is your chance. And you've got to sign your real name. No more 'Bob White.' That's better than trashing armbands and leaving a noose on my locker door."

"I didn't put that there," Curtis said quickly.

"You said you didn't care!" protested his friend.

"Shut up," said Curtis. He fished in his pocket for another cigarette and lit it. "I say whatever I want, I'd get kicked out."

"Not if you can write it without name-calling. You heard what Beck said: Every student has a right to free expression. You do believe in freedom, don't you?"

"For the people who founded the U.S. of A., yeah," said Curtis. "Not the ones who came after."

I decided not to argue the point here on a windy field with no help in sight. "So you'll do it? Write an article?"

Curtis shrugged and turned sideways, looking off into the distance.

"It would be short," I said. "About two hundred and fifty words. But you can say a lot in two hundred fifty words. Deadline noon tomorrow?"

"Front-page article? Just as I write it?"

"If you keep it clean."

"I'll think about it," said Curtis.

They walked on past me, and I continued toward the strip mall, perspiration trickling down my back, a desperate urge to pee. Any moment I expected to feel an arm around my neck from behind. But I didn't.

When I reached the doughnut shop, Phil was already there at one of the small tables.

"Alice!" he said when he saw me. "What's the matter?"

I was breathing hard and went immediately to the restroom. When I came back, I collapsed in the chair across from him. "I think my heart stopped temporarily. Actually, I've been scared half out of my mind." I was still breathing jerkily.

"*What?* What happened?"

"I just ran into Curtis Butler and one of his buddies on the football field. I was stupidly taking a shortcut. They were smoking on the bleachers and came toward me."

"Jeez, Alice! You were alone?"

I nodded. "I couldn't think of what to do, so I told Curtis I wanted him to write an article for *The Edge*."

Phil squinted in disbelief. "You . . . *what*?"

"It was fight or flight," I said. "I couldn't take on both of them."

Phil just sat there staring at me. Then, "What's he going to *say*? You trying to get us both booted off the staff?"

"I don't know. I told him this was his chance. To express himself, I mean."

"Alice, what exactly did you promise him?"

I took a deep breath. "Front page. Next issue. Two hundred and fifty words. But he has to use his real name and write it without racial slurs. I told him we'd publish the responses in the following issue."

Gradually, as Phil's stare became less fixed, I saw his shoulders begin to relax, his face to soften. Finally he said, "You know, it just might be the best idea you've ever had."

I don't know where I got the courage to face Curtis Butler as I did. Maybe from Amy's example.

When I told Miss Ames all that had happened and how I'd come to request the front-page article from Curtis, she smiled and shook her head in disbelief. "You just can't help saving the world, can you, Alice?"

"It was me I was trying to save," I told her. "It was all I could think of to do."

"Well, we don't know where this will lead. But we hadn't figured out until now who was behind all this, so you may have opened the door for some real dialogue here. Better than nooses hanging from lockers," she said.

I couldn't have agreed more.

21

WRAP-UP

Our next-to-the-last issue before Christmas vacation:

> The staff of *The Edge* thinks it might be important to present a minority view from time to time and has therefore asked for a short essay from a junior student which follows below. It goes without saying that the beliefs presented here are neither those of the administration nor of the newspaper staff, but because there seems to be an undercurrent of anger in this school, we feel it might be helpful to get these views out in the open. Your responses will be

published in our "Sound Off" column next week.

—Alice McKinley, Features Editor

STANDING UP FOR THE WHITE RACE
by Curtis Butler

A lot of you may not agree with me, but I'm trying to save a dying race. The USA was created as a homeland for people of European descent and not as a melting pot or refuge for non-Europeans, because what we're becoming is a third world ghetto.

White people in their very own country get a raw deal. Africans come here and are treated like some kind of royalty—scholarships and free housing and food, and all they have to do is show up at school and dances. Mexicans sneak into the U.S. of A. and get the jobs that decent white Americans should have, and everybody knows that Jews get all the money, one way or another. Just look at the names of investment firms and you'll see they're all Jewish.

If our nation keeps this up, mixing together and even marrying, we are all going to end up the same color and not believing in God and probably not even having children because we'll all be homosexual.

I personally don't believe in violence because that only hurts our cause. I, and others like me, believe that white teenagers should band together—free of drugs, homosexuality, and race mixing, not believing the Zionist-controlled TV and radio. Our goal is to promote racial awareness and pride, and it's about time we started taking care of ourselves.

Note from the Faculty Adviser: If these, and opposing, views can be discussed without name-calling and slurs, if we can express emotion without violence, we can show the community that this is a school in the truest sense, where even ideas that are repugnant to many can be discussed as to their cause and resolution. It is the hope of the newspaper staff that prejudice—in the act of being examined and questioned—can be healed.

—Shirley Ames

The day the paper came out, we felt as though we may have planted a time bomb in it. I'd had to edit Curtis's article, of course. I'd changed *Mexicanos* to *Mexicans*, and *mud-colored* to *the same color*.

Nobody knew what would happen, though. Miss Ames had alerted Mr. Beck and Mr. Gephardt, and we noticed there was an extra security man on duty that Thursday, just strolling around the halls. We didn't expect a rock through the window of the newsroom or anything, because it wasn't considered "cool" to get emotional, but those of us on the newspaper—and Miss Ames in particular—wondered if we'd done the right thing; if we'd started something we couldn't control.

Because of the noose threat, Phil and Tim and Sam made sure that one of them walked me to and from classes each day if I wasn't in a group. I noticed that Curtis went around school flanked by two buddies—one of them the guy I'd met out on the football field. There was a wary macho air about them, as though expecting trouble. But Mr. Gephardt was everywhere, talking with everyone, and surprisingly, the day went off without incident.

A lot of kids hadn't read the article yet, of course, and of those who had, a lot looked upon it with ridicule. There were a few jeers, some condescending remarks, but so much was going on with Christmas coming up and semester finals to take that most of the kids probably dismissed it and moved on.

There was a lot going on in my life too besides school—Lester's graduation, for one. Why the U of Maryland thinks the weekend before Christmas is a good time to hold a graduation escapes me, but there we were in the Comcast Center—Dad, Sylvia, and me (and several ex-girlfriends of Lester's), cheering him on. I was coming down with a cold, but I would be at Lester's graduation if I had to crawl there on my hands and knees. I stuffed my bag with Kleenex and throat lozenges and waited for his turn on the stage.

We didn't know what Les would be able to do with a master's degree in philosophy, but it pleased me to see the pleasure and relief on his face when the dean read his name and shook his hand in congratulations.

"Way to go, Les!" I yelled amid the general applause, and Les grinned in my direction and waved.

"Les," Sylvia told him afterward, "I'm only your stand-in mom, but I'm as proud of you as a person can possibly be."

Dad hugged him, and Les hugged back. "It was a long road, but you made it," Dad said. "I knew you would."

"Then you're psychic, Dad, because I wasn't always sure," Les said.

We took him out to dinner at his favorite steak house, and I tried to think what the day would be like if Mom were here—what she'd say. She was tall, Les always told me. Strawberry blond hair, lots of it. She sang. She liked to laugh. To swim. To camp out and hike.

She'd be smiling, of course. Maybe she'd be sitting with her arm around Les. Or maybe she'd just lay one hand over his on the table. She'd probably have a funny story to tell us about Les when he was little, and maybe she'd have her other arm around me.

I wondered if Les was thinking of her just then. Wondered if Dad was thinking of her. And when he said, "Marie would have been so proud," I was sure of it.

Maybe more people read *The Edge* than we'd thought. We got so many responses to Curtis's article that we had to give "Sound

Off" a full page in our last issue before Christmas. I knew we'd have even more waiting for us when we came back from winter break.

Miss Ames wrote the introduction:

> These are the first responses to Curtis Butler's essay in last week's *Edge*. We recognize that emotions run high on this subject, but we believe that as civilized people, any debate is preferable to keeping our feelings under wraps. We will take him at his word that he doesn't believe in violence. *The Edge* will print all responses as long as they are signed by students attending this school and do not resort to profanity, threats, or slurs. Your ability to write in this manner will demonstrate your maturity.
>
> —Shirley Ames, Faculty Adviser

> Was that essay by Curtis Butler a joke? Do we really have Nazis in our school? Somebody say it ain't so! I can't believe what I read!
>
> —Emma Cortez, sophomore

> How far back can this dude trace his ancestors? Does he realize that the first humans originated in Africa?
>
> —Jack Berg, senior

How did that diatribe by Curtis Butler get front-page space in our newspaper? We don't need racists in this school. I threw the issue in the trash, where it belongs.

—Sean Farmer, junior

What Curtis said in last week's paper may have seemed pretty racist, but I'll bet a lot of people feel the same way and are afraid to speak up. When you see people who aren't citizens getting free medical care and their kids go to school while your own family has to pay every time you go to the emergency room and pay taxes and stuff, you get a little pissed.

—Jon Klaybrook, freshman

I can't believe you would print that article "Standing Up for the White Race." What are you trying to do? Start a race war?

—Christy Lavies, senior

You tell it, bro! Just go live in Germany and take your prejudice with you.

—Aaron Truitt, junior

Let's have a school debate and invite Curtis Butler to be on the panel. Here's a question for starters: Since all the explorers who discovered

America were men, should only men have rights of citizenship in this country?

—Zachary Murdo, senior

Hitler was right, but history got it wrong. If he really had managed to weed out the misfits and create a superrace of strong people with superior minds, the world wouldn't be having the problems we have today.

—Eric Haller, sophomore

If we really want to be fair and just, the United States should belong to the Native American tribes who were here first, and the rest of us should get the heck out.

—Jacob Early, senior

Congratulations to *The Edge* for printing what will undoubtedly cause a lot of flak, but hopefully a lot of good discussion. Keep it coming. That's where our paper gets its name.

—Shauna Perkins, senior

The security guards were very visible the day this latest issue came out, the last day of school before Christmas vacation. Some of the GSA members wore their rainbow armbands to show their solidarity. A few guys and one girl painted double eights on their foreheads, and there was a shoving match near the gym, but it was broken up in a hurry, not by security, but by students themselves.

The newspaper staff was nervous, I'll admit. Beck and Gephardt had only halfheartedly endorsed our approach at the start, but once the racist views in our school rose to the surface where we could now touch them, the administration seemed to think the newspaper coverage might help turn things around.

I was miserable regardless. My throbbing head and stuffed-up nose used up my energy. I knew that with all the tension of the last couple of weeks, my resistance was low, but why did I have to have a cold at Christmas?

One good thing happened, though. Mr. Beck paid a visit to the newsroom.

"However this plays out, I think you've done the school a service," he told us. "This is only the beginning of a dialogue we need to get started in this school. We're thinking of organizing a periodic 'talk-out' in January, where we divide students in groups of ten, with a moderator, and everyone can express their feelings as long as they can do it with respect and consideration for all points of view."

"Fingers crossed," said Phil.

Patrick called me that night.

"Just got in," he said. "I've been doing research for one of the poli-sci profs, and he wanted me to stay one more day. I told him there's a certain girl I have to see. Can I come over?"

"Of course!" I said. "But I've got a cold!"

"You sound like it," he said. "In fact, you sound really awful."

"It's been coming on for a week. Just all the uproar at school. I don't want you to catch it."

"It wouldn't matter if you had the plague. I'm coming," he said.

We hugged there in the hallway. I tried to keep my germs away from him, but it was difficult. He kissed my forehead, not my mouth, and seemed to be even taller than he'd been when I visited him in July.

"Of all times for me to be sick, Patrick!" I wailed. "I've waited for this for so long."

"Remember the time I got sick and couldn't take you to the eighth-grade semi-formal?" Patrick reminded me. "You were pretty understanding then, if I remember correctly."

"But I didn't love you half as much then," I whispered. Was this the first time I'd actually said *love*?

"Then let's just enjoy now," he said, and held me tight.

"Maybe your mom will change her mind about leaving and will talk your dad into staying here another few years," I said hopefully into the collar of his shirt. A really stupid comment. The movers were coming in—what?—five days.

"No. They've made up their minds. I'm just supposed to see them through it." He held me even closer. "It would be different if I were still in high school, Dad said. But I'm there at the university, about an hour from my uncle's."

"Can we get together with the gang while you're home?" I asked. "Are you going to tell them good-bye?"

"It's not like I'm saying good-bye, Alice. I'll be coming back for your prom. You'll be coming to visit me. You've got an aunt in Chicago." He held me away from him for a moment and shook me gently. "You worry too much."

"And you don't worry enough," I told him. "A lot can happen when two people are apart."

"A lot can happen when they're together," he said. "Look at Jill and Justin. They broke up."

"They're back together," I said.

"So there you have it!" he joked as I guided him to the family room.

We spent part of Christmas Eve with each other. Patrick was here for dinner and helped me wrap some last-minute gifts for my family because I was continually holding a tissue to my nose. My head felt as heavy as a pumpkin, and either my nose was running like a faucet or it was stopped up and I had to breathe through my mouth.

"I don't want you to catch this!" I insisted. "You'll be miserable if you have to fly back with a cold. You *are* flying, aren't you?"

"Yeah. I have to go back on the twenty-seventh, but Mom and Dad will leave in the car as soon as the movers are gone the next day. I'll be working for this professor all through winter break. He's paying minimum wage."

"What's he doing that's so special?"

"He'll be teaching a course in Spain next year, part of a foreign studies class for upperclassmen. Wants to have his lesson plans all done before June."

"And you're an expert on Spain?"

"Hey, I'm an expert on everything," Patrick joked, and kissed the back of my neck, about the only safe spot.

We opened our gifts to each other. Patrick gave me a gorgeous scarf of lamb's wool, soft as a breeze, in graduated shades of green.

"It's beautiful!" I said, holding it out at arm's length, afraid I'd drip on it.

I guess we both had the same theme in mind—something to keep the other warm when we couldn't be together—because I gave him a gray sweater with narrow black stripes.

When he left later to go to a midnight service with his parents, I lay in bed, Kleenex stuffed in one nostril, a box of Tylenol PM on my night stand, and wondered what Fate had against me that I'd had to wait three months to see my boyfriend and then couldn't even kiss him properly.

We spent Christmas Day alone with our families, and Christmas night with the gang over at the Stedmeisters'; we'd told Mark's mom we were stopping by, and she begged us to stay for supper, so we did. Eleven of us crowded into their living room, some bringing tree ornaments with Mark's name on them, some of us with brownies or Christmas cookies, and I could tell how pleased his parents were that we had come. I tried to sit apart from the others so I wouldn't infect anyone.

Mr. Stedmeister showed us Mark's room, which he had turned into a photo gallery almost, having framed about every photo he'd taken of his son. Moving left to right, you could follow

Mark from the day he came home from the hospital, up through his toddler years, Cub Scouts, his first dance, first car. . . .

"God, I miss him," his dad said as we neared the end of the photos, and there was a tremor in his voice. "But he'll always be a part of this house, this family."

Just like the Fourth of July, when rain had kept us from going to the fireworks celebration, we hunkered down on their living room rug to watch a Christmas special at the Kennedy Center on TV, the Stedmeisters moving in and out of the room with leftover turkey and ham, homemade mincemeat pie and coconut cake, each of us having pigged out already at Christmas dinners with our own families.

Brian Brewster, in what had to be the most insensitive gesture of the evening, came by in the new yellow Toyota his dad had bought for him now that his license had been restored and invited us to come outside to admire it. As though Mark's accident had never happened. As though the Stedmeisters didn't have to live with the knowledge that their son reached the end of his life crushed between an SUV and a delivery truck.

"Brian . . . ," I said, as he stood just inside the door, beaming and jiggling his car keys.

And it suddenly took.

"Hey, I'm sorry," he said, shoving the keys back in his pocket and coming on in. "Sometimes I get carried away. Merry Christmas, everybody. How's it going?"

Mrs. Stedmeister offered him a plate. "Just help yourself to what's on the table there," she said. "It's so nice to see you, Brian."

* * *

Patrick spent his last night, the twenty-sixth, with me. Not the *whole* night. Not even a whole evening. My nose wasn't running quite as much, but it was still red and sore. Dad and Sylvia came in to chat awhile, then left the family room and the fire to us. But we heard Dad rummaging around in the kitchen a few times, and Sylvia went into the office next to the dining room to get something. We put our feet on a hassock and let the fire warm our legs, my head on Patrick's shoulder, his arms pulling me close.

"How am I going to get through the next semester without seeing you once?" I asked. "It's a long time until May."

"It won't be easy for me either," he said.

"Patrick, *everything* is easy for you!" I protested.

I could feel his body stiffen. "We've had this conversation before, Alice. You know it's not."

I was instantly sorry. "You're right. I want a perfect life, I guess. I want you here, not in Chicago. And if I can't have you here full-time, I want you back for vacations. And if I can't have you back for vacations, I want . . . I don't know. To stow away in your suitcase and let you smuggle me back to your dorm."

He nuzzled my hair. "To sleep in my dorm room with Jonah and me?"

I sighed. "There's always a spoiler, isn't there?"

We talked a long time about what had gone on at school—about Curtis Butler and his white-power views; about Dennis Granger, now that his case had gone public; about the Stedmeisters and Molly and Keeno and Brian—and finally we took the lap robes Sylvia keeps around the family room and tiptoed out onto the back porch, where the two-seater glider rocked slightly in the wind.

The cushions were dusty and cold, but we put one of the lap robes beneath us, and in time the warmth of the robes and the heat of our own bodies replaced the chill. We clung to each other.

"I wish . . . we could have each other," Patrick whispered in my ear.

My heart was racing. "So do I," I whispered back. "But this isn't a good place."

"I know. Just wishing," he said, and stroked my breasts.

"Patrick," I said, my head against his chest. "When we do . . . I don't want it to be a one-time thing. . . ."

"A one-night stand? Why do you think it would be?"

"I mean, I want it to be the best place, the best time . . . when we could have each other again and again. I don't want you going off somewhere when . . . things . . . are still sort of . . . new."

"Okay."

I pulled away from him. "You understand?"

"I think so." He pulled me down on his chest again. "But . . . God! I do want you."

I guided his hand beneath my sweater, and wordlessly, we unbuttoned buttons, unzipped zippers, and explored each other's bodies under the blankets, listening to the sound of our breathing and our pleasure in each other.

Three days after Christmas, the same day the moving van came and the Longs left for their new home in Wisconsin, I got early acceptance from the University of Maryland.

"Yay!" I said, opening the envelope there in the kitchen where Dad and Sylvia were making kebabs for dinner. "I'm in! You won't have to mortgage the house!"

"Well, that's good to know!" Dad said. "I didn't think you'd be hearing from colleges so soon, Al. You applied for early acceptance? This doesn't obligate you to go there, does it?"

"No, but it means I'm pretty serious about it."

"Well, let's don't make a final decision until you've heard from the others," Dad said. "You might like being farther away—a whole new community to explore."

"Or not," I said. "If one of you got sick . . . or the store closed . . . I could live at home and commute, and it would save you a bundle."

"Al, you're not going to choose a college on a bunch of what-ifs. I want you to go to the college of your choice. But if you decide on the University of Maryland, you've got to live in a dorm. I'm willing to buy you a used car when it's time so you can get home now and then, but you have to live there during the school year. That's a must."

"I . . . have to?"

"That's my condition. You've got to have the experience of living independently, learning to trust yourself, getting along with roommates . . . That's as much a part of college as the courses."

I silently began setting the table for dinner. The thought of having a car helped considerably. Still . . . were they kicking me out? Had they been waiting for the chance to have the house to themselves for so long that all they could think of was having me gone? What if Patrick . . . ?

And suddenly I realized that if I was living in a dorm, Patrick could visit me *there.* I could arrange for my roommate to be out for the evening. *I* could smuggle him into *my* bed. We wouldn't have to sit out on a cold glider on a freezing porch in December. We wouldn't have to talk in a family room with parents close by. And it didn't matter which college I chose, I could still invite Patrick.

"Okay," I said with finality. "If I choose Maryland, I'll live in a dorm."

22
TO LIFE

On the twenty-ninth I was feeling well enough to make a short visit to the mall. I had just used a gift card from Aunt Sally when I almost bumped into Curtis Butler. He was coming out of a Sports Authority store, bag in hand.

"Hey, Curtis!" I said, backing up to avoid a collision.

"Hey," he said, looking at me uncertainly. "How ya doin'?"

I think he was going to walk on by, but because I stopped, he did. It was awkward.

"How was Christmas?" I asked.

"It was okay. How about yours?"

"Nice. My brother graduated from Maryland, so it was sort of special," I told him.

"I guess." He looked about hesitantly, took a few steps toward the escalator, then stopped and came back. "Listen. I just wanted you to know that some of that stuff—and a couple of letters—I didn't do. Sometimes the other guys get carried away."

"Okay," I said. "Glad you told me."

We fell silent again. I nodded toward the ice-cream tables in one of the side corridors. "Want to sit down for a minute? I've got some questions."

He shrugged. We walked over to a table, and he put his bag on it. Shoes, I guessed. He sat perched on the edge of his chair as if to say, *A minute's all I've got.*

"*The Edge* has been getting a lot of letters since we published your piece, and one of them, as you probably know, suggested a debate. The newspaper would be glad to sponsor it." *Here I go again*, I thought, *climbing out on a limb all by myself.*

"We're . . . really not into that," Curtis said.

I studied him. "Who's *we*, exactly?"

He looked away. "Different groups. Different names."

"Do you consider yourselves racist?"

"Yeah, I suppose so. In a good sense."

"Good how?"

"We're not saying that other races shouldn't exist. I'm not, anyway. We're just saying that the white race has been getting a bum rap, and it's time we took the country back, that's all."

"You want some ice cream while we're sitting here?" I asked, hoping to prolong things. "I'm buying."

"No, thanks. I gotta get going."

"I just wanted to tell you that after I read your essay for the paper, I realized it sounded as though you'd memorized some of those hate group sites on the Web."

He shrugged again. "They say it better, that's all." And then he added, "But . . . after I read some of those responses in *The Edge*, I asked Vance—"

"Vance?"

"He's twenty. Sort of in charge of our unit. I asked him if he'd give a talk . . . anything . . . at school. I mean, now that we've got an opening. . . ."

"He agreed?"

Curtis shook his head. "He said we don't get mixed up in that. We are what we are."

I didn't say anything. Curtis shifted uneasily, then leaned forward, resting his arms on his knees. "Well, that sort of got to me, know what I mean? You let me write that essay, and I put myself on the line. I'll pick up a lot of crap. And now that we've got a chance, Vance says no."

"Did he say why?"

"He says they always try to trick you, and when we're right, we're right, and you don't have to explain it."

I smiled. "That's what they told Galileo when he insisted the earth revolved around the sun."

Curtis didn't return the smile. "Well, I'm just saying that I've sort of been thinking this over, and I figure if we believe it, we should be able to defend it."

"You could always debate it on your own. Get some of your friends to be on the panel too." I could only imagine how this would go over.

"I don't know that I'm ready for that yet," he said. "I just joined last summer. Anyway, Vance sort of nixed the idea. His solution is that everybody should get a free ticket back to where he came from. Keep it simple. It'll never happen, but it should."

"Then we'd *all* disappear."

He shrugged my comment off as though it weren't worth arguing about.

"Curtis, did you ever get to know—really know—someone from another race? Another country? Make a real friend, I mean?"

"Hey, I don't need to *know* the bean eater's family. I don't need to *know* the blacks who got the jobs we could have had. I know what they got, and that's enough." Curtis turned away again, his face angry.

"Did you ever think that the United States is the only home most people here have ever known?"

"Not our boy from Sudan."

"No. Africa's his country and eventually, he *is* going back. He's here to see how the real America works."

Curtis didn't answer for a moment. Then he said, "Okay, so his village was burned down. I didn't do it. The U.S. didn't do it. But here they are in this country, getting all the breaks."

"Some people risked their lives to get here," I said.

"So? The answer isn't to give them what's meant for red-blooded Americans either, that's for damn sure." He shook his head. "I don't know. Some of the things the guys are doing . . . I don't see it. 'For the cause,' they say."

"And the cause is . . . ?"

"Helping the white race see blacks and Hispanics for what they are."

"I don't see any of it, frankly. I don't know where all that hate comes from."

He went on talking as though he hadn't heard me. "Vance says my heart isn't one hundred percent in it. He wants to try our operation in a different school."

"Scare tactics? Is that what you're telling me?" I asked.

I could sense that Curtis was ending the conversation. "I'm not telling you anything. I'm just saying that's how some groups operate. To each his own. Vance can do without me? Fine. I'll find a group I like better. But, anyway . . . I do my job, you do yours. You're features editor, aren't you?"

"Yeah. By the skin of my teeth. I've made some mistakes this year."

"Like asking me to write that article?"

I gave him a questioning smile. "Guess we'll have to see how this one plays out. We've got a dialogue going—in print, at least—and that's good."

"Yeah. Well . . ." He stood up and picked up his bag. "I gotta go. See you around."

"See you," I said.

It was only two days later that I saw Curtis again.

In return for Sylvia's help with altering our dresses for the Snow Ball, I told her I'd fill her gas tank and pay for it this time—wash the windshield and check the tires, too, a job she hates.

I put a hoodie on over my sweater, pulled on a pair of

gloves, and drove to the gas station. Other drivers were there, filling their tanks for their New Year's Eve destinations before the storm that was to blow in that night. Hard to believe when the air seemed unusually warm for December and the sun was out. But a cold gray mass was coming in over the horizon, and I figured that Fate, which had assigned me a cold over Christmas, was planning to ruin New Year's Eve for a lot of people too.

After I filled the tank, I moved the car over to the air hose and began checking each tire. I noticed Curtis and two older men standing next to a pickup truck outside the service bay area of the garage. They were joking around about something, and a mechanic came out to talk with them. Curtis strongly resembled both men—same deep-set eyes, same shape of the jaw, same build—father and uncle, I guessed.

I was crouched down on one side of the car with the tire gauge, in no hurry to stand up as I watched the tableau unfold. Curtis was evidently the butt of some joke, because one of the men took little not-so-playful jabs at his stomach to punctuate a point.

"Cut it out, Dad," Curtis said at last, his face a dull shade of pink.

His father laughed and said to the mechanic, "Thinks he's going to join the Marines."

"That a fact?" the mechanic said, pulling a rag from a back pocket and wiping the grease from his hands.

"He doesn't drive an ATV better'n he drives that Chevy in there, he's gonna make one sorry-ass Marine," said the uncle.

"Make a better Marine than you would," Curtis said.

With lightning speed, his father kicked one foot out from

under him, and Curtis tottered, almost falling to the ground. He righted himself just in time and now his face was crimson. Both men laughed.

"Why the hell you do that?" Curtis said hotly.

His dad was still laughing and drew up his fists. "Wanna fight? Wanna fight?" He threw a fake punch at Curtis's jaw.

"Hey, son," the mechanic said. "Come on in here and let me show you what we did for the Chevy."

"Never could take a joke," the dad said as Curtis sullenly followed the mechanic inside.

"Toughen up the little shit, make a man out of him before he can be a Marine," said the uncle.

I checked the pressure of the fourth tire, slowly hung up the air hose, and drove away.

Patrick called me from Chicago that evening. The cold rain that had come in during the afternoon was already turning to ice in our area, and people were staying off the roads. You couldn't even get to a neighbor's without falling down, so people were advised to stay home. We were texting like mad and calling all over the place. But it was Patrick's call I'd been waiting for.

"So how are you spending the evening if you can't go out?" he asked. "I'm going to a triple feature at Ida Noyes Hall. I'll probably fizzle out after watching two films back-to-back."

"I'm writing the article in memory of Mark that I promised myself I'd do last September," I said. "It keeps morphing into something else, and I'm not sure of where it's going, but I'm giving it a try."

"I'm glad we visited the Stedmeisters on Christmas. Did you get the feeling Mark's mom was just waiting for a crowd to come? That somehow she knew we'd show?"

"Yeah," I said. "I kept thinking, what would she have done with all that food if nobody came?"

I'd already e-mailed Patrick that I'd been accepted at the U of Maryland next year, and we talked about the two other colleges and about how Patrick was liking their new house.

"Funny, but my dorm room seems more like home to me than the house," Patrick said. "I don't know the new neighborhood. Don't know any of the people, don't know the yard, the street, the trees. . . . I was thinking about that last night: how maybe the new house will always be my parents' house, not mine; that home for me, from now on, will be wherever my stuff is. Weird."

"I wonder if I'll ever feel the same way," I said. "Is it . . . have you ever felt homesick when you were away? Missed your folks, I mean? Or have you traveled so much that living out of a suitcase is old hat?"

"I was homesick a couple of times when I went to camp, but that's all. I guess I see life more as an adventure. Always wondering where I'll be a year from now. What I'll be doing."

For me, I thought, I was getting to a place that wherever Patrick was, that's where I wanted to be.

I had been delaying the writing of Mark's memorial tribute because there was both too little and too much to say. When September became October, and that turned to November,

I'd put it off once again, thinking I'd write the piece and, after it was published, slip it in a Christmas card to Mr. and Mrs. Stedmeister. Now Christmas was over, and here it was, New Year's.

Mark was a good friend—not a close personal friend who confided in me, but a "group friend" I'd watched grow up ever since I met him in sixth grade.

The summer after, I'd been there when he became Pamela's first boyfriend. I was with Pamela when he and Brian stuck gum in her hair and she had to cut it. As one of the best-looking guys in seventh grade, he was dubbed one of the "Three Handsome Stooges," and we commiserated with him in eighth grade when, in a Critical Choices class, the "problem" he was assigned to solve was how—working two jobs and with no college education—he could possibly provide child support for eighteen years to a "baby he had fathered with his girlfriend."

By tenth grade the Stedmeisters' pool was the gathering place for our crowd on Monday nights during the summer. We worried about Mark when he fell too much under Brian's influence, then watched him become more self-confident as he and Keeno worked on old cars.

Though Mark was never particularly outstanding in any accomplishment, he was a necessary part of our scene. If he was missing, we were incomplete, but I couldn't say why.

I was thinking about the uniqueness of stars. I was thinking about snowflakes. And then my mind drifted back to the discussion we'd had at church about the odds that any of us had been born at all, and I sat down at my computer to write.

IN MEMORIAM

Mark Stedmeister would have described himself as a "regular Joe." I never knew him to volunteer for a special project, because he didn't think his abilities were special. If you asked for his help, however, he was right there. He was on the quiet side—didn't often tell jokes or stories—but in our crowd Mark was as essential as air.

Sure, he was one of the first guys to own a car and he drove us around. When he wasn't going out with a girl, he was always available to make up a foursome. But it was his presence we needed to make us complete. When one of us told a joke, he was right with us, all the way, his eyes bright with anticipation from the start. We watched those familiar laugh lines deepen on his face as we approached the punch line, and he was the first to throw back his head and let out the series of chuckles that became his trademark. If we had a story to tell, he'd settle back and grin like he'd paid good money for our entertainment and knew it would be good.

Summers we met weekly, sometimes more, at the Stedmeisters' pool, horsing around, eating his mom's food, often leaving our wet towels in their bathroom, treating their place like our own. He never said we were a pain, never asked us to leave, never complained when he carried in all our glasses and plates and scraps of pizza when we forgot our manners and didn't offer to help. If Mark couldn't make one of our parties, we felt it. If his laughter was missing, jokes weren't the same.

I'd met Mark in sixth grade and figured he'd be part of our lives as long as we went to this school. As long as we lived in this neighborhood. We danced with him, swam with him, argued with him, studied with him, and finally, mourned for him when he was killed in a car accident last August.

We missed him at homecoming in September. He would have worn some crazy getup at Halloween. Over the Thanksgiving holidays we would have gotten together, and when we stopped by his house this Christmas, only his parents were there.

He'd say he was nothing special. But Mark was the one—out of the four hundred million sperm racing for the egg just before he was conceived—that got there first. If it had been any other sperm that won the race, it wouldn't have been the same Mark.

Like stars, like snowflakes, Mark was unique. Losing him created a hole in our crowd, our family. He'd been part of everything we did, and he will be remembered in everything that happens next.

—Alice McKinley, a friend

Incredibly Alice

To Hannah, Becca, and Melissa,

who love the Alice books

Contents

1
PLANS

If I could characterize my last semester of high school, I think I'd say it was full of "might have known," "should have thought," and "wouldn't have guessed in a million years." Surprises, that was it, and decisions like you wouldn't believe.

When I woke on New Year's Day, I thought it must be ten in the morning, it was so light out. But when I got up, it was only five after six. A fresh blanket of snow had fallen after the ice storm of the evening before, and everything looked untouched, untested. Like it was up to me what to make of it.

I used the bathroom and jumped back into bed, pulled the comforter up under my chin, glad there was nowhere I had to go, no special ritual connected to this particular holiday. And though I don't much believe in New Year's resolutions because

I so seldom keep them, I wondered if there was anything I really wanted to do before I graduated. Come June, I didn't want to look back and wonder why I'd missed the chance for something big.

Yeah, right. As though I weren't overscheduled enough as it was. But I went through the exercise anyway. Sports? I'd never been especially good at them, so I didn't crave to be on the girls' soccer team or anything. Student government? I'd served on Student Jury last semester, and that was all the student government I needed. Journalism? I was already features editor of *The Edge*. I had no regrets.

I opened my eyes again and stared at the light reflected on the ceiling. Maybe I was comparing myself with my friends and what they had done—Gwen on Student Council, Pamela an understudy in *Guys and Dolls* last year, Liz in a folk dance group. I suddenly realized I had never really competed for anything. *Anything*. I didn't try out for girls' track team—I did my solitary running a few mornings a week before school. Stage crew? You didn't have to try out to be on the props committee. Student Jury? I was appointed. Features editor? I'd started out as a lowly roving reporter, no experience necessary, and worked my way up.

It's weird when you discover a new fact about yourself. Like a birthmark you never knew you had on the back of your thigh. Was it unnatural somehow not to be competitive? My grades were reasonably good, but I was only competing with what I'd done before. Was I *afraid* to compete, or was I just genuinely not interested?

Who knows? I concluded finally. It was too late in the year for any kind of team I could think of, and I wasn't going to join something just to be joining. I decided to hunker down under the covers and wait for the impulse to pass, and after a while it did.

Sitting in the hallway outside the cafeteria on Monday, our legs sprawled out in front of us, lunches on our laps, Gwen said, "I've got an idea for this summer."

I lowered the sandwich I was eating and stared at her—at the short brown fingers with magenta polish that were confidently peeling an orange without her even looking. Here was someone ready to sail through the next few months of assignments without a care in the world, already planning her summer.

"You're going to intern for a brilliant scientist in Switzerland?" Pamela guessed.

"Nope. This time it's something fun," said Gwen. "I'm going to apply for a job as a waitress/housekeeper on a new cruise line, the Chesapeake. Why don't we all do it?"

Now she really had our attention.

Liz had the look of a puppy who thinks someone just said the word *walk*. Her head jerked up, blue-violet eyes fixed on Gwen. "We can sign up just for the summer? We could still make the first day of college?"

"Depends on the college, I guess, but I've got the dates already. I think they rely on college help, because the summer cruises end in mid-August and the fall cruises begin with a new crew."

"Where does it go?" I asked.

"Mostly the Bay. A sister ship will be ready in a few months, but for now, this is the maiden voyage of the Chesapeake *Seascape*. A hundred and forty passengers."

I tried to jump forward to summer. Patrick's folks had moved to Wisconsin, so there wouldn't be any house here in Silver Spring for him to come back to. If he was there, and I was here, and there were 750 miles in between . . . Why *not* work on a cruise ship?

"Sounds *great*!" I said. "Providing it doesn't interfere with the prom."

"It doesn't. Training starts the day after graduation," Gwen told us. "I tried to get Yolanda to come too, but she doesn't want to leave her boyfriend. They're going at it hot and heavy."

"You make it sound like a wrestling match," said Liz.

"You might call it that," said Gwen. "Anyway, we could have a blast, just the four of us."

Pamela was leaning forward, elbows resting on her thighs—*shapely* thighs, I might add, because everything about Pamela is shapely. "Will there be guys?"

"Of *course* there will be guys," Gwen said. "There are deck-hands, you know, plus the regular crew. Bare-chested, sun-glazed, bronze-colored, muscle-molded, heat-seeking—"

"Stop! Stop! I'm burning up already!" Pamela cried, clutching her heart. And then, singing, "I'm in the moooood for love."

Gwen laughed. "Puh-lease! Not a summer romance."

"Why not? That's how you and Austin met, isn't it?"

"Austin's here! We can see each other as much as we want."

"Well, remember what happened to Liz and Ross," I said, thinking about the great guy she had met when we were camp counselors, the summer after our freshman year.

"I still miss him," Liz said in a small voice. How any guy could keep his distance from Liz, with her long dark hair and creamy complexion, was beyond my understanding.

"You never hear from him?" Gwen asked.

"We text now and then. But he's got his life to live there in Pennsylvania. We just decided it wouldn't work."

"But you have Keeno!" Pamela chirped, hoping to get us back in a happier mood. Liz and Keeno really had seemed to be hitting it off in recent months.

But Liz gave a little shrug. "I like him. He makes me laugh. But I don't *like* like him, know what I mean?"

"Aha! Somebody else is looking for love!" Pamela crooned. "Go ahead and get the applications, Gwen. I'm in."

"Me too," I said. "Sounds like a great summer. At least Patrick's coming for the prom."

"You've got the best of all possible worlds, Alice," Liz said, breaking a huge cookie in half and holding up one piece. Gwen and I grabbed for it at once. Gwen won. "He's in Chicago, you're here, he comes back for the big stuff. Meanwhile, you're free to date other guys. . . . *There's* a long-distance romance that's working."

"He's only been gone for six months," I reminded her. "And now that his parents have moved to Wisconsin . . . Well, I don't even want to think about it. No, I *do* want to think about it. We've got this understanding that we're special to each other, but . . ."

This time nobody jumped in with assurances. No one made a joke.

"It's rough," said Gwen. She broke off one bite of the cookie half and handed the rest to me, like a sympathy card, and I accepted. "This is make-each-moment-count time, everybody, because who knows where we'll be a year from now?"

That was to be our motto, I guess. Make each moment count. I remembered that a long time ago, when my brother and I were quarreling a lot, I'd decided to live each day as though it were the last time I'd ever see him, and it worked. It stopped the quarreling, but it got so real that I was always imagining Les choking on a chicken bone or something. There had to be some kind of balance here, but I wasn't sure what it was.

And I wondered why, just as in physics, for every action, there's an equal and opposite reaction; for every new thing I looked forward to after high school, there seemed to be some opposite feeling I could hardly describe. Anxiety? Sadness? *Don't be a basket case,* I told myself, and meant it.

It was Phil's idea. Phil—as in editor in chief of our school paper, *The Edge*. Phil—as in tall, once-gangly, now-square-shouldered head honcho.

"Let me handle the neo-Nazi stuff if it keeps kicking around," he told me that afternoon. "With all that's happened at our school, we—and you in particular—need some R and R."

He was talking about the death of two students last summer, the white supremacy stuff, the prejudice against our Sudanese student, Daniel Bul Dau, and Amy Sheldon's molestation by a substitute teacher. That was a lot for any of us to handle, but I wasn't sure what Phil was getting at.

"You want me to do R and R as in . . . writing about spring fashions? Healthier food in the cafeteria? The summer plans of graduating seniors? Serious fluff?"

"Get off it, Alice," Phil said, giving me that you-know-what-I-mean look. "Write anything at all, something people can sink their teeth into, but different from all the Sturm und Drang of last semester."

I did know what he meant, and I did need a break. I'd think of something, I figured. In the meantime, I checked the school calendar for coming events. Last year we did a girls' choice dance. This year we were going to put on a 1950s-style sock hop, and when I got all the details, I wrote it up:

February 11—Save the Date!
Ask Gram for those poodle skirts, those Elvis wigs, those 45s,
those glow bracelets, 'cause this school is gonna rock!

Last year we did Sadie Hawkins, but this year it's Sock Hop.
We're going to go back sixty years and have a dance marathon.
We're gonna have root beer floats at a drive-in. There will be
inflatable instruments, a jukebox, a balloon drop, pizza, pom-poms,
pastel pearls, and bouffant hairdos galore.

Get a photo of you and your friends in a '57 Chevy. Leave your shoes at the door and buy a pair of bobby socks for charity. Watch *The Edge* for more details.

"This fluffy enough for you?" I asked Phil, handing him my copy.

"Perfect!" He grinned. "Now go find a poodle skirt to show your heart is in it."

I did better than that. I assigned one of our senior reporters to write up instructions for making your own circle skirt out of a piece of felt. I asked another to research places where people could buy an Elvis wig, rent a guitar, learn to jitterbug, make their own pom-poms, and we had all our girl reporters do up their hair beehive-style so that Sam could take a picture of it for the paper.

"You guys are *rockin'*!" Miss Ames told us. "Good show!"

Patrick called me that evening.

"So how was your first week back?" he asked.

I lay on a heap of pillows, cell phone to my ear. "Interesting," I told him. "Remember the white supremacist guy I told you about, Curtis Butler? The one who was writing those letters to *The Edge* last semester? He transferred to another school."

"Well, that should make life easier for you," Patrick said.

"And worse for the school that got him, probably," I said. "But . . . in other news . . . Jill says she and Justin 'have big plans'—I'm betting they'll elope; Gwen wants us to get jobs on a cruise ship this summer; and the school's having a sock hop."

"Whoa," said Patrick. "What cruise ship? To where?"

"The Chesapeake *Seascape*, cruising the Bay. A new line. Gwen thinks it would be fun."

I was about to ask if he wanted to apply too when he said, "So you'll be on the Bay and I'll be in Barcelona."

It took a moment to sink in. "Spain?" I gasped.

"Yeah. This professor I'm working for—he wants to go get settled before the fall class he'll be teaching there, and he's offered to take me with him. He wants to finish his book this summer—that's mostly what I'm researching for him. And . . . here's the really big news . . . only you won't like it . . ."

"Oh, Patrick!"

"He's going to see if he can arrange for me to do my study abroad in my sophomore year instead of my junior, so I can stay on in Spain when the fall quarter begins. I'll be living with a bunch of students all the while."

Why was I not surprised? Why didn't I know I couldn't fence Patrick in? And why did I realize that even if I could, I shouldn't? Patrick had the whole world ahead of him.

"I . . . I guess I didn't know you *wanted* to do a year abroad."

"I have to. Part of my major. But here's another way to look at it: The sooner I put in that year abroad, the sooner I'll be back."

That was comforting in a strange sort of way. It seemed to mean that Patrick was looking ahead. Way ahead. That the two of us had plans.

"I want the best for you, Patrick—you know that," I said. "But I'm not sure I can stand it."

He chuckled. "I think you'll stand it very well on a cruise ship with a lot of hunks around."

"You won't be jealous?"

"Of course I'll be jealous. You could fall for the first mate and get married on Smith Island and be raising a little deckhand by the time I get back."

"I'm not laughing," I said.

"It's not like I'm leaving tomorrow," he told me. "There's still your prom."

"You *will* be here for that?"

"I'll be there."

That was reassuring, but . . . Spain? For a whole year? Still, after we'd talked and I put my cell phone back on my nightstand, I wondered why I didn't feel worse. Maybe I felt safer with Patrick in Spain for a year than on the University of Chicago campus, surrounded by all those free-thinking college girls. Now that there was no home here to come back to, I had wondered how he'd spend his summer. And since I'd be on a cruise ship . . .

Okay, I told myself. *Make the most of it. Quit worrying*. When I made new friends at college and they asked, I'd be able to say, *Oh, yeah. I have a boyfriend in Spain.*

2
THE UNEXPECTED

I rode in with Dad when we went to the Melody Inn on Saturday.

"Are you going to hire a part-time clerk after I go to college, or do you want me to drive back to Silver Spring once a week?" I asked.

I could tell by Dad's expression that the question took him by surprise.

"If you go to the University of Maryland, you mean? I don't know," he answered. "But I doubt you'd want to get up every Saturday morning and drive all the way over here."

"I'll need to work somewhere if I want some spending money," I said.

Dad slowed as we approached the small parking lot behind the Melody Inn. "Won't be the same without you in the Gift Shoppe."

"Should I take that as a 'yes'—that you'd still want me to drive over?"

He pulled into the space marked MANAGER. "That's nine months from now, Al," he said. "Let's see how it all plays out."

Kay Yen, our new full-time clerk, was hanging up her coat as we walked in. Marilyn Roberts had already opened the store and would be turning the key over to Kay after her baby came. It was due February 17, but Marilyn looked as though she could deliver any day.

"Kay and I are working up a special display for Valentine's Day," she told Dad. "DVDs and CDs of all the great songs, operas, ballets—anything that has to do with love."

"I'm all for that," Dad said. In retail, the minute one holiday is over, you start marketing the next one.

"I've already ordered some valentine stuff for the Gift Shoppe," I told them. "Heart-shaped music boxes, red coffee mugs—I wanted to include a lacy red thong with sixteenth notes on it, but I figured that was going a little too far."

"Correct," said Dad, and gave me a look.

"We could even have a drawing for a strolling violinist," Marilyn said. "Kay and I were talking about it yesterday. Like, from February first to the twelfth, all cash register receipts would go into a box, and on the twelfth, you draw one and the lucky winner gets a dinner for two on Valentine's Day, with a strolling violinist."

"It would be a big hit, Mr. M.," Kay said.

"Yes! Do it, Dad!" I chimed in.

"I *would* have offered Jack to play and sing his love songs for free," said Marilyn, "but with my due date so close, we'd better not chance it."

"Well, I think the Melody Inn can spring for both a dinner and a violinist," Dad said. "Great idea! Keep 'em coming."

I set about opening up the Gift Shoppe—a cubbyhole beneath the stairs to the second floor. Up there, instructors give lessons in soundproof cubicles, and on Saturdays kids troop up and down the stairs with their trumpets and saxophone cases. But here, I slide a drawer into the cash register, open up the little cylinders of nickels and dimes, recount and record the bills. Then I wipe off the glass countertop and turn on the light in the revolving case where we keep the music-themed jewelry. On the shelf behind me, I straighten the Beethoven sweatshirts, the keyboard scarves, the Bach notebooks, and the dancing bears, and I keep an eye on the sheet music department so I can help out there if I have no customers.

This particular Saturday, Kay seemed distracted. I caught her standing with palms resting on a counter across the store, shoulders hunched, staring at nothing. She answered the phone, then flipped through a box of index cards, paused, stared into space some more, and started all over again.

Around eleven, when Dad brought by a box of heart decorations, Kay saw us together and came over.

"Mr. M., your family was so nice to invite me to your house at Thanksgiving, I'd love to take you two and Sylvia out to dinner.

Or I could even bring food over if that's more convenient. Would you be free tonight?"

"Why, Kay, you don't have to do that," said Dad. "We were glad to have you. You're part of the Melody Inn family."

"I know, but I'd really like to do it. How about tonight?" she insisted.

"Actually, Sylvia has me programmed all weekend," Dad said. "We're eating with some of the faculty from her school tonight, then joining another couple at a concert tomorrow."

Kay looked not only disappointed, but somewhat desperate. "Well, another time, then?"

"Of course!" said Dad.

After he moved on, though, she turned to me. "What about you? Are *you* free tonight? I'd really like to make it tonight."

"I don't have any plans yet," I said. "Sure."

She looked a little embarrassed. "Alice, would it be all right if I got some takeout food and brought it over?" As though I were doing *her* a favor.

"Whatever you want. Sounds great!" I said.

Dad and Sylvia went out around six, and Kay arrived at six thirty with a bag of little cartons of Chinese food from a restaurant I'd never heard of. I put place mats and silverware on the table while she heated water for the tea. The whole thing seemed sort of weird, but I figured this night must be special somehow. Maybe she had an announcement to make or something.

I was half right.

We'd just started eating—Peking duck, cashew chicken—when her cell phone rang. I heard the music coming from her bag in the living room.

At first I thought she wasn't going to answer. Then she suddenly excused herself and leaped from her chair. I saw her check the caller ID before she answered in Chinese. The conversation was short and, as far as I could tell, polite.

When she returned to the table, she gave a big sigh and leaned back in her chair. "Yi, yi, yi, yi, yi," she said, and looked across at me. "I'm going a little bit crazy. My parents are back from China. . . ."

"They just got in?" I asked.

"No. They got home yesterday. They apologized all over the place for interrupting our dinner just now. They thought it was for later this evening."

I didn't understand, so I waited.

"But . . . you know that man they wanted me to meet? The reason they wanted me to go to China with them last November?"

"Yeah," I said, remembering how she had refused, how she'd told them Dad needed her at the store over the holidays.

"Well, they brought him back with them. They want me to have dinner with him."

"Now?" I said.

"No. They *wanted* me to have dinner with them tonight, and I . . . told them I had to eat with my boss. So they invited me to dinner tomorrow night. I made up another excuse. I don't *want* an arranged marriage."

"Oh, wow," I said. "Have you . . . even seen this man?"

"Only photos. But once we meet, and *then* I say no . . . His parents and my parents have been friends for decades, they tell me. Before I was born. They say we'll learn to love each other once we're married."

"What about your boyfriend here? Can't he do something about this?" I asked.

Kay buried her head in her hands. "We broke up after Christmas. He could see that—with all the pressure from my parents—I come with too much baggage. He wasn't even thinking of marriage, and neither, really, am I. I've got grad school coming up next year, and I'm saving for that."

I smiled as I helped myself to more rice. "So you're having dinner with your boss's family tonight, right?"

She smiled a little. "Yeah."

"An invitation you couldn't refuse."

"I hate to lie to my parents."

"Well, this takes care of one evening, anyway. How long is this man going to stay?"

"A few months. He's supposedly here on a consulting job. The whole thing is just so phony. I know why he's here and he knows why he's here and he probably knows I know why he's here and—"

"Do you even know his name?"

"James. James Huang. My dad thinks he's perfect for me, but I want to choose my *own* husband. I want a man who chooses me; I don't want his parents to do it."

It was sort of exciting being in the middle of all this intrigue, but it didn't ruin my appetite. I took another bite of duck. "What did you tell your parents just now?"

"I said we were right in the middle of dinner and I'd let them know later. They apologized, by the way, and begged you to forgive them for interrupting our meal. My friends are arranging all sorts of things to keep me busy, but I can't put this off forever."

"You've got my sympathy," I told her.

Over the weekend Sylvia was in her "nesting mode," as Dad calls it—making soup and meat loaf and spaghetti sauce for the freezer. Dad says if we got snowed in from now till May, we wouldn't have to buy groceries once.

Sunday afternoon she asked if I'd take some over to Lester. When I called to see if he was home, he said that he and his roommate had been advertising for a third person, now that George had married and moved out, and that someone named Andy was coming by to see the place that afternoon. So he'd be home all day.

I like to play "rescuer" to my brother, even though he doesn't need it. When he was still in school, he sponged meals off us a lot. But now that he's got his MA and is working in the admissions office at the university, he takes *us* to dinner sometimes. Sylvia still can't resist the impulse to send him home-cooked food, though, and he doesn't exactly refuse it.

I parked outside the large old house in Takoma Park, its

yellow paint beginning to peel a bit on the porch railing, and took the side staircase up to the apartment on the second floor.

Les has a good thing going and he knows it. He and the other two roomies got the apartment as grad students, rent-free. Elderly Otto Watts, who owns the place and lives downstairs, has a caregiver during the day. But he lets Les and his buddies have the upstairs on the condition that one of them is always there during the evening and all night, should he have an emergency, and that the men help maintain the house and do minor repair work about the place.

I knocked and heard Les yell, "It's open," so I went inside.

"Care package for Les McKinley," I called, taking the bag to the kitchen down the hall.

"Sylvia send any of her chili?" Les called from the living room.

"A little of everything, I think," I told him, and began arranging the stuff in his freezer compartment to fit it all in. "That guy come by yet?"

"No. He said he'd be here before five."

"Hope he's hot," I said. "I'll bring you more stuff if he is."

Les was reading the sports section with one leg thrown over the arm of the lounge chair. Even when he doesn't shave, he's handsome. Dark brown hair (with receding hairline), dark eyes, square face, square chin. He was dressed in sweats and a tee and socks so old, they had holes on the bottom.

"I thought there would be a line halfway down the block," I said. "Nobody wants a rent-free apartment?"

"We have to pay for our phone and utilities," Les said. "The real drawback is taking turns being here in the evenings and caring for Mr. Watts when he needs it. Most grad students don't want to commit to staying home two or three nights a week, and at least half of them have never picked up a hammer, much less helped an old man in the bathroom."

"This guy okay with that?"

"Says he worked in a nursing home one summer—can handle anything. I said great, if he likes the place, he's—"

The doorbell rang just then, and since I was leaving anyway, I answered. There stood a woman in her late twenties, I'd guess, with a purple streak in her long copper-colored hair, red-framed glasses, wearing a fake-fur parka, jeans, and ankle boots.

"Hi," she said, and I knew from her voice how Les got the wrong impression. Tenor. Not alto: tenor. Baritone, even. "I'm Andy," she said. "Came to see the apartment."

"Oh, yeah!" I said cheerfully. "I'm just a relative. Come on in."

I led her down the hallway, trying hard not to smile too broadly. I'd been thinking of going to the mall, but now I decided to stay and watch the show. "Les," I called. "Andy's here."

Lester put down the paper as we came in, and his mouth froze in an unspoken exclamation, his leg sliding off the arm of the chair. "You're . . . Andy?" he asked.

"Yes. Andy Boyce." She had a wide face—somewhere between plain and pretty—and she smiled as she shook his hand. "Nice," she said, looking around.

I took off my jacket and plopped down on the couch,

wishing I had some popcorn. I locked my face into a friendly smile to keep from laughing out loud.

"Which room is mine?" Andy asked. I'd only heard one or two women in my life with a voice as low as hers, but Andy's was more sultry. Maybe she was a nightclub singer or something. There were three piercings in each of her earlobes.

"Uh . . ." Les let the newspaper fall to the floor, and his feet fished around for his loafers. "Mr. Watts has the final say," he said quickly. "A caregiver's a pretty personal choice, so you'd need to meet him." Then he added, "The room to the right of the entrance."

"Thanks. I'll look it over," Andy said, and started back up the hall.

Les stared at me with wide eyes, and I covered my mouth. He lifted his hands helplessly, palms up, his mouth in the shape of *Wh . . . ?*

"You're in for it now, bub." I giggled.

Les went out in the hall. We could hear a closet door opening and closing.

"Cross circulation. That's good." Andy's voice, checking out the windows.

"Bathroom?" she asked, coming back.

"End of the hall," said Les, following after her. "But, you know, you might want to see Mr. Watts first before we go any further. . . ."

"And this is the kitchen?" Andy stopped at the makeshift kitchen, with appliances along one wall, the sink on another. "Well," she said, "I've seen better, but it'll do."

In the bathroom she checked out the medicine cabinet and the space under the sink. "This Mr. Watts—he have any specific issues?"

"Quite a lot of them," Les replied. "Takes a ton of medicines."

"Is he ambulatory?"

"In a matter of speaking, I suppose, yes. But he's old and frail. And he also has male problems—you know, urinary incontinence. Needs assistance in that area, so I don't know how he'd feel about a woman—"

"No sweat, I can handle it," said Andy. "Who's the other renter here? What's he like?"

"Paul Sorenson?" I could almost see the wheels spinning in Lester's brain. "Eccentric. Very eccentric. An odd duck, actually. Hard to get to know at first."

"I think we'll get along fine," said Andy. She thrust her hands in the pockets of her parka and looked straight into Lester's eyes. "Well, I can move in anytime. Let's go meet Mr. Watts."

I waited while Les took Andy down the outside staircase and heard the doorbell ring far below. Les was back in a matter of minutes and leaned against the door once he got inside.

"What's happening?" I asked.

"I'm probably having a heart attack or something," he said. He walked slowly into the living room and sprawled on the couch. "He's interviewing her now. He said he'd give me a call."

"He wasn't surprised she was a woman?"

"I don't know. How the hell will I explain this to Paul?"

I pressed my lips tightly together to hold in the laughter. "You didn't specify you wanted a guy?"

"I guess not. Just said we wanted a nonsmoking grad student and gave the conditions. Oh, man, I'm dead."

"Yeah," I said. "What if Paul bolts and it's just you and Andy?"

"Don't *say* that!" he yelped. "Can't you see I'm suffering here?"

"Where *is* Paul?" I asked.

"Ten-day ski trip. Which means I can't go out at all in the evenings until he comes back. He said to go ahead and get a roommate—he'd trust my judgment. Oh, brother, am I fried!"

"Well, let's try to look on the bright side. What's her major?"

"History . . . English lit . . . I forget."

"Smoker?"

"No."

"Drinker? Did you say you didn't want wild parties?"

"Why would I say that? What am I going to do if I want to invite someone to stay overnight?"

"Oh, the two girls will probably get along famously. They'll spend the whole evening in the kitchen talking," I said breezily.

Les jumped to his feet and ran one hand through his hair, then paced back and forth, taking deep breaths. "*Why* didn't I tell her the room was taken? I hadn't even met her before! I must have been out of my mind to let her see the place."

"Relax," I told him. "Watts won't want a woman in the bathroom with him."

Lester stopped suddenly and peered out the window. "Hey! There's hope! It's Andy, heading for her car."

I leaned forward.

"Hold it," Les said. "She's opening the passenger-side door. Taking something out."

"A suitcase?" I jumped up and joined him at the window, but it wasn't a suitcase. Something Andy held in both hands. She disappeared again under the roof of the porch.

Les and I sat down opposite each other. He looked so miserable, I almost wanted to give him a hug. We waited two minutes. Five.

The phone rang and Les picked it up. Mr. Watts was yelling. He's stone-deaf without his hearing aid, but always takes them off when he's on the phone.

"Lester?" I heard him yell. "She brought me some apricot strudel! She's in!"

Two days later Les was sitting at our kitchen table with the news that Andy had moved in, books and all.

"So? How goes it?" Sylvia asked.

"I don't know. We don't have much to say to each other, which is probably good," Les said. "She doesn't ask, she announces: 'I'm taking a shower now,' not, 'Need the bathroom before I shower?' Or she'll say, 'I used the last of the milk.'"

"You should be able to work that through. Set some ground rules," Dad said.

"It's just weird having her around, Dad. I walked in the bathroom yesterday and knocked over a shampoo bottle turned upside down on top of another, draining out every last drop of shampoo."

"That's called being frugal, Les. And it's not a crime," Dad said.

Les looked helplessly around the table. "Look. She washes her underwear in the tub with her feet."

I burst out laughing. *"What?"*

"How would you know that?" asked Sylvia, amused.

"Because I found sopping wet pants and a bra in the tub that she forgot to wring out after she showered. I could hear her stomping around in there. I figure she saves on detergent by letting her soap and shampoo rain down on her underwear while she washes her hair."

"Marry the girl, Les! She'll save you a ton of money!" Dad chortled. "Look, Les, every person has idiosyncrasies, you included."

"She's loco, and Paul's going to hate her."

"Mr. Watts likes her?" Dad asked.

"He's crazy about her. Her strudel, anyway, which I happen to know came from the Giant."

"Oh, boy, you're in it for the long haul, Les," said Sylvia.

Scary, I thought. Kay Yen would be starting grad school next year, and Les had already received his master's. The first four years of college were behind them, but problems just kept coming, no matter how much education you had.

There ought to be a recess. A time-out. Some plateau you could count on where absolutely nothing happened, good or bad, and you could catch your breath. When did that happen? After you married? Had your children? Retired? Never?

3

BODILY PERCEPTIONS

Gwen invited Liz and Pam and me for a sleepover and included her friend Yolanda from church.

We propped ourselves up on pillows around the living room floor with a bowl of dip and Fritos and traded catalogs from many of the colleges we had applied to—Frostburg, William & Mary, Clemson. . . . Gwen's parents and brothers were out for the evening, and her grandmother was asleep in a back bedroom.

With rings on every finger, some with two, and her finely arched eyebrows rising and falling with every word, Yolanda read aloud the names of courses that sounded interesting.

"Here's one for you, Pamela: Theater of Revolt," she said.

"I like it! I like it!" said Pamela. "No, wait a minute. I'll take Sensory Exploration Lab. Woo! Hope it's coed."

"What about Witchcraft and Magic in Premodern Europe?" said Liz, reading from her Bennington College catalog.

"Hand Percussion and Dance Accompaniment. That's for you, Pamela," I said. "And this is for Gwen: The Nature of Moral Judgment."

"Naw, I'm taking judo or scuba diving," Gwen told us, checking the catalog in her lap.

It was amazing. The depth and variety of college courses made high school look like kindergarten. It was almost embarrassing to think about going back to physics and economics on Monday. We, here on the floor, were a huddled mass, yearning to breathe freely of the intoxicating air of adult discussions and debates: Advanced Logic; American Humor, 1940–1965; The Psychology of Sexual Response; Storytelling and Film. . . .

I saw Gwen nudge Yolanda and point to a course. "Reading the Body," she read. "'Our bodies and our perceptions about them constitute an important part of our sociocultural heritage . . .'"

Yolanda only shrugged.

"I've *got* to get into Bennington!" said Liz. "I've practically memorized the map of the campus. You know how sometimes a place just seems like home?"

"That's sort of the way I felt about William & Mary," I said. "But . . . I feel the same about the University of Maryland. I applied for early admission at Maryland, but I've got until April first to make a decision."

"I'll take anything as long as it's in New York," Pamela told us. "I've applied to four schools in Manhattan."

"How are we going to stand waiting until April to find out?" said Liz. "This is absolutely the worst part of senior year."

"What's the best part?" asked Yolanda.

"Prom," said Pamela.

"Graduating," said Gwen.

"I think it's being together, like this," I said. "We've only got four more months."

"Seven," said Gwen, "if we work on that cruise ship together this summer. Speaking of which . . ." She reached around behind her for a manila envelope and waved it in the air. "Applications, everybody. They have to be in by March first."

"What's Lester doing this summer?" Pamela asked. "You should talk him into coming, Alice. Really! He'd make a great deckhand. Now that he's got his master's, he can do something different for a change. Can you imagine how wild it would be if he was on board?"

"He's got his hands full," I said. "He's sending out résumés for a new job. And he's also dealing with a new roommate he thought was male, because she had such a low voice over the phone."

"Is she hot?" asked Pamela.

"I wouldn't call her that, no. But her low voice certainly doesn't seem to bother her; she's obviously lived with it all her life."

"I don't know how you could change your voice even if you

wanted," Liz said. "If I could change one thing about myself, though, I'd have curvier legs. My calves are too straight."

Gwen shook her head. "It always amazes me how some of the most beautiful girls don't even know they're gorgeous enough."

"You've got to be kidding," said Liz, frowning down at one leg.

"See? I rest my case," said Gwen.

"If I could change one thing about *me*, I'd take a pound off each of my thighs and put them on my breasts," I said, dipping another Frito in the sour cream dip.

"A whole pound? Like a pound of butter?" said Pamela, laughing. "Alice, you'd be falling out of your bra."

"I wish my fingers were longer," said Gwen, placing both hands on one of the cushions and studying them. "Mine are too short and stubby. I've always wanted long, elegant fingers with tapered nails."

"Well, I wish I could tan more easily," said Pamela. "If we get that job on the cruise ship, I'm going to look freakishly white in shorts. I hope we get hired, though. I'm getting psyched for it."

"Me too," I said, and looked around the group. "Are we all in?"

Gwen glanced at Yolanda.

Yolanda hugged her knees and rested her chin on top of them, a black coil of beaded hair on one side of her face dangling down her leg. "I don't know," she said.

"She doesn't want to leave her boyfriend," Pamela teased.

"It's not just that. I'm probably earning more waiting tables than I would on a cruise ship. Summers I work full-time, and those tips really add up."

"Oh, come on, Yolanda. It would be fun! Money's not everything," I coaxed.

"I really need it, though," Yolanda said.

It was the way Gwen was looking at her sideways that cued us there was more to the story.

"College fund?" I asked.

Gwen raised her eyebrows, still looking at Yolanda, waiting.

"A little surgical procedure," Yolanda said finally, and sat back against the couch, her eyes on the floor.

Okay, so we were probably all wondering the same thing—abortion? Why else wouldn't she discuss it? My mind went through a simple calculation I'd been through before: Of me and my original two best friends, Elizabeth and Pamela, only Pam had had sex. Intercourse, I mean. Two virgins, one non. Once we added Gwen, that was two virgins, two non. Add Yolanda from another school, two virgins, three non. Add Jill from our school, two virgins, four non. Add Karen and Penny . . . I had no idea.

When the silence got heavy, Liz asked, "What's wrong, Yolanda? Tell us."

"*Nothing's* wrong," Gwen said emphatically, continuing to frown at Yolanda. "She only *thinks* something's wrong, and I'm about to beat bumps on her head if she goes through with it."

Yolanda gave her a defiant look. "Everybody has something

they'd like to change, including you. You said so yourself. Well, I want to change something else." She glanced around at us. "It's just a girl thing."

"Boobs?" Pamela prodded. "Are you serious?"

Yolanda sighed, knowing we wouldn't give up. "It's personal. . . . I sort of stick out down there, and there's a surgery you can have . . ."

I think each of us cringed, wondering exactly what she was talking about but too embarrassed to guess. Not Gwen, though. It had gotten this far, and Gwen wasn't about to give up.

"Her labia. It's got a name, Yolanda," she said, and then, to us, "I keep trying to tell her that this is a normal sexual characteristic, and every girl's different, but she won't listen."

I finally thought of something to say. "Yolanda, have you read Maya Angelou's *I Know Why the Caged Bird Sings*? She was worried about the very same thing until her mother persuaded her it was natural."

"Well, some doctor advertises that he does this kind of surgery, and Yolanda's borrowing four thousand dollars from a cousin to have it done," said Gwen.

"Four thousand!" we spluttered in unison, and Liz choked on her Sprite.

Gwen turned to Yolanda again, and her voice was more gentle, almost pleading. "Listen, Yolanda. Some girls have labia all tucked up inside them like . . . like petals on a carnation. Other girls' are more like rose petals, half in, half out; and some are like . . . the open petals of a tulip."

We laughed, and that helped relieve the awkwardness, if not the embarrassment.

"Gwen, you should write for Hallmark," I said. "'Ode to the Labia' . . . a rose is a rose is a labia."

"I guess I'm a tulip too," said Pamela thoughtfully, making us laugh again. "I never thought much about it. But Tim sure liked the way I looked. In fact, I heard a guy say once that girls with big ones are supposed to be more sexually responsive than girls with small ones—like pouty lips, I guess. Next, girls will be getting collagen injections in their labia to make them pouty."

I was all for changing the subject at that point, but I realized we had Yolanda's attention.

"Where did you get the idea that something was wrong with you?" Liz asked her.

Yolanda hugged her knees again. "My boyfriend said I didn't look like the girl in a movie we watched."

"Must have been some movie!" said Pamela.

"Okay, so it was porn, but we got a good look, and he's right. I *don't* look like the girl down there."

"So you're going to have surgery? Lop them off just for your boyfriend?" said Gwen. "To look like a *porn* star?"

"It's a regular surgery, not a back-alley kind of thing," Yolanda said. "This doctor's done hundreds of them."

"*Listen* to yourself!" said Gwen. "If hundreds of women think they 'stick out down there,' as you put it, it only proves it's normal! Somebody's feeding them a bunch of crap. And it's risky. What if you went through with it and found you didn't feel as much as you did before? That there was nerve damage. What would your boyfriend think about that?"

Liz was trying to comprehend it. "How . . . I mean . . . does your boyfriend . . . like . . . *examine* you all over? 'I like this part' and 'I don't like that'?"

More embarrassed laughter, but a little louder.

"Well, he sees what I look like down there. Any guy would when you've been having sex."

I shrank back against the cushions. "Arrrrggghhh! I want a guy who loves all of me, not just a part. 'It's a package deal,' I'd tell him. Yolanda, what if you go through with this and he decides he doesn't like something else? What if he says your belly button should poke in instead of out? Would you fix that, too?"

"Then he'll want a boob enhancement," said Pamela. "I think it's a control issue."

"Yeah. What if you go to all the trouble to make your labia smaller and the next guy who comes along wants them larger? You going to have them stretched?" I said. "I've got a better idea. The next time your boyfriend wants to do a clinical exam, tell him you'll trade places. Put *him* on the table."

"Yay!" the others cheered.

"Yeah, stretch him out buck naked and tell him all that body hair has to go," said Liz.

"And *that* thing could be a little . . . uh . . . thicker," said Gwen.

We shrieked.

"And *those* could be a little tighter," said Gwen. "'How about doing a testicle tuck just for me?'" she suggested.

We howled.

Yolanda was laughing so hard, she had tears in her eyes. In fact, I wasn't sure if she was laughing or crying. Relief, maybe.

"Now tell me something good about yourself," Gwen urged her.

Yolanda just wiped her eyes and gave a half smile.

"Well, I may not like my fingers, but I like my hair," Gwen continued. "If I want to press it out and get it straightened, I can do that. If I want to go natural, I can. I can dread it and twist it. I've got great hair."

"I like my arms," I said, holding one out. I don't know that they're different from anyone else's, but they're pretty arms. "I've always liked my arms and elbows."

Pamela jumped up and paraded around. "I like my butt!" she said, and gave herself a slap on the behind, and we applauded.

We all looked at Yolanda. "I like my feet," she said finally, wiggling her toes with their bright red polish.

"The only part of you that's got any sense," said Gwen.

4
AN UNTIMELY OFFER

After AP English on Monday, Mrs. Rosen asked if I could stay for a few minutes after class. I figured there was something she wanted me to cover for *The Edge*, so I had my pen in hand when I went up to her desk.

She waited until the other students had left the room, then said, "Thanks for staying, Alice. I wonder if you're familiar with the Ivy Day Ceremony here at school?"

"A little," I said, remembering that a few days before graduation each year, I'd seen the seniors, in their caps and gowns, gathering in the hallways and going outside for a procession around the block—around our ivy-covered building—for some kind of ceremony in the courtyard.

Mrs. Rosen motioned for me to sit down and sat in the

chair opposite me. In her white turtleneck and black pants, she looked more like an usher than a teacher, but I liked her shoes—really great purple and black shoes with a little curved heel.

"Each year the teachers choose an Ivy Bearer—usually a girl who is deemed to be one of the most focused, well-rounded seniors. This is a seventy-year-old tradition in our school. Each class plants a little pot of ivy in the courtyard, symbolic of the senior class having planted its roots in this school. Walking along with the Ivy Bearer is the senior class president on one side and the Ivy Day Poet on the other. The president gives a short dedication as the ivy is presented, the principal accepts it, and then the poet reads an original poem. I'd like you to try out for the poet."

My eyes moved from her shoes to her face, a small face, deep-set eyes. I'd had the vague hope as she talked that perhaps I was going to be the designated Ivy Bearer—that focused, well-rounded girl. Had she really said "poet"? Had she said "try out for"?

"Here's the way it works," Mrs. Rosen explained. "The English teachers invite four or five students to write an Ivy Day poem—about our school, their class, the meaning of Ivy Day to them—and each of the students reads his or her poem aloud at a faculty luncheon in early April. That week the faculty votes on which of the poems should be read at the Ivy Day Ceremony, and the author is appointed the Ivy Day Poet. I'd very much like you to be one of the contestants."

I was still staring at her. "I . . . I don't really write poetry," I said, stupefied.

"Well, many of our previous poets hadn't either, until they were asked. You write some very fine articles for the school paper, and poetry is an excellent way to learn to distill your writing down to its essence. Whether you win or not, you'll have a chance to perform before the faculty, and that's both an honor and good experience for college."

My pulse was going ninety miles an hour and my throat was dry, but not, I think, from excitement.

"I just . . . I don't know," I said. "I've never thought about it."

She reached out and touched my arm. "Well, will you think about it for a few days, then? You don't have to decide this minute. Take a week if you need to. But I know several teachers who would be very happy if you agreed."

I ended up in Mrs. Bailey's office the next day. The minute I saw a free space on her sign-up sheet for after school, I wrote in my name.

"I've never written much poetry, nothing I really liked," I lamented. "I don't do abstract very well. I mostly enjoy writing about people. What am I going to tell Mrs. Rosen?"

My guidance counselor had made each of us a cup of chai tea, and she nodded as she listened, letting the steam warm her face. She was a sixty-something woman with gray hair, still brown in places, gently curled. Soft skin. Laugh lines at the corners of her eyes.

"I've already got loads of stuff to do—things I *want* to do—

and I feel sure that there are other people who write poetry better than I could," I continued.

"Is it possible you might surprise yourself?" Mrs. Bailey asked.

"It's possible I'd surprise myself; it's possible I'd spend the next three months writing and rewriting a poem that isn't very good, and I'd stand up at the faculty luncheon and humiliate myself," I said.

"Well, you've given some reasons why you feel you shouldn't accept. Can you think of any reasons you should?"

"I really tried to do that," I told her. "The only reasons I could think of were that Dad would be proud of me and Sylvia would be pleased, simply because she loves poetry."

Mrs. Bailey was quiet for a few moments. "And you?" she asked finally.

"I don't want to do it, Mrs. Bailey. I wouldn't enjoy it, I'd obsess over it, and I'd rather be doing other things."

"So . . . ? Where's the problem?"

"Mrs. Rosen really wants me to try out for it, and evidently, some other teachers do too. I feel I'd be letting them down. I just . . . what if I'm saying no because I'm afraid I'll fail? Actually, in this case, I'm sure I would. But how do I know if I might be refusing for the wrong reasons?"

"Ah! A question for the ages, Alice."

"For the aged?"

"No, my dear, I mean, this is a question we all wrestle with each time we make a decision."

"But how do we ever *know*?"

"We don't. Each time you make a decision, you have to factor in everything you know at that moment. And later, if you see you chose wrong, you remind yourself how it seemed the best choice at the time. Some decisions are reversible, while others aren't."

"I keep telling myself that if I say no, I'm closing a door. They'll ask someone else and I will have lost the chance to be class poet, to have that honor."

"And if you say yes?"

"If I say yes, I will probably be miserable for the next three months and fool around over and over again with verses I don't even like. There's just no *joy* here, except to think how proud Dad would be."

"Did it ever occur to you that by saying no, you could also be opening a door? That there are other ways to win the praise of your dad?" And when I didn't answer, she asked, "Isn't he proud enough of you as you are?"

I slouched down a little and smiled at her. "I think you just talked me into saying no."

"My job isn't to talk you into anything—just to help clear up the picture a bit," Mrs. Bailey said.

"Well, it really helps," I said, but made no move to leave.

Mrs. Bailey sipped her tea again. "How are other things going in your life right now?"

"Mostly good," I said. "I'm excited. Happy. But, well . . . a lot of the time I also feel sort of . . . lost."

"Lost? As in . . . ? Can you put your finger on it more specifically?"

"Well, sad in a way. Scared in a way. Like . . . all along I've had a good idea of what was coming next. When I was a freshman, I'd watch the sophomores, and so on. Suddenly I'm a senior, and stuff like this starts coming at me. *Be the class poet.* My last chance to do something big in high school. Graduating's like . . . like jumping out of a plane, doing something I've never done. I don't know what to expect after high school, not really."

"You said you'd decided on the University of Maryland?"

"Well, not exactly. I'd like to see if I'm accepted at William & Mary. It would be great if I could go there. But Maryland would be good too. It's not just school, though."

I let out my breath, then inhaled again and blew on my tea. She waited.

"It's like I'm leaving one whole life, almost, and starting another. Leaving one part of me behind," I said. "I guess that's the sad part, and yet . . . I mean, it sounds crazy . . . ,"—she smiled at that—"but for as long as I can remember, I've had this beanbag chair. Even after we moved from Chicago to Maryland, even after I redecorated my bedroom, I kept that beanbag chair in one corner because I was so comfortable in it. I curled up in it when I was sad, when I was happy, when I was scared. I always wondered if it was a substitute for my mom's lap. I never wanted to give it away even when it looked out of place, which it does.

"And the other night . . . I don't know why . . . I just got the urge to go sink down in it, and . . ."—my voice actually quavered a little—"I didn't feel comforted, I felt ridiculous. And I'd always believed I'd take it to college with me and keep it in my dorm. All it's good for now is a footstool, and I . . . I . . . m-miss it."

I tried to laugh through my tears, and Mrs. Bailey nodded and smiled.

"Alice, if you only knew how common this feeling is. Not everyone expresses it as easily as you have," she said, "but I've almost come to expect this of seniors the closer they get to graduation."

"Expect what? Everyone missing a beanbag chair?"

"The blues. The uneasiness." She put down her cup and folded her hands in her lap. "It's a kind of mourning, actually, the way I see it, because you really are experiencing a loss. Loss of your childhood, even though you're glad to be growing up. A certain loss of security, a familiar routine. The pattern of high school life."

"But I've always looked forward to college! I thought I *wanted* to be on my own."

"And you do. But right now, as you put it, you're preparing to jump into your future, and you don't know exactly what you'll find when you land. You've never been there before, only heard about it. And sometimes you just want to fly back to home base, where you feel safe and loved."

"Everyone else seems so excited about college, about graduating."

She laughed. "They'd probably say the same thing about you."

"Really?"

She nodded. "You guys are good at hiding feelings from each other."

I took a minute or so to think about that and sip the tea.

"So . . . how do I deal with it? When I get this . . . sadness?"

"Acknowledge it. Take time to say to yourself, 'I'm feeling really sad'—or nervous or scared, you supply the words—'and I'm wondering how I'll get along in college.' This much I can promise you: It's a lot less scary when you recognize what you're feeling instead of trying to hide it from yourself."

"I'm not sure that will be enough."

"It may not be. You also need to talk about it with whomever will listen, and you know I'm always ready to listen. Remind yourself of the things you've faced in the past and how you managed to get through them."

"Not exactly like this, though."

"No?" She waited.

"Well . . . losing my mom, maybe. That was worse."

"Really major."

"And moving a couple of times."

"Uh-huh."

"And Mark dying." Somehow the things I'd had to deal with before seemed a lot scarier than just going off to college. "I guess you sort of have to take a deep breath and tell yourself to get over it," I said.

"No. Not get over it. Get through it. Go into it staying up front with yourself and remind yourself of all the ways you have of coping. When you get to college, make friends with your counselor early on. Tell her what we've talked about here, so that when you come to a bump in the road, you're already friends."

I could feel my panic, like a gas bubble in my chest, slowly evaporating.

"In the meantime," Mrs. Bailey said, "why don't you write about this?"

"Write it?"

"A feature article for the paper. You'd be helping a lot of people who, like you, think they're the only ones who feel this way."

"Wow!" I said. "I'm not sure I'm the one to do it."

"If not you, who?" Mrs. Bailey asked.

She was right. It couldn't be someone from outside the pain and panic, looking in. It had to be someone inside, looking out. And better this than a poem about ivy.

"Okay," I said. "I'll think about it."

5

NEW LIFE

Sylvia and I went to a baby shower for Marilyn after work on Saturday. I'd known Marilyn since I was in sixth grade. Of all Lester's old girlfriends, she was probably the one I liked most.

I'd always thought of Marilyn as the original "flower child," like the ones we read about back in the sixties. She was earthy and natural and sweet—as close as I could get to an older sister—and I'd always hoped she and Les would marry. But it never worked out, and she and Jack were happily married, playing their guitars, composing folk songs, and playing at weddings and anniversaries and stuff.

The shower was supposed to have been at the home of one of her friends, but Marilyn had been having back trouble, so they were bringing the shower to her. I had her address, and Sylvia was doing the driving.

It's sort of fun to be invited to an adult thing with your mom—stepmom or otherwise. Like you're accepted now as a woman. An acknowledgment that this would be happening to you—love, marriage, sex, a baby, not necessarily in that order.

I was wondering how Sylvia felt, going to baby showers when she'd never had a child herself. It was something I didn't feel I could ever ask. And then Sylvia answered it herself.

"I used to dread going to baby showers," she said, steering with one hand as she turned the radio down with the other. "It was the way the women looked at me, or I imagined they were looking at me—their side glances—when little sweaters and booties were held up to be admired. As though I might cry or something. They even said things like, 'Well, it's not all baby powder and cooing, you know. There are diapers.' To make me feel as though I wasn't missing much."

I couldn't believe Sylvia was telling me all this, things she'd probably never told her friends.

"So that . . . wasn't the way you felt—that you were missing something?" I said hesitantly.

"Of course I'm missing something. But I've never seen the Taj Mahal either. I never played the violin. I never wrote a novel or learned to fly or met a president. When people infer I'm incomplete somehow because I haven't given birth, I think, 'We're all incomplete in some way.' I don't know anyone who has done *every*thing she wanted to do in life."

"Well, I guess I'd like to have children if it works out," I told her. "I'm just not sure I'd like the birthing part."

She laughed. "That wouldn't have held me back, but I wanted any children of mine to have a dad they loved as much as I did, and until I met Ben, that just hadn't happened."

I didn't say, *And now you've had a hysterectomy, so it's too late.* I didn't know what to say, but finally I managed, "Well, if you *did* have children, I think you would have made a good mom."

She didn't laugh out loud, but even without looking at her, I knew she was smiling.

"And now that I *am* a mom?" she asked.

"I think you're doing pretty good, considering what you inherited," I said.

Sylvia glanced my way and gave me a grin. "*I* think I was pretty lucky with what I got."

"I'm not out of the nest yet," I told her. "Eight more months before college. But there's a possibility I'll be out of your hair this summer. A bunch of us are applying for jobs on a new Chesapeake Bay cruise line—waitressing and making beds."

"Really!" she said. "Now, *that* would be fun. See? That's another thing I always wanted to do and never did."

The Robertses' rental house was a little Cape Cod off Route 28 out in Rockville. It was on a dark winding road, set back from the street, the trees much larger and older than the houses.

We saw Kay Yen's Toyota parked in front, and it was Kay who answered the door. We could hear the chatter of women's voices as we came up the steps.

"They put me in charge of the door," Kay said, grinning, and held it wide open. "I don't know—is there some symbolism in this?"

"Like catching a bride's bouquet?" Sylvia said, and laughed. "I doubt it."

I gave Kay a hug as I stepped inside, conscious of how slim she felt, in contrast to how Marilyn looked, sitting on a straight-backed chair, her abdomen huge and resting, it seemed, on her thighs. At the store she was mostly standing or perched on a high stool behind a counter. Now, sitting down, her knees apart, she looked as though she could deliver any minute, and she still had a month to go. I guess on smaller people, an eighth-month pregnancy resembles a basketball under the clothes, but every time I tried to imagine that baby pushing its way out, I had to remind myself that everything stretches.

"I know," Marilyn said when I hugged her, as though she could read my thoughts. "I look huge."

"You look mama-ish," I said. "It's exactly how you're supposed to look."

"Well, I'm ready," she said, and patted her tummy. "But I guess this little person still has some finishing to do yet."

I sat down on the floor beside her chair as the other women gathered around, each of them with a photo of herself as a baby pinned to her shirt, as requested on the invitation. Sylvia's photo was of a newborn, lying on her back, fists clenched, legs in the frog-kick position, a little red-faced, hairless wonder. It was impossible to see in that baby the beautiful woman she was now.

For my photo I'd chosen a picture of me in a sundress at around fifteen months, sitting on the curb with an ice-cream cone. It was fun to look at each other's baby photos and try to see something of the woman-to-be in them, even women I didn't know.

Along with the stroller and bottle warmer, the diaper pail and mattress cover, Marilyn received some novel gifts as well. The Melody Inn gave her a crib and a fancy mobile to hang above it. There were five different sound tracks a parent could choose to put her baby to sleep—Bach, Mozart, Beethoven, Brahms, and Liszt—while colorful little birds, with tiny lights in their wings, swirled around and around with the music. Kay's gift for the baby was a tiny hand-embroidered robe from China, with little silk slippers to match.

"This is fun," I said to Marilyn as she held up each outfit for inspection. "Aren't you excited?"

"Excited, scared, impatient, eager . . . ," she confirmed, and the other women laughed.

"Don't forget tired," someone reminded her, one of Marilyn's friends with a platter of little frosted cakes that looked like baby blocks.

Another friend, who had been working in the kitchen, pulled a chair into the circle next to Sylvia. "Hi, I'm Julia," she said.

Sylvia smiled and shook her hand. "Hello, I'm Sylvia," and, nodding toward me, she said, "and this is my daughter, Alice."

"Hi," Julia said, smiling at me. "Yes, I see the resemblance," she added, looking back at Sylvia again. Then, "I'm glad we moved the shower here. When your back hurts, you just seem to hurt all over," and she made room for still another woman to join the circle.

I sat flushed with . . . what? Surprise? Astonishment? Was I offended that Sylvia had claimed me as her daughter? As much as I'd always wanted her to marry Dad, there was a part of me that held back, that told me I belonged to Mom. I tried hard to concentrate not on how I thought I *should* feel at that moment, but on how I truly did feel. And I was pleased.

Did we have to go on saying *stepdaughter* and *stepmother* forever? I could never deny my true mother, never remove her picture from my dresser or forget the few years I had with her, but if Sylvia wanted me to be the daughter she never had, then whenever I was with Sylvia, she could call me her daughter. And I found I was smiling.

I handed Marilyn each gift and helped unwrap them if they were large, stacking them all behind her when she was ready for the next one. When the last present had been opened and I was gathering up wrapping paper, Marilyn asked, "Alice, would you mind going up to our bedroom and bringing me a little green pillow to go behind my back? You may have to hunt—I use it during the night, and it could be under the covers or even under the bed—a small flat pillow. Top of the landing to your left."

"Sure," I said, getting up and stepping over boxes. I went up the short flight of stairs and into the bedroom on the left.

It felt sort of strange walking into a couple's bedroom. I turned on a lamp on their nightstand. The bed was unmade, the covers awry. The usual bedroom scene—a T-shirt hung over the closet's doorknob, a pajama bottom and shoe on the rug. I looked around for the pillow but didn't see it, so I crouched down and found it poking out from under the bed, just as Marilyn had guessed.

As I stood up again to turn off the lamp, I hesitated. The drawer of the nightstand was slightly ajar, and it occurred to me that if I just took a peek, no one would ever know. It wasn't as though I had come into Marilyn and Jack's bedroom as a spy. But people often kept their most intimate stuff in their nightstands, and it was normal to be curious, wasn't it? It would only take a second to peek.

But I didn't. Marilyn had trusted me to go into her bedroom as an adult, and I wanted to come out the same way. As my fingers groped for the light switch once more, I took one last look at the bed. Both pillows were there in the middle, touching, sort of turned toward each other, as though Jack and Marilyn were used to talking together in the night. It gave me a happy feeling, and I was still smiling a little as I went downstairs and tucked the pillow behind Marilyn's back.

There was an empty chair beside Sylvia, and she was holding a little dessert plate of cream puffs.

"I know you like these, so I saved some while I could," she said, handing it to me.

"Thanks, Mom," I said, and sat down beside her. We grinned at each other, and she patted my knee.

Jack came in a little later, a light dusting of snow on his cap and sprinkled in the dark stubble of his face. He went around the room greeting the women, hugging the ones he knew. Someone begged him to take a plate and join in, but Jack said he had a present first for his wife. Then he brought out his guitar and sang a song he had composed for their baby. He said he was performing it for the first time here at the shower, the first time Marilyn had heard it too:

"Been waitin' for you, baby child,
Wonderin' when you'd come.
Mama gettin' bigger,
Pacing to and from.

Bedroom's been all painted,
Car seat's set to go;
Daddy's growing restless,
Mama gettin' slow.

Once you're here, we'll hold you,
Kiss your downy head,
Count each chubby finger,
Keep you dry and fed.

Breathe upon my shoulder,
Sleep upon my chest.
You're the little sweetheart
Gonna make us blest."

When he had finished and strummed the final soft chords, we all had tears in our eyes, and Marilyn reached over to hug him.

"It's so beautiful, Jack. So beautiful!" she kept saying, and the woman named Julia made us laugh by passing around a box of tissues.

Jack broke into a lively song next, as the women gradually started straightening up the living room, gathering coffee cups and plates to wash, collecting the gift bows. Sylvia and I worked side by side, and it felt incredibly good.

I couldn't put it off any longer. I had to give Mrs. Rosen an answer. For a week my mind had toyed with the same dull phrases, and then, like a balky horse, it just stopped working. *The ivy grows / it climbs ever upward, / reaching higher.* So what? Nothing profound about that. *The ivy in the early spring / is colored like the evergreen* . . . A thousand yucks.

I delayed gathering up my stuff at the end of class on Monday and waited till everyone else had gone.

"Mrs. Rosen," I said, "I've been thinking it over, and I just don't feel I'm the right person to compete for Ivy Day Poet."

"I know others have felt the same way, Alice. Are you sure you don't want to try for it?"

"I'm sure," I said. "I really don't. But I appreciate your thinking of me. And I hope you get a great poem."

I called Les that weekend to see how things were going. His voice sounded tired and pained.

"Paul says it's either him or Andy—one of them has to go," he replied.

"Paul would leave? He actually said that?"

"Not in so many words. He says with her around, everything's changed. No more breakfasts in his shorts. No more gratifying belches with our beers. She tutors, she tells us, but as far as we're concerned, Andy's about as social as a mole. Shuts herself up in that bedroom and even takes her meals in there from what we can tell. Students come in and out occasionally, but even then, her door's closed. Food appears and disappears from the fridge, bathwater turns on and off. Once in a while we get a fleeting glimpse of her in the hallway."

"So what does it matter if you belch or not, if you never see her?" I asked.

"It doesn't feel like home to either of us. She's like a spook when she's around, and all we do is plot to get rid of her."

"But at least you and Paul can go out on the same night."

"Yeah, and don't think we don't take advantage of it. We told her Paul and I each stay home two evenings a week and she stays home for three. She asked why she got the short end of the stick, and Paul said because she was the shortest."

I laughed. "What did she say?"

"I quote: 'You're so full of human kindness, it's coming out your ass.' I think it was meant to be funny."

"Whew!" I said. "The temperature's rising already. Why don't you and Paul just tell her it isn't working out?"

"Because we need to have at least one person here who

knows how to care for Otto in case we get jobs somewhere else. We've both got résumés circulating, and we'd still have to find two other people to take care of Mr. Watts if both of us moved out."

"Of course, the next two people could not only have purple streaks in their hair and hide in their rooms, but they could be making counterfeit money," I said, enjoying myself.

"Not to worry. Nobody else gets a room up here without a shakedown, fingerprints, and an FBI check," Les said.

6
CALL FROM AUNT SALLY

Gwen drove us to school on Monday because her brother was buying another car and she was negotiating the sale of his old one to her.

"I just want to see how this really drives before I commit all my earnings," she said, testing the brakes. Liz and I were glad to give our opinion, which was that any car that ran was a good car.

After we picked up Pamela, Gwen said, "You'll be glad to know that Yolanda's filled out an application to work on the cruise ship. And I think we've talked her out of her little procedure. That's the good news."

"Yay!" we said. "What's the bad?"

"She's trying to talk her boyfriend into applying too."

"Boo!" we hissed.

I went to the newspaper office when we got to school and had barely walked in when Phil said, "There's some protest going on outside the library, Alice. Would you check it out for a story? When Sam gets here, I'll send him down for a photo, if it's worth it."

I had a half hour before first period and had planned to proof a couple of stories, but Phil said he'd do it for me, so I headed for the library. I could see a line of protesters as soon as I turned the corner.

A few of the students were carrying homemade signs: FREE THE CAGED BIRD, read one. BAN BONEHEADS, NOT BOOKS, another. And DON'T CENSOR THE INDIAN'S DIARY.

Now what? I wondered.

The protesters seemed to be mostly juniors, a few sophomores, their faces serious and defiant. The library itself was empty.

"What's up?" I asked a guy, falling in step beside him as he picketed back and forth. "Is the library closed?"

"Close-minded," he said, and pointed to a large sheet of paper they had stuck to the door: NOW RESTRICTED READING. MAKE YOUR VOICES HEARD.

I got out my notebook and wrote down the titles that were listed below: *The Color Purple*; *The Absolutely True Diary of a Part-Time Indian*; *Catcher in the Rye*; *I Know Why the Caged Bird Sings*; *The Kite Runner*; and *The Diary of Anne Frank (Definitive Edition.)*

Through the window of the library, I could see Miss Cummings back in the workroom, peering tentatively out at the gathering crowd. I stopped another girl who was handing printouts to anyone who passed by. "When did this happen? These can't be checked out?" I asked.

"Not without a note from mama," she said. "Some parent wants them removed from the library, so Miss Cummings put them on a restricted shelf. Mrs. Garson would never do something like this. I don't even remember a restricted shelf."

Mrs. Garson, I knew, was on medical leave for a month.

Someone started a chant: "We want books! We want books!"

Sam appeared with his camera. "Any idea what's going on?" he asked me.

I motioned toward the sign on the door. "All those authors are restricted reading. Parent's signature required."

"Are you kidding? Alice Walker? Maya Angelou? What did Maya do to deserve this?"

"Got raped," I said. "Probably some mother doesn't want her daughter to read about it."

"Is this high school or grade school?" Sam murmured, taking a picture, then another of the protesters.

"It's sure not college," I said.

Someone tried the door of the library and found it locked. He rapped on the glass. Miss Cummings was on the phone.

Then Mr. Gephardt was coming down the hall, a puzzled, bemused expression on his face. When the protesters saw him, they began chanting in earnest. "We want books! We want books!"

"Whenever we want," added a loud voice.

"Whenever we want." The crowd took up the chant.

Miss Cummings came to the door of the library, now that she saw the vice principal. She unlocked it.

"What's going on out here?" Gephardt asked her.

Miss Cummings tried to put on a brave front. "I think this must be about the books I've placed on the restricted shelf, waiting a final decision," she said.

"Just because a parent wants them removed from the library doesn't mean that *no* one can read them!" a girl said, speaking above the chants.

Mr. Gephardt looked at the sign. "You took all these out of circulation?" he asked the librarian.

"Only until a decision is reached. I promised the parent," Miss Cummings said hesitantly.

"Let's go inside," he said, and followed her back to her office.

While Sam took a few more photos and I made some notes, the students milled around, making up new chants, and Mr. Gephardt came back in five minutes. "A simple misunderstanding," he said. "We have a procedure in place for anyone making a complaint, and the parent will have to come back and put it in writing. Then it goes before a faculty committee. But for now, I think you'll find those books back where they were."

I figured the answer would be something like that, but everyone cheered. Actually, I think they would have preferred a larger battle. The leaders looked a little crestfallen, reminding me a bit of myself in earlier semesters.

"It just goes to show that we keep fighting the same battles," said Phil when Sam and I got back to the newsroom.

"Yeah, but maybe it's a good thing that each class learns something from the one before," I said. "Last year it was us having a protest march because a parent complained about Mrs. Cary. Remember?"

"Yeah. Wonder what we'll protest when we get to college," said Sam.

"The food," said Phil. "What else? Start with food and work your way up to Wall Street."

Wouldn't you know, Aunt Sally called that very night? She likes to make sure we're all living and breathing and eating our vegetables. When she promised my mom she'd take care of us, she'd meant what she said. Never mind that Dad married again and Les lives in an apartment and I'll be going away to college soon; Aunt Sally keeps her word.

"Hi, Aunt Sally," I said. "How much snow did you get in Chicago so far?"

"Oh, it's not as bad as last year," she said. "How are things in Maryland, dear? I haven't heard from anyone since Christmas."

"We're doing fine," I told her. And added, "Lester's living with a woman now, you know."

Why do I do these things? Aunt Sally cared for us for a long time. She washed our clothes and cooked our meals and braided my hair, and I still can't resist the urge to set her off.

I started counting the seconds of silence. Finally Aunt

Sally said, "Just tell me this, Alice. Has she reached the age of consent?"

"Oh, she's beyond that," I said. "I think she's in grad school."

"Did he choose her for her looks?"

"Not likely," I said.

"Her body?"

"Doubtful."

"Is she wealthy?"

"Not at all."

"Are we talking about the same person—your brother Lester?" she asked.

"One and the same."

"Then she must be quite a catch," Aunt Sally said.

"Oh, he's not chasing her," I said. "They're not even sleeping in the same room." And then I stopped tormenting her. "They're just roommates. She's moved into George's room."

Aunt Sally gave a long, loud sigh of relief. "Well, tell me what's going on in your world, Alice," she said.

"For one thing, I covered a protest today," I said.

"Good heavens, what was that all about?"

I told her about book censorship and the restricted shelf, the people with signs and chants.

Aunt Sally listened quietly, and then she said, "Alice, you have pierced ears, don't you?"

I wondered if I'd heard right. *"What?"*

"In the future take off your earrings before you go to a protest. It's important!" Her voice was grave.

"Why?" I croaked. "No one's against earrings."

"Earlobes can get torn in protest marches. I read that women should always remove their pierced earrings if they take part in riots."

"It wasn't a riot, Aunt Sally," I told her. "I guarantee there isn't a person in school who wants books banned from the library. We're all on the same page."

"Oh." There was another sigh from Aunt Sally. "Alice," she said finally, "did you ever feel that you were out of step with all the women who came before you, the women who were the same age, and the women who came after?"

I thought about that a minute. "I'm only seventeen, Aunt Sally. I guess I haven't."

"Well, I have, and I do. When my mother used to tell us about the twenties, I could never understand why women would want to bob their beautiful hair. When I became a woman, I couldn't understand how some of us wanted to burn our bras. And now I can't understand why girls who are crazy enough to punch holes in their ears would risk having their earlobes torn off by taking part in a riot."

I sort of ached for my aunt just then. I guess I always do when she gets personal and lets me in on her world a bit.

"Aunt Sally," I said, "I probably won't ever understand the world that you and Mom grew up in, but I love you for it just the same. How's Uncle Milt?"

"Not so good, Alice," she said. "He takes so many medications he hardly has room for lunch. And he's slower than he used to be. He says that everyone walks too fast, talks too fast, eats too fast, and he can't keep up."

"Well, give him an extra hug from me," I told her.

"We need all the hugs we can get," Aunt Sally said.

The next day I was coming out of a restroom stall just before first bell when I heard someone vomiting in the handicapped stall at the end of the row.

As I washed my hands at the sink, I studied the stall in the mirror and realized there were two people in it. I was drying my hands when the stall door opened partway and Karen came out for a paper towel. She moistened it at a faucet and, with a secretive glance at me, took it back inside. A moment later Jill came out and rinsed her mouth at the sink.

When she stood up at last and wiped her mouth, I saw her eyes fasten on me in the mirror.

"You guessed it," Jill said. "I'm pregnant."

I stared. "Oh . . . wow! I—I'm—"

"She's happy!" Karen explained. "Don't be sorry."

"Well, I . . ." I didn't know what to say.

But Jill had a satisfied look on her face. "It's all part of the plan," she said.

7

A PIVOTAL MOMENT

I couldn't believe what I was hearing. All I could manage to say was, "Well . . . when is it due?"

"September, I figure," Jill said, cupping her hand under the faucet again, then splashing water into her mouth.

I don't know how anyone can look gorgeous right after she's barfed, but Jill did. Cheekbones, hair, figure, everything done up neatly in a package of denim and rose-colored wool.

Karen was grinning. "Nine months from the night of the Snow Ball. The way she looked in that dress, Justin couldn't help himself."

It could have been nine months from almost any time at all, because Jill and Justin had been having sex for years. I started to ask about college, but I knew how ridiculous that was now.

The first bell rang, but I didn't make any move to leave, and neither did they. Jill fished a little bottle of mouthwash from her bag, took a sip, and rolled it around in her mouth before spitting it out.

"Well . . . I guess congratulations are in order, then," I said, sounding too nerdy for words. Nothing I ever say to Jill and Karen sounds smart and sophisticated. But I was still too curious to leave. They hung out with my crowd occasionally—often came to the Stedmeisters' pool with the gang when we'd gathered over the summer. But Jill and Karen had their own inner circle of friends here at school, and I never had felt welcome in that. Yet here they were, letting me in on a secret.

"Justin knows?" I asked. Stupid comment number two.

"Duh!" said Jill. "My mom said once that she didn't really start to show till the sixth month, so I can probably hide it till May. If Justin's folks agree to a church wedding, fine. If they won't, we'll go to a justice of the peace. One way or another, we're getting married right after graduation. We'll both be eighteen by this summer, and then Justin will have access to the trust fund his grandfather left him."

"But . . ." I winced. "From all you've told us, won't his parents be furious?"

Jill gave a little laugh. "Of course! But Mr. Collier has always wanted a grandchild. A boy, preferably, to take over the business. Justin's their only child, and this baby may be the only grandchild he's going to get. Justin thinks they'll come around." She glanced at her watch. "Jeez. Lab day. All those chemicals.

See ya." And she headed for the stairs and the science labs below, arm in arm with Karen.

Gwen and Liz and Pamela and I sat at a corner table at lunchtime. It was sleeting out, and the halls still had muddy traces of boots tramping, bringing in the damp. All we wanted to talk about, of course, was Jill and Justin. It was obviously not a secret any longer, because Pamela had already heard, and I think the reason Jill told me was so I would spread it around. I figured that Jill wouldn't mind if the word reached the Colliers, if Justin didn't get up the nerve to tell them first. The sooner Jill could start planning her wedding, the better.

"I just can't understand it," I said. "I believe in planned parenthood, but *this* . . . !"

"Desperate people do desperate things," said Liz. "I think they were simply sick of all the fighting with Justin's parents and decided that having a baby would settle the whole thing."

"But to put a *baby* in the middle of that mess?" I said. "It's only going to add more tension."

"And a mother-in-law who hates you like poison," said Gwen. "Who wants to start a marriage with all that baggage?"

"I didn't even know that Jill wanted a baby," said Pamela.

"She wants Justin," said Liz. "Who wouldn't?"

We pondered that for a while over our grilled cheese. "Isn't it weird that you can't drive a car until you've taken lessons and passed a test, but you can have a baby without any preparation at all?" Gwen said. "Even murderers and child abusers can have babies, and nobody stops them until something happens."

"But how do you ever know you're ready to be a mother?" I asked. "I still feel sometimes like I need to be taken care of myself, and if I'm a mom, *I'm* supposed to be in charge. What if my baby got really sick or something? I'd be a basket case. I'm not the least bit brave."

"But sometimes we find out we're a lot braver than we think," said Gwen.

I wondered what Pamela was thinking during our conversation. About her own miscarriage. About Tim. About the two of them miraculously dodging the bullet. About how a baby is a blessing for some couples, but for others, it's a bullet.

On Saturday, Kay hung up her down jacket in the storeroom and let out a prolonged sigh. Then she realized I was back at the mailing table and gave me a wan smile. "Sorry."

"For what? Sounded like something that needed to come out," I said.

"It was the sigh of a half-deranged daughter who has upset her parents and, according to them, shown them the greatest disrespect."

"They still want you to meet this guy, huh?"

"I did! I went home for dinner." Kay sat down on a folding chair and tucked her hands beneath her thighs, shoulders stooped.

"How did it go?"

"Awkward. Very, very awkward. I'm convinced James could tell I didn't want to be there. My parents certainly could."

"What's he like?"

"Mr. Great Stone Face, that was him. I'm sure he's got the same mind-set as my dad, that I'm supposed to be the dutiful daughter and marry whomever Dad says. Oh, the room was full of artificial smiles, mine included. Frozen smiles. I tried not to look at him and let my dad do most of the talking. I asked James once how long he planned to be in the States, and he said he didn't know. Then Dad asked if I was going to have a free weekend soon so we could show our guest around the capital, and I said *I* didn't know. All Mom did was sip her tea and stare right through me for not helping out more with the conversation."

"Is he staying at your parents' place?"

"No. Some hotel. He's supposedly here as a consultant for some networking firm. That's the story, anyway."

"Interesting," I said. "There's a girl at school who's going all out to marry her longtime boyfriend, but his parents are against it; and you're giving it all you've got *not* to marry someone your folks like."

"So what all has she tried?" Kay asked.

"She just got pregnant. That's the latest."

"Great. I'll find some guy to impregnate me, and then neither my parents nor James will want me," said Kay.

Wouldn't it be wonderful if we could shift problems around? I was thinking. I'll take yours for a day, you take mine? On the other hand, the biggest problem I had faced in the last few weeks was saying no to Mrs. Rosen, so I wouldn't want to trade places with Lester or Kay. And I certainly wouldn't choose to trade places with Jill.

On the first Monday in February, Drama Club had its first meeting of the semester. Everyone comes to this one—both backstage and onstage members—because it's the first announcement of the spring production. Last year it was a musical, so this time it would be a play. That's how our school does it—we alternate. I hoped it would be something exciting or racy or funny or wild. *Noises Off*, maybe, or *A Streetcar Named Desire.*

Mr. Ellis smiled as he held up a manila envelope, like this was the Academy Awards or something. "As you know," he said, "we strive for variety in our spring productions, and every so often we do a period piece—always popular with the community."

Our faces dropped. We knew we needed ticket sales to keep the productions going, and we needed to have the community behind us. But period pieces didn't raise the heartbeat much.

"Last year," Mr. Ellis continued, "we did *Guys and Dolls*, with a lot of scene changes. This year we'll have only one set to worry about—the living room of a Victorian house. It has a lot of features, though: a stairway with a landing, two doors, a window, wallpaper, the works. It's a family story."

"What's the name?" someone asked.

Ellis reached into the envelope and pulled out a green script book. "*Cheaper by the Dozen*," he said. "An old favorite."

Most of us had heard of it, but some hadn't, so Mr. Ellis explained that it was the story of Frank Gilbreth, a motion study engineer back in the twenties, who believed that the same time-saving methods he devised for factories in World War I could be used in the home with his twelve children. A comedy. Well, at least it wasn't *Our Town*.

Ellis passed out scripts so we'd be familiar with the play. Mrs. Cary, the speech teacher, would be designing the set.

I figured I'd be on props again, but I didn't want to be in charge and was glad when a guy named Joel volunteered. Those of us on stage crew read off the list of things we had to find for this play—stopwatch, umbrella, large floppy hat—and when we came across *flimsy underwear*, Joel said, "I'll get that one," and we laughed.

I'd tucked my copy of the script in my backpack and was preparing to leave when Mrs. Cary came over. "You've worked on props before, Alice. How would you like to be on my set design committee? Love to have you."

"Sure," I said. Why not? It would be something new. I didn't have to say no to *everything*.

Seniors began forming themselves into separate crews—props, lighting, set, sound—our last chance to strut our stuff; and the lower classmen waited around to be chosen for a crew. If we went into theater in college, we'd be at the bottom of the totem pole again.

The play was officially announced the next day during morning announcements, and a list of the characters, with a brief description of each, went up on the door of the dramatic arts room, along with the dates for tryouts. Other students could sign out a script overnight, and that afternoon there was a swarm of students waiting outside the classroom.

Pamela called me that evening and said she was going to audition for the part of Ernestine, the second-oldest daughter.

"Is she the one who wears the flimsy underwear?" I asked.

"What? Oh, man, I hope so!" Pamela said excitedly. "Where did you hear that?"

I laughed. "Someone mentioned it at the meeting yesterday."

"I'll read the whole script tonight," Pamela said. "But I noticed that Ernestine and Frank Jr. open the show. Don't you love it? The curtain opens and there I am! I want to talk Liz into trying out for one of the other five daughters."

"Who's trying out for the part of Frank Jr.?" I asked.

"Somebody hot, I hope," Pamela said.

"He's supposed to be your brother, Pamela."

"So?" she said. And laughed.

I'd scanned the script a few times, trying to picture the stage set in my mind, the way it was described, but I was feeling strangely unsettled. When I detected the scent of cinnamon in the air, I knew that Sylvia was making Dad's favorite snack. She takes a piece of thinly sliced bread, butters both sides, sprinkles them with cinnamon and sugar, and then browns each side in the toaster oven, just enough to melt the butter and caramelize the sugar a little. I didn't know if I was more hungry for cinnamon toast or for company, but I went downstairs and joined them in the kitchen.

"Somehow I knew you'd be down, so I made some extra pieces," Sylvia said, pushing the plate toward me.

I poured a glass of milk and sat down across from her.

"Homework all done, or are you taking a break?" Dad asked.

"I'm actually done for a change." I bit into the warm toast and savored the buttery taste. "Sylvia," I said, "when you think about your senior year, what was your favorite time? The most exciting thing you did?"

She thought about that a minute. "I guess I'd have to say it was the solo I sang in the choir concert. It's the first thing that comes to mind, anyway. I worried I'd get a cold or something, but after I sang the first couple of notes, I knew I was going to be fine." She shrugged. "I don't know where it came from, but I really sang beautifully." I was surprised to see her blush a little. "Now, didn't *that* sound conceited."

"Not at all," Dad told her. "I don't know why people who do things well can't just say so."

"Was it the singing itself or the applause that made it special?" I asked.

"Both. Obviously, if I'd been singing in the shower and nobody heard it, it wouldn't have been nearly as exciting. But . . . well, it wasn't quite a standing ovation, but I could tell by the applause afterward that I'd done well."

I smiled and looked at Dad. "What about *your* best moment?"

"Next to kissing Joanna Lindstrom, you mean?" We laughed.

"Probably the game against North High. I was a second-stringer on the basketball team, and one of our players fouled out, so I was put in for the last six minutes or so. I wasn't anything great—not like Ed Torino, who got the three-pointers. But it was the next-to-last game of the season and we were tied—the usual story. Ed missed a jump shot, we had about thirteen seconds left, and I retrieved the ball. I jumped and put it in."

"Wow!" I said.

"The crowd went nuts. Of course, North High could have made another shot in those last seconds, but they didn't. Everyone was pounding me on the back and yelling my name and crowding around me, and it was like . . . I don't know. It wasn't that my shot won the game, because everyone's basket counted. Just that mine was the last shot, so I got the glory. Silly, but that was my big moment, something I'll always remember."

They both turned to me. "What about you?" they asked.

"Well, I still have a semester to go," I said. "It's not any one thing. I like it when people comment on my feature articles."

"And well they should! They're excellent!" Sylvia said.

"And they have depth. You always have something to say," Dad told me.

I half sat, half lay on my bed, surrounded by pillows, swathed in a fleece blanket, with the script of *Cheaper by the Dozen* in my hands. It wasn't racy, like *Guys and Dolls*. It wasn't heartrending, like *Fiddler on the Roof*. But it was funny, had its poignant moments, was based on a real family, and I certainly knew about family.

I opened the green script again, and this time I felt my mouth drying up, my pulse racing. I read each page hurriedly, then found myself going back and reading them again. I leaned back against the pillows and closed my eyes.

I started to reach for my cell phone, then stopped. Reached for it again and put it in my lap, breathing out of my mouth, my heart thumping.

Finally I punched in Pamela's number, and when she answered, I said, a quaver in my voice, "Pamela, tell me if I'm crazy, but I'm going to try out for the part of Anne."

8

GETTING READY

A long squeal came through my cell phone.

"Alice! That would be so cool! If Liz got the part of Martha, we could all be the older sisters and—"

I laughed. "I didn't say I was getting the part. I said *maybe* I'd try out for it."

"No, you didn't!" Pamela said fiercely. "You didn't say 'maybe.' You *are* going to try out for it. This will be great. We could all go to rehearsals together, the cast party . . ."

I got that sinking feeling. Wasn't this just like our old dream of going to the same college, getting married the same summer, helping raise each other's kids?

"To tell the truth, I'm scared half out of my wits," I told her.

"Alice, this might be our last chance to do something like

this ever again," came the determined voice over the phone.

"Did you see the crowd waiting for scripts this afternoon?" I asked.

"So? Not all of them want to be Anne."

"What if I bomb? I've never done acting, even in grade school."

"What do you mean? You were in the sixth-grade play with me."

"I was a bush, Pamela. A bramble bush, and you were Rosebud, tripping around the stage in a long dress, singing."

"Well, nobody has to sing in this play, and if you don't try out, I'll kick your butt," said Pamela. "Hard! How's that for motivation? And besides," she added, and I could hear the change in her voice, "if you try out for Anne, *you* get the flimsy underwear."

That made me laugh. "She doesn't *wear* it, though."

"I know. If she did, *I'd* be trying out for the part."

I lay staring into the darkness long after I'd turned out the light. I shouldn't have told Pamela. Now I'd really committed myself. How would my audition go? What would Ellis ask me to do? Was I really going to audition in front of other people or could it be private? Omigod. I'd already told Mrs. Cary I'd work on set design with her. How was I going to get through the next week when I was so miserable already?

Most of the talk at school was about the sock hop that coming Friday, but among seniors, the buzz was about who was trying out for the play and predictions on who would be chosen for each part. Seniors always got priority. A few people, like Pamela, were candid about the roles they wanted, but most of us held back and said, "Oh, I don't know. I'm just going to tryouts and see what happens."

Wednesday evening, when Dad and Sylvia were out to dinner with friends, I took over Dad's big armchair in the family room, wrapped in a robe and a blanket, and carefully reread all of Anne's lines.

It was the story of a teenage girl's relationship with her father. In some ways I was like Anne, and in some ways I wasn't at all. She was the oldest child in her large family; I was the youngest in my small one. She was from a wealthy background, her father famous in his field. Mine wasn't rich at all, and except for musicians in the Washington area and our friends at church and in the neighborhood, no one except relatives knew of Dad outside of Silver Spring.

We were alike, though, in that Anne had to be the trendsetter, the scout, the pathfinder for her siblings. She had to pave the way for wearing lacy underthings and silk stockings and for having a boyfriend. I didn't have any sisters, but I had to fight my own battles. And while both Anne and I loved our fathers and knew they loved us, they could be so stubbornly old-fashioned at times.

I remembered how, after Dad saw Patrick kissing me once on the front porch in the dark, he always had the porch light on after that when I was out with Patrick during junior high school. I remember how I had to argue and argue with him to go to a coed sleepover. Strange how life turns out sometimes. We ended up having the coed sleepover here at our house. And that was the night of the fake kiss between Patrick and Penny.

The more I thought about it, Anne's disobedience in buying underwear her dad disapproved of wasn't much compared to my riding on the back of a motorcycle with a guy I didn't know, and even that was mild. So yes, I knew how desperately Anne felt about the rules in her household, the way her father interfered in what she wanted to do and where she wanted to go, even though her story took place in the 1920s.

I was breathing through my mouth again, and I felt the strange thumping in my chest. I realized that I wanted to play the part of Anne in this play in my senior year almost more than anything I'd ever wanted.

Being on the props committee, standing behind the curtain and waiting for a scene to end so I could replace breakfast dishes with a book and reading glasses, didn't make my heart race. Coming onstage with the rest of the crew for a curtain call, all of us dressed in black, wasn't something people would remember me for.

I didn't want to be the girl behind the curtain helping Pamela change costumes, or the girl in the gym cheering Liz on as she played Stupefyin' Jones, or the friend in the auditorium clapping for Gwen getting her scholarship award—proud as I was of all of them. For once in my life, *I* wanted to be center stage, the spotlight on *me*. *I* wanted to be the one the audience was applauding.

But my chances! Charlene Verona could probably get the part of any character she tried out for. I'd seen a couple of cheerleaders waiting in line for a script. *Face it, Alice!* I told myself. *The odds are against you. Understand that!* I did. I think. It was just that I was burning bridges behind me. I'd said no to Mrs. Rosen about trying out for class poet. I was about to say no to Mrs. Cary for set design.

I closed my eyes and took another deep breath. *Just do it!* I told myself. *Get up there and take a chance.* If my only big accomplishment in high school was features editor of the paper, that wasn't so bad. I was doing this for me. I'd made a decision and, right or wrong, it was mine.

Beside the tryout schedule posted on the door of the dramatic arts classroom, there was a sign-up sheet. Auditions would start the following Monday.

I wished I could just concentrate on Anne's lines over the weekend, but Phil had assigned me to cover the dance Friday night. Seniors seemed divided between those who wanted to squeeze in every possible activity they could to remember always and those who were losing interest in high school stuff. Some who had already been accepted for admission had even sent away for college sweatshirts! Gwen was going somewhere with Austin but said they might drop in later. So Pamela and Liz and I went together in the matching poodle skirts Mrs. Price had sewn for us. Poodle skirts and saddle shoes, our hair in the strange pompadour style of the fifties that Sylvia helped us with.

The junior class had done the decorating this time, and Sam was taking pictures, of course. The school had rented a jukebox with a Plexiglas window so you could watch vinyl records drop onto a turntable for the next song.

The cheerleaders were there in their own poodle skirts, demonstrating the jitterbug and getting people to try it. There was even an Elvis Presley impersonator sitting at the wheel of a '57 Chevy, waving to people, then getting out and strolling around the gym, signing autographs as though he were really Elvis.

Amy Sheldon arrived with two other girls, and though her "Hi, Alice!" could be heard halfway around the gym, I waved and laughed along with her when Elvis gave her a hug as he made another tour of the gym.

"Do you know what I feel like?" Liz asked as we circled the dance floor for the third time, looking for people we knew. "I feel like somebody's mother, here to chaperone. I used to be wild for things like this. And it *looks* like fun, but . . . What's the matter with us, Alice? Have we suddenly grown too old for this?"

"Speak for yourself," said Pamela.

"Maybe it's just overload, everything piling up on us at once. Are you trying out for the play?" I asked Liz.

She shrugged. "I might. But it's no big deal if I don't get a part."

I guess that was a major difference between us. For me, it was. I wanted to be tested. I didn't want to go on dreading things like this forever.

There were little tables off to the side of the gym where people could sit down, and a couple of girls on roller skates with rubber wheels came out of a shed, taking orders for root beer floats.

Penny was at a side table with one of the cheerleaders and waved us over to join them, so we ordered floats too.

"Isn't this fun?" the cheerleader said. "The decorations committee did a great job. But it was one of the sophomore dads who got the Chevy for us."

Penny, as always, looked great. She probably wears size two jeans, and she paired them with a short-sleeved sweater with a Peter Pan collar, fifties-style. I wondered if I would ever get to the place where I could look at Penny without feeling even an ounce of jealousy. Sometimes I felt I was *almost* there, but not quite.

The fact that Patrick had once—for a while, anyway—liked her best . . . liked her, held her, kissed her . . . would always keep us a little distance apart, like two polarized magnets, I suppose. If it weren't for that, we might be close friends.

"Do you ever wish you lived back in the fifties, when they had drive-in root beer places and drive-in movies?" Liz asked.

"My grandmother says life was a lot simpler," Penny told us. "Girls were either 'good girls' or 'bad girls,' and basically they had four career choices—secretary, housewife, nurse, or teacher—though if you were really adventurous or talented, you could become an airline stewardess or an actress."

"Yeah, but you got to wear these cute poodle skirts and dance to Frank Sinatra and Bobby Darin," I joked.

"Or be one of the girls who marched with the ROTC and carried a flag," said Liz.

"Hey, you can still be the lucky girl who gets to be the Ivy Bearer on Ivy Day," said the cheerleader, rolling her eyes. "Or even the Ivy Day Poet! Whoopee! Mom says they had that ceremony when *she* went to our school. Somebody left an annuity or something, and we have to do it."

I took a deep breath. Close call.

About an hour into the evening, the jukebox stopped playing and the junior class president made a short announcement. He said that "The Shack" would be selling hot dogs for the next twenty minutes and that the dance committee had worked up a special combo to play during that time.

"Combo?" said Liz.

"A band," the cheerleader explained. "Oh, here they come."

We watched some guys cross the floor with their instruments—saxophone, clarinet, the same instruments people played in the fifties—but there, walking along with them, was Daniel Bul Dau, our Sudanese student who's been in the United States for only eight months or so.

"Hey, Daniel!" Liz and I yelled.

The tall, thin guy with the high cheekbones looked our way, smiling, and when his eyes found us, he grinned.

He took his place with the others on a glittering makeshift bandstand, and for the first two numbers he didn't do much, mostly sat with the school drummer, his own drum between his knees, and accompanied a little. But when they started a third number—I didn't know what kind of dance it was, a Latin beat, I guess—he began drumming out his own rhythm as an accompaniment.

As the music went on, his fingers began to fly on the drumhead, a complicated beat that none of us could identify. We couldn't even copy it. The other musicians just grinned and shook their heads. Daniel grinned too and went on playing, his rhythm intricately bound up with the music. At one point the other guys stopped entirely and let him have the spotlight. Students gathered around to watch. It was a rhythm all his own, and Daniel played with his eyes closed now, his head tilted back in concentration, his fingers just a blur over the drum.

It was as though his hands were playing two different rhythms at the same time. Sweat broke out on his forehead, and his head began to nod in time with the beat. Daniel was off in Sudan somewhere far away, and we could hear, through his drumming, his missing of home.

9

READING FOR MR. ELLIS

I did want to hear how things were going with Lester, though, so on Sunday morning, after I'd done my homework, read over Anne's lines again, and plucked my eyebrows, I finally called him. Too late, I discovered I'd punched in his apartment phone instead of his cell.

"Hello," said a low voice, and it wasn't Lester's or Paul's.

"This is Alice. Is Les in?" I asked.

"Hold on," said Andy.

I could tell Les was grumpy the moment he said hello.

"How are things?" I said.

"Don't ask," he told me. "I'll call you back on my cell," and he hung up.

A few minutes later he called.

"Where are you? Barricaded in your room with your dresser against the door?" I asked.

"One of the worst mistakes I ever made, not checking Andy out before she got here," he said. "She's not only a recluse, but when she *does* come out, she's got to be the pushiest female I ever met. She never says, 'Would you mind turning the TV down?' She waits till you go get a beer, then turns it down for you. Throws out any food over the sell-by date. Suddenly the corned beef you were saving for those last two pieces of rye bread is gone. And she'll make a grilled cheese for herself with the bread. You don't take your clothes out of the washing machine, you'll find them in a bucket. She wouldn't think of tossing them in the dryer for you. Whatever Andy wants, it seems, Andy gets, including a rent-free apartment with the jackass who let her in."

"That would be me," I said. "I opened the door."

"You know what I mean. The advertisement I wrote without mentioning gender and letting her go meet Mr. Watts. I refer to her as Nurse Ratched because she thinks she knows what's best for us, but Paul calls her Mother Superior because of the mystical way she eats our corned beef or throws our clothes in a bucket without our ever seeing her do it."

"Well, maybe you'll be moving yourself one of these days," I said to console him. "Any interviews yet?"

"Only one, and you wonder why they bothered. I've got a major in philosophy, a minor in psychology, and I'm looking for a job working with people, I tell them. So I get there, and what do they want me to do? Digitalize all their records."

"Well, it's a job," I say.

"I'll stick with the university till I get something more my line," he said.

"Meanwhile," I told him, "what you need is some fun in your life."

"Yeah, all the babes are in hiding," he said. "Seems like all the girls I used to know have moved away."

"Well, I'm doing something sort of fun," I told him. "I'm going to audition for a part in the spring play."

"No kidding? It's not a musical, is it?"

"No, Les. I don't torture anybody by trying to sing. But there are dozens of other people trying out."

"So you give it your best shot, that's all," he said.

Tryouts for the female roles were scheduled for Monday and Tuesday, male roles Wednesday and Thursday, and the cast would be posted on the door of the dramatic arts classroom Friday morning at eight o'clock. Charlene Verona, the perpetual diva, let it be known that she'd be there "with bells on," as she put it. Petite Penny said she was going to try out for the part of Lillian, the youngest daughter being cast.

As it grew closer and closer to the last bell on Monday, and other names came floating by of people who were trying out, I could feel an uproar in my insides and panicked when I had an attack of diarrhea in the restroom. Never mind expression and diction and whether or not I could memorize the lines. If I couldn't even control my bowels, what business did I have getting onstage at all?

At last I got myself in shape and went out in the hall, where Pamela and Liz were waiting.

"You okay?" Pamela asked.

"No, but let's get it over with," I said.

She grabbed one arm, Liz grabbed the other, and we set out for the dramatic arts room.

"What's the worst that can happen?" Liz asked me. "We don't get parts, that's all. Life goes on. The prom's coming up. College . . ."

Pamela was in her wiseacre mood, though. "No, the worst is that we could all get parts and throw up together onstage."

"Pamela!" Liz scolded.

We passed the water fountain and turned the corner. Just as I suspected, a dozen or more girls were moving through the doorway of the classroom, scripts in hand. From the noise inside, we knew there were even more already there. I heard an audible gasp from Pamela on one side of me, from Liz on the other.

"Oh, Pamela, I don't have a chance," I said, feeling weak in the knees.

She squeezed my arm. "You have as much of a chance as anyone else. Just be yourself."

Why do people always say that? As though anyone's self is everything good, just naturally funny and clever? What if *my* self was mousey, silly, plain, ordinary, and boring?

Only the people actually trying out were permitted inside, so some of the girls had to leave. There were nineteen left. Nineteen girls wanting the same female roles, and there were two days of tryouts. Thirty-eight girls, maybe, wanting parts? The best parts?

We went up to the blackboard, where sheets of paper were taped in a row—one sheet for each of the seven roles: Mother; Miss Brill, a teacher; Mrs. Fitzgerald, the housekeeper; and four of the daughters—Anne, Ernestine, Martha, and Lillian. We were to sign our names under the character we most wanted to play.

The longest lists were for Ernestine and Anne.

I picked up one of the pencils in the chalk tray and signed my name under *Anne*, my eyes roaming the page for the other names on the list. And then my stomach churned in earnest when I saw Jill's name near the top.

I turned, and there she was in the second row, beautiful and demure-looking in a white cashmere sweater.

How could this be? Maybe she wasn't pregnant after all. Maybe she'd had a miscarriage. Maybe the whole rumor was just a big joke, and now that I'd gotten my nerve up to do one of the most difficult things I'd ever done, Jill would do it for me, ten times better.

I wondered if this was how it felt to enter a beauty contest—all the girls smiling at everyone, secretly sizing them up. I wished the auditions could take place in private, just a solitary room where Mr. Ellis could ask me to read a page and then tell me, *Sorry, Alice. I don't think so,* and I could leave without a gaggle of smirking girls watching me go.

We were all sitting in chairs scattered about the room, and there was a lot of nervous chatter. Liz leaned over to whisper, "Is she *serious*? Jill, I mean?"

"Maybe she'll play the mother," said Pamela. "If she's already had a dozen children, what's one more?"

Yeah, right, I thought—as though Jill looked like she'd had a dozen children. And if she wasn't due till September, she'd hardly even be showing by the time of the performances in April.

The door opened and Mr. Ellis came in with Mrs. Cary. *Oh, great!* I thought. Mrs. Cary was going to be in on the casting, and I still hadn't told her I was trying out for a part and wouldn't do set design if I got it. What were my chances now?

Mr. Ellis was carrying a clipboard and the script, and he smiled at all of us.

"Good to see so many of you here," he said, and walked along pulling the sheets of paper off the board, attaching them to his clipboard. "Here's how it works, girls. I'll have two of you reading at a time, maybe even three or four, switching parts around. Don't try to figure out what I'm up to." He grinned. "You'll definitely have a chance to try out for the part you want, but Mrs. Cary and I will be listening and watching for a number of things. The best advice I can give you is to play each part we assign you with as much honesty and feeling as you can."

Charlene read first for Ernestine, the role Pamela wanted, and, as usual, Charlene was good. Very good. I could feel my stomach tightening up for Pamela. Charlene had been taking acting lessons since she was nine, she'd told us once. Pamela gave me a helpless look, but I mouthed *Go, Pam, go!* when it was her turn, and she took the high stool that Charlene had vacated.

"Take it from the top, Pamela," Mr. Ellis said. "I'll read for Frank Jr. Go ahead."

Charlene had cupped one hand to her ear on the first line, but Pamela read it straight, with a touch of nostalgia: "Can you hear the music, Frank? I think it's coming from down the street."

"I thought I heard something else," Mr. Ellis read.

Pamela smiled faintly. "Songs like that make you remember . . ."

Mr. Ellis had her read another page, and then he chose a third girl to come up and try out for the same part. Every time a new girl auditioned, we tried to read Mr. Ellis's expression. We watched Mrs. Cary's face. Mrs. Cary smiled encouragingly at everyone, and Mr. Ellis looked pleasant enough. Now and then I detected a smile on his face. Sometimes he dropped his eyes to his lap. But he'd just say, "Good, thank you," after someone read a part, and then he'd call on someone else.

"Alice?" he said at last. "You signed up for the part of Anne."

I got up and took my place at the front of the room, my palms wet, mouth dry.

"Let's try . . . um . . . start at the top of page twenty-five," Mr. Ellis said. "Pamela, read Ernestine's part for now, will you?"

We didn't even exchange looks, afraid it would spook one

of us. In this scene the sisters were arguing with their dad about silk stockings.

Holding the playbook in one hand, Pamela said, "But that's the way everybody dresses today."

And I read, "Boys don't notice when everyone dresses that way."

Ellis, reading the father's part, said gruffly, "Don't tell me about boys. I know all about what boys notice." The rest of the girls laughed.

"You don't want us to be wallflowers?" I read.

"I'd rather raise wallflowers than clinging vines," Mr. Ellis retorted.

I studied the script. It said that I clutched my package with determination. The flimsy underwear package. "I'm *going* to wear these," I said, hugging my script to my chest for moment. "I'll not be a wallflower anymore!"

And Pamela read, "And I'm going to buy silk stockings too!"

"And me!" Mr. Ellis read in a high voice, imitating a younger sister, Martha. Everyone laughed but Pamela and me. We knew enough to stay in character.

"I won't let you out of the house with them!" Mr. Ellis boomed.

He skipped a few lines after that, looking at me and pointing to the bottom of the page: "Listen to me, Anne. When a man picks a wife, he wants someone he can respect."

This was so weird, acting out a scene with a teacher. I was supposed to brush past him then and start up the stairs. But I just read my lines with passion: "They certainly respect me," I said, and my voice quavered a little. "I'm the most respected girl in the whole school. The boys respect me so much, they hardly look at me."

"Come back down here!" Mr. Ellis shouted. "I don't want you wasting your time with a lot of boys: Look at the fun we have right here at home with our projects."

"You don't understand!" I said. "You don't understand at all. I wish your job was selling shoes and you only had one or two children"—*voice rises to a wail*, the script directed—"and neither of them was *me*!"

I wondered if I'd overdone it when I got to the end. Mr. Ellis just smiled and nodded and said, "Okay," and read the next name on the list.

"Jill," he said, "would you come up here and read Anne's part? And, Alice, please read the mother's lines. Page seventy-eight, where the mother enters."

I felt stones in my stomach. *No!* I didn't want to play the mother, especially Jill's mother! I tried to close her out as Jill came up to the front of the room and took Pamela's stool. Tried to ignore the scent of her haunting perfume. That would do Mr. Ellis in, if nothing else.

"Okay, begin," Mr. Ellis said.

Should I play this flatly so he couldn't possibly assign the part to me? I wondered. He had said to play all the parts as well as we could. . . .

I decided to do as he'd asked and took a maternal tone as I read my lines: "Aren't you going to eat any ice cream, dear?"

Jill shook her head and looked petulant. (*Choked*, the script read.) "I don't have much appetite," she said, and there was a trace of anger in her voice.

"Are you worried about the test?" I read.

"The test—and *everything*."

A little further on, when the character discovers that her father has heart trouble and no one told her, Jill put fire into the part. She was the teenager I wasn't.

"Okay," Mr. Ellis said. "Thank you both. Let's move on to the next person."

We waited while Liz read for the part of Martha. Mr. Ellis asked her to read for the mother, too, and Penny was asked to read for three parts—the mother, Lillian, and the housekeeper. Penny seemed to get in the spirit of all three, and everyone laughed, even Mr. Ellis, when the housekeeper, grumbling over the father's motion study tips for her work in the kitchen, leaves the room muttering loudly, "Lincoln freed the slaves . . . all but one . . . all but one."

Most of us stayed to the end of the audition just to see what the competition was like. As Mrs. Cary stood up to stretch and Mr. Ellis stuck the clipboard in his briefcase, he said, "Check the list tomorrow, girls. Some of you may be called back to read again."

Out in the hall, Charlene said knowingly, "It's a good sign if you get a callback. If you don't, just forget it; you didn't get a part."

And then she added, "I've got to decide between *Cheaper by the Dozen* and a part with the Montgomery Players. They held auditions for *The Wizard of Oz* last week, and I tried out for Glinda. I guess it depends on what part I get here."

It must be great to be so sure of yourself, I thought.

"Well, I only want the part of Anne," said Jill. "I think I could add a lot to the role. She's too passive in the script."

Charlene nodded. "Directors are looking for someone who can take a role and put herself in it. I mean, *anyone* can read words on paper."

Karen had been waiting for Jill in the hall, and as they headed off, I heard Karen ask her, "Do you really think you should go out for this?"

"Why not?" Jill replied. "By afternoon, I'm feeling fine."

I had Sylvia's car—she gets a ride to work when I need it—but I'd promised to get home so she could go to a meeting. Liz was riding with Pam. You shouldn't drive when you're distracted, I know, and when I pulled in our driveway, I was scarcely aware of getting there. Thoughts were ricocheting around in my head like Ping-Pong balls, and I had the feeling I was going to do something impulsive.

Why *not* go in early tomorrow and tell Mr. Ellis that there was something he might want to know, that I didn't mean to be a gossip, but I was sure he wanted the play to be the best it possibly could be. . . .

My hands dropped from the steering wheel into my lap. If I were the drama coach, wouldn't I want to know? Wouldn't any director want to know whether one of the actors might be sick on opening night? If one of the actors was *pregnant*?

Then I thought of the impulsive way I had written up a Student Jury session last semester. Of all the spur-of-the-moment things I'd regretted later.

You don't have to decide this right now, I told myself. *You sure don't have to call him tonight.*

But I knew that tomorrow I would feel the same as I did right now: that Jill might get the part of Anne unless Mr. Ellis knew she was pregnant, and who else was going to tell him?

10
THE LIST

Things look different in the clear light of morning. It wasn't all that bright, actually, but as I lay there, imagining myself going to school early, tracking down Mr. Ellis and telling him Jill was pregnant, I knew I couldn't do it. Shouldn't.

If he *was* going to give Jill the part of Anne—and I would get it only because she was out of the picture—did I really want it by default? And how did I know I was even in the running? Six girls had tried out for Anne's part the first day, and there would be more coming that afternoon.

I didn't have any appetite for breakfast and ate only part of an orange. Was I more disgusted with my impulse to squeal on Jill or with my lack of confidence?

I felt alternately hot and cold as Dad drove me to school and let me off at the north entrance.

"Hope the rest of your day's a little better," he commented as I turned to open my door.

"It shows, huh?" I said.

"A little."

I went to the newspaper room to help Phil decide which photos from the sock hop we should print in *The Edge*.

"Definitely one with Daniel playing his drum," I said. "Ditto for one of the waitresses on roller skates."

When we'd marked the photos for Sam, Phil said, "Saw you got a callback."

I'd just gathered my books and had started to stand up. "What?" I said, dropping back onto my chair again.

"The list for the play. You're on callback. Didn't you check?"

"No! Who else was on it?"

"Uh . . . Penny. Jill, I think. I just walked over to see what everyone else was looking at and saw your name."

"It doesn't mean I'll get a part," I told him, trying to hide my excitement.

"No, but it means you've made an impression," he said. And then, "You know, if you're in the play, you've got to give up yearbook. You can't do the yearbook, the newspaper, and the play, too. That's too much. If you can't read proofs by deadline, you can't be listed on the yearbook staff."

I winced. "It would mean extra work for everyone else if I dropped it, right?"

"Yeah, but I think one of the reporters could fill in. In any case, if you get a part, go for it. You're only a senior once."

"Thanks, Phil," I said, but it unnerved me a little. If I wanted to work on a college paper, being on a high school newspaper *and* the yearbook staff would be a huge plus. But these were safe places for me; I'd already proved I could research, interview, write, edit. Acting was something new. Something entirely different. And scary. Decisions, decisions . . .

I hurried over to the dramatic arts room, where a little crowd had gathered, checking the list. All three of us—Pamela, Liz, and I—were on the callback list, but so were Jill and Charlene and Penny and a few others. And there were still girls waiting to try out.

Pamela came up behind me and gave my arm a squeeze. "Getting closer!" she said. "Fingers crossed!"

There was a smaller crowd at auditions that afternoon, but the atmosphere was even more tense. Jill and Charlene were sitting together this time by the windows, chattering like pros. Eight other girls were trying out, and Mr. Ellis and Mrs. Cary listened to each of them read before any of those on callback were asked to read again. Ellis had Jill read for the parts of both Anne and Miss Brill, and I read for both the mother and Anne.

It wasn't one of Anne's best scenes, and I was disappointed I couldn't do one with more emotion. It was a rather dull scene, actually, which made me feel Ellis didn't much care how I did it. He asked still another girl to read Anne's part twice, and I reluctantly gave her my place. Then he asked me to read again, but not for long.

When he called it a day and said he'd post the list on Friday after the boys' auditions, I hung back. Could he let me read just a little bit more? I wanted to ask. Couldn't I read some of the lines Anne had with Joe Scales, the cheerleader? A few with Larry, the boy she really likes?

But Charlene got to him first, and she and Mr. Ellis were having a serious conversation at the back of the room. I dawdled just a little to see if I should stick around.

"I haven't cast anyone yet," I heard him tell her, "but the school frowns on any one person getting major roles in two productions, so I want you to know that. You had a great part in *Fiddler*."

"But I was only a freshman when I played the part of Tzeitel!" she said. "If I'd known then that I couldn't have a major role in my senior year, I might have refused it."

"Come on, Char," he said. "I don't think so. That was a great part and you were the only one who fit the role that perfectly." He reached for his jacket and slipped one arm in the sleeve. "I haven't made up my mind about anyone yet."

I could tell he was eager to leave, and I figured I could only hurt my chances by begging to read more, so I left the room ahead of them, but my heart was down in my shoes.

Gwen met us after school, and we stopped at a chocolate shop for some Mexican hot chocolate, thick and spicy. The small table had barely enough room for eight elbows and four cups, but we managed. Ordinarily, I love Mexican chocolate, but it tasted bitter today.

I told them what I'd overheard from Ellis, that those who'd had major roles in another performance couldn't expect a big role in this one.

Liz looked at Pamela. "Would that apply to you? Because you were an understudy in *Guys and Dolls*?"

"Understudies don't count," Pamela said. "I already checked."

"Which guys are trying out? Does anyone know?" Gwen asked.

"I heard that Sam was interested," said Liz.

"Sam? Really? He didn't say anything about it to me," I said, but Sam does sort of go in for drama. I used to date him. I should know.

"How many guys' parts are there?" Gwen asked.

"Well, there are nine male roles, so this is a good way to meet guys," said Pamela.

"That's what Mom always tells me," Liz said. "If you want to meet a guy who shares your interests, get involved in things you love."

"Chocolate," I said, looking around the shop. "Don't see any chocolate-loving guys in here."

"Yeah, I hang out at libraries, but I can't say anyone looks at me with lustful eyes in the nonfiction section," said Gwen.

Strangely, I was missing my own mother right then. What wise thing might Mom have said to me about the play? What comforting words would she have for me if Mr. Ellis chose someone else and I lost the one big thing I wanted in my senior year? Would burying myself in Sylvia's arms be the same?

* * *

Patrick phoned me that night.

"How'd it go?" he asked.

"I got a callback, but Ellis had other girls reading too."

"Still, it means he's interested in you. When do the guys try out?"

"Tomorrow and Thursday. Why? Are you sorry you were never in the school play?"

"I would have had to give up eating and sleeping," he said, which was probably true, because Patrick went through four years of high school in three.

I started to ask if he was coming home for spring break, then remembered, with a pang, that "home" for him now was Wisconsin. So I reworded it: "Are you going home for spring break?"

"Yeah. I have to. Mom and Dad want some time with me before I leave for Spain."

"They're not the only ones," I said, then realized how whiny that must sound. So I added quickly, "But I'll have you for the prom."

"Right," he said. And then, "Don't plan for anything after. I'll take care of that."

"Okay," I told him, and liked the sound of it. Liked it very much.

Waiting. That was the worst. There were all sorts of rumors going around—one was that Ellis was choosing the cast based on height. The tallest ones would be the oldest children, and so on. Jill was taller than me. I even heard that Mrs. Cary suggested choosing the cast based on hair color.

I was restless and miserable Thursday evening. The cast list was going up the next day. What would I say, what would I do, if Jill got the part of Anne and I was given the part of her mother? I'd almost rather not be in the play at all.

The four of us—Gwen, Pamela, Liz, and I—went to school early on Friday. There was already a small crowd gathered around the doorway to the dramatic arts room. But the list wasn't posted yet.

I didn't think I could stand it. Jill was there in the crowd, leaning back against Justin, who was nuzzling the side of her face, arms wrapped around her midsection, hands on her belly. Charlene stood with her back to the door as though she was going to read off the names when they came through. Several people were looking out a window at the end of the hall, trying to determine if Mr. Ellis drove a Prius or a Honda and if his car was there yet.

"Remember," Charlene was saying in a voice loud enough for everyone to hear, "at least half of us could be understudies."

That was something I hadn't taken into account. What if I had to learn all the lines for a part, be dressed and everything—two nights a week for two different weekends—and never got to be onstage? Did understudies secretly hope that their leads broke a leg? Is that where the saying came from?

At 7:17, Mrs. Free from the office came down the hall smiling, holding two sheets of paper and a roll of tape.

"Excuse me," she said to the crowd. "If you'll just let me through, I've got some information for you."

We all made room and watched her red-painted nails press down on the first sheet of paper.

"Male roles," someone called out. "Hey, Broderick, you're the dad."

Cheers and backslapping among the guys.

The second sheet of paper went up, and Mrs. Free quickly moved back as students edged forward. I could see between the heads of the two girls in front of me.

Female roles, it read.

Mother: Elizabeth Price.

"Liz!" Gwen shouted.

Anne: Alice McKinley.

I stared, absolutely stunned.

"Omigod! Alice!" Pamela gasped.

Ernestine: Pamela Jones.

We screamed. The parts of Martha and Lillian were given to a junior in my gym class named Chassie and a sophomore, Angela, I didn't know. The part of Miss Brill went to Charlene, and the housekeeper was to be played by Penny.

Below the cast roster was the list of understudies. Jill was the understudy for me.

11

CARRYING ON

I was almost afraid to turn around. The right thing to do, probably, was to hug Jill and say, *Looks like we're a team!* but in all the excitement, I heard a girl's voice saying, "Well . . . shit!" And when I did turn around, Jill was gone.

I was too delighted and shocked to worry about it for long, and when Pamela grabbed Liz and cried, "Mo-ther!" we all broke into laughter.

"We'll be going to rehearsals together and everything!" Pamela said. "Did you ever . . . ?"

"No! I never dreamed it! I can't believe it!" I said.

It was funnier still when Brad Broderick looked around to find the rest of his family, and Pamela and I together yelled, "Daddy!" Everyone laughed, and he came over and hugged us both at the same time, then turned to Liz and said, "Well, Ma, looks like we created quite a clan!"

Sam Mayer got the role of Dr. Burton; Jay, an intense guy from my speech class last year, got the part of Frank Jr., whose dialogue with Pamela opens the play; Tim Moss, Pamela's ex, would play Fred, one of the sons; and a guy I didn't know, Ryan McGowan, from my physics class, won the part of Larry, my crush.

"Looks like *we're* going to get better acquainted," he said, smiling down at me as we studied the list again, checking out all the actors.

"First reading today!" I said, looking at the note at the bottom. *Read for characterization: Friday, February 18, 3:00 p.m.*

All morning people congratulated me on getting a part in the play. "Is that the part you wanted?" some of them asked. And "Were you disappointed you didn't get the part of the mother?" as though if the dad were the star, the mom was also.

"It's exactly the part I wanted," I told everyone, and drifted from class to class in a happy daze.

Mrs. Cary stopped me in the hall, smiling, and said, "I guess you won't be part of the set design crew, Alice. Congratulations!"

"Oh, I'm sorry, but . . . ," I began babbling.

"Of course you're not! You should be excited. It's wonderful!" she said.

I called Dad over the lunch period and told him the news.

"Terrific, Al!" he said. "You think you can handle this now, with all you've got on your plate?"

"Sure," I said, and didn't repeat Patrick's line about how he'd have had to give up eating and sleeping if *he* took on something like this. "I'm giving up yearbook to do this. I'll work it in."

The whole cast, including understudies, was supposed to show up at three o'clock, but Jill wasn't among us. Charlene Verona, though, was there with an announcement. She waited until we were all seated and then, before Mr. Ellis could even start the reading, she said, "I didn't want to leave without explaining, so I just came by to say that I got the second best part in *The Wizard of Oz* with the Montgomery Players, so I'm going to have to give up the part of Miss Brill. If it wasn't for that, I'd have loved to work with all you guys, but I know you'll do a fantastic job. So break a leg, everybody!"

Penny and I rolled our eyes at each other, and we each looked so funny, we almost laughed out loud.

Mr. Ellis smiled a little. "Good luck, Charlene," he said. "Thanks for letting me know." Then he looked at the understudy who had been sitting beside Charlene and said, "Well, Jenny, looks like you're Miss Brill."

Charlene smiled around the circle, picked up her backpack, and even waved to us as she went out the door. People ducked their heads to hide their laughter, and Mr. Ellis began reading stage directions.

Things still seemed unreal. When I went to my locker later, I thought, *When I was a freshman, I never would have believed I'd get one of the lead roles in the play*. I marveled at the coincidence that Pamela and Liz were in it too, even though it wasn't quite the way we had pictured it. Maybe, because we knew each other so well, the familiarity showed in our readings.

Liz had read her lines in the same comforting tone she used with her little brother when he was upset, and Pamela's voice was just right for Ernestine when she related some of the family's funniest memories, like the two noisy canaries—one that the father named "Shut Up" and the other, "You Heard Me."

But the biggest mystery of all: How did I get the part of Anne? Was I really that good at it? Jill had added some anger to the role—more than I had—and that was good, wasn't it? Original? Another girl had played it with more sadness, and that seemed real too. Anne seemed conflicted to me—love for her dad along with dismay and resentment, a subtle mix. Was it possible that this was what Ellis was looking for and that somehow I had pulled it off?

I called Patrick that night.

"Hey!" Patrick said.

"Hey!" I responded. "This is Anne."

There was a moment of silence, and then he yelled, "*Hey!* You got it?"

"Got it."

"Way to go!" Patrick said. "You *did* it!"

"And guess who's my understudy."

"Pamela?"

"No. Jill."

"Huh?" said Patrick. "I don't quite see that."

"I don't either, and neither, evidently, does Jill. She didn't show up at rehearsal. But Pamela got the part of the next-oldest sister, and Liz is the mother. Can you believe it? That all three of us are in the play?"

"You guys hit the jackpot," said Patrick. "Anyone else that I know?"

"Penny as Mrs. Fitzgerald, the housekeeper."

"The *housekeeper*? And what about the guys? Aren't you supposed to have a boyfriend in the play?"

"Yes. A guy in my physics class, Ryan somebody. Sam got a part. So did Tim."

"Uh, let's get back to Ryan. What's he like?"

I laughed. "Are you jealous?"

"Sort of. Is he hot or not?"

"Well . . . yeah. I'd say he is."

"Tall, dark, and handsome?"

"Tall and handsome, anyway. Sort of a brownish blond."

"Hmmm. Maybe I should come back for the play."

"Maybe you should," I said.

When we finally finished our conversation around ten, I reached for the schedule Mr. Ellis had passed around before rehearsal. Every single day except Saturdays and Sundays. Performances Friday and Saturday, April 8, 9, 15, and 16. I had to squeeze the rest of my life into what was left.

The home phone rang around ten fifteen as I was collecting

my papers and books and putting them in my backpack. Dad and Sylvia had already gone to bed, so I hurried out in the hall to pick it up. "Hello?"

At first I didn't think that anyone was there or that someone was playing around with the phone—the fumbling, the breathing, the background noise—but then a man's voice said, "Alice?"

"Yes?"

"It's Jack."

Which character was that? I wondered. It was a voice I knew but couldn't place. Then I realized it was Marilyn's husband.

"Yes?" I said eagerly.

"Just wanted to tell you about our new baby daughter," came his excited but weary voice.

"Oh, Jack! Wonderful! How's Marilyn?"

"More tired than I am, that's for sure, but she and Summer Hope are doing just fine."

Summer Hope. It was so right. So . . . Marilyn!

"What a beautiful name. What's the baby like?"

"Scrunchy-faced and scrawny, but already sucking her fist," he said. "We'll e-mail some photos when we all recover. It was a long labor, but Marilyn's doing fine. I've got a list of people to call, and you and your dad were on it. Just wanted you to know."

New life, I thought as I put down the phone. I guess that's what I was feeling right then. New everything.

When Jill didn't show up at rehearsal on Monday either, Mr. Ellis announced a new understudy for me, someone I didn't know. He gave no reason for Jill dropping out, but on Tuesday, when Jill and Karen condescended to eat with us at lunchtime, Jill explained in an offhand way:

"I'm just going to be too busy planning my wedding," she said.

"Wow! You're really going to do it?" said Liz.

Jill popped a cherry tomato into her mouth, closed her lips to crush it, then leaned back and folded her arms across her chest.

"Of *course* we're going to do it! If the Colliers won't agree to a church wedding, we'll just have a civil ceremony. And I don't think Justin's parents would care for that. They have to do everything up big."

"Have you told them? About the baby?" Pamela asked.

"Justin did last weekend. He said it would be better if I wasn't there, that his mom might say something she'd regret. She freaked out as it was. Kept screaming that she *knew* it, she *knew* I was going to pull something like this, and how did they know the baby was his?"

"She actually *said* that?" Gwen exclaimed.

"Yeah, before Justin's dad shut her up. He said why didn't they all just try to calm down and not make any big decisions for the next month." Jill stared out the window a moment before she picked up her club sandwich and took a bite. Tore at it, really, with her teeth, hardly letting it touch her tongue.

"He's at least trying to be reasonable," Liz said, in her usual soothing manner.

Jill gave a sarcastic laugh. "Yeah, like maybe I'll miscarry or something."

"I thought you said he wanted a grandchild," I reminded her.

"He does. I'm probably not being fair, but he's not wild about me either. It's the witch who runs that household, and he's probably under her spell."

I couldn't help myself. "Jill," I said, "how can you . . . I mean . . . manage with all that hostility? I'd be a wreck."

"Well, we're not moving in with them, that's for sure," she said. "Justin and I love each other, and we're not going to let them break us up. Justin says his dad will support us till he gets through college—he's not worried about that. But his mom will pull every trick in the book to make it hard for us. You can count on it."

We were sprawled on the floor by the window in the hall. The only reason I could figure that Jill and Karen were eating with us was because we had one of the few spaces left. No, I think there was a bigger reason: Jill wanted the largest audience she could get whenever she talked about her wedding. If she couldn't have a zillion bridesmaids, she wanted an envious crowd of enthralled girls listening to her every word, and that was us.

For a minute or so the only noise came from the cafeteria at the other end.

Then Pamela asked, "You're still planning a June wedding?"

"May or June."

"But . . . like . . . won't you be showing?" Pamela asked.

"Probably. A little. But I've already picked out my dress. It's gorgeous," Jill said, and her eyes were alive again. "Lace over satin, neck to hem. We'll make it work. Everyone knows a baby's coming anyway. Justin and I are even going over names:

Isabella Paige and Ethan Alexander." She gave a satisfied smile and took a bite of cookie.

"Do you ever expect to go to college?" I asked, and immediately wished I hadn't. Jill's expression went from day to night, and there was the slightest downturn at the corners of her mouth.

"Do you expect me to plan my whole life right now?" she asked. "Don't you think I have enough to deal with?"

"Sure," I said quickly. "That's me—always jumping ahead."

Amy Sheldon had just joined stage crew, someone told me. And I heard it firsthand from Amy the next morning.

"Alice!" she called when I was heading to second period. "I'm doing what you did last year!" When people turned to look at her, she waited till she'd caught up with me to tell me the rest. "I signed up for stage crew," she said, walking along beside me, several feet away.

"Yeah, I heard!" I told her. "That's great, Amy. I think it'll be fun for you."

"I'm on props," she said, and dug one hand in the side pocket of her bag, then pulled out a sheet of paper. "Here's what I have to get: a book—that one's easy; a manicure set; handkerchief—my dad uses handkerchiefs. Mom and I use Kleenex. A sofa pillow, a plant, and a sandwich. Only I'll wait till the last day to get the sandwich on account of it would be spoiled if I got it now. There's lots more stuff, but the other kids will get that. One boy has to find a dog."

I laughed. "Yeah, I wondered about that."

"It's a good thing a large lollipop was on someone else's list because if it was on mine, I'd probably eat it. They're bad for your teeth, though, because the sugar stays in your mouth for so long. I've had two cavities, but I don't get them anymore. Do you?"

"Not often," I said.

"We're both working on the same thing, only you'll be onstage and I'll be behind the curtain, but I'll be cheering for you. I won't make any noise, though. If you're on stage crew, you can't make any noise."

We turned the corner, and I stopped to get a drink of water at the fountain.

"And I have to dress in black. I don't like black, do you, Alice? Am I talking too much?"

"Sometimes you do rattle on, Amy," I said, grinning up at her.

She looked confused. "I don't rattle. Dishes and pans rattle."

I realized how difficult it must be for Amy when speech is inexact. Amy's world is so black-and-white, so either-or.

"You're right. And yes, sometimes you do jump—I mean, switch—from one subject to another without waiting for an answer. And sometimes I just use the wrong words. You'll have to stop me when I use the wrong words," I told her.

"I'll just give you a signal," said Amy. "Like, maybe I'll hold up my hand or something. Or maybe just a finger on one hand."

"Got it," I said. "I mean, I understand."

12

ROOMMATES

I had only been home fifteen minutes, and was eating the dinner Sylvia had left for me, when my cell phone rang. I swallowed a bite of lasagna and pushed away from the table, ambling into the living room in my socks to check the caller. It was Pamela, so I took it.

"What's up?" I said.

Her voice was almost a scream. "I'm *in*! Alice, I've got a scholarship to the Theater Arts College in Manhattan!" She *was* screaming.

"*What?*" I cried.

"The letter just came! Dad's at Meredith's, so you're the first one I've told! I went to New York and auditioned, and I'm *in*!"

"Pamela! My God!" I said. Why hadn't she told us she'd

applied for a scholarship? Why hadn't she told us she'd been in New York? I might have known that theater arts people had to appear in person, but . . . What was I, jealous? Shouldn't I be congratulating her? "It's wonderful! It's amazing! It's incredulous, Pamela! When did you audition?"

"Remember last December when I stayed home because of a sore throat? I was really in New York that day. Dad gave me the money."

"And you've kept it secret all this time?"

"I didn't want everyone feeling sorry for me if I failed, Alice. I mean . . . all that grief over my pregnancy, then the miscarriage . . . I was tired of people feeling pity for me. It's only a half-tuition scholarship, but . . ."

"Well, I don't feel sorry for you, Pamela, and I think it's great! Really! What did you do for your audition?"

"That ditzy Adelaide scene from *Guys and Dolls*. I guess I nailed it, Alice! Yay!"

All I could think of was that the University of Maryland had been her safety school, and down deep, I had imagined her being my roommate if I couldn't room with Gwen. Next selfish thought: "Does this mean you won't be working on the cruise ship with us this summer?"

"It means I absolutely will. Do you know what it *costs* to live in Manhattan, Alice? I'll need the money more than ever. Of course I'll be on that cruise ship."

And so I loved her again, but I wondered if I'd ever look at her the same. The girl whose grades were good but not remarkable, who had been careless enough to get pregnant, had somehow gotten her act together and was accepted into a theater arts school in New York City. . . . Maybe someday I would quit pigeonholing people—would realize how much they can change.

"I'm standing here listening to all of this and feeling so . . . *proud* of you, Pam!" I said. "Listen, call your mom. Let her in on it."

"I will. Right after I call Dad," she told me, and gave a little shriek again of pure joy.

It was hard to be as excited about the school play with Pamela destined for New York. I'd made a decision: If William & Mary would take me, I was going to go there. I could be adventurous too. But getting the part of Anne was still a big step for me—strange to be one of the cast, no longer part of the stage crew. I was so used to staying in the shadows, never venturing farther out in the wings where the audience might see us.

Now, after a week of reading the play together in the drama classroom, Mr. Ellis moved rehearsals into the auditorium and up on the stage, facing rows and rows of seats that morphed into darkness at the back of the cavernous hall. I was part of the curtains and lights now, not just the paint and the props.

When the actors weren't needed in a particular scene, we sat in the seats below. Ryan sat down beside me while Pamela and Jay were rehearsing onstage.

"The only time I can take a break is when you do," he said. "I'm never onstage if you're not."

"Ah! Power!" I whispered back, smiling at him.

His knees almost touched the seat in front of him and his jeans stretched tightly over his thighs. The body of an athlete, I thought, or maybe a dancer. I didn't know much about him except that he was playing the part of Larry, my boyfriend.

"I was surprised Ellis dug out this old play," Ryan went on. "My cousin said they did this nine years ago."

"Why did you try out if you don't like it?" I asked.

"Experience," Ryan said. "Don't you know that everything we do in senior year counts as 'experience'?"

Mr. Ellis, in the front row, looked around to see who was whispering, and we immediately faced forward, totally focused on Pamela and Jay.

Becoming a part of my stage family made me feel even closer to my own. The dialogue between Anne and her brothers made me think more about Lester and something he'd said in our last phone conversation, about how so many of the girls he used to know had moved away.

I called him that evening.

"How are things?" I said.

"Need you ask?" he answered. "Andy's here, the weather's lousy, we're out of cheese, and the Super Bowl's over."

"Want some company?"

"You could come by Friday night, if you want. We had some guys in last week, but I'm the designated sitter for Mr. Watts this Friday."

"Sure, I'll come," I said.

"Bring food," said Les.

As soon as I ended the call, I punched in Kay's number and asked if she would be needing any rescuing Friday night.

"I need it twenty-four/seven," Kay said. "If I don't have something planned every night of the week, my parents invite me over. I asked them the other day if they didn't agree this was a hopeless cause, and Mom just said that as long as James was in the States, it was our obligation to entertain him. And then I really made my dad angry, because I said, 'But is it necessary to involve me?' And he said, 'Since you are determined to do the least possible to help, yes, it is necessary for you to come along.' It's so miserable. James and I hardly even talk to each other. I don't think he can stand me."

"How would you like an excuse not to go to their place this Friday?" I said. "Could you get some girlfriends together and come with me to Lester's apartment? He's got to stay home that evening and needs cheering up."

"Great! I'll do it!" Kay said. "I'll say my boss's son is giving a party. They don't like to interfere in my work."

Asking Kay Yen to bring some of her friends to Lester's apartment Friday night was one of my more inspired ideas. The two other girls were about Kay's age—early twenties—fairly attractive, one Asian, one Caucasian, friendly and full of life.

"I've got food, but I figured friends were welcome too," I said, brushing past him with a grocery bag in my arms.

"Hi, Les," Kay said. "Nice to see you again. This is Lee and Judith."

"Well, come in! Come in!" Les said, holding the door open wide, obviously taken by surprise. I wondered if he even remembered he'd invited me.

"We were going to get together for dinner, and Alice said you were home alone, so we thought, 'Why not have dinner there?'" Kay explained, following me to the kitchen.

"Yeah, dirty up your kitchen instead of ours," I joked.

"Be my guests!" said Les, still puzzled but looking pleased. "I'll even put on shoes for the occasion." He went into his bedroom while we set out some stuff. Nothing fancy. Kay had bought a cheesecake from the supermarket, and I brought a jar of spaghetti sauce and pasta. The others purchased green beans almondine and garlic bread. A feast.

We put on water to boil for the spaghetti, and Les emerged from his bedroom. He had put on a clean shirt over his tee and combed his hair a little.

"Too bad Paul isn't here. He'd love this," he said.

"So we'll do it again," said Kay.

"You have a roommate?" Judith asked.

"Yeah, two of them, both out for the evening. I'm on duty," Les said. As we set the table, he told them about the arrangement with Mr. Watts, and they laughed during dinner at his account of how Andy got in on the deal. Lee found a soft-rock station, Les opened some beer, and as the evening progressed, it seemed as though we'd all known each other for a long time.

Judith entertained us with stories of her and Kay's canoeing adventures on the Potomac, especially the time they managed to collide with a kayaker, who threatened to sue.

"Can you believe it?" Judith said, imitating the man in the kayak, waving his paddle in the air and demanding to see their IDs.

We were still laughing when we heard the door click. I hoped it was Paul, that he could join the party. But a moment later Andy appeared in the kitchen doorway, her red-framed glasses fogging up slightly as she surveyed us there at the table.

"Hi," she said, and I was about to introduce her to the others when she turned and walked back down the hall to her room. We heard voices, and even though Andy's is low, we could tell that the other voice was male. And then she shut her door.

"She tutors," Les said in explanation.

A TV set came on in Andy's room, and the volume was turned down. A man's laughter. The women exchanged smiles.

"What subjects?" Kay asked.

"English, history . . . ," Les said, and then, catching their drift, "physiology, maybe? Hey, she's allowed to have friends, you know." We laughed and talked of other things.

13

SOUND OF THE WHISTLE

After work the next day, Kay and I went to visit Marilyn. Actually, we volunteered to go over and make a big pot of chicken and corn soup, and Jack said the kitchen was ours to do with as we liked. I brought along Sylvia's recipe for blueberry muffins and all the ingredients I'd need.

But first we wanted to see the baby.

Marilyn was sitting on the couch in an old pair of baggy jeans and a sweater, folding laundry, the baby snoozing in the narrow dip between her knees. All I could see when I came in was a wisp of fine golden hair over a pink scalp and two tiny fists clenched tightly.

"Oh, Marilyn!" I said, pushing some towels out of the way and sitting carefully down beside her.

Marilyn beamed as she studied her baby. "Isn't she the sweetest thing you ever saw?" she whispered, gently edging her fingers under the baby's back and neck, lifting her from her lap and handing her over to me.

The small body was so light! How could a baby weigh so little? The pink lips barely opened as the head tipped back a bit. But when I cradled her in my arms, she gave a soft sigh and the yellow flannel shirt she was wearing rose and fell again ever so slightly as she breathed.

Jack and Kay were hovering over the back of the sofa behind us. He chuckled as a tiny bubble of spit formed at the baby's mouth.

"She's adorable!" said Kay. "Oh, I want one of those!"

"Get a husband first," said Marilyn. "A *good* one, like Jack. They don't come any better."

I watched the baby's mouth twitch, the lips forming an *O*, almost a smacking motion, and she stirred slightly.

"She'll be getting hungry pretty soon," Marilyn told us. "Every three hours, she lets us know she's alive."

I stroked the side of Summer's face with one finger, marveling at the fine hair of her eyebrows, the dark lashes, the chrysanthemum-colored lips. "Grow up like your mama," I told her.

"Next?" said Kay, coming around the sofa to sit beside me, and I gently placed the little sleeping beauty in her lap.

Jack went off to run errands, and while Marilyn nursed her baby, Kay and I took over the kitchen. We'd brought a fruit salad that

Sylvia had made, and Kay set to work on the chicken soup, her grandmother's recipe from China.

The Robertses' house was small, but it had a large old-fashioned kitchen. It was a welcoming place, with a rocking chair in one corner on a braided rug, where the cat was sitting now. There were plants at every window and a big round table in the middle of the floor.

We soon had the windows steamed up, and as Kay followed the soup instructions, I concentrated on greasing the muffin tins and paid extra attention to the lines on Sylvia's recipe card that she had underlined in red: *Stir only until moistened. Batter will be lumpy. DO NOT OVERMIX.*

Once we had the soup simmering and the muffins in the oven, we allowed ourselves to talk to each other, and Marilyn, hearing the chatter, came out to the kitchen to make us some tea.

"Summer's sleeping," she said. "Now we can visit."

I couldn't keep my eyes off Marilyn. She was still a little thick at the waist, but even so . . . !

"You can go through having a baby, and two weeks later you're walking around like this?" I marveled.

"What do you mean, two weeks later?" Marilyn said. "I was walking around the very next day."

"Amazing!" I told her. "I figured you'd be all sore and bent over and—"

"Alice, it's a normal bodily function, having a baby," she said. "I take a nap each day. But the more I move around, the stronger I feel." She looked about the kitchen and inhaled.

"Mmmm. Everything smells so good. You guys are the best!"

We sat at the round table, drinking our tea, letting the steam moisten our faces, waiting for the muffins to finish baking so we could taste them.

"So how are things going with your parents?" Marilyn asked Kay.

"Nobody's budged," said Kay. "They invite James over for dinner twice a week and expect me to be there at least once. James sits there with a stoic look on his face, and more than once I've caught him checking his watch. I think his consulting job is over in April, so this can't last forever. I escaped last night's dinner at least, thanks to Alice—rounded up some girlfriends and took dinner to Les."

"Lucky Les," said Marilyn. "What's the latest with that new roommate of his?"

We told her how Andy's "student" turned out to be a boyfriend.

"And they didn't come out of her room all evening," Kay said.

Marilyn laughed. "Well, at least she has friends."

"Anyway," Kay continued, "Andy's on duty next Friday night, so Judith and I are going to take Les and Paul to a club. We promised them a canoe trip when the weather gets warmer."

"Les always lucks out, doesn't he?" Marilyn said.

"Not always," I said, but didn't say more. Jack was the lucky one here.

The rehearsal schedule for March was unrelenting. No holidays, no time off. Some were late rehearsals, which meant we worked through the dinner hour, ate alone when we got home.

On Friday there was an assembly right before lunch.

"Now what?" said Gwen, as she and I filed in with a couple of friends from physics. I knew what it was about but had to pretend I didn't.

"I think it's supposed to advertise all the spring activities," one of the girls said.

"Just so it's not another lecture on drunk driving or STDs," someone else said.

Principal Beck came to the microphone first and gave a two-minute history of all the awards and honors our school had won in the past, then talked about what a bang-up year this one was turning out to be.

When he mentioned the orchestra concert in May, three violinists in their white shirts and black bow ties emerged from behind the curtain and, playing a schmaltzy tune, crossed the stage and exited the other side. When he mentioned the coming band concert at the end of this month, a trumpet player, oboe player, bassoon player, and drummer came marching across the stage from the other direction, playing a polka.

The basketball team dribbled a ball across the stage when Mr. Beck gave a shout-out to the high school finals that weekend. The girls' soccer team followed, then the cheerleaders, and finally the madrigals, singing a short piece to promote the choir concert in April.

Gwen, a seat away, leaned forward and gave me a puzzled expression, like, *Where's any mention of the play?*—and I just shrugged and gave her a woeful look.

Then, as Mr. Beck walked off the stage, Brad Broderick entered, dressed in an old-fashioned three-piece suit, obviously padded around the middle. His dark sideburns had been grayed, he wore his round-rimmed spectacles halfway down his nose, and there were lines drawn on his forehead and around his mouth.

Without a word, Brad stood in the center of the stage. He pulled a stopwatch out of his vest pocket and held it out in front of him. Then, lifting a whistle to his mouth with his other hand, he blew a loud blast and pressed the button on the stopwatch.

Instantly, I leaped to my feet and yelled, "Coming!" and the girls in my row shrank back, staring at me wide-eyed. But all over the auditorium, the scattered Gilbreth children were climbing over legs in their rows, all heading for the stage, all yelling, "Coming, Dad!" and "Wait for me!" and "Just a minute!" as our classmates began to get the picture and broke into laughter.

Using the side steps of the stage, up we went, dropping our books in a heap and quickly forming a row in front of the footlights, from oldest to youngest, as our father clicked the stopwatch once more.

"Fourteen seconds!" Brad boomed, looking us over in disgust.

"That's pretty good!" said Jay cheerfully, playing the part of Frank Jr.

Brad glared at him.

Tim, as Fred, said, "Only eight seconds off the record."

"Where's your mother?" Brad asked.

"Upstairs with the babies," I told him.

Turning toward the audience, Brad said gruffly, "I had so many children because I thought anything your mother and I teamed up on was certain to be a success. Now I'm not so sure." He wheeled about abruptly. "Let me see your fingernails."

And as Brad moved down the line, all of us wincing, drawing our hands back or quickly buffing our nails against our clothes, the school principal returned to the microphone and said, "And you won't want to miss this year's spring production, *Cheaper by the Dozen*, to see what happens when two efficiency experts raise a family of twelve children and there's an uprising brewing over—you guessed it—romance . . . freedom . . . silk stockings and other unmentionables! Bring your family! Bring your friends! April eighth and ninth, fifteenth and sixteenth." And then all of us onstage shouted together, *"Cheaper by the Dozen!"*

And the assembly was over.

It was so much fun. Liz and Gwen and Jill and Karen were waiting for me out in the hall, and we all collapsed in laughter. Even Liz hadn't known it was coming, not being in that particular scene.

"You almost gave me a heart attack!" said Gwen. "I thought you were having a fit or something."

"It wasn't till we saw the other actors jumping up that we realized it was staged," said Karen.

"Yeah, Alice will do anything for attention," said Jill, but she said it jokingly, and for maybe the first time, I sensed that perhaps she was relieved she hadn't gotten the part of Anne after all.

"Even scared the wits out of me," Ryan McGowan said as we were leaving the physics lab last period. It was hard for me not to call him "Larry." "Pamela was in our row, and when she jumped up, I thought she was choking or something."

I laughed. "Mr. Ellis wanted us to keep it secret from everyone, even the rest of the cast. Have you done theater before?"

"Back in Illinois," he said. "My dad was transferred here last year. I had bit parts in community theater. How about you?"

"My first time, unless you count my sixth-grade production."

He smiled a little. "What part did you play?"

"A bramble bush with branches thick," I said, and he chuckled.

"Well, I'll bet you were a darned good bramble bush."

"Not really," I told him. "I tripped up the star of the show, who happened to be Pamela, by the way, and she was furious. I was so jealous of her."

"The tragedies of life," Ryan said. "I'm thinking of majoring in theater. I've been getting some coaching."

"Really?"

"I'll see how it goes at college. Either theater or a fine arts degree. Publishing, maybe. You?"

"I want to be a school counselor."

He glanced down at me. "Yeah?"

"Yes." And when he didn't respond, I added, "I've been accepted at Maryland. I'm waiting to see if two other schools come through, William & Mary in particular."

"I've applied to Columbia and the University of Iowa. Also, a little college in Minnesota where my mom went, just to make her happy," Ryan said. "But I want to do my grad work at the University of Iowa, if I make it that far. It's the best writing program there is, if I go into that."

We reached the corner and I had to turn. "See you at practice," I said.

"I'm heading for the doughnut sale," he told me. "Can I get you something?"

"Yeah. One glazed. Thanks," I said.

Seemed strange, somehow, that I was sounding more and more like my life was on track and that it was other people's lives that were question marks. As Dad was fond of saying, though, "Life is what happens when you're planning something else." In fact, every new person you meet introduces a question mark. And Ryan was no exception.

14

NEWS

March Madness was going on, and I hardly got to watch any of the games. By the time rehearsals were over, I still had homework to do and didn't have much evening left, even for watching TV.

On Sunday, though, with Maryland poised for a slot in the Elite Eight if they beat Virginia Tech, I called Les to see if he and Paul were going to watch it and ask if I could come over to join them. It's always more fun to watch a college game with a Maryland student or, in Lester's case, two former grad students, him and Paul.

"Sure," he said. "Couple buddies are coming over, and Kay's dropping by. Join the crowd!"

Hmmm, I thought. Was it just possible that Les and Kay

were hitting it off? Was there remotely, conceivably, incredibly a chance that under the guise of rescuing each other from Andy and James, respectively, an attraction between them was blossoming under our very noses?

I had some errands to run first, and when I finally got to Lester's apartment, the place was rocking. The game had started, Maryland had the ball, and there were guys I didn't know on every available chair and couch cushion. Paul was lifting a couple beers out of a cooler and passing them around. Kay said that Judith would be coming too, but right now she was sitting cross-legged on the floor in front of the couch, between Lester's knees. I tried not to smile. I had managed to hook up Dad and Sylvia, hadn't I? Was I a matchmaker or what?

When I went to the door later to let Judith in, I noticed that Andy's door was shut. I took Judith's chips to the kitchen to get a bowl, and when Paul came out for more ice, I asked, "Nobody invited Andy to join in?"

"We did! We did! But she's doing a tutoring session," he told me.

I shrugged.

It was during the third quarter, when I was taking some bottles to the trash, that I saw one guy leaving Andy's room and another coming in from outside. They passed without speaking. Andy was waiting in her doorway in a knit top and silky leisure pants, purple dangly earrings at her ears.

"Hi," I said.

"How you doing?" she answered, ushering the new guy into her room and closing the door behind them.

Les came out to the kitchen to get more dip.

"How many boyfriends does she have?" I asked, nodding toward Andy's room.

"Haven't asked," said Les.

Maryland lost and was out of the play-offs, but it was a close game and the team played well. I love basketball because it's so easy to follow: If the ball goes through the basket and there's no whistle, the team scores. You don't have to know the rest of the rules.

But the play was taking my full concentration these days, especially now that the costume committee was beginning to outfit the cast. I hated what I had to wear for the first act, but Mrs. Cary thought it was just right, so I wore it—a black pleated skirt that came just below the knee, a long green sweater that fell halfway down my thighs, and a black belt a few inches below the waistline. Worse yet were the black cotton stockings that made my legs look fat.

Pamela and Chassie, as Martha, the third-oldest sister, got to wear white sailor tops with navy blue kerchiefs around their necks; and Angela, as Lillian, the youngest, got to wear a pinafore, white knee-length stockings, and Mary Jane shoes. But in the final act I would be wearing a thin, filmy sleeveless dress with silk hose. They made my legs shine, but it was still a beautiful costume, and I guess the audience was supposed to see how much I'd managed to improve between the first and third acts of the play.

The rehearsals were wearing me down, though, and by the last weekend in March, when Karen called and said a bunch of girls were going to Clyde's restaurant for dinner Saturday night, I said I'd go. I was so amazed to be invited that I was going mostly out of curiosity. Liz and Pamela were going too, but Gwen was singing in a concert at her church.

Pamela drove this time—her dad had finally let her use his car—and she said if I'd quit gasping every time she reached a stop sign, she'd drive more often.

"It's just that you never brake till the last minute," Liz told her. "Your passengers think you're going to sail on through."

"But I *do* stop, don't I?" said Pamela. "Do I have to sing an overture before I stop?"

"I'd settle for just taking your foot off the gas pedal," I said.

We drove to Clyde's at Tower Oaks in Rockville—a great place for crab cakes, a sort of safari-themed restaurant with animal trophies and canoes on the walls. Lots of couples go there before proms, but we like to go as a group because half of us order a plate dinner and the others order appetizers. Then we share, and we can stay as long as we like.

Jill had reserved a large table, and some of the girls were already there when we arrived. One of them was talking about receiving an acceptance from Towson State.

"It's so great to know that at least *some*body wants me," the girl was saying, and the discussion turned to how many colleges—four? five? six?—you should have applied for to be on the safe side.

"And what about Pamela here!" I said. "Isn't she amazing?"

We clinked our glasses in tribute, and Pamela made a funny face.

"She auditioned as Adelaide from *Guys and Dolls*," I said, in case anyone hadn't heard. "Just goes to show that even an understudy has possibilities."

I realized too late that Jill may have thought I was taking a dig at her for backing out. But Jill was biding her time, I guess, because she listened with a sort of condescending air, and then she said she had an announcement: "We're getting married April twenty-third."

We stared. "Whaaaaaat?" we said, almost in unison.

Jill basked in the limelight and smiled coyly around the table, her elegantly manicured fingers splayed out in front of her. Without a ring, however. "The Colliers gave in. Justin told them we were marrying as soon as school was out, and it would be either in a church or before a justice of the peace—it was up to them. When they realized that we were serious and, probably more to the point, that I hadn't miscarried yet—I'm in my second trimester now—Justin's mom caved and said they'd pay for the wedding. But, of course, there are conditions. . . ."

"Wow, Jill! Right in the middle of the semester?" said Liz.

"It'll be spring break. Mrs. Collier doesn't want me walking down the aisle obviously pregnant, and there's to be no civil ceremony for their son. Like I said, whatever they do, they do *big*."

"This is unbelievable," I said. "I never thought they'd give in."

"That's what Mom said," Jill went on. "She had the invitations engraved and in the mail before the Colliers could change their minds. And I wish we could invite you all, but the witch is in charge of the guest list."

"Where's it going to be?" asked Pamela.

"The Episcopal church near Chevy Chase Circle. That was one of the conditions. They'll pay for most of the wedding if we agree to the conditions."

"What are the others?" asked Liz.

Our drinks arrived and Jill leaned back, waiting for our server to leave before she continued. Then she began counting them off on her fingers: "Number one: We marry in April. Number two: We marry in their church. Number three: Justin finishes college no matter how many children I 'manage to produce.' His mother actually wrote that down. She crossed it out after and inserted 'you have' instead of 'Jill manages to produce,' but she left it in so I'd know she suspects I planned to get pregnant."

"Well . . . it *was* a plan . . . I mean, both of you planned it," I said.

"Damn right," said Jill. "And I don't care if she *does* know it. Number four: that we pay for the honeymoon ourselves. Ditto, the ring. Numbers five, six, and seven: Justin works summers for his dad's company until he's through college, we have to live in this area till he graduates, and we don't deny the Colliers access to their grandchildren."

Jill took a deep breath, held it, then let it out.

"Wow. She forgot to add the pound of flesh. She didn't put that in," somebody said. "And you don't have to name your first daughter after her?"

"Yeah, I know. They more or less own us till Justin's through college, but at least they didn't insist we live with them. They're paying for everything except the ring, our honeymoon, and our apartment, and Justin says we can pay the rent out of his trust fund. But Mom could never afford the kind of wedding the Colliers want for Justin."

The appetizers came and we began dividing them up—a bit of crab cake on each saucer, a wedge of fried onion. . . . Jill held up the chicken satay on a stick: "This is one of the appetizers we've chosen along with the shrimp," she said. "The dinner menu, of course, is completely Mrs. Collier's, but she did run it by Mom first."

"How do they get along—Mrs. Collier and your mom?" Liz asked.

"It's all surface, you know? Mom was terrified to meet her, actually—she'd heard so much about her from me. All bad. Mr. and Mrs. Collier came over on a Sunday afternoon—the usual courtesy call—and said that a spring wedding would be so much more appropriate than a summer one, didn't Mom agree? And asked how long we'd lived in the Washington area, meaning: Where are your 'people' from? Since then, everything's being arranged by a middleman—woman, I should say. Mr. Collier's secretary relays messages to Mom and she replies to the secretary.

Every day Mom gets a memo on something else that's been decided for us."

"And . . . you don't mind?" another friend asked.

"Of course I do. But I'm going to keep my mouth shut as long as they don't try to break us up. I've just been really, really tired lately. If they want to do all the planning, so be it. It'll be an even fancier wedding than I could ever afford, and I'm just going to pretend the Colliers aren't there. The parents, that is."

The dinners arrived and we divided those up too, and afterward Jill passed around photos of what the wedding cake would look like, the place settings and favors and flowers. I guess when you put everything in the hands of a wedding planner and money is no object, you can put together a wedding in six weeks and make it look like you've been thinking about it for a year or more.

"When you *do* go on a honeymoon, where do you think it will be?" Pamela asked.

"Hawaii. We're going as soon as school's out. We have to decide between a honeymoon and a diamond, though, and I don't want to start out with something small, so we'll put the engagement ring off till later," Jill told us. Then she reached in her bag and pulled out a brochure of a resort hotel on Kauai, tucked in a cove with palm trees and flowers and blue waves beyond a white sandy beach.

Jill was right. She did look tired. Just as pretty, just as svelte as she always looked, but tired. Just thinking about her next four years with a baby while Justin was in college made me tired too.

15
INSOMNIA

The feathery green of spring.

The star magnolias had blossomed in the middle of March. Crocuses came up next, then daffodils, and the forsythia was a brilliant yellow against the new green of the lawns. Near the end of the month, cherry trees had burst into bloom, and on every tree in the neighborhood, little feathers of leaves appeared, trembling in the breeze.

But I felt like I was trembling too. I had to give the University of Maryland a reply by April 1 as to whether or not I was going to attend. And every day I waited to hear from William & Mary. I couldn't believe that everything was coming at me at once, with the first play performances beginning the following weekend.

I wanted so much to be able to call Pamela and say, *Guess*

what? To tell her that I, too, was striking out in a new direction. And then, on March 29, after a late rehearsal, I got home to find that Dad and Sylvia had gone to a movie. A pile of mail had been dumped on a chair, unsorted, and there, near the bottom, was an envelope from William & Mary. My heart began to race. I pulled it out from among the stack.

But it was not a large manila envelope. It was a white business-size envelope, and I felt my throat constricting even before I opened it, my eyes filling with tears. I sat down on the bottom step of the stairs and balanced it between the palms of my hands. Then, furiously, I ripped it open and read the first two lines—*Dear Alice McKinley: We are sorry that we will be unable to admit you to our college this coming fall. We know that . . .*

I ran upstairs like a crazy person, sobbing loudly, and threw myself on my bed. Why? What was it about me that they didn't like? Wasn't I a B+ student? Didn't I have a lot of extracurricular stuff on my application? Hadn't Mrs. Bailey written an excellent recommendation? I loved the place; why didn't they love me back? And why did Dad and Sylvia go off to a movie when if ever I needed somebody's shoulder, it was now? Even though I knew that wasn't fair, that Dad and Sylvia hadn't even looked at the mail, I needed someone to listen to me, comfort me, and because there was no one there, I impulsively called Patrick.

Even as I punched in his number, I knew I was in no condition to carry on a conversation. At the same moment I was afraid he might answer, he picked up. "Hey, Alice!" he said.

"P-P-P-Patrick!" I sobbed.

"Alice? *Alice?*" His voice was instantly tense, concerned. "Alice, what *is* it? Where are you?"

"Oh, P-Patrick," I wept. "They d-didn't . . ." I couldn't stand the childish sound of my voice, the stammering. I could feel my cheeks blaze, and I suddenly pressed END and dropped the phone on my rug, doubling over in anguish.

Almost instantly the phone began to ring, and I stared at it there on the rug. Stared at it through the flood of tears dripping off my lashes. There was something steadying about the insistence of its ring, and I realized that if I had been childish calling him in the first place, I was even more childish not to answer now. So I picked it up and tried to get hold of myself.

"Patrick?" I mewed.

"Alice, don't hang up. Are you listening?" he said. "Don't hang up, no matter what. Where are you?"

I spoke so softly, I could hardly hear myself. "I'm home."

"Okay. Just take a couple breaths or something. I'm listening. I'm not going away."

"I'm s-so sorry," I said. "I knew I shouldn't have c-called. Are you busy right now?"

"I was watching TV with the guys. I'm out in the hall now, sitting on the floor, and nobody's around. What's the matter?"

When I remembered what the matter was, the tears came again. "William & Mary rejected m-me."

"Oh, man. I'm sorry, Alice. I really am."

"But—but that—that makes me even sadder," I wept. "Because I know y-you wanted me to g-go there."

"It's what *you* want, Alice! Why should I—?"

"It's true, Patrick," I said, wiping my nose on my arm. "You're going to Spain and Gwen's in a pre-med program and Pamela's going to New York and everybody's going places and doing things . . . and . . . and . . ." I was sobbing again. "Why do you even b-bother with me? Why do you like me at all? There are all kinds of girls who know m-more than I do and travel all over and speak Russian and Japanese, and I—I—All I know is here, P-Patrick! The only places I've l-lived are Chicago and Maryland. All . . . I really know . . . is . . . m-m-me!"

Patrick was quiet for so long I thought he'd hung up on me except that I didn't get a dial tone. And then I heard his voice, firm and steady.

"Alice, before we moved to Maryland when I was in sixth grade, I'd already lived in four different countries—"

"I *know*!" I wept, my voice high and tight. "That's what I'm talking about!"

Patrick continued: "There wasn't any one place to call home. And when we moved to Maryland and Mom said we'd be there for a while, it was the first place I started to make friends . . . I mean, friends I knew I'd see for more than a year or so. And yet, even there in Maryland, my dad traveled so much and was home so little that it never seemed like a real home, not the home that other kids had, and certainly not your home, the way you feel about it, the way you and your dad and Lester made it home. And *that's* what I love about you. Among other things," he added quickly.

"You love me because I stay home?"

"I love you because you *love* home. It doesn't mean you're never going to get out. It doesn't mean you're not curious about other people and places. You *are*! You care about people who are different from you—Amy Sheldon, for example. Lori and Leslie. That Sudanese guy you told me about. You want to know what it feels like to be them. You don't have to live somewhere else or go to William & Mary to do that. You open your mind to the world, Alice. That's what makes you you."

"Oh, Patrick. I wish you were here," I said, still crying, but managing it now. "I'm just so keyed up over everything and rehearsals run late and I'm behind on my homework and I've got to let Maryland know I'm coming and—"

"And it will all work out. Trust me. It will."

"I trust you," I said.

Patrick's phone call helped more than he knew, and I soldiered on, grateful for Dad and Sylvia's reassurance that Maryland was a fine school, which of course I knew. For the next week, I focused entirely on the play and got caught up in the excitement of our final round of rehearsals. *Too* caught up, because I started having trouble sleeping. I'd lie awake till two or three in the morning, then the alarm would go off at six thirty, and I'd feel half dead.

When I woke on Wednesday, though—just two days before

our first performance—there was no alarm sounding on my nightstand. The sun was already shining full on my bedspread. I rose up on one elbow and stared at the clock. Nine fifteen! I leaped out of bed, then saw the note stuck on the back of my door.

> *Alice, you've been exhausted, and we don't want you sick for opening night of the play. I've called the school and told them I'm letting you sleep in. They understand. Sylvia*

Omigod! I thought. *I don't want anyone to think I can't handle this!* I showered, but I let my hair go, pulled on my jeans and a knit top. Sylvia had left two blueberry muffins on the table along with her car keys, but by the time I got to school, I'd missed the first two periods.

"Somebody was up late last night," Gwen said diplomatically when she saw me at lunch. Saw my hair.

"I'm not sleeping well," I told her. "I haven't been falling asleep till around three, and I'm exhausted when I try to get up. Sylvia turned off my alarm and let me sleep in."

"Best thing she could have done," Gwen said.

"Does this ever happen to you?" I asked her.

"Once in a while. I go through spells. I find that if I take a warm bath, read a while, drink some milk, and let my mind wander over old movies or books or dreams after I lie down—never what I have to do the next day—I eventually fall asleep.

The secret is to make a list before you turn in of all you have to do the next day so you won't forget something. Then tell yourself that those things are off-limits once you get in bed. You'll deal with them tomorrow."

"Gwen," I said, "you're a walking Google. No matter what I ask, you have an answer."

Pamela put my hair in a French braid in gym, and I felt reasonably recovered when I walked into rehearsal at three. But Ryan took one look at me and said, "You look tired. You getting as little sleep as the rest of us?"

"Even less," I said. "But this morning they let me sleep in. I didn't get to school till around ten."

Every rehearsal this final week was a dress rehearsal, and Penny waylaid us when we got to the dressing rooms and had a thin little paste-on mustache she wanted Ryan to wear for his part as Larry. "C'mon, just for a joke," she laughed, grabbing his arm. "See what Ellis thinks."

He was still fending her off when I went in the girls' dressing room and took off my shirt. It was stuffy in the room—the one window didn't open, and the lights over the long makeup table were hot. We took turns sitting on the worn stools in our underwear and bras, brushing color on our cheeks, darkening our eyebrows, going heavy on the eyeliner and mascara. Occasionally, we could make out bits of conversation from the guys' dressing room on the other side of the wall, and we'd grin.

Once in a while, when one of them raised his voice, we figured they wanted us to hear, and at some point I heard one of the guys say loudly, "Hey, dudes! Did you know there's a hole in the wall and I can see the girls half naked?"

We looked at each other and giggled.

I turned to Liz and said, just as loudly, "Well, if they haven't seen it by now, it's time they did."

Liz's eyes opened wide, and the other girls stifled their laughter.

"Who said that?" we heard one guy ask, both surprise and excitement in his voice. "Could you tell who that was?"

"Maybe Penny," said someone else.

"Didn't sound like her," another guy mused. "Sounded like Alice."

"*Alice* said that?"

We shook our heads, still grinning, and went on doing our faces.

Strange, the satisfaction I got out of that. Alice, playing the thoughtful, older, dutiful daughter, could be a little risqué now and then. Sometimes I surprise even myself.

I overslept on Thursday morning too. I was simply too wound up after late rehearsal, and when I got to the breakfast table, Dad was waiting for me with a note he was writing the office to excuse my missing the first two periods again.

"Dad, this is the second time it's happened. They won't let me keep skipping classes!" I protested, frantically trying to get my shoes on.

"Al, sit down," he said. "You're not leaving this house till you've had some toast and juice. I'm telling the school that the overload has given you temporary insomnia and that you will make up any work you've missed after the play is over."

"It makes it sound like I can't handle stress. The other actors show up."

"How do you know you're the only one coming in late? This will blow over, trust me. But when you get as tired as you've been, your resistance is down, and that's when you can easily pick up a bug that will knock you flat. You've worked too hard on this play to get sick for the performances."

That was the only part that stuck with me, that I might miss a performance, so I sat down and ate the slice of toast he had buttered.

"It's so scary," I said, reaching for the marmalade. "I've never done anything on a stage before. Not like this."

"Of course you have. You've been practicing on that stage for two months."

"Not in front of a zillion people. What if I forget my lines?"

"That's what prompters are for."

"What if I get so nervous that I throw up?"

"That's what custodians are for, Alice. Will you please finish your toast and let me drive you to school?" he said.

There was no dress rehearsal Thursday night. We were told to go home, have a normal dinner with our families, and get a good night's sleep. Nobody argued.

Dad and Sylvia were delighted that we could all have dinner

together, and I could tell they were keeping the conversation light. They seemed to move about the kitchen in slow motion and to prolong the meal just to keep me at the table, getting nourished.

"I won't need you at the store for the next two weeks, Al," Dad said. "I want you to take these two Saturdays off and sleep in."

"Dad, are you sure?" I asked. "Easter's coming. All that Easter Sunday music!"

"Churches bought that ages ago," Dad said. "Besides, I've hired two temps to help out."

"Wow! *Two* temps to replace me? I must be a real workhorse!" I said.

Dad grinned. "You'll do."

I didn't want to wait to see if Patrick would call that night, so I called him around nine, but he didn't answer. I wondered if I should try again and leave a message. What if he didn't call back? Would I worry and not sleep again? I spent the next hour getting more and more uptight. If his cell phone was ringing and he checked it, he could tell it was from me. Why wasn't he answering?

I called him again at ten fifteen, and this time he picked up.

"Alice? You okay?" he asked.

"No, but just hearing your voice helps," I told him. "It's the night before the play and we're supposed to be relaxing, but I've had insomnia and I've got the jitters and two mornings I've gone to school late and—"

"Hey, hey," he said, to slow me down.

"What are you doing, Patrick? I'll bet I've interrupted a great conversation, or you're at the Medici with friends, or—"

"Actually," said Patrick, and I could tell he was moving around as he talked, "I just saw a movie at Ida Noyes and came back to my dorm to get a jacket. I'm meeting some guys at a club over on Fifty-ninth."

"Oh, I don't want to hold you up. Go on and we'll talk tomorrow . . . or . . . sometime," I said.

"The club doesn't close till one, and the guys won't miss me for a while. So . . . talk. About anything at all."

"I just wanted to hear your voice. I called before and you didn't answer."

"I had my cell phone turned off during the movie. Okay . . . now I'm sitting down on the couch in our tiny living room—the couch you slept on when you were here—and I'm looking at an empty Pepsi can on the bookcase and somebody's sneakers on the floor, and my roommate's plant is dead, so almost *anything* you say will be more interesting than this," Patrick said, and that made me laugh.

"Tomorrow's the big night," I told him, "and I've never been onstage before in front of a lot of people—lights and everything—except for our little skit at assembly. I've done okay at rehearsals, but what if everything falls apart once it's for real?"

"Why would it? You won't be able to see past the first couple of rows. Pretend they're all from Pergatoria or something—"

"From *where*?"

"Never heard of Pergatoria? Yep, they're all from there, and none of them can speak English."

I was grinning now. "So it will be completely unimportant—the play?"

"Completely."

"And how we perform is totally irrelevant?"

"Totally."

"So it makes no difference if I show up or not?"

"Uh . . . not exactly," said Patrick.

"Oh, Patrick, just talking with you makes me feel better. I really wish you were here."

"I wish I could be in the front row cheering for you," he said. "But then, I wished you were here with me last night."

"What happened last night?"

"Nothing," he said. "That's why I wished you were here. It was great weather in Chicago. I was at the library till late, and on the way back I walked by Botany Pond. And I thought of you."

I felt warm all over. A rush of warmth in my chest, a throbbing warmth between my legs, thinking of Patrick's hands, his fingers . . .

"Patrick . . . ," I said, and was almost embarrassed, it sounded so much like the *Patrick* I had said back then.

Neither of us said anything for several seconds. Then, Patrick's voice, husky, "Two more months till the prom. . . ."

16
OPENING NIGHT

It helped that everyone else in the cast seemed as jumpy and excited and nervous as I was on Friday. Even more so. Angela confessed she really had been sick and lost her breakfast shortly after she got to school that morning. I found myself comforting her.

"Break a leg," people kept saying to us in the halls.

The short guy who played Jackie had a breakout of acne, not quite what you'd expect on the youngest son in the play. But when we got ready for the performance that evening, Mrs. Cary covered his face liberally with makeup and gave him rosy red cheeks. Unless you were in the first three rows of the audience, you wouldn't have noticed.

Some of the ushers were stage crew members, selected to give out programs at the door, and Amy was one of them. I passed her briefly in the hall, and she looked rather elegant in black jeans and a black turtleneck with dangling silver earrings.

Because this wasn't a musical, there was no orchestra. But when the houselights dimmed, the chatter and laughter in the auditorium died down, then stopped abruptly as a recording began of "Love's Old Sweet Song."

There were not only butterflies in my stomach, there were horses galloping and gorillas in hiking boots. My heart pounded, even though I didn't make an appearance until page 12 in the script.

Ryan saw me hyperventilating back in the wings. He smiled and came over to give me a quick back rub, and that helped. His fingers lingered up around my neck and cheek. *Whoa!* I thought. Too much coming at me at once. I was both relieved and sorry when he moved away.

I couldn't see the stage from where I was standing, but I saw Pamela and Jay move toward the front of the curtain where the spotlight would find them. And finally, when I heard Pamela's voice, as Ernestine, saying, "Can you hear the music, Frank?" I knew that the performance had begun.

I had an easier entrance than some, because I came on with the rest of the Gilbreth clan when Brad blew the whistle and we all lined up to have our fingernails inspected. By the time I *did* get some lines, I was eager for my part, more than ready to show how Anne was changing from a dutiful daughter to a more adventurous girl, ready for a boyfriend.

Mr. Ellis had told us to expect it, but I was still surprised at how the audience reaction helped us along. When "Dad" announces that he has bought two Victrolas—one for the boys' bathroom and one for the girls'—the subject of dance music comes up. And the father admits that the Victrolas are not for music, but for language lessons, French and German.

"Just play them, and finally they'll make an impression," he pleaded.

And when I cried, "Not every morning in the bathroom!" the audience broke into laughter. We'd never laughed at that line before.

One of my favorite parts comes halfway through the first act. The family is having a council meeting, and the father has been outvoted on whether or not the kids can have a dog. Outraged, he says, "I suppose next you want ponies, roadsters, trips to Hawaii—*silk stockings*!" And at that, I stand up, go to a table at one side, open a drawer, and take out a small package.

"I'm not hiding a thing," I say determinedly. "I want the entire family to see." And I unwrap a short, flimsy piece of underwear, a teddy, like the top of an old-fashioned lacy slip while the bottom part was lacy panties. "I'm going to wear them," I say, at which point Brad Broderick goes bananas. On top of that, I announce I also bought silk stockings.

This time I was amazed that the audience clapped after I disappeared. I didn't know if they were clapping for me as an actress or for the script—that I'd finally told my father off. But either way, it was a heady moment. When I reached the platform behind the curtain where the stairs ended, my heart was racing with excitement, and Ryan, down below in the wings, gave me a thumbs-up. I smiled back and let out my breath to show him I was glad it was over, and he winked.

I got through Act II without a hitch, and it ends with my character in tears after her father vetoes going to a dance with the boy she really likes, Larry.

The play was short enough that there was no intermission, but I didn't have to go on right away in Act III, so I found a box to sit on where I could still hear my cue. I knew that Dad and Sylvia were out in the audience somewhere, but I didn't try to find them when I was onstage. I wondered how Dad felt about the play—wondered how deeply it hit home. We got along pretty well together, but I remember times it seemed he said "no" for no good reason. About letting me dye my hair green, for example. It was only for a day or so, not forever. It wasn't like I'd asked for a full-body tattoo. I remember how angry he was that I did it anyway. I knew too that I hurt him when I had arguments with Sylvia, but he was really good about keeping out of it and letting us work things out.

"Alice," Pamela whispered, "we're on—next scene."

I jumped up, afraid I'd missed my cue, but then I heard Brad Broderick say, "I . . . I just don't much feel like . . ."

I entered and stood just inside the door.

Later in the play, Anne redeems herself in her father's eyes by passing a test with flying colors; the dad relents about her having a boyfriend; Ryan, as Larry, takes me to the prom; and the dad leaves for a speaking trip overseas while the family has a council meeting in his absence. Carrying on . . . Curtain.

The ushers came down the aisles bringing small cellophane-wrapped bouquets of flowers, which were distributed to some of the main players. Mine were from Dad and Sylvia, and I finally spotted them about halfway back in the auditorium, smiling at me and still clapping.

"One down, three to go," Tim sang out as we milled about backstage, friends gathering outside the dressing rooms, beaming parents hugging their offspring, all of us talking excitedly about the lines almost missed.

Penny was hugging everybody, including Ryan, who had just hugged me. But I saw Sylvia waiting in the hallway, and I squeezed through the crowd to get to her and Dad.

He pulled me over and gave me a bear hug. "*So* proud of you!" he said. "That was marvelous, honey."

"We could hear every word," Sylvia said, joining our hug. "Mr. Ellis must have really emphasized diction."

"Did he ever!"

"That little speech of yours from the stairs . . . I even felt myself tearing up. Well done, Alice. I really enjoyed it," Sylvia said.

"Alice!" Sam called. "We're going to the Silver Diner. Want to come?"

"As soon as I change into jeans," I called back. And to Dad, "Someone will drive me home."

He gave me a final hug. "Go on, honey. It's all downhill from here."

17
GETTING CLOSER

Saturday morning, I slept like the dead. I was in the process of waking up about one in the afternoon when my cell phone rang. Sleep was too delicious, so I didn't pick up at first, but then I realized it might be an unscheduled rehearsal. I swung my legs over the side of the bed and reached for my bag.

" 'ello," I said hoarsely.

"Omigod, you *were* still sleeping," said Lester.

"I'm awake," I said, but the frog in my throat gave me away.

"Sorry, Al. I knew you had today off work but figured you'd be awake by now. How'd the play go?"

"Fine," I croaked, and tried to clear my throat. "No big boo-boos. The audience clapped like they meant it."

"Well, I'll be there tonight," he said. "Listen. Has . . . Kay told you anything?"

Aha! I thought, and now I was really awake. *Here it comes!* Les and Kay were going out. I mean, really.

"No," I said curiously. "What's happening?"

"Well, that's what I'm trying to figure out," said Les. "We were supposed to go out last night, and she stood me up."

My eyes were wide open now. "She . . . didn't show or what?"

"I went to pick her up, and she wasn't there."

"Have you called her?"

"Yeah. She doesn't answer. I used Dad's direct line at the store when I called just now, so that I wouldn't get Kay on the phone in case she's teed off about something, but I don't know what that would be."

"Have you tried calling her parents?"

"Are you insane? No, I asked Dad who was working today, and he said that Kay was there and a couple clerks."

"So we know she's all right," I said. "Well, there's probably a good reason she wasn't home, and my guess is she'll call you sometime today when she gets a chance."

"That's sort of what I figured. Listen, I'm washing windows for Mr. Watts this afternoon, so I'll be here . . . if you find out anything."

"Sure."

"And . . . about tonight . . . have fun. I'll be out there applauding like mad," Les said. "If you deserve it, that is."

I went back to bed to finish waking up slowly, the way I like, but after three or four minutes I realized I was as awake as I was going to get, so I took my shower.

Two o'clock already. I had to be at school by six thirty. I had slept through most of the day.

Ryan called next and said that some of the cast was going bowling after tonight's performance, did I want to go? Of course, I told him. And I felt that old excitement you feel when a guy is interested in you.

I decided I was probably having more fun right now than I'd ever had before, and there were already a lot of great things to remember about my senior year. A few things to regret, of course, but being Anne in the play helped cancel out some of those.

Pamela and I peeked out about fifteen minutes before curtain time, and there seemed to be about as many people as there had been the night before.

"I see Les and Kay," I said excitedly, watching them sliding in the seventh row and getting two seats near the center. Both were smiling. Good sign.

Dad was right that having had one successful performance, I wasn't as nervous this time. Just as excited, though, maybe even more, because I knew how much the audience had liked certain scenes—Anne on the stairs, for one—and I was eager to do them again.

Ryan forgot one of his lines, though. It was the scene where we're having an argument. He suspects I'm seeing other guys and doesn't realize I'm worried about my father and responsibilities at home.

"You don't have to pretend with me," he says as we're face-to-face there on the stage.

"I'm not pretending," I say earnestly, taking his hands. "I wouldn't pretend with you. I don't think people should pretend with people."

I don't know whether Ryan forgot his next line or just forgot to say it. He was supposed to say, "I don't either," which is Bill's cue—one of Anne's brothers—to say, seeing us holding hands, "So you're at it again."

But Ryan was just looking at me. I gave his hands two quick squeezes. He blinked, looked panicky for a minute, then Bill came in with, "So you're at it again!" and we quickly dropped hands.

"He certainly has a wonderful sense of timing," Ryan said, and the play went on without anyone knowing he'd missed a line.

Les and Kay came backstage when the play was over, and Kay handed me a single rose.

"Hey! A budding actress!" she said, and gave me a hug, laughing at all my eyeliner and blush. "Wow, Alice! Look at you! *So* twenties! You were great."

Les looked happy, and I decided that whatever had happened the night before was explained and forgiven.

"Did you like it, Les?" I asked.

"Yeah, especially that Joe Scales guy."

"The cheerleader? You liked *him*?" I asked.

"Sure. You should have gone out with him, Al," Lester said, grinning, and imitated the cheer that Joe Scales teaches my younger brothers in the play. "Hoo, rah, ray, and a tiger!" We laughed, and then he said, "You were good, Al. Loved those black stockings."

"Oh, weren't they hideous!" I said.

"We're off to meet some friends," Les explained. "I'll drop by tomorrow, Al. Sylvia invited me to brunch."

"See ya," I said, and turned to look for Pamela and the others.

The whole cast went bowling afterward. I guess I was surprised how many people went bowling at eleven o'clock at night, but we had to wait for a couple of alleys, and then we got two side by side.

Ryan was an excellent bowler, and he knew it. Just the way he paused after letting go of the ball, the angle of his body, the tilt of his head, the position of his arm showed a guy who expected a spare, if not a strike, and he usually got one.

When I asked how he got to be so good, he said, "Hey, I was born in Bowling Green, what do you expect?"

I found myself studying his body, and I wondered if that was the way guys studied girls. I wasn't exactly undressing him with my eyes, but I did imagine the way his thighs must look in swim trunks, the V shape of his upper body. I think he caught me watching him once and paused just a nanosecond, watching me back, and I felt my face flush.

What was happening here? I wondered. My guy goes off to college, so I'm suddenly attracted to my "leading man"? Was this the Hollywood syndrome or something? Was I not to be trusted? Still . . . Where was *Patrick* tonight? How did I know what *he* was doing?

Penny was the real cutup. Because she's petite, you might expect her to be "one with the ball," since she's closer to the ground, and I guess she was, in a way. The ball was too heavy for her, and the first time she let it go, she sat down with that surprised look on her face that cracked us up.

The guys were teasing her, of course, but Ryan seemed more interested in showing me how to position my hand when I released the ball and had to wait till I quit laughing at Penny so he could demonstrate.

He drove me home afterward, dropping Penny off first, then Pamela. Liz was riding with someone else. When we got to my house, I reached to open the car door, but Ryan turned the engine off and gave me a little more than friendly hug—a sort of prolonged friendship hug—which is difficult to do in bucket seats.

"What are you going to do over spring break?" he asked.

"Recuperate," I told him, and he released his grip a little. We both sank back a few inches. "Catch up on sleep. I feel I could sleep for a week."

"Well, when you do wake up, maybe we could get together," he said.

"Maybe we could. If I ever catch up with homework. And I've got an article to write for *The Edge*." I knew I was making excuses as fast as I could think of them. Why? Hadn't Patrick said to enjoy my senior year? Hadn't I been having the time of my life? As he'd told me, we both knew how we felt about each other. "But I know I'll have some free time," I added. "Yeah, let's get together and do something."

He kissed me then. It wasn't a long, slow kiss or a quick peck on the cheek. If there was ever an in-between kiss, that was it—one hand cupping the back of my head, a soft kiss on the lips, both of us leaning over the center console.

Then he was smiling at me. "Okay," he said. "See you Monday."

"Thanks for the ride," I said, and got out of the car, my face warm, my head spinning.

Once inside the house, I waited for his car to pull away, then leaned against the wall and waited for my pulse to slow down. Oh, man! *Now* what?

18

HOLDING BACK

Sylvia made crêpes for brunch on Sunday. Crêpes with powdered sugar and strawberry sauce. When I got up around noon, I pulled on a pair of sweatpants and a long-sleeved jersey, tied my hair back with a scrunchie, splashed water on my face, and came to the table to find Les already eating a mound of scrambled eggs with cheese on his plate.

"Awwwrrrk! What is it?" Les cried when he saw me, but I only stuck my face up close to his.

"Here's what a female looks like without makeup," I said. "Be grateful I brushed my teeth."

"Lester thought you were great last night. He told me so," Sylvia said.

"How did Kay like it?" I asked.

"Loved it," said Les. "Kay said she'd always wanted to be in a play or sing in a musical, but her parents wouldn't allow it. Too frivolous. Anything she did had to be 'academically oriented,' as she put it."

"Seems like a very controlling atmosphere to grow up in," said Sylvia, resting her elbows on the table and tucking her hands in the opposite sleeves of her kimono.

"And they're still at it. She called me yesterday and said that there was some big hassle at the last minute Friday night, and she apologized for standing me up."

"I'd think her parents would take the hint by now," said Dad.

"Oh, they get the hint, all right. They just don't seem to feel it makes any difference. They feel she *owes* them this, to marry into a respectable Chinese family that they've known for a long time. Her mother told her that after all they've done for her—bringing her to this country so she could get a good education—she's being disrespectful to her father by not marrying into the family of their friends."

"Wow," said Sylvia. "That's a lot of baggage to have to carry around."

"You know it," said Les.

"Any more news on the job search?" Dad asked him.

"Not much. I'm holding on to the one I've got until I find something better. I'd like something here in the area, but I'm beginning to send my résumés farther and farther out."

"Just make it something you love," said Dad.

"Meanwhile, what's happening back at your apartment?" Sylvia asked.

"With Andy?" Les shook his head. "That's what *we'd* like to know. For a woman who takes most of her meals in her room, she certainly has a lot of visitors. Mostly male, though not always."

"Maybe she's feeding them, and that's where all the food goes," I said, happy to probe around in the mystery.

"And Otto Watts likes her?" asked Dad.

"Seems to. No complaints there."

"Does she pay her share of the utilities?"

"Yep. First of the month. Cash. People come, people go. . . . Some stay a long time, some a little. Except for the man on Friday nights who turns on the TV, it's generally pretty quiet in there. Low voices."

"So there really is more than one boyfriend?" I asked.

"I can't tell. Maybe guys need more tutoring in English and history than women do. Or maybe she's just . . . uh . . . unusually attractive to men."

I couldn't help laughing. "What are you going to do? Evict her for corrupting the morals of a minor?"

"Too late for that," he said. "No, I guess we're just going to sit tight and see what happens. See where Paul and I get jobs, that's the main thing."

I should have spent the whole afternoon catching up on homework, but I took a couple hours off to go to the mall with Gwen and Liz and Pamela. We'd received invitations to a surprise baby shower for Jill on the eighteenth.

"Isn't this a bit early for a baby shower?" Sylvia had asked me when I'd opened the envelope. "I mean, even before the wedding? Is this done?"

"I don't know, but Karen's doing it," I'd said. "She figures that so few friends from school have been invited to the wedding, thanks to Mrs. Collier, that she'll give some kind of party they can attend now."

"Well, I didn't want to sound mean. It's just that sometimes a pregnancy doesn't go well, there isn't a baby, and then there are all those baby things sitting around to remind you. . . ."

I'd never thought of that. But this was a chance to be magnanimous, so we all decided to go along with it.

"When I get married, Sylvia, please don't shut out my friends," I'd said dramatically.

"I promise, but try to have your baby after, not before," she'd replied.

As we drove to Bloomingdale's at White Flint Mall, Liz said, "It's more fun buying baby gifts than towels. Besides, Jill and Justin are getting a bunch of hand-me-downs from Mrs. Collier, Karen said."

"That's what I heard. Things from their attic and odd pieces of furniture from their summer place at Hilton Head," Pamela told us. "Jill's not real happy about starting out with secondhand stuff. She thinks Justin's dad talked to the trustee at the bank, because she was all set to go furniture shopping, but then the bank told Justin the trust would cover only apartment rental, not furniture," said Pamela.

"Ouch. No shopping spree for Jill," I said. "That must have hurt."

We were being incredibly catty about someone we were about to spend more money on than we cared to.

"Do you realize that our main social activity for the next ten years will be showers?" Gwen said, turning into the parking lot off Nicholson Lane. She was driving the car she'd bought from her brother, and we were all impressed that she was the very first girl in our crowd to have her own car. "I've been to showers for three cousins and one aunt all within the last eight months," she said. "And I've been a bridesmaid at three of those weddings."

I found myself counting too. So far I'd been to a bridal shower for Crystal, one of Lester's old girlfriends. I'd been to Marilyn's wedding and a shower for her baby. I was a bridesmaid at both Carol's and Sylvia's weddings. . . . "Wow!" I said "We need to set aside a special account just for showers, I guess. They really start adding up. Jill is going to expect something exquisite, you know that."

"Why do you think we're going to Bloomingdale's?" said Pamela.

As we got out of the car, Gwen said, "I suggest we all go in together and get one gift from all four of us. Then, if she doesn't like it . . ."

". . . she can't pick on any one of us," I finished.

"No. Then she'll simply return it and buy a fantastic negligee for her wedding night," said Pamela, and we laughed.

It was easier knowing that all four of us would make a decision together and that the strain wouldn't be quite so heavy on our wallets.

Walking into the baby section at Bloomingdale's was like entering an imaginary land. There was a different stuffed animal beside each sign—BABY BOY, BABY GIRL, INFANTS, TODDLERS. . . . Some counters were arranged by color, others by article of clothing, and we milled about with young mothers and grandmothers, some with toddlers in tow and an occasional husband.

"This is more fun than looking at shoes," said Liz.

"Not quite, but close," said Gwen.

I held up a ruffled print top and matching leggings by Juicy Couture. "Did we ever wear anything this cute when we were babies?" I asked.

Gwen checked the price tag. "At seventy-eight dollars, no."

I dropped the outfit as though it burned me. "There's hardly anything to it!" I protested. "A yard of material at most."

"The smaller the package, the higher the price. First rule of retailing," Gwen said.

We proceeded toward the boutique section, where an elephant rocking chair had caught our attention. "Something like this, maybe, from all of us?" Liz said. She checked the tag and shook her head. "A hundred twenty, plus tax. Too steep for me."

"Let's decide what each of us planned to spend," said Gwen. "Twenty-five dollars is tops for me."

I was too embarrassed to say I was thinking more like fifteen. Liz and Pamela offered twenty. That made the ruffled top and matching leggings about right for our price range, but it seemed a rather puny gift coming from four girls. We kept looking.

"Look!" said Gwen, holding up a pair of UGG infant booties. We oohed and aahed until we checked that price too. Fifty bucks.

"I can buy a pair of stiletto heels for less than that," said Pamela.

Liz found a package of infant sneaker socks for twenty-eight dollars.

"Maybe we should buy a diaper bag and fill it with small items," she suggested, and we all were in favor of that. We checked out a Rebecca Minkoff baby bag and gasped at the price: three hundred ninety-five.

"I've got a better idea," said Gwen. "Why don't we buy the largest but least expensive thing they have here, ask for a gift box, then go to Old Navy and buy some more stuff to add to it. I was shopping with my aunt last month and we got a pair of baby fisherman sandals for eight dollars. A newborn pajama set for ten."

We considered that a moment.

"Yeah, but if she tries to exchange them, they'll tell her that most of the stuff wasn't from Bloomingdale's," said Liz.

Pamela had wandered off and was looking at a little pair of cotton jeans for seventy-nine dollars.

"You're not serious?" I asked.

She didn't answer, just pointed to the size tag: 3 MONTHS. I looked at her quizzically.

"That's how old my baby would have been . . . if I hadn't miscarried," she said.

That was about right, I figured. Three months. What is a baby doing at three months? Are babies rolling over yet? Laughing out loud? Sleeping through the night or not? What would *Pamela* be doing if she had a three-month-old baby? Nursing? She certainly wouldn't be thinking of working on a cruise ship come summer.

Two aisles up, a woman carrying a baby in a baby sling was comparing two packages of knit shirts. Her husband, who might have been slightly younger than she, stood with hands in his pockets, a diaper bag over his shoulder. Neither was smiling, though that said nothing about who they were or what they were feeling. Not everyone smiles when they're shopping.

But Pamela had seen the couple too, and as she put the little blue jeans back on the shelf she said, "That would have been Tim right now, and he'd hate me."

"Why do you say that?" asked Liz. "I don't think Justin hates Jill because she's pregnant."

"They'd been planning to marry," Pamela said. "Tim and I hadn't. And even if we had, who wants to start married life pregnant? Puking in the mornings? Jill probably won't end up hating Justin either, but I bet she'll hate living in an apartment with his parents' cast-off furniture. You know"—she looked around at us—"for the first time in my life, I sort of feel sorry for Jill."

I couldn't go that far. "Let's just hope they bring up a happy kid," I said. "So . . . what are we going to buy?"

We ended up purchasing a Ralph Lauren reversible blanket for twenty-five dollars, a Spunky dog for twenty, a white Ralph Lauren beanie hat and booties for twenty, and the infant socks that looked like sneakers for twenty-eight. It all came to ninety-three plus tax, more than we'd wanted to spend, but it all fit in a Bloomingdale's box and didn't look too bad for a present.

Patrick called me that night to see how things had gone. I told him everything . . . except that Ryan had kissed me. And that we were going out over spring break. I told myself that it had just been an affectionate kiss—that we were feeling close because we were in the play together, that it was our senior year—you can't help but feel a certain closeness, but it didn't necessarily mean anything.

"So how are you going to celebrate when it's all over?" he asked.

"I don't know," I said. "The first night we went to the Silver Diner, and the next night we went bowling. We'll probably do the same—a good way to get rid of tension. I don't think you need to worry that we're going skinny-dipping or anything."

"Here in Chicago they celebrate by jumping in Lake Michigan," Patrick said.

"What? In April? In the nude?"

Patrick chuckled. "Okay. I made that up. I'm not part of theater, so I don't know what they do. Something crazy, probably. You sleeping any better?"

"No, but I will by this weekend. I'd be okay if I didn't have to get up early for school."

"Well, I'll be thinking of you Friday and Saturday nights. Wondering what you're doing, who you're with. . . ."

"You already know most of the cast, Patrick."

"That's true. I know they'll take a lot of pictures for *The Edge*. Save a set for me."

"I will," I told him.

After I signed off, I sat on my bed, my arms locked around my knees, and stared at the wall. What does it mean when you hold something back? What does it say about a relationship? After all those wonderful things Patrick had said to me just over a week ago when I called him, crying, why would I even be *thinking* of going out with someone else over spring break?

Because we weren't engaged, that's why. Because we were expected to go out with other people till we could be together full-time. Would Patrick have told me if he'd driven a girl home and kissed her? If he had a car, that is? Would I be understanding if he did? Would I realize this was a temporary situation? How on earth did you ever know for sure?

19
MAIL

It was a surreal week. We had rehearsals again Monday through Wednesday, and I had trouble sleeping again; missed two more mornings of school because of it. But I went to the rest of my classes and did the best I could, light-headed for lack of sleep, excited, nervous about Ryan, thinking about Patrick. . . .

In physics Ryan told me he'd been accepted at the University of Iowa, that this might push him in the direction of becoming a writer.

"You've heard from them already? That's great," I told him. "I'm surprised you never got involved with the newspaper here. I mean, if you like writing so much."

"Small potatoes," he said. "And I've only been here a year. Where are you going to go?"

"Probably the University of Maryland," I told him, not wanting to admit it was a done deal, "though I'm still waiting to hear from UNC. I like the idea of being able to come home whenever I want."

"Yeah?" said Ryan. "Well, if you're going to major in counseling, I suppose you could go almost anywhere."

"Uh . . . not really," I said, but the screen lit up at the front of the room and we settled back to watch a video on quantum gravity, our minds on anything but.

More and more people were hearing from colleges—Liz got accepted at Goucher, her second choice—but even that took a backseat to the buzz about Jill and Justin's wedding. It was all Jill talked about when we saw her at lunchtime. It was less than two weeks away, and there was *so* much to do, she kept saying. The Colliers had worked out an agreement with the church that they could have the wedding the day before Easter if they left all the flowers for the Easter-morning services and had vacated the building by three.

Penny said what none of us dared say: "I'd think you'd want the wedding at the *start* of spring break, so you could have a week to yourselves."

"Not enough time to get ready," Jill said woefully. "Mrs. Collier is moving this along at the speed of sound as it is, and she needs every extra day she can get. We'll be spending the weekend at the Hay-Adams, though—forty-eight hours of pure luxury."

I'd been noticing the little "fault lines" that had appeared on Justin's forehead the last few months—all the bickering and tension with his folks, I guess. I thought *I* had problems making the leap from high school to college, but what if I had to throw in marriage and a baby too? If anyone should be at the breaking point, I'd think it would be Justin.

Some of us had received invitations and some had not. We couldn't quite see the reasons for the selection. Karen, of course, as one of the bridesmaids, got an invitation. Penny did not. Gwen got an invitation, Pamela did not. *I* got an invitation, Liz did not. All Gwen and I could figure was that Gwen, as class valedictorian and med-student-to-be, would be a prestigious addition to the guest list, and that I, as features editor for *The Edge*, might do a write-up of the wedding. Fat chance.

"Did I tell you that Justin and I have an apartment now?" Jill was saying. "We move in over spring break."

"Where?" we wanted to know. "What's it like?"

Jill toyed with a coil of her hair that had recently got new highlights—glorious strands of gold and brown. "Sixteenth Street in D.C.," she said. "I wanted one overlooking Rock Creek Park, but Justin said we couldn't afford it. This has to come out of his education trust fund. It pays for room and board while he's in college, and the trustee will stretch the meaning to include a basic apartment off campus, and I do mean 'basic.' Ha! I'll bet if Justin was marrying into one of those families in Capitol Hill real estate, the Colliers would spring for a gorgeous apartment we could show to all our friends."

"You can still show it to us!" I said.

She gave me one of her condescending looks, as though I didn't count, and continued: "First they said Justin had to buy the diamond ring himself if I wanted an engagement ring. Well, we'd already decided on that. I certainly didn't want to wear one of his mother's cast-off diamonds. Then they said we had to pay for our own honeymoon. I guess that's okay too, because if Mrs. Collier paid for it, she'd have Justin going to Paris and me to Siberia. But to make him pay for so much other stuff while he's in school . . . I mean, she'll do everything she can to break us up, I'll bet, even after we're married."

"It just might be . . . that they're doing everything they can to help you two become independent," said Gwen, and I was glad Gwen said it, not me.

Jill ignored her. "They didn't even mention baby expenses, but that's okay. Mom says she'll buy the car seat and stroller. The one good thing about our new apartment is it's on the top floor, so we won't have to listen to footsteps overhead. It's a one-bedroom with a den, but we'll do the den over for the baby. The living room faces the courtyard, so we're directly across from another apartment, and there are no balconies, but there's a little playground not too far away, so I can take the baby there." Jill seemed on a talking jag she couldn't stop. "Mom says fall's a good time to have a baby because the weekends are unusually good, and of course Justin will be studying a lot, but—"

"I can come over on weekends and keep you company," Karen said.

"Oh, we'll be fine," Jill said hurriedly. "And I love, love, *love* my dress!"

On Thursday, just as he did last week, Mr. Ellis said there would be no rehearsal—that all of us should have a relaxing evening with our families before the weekend performances. Gwen let Liz and me off at the corner, and we walked the half block to Elizabeth's house in the sweet April air.

"I think Ryan's hot for you," Liz said as we sauntered along, elbows bumping occasionally. There was a delicious scent of blossoms, and I realized how little time we'd had just to stroll like this.

"Oh, really?" I said, and we exchanged smiles.

"Yeah?" she said, studying me closely. Then, "Yeah?" a little louder. "And you . . . ?"

I continued facing forward "Oh, it's just a . . . fling."

"A lot can happen in a fling," said Liz. "How do you *feel* about him?"

"I don't honestly know," I said. "He's . . . hot, like you say. He's interested in me. We've actually kissed—"

Liz came to a complete stop. "*My God*, Alice!"

"Oh, it was sort of a cross between friendship and . . ."

"Passion?" she asked.

"Something like that. Not that much. He wants us to go out over spring break."

"Are you?"

"Yeah. I suppose. Patrick wouldn't want me to just sit around."

"Hmmm," said Liz. "Well, I guess you're never going to know if Patrick's 'the one' unless you experience other guys."

"*Experience?* Uh . . . as in all forty-nine flavors?"

"I don't know about that. Come on in. We've got some passion fruit sorbet. Just what you need."

It seemed perfectly wonderful to hang out like this, as though all the hurry and worry of senior year was behind us. Felt like it did back in eighth grade when we hung out on each other's porches after school.

There was mail in the box, which meant Mrs. Price was out somewhere with Nathan. Holding the envelopes in one hand, key in the other, Liz let us in.

Inside, she dumped her backpack on the sofa beside the mail. And then she gasped and grabbed for an envelope that had landed on the floor.

"Alice!" she cried. "It's from Bennington!"

"Omigod!" I said. "Open it! Open it!"

"They rejected me," said Liz, staring at the white business envelope in her hand.

It was déjà vu, but I managed to say, "Liz, you haven't even looked."

There were already tears in her eyes. "Everyone *says*! If it's an acceptance, it comes in a large envelope with a whole bunch of forms to . . ." The tears were spilling onto her hand.

She gave the envelope to me. "You read it. Just tell me."

We pushed the books and mail off the couch and sat down together. I opened the envelope, and Liz closed her eyes. I scanned the letter. "You've been wait-listed," I told her, trying to put some hope in my voice. "That's not a no."

"Wait-listed!" Liz wailed, her eyes filling up again. "That's even worse! That means I go on not knowing. And even if I get in eventually, it means I'm second choice." She was crying again in earnest. "Alice, I had my sweatshirt all picked out and everything! I have a map of the campus and a map of the town and . . ."

I put my arm around her, but oh, I knew the feeling. "This isn't the only place you applied. And you've been accepted at Goucher."

"But I don't want to go anywhere else! I w-want to be a Bennington Girl!" she wept. "How can I go all summer not knowing where I'm going to college? How will I know if I should buy ski clothes for Vermont or sundresses for Georgia?"

"Did you apply to a college in Georgia?" I asked.

"No," she said, and cried some more. I almost wished I had taped this so I could play it back to her when she was sane.

"Liz," I told her, "this is the final weekend of the play, and you have a leading role. No matter what happens, an actress dries her tears and the show goes on. You're going to put on a magnificent performance because you know you must!" I was putting on a pretty good performance myself.

"The play!" Liz said, and her eyes got huge. She wiped one arm across her face. "My eyes are going to look swollen, aren't they?"

"Everything that happens to an actress is something she can

use onstage, remember? Laughing on the outside, crying on the inside? Think of the play, Liz, and we'll worry about Bennington later," I said.

Liz hugged me, still sniffling. "What would I do without you, Alice?"

After we each ate a dish of passion fruit sorbet, I went across the street to our house, part aching for Liz, part smiling at her "Bennington Girl."

We have a mail slot in our front door, and some days there are so many catalogs on the other side that I can hardly get the door open. This was one of those days. Crate & Barrel, JC Penney, J. Crew, Territory Ahead . . .

And then I saw the words "University of North Carolina" peeking out from under the Crate & Barrel catalog. What was this—National Letdown Day? But the envelope from UNC was large. Heavy.

Mechanically, I opened it. *Dear Miss McKinley: We are pleased to inform you . . .*

Too late. But I wouldn't have gone anyway. I was a Maryland Girl now.

20

IN THE DINER

I guess actors always keep the possibility of disaster in mind—a set falling over on someone or actually breaking a leg onstage. Nobody thought of the possibility that college rejections the day of a show could affect a cast. At school on Friday, a few other people had heard from colleges, and someone referred to the hall outside Mrs. Bailey's office as the "wailing wall." I was pretty much over my own disappointment about William & Mary—it was just a dull ache in my chest. And even though I'd confirmed with Maryland that I was going there, I could still say, *Oh, yeah, well, I was accepted at UNC too, but . . .* And it *was* nice to know I was saving Dad a heap of money.

Liz came to school subdued, and I let her talk about Bennington when she felt like it. It was her story to tell, if she wanted to. By the time we gathered for the evening performance, she wore a stoic, determined look on her face, a "bravely carrying on" sort of look that made Mr. Ellis say, "Mrs. Gilbreth, your husband dies at the end of the play, not the beginning," and somehow Liz took on the warm maternal glow we needed, *she* needed, to see the play through.

Then the unexpected happened. Maybe what did it was a number of people saying "Break a leg" before the play instead of *Watch out for the dog.*

I don't think any of us in the cast were particularly nervous. We'd had two good performances the weekend before, and we arrived at the dressing rooms to find that someone had steamed the wrinkles out of our costumes, so everything was fresh and ready to go. Gwen came with a bunch of friends. She was sitting with Daniel Bul Dau and Yolanda. I could see them in the second row. Phil Adler and some of the other people from the newspaper were behind them.

In the play two of the Gilbreth boys are coming down the stairs holding their dog—the dog their father didn't want—and the audience hears Mr. Gilbreth shouting, "Get him out of here!" from above.

Dan had just said, "Of all the dumb dogs," and Fred had replied, "What do you expect for five dollars?" when the dog wriggled loose and began running from one actor to another onstage, tail wagging, leaping up, and putting its front paws in people's laps.

It was total chaos. "Guinness, no!" people were hissing, but the two-year-old Lab upset an end table and scrunched up the rug. When Jackie, his true owner, who wasn't even supposed to be onstage, came running in to get him, the dog thought they were playing and barreled away to the delight of the audience, which screamed with laughter. What could we do but pretend it was all part of the play? When Jackie finally belly flopped on the dog and dragged him off the stage, I managed to say, "That dog! Where was he this time?"

And Bill answered, "Up on Dad's bed again. The basement window . . . across the coal bin . . . up the back stairs . . . Dad's bed!"

"Dad was right about the dog," I said, continuing on. "Now he'll think he's right about everything."

"Clothes, makeup, everything," Pamela said, and we were finally back into the script.

When the phone rang, right on cue—Joe Scales, the cheerleader, calling to ask my character out—the scene played without a hitch, and I loved that a low chuckle went through the audience as I said innocently into the phone, "Where have I been all your life? Mostly, I've been right here. . . ."

Afterward, everyone was talking and laughing about the dog, and if Liz was still depressed over Bennington, she didn't show it. Mr. Ellis said we'd played it well. "Good show, guys," he said. "But tomorrow night, hang on to that dog!"

Mrs. Cary came out of the girls' dressing room just then to report that a water pipe overhead was leaking and it would probably be morning before anyone could fix it. She suggested we take our costumes home in case the drip got worse during the night.

So, still wearing our makeup and third-act costumes, we stepped around the wet newspapers on the floor, collected the clothes we had worn in Acts I and II, and with Gwen and Yolanda helping, carried them out to the car.

When the waitress at the Silver Diner saw us coming this time, in costume, she began hastily clearing tables as fast as she could, and we swarmed in, taking up half the booths.

"It's on him," Sam said, pointing to Brad Broderick, who was still in his three-piece suit and who, with lines on his forehead, gray powder in his hair, and a padded potbelly, looked at least sixty-five.

"Me?" cried Brad, standing regally by the counter. "Why, children, I'm sailing for Europe tomorrow. I thought this was my send-off party."

Everyone in the diner turned to watch now, some of them smiling, others just looking puzzled. But Brad hadn't been cast as the star of the play for nothing. He looked around the diner and said, "But I think we've got time for one last check." He pulled his stopwatch out of his vest pocket, then his whistle, and gave a loud blast.

Now all the customers had stopped eating and were staring at us, and the manager came out of the kitchen, curious. All nine of us children scrambled out of the booths crying, "Coming" or "I'm here, Dad," and we lined up in front of the counter, holding out our hands for fingernail inspection.

The manager watched, grinning, as Brad went down the row,

making up his lines: "I've seen better" and "What have you been digging?" When he got to young Jack, he bopped him on the head with a menu and said, "Filthy! Utterly filthy! Shame on you!"

The customers were laughing, enjoying the show, even though they didn't know who we were or what the play was about.

When Brad got to me, though—he'd started at the younger end of the line—he said, "Oh, Anne, Anne. You always were my favorite daughter, and since I'm leaving forever, I think you ought to know a deep family secret."

I played along. "Oh, what, what?" I cried. "Tell me!"

"Anne . . . ," Brad said, holding me out in front of him, hands on my shoulders. I could tell he was still in the process of making this up. "Anne . . . I'm not your real father."

The cast was hooting and laughing, and customers had turned in their seats to give their full attention.

"Oh, Daddy," I cried. "What are you saying?"

"That I am your lecherous Uncle Harry in disguise," Brad said, and with that, he pulled me to him, tipped me over backward, and gave me a movie-star kiss while everyone cheered and applauded.

The guy playing Bill, one of the brothers, yanked the cap off his head and went around to the tables, holding it out for tips, but not long enough for anyone to put anything in it, and the whole diner was laughing and clapping.

I couldn't tell if Ryan was all that amused when I went back to our booth. He was smiling, anyway. But I knew I'd remember this night forever.

* * *

Dad and Sylvia came to the final performance just to see it again. I think all of us in the cast had a catch in our throats when we said our lines for the last time. We wanted this performance to be our best, and so we probably overacted some of the scenes. When Penny recited the line, "Lincoln freed the slaves . . . all but one . . . all but one," friends in the audience cheered wildly, simply because Penny was so popular herself.

When the curtain fell at last, then opened as we all joined hands and stepped forward for our bow, a lot of us had tears in our eyes. A couple of the guys, even. Elizabeth and Chassie were smiling even as tears ran down their cheeks, and when we looked at them and laughed, they laughed with us.

Dad and Sylvia were still clapping along with the rest of the audience—a rhythmical clapping now, as though nobody wanted the evening to end—and ushers made their way down the aisles with bouquets of flowers, more flowers than usual because it was the last night. I could see a huge bouquet of red roses bobbing down the center aisle, but I couldn't see who was carrying it till Amy's head came into view. She came right up to the footlights and handed them to me.

Surprised, I bent to receive them, a little embarrassed. Most of the other bouquets were wrapped in cellophane, held together at the base with a rubber band, but these were exquisite, and I gave Dad a fond but surprised smile as I accepted them.

The curtain closed again, and everyone was hugging everyone else. Liz and Pamela gathered around me, however, and asked, "Who sent those, Alice? Who are they from?"

"My dad, I think," I said, and found the little card attached to one stem. I turned it around to read it. There was just one word: *Patrick.*

Mr. and Mrs. Ellis invited us all to their house for the cast party, and Mrs. Ellis herself wore a 1920s beaded dress. It was an exceptionally warm night, and some of us had opted for dresses instead of jeans. Sylvia had taken Patrick's flowers home with her, and she and Dad had brought both cars so that I could drive Liz and Pamela to the party.

The Ellises' house was even more Victorian than Mr. Watts's. It looked like something out of a Charles Addams cartoon, with little nooks and crannies at every turn, lace curtains, flocked wallpaper, overstuffed velvet furniture, old photos covering the walls, and pillows you could get lost in.

Mrs. Cary had changed her dress for the occasion, and she and her husband came looking like Daisy and Jay Gatsby themselves. On one side of the parlor, Mrs. Ellis had an open trunk filled with old costumes—tall silk hats, capes, corsets, vests. . . .

"Alice, this is for you!" Pamela cried, holding out a luscious black lace teddy, and of course everyone urged me to try it on, which I didn't. But I did pull on a pair of ruffled knee-length bloomers under my dress, the ruffles gathered at both knees. And when someone handed me a fitted corset, circa 1910, I put that on too over my dress, and Liz and Pamela were screaming with laughter as they stood behind me, tightening the laces to see how much tighter they could go before I passed out. Sam even took a picture for *The Edge*.

What surprised us all was watching the stage crew get in the act. When Mrs. Ellis put on a CD of the Charleston, a couple girls and one of the guys from the crew did an impromptu dance for us. We kept finding things in the trunk and putting them on their heads—strings of pearls, a boa—and it seemed the more we dumped on them, the faster they danced.

Amy Sheldon was there in her black pants and a black tee. Mostly she watched from one of the straight-backed chairs, laughing at the antics of the dancers, happy to be part of the celebration. I sat on a hassock at her feet as we ate the little meatballs and tiny hot dogs Mrs. Ellis had made for us, and I asked Amy if she was having fun.

"It's a silly party, isn't it?" she said. "I think you have your clothes on wrong. Your dress should be on the outside."

I laughed. "You're right. I wouldn't wear a corset like this in a million years, but tonight it's just for fun."

"It makes people laugh," said Amy, trying to analyze it.

"Exactly."

She smiled then. "I'm going to be on stage crew next year too. I already got invited," she told me.

When the party broke up a little after midnight and I drove Liz and Pamela home, we went over all the details of the party—who did what, said what, wore what. . . . And just before Pamela got out, she said, "Ryan asked me who sent the roses, Alice."

"Yeah?"

"I told him they were from your brother."

"My *brother*? Why?"

"Dunno," she said as she opened the door. "Just to make things more interesting, I guess."

21
TALKING WITH PATRICK

Spring vacation couldn't have come at a better time. Sylvia said that I slept until two thirty the following afternoon. That wasn't entirely true, because I woke around noon and debated getting up—then thought better of it and went back to sleep again.

When I finally stumbled into the bathroom, I felt as though I had molted into a new person, refreshed and alert. If spring hadn't always been my favorite season (I like fall), it was for today.

Dad and Sylvia didn't ask anything of me. There was a slice of quiche waiting for me in the fridge, some fruit salad, some ham. Dad was watching an NBA play-off game, Sylvia was altering a skirt, and the house had a blissful, contented sound—the low hum of the sewing machine, the sports commentator's monologue. It all just made me happy and totally absorbed in the deep red of the roses on our coffee table. I was thinking about the best time to call Patrick to thank him when the phone rang.

It was Ryan.

"Hi," he said.

"Oh, hi!" I said, wishing I could have talked to Patrick first.

"Tried calling you on your cell phone, but you didn't answer," he told me.

"It's in my bag upstairs and I didn't hear it," I explained.

"Just get up?"

I laughed. "About a half hour ago. How long did you sleep?"

"I've been up since eleven. Told Dad I'd wash the cars this afternoon, get the pollen off."

"It'll only get worse in May," I said.

"I know, but it'll give me something to do. I was wondering if you wanted to go out tonight. Take in a movie, maybe. . . ."

This was too much too soon. I wanted some downtime. I wanted to talk with Patrick, try on some summer clothes. . . .

"I sort of promised to hang with my family tonight, Ryan," I said, searching for an excuse. "They've hardly seen me at all the last several months." What was the matter with me? I couldn't say I wasn't interested, because I was.

"Understood," he said. "Tomorrow?"

"Oh, I'm sorry, I'm going to a shower for Jill tomorrow."

"She the one getting married?"

"Appears that way."

"Sort of weird, isn't it? Spring vacation and all," Ryan said.

"Well, there's a history to it," I told him. "What about Wednesday?"

"Okay. Wednesday afternoon or evening?"

"You decide. Whatever you want to do," I said.

"Till Wednesday, then," he said. "I'll let you know."

My heart was racing when we ended the call. I felt a certain excitement I hadn't felt for a long time—the growing certainty that a guy likes you and you maybe like him. The beginning of the flirtation dance, back and forth, where you're edging into unknown territory, and each question, each answer, is a clue.

I finished my breakfast, looked over the comics without really concentrating on them, then went straight up to my room and called Patrick. It was a while before he answered. I was afraid I'd have to leave a message, but then he picked up.

"Hi, it's me," I said. "You weren't sleeping, were you?"

"Sleeping? No. I'm here at the tennis court waiting to play," he said. "It's a gorgeous day in Chicago."

"Here, too," I told him. "Patrick, those roses are beautiful. I was bowled over."

"Glad you like them," he said. "I'd rather have been there, but I had to work for my prof yesterday. And I'd barely see the play before I'd have had to fly back again. This will be the first time I've had in a week to get some exercise. How'd the play go?"

I started to tell him about the dog getting loose onstage, but Patrick was saying something to someone else.

"I'm up next, Alice," he said. "I'll call you later, okay? You going to be in this evening?"

"Yeah, I'll be home," I said.

"We'll talk then," he said, and we signed off.

I sat on the edge of my bed, staring at my toes. The nails needed trimming, but I didn't make a move to go get the manicure set. What did I want from Patrick? I asked myself. His blessing? Permission? His telling me it was okay to go out with Ryan during spring break? Even after spring break, maybe? Did Patrick ask me if he could go out? He might even be playing tennis with a girl—how did I know? Why hadn't I told Ryan I'd go out with him tonight?

The truth was, I wasn't sure how I felt about Ryan. But another truth may have been that I was trying to think up reasons *not* to like him. What did it say about a relationship if I said no to other guys because I wanted to convince myself that Patrick was "the one"? Or why couldn't it be that Patrick really *was* special and I was protecting the relationship? Isn't that what people did when they were married? Committed themselves to the marriage as well as to the person? But who was talking marriage? We weren't even engaged. And Patrick was going to Spain in a couple of months.

I stood up and went to get a basin to soak my feet so my toenails would soften. That's me—always jumping ahead. Planning my life weeks, months, years ahead instead of savoring each minute of every day.

When Molly Brennan called later and said she was having a hen party cookout in her backyard Tuesday evening, I almost leaped into the phone saying yes.

"I'm inviting you and Gwen and Pamela and Liz and a few others," she said. "And guess who else will be there?" I tried to think, but before I could answer, she said, "Faith."

I squealed. "Oh, I'd love to see her. She's not—"

"Back with Ron? Nope. She's moved on—*way* on."

"Okay. What can I bring?"

"How about crackers and dip?" said Molly. "Hey, if I play this right, everyone wanting to bring something, I won't have to cook a thing."

Les took us to a steak house for dinner that night, so I obliged him and ordered a T-bone.

"Heard from any colleges yet?" he asked me after he'd ordered the drinks.

"UNC and George Mason said yes. William & Mary turned me down. I'm going to Maryland," I said.

He didn't say anything for a moment, just watched me. "Well, three out of four ain't bad, kiddo."

I gave him a fake pout. "I wanted *everyone* to love me."

"You'll be going to a good school, Al, and we're proud of you," Dad said.

"I just want to know *why*," I told him. "It's like when you break up with someone. You need to know why. You need closure."

Les reached for the pepper mill and ground away. "I broke up with a lot of girls and never said why, mostly because I didn't quite know myself. Just wanted to move on, I guess."

I hate that phrase, *move on*. Like no matter what happened or what you did, you just "move on," and that's supposed to make everything all right.

"I feel like writing the admissions office back and asking, 'Was it something I said? Something I wrote? My SAT scores? Not social enough?' *What?*" I told him.

"Just let it go, Al. There's a lot more to life than school."

"Yeah? So how is your life going? How's Kay?" I asked.

"How should I know? You probably see more of her than I do," he answered.

"Les, I haven't been to work for two weeks."

"Well, Paul and I had invited her and Judith to hear a new band in Georgetown last night, and only Judith showed. She said that Kay called her at the last minute and said she couldn't make it, she'd explain later. Something to do with her parents. Judith thinks she's starting to cave."

"No!" I said. "That would be horrible!"

"It's her life. And we had a pretty good time with Judith, though I cut out early."

"And Andy? What's happening there?" asked Sylvia.

"Same traffic, up and down those side stairs. Somebody every night. Often two."

"Les, is this something you should look into?" Dad asked after the waiter placed our orders in front of us and left. "She's using Mr. Watts's house, after all."

And I said what the others didn't: "You think she's a *hooker*?"

"Oh, Les!" Sylvia said.

"I've already been looking into it, doing a little checking at the U," Les told us. "Andy calls herself a grad student, but that was a couple of years ago. She claims she's tutoring, so I've got to be careful here. . . ."

"Just don't you and Paul get yourselves arrested if the police raid the place," Dad said.

After Les had gone that night and Sylvia and Dad were going to bed, I propped myself up on pillows in my room and called Patrick. I told him about how the dog got loose onstage and how Brad had kissed me in that funny act we put on in the Silver Diner, and I loved hearing Patrick's deep chuckle at the other end.

"You found out you had talents you never knew you had," he said.

"Kissing, you mean?"

"I mean the whole thing. Acting, being onstage . . ."

"Yeah, I guess I did. But I'm not thinking of making a career of it," I told him. "How did the tennis game go?"

"Got creamed. We were playing doubles, though, and I'd have to say that my partner wasn't quite up to it."

"Who was your partner?"

"Fran. We were playing Adam and John. You met them when you were here last summer."

My stomach did a flip-flop.

"Last week Adam was my partner and we won, so I don't think my own game was off. But, as I said, the weather was glorious."

I decided this was an incident I didn't have to file in my worry bank. Patrick's spring break hadn't coincided with mine, and he'd spent his with his parents in Wisconsin. Now he was back in school, and he needed all the relaxation he could get.

"What do you have planned for your spring vacation?" he asked me.

"R and R," I said. "I have a couple papers due and an article to write for *The Edge*. Tomorrow night there's a surprise shower for Jill, Tuesday night I'm going over to Molly's with a bunch of girls, and Wednesday I'm hanging out with Ryan. He was Larry in the play."

"Oh? Going anywhere in particular?" Patrick asked.

Is that all he's going to say? I wondered. *No surprise? No jealousy?*

"I don't know yet," I said flatly. "We just said we'd get together. Maybe he's invited some other people, I don't know."

"Maybe," said Patrick. And now I could tell by the tone of his voice that he was smiling again. "Or maybe he just wants you all to himself."

"We'll probably just talk about the play," I said. "Don't worry. He's going to the University of Iowa next year. He'll be even farther away than you are."

"Correction," said Patrick. "I'll be in Spain."

"Yeah, that's right," I said. I *wanted* to say, *So whose fault is that?* but I didn't. I told him I'd been accepted at UNC and George Mason but had confirmed with Maryland I'd be going there.

"Well, it's a relief to have that decided and out of the way," Patrick said.

"I suppose," I said. "All these decisions I've had to make this year, Patrick—whether to try out for the play, whether to try out for Ivy Day Poet, what colleges to apply for . . . they must seem so small compared to all the things you've done in your life. You've had a lot of great moments, but one of the biggest moments for me was receiving that bouquet of roses onstage." I felt as though I was going to cry again.

But Patrick said, "Then I'm glad your biggest moment was from me."

How could I go out with Ryan after that?

22
CATCHING UP

The surprising thing about Jill's baby shower was that she really was surprised. I could tell partly from her reaction and partly because she hadn't fixed herself up especially—just came to Karen's in a wrinkled shirt without mascara, thinking she was going somewhere with her mom. I almost thought she was angry at first, like she'd been set up to humiliate herself, but then I think she was genuinely moved that so many girls had shown up. Maybe even Jill, homecoming queen, had insecurities too, I decided, watching the number of times she tried to pin her hair back, hair that could have used a washing.

Her mom was there, looking lovelier than Jill, actually—a former model, I'd heard. As each gift was opened, it was placed inside the crib Karen had borrowed for the occasion.

"Did you ever see so much white and yellow?" Jill said, laughing as she opened a little romper set. "Nobody dares buy pink or blue till after they find out the sex of the baby. I want a little girl. I know just how I'll dress her."

"Just wish for a healthy baby, Jill," her mother said. "Little boys are nice too."

"Hmmm. Big boys are better," Jill said, and we laughed.

I noticed how frequently there was a snide remark about the person who wasn't there. When the doorbell rang a half hour into the party, one of the girls arriving late, Jill murmured, "Please don't let that be you-know-who." When the tiny cakes were passed around, Jill said, "I'm going to have two, even though the witch would frown at me."

I guess she liked the gift from Gwen and Pam and Liz and me. "Oh, Ralph Lauren," she said, more about the labels than the little booties and cap. I saw her peek beneath the tissue paper for a gift receipt, and when she found it, she smiled and said, "Thanks, guys! Cute!" and passed the box along to her mom.

Something was missing here, I wasn't sure what. I kept hoping the door would open and Justin would appear with a guitar, if he played a guitar. That he'd sit down and sing a song to her and the baby. That Jill would caress her tummy, even, and say, *It's okay, little man*, or something.

But the evening ended with people carrying cups and saucers to the kitchen, and Jill saying we were all invited to see their apartment after they'd fixed it up, and then we were in Gwen's car again, going home.

For the first minute or two, no one said anything. We were each struggling for something positive or kind or generous to say, but somehow words were hard to come by.

It was Pamela who finally spoke. "It would be nice if all mistakes were reversible, wouldn't it?" When no one dared take it further, she said, "If you marry the wrong person, you can get a divorce; if you believe in abortion, you can get un-pregnant; but the one thing you can never change is the father of your baby."

I was about to protest that Jill and Justin had wanted to marry, that they'd wanted—I hope—the baby for its own sake, that Justin was not a bad guy. Then I realized that Pamela wasn't, perhaps, talking about them at all.

"Well, you lucked out, Pamela," Gwen said, speaking for all of us. "You didn't have to make any of those decisions."

"That's what senior year is all about, isn't it?" said Liz. "One decision after another. Do you remember when we were little, and all we had to do was get out of bed in the morning and our moms had our clothes all laid out for us? They arranged our playdates. Drove us wherever we needed to go."

"I don't know," said Gwen. "I sort of like driving my own car, buying my own clothes, and I certainly want to arrange my own playdates."

There was something to laugh about at last, and we said we'd see each other the next day at Molly's.

I couldn't take my eyes off Faith. The last time I'd seen her, she was thin as a broom and was having some of her teeth replaced after her abusive boyfriend slammed her face down on the hood of a car.

Now she had gained about ten pounds and looked so much better—more curvy, more friendly, more . . . happy. Her hair was especially shiny, and even her skin looked better. Amazing what being healthy will do for your looks, I thought. I noticed she was wearing a lacy chemise, cut low enough to show her cleavage, now that she had breasts again.

"You. Just. Look. Fabulous!" I told her. "Really, really!"

"You know what?" she said as we hugged. "I *feel* pretty fabulous."

I thought of the guy she was going out with after she booted Ron. A nice guy. "Are you and Chris . . . ?"

"No. He went to Virginia Tech, and I'm getting my associate degree from Montgomery College in June. We still e-mail each other from time to time, but I'm going with a navy guy now. He'll be out of the service soon, and then we'll see what happens."

"Well, you're beautiful," said Pamela. "And you deserve the best."

So did Molly, come to think of it, and from all appearances, she was healthy too. She and Faith had seen the play the last night, but there was such a crowd at the stage door that they hadn't stuck around.

"The loose dog scene was a scream!" Molly said. "You guys played it so well, we weren't sure whether it was in the script or not. I'll bet Ellis was sweating bullets backstage."

"We were sweating bullets *onstage*," I said. "It was unrehearsed, believe me!" And of course she and Faith and Pamela and I had to reminisce about the plays and musicals that had gone on before: *Fiddler on the Roof*, *Father of the Bride*, *Guys and Dolls*.

"And guess what?" Pamela told them when we stopped for breath. "I got accepted at a theater arts school in New York."

We cheered all over again, stamped our feet, and Faith pounded on the patio table. "Pamela! Yay!" she cried.

I felt a twinge of jealousy again—would we ever stop celebrating Pamela?—but refused to dwell on it. I concentrated instead on what Patrick had said—about how you can be curious and intellectual and all the rest right where you are at the moment. You didn't have to go to someplace big.

I raised my glass of Sprite. "To *us*!" I said.

"To us!" the others chorused.

To all the bad things that could have happened that didn't, all the mistakes we almost made, but didn't. I marveled that Molly was sitting here cancer-free, that Faith had dropped Ron out of her life, that Pamela had miscarried, that . . . the list went on and on. What about the mistakes that were yet to come? I wondered. And I immediately thought of my date the next day with Ryan.

"What's this I hear about Jill getting married on Saturday? Is that for real?" Molly asked.

"It's for real."

"And is she pregnant? That's the story I got."

"It's no secret. They're expecting in September," Pamela told her.

"Is . . . is this a good thing . . . or what?" Faith asked uncertainly.

"Who knows?" Pamela said. "They planned it, and they've been going together longer than anyone else in high school. She's marrying a nice guy, anyway."

Who knows what's going to happen with any of us? I thought, looking around the group. If I had to make a guess about what any of us would be doing five years from now, I could be so far off. Who knew that Les would be going out with Kay? Who knew that Patrick would be spending a year in Spain? Who knew that Faith would be looking so great, completely leaving all that pain behind, or that I would have starred in the school play?

Wednesday morning, I started my next article for *The Edge*:

WHAT WE LEAVE BEHIND

You've felt it. So have I. I can't quite explain when it happens, but with college getting closer, I'm more conscious when it happens. Much as we've wanted to grow up, move on, move out, we're saying good-bye to something we thought we'd never miss: being kids.

I felt it a year ago when I was driving by a county fair and stopped to watch the kids on a merry-go-round, the calliope playing "The Sidewalks of New York" as the painted ponies rose and fell on their shiny poles.

I used to *love* that ride. I loved the summer my dad decided I was big enough to go on all by myself, but every time my horse got around to the gate, there he'd be, smiling, and I'd feel brave enough to let go with one hand and wave back. And though big people do ride the merry-go-round sometimes, even teens, it will never be the same as it was then—my dad waiting for me at the gate, smiling.

I remember promising myself, when I was nine, that I would never, ever stop doing the two things I enjoyed most: reading the comics and hanging upside down by my knees on the jungle gym. I've already stopped hanging by my knees.

The beanbag chair in the corner of my room—the chair that's been a refuge for me through all the hurts and disappointments of grade school, and even some in high school—is getting too small for me. The furry little monkey with the missing eye that has been a fixture on my bed for as long as I can remember will not be going to college with me.

The shoes I once loved, my favorite books, reading the newspaper over Sunday brunch with my parents—that'll all be left behind when September comes; and along with the excitement of living on my own, there's an emptiness deep inside me, and I wonder what will take its place.

Saying hello to something new means saying good-bye to something old and loved. Much as we seniors are looking forward to college or work, to moving out and moving on, we have a little grieving to do, and it takes us by surprise. We're leaving a part of ourselves behind. And it's okay to feel sad along with happy, loss along with gain, regret along with excitement. It's part of the process. Expected, in fact.

—Alice McKinley, Features Editor

23
EATING OYSTERS

When Ryan called around noon on Wednesday, he had the rest of the day mapped out, and I was glad I didn't have to make any decisions. I just wanted to drift, to float. I wanted someone to give me a nudge, and my body would move in whatever direction I was pointed.

"I'll pick you up about three and we'll play some miniature golf. Then we'll head for the marina on Main Avenue for dinner and maybe pick up some improv theater. How does that sound?"

"Very ambitious," I said. "What kind of theater?"

"You don't know improvisational theater?" he said. "Alice, you haven't lived till you've seen what a cast can do!"

"I guess I'm about to be born, then," I said. "Sounds fun. I'll be ready."

Actually, I did know what improvisational theater was, I just hadn't seen any professional performances. But Ryan seemed so gung ho about instructing me that I'd let him take the credit.

April in Maryland can be cold and rainy, and we'd probably get that yet. But the sun smiled down on our spring vacation and gave us a couple of beautiful days. I dressed in a good pair of jeans and a black tee, a yellow sweater, and went out to Ryan's car when I saw him drive up.

"How's your golf game?" he asked as I slid in the passenger seat.

"Even worse than my bowling," I told him.

"We'll have to do something about that," he said, and smiled as we started out. Then, "It doesn't bother you?"

"What?"

He shrugged. "Not being very good at either one?"

"No. Not particularly. Why?"

He turned down the music a little. "I don't know. It would bother me. I'd want to be fairly good at something or I wouldn't want to do it."

I gave him a quizzical look. "How could you ever try anything new if you had to be good at it first?"

"I mean, whatever I try, I keep at it till I'm . . . well . . . at least competent."

"You don't do anything just for fun? Just to be with a bunch of friends, having a good time?"

Ryan seemed to mull that over. "Not really, I guess. If I'm going to spend time at something, I want to be good at it."

Who was I dating here? I wondered. Another Patrick? Patrick—who was good at everything, it seemed?

"Well, I can't see that my life would change much if I got to be a good bowler or a good golf player, since I don't have time for either one," I told him. "But maybe we make time for the things that we like best."

"You're probably right," he said as he headed onto the beltway.

As it happened, I wasn't bad at miniature golf. Ryan beat me by four points, and when we played a second game, I beat him by two. It surprised us both.

"See? You're better than you thought," he said. "If you keep at it, you'd probably want to try real golf."

"It's not on the agenda," I said, laughing, as we turned in the clubs and walked back to the car.

"Why not?"

"I don't know. Doesn't appeal all that much."

"What sports do you like?"

"To watch or to play? I love watching basketball and football, but I'm sort of a loner when it comes to playing a sport. I like to run by myself in the early mornings. I like to swim when I get a chance. I like playing badminton with my girlfriends. I guess I'm not very competitive when it comes to sports."

We drove into D.C. and over to the marina along the Potomac. At one end, near the bridge, the road was lined with little shops selling fish, and farther on there were restaurants catering to the boating crowd.

We were early enough to get a table by the window, and it was fun watching the boats come in and out, unfurling their sails or making their way into their slots along the dock. Nice sitting there with Ryan, who looked especially handsome in an olive T-shirt that strained at his biceps.

"You ever sail?" he asked me.

"I've been on a sailboat—well, a boat with sails, anyway—but I didn't have to do anything," I said.

"You ought to try it. It's like nothing you've ever experienced before—just moving across the surface with the wind, the only sounds being the water rippling, the sails flapping now and then, the gulls calling. No one should reach his twenty-first birthday without learning to sail."

"There are a lot of people who don't live near water," I reminded him.

"Well, the ones who do, then," Ryan said. He scanned the menu. "What are you going to have? I recommend oysters on the half shell. Ever try them?"

"Nope."

"You should. How do you know you wouldn't like them if you've never tried them?"

"I didn't say I didn't like them. But other things interest me more," I said. And when the waiter came, I said, "I'd like the shrimp basket, please, and a glass of iced tea."

"Oysters on the half shell for the appetizer," said Ryan, pointing to the menu. "Then I'll take the crab Newburg with fries."

We didn't say much waiting for our dinner, just watched the people moving about on the dock outside the window. Some were hosing down their boats, and others were carrying ice chests aboard, ready for an evening's outing. They were all expensive-looking boats, with decks and cabins and helm seats—at least that's what Ryan called them. There was a dog on one of the decks, wagging its tail and excitedly running from one side of the boat to the other, eager for its master to get on board.

"Well, this is pleasant," Ryan said. "And we can take our time over dinner because I wasn't able to get tickets for the Capitol Steps. They don't have a performance tonight."

I was sort of glad, because Ryan had paid for miniature golf, and this dinner was going to be expensive. I didn't want the evening to cost him any more.

When the oysters arrived—glistening, semitransparent blobs in gray shells—Ryan immediately began giving instructions: "First," he said, picking up a bottle of hot sauce, "you give your oyster a quick shot of this or whatever you have handy. Then"—he glanced over to make sure I was watching—"you lift up the shell between thumb and forefinger . . . like so . . . then you tip your hand and slide the oyster and juice into your mouth without letting the shell touch your lips."

He showed me how to find the best place on the lip of the shell to pour from. "Once it's in your mouth, hold it there, savoring the fresh, briny taste, then mash the oyster a couple of times and swallow it down. You don't want to swallow it whole and you don't want to chew it to pieces—just enough to swallow it easily." He tipped back his head, slid the oyster in, chewed a couple of times, and swallowed.

I wondered what Miss Manners would say about insisting that your dinner guest try your food. I really didn't want a raw oyster. But I wanted to be a good sport, so I did as he told me, trying not to look at the oyster as I picked up one of the shells. I held it up to my lips, tilted my head back, tipped the shell, trying not to touch it with my teeth, and felt the slimy blob slide into my mouth and some of the liquid dribble down my chin.

Holding the oyster in my mouth, afraid to chew, I reached for my napkin and wiped my chin. And then, feeling as though I might gag, I chewed once and swallowed the thing, my mouth tasting like seaweed.

"Good, huh?" said Ryan. "But you forgot the hot sauce."

I reached for my iced tea and took a long drink, wishing I could swish it around in my mouth a couple of times and spit it out.

"Well," I said, "it's different. I suppose it's an acquired taste."

"You'll end up loving them," said Ryan. "Have another."

"No thanks," I told him. "They're all yours. I'm saving room for my shrimp."

I wanted to split the bill with Ryan, and offered, but he wouldn't let me.

"Tonight's on me," he said. "You can take the next one."

We ambled along the concrete walkway behind the line of restaurants, watching some of the boat owners, who actually lived on their boats, come home from work. Several men were in suits, carrying briefcases. They fumbled in their pockets for keys to the padlocks and opened the gates leading to their particular dock. A woman with a dry-cleaning bag thrown over one shoulder greeted a cat that waited for her on a deck chair.

"Are you going to miss the water when you go to Iowa?" I asked Ryan.

"Probably," he said. "We have some relatives in Maine, though. Chances are I'll go up there a lot over summers. I'll be busy in theater at Iowa, though. That and writing. Hope so, anyway. I want to keep my hand in theater in case writing doesn't work out and vice versa. What did you say you're going to major in?"

"Counseling," I told him. "It's part of the education curriculum."

"Why do you want to do that?" he asked.

"I think I'd enjoy it, and I might be good at it, I don't know. I think it would be satisfying work, if I am."

"For some people, maybe," said Ryan. "After getting a taste of the limelight, though, wouldn't you like to be more . . . well, visible?"

"Writing's rather invisible," I countered.

He chuckled. "Not if you get published. Get your picture on book jackets. Like I said, I'd like to see where I can . . . well . . . make a splash. I don't want to get stuck playing bit parts the rest of my life, but I don't want to end up just writing obituaries, either."

The breeze picked up, and I wished I hadn't left my sweater in the car. Ryan pulled me closer and covered my bare arm with one hand. It was warm. If this had been Patrick, I would have snuggled up against him. Maybe we would each have thrust one hand in the hip pocket of the other. I couldn't quite imagine doing that with Ryan.

We sat on a bench in a little plaza and watched the boats and the sky, talking about what Ryan would be doing over the summer—working at an uncle's hardware store when he wasn't up in Maine.

At one point, when the wind blew a lock of hair in my face, he reached over and tucked it behind one ear. "I think I liked your hair better the way you wore it in the third act," he said. "Back away from your face."

"I sort of like it the way it is now," I told him. "Long and loose."

He asked if I wanted to go somewhere and get some coffee and dessert, but I could feel the evening petering out, so I said I was still catching up on sleep and was getting a little tired.

"When can we get together again? Friday?" he asked as we drove along the parkway.

"Let me get back to you on that," I said. "The girlfriends have something planned that night, I think."

"Saturday?"

"That might work. I'll call you," I said.

He must have felt the way girls have felt for decades when a guy says "I'll call you" but has no intention of doing so. I could tell by his silence that he was already getting the picture.

If he was, then I was glad that somebody knew what was happening here, because I sure didn't. Ryan was good-looking—Penny had called him hot—he was smart, talented, motivated, and . . . ?

I don't know. Is there a term for when your chemistry just doesn't click? I guess I wasn't that into him because I could tell he wasn't that into me—into me as I am right now, anyway. The more I thought about it, the more controlling I realized he was. Not controlling in the way Ron had been with Faith, but he sure had a list of things he wanted to change about me—my bowling, my golf, my diet, my career, my hair. . . .

"Well," he said when he pulled up to my house, "I guess whether we go out again depends on you."

"Thanks so much, Ryan," I said. "It was a beautiful evening, wasn't it? And the dinner was delicious. If I see that Saturday night's open, I'll call, okay?"

"Yeah, I guess so. Good night," he said.

"Bye. Thanks again," I told him.

He pulled away from the curb the minute I closed the door, and for a moment I felt awful. Would it have been kinder to string him on for a little while? To at least have gone out one more time and paid for some of it myself? Let him know gradually that . . . ? That what? Had I even given him a fair chance, or had I been subconsciously making up my mind about him before we'd even gone out so I could stay true to Patrick? That was my biggest question.

Why is life so complicated? I wondered as I went slowly up the walk and into the house. I hoped that Dad was still up so I could talk to him. It was only nine thirty. But a note told me that he and Sylvia had gone to a concert at the Kennedy Center. I had to get used to the idea that once I went to college, there wouldn't be a Dad or a Sylvia in my dorm room, waiting for me to unload on them.

24

DEARLY BELOVED

Strangely enough, Penny called that evening because she'd heard from Liz that we'd applied for jobs on a cruise ship over the summer and wondered if she could get in on it too. Liz didn't know. I gave her the number to call, but explained that the cutoff date for applications had been March 1.

"Check with Gwen," I told her.

She sighed. "I'm always on the losing end."

"You *what*?" I asked incredulously.

"You and Patrick. You and Ryan. You and the cruise ship," she said plaintively.

I heard what she was saying, but the words didn't compute. "You're joking," I told her.

"No, I mean it, Alice." She sounded sincere. "I think the

whole time Patrick and I were going out, I knew it wasn't the same as his being with you. Oh, we had fun and a lot of laughs, but . . . It was hard to be serious with him, you know? Like, to find out how he really felt about me?"

"I can't quite believe that, Penny, but it's all in the past," I said.

"No, really."

"Well, you could have fooled me, then. You sure looked pretty close when I saw you together in the halls," I said, wondering why we were talking about this now, and over the phone no less.

"We were attracted to each other, Alice, but . . . even our kisses were playful. I always felt like, 'This is fun, but it's not the real thing.' Am I making any sense?"

"Maybe," I told her. "I guess the only two people who are banking on 'the real thing' right now are Jill and Justin." Why had I changed the subject? I wanted to hear more, more, more of how Patrick maybe liked me better all the while. But it was making me uncomfortable too.

"Yeah, seems that way," she said. "I know you and Gwen were invited to the wedding. We're all waiting to get an eyewitness account. When the minister asks if anyone knows of a reason those two should not be united in holy matrimony, I'll bet Justin's mother will have a speech all prepared."

We laughed a little.

"Anyway, thanks for the phone number," she said. "I'll call the cruise line and see if they'll still take an application. It would be more fun than babysitting my cousins, which is probably the only job I can get this summer."

"Good luck," I said. "And, Penny, just so you know, Ryan's available."

There were a few seconds of silence.

"I thought you were going out with him over spring break. That's what I heard."

"We did go out, but . . . like I said . . . he's available. Just so you know."

"Hmmm," said Penny. "I wonder if he's ever been to the U Street Music Hall."

"Ask him," I said. "I know he's got Saturday night open."

"Thanks, Alice," she said again. "Really."

"You're welcome," I answered. "Really."

Jill and Justin got married on April 23. It wasn't a sunny day, but it wasn't raining, either—one of those overcast April days when it looks as though it could rain but doesn't. Sort of like the wedding, where it might be happy for some people but not for others. Gwen and I had sent them a pretty ceramic picture frame and wore our very best dresses to the ceremony.

We sat together on the bride's side of the church. Like everyone else, we were watching for the entrance of the mothers. Jill's mom came in a purple dress, covered in lace, and Mrs. Collier, not to be outdone, wore a mauve creation that had "designer" written all over it. But they smiled at each other and took seats on their respective sides. Jill's mom, being divorced, was escorted by one of her brothers, and Mr. Collier had the stoic look of a man who knew that the next six hours were going to be devoted to shaking more hands and chitchatting more than he liked, but whatever was required or expected, he would do.

And Jill did make a beautiful bride. Her body was a little thickened around the waistline, and there was the beginning of a baby bump, but the gown was gorgeous.

"Wow!" Gwen whispered. "One look at her . . . and no wonder the groom and best man have their hands folded in front." I poked her with my elbow.

Jill looked a bit more anxious than I expected. She was smiling as she came down the aisle on her father's arm, but I saw her run her tongue over her lips a time or two as though her mouth were dry. When she reached the front of the sanctuary, her dad kissed her cheek and handed her over to Justin, who escorted her the next few steps toward the altar.

It was a traditional ceremony, not the kind that brides and grooms write themselves. No personal references to "overcoming obstacles" or "a ceremony of healing." Just "love, honor, and cherish" and "till death do us part." We were sitting close enough to the front of the church to look over and notice that when Justin took his vows—"I, Justin, take thee, Jill, to love, honor, and cherish . . ."—there were tears running down Mrs. Collier's cheek. But her lips never moved when the tears reached them. No hand came up to wipe them away. When the minister asked if anyone knew why Jill and Justin shouldn't marry, she sat like a sphinx and didn't move a muscle.

Then, after the magic words "I now pronounce you man and wife," Jill and Justin kissed. There was no clapping or cheering as there might be in some churches. I think all of us sensed that in this congregation, it wasn't appropriate. We were relieved when the organ peeled out the recessional and Jill and Justin, looking relieved themselves, went happily back up the aisle, followed by the parents of the bride and groom. I detected a thin line of mascara on both of Mrs. Collier's cheeks.

The bridal party retired to the minister's chambers for the official wedding photos after the church was cleared, and Gwen and I drove to the club where the reception would be held, sipping the champagne punch and sampling the shrimp, till Jill and Justin got there.

When they came in at last and formed a receiving line, we said all the right things to Jill and took the opportunity to hug Justin, laughing at the moisture on his forehead.

"Well, we did it," Jill murmured to us.

"We really pulled it off," said Justin.

We moved on down the line, telling Jill's mom it was a beautiful wedding, shaking hands with the father we'd never met, and on to the Colliers.

"So glad you could come," Mrs. Collier said, giving us her hand but scarcely looking at us or asking our names. Her makeup was repaired and her manners faultless. She turned to the next guests, her smile never wavering.

We sat together at the lavish dinner farther down the hall, behind a set of mahogany doors, and didn't know a single other guest. We were glad we had each other to talk to, because the rest of the people at our table were younger cousins of the groom who fidgeted in their seats, arranged lemon wedges in their mouths like tooth protectors, then grinned menacingly at each other and received glares and threats from their parents. We stuck it out through the introduction of the new Mr. and Mrs. Justin Collier, the toasts and the dancing, and as soon as we comfortably could, we said our good-byes and went out to Gwen's car.

"Well," I said, "what do you think?"

"I think she looked beautiful, I think Justin looked relieved, and I think Jill's mom is glad it's over. And I think Mrs. Collier is saying to herself, 'This is only the beginning,'" Gwen said.

"Really? You think she'll cause trouble?"

"I think Jill married into trouble. But you know, somewhere down the line, Mrs. Collier could end up crazy about her grandchild. Who knows?"

"No one," I said.

I helped Elizabeth hide Easter eggs on their lawn Easter morning after her family came home from Mass. Then I sat on the porch steps with her, and we laughed as Nathan, her little brother, found another egg, screaming at the top of his lungs.

"That's something else I miss," Liz murmured.

I looked over at her. "What?"

"Oh, just one of the things I used to love that has lost its pizzazz. Remember how exciting that used to be—knowing your mom or dad had gone out when you weren't looking and hidden all those eggs? What do you suppose we'll outgrow next?"

"Not guys, that's for sure," I said. "Speaking of which, what's the latest with you and Keeno?"

"Not much. But we're going to the prom. I asked him last night," she said.

"Yay," I said.

"But . . . everything's up in the air right now. We don't even know whether or not we have jobs this summer. I don't know which college I'm going to in the fall, and wherever it is, who knows whom I'll meet there?"

"Right," I said. *And Patrick will be in Spain*, I was thinking. *Who knows whom* he'll *meet* there?

25
LOOKING AHEAD

I was still sitting on Elizabeth's steps when I saw Lester drive up. I don't think he noticed me over at the Prices' house, because he got out, slammed the door, and walked soberly up the walk to our house.

"What's up with Les?" Liz asked me. "No maple creams in his eggs?"

"I haven't the faintest," I said. "Usually he can't wait to get to Sylvia's cooking. We invited him for Easter dinner. I'd better go see if I can help."

She didn't look very sympathetic. "Tell him Nathan will share his candy, if that's his problem," she said, and grinned.

I crossed the street and went inside. Les was leaning against the kitchen doorway. He'd obviously got a haircut recently, because the sideburns were neatly trimmed, the back tapered. He was also wearing a new shirt.

"Happy Easter, Les," I said, coming up behind him and giving him a hug. "What's up?"

He reached around and swatted at me, not even bothering to turn. "Got any candy?" he asked.

"No, but the little boy across the street might share some with you," I said, and moved where he could see me. "You look like someone the Easter bunny forgot."

"Well, it wasn't a bunny," he said, and when Sylvia paused as she sliced the ham, he said, "Kay hasn't answered my last two phone calls. Can't figure her out."

Dad looked up from the sink, a bowl of spinach leaves in his hands. "That's really strange, Les. She's been having some dental problems, but nothing serious that I know of."

"Was she at work yesterday?" Les asked. "Because I left a message there."

"No. She was at the dentist having a wisdom tooth extracted. I told her to take the rest of the day off," Dad said.

"That probably explains it, then," Les said.

"She's seemed in a good mood lately," Dad went on. "I think James is going back to China at the end of the month."

"That's good," said Les. "I just get annoyed when people aren't honest with me." He took off his jacket and moved to hang it up in the hall closet. The thin brown stripe in his shirt brought out the brown of his eyes, and I realized again how handsome he was. Not surprising he's had a long string of girlfriends. When he came back in the kitchen, he said, "Nothing serious between Kay and me—we've just gone out a few times. But it would be nice to know I didn't make some cultural gaffe or something."

"I don't know what that would be. She's not easily offended, as far as I can tell," Dad said.

"Well, if any hot babes happen to ask, I'm available," he said, and raised an eyebrow at me. "Any hot babe my own age, Al. Don't give Pamela any ideas." Pamela's had a crush on Les forever.

I went out to the buffet in the dining room for the good silverware, placing it around our china there on the table. It was Easter, and we were all together, and that was reason enough to celebrate.

We were halfway through the meal when the doorbell rang. Dad had gone back to the kitchen for the butter. "I'll get it, Sylvia," he called. "Stay put."

I heard the front door open and then Dad's voice saying, "Why, Kay! Come on in."

We stared at Les, then turned toward the doorway.

"Oh, my goodness!" I heard Kay exclaim as she entered the dining room. "You're still eating. And . . . it's Easter! I forgot! We don't celebrate Easter. I'm so sorry."

"It's okay. Please pull up a chair," Dad said.

But Kay looked uncomfortable as Les gave her a puzzled smile.

"I drove over to Lester's apartment, and Paul told me he'd be over here," Kay said. "I wanted to talk to him face-to-face and . . . Oh, this is so embarrassing."

"You . . . uh . . . want some privacy?" Dad asked.

"Come on, sit down," Les said genially, and reached around to pull an empty chair to the table.

She sat. "Les . . . well, you know, two weeks ago, when I didn't keep our date?"

"Yeah?"

"That really wasn't my fault. I hadn't planned it. Someone knocked on my door, and when I opened it, James was standing there. Alone. He looked really miserable and asked if he could talk to me for a few minutes, so I let him in. He was sort of . . . well, bowing and scraping, I guess you'd call it, and said he just wanted me to know that he was as embarrassed over this whole thing as I was, but that both sets of parents were making unreasonable demands of us and he was going back to China in a week.

"I told him I knew it wasn't his fault. Since we both had made excuses for not being at my parents' house for dinner that night, he said he didn't want my dad to drive by and see his rental car and know we were in the apartment alone. He asked if there was anywhere we could go to talk. So I suggested a sandwich shop, and we drove there. We just got talking, Les, and there was so much to say. His parents practically ordered him to come back with a wife. A wife-to-be, that is. Namely, me. He just wanted me to know that this wasn't his idea of marriage and would tell his parents so when he got back."

Lester had stopped chewing now, and we were all sitting there entranced. Kay let her jacket slip off her shoulders because sunlight was pouring through a side window now, warming the room and making her black hair positively shine. She turned to Lester.

"Les, we . . . I had no idea we had talked so long, and when I realized it was an hour and a half past the time I was to meet you, I was . . . I was just too embarrassed to call. I made up some story the next day about my dad. I shouldn't have, but I was too confused to explain. Well, James called me a few days later to say he was on standby for a flight to China, and maybe we could talk once more, just for friendship's sake, so . . . we met again at the sandwich shop."

I think we all guessed the end of the story.

"We've . . . been to the sandwich shop six times now, and tonight we're going on a for-real date."

We all started to smile. Even Lester.

"The thing is, we don't want anyone to know. We want to see how this goes completely on our own, without any pressure from our parents. If . . . if we 'click,' as you'd call it, then we'll decide all the rest. I'm *really, really* sorry I didn't tell you sooner, but . . . I wasn't sure of anything."

Les gave her a real smile now. "Hey, babe, no problem."

Kay giggled a little, but then grew serious. "James has declined my parents' dinner invitations, and my parents are furious with me. They say he'll go back to China and tell everyone what a disrespectful daughter I am, unfit to be his wife."

"You're not telling them anything?" I asked.

"Not yet. If this works out between James and me, it will

be on our own terms. We've been miserable enough on theirs. Now it's like we just met and know nothing about each other, so we're starting at the beginning. Mr. Stone Face, I tease him, and he calls me Miss Nose in the Air."

This was better than any romance book.

"Kay, I've got lemon pie for dessert," Sylvia said. "Won't you have some with us?"

"I'll just take a glass of water," she said. "We're going out for dinner tonight."

"I hope you have reservations," said Dad. "It's almost impossible to get in a restaurant on Easter without a reservation."

"A Chinese restaurant," Kay said, laughing. "You can always get a table at a Chinese restaurant on an American holiday."

I just sat there grinning at Kay. "Wow!" I said. "Who would have thought?"

"Not in a million years," said Kay. "But my *parents* are going to be the last to know."

We got our letters on May 2. Gwen, Liz, Yolanda, Pam, and I were tentatively hired for the cruise ship. Five two-week cruises on a new line, providing we passed our interview and the training session.

Everyone else at school was envious of us, including Penny, who hadn't got her application in on time. It was hard enough to find a summer job, not to mention one that began after graduation and ended before any of us had to start college.

Sometimes I'm blown away by how coincidental life is. If

Gwen's mom hadn't worked for the Justice Department, she wouldn't have been having lunch with a woman whose brother-in-law had just been hired to be the assistant cruise director for a new Chesapeake Bay line, and we wouldn't have summer jobs.

I was trying to explain this to Liz and Pamela as we ate our lunch outside under the oak tree at the side of the school. But Pamela can take just so much philosophical thought before she barfs.

"Alice," she said, "did you ever consider that in spite of all the twists and turns of fate, there is only one reason why you are here on this earth?"

"No," I said. "What?"

"Your parents had sex," she told me.

And who would have thought that the senior prom would be scheduled on my eighteenth birthday, May 14!

"Now, *that's* pretty incredible!" said Sylvia.

My gift from them would be any prom dress I wanted, with shoes to match, she said, and she went with me to try some on. She said as long as we stayed out of the designer collections, I could have whatever I wanted. I chose a gorgeous gown in a deep, brilliant yellow. The long, full skirt was covered with a layer of white chiffon that made the whole dress look sort of ethereal, cloudlike. It almost seemed to shimmer with every step I took.

But somehow I couldn't find the right shoes to dye. I already had a pair of neutral sling-back heels that I loved because the flesh color seemed to elongate my legs, and a pair of bright yellow shoes would give my legs a chopped-off look if I lifted my skirt. And where would I ever wear bright yellow shoes again? So I decided to wear what I had, and Sylvia bought me a cute little clutch purse instead.

Patrick called the Wednesday before the prom to give me his itinerary.

"I'm winding up some research for the professor—a graph to go in his book—and I should be finished by Friday," he said. "*Late* Friday, probably, but I'll have it done. I'll fly into National at eleven forty Saturday morning, and I'm staying with the Stedmeisters."

That was no surprise, because I'd heard Mark's parents offer their home to Patrick whenever he came back for a visit. Patrick was good company for them, having been one of Mark's best friends. He always did converse easily with adults—maybe because he was an only child.

"Mr. Stedmeister's picking me up at the airport and taking me to get my tux. I pretty much guessed at the measurements. You and I are going to have dinner before the dance with the gang. But I've made our own plans for what we do after. It's your birthday, you know." As though I'd forgotten.

I felt my heart speed up. Patrick may have had plans, but Dad also had rules. And the one big nonnegotiable rule of the evening was that I could not go to a hotel room after the prom was over. I tried to explain to him that people just got together and rented a room to have an all-night party, not an orgy, but Dad held firm.

"It's a lot safer than driving around with all the drunks on the road at three in the morning," I had said the week before, pulling out all the stops.

"Not necessarily," Dad had answered.

Patrick continued: "Just wanted to make sure you weren't counting on the after-prom party at the school."

"No, I wasn't. But my dad's just being a dad, Patrick, and there's a nonnegotiable rule: I can't go to a hotel room, even if there are twenty people there."

Patrick was quiet for several seconds, and I wondered if his plan for an intimate evening had just gone up in smoke. "Tell your dad that there's no hotel room in the picture and that you'll be perfectly safe with me," he said.

I wasn't sure I wanted to hear that, either, especially after what came next: "I have to fly back Sunday, Alice. I have a huge—and I mean *huge*—test on Monday."

I know that for some girls, prom night is when you're supposed to lose your V card—the atmosphere, the romance, the glamour, the gown. Something to make it special, to remember it by. And this was already special, being my eighteenth birthday, with a boyfriend who was leaving for Spain for a year.

But I had already decided that wasn't the way I wanted to have sex my first time—intercourse, I mean. That would seem so . . . so stereotypical. Everybody dressing up and expecting to get laid afterward. I wanted Patrick so much, it almost hurt to think about it, but I didn't want it to be a single night. I wanted us to be someplace really private with all the time in the world—before, during, and after.

It didn't look like that was going to happen anytime soon, though, and Patrick didn't live here anymore. He would be leaving for Spain the minute spring quarter ended at the University of Chicago. He would be in Spain a whole year—four quarters. Maybe this night was all I was going to get, I thought nervously. Maybe it was now or never.

But what if we tried to make love and it was terribly awkward? What if it really hurt, or he came too soon, or I bled and was too sore to try again? I'd heard accounts of other girls' "first times." I'd read articles. I knew the old joke about how Niagara Falls was a bride's "second biggest disappointment." Did I really want Patrick and me separating for a year with an awkward, hurried "first time" to remember?

Patrick had just asked a question and was waiting for an answer.

"What?" I said.

"What color is your dress?"

"Yellow," I said. "Daisy yellow."

"I can get you daisies, then?" he teased.

I smiled. "Even dandelions would do if they're from you."

"Till Saturday, then," he told me.

26

MAY 14

Sylvia did my hair and nails and even gave me a pedicure (still part of my birthday present, she kidded). I wondered if this was a setup where she'd ask me personal questions about what Patrick and I would do after the prom, seeing as how I was a prisoner of sorts, with one leg on a towel in her lap. She didn't, though.

But she did say, "It must be hard to have Patrick so far away."

"It is," I said. "And he'll be gone all summer."

"So will you."

"I know, but when I come back from my summer job, he still won't be here. He won't even be in Chicago. I wouldn't be able to see him if I visited Aunt Sally or Carol. He'll be half a world away."

Sylvia carefully buffed the heel of my foot with a pumice stone. "Thank goodness for e-mail and cell phones," she said. "Maybe he'll get an international phone card and call you now and then. Maybe you won't be quite as lonesome as you think."

I didn't tell her I wanted more than that. Didn't say that maybe I'd make enough on my cruise ship job to fly over and see him in Spain. Didn't say that maybe with the money Dad was saving by my not going to an out-of-state college, he could afford to send me to Spain and back a couple times a year. And it was that idea that made it bearable.

Austin and Gwen drove up with Patrick around six o'clock. I could feel my excitement building as I watched the passenger door open and Patrick stepped out. He seemed even taller than when I saw him at Christmas. He'd be eighteen in July. Wasn't a guy supposed to have attained his full height by eighteen?

I rushed to the door and opened it before he got to the porch, and then we were in each other's arms, lips together, and I think he even dropped the corsage box, but we didn't care.

When we finally stopped to breathe, we smiled at each other sheepishly, then kissed again, a short kiss this time—it was mostly a hug—and then Patrick picked up the box.

"Happy Birthday," he said, his eyes smiling down at me.

"I'm so glad you're here," I told him, pulling him inside the house.

Sylvia hugged him too, and he and Dad shook hands. I opened the corsage box. The flower must have been something from the orchid family, it was so delicately shaped. A very pale yellow, with sprigs of white baby's breath. Patrick fastened it to my wrist, and we posed for pictures in front of the stone fireplace in the family room.

"Come by for lunch tomorrow, Patrick, and we'll drive you to the airport," Dad said.

"That would be great," Patrick said. "I was planning to come by anyway."

I tucked my cell phone in one of Patrick's pockets so we could take pictures of our friends. I had Sylvia's wrap over one arm, but as we were about to leave, I asked, "Anything more I should bring, Patrick? A change of clothes or something?"

"No. What you're wearing is fine. But . . . well, sneakers, maybe, in case you want to get rid of those high heels."

I went back upstairs to get them, Sylvia fetched a bag, and after the obligatory "Be safe" from Dad, we went out to the car.

"Have a great time," Sylvia called as they watched us go.

We drove to Normandie Farm in Potomac, where we met the others, and everyone greeted Patrick with hugs and cheers.

It was an old establishment with huge fireplaces at each end of a great hall and geese roaming the grounds. No fire was needed on this evening, but the hall was half filled with prom couples. Pamela was already there at our table with Jay, the guy who had played Frank Jr. in the play. Throughout rehearsals, I'd wondered if something wasn't clicking between them, so I hadn't been at all surprised when she'd told us that he invited her to the dance the night of the cast party.

We all looked positively great. Gwen was in red, Pamela in white, and Liz in lavender. Along with my yellow, we looked like a summer bouquet. It wasn't long before our table of eight was buzzing with happy chatter, questions zinging back and forth, talk of game scores and vacation plans. All I could think of was how normal, how comfortable, how familiar it all was, having Patrick back again, and yet . . . how different, because we were all going off in different directions, like seeds from a dandelion—Patrick going farthest of all.

"Patrick, college must agree with you," Pamela told him. "When you get back from Spain, you'll probably be doing the rumba or something."

"That's Cuba, Pamela," said Austin.

"Well, the tango, then," said Pamela.

"That's South America!" said Liz, and we laughed.

There was so much to talk about. Both Austin and Keeno went to different schools from ours. Austin was in his second year at Howard University in the District, Keeno would be entering the naval academy in Annapolis, and Jay would be going to Montgomery College after graduation. I told them how long Patrick and I had known each other—as long as I'd known Liz and Pamela—and how we had all been in Mr. Hensley's seventh-grade World Studies class together, when we'd buried a time capsule and were supposed to come back when we were sixty to open it.

"Old 'Horse-Breath Hensley,' we called him," Pamela said.

"And could that man spit!" Patrick put in. "You almost needed an umbrella if you sat in the first row."

"But we liked that time capsule," I said. "Hensley won't be around when we open it, but I plan to be here."

"We'll all come," said Liz. "From wherever we are, we've got to be here. And that means you too, Patrick, even if you're in Samoa or someplace."

"How do you know the time capsule will still be there?" Austin asked. "That the *school* will still be there? I'll bet there's a town house development over the playground."

"Don't be so pessimistic," Gwen told him. "The school undoubtedly recorded it somewhere. What did the class put inside it?"

"All I remember is that we were each supposed to write a letter to our sixty-year-old selves," Liz told them.

"Won't *that* be a scream!" said Pamela.

We rode to the Hyatt, where each end of the ballroom had been decorated like an Arabian tent, with huge pillows and rugs and an artificial sky above. In between dance numbers, seductive belly-dance music came from the tents, along with wafts of incense from elaborate copper burners. We took turns posing in front of the tents and took pictures of each other.

During some of the numbers we walked around the halls, Patrick greeting old friends, and I felt as though I were showing off a movie star or something—Patrick in his black tux, the yellow boutonniere in his lapel; Patrick looking down at me, smiling; Patrick shaking hands with some of his former teachers, telling them where he was going to school now. But every time there was a slow number, we were in each other's arms again, gently rocking on the dance floor, my cheek against his chest.

"Well," he said, "Happy Birthday. I guess I can say I spent the evening with an older woman."

I laughed. "Only by two months."

"Yeah, I was probably building block fortresses before you even learned to crawl."

"Yeah? I'll bet I was potty trained before you," I said, and when a couple next to us overheard and turned to stare, we laughed out loud and Patrick whirled me away. I danced once with Austin and Keeno too, and even once with Sam, who looked especially nice in a gray tux with a wine-colored cummerbund and boutonniere. We danced like old friends, which, I guess, we were.

Ryan, I noticed, was there with Penny; Phil and another guy from the Gay/Straight Alliance had come together; and Lori and Leslie were still partners, both in white tuxes and looking smashing. When Lori saw me and cut in on Sam, I danced with her, and we laughed when the spotlight—which was focusing for a few seconds on one couple, then another—shone on us.

"You look great, Lori," I told her as she turned us so the glare wasn't in our eyes.

"You know what? This has been the happiest year of my life so far," she said. "Everything's going good."

"I can tell," I told her as she swung me around again. "It shows."

"You look pretty happy too," she said.

"For a girl whose guy is going to Spain for a year, I guess I am," I said. "Trying to focus on the here and now."

"It's all any of us have got," said Lori.

Patrick claimed me again as the lights went even lower and artificial stars overhead began to twinkle. Patrick's hand was firm on my bare back, and I leaned into him, my face against his neck, hand resting on his chest as he enclosed me in both his arms. I felt so safe, so secure, so loved.

We were barely moving to the music now, our bodies pressed against each other. One of his fingers caressed my back, my lips brushed his throat. *If only the here and now could last forever,* I thought. *If I could just stay wrapped in his arms like this . . .* When we kissed, I was conscious once more of the spotlight. I just closed my eyes and moved with him to the music, enjoying the warmth of his hands, the caress of his thumb on my back, the feel of his breath in my hair.

The spotlight stayed, and some of our friends were applauding. I realized they had stepped back to give us a small space on the floor as long as the spotlight was there, and then the moment was over—we were in shadow again. The crowd moved away, and we lingered over a long kiss.

About eleven Patrick said we were leaving, and he suggested I use the restroom first. Where would we be going that we wouldn't have a restroom handy? I wondered. And who was driving? But I did as he said, then picked up my wrap and sneakers at the coatroom. When I got back to the main entrance, where Patrick was waiting for me, he held open the door while I went outside. There in the hotel driveway was a black limo. When he saw us, the driver immediately hopped out and opened the door.

"Patrick!" I said breathlessly, staring up at him, but he just smiled and helped me get in. Then he slid in beside me.

It wasn't a large limo, but the seats were soft and spacious, with a small bouquet of fresh flowers at one side, along with a DVD player, chilled bottles of mango and lime juice, a jar of chocolate-covered raisins, and some macaroons. A sliding panel of dark glass separated us from the driver.

"The next few hours are for you," Patrick said, putting one arm around me. "Happy Birthday."

"What?" I said. "Where are we going?"

"We have the limo for three hours, so I thought we'd just go to all your favorite places. You know, drive around."

I stared at him in astonishment.

"Patrick, all my favorite places are within five miles of my house. We could do the whole tour in a half hour."

"Oh," said Patrick, looking dumbfounded.

Was it possible that Patrick Long, who could speak at least three languages and had traveled all over the world, hadn't thought out what to do with a limo in Maryland for the next three hours?

"Well . . ." he said at last, as the driver waited. "Hmmm."

I broke into laughter. "Patrick! Every minute we sit here is costing you money! Are you sure you want to do this? I mean, whatever it is we're doing?"

"There's got to be some place you'd like to go," he said. "I mean, dancing, dining . . ."

We'd already dined and danced. I knew that all my friends who had watched us leave were wondering what we were doing. I knew that Pamela's question to me would be, *You won't be seeing Patrick for a year, right? So . . . tell all. How far did you go?*

"Patrick," I said, "how far have we been together? Away from here, I mean."

"Chicago?" he said, thinking.

"Well, we can't get to Chicago and back in three hours. What about Ocean City? Remember that summer Lester brought you out there when Dad rented a house?"

"It's a three-hour drive just to get there," Patrick said. "The farthest we could get would be the Bay Bridge and back."

"Okay," I said, settling myself into the plush seat. "I want to drive to the Bay Bridge with you."

His face spread into a grin. "Really?" he said, laughing. "Okay, you got it." Leaning forward, he slid the dark glass to one side. "Bay Bridge and back," he said.

I suppose limo drivers are used to all sorts of directions. There was no answer that I could hear. Patrick slid the window closed again, and the limo rolled out of the circular drive, heading for the beltway.

27
VIEW FROM THE BRIDGE

I think we laughed all the way to the Bay Bridge. It was such a crazy idea, and we had to go over every detail of the evening—the tents and the incense; how great Gwen looked with her hair coiled on top of her head, a silver thread in the braids, how comfortable she and Austin seemed together; whether Keeno would make it through the academy; whether Liz would get to Vermont. . . .

After we'd passed the Annapolis exits, I wanted to roll down the windows and look for the bridge, but all I could see was night.

"It's dark!" I said.

"Duh!" said Patrick. "What did you expect?"

I guess I'd never been over the Bay Bridge at night that I could remember, but when at last we spotted those high towers holding up the long span, the lights illuminating the miles of cable, the limo slowed and we heard the intercom come on and the driver ask, "You want me to cross?"

"Yeah. Go across and find a place to turn around. Then we'll head back," Patrick told him, but he kept the sliding window open now so he and the driver could talk.

We rolled down the rear windows so we could stick our heads out both sides of the limo. Even though we couldn't see the water, we could sense the salty air. It was after midnight, and there were only a couple of cars at the tollbooth. Usually the traffic was going east on one span, west on the other. But on this weekend night, two lanes of one bridge and one lane of the other were all heading toward the ocean. The bridge we were crossing had lanes going both ways.

I grabbed Patrick's hand. "This is the farthest we've ever gone together, Patrick. I mean, in the same car. Both at the same time."

He smiled. "So, what do you want? A souvenir or something?"

"Yes, I wish we could."

I crawled over on Patrick's lap so we were both leaning out the same window, the wind blowing in our faces. Patrick said the bridge was almost four and a half miles long. We figured when we got to the very center that we were probably higher than we'd ever been before, since we'd never been on a plane together.

"So this is a first," I said.

Finally, when we reached the other side, the driver pulled into a restaurant parking lot to turn around.

"Patrick," I said, "when we get to the top going back, I want to get out and take our picture."

"You can't stop on the bridge," he said.

"What if you blew a tire or something? You'd have to be able to stop."

"Not for a picture, though."

"So what would they do? Arrest us? It would only take half a minute."

He laughed. "You're crazy."

"Please?"

He had a low conversation with the driver, but I could only hear his voice, not the driver's. Finally Patrick settled back beside me. "He says he's going to wait until there are no cars coming in the opposite lane, then he'll pull out and head back across. He'll slow down and stop just long enough for us to get out and will move on very slowly, but we'll have to take a picture in about five seconds and run to catch up. If we dawdle, we'll have to walk back and he'll wait for us at the other end, at which point they'll probably arrest us."

I didn't know if the man was kidding or not, but this was about the most exciting thing I'd ever done.

"Okay!" I said, and immediately took off my sling-backs and pulled on my sneakers.

There were few cars heading away from the ocean at twelve thirty on an early Saturday morning. When there were no cars at all coming as far as we could see, the driver pulled out and crossed over into the return lane.

"There aren't any sidewalks on the bridge," Patrick murmured, studying the span out the window. "If we had to walk back, we'd be right on the roadway. We *have* to ride back."

"Get my camera out, Patrick," I said.

When we reached the top of the span, the limo slowed and stopped. Patrick jumped out first, helped me out, closed the door, and we climbed over the low wall and moved to the cable railing, laughing wildly.

"Ready," Patrick said, holding my cell phone out in front of us. It flashed.

"Take another one," I begged, as the wind blew my hair in my face and I could see only a reflection of the moon on the water.

The limo was slowly moving away. Another flash.

"One more?" I cried. "Please!"

"Alice, we have to go!"

"Just one more?" I pleaded.

"You crazy person!" Patrick said, but he held out my cell phone once again, and the moment it flashed, we scrambled over the parapet again, my skirts billowing out above my knees, and went racing along the grid surface to the limo, which barely stopped as we climbed in and closed the door, shrieking like maniacs.

We were trying to see our pictures in the backseat, but the driver told us to fasten our seat belts, so we did, and it wasn't long before we started down the long incline where, we saw with pounding hearts, that a patrol car waited, an officer standing outside it.

There was no tollbooth at the bottom of the return span,

but the driver slowed anyway and obeyed when the officer motioned him over.

"Oh, man," said Patrick.

"You'll bail me out?" the driver said sardonically.

A car behind had caught up with us, the passengers rubbernecking as they passed to see what we had done. The officer walked over.

"You are aware that only emergency stopping is allowed on the bridge?" he asked. They must have had motion detectors or cameras along the span, I decided.

"Yes," the driver said, "but I wanted to make it special for the young couple here on their prom night. I wouldn't have tried if there had been cars behind us."

"Sorry. No dispensation for being the only car on the road or for prom nights," the officer said. "License, please?"

The driver presented his credentials.

Patrick spoke up. "I'm the one who asked him to stop. If there's a fine or anything, I'll pay it."

The officer didn't answer for a moment. Still checking the driver's ID, he said, "I'll get to you next."

He did. He moved to the back window and asked us to get out of the car. We obeyed. I was still wearing my sneakers and almost tripped over my dress till Patrick caught me.

"It's my fault!" I cried. "It was all my idea, and I just wanted a picture before Patrick goes to Spain, and it will be a year before—"

Patrick squeezed my arm and I shut up.

The officer turned on his flashlight and checked the backseat to be sure there was no one else inside. No beer bottles on the floor.

"ID?" he asked.

Patrick fished around in his pocket. "I left everything back at the Stedmeisters'," he murmured to me. And then, to the policeman, "This is all I brought with me," and handed the officer a credit card. "It's my dad's."

"Stay here, please," the officer said, and went back to his car. He slid in, and we could see him calling in the numbers on his radio. He waited. We waited.

"Patrick, I feel horrible! I got you into this," I said. "Do you think we'll go to jail on our prom night?"

"I'll ask if we can share a cell," Patrick said, but he wasn't smiling.

"There's going to be a heck of an extra charge for this," the driver complained.

"I know. It's okay," Patrick told him.

"Not if I lose my license," the driver said.

I was feeling worse by the minute. The old impulsive me again. I just don't think!

Finally the officer got out of his patrol car and walked over. He handed the credit card back to Patrick.

"Okay," he said. "Move on. But don't try this again. Not in this high-security age."

"Thank you," said Patrick. "We won't."

"Thank you so much!" I burbled. "We really didn't mean to cause any trouble. I just—"

"Get in the car, Alice," Patrick muttered, steering me through the open door.

The officer didn't answer. He waited till another car went by and walked back to his patrol car. Then we were moving forward, on the road again.

"No tickets? No fines?" the driver asked over the intercom. "You guys must have a guardian angel or something."

"Or something," said Patrick. "Maybe it's just this crazy lady I'm with."

"This has been the most amazing night!" I said. "I was sure he was going to arrest us. He didn't fine us or anything. Why?"

"All I can figure is that it was Dad's credit card I gave him. Dad said I could use his this weekend. Maybe it was diplomatic immunity or something."

"But I thought your dad retired from the State Department?"

"He did. But I'm sure his history is all in his records."

"Wow, Patrick!" I said.

"Roger that!" said the driver from up front, and we laughed as Patrick closed the little glass window again and the intercom clicked off.

We checked out the photos Patrick had taken and laughed at the camera angle of the first one. We were on a slant, and the left side of my face was missing, Patrick's eyes were wide and goofy. The second photo got us both in, my hair tossing in the wind, me smiling a little too broadly, Patrick striking a moody movie-star look. In the last photo I'm looking away from the camera at the receding limo and Patrick's chin was cut off.

"The second one's best, Patrick," I said. "*Look* at you!"

"Look at your hair." He laughed.

"We're like that couple at the prow of the *Titanic*."

"Except for your grin."

"That's a smile, Patrick."

"Whatever it is, I'll take it," he said.

The lights of the bridge had disappeared far behind us and the dark of the trees closed in. And then we were in each other's arms again.

The driver cut through D.C. on the way back, and we had almost every street to ourselves. He drove us by the Jefferson and Lincoln Memorials, all lit up. Past the reflecting pool, where tourists walked when cherry trees were in bloom, around the Washington Monument. It was like we were the only ones in Washington. Like all the lights were on just for us, celebrating my eighteenth birthday.

Finally we were on our way home again. Patrick asked the driver to take the scenic route—the slow lane along Beach Drive. We didn't see any of the rest. Patrick and I were entwined together on the backseat, caressing each other and kissing the parts we couldn't see.

"Patrick," I whispered, "when we're together again, I want it to be for a week, at least. I want seven days and seven nights. I can't stand wanting you so much and never having time for more than a taste."

His lips were buried against my neck. "If you only knew how much I've wanted you. . . ."

When the limo pulled up to my house, the driver turned off the engine and sat, unseen, in his seat up front while we gave our good-night kisses. At last, when we heard him open the door and get out, we knew we had reached the end of our magical evening.

"I love you," Patrick said.

"I love you," I whispered back.

28
BY THE HOUR?

Pamela invited us over the following night so we could relive the prom in slow motion, dissecting every incident, commenting on every dress, reflecting on every couple, every expression, each word. . . . Her dad and his fiancée were out for the evening, so we had the place to ourselves.

Liz and Pamela and Gwen, of course, wanted to know what happened after Patrick and I left the prom, and Pamela's ears were like antennas, practically vibrating, wanting to know all the passionate details.

"Well," I said, "Patrick and I went farther than we've ever gone before."

"You . . . ?" Liz said, eyes huge.

"Together," I added.

"Meaning?" said Pamela.

I told them about the limo ride to the Bay Bridge and how we stopped and got out and how a policeman was waiting at the other end. Everyone loved hearing about it, but Pamela was getting impatient.

"Meanwhile, back in the limo . . . ," she prompted.

"We were about as close as we could get," I said, skirting the question.

Liz studied me. "No waves crashing? No earth moving? No violins?"

I sighed. "Not in the way you're thinking."

"And don't expect it either," Gwen said. "It'll be a while before you get violins."

"What about you and Austin?" I asked.

"I don't know," she said. "Eight years is a long time for me to be in school, and who knows where he'll get a job? We're just enjoying what we have. But guess who I saw at the prom?"

We shook our heads.

"Legs," she said.

"Leo? The guy who—?" Liz began, and stopped.

The guy she'd had sex with way back when. The guy she finally broke up with when we were counselors together at camp. The guy who had been cheating on her all the while.

"Did you talk to him?" I asked.

"No. I'm not sure he even knew I was there. I was trying to see who invited him, but I couldn't. He and Austin are so . . . It's like they're from different planets. I'm dancing with Austin, wondering what I ever saw in Legs. Just the fact that he liked me, I guess. I figured that he must think I was really special if he wanted to have sex with me."

We all groaned at that, even the two of us who were still virgins.

Pamela told us how much fun she'd had with Jay, and Liz said she and Keeno were going out a few more times before we left for the cruise ship. But while they chattered on, I settled back against the cushions, remembering the way Patrick and I had said good-bye at the airport that morning. Mr. Stedmeister had driven him over to our place around noon so Patrick could have lunch with us and talk with Dad and Sylvia. Then Patrick and I got in Dad's car, and Dad drove to Reagan National, then around and around the traffic circle while I walked with Patrick as far as the security gate.

What do you say when you know you won't see someone for over a year? Call me? E-mail me? Think of me? Love me? All the above? All those promises. . . .

When we embraced for the last time, I felt as though if I held him tightly enough, he wouldn't leave. Like I was imprinting him on my body. But finally he gently pulled away, squeezed my arm, then picked up his bag and went through security.

We waved for as long as we could see each other, Patrick heading down the long hall. Then another passenger came between us, and he disappeared.

I hadn't wanted to talk on the way home. I'd looked around twice, thinking Patrick might possibly be running after our car.

That he might have forgotten something—left something in it and I could see him one more time. But then we were turning onto the George Washington Parkway, Dad had the radio playing, and I just closed my eyes, drawing in my breath, trying to detect Patrick's scent. But it was gone.

I was like a robot the following week, partly because there was so much to do before graduation and partly to keep from missing Patrick. I had a checklist of things I needed to complete for every class before finals, and I set myself on automatic. I put in eight hours at the Melody Inn on Saturday, catching up on the work I needed to do there, and Dad let me have his car afterward for a whole evening of errands if I'd take some insurance papers over to Lester while I was at it.

I picked up Sylvia's dry cleaning, stopped at the shoe repair shop, returned a book to Silver Spring Library, bought some stuff at the drugstore that I'd need on the cruise, and by the time I got to Lester's apartment around nine thirty, the evening had turned from cool to cold—typical, unreliable May weather.

He was waiting for me in the living room, watching an ESPN sports special that not even he seemed especially interested in.

"You're on call tonight?" I said, giving him the insurance papers and throwing my jacket on a chair. "What are you eating?" I asked, looking at what appeared to be brownie crumbs on a saucer.

"Well, make yourself at home, why don't you?" he said.

"I'm trying. I've been running errands all evening and I'm hungry."

He motioned toward the kitchen. "Rubbermaid container," he said.

I got a couple brownies, checked the milk to see if there was enough for me, and poured a small glass. Then I came out to sit beside him. "You going to miss me when I'm gone all summer?" I asked, savoring the first bite of chocolate.

"I'll save some on food," he said. "Though Andy will probably eat your share."

I'd noticed her door was closed when I came in.

"Still in business, huh?"

"It's a mystery. I'm doing all the checking I can, and things keep turning up. She evidently was a straight-A student when she was at the university. No evidence that she took part in any extracurricular stuff—no clubs or sororities—all nose to the grindstone. But she . . . and those students . . . just don't add up somehow. I've got a call in to a friend in the finance office. He says there was a memo going around a month or so ago about an Andrea somebody or other, but he couldn't remember what it said. He's checking."

"I almost wish I were staying home this summer. Alice, Girl Detective."

"Naw. You'll have a ball. Where does that cruise ship go, anyway?"

"Just around the bay. All the little towns and byways. Passengers explore some on rubber dinghies, and there are picnics and stuff. Sometimes we get to help at cookouts. I'm going to come back with a toned body like you wouldn't believe."

"You're right, I don't believe it."

"Les," I said, "if you were going to be separated from a girl you really, really liked—okay, loved—for a whole year, what would you do to make sure the . . . romance stayed alive?"

"Hmmm," said Les. "Well, first I'd make sure we both tattooed the other's name on our foreheads—"

"Les . . ."

"And we could each wear a tiny vial of the other's blood around our necks."

"Seriously . . ."

Lester turned the TV down so we could talk. "It's easier to say what you shouldn't do than what you should. You shouldn't make each other promise anything—that you won't see other people or fall in love with anyone else. You want Patrick to come back to you because he *wants* to, not because he said he would. And you don't fill your letters and phone calls with woeful tales of how much you miss him or whine about how boring your life is without him. He doesn't want to come back to that. Tell him about all the exciting things you're doing, places you're going, books you're reading, people you're meeting. He wants to come back to somebody interesting, not boring."

I was barely chewing my brownie. I'd done a lot of whining and wailing already about how much I'd miss him, and here he was, going to Spain!

"I don't know if 'Life on the Bay' can equal 'Life in Barcelona,'" I said.

"It will if you're on the lookout for adventure. Use the time he's away to really broaden yourself, try new things. You've already made a good start."

"I'm thinking about going to visit him in Spain, if I can save enough for the plane ticket."

"*There* you go!" said Les. "Now, that's positive thinking."

I divided the second brownie and gave him half. "Thanks, bro," I said. "You're a good listener." I took my glass out to the kitchen, then picked up my bag and said, "Dad says to sign the three places he's marked on that insurance policy. But *read* it first, he says. You can get it back to him next week."

"Will do," Les told me, and I went on outside and down the steps. The full moon made my shadow on the path to the street. It was only when I fumbled for my car keys that I realized I'd left my jacket back in the apartment. That was exactly the hoodie I needed for my summer job. I retraced my steps across the lawn and had just reached the evergreen at the bottom of the outdoor staircase when I heard footsteps coming down and a man's voice saying, "Be good, Andy, but not too good."

I paused.

Andy's voice: "Hey, Bob, aren't you forgetting something?"

"Oh, yeah," the guy named Bob said. "Sorry."

A couple more footsteps. Another pause. I wasn't about to go on up in the middle of this.

Andy's voice again: "This is only a fifty."

"Well . . . listen, I don't have any more on me."

"Come on, Bob. I gave you the full treatment. I did everything."

"Honest! Here. Check my wallet."

"We've been through this before."

"Aw, I'll get it to you, Andy. I'm just—"

"No, you won't. Don't call me again. No more jobs. That's final."

And then the guy saw me.

"Uh . . . company," he said over his shoulder, and came on down, passing me at the bottom of the steps.

Andy moved out a little farther on the second-floor landing so she could see me, and we stared at each other for a couple of seconds.

"Oh, Alice, hi," she said. And then, "Just a business transaction, sweetie. Students always claim poverty, you know."

I didn't like the patronizing tone in her voice. I didn't like being Alice the Innocent, lectured by Woman of the World. I headed back to the car and sat behind the wheel hyperventilating. At last I turned on the engine and headed home. I could pick up my jacket another day.

I'd intended to call Les when I got home and tell him what I heard on the stairs, but Pamela called and wanted me to check out some new prom photos on Facebook. And when I finally remembered to call Les, he didn't pick up. So I went to bed.

Around noon on Sunday, I reached him and said I wanted to stop by again—I'd left my jacket.

"How about right now?" he said. "I want to show you something."

I wondered what that could be as I drove back to Takoma Park. Show-and-tell, that's what, not that what I had to tell was all that conclusive. Andy could have loaned this friend some money and he was supposed to pay her back. She could have bought something for him, and he'd forgotten to pay her.

I pulled up in front of the big yellow house with the brown trim and climbed the side steps.

"Come on in!" Les yelled when I knocked, and I opened the door. He was coming down the hall in his stocking feet.

"I got up about fifteen minutes ago, and Paul's at the gym," he said. "Take a look at this."

Now what was Andy up to? I wondered as he opened the door to her room. Cautiously, I peeked inside. Then I stared. Except for the curtains and furniture, the room was empty. The dresser, the bookshelves, the desktop . . .

I looked all around before I spoke, as though Andy might be in the closet or something.

"When?" I asked.

"While I was asleep this morning, I guess. It's like the wind blew in and whisked her away. And just in time, because I got an e-mail from my friend at the U. He found the memo he was telling me about. Andrea Boyce has been a ghostwriter for more Maryland students than you could count. Her 'tutoring' consists of not just helping them write essays and term papers, she does the whole job, and charges accordingly. And she's good at it."

"So she's not a hooker?"

"Don't think so. Wasn't selling her body so much as her brain. My friend said they haven't been able to trace any of these students' essays to the Internet, but there were just little phrases that seemed to turn up often enough to let them know they were all being written by the same person. She's original."

"And this is a crime?"

"It's aiding and abetting cheating. Mostly it falls on the shoulders of the students who pass it off as their own work, but it's been worrisome enough that some professors have talked about grading almost entirely by test results, not essays, just to shut her down. It means that students who don't really know their subjects are passing their courses, and this reflects on the whole school."

"Did you tell her what you'd found?"

"Yeah, tried to. I knocked on her door around eleven last night and said, 'Andrea, we need to talk,' and she didn't answer. First time I'd called her Andrea—first time I *knew*—and that must have spooked her. This morning she was gone. No forwarding address."

Whoa! I couldn't believe it!

"You've been harboring a fugitive, Les!" I said excitedly. "Have you told Mr. Watts she's gone?"

"No. I've got to break it to him today. Thought I'd pick up some apricot strudel to take with me."

"And now you've got to rent her room all over again. Well, you have to admire her entrepreneurial spirit."

"Or not," said Les.

29
PRANK DAY

It was as though everything between prom and graduation had a good-bye tag on it—everything said, *This is your last* . . . The Ivy Day Ceremony (a guy from my history class was the poet and a girl from choir carried the ivy); the senior class gift to the school—(two more armchairs for our library); the arrival of our caps and gowns. . . .

If I thought I'd been busy with the play and homework and articles for *The Edge*, I'd had no idea what the last weeks of May would be like. Not only did I have to get through all my final exams while simultaneously doing all my packing for ten weeks of work on a cruise ship, but when I got back from that, I'd have only a few days before I left for the University of Maryland.

I was frantically going through my closet, my dresser drawers, my chest like a madwoman, tossing stuff into three different piles: "Keep," "Toss," and "Maybe." Every so often I'd have a change of heart and pull something out of the "Toss" pile and add it to the "Keep" pile or vice versa. It was the "Maybe" pile that grew higher by the minute, meaning I was only deferring the decisions until later.

"I hate to even suggest this," Sylvia said, looking in on me, "but since you'll be living only forty minutes away come fall, you'll be able to do a little of this on weekends once you start college."

"Don't even think it!" I wailed. "I need all the motivation I can get."

At school people were carrying their yearbooks around from class to class so friends could write sentimental, embarrassing, or crazy stuff in them no one else would understand. Luckily, I didn't have to show mine to Dad and Sylvia. Some of it they'd understand and approve: *To a talented girl who helped make* The Edge *what it is today: controversial. Phil.* And *To one of the best friends I ever had. You've got my shoulder to cry on whenever you need it if I can use yours. Hugs, Gwen.* From Pamela: *To Alice, the girl who can't wait to lose her V card. Pamela Jones.* Some people wrote the usual *HAGS* (Have a great summer) or *Yours till the chocolate chips.* I was taken aback when Sam wrote, *To the only girl I really loved.* But when I found out he wrote, *My love goes with you* in Jennifer Sadler's yearbook—another of his ex-girlfriends—and *A piece of my heart will be with you always* to the girl he was dating now, I decided that Sam was in love with love. I hope he goes into theater someday.

There were all these grad parties also—so many that there might be three or four scheduled on the same Saturday afternoon, a few more in the evening. I was picky about the ones I'd attend, and even then, I dropped in for maybe an hour at each one. I avoided the ones where people were most likely to be sloshed, went to the parties of my best friends, had a party of my own on a Sunday afternoon just so I could attend Gwen's that night. . . .

At one party Sam's cheeks were brighter than I'd ever seen them, and Liz and I were laughing at how red they got when he drank. "Hope he doesn't have another one," I said. "They'd pop." At Tim's the keg was disguised under a scarecrow costume. To reach the tap, you lifted the shirt, and that was a lot of fun.

I didn't go to Ryan's—it would just have been too awkward—but it still was a week of saying good-byes and forgiving faults and truly wishing everyone good luck.

At our school Senior Prank Day usually falls on a Thursday, the day before Senior Skip Day, when students take off en masse, many of them heading for the beach. Because the forecast for Friday was chilly and rainy, and I'd be on a cruise ship all summer, I decided to save my money and skip both school and the beach. Gwen, Pamela, and Liz planned to do the same. I wouldn't miss Prank Day, though. Usually a bunch of seniors put their heads together and come up with some big joke. But somehow, when we got to school on Thursday, a week before graduation, we knew this was going to be a day like no other.

Phil had got word of it first and had told us the jocks were in charge of Prank Day this year. He alerted the newspaper staff to take notes or photos for our last hurried edition of *The Edge*.

I was driving Dad's car, and as I approached the school, I could see the racing lights going around and around our school billboard like the lights on a marquee, and instead of our school's name, followed by the principal's, followed by the words *Spirit Week* or *Cheaper by the Dozen* or any of the other themes or productions we'd promoted, there was a huge full-color advertisement for Budweiser Light.

Drivers were already honking with amusement as they turned into the student parking lot, and I knew that Mr. Gephardt must have okayed this one, as it couldn't have been rigged up electrically without his consent.

What really made me laugh, though, was the big maple tree in the center of the circular drive, because it had been lavishly decorated during the night with bras and jockstraps, hanging from almost every branch.

So I entered the building knowing that almost anything could happen, and almost everything did. As the news traveled around that each athletic team had been assigned to pull one prank, we looked for signatures—a football was dangling from the billboard out front, and a bra on the maple tree had a softball in each cup, signed by members of the girls' softball team.

It was hard to settle down to anything like a normal school day, and at first, when we heard the microphone click on in homeroom for morning announcements, no one was paying attention. Then someone said, "Hey! Listen!" And suddenly everyone grew quiet.

There was something like a moan, followed by deep, heavy breathing and a husky male voice saying, "Oh, baby . . ."

Half the class was shrieking with laughter and the other half was saying, "Shhhh. Be quiet!"

We were all giggling, trying to figure out which guy and girl were doing the vocals. The breathless female voice said, "This . . . is your . . . morning . . . wakeup call, all you hot-blooded, hard-bodied dudes and chicks out there—(*oh, yes, baby, yes!*)—and [pant pant] we wanna give you . . . the news . . . of the . . . day." At this point we got a recording of bedsprings squeaking loudly and then the guy and girl moaning together, "Oh, yeeeeeessss!"

There was so much laughter, we could hardly hear what the daily announcements were. I guess most of the teachers were resigned to the fact that not a lot was going to be accomplished on Senior Prank Day because as the morning went on, some were already prepared with short documentary films to show in class or fun quizzes, played like a game show.

When we heard a commotion in the hall outside the conference room next to the office, we got there just in time to see a life-size blow-up doll in a black negligee being carried through the doorway on the hands of students, while our laughing but red-faced principal tried to explain to the budget committee why she had been lying on her side on the conference table. *See you around, big boy,* said a note tied to her toe, signed by the captain of the basketball team.

"This is wild!" Liz exclaimed when we found a couple of goldfish swimming in a bag of water submerged in the iced tea canister in the dining room, courtesy of the swim team.

"Who did the voices on the morning announcements?" everyone was asking, and it turned out to be one of the girls on the gymnastics team and a guy from tennis.

Things got even wilder that afternoon when the inflatable doll was found seated in a history teacher's chair when he entered and later in the chem lab. I think all the teachers had their eyes on the clock, waiting for the day to be over, but it didn't end the way everyone hoped.

It was still fun when someone looked out the window and saw that all the cars in the student parking lot had *For Sale* soaped on their windshields. But shortly after the last bell, we could hear a banging and rattling from the sophomore corridor, angry yells, and when I went to check, notebook in hand, I found that someone—many someones—had glued all the handles of the sophomore lockers in place. They wouldn't move up or down and the doors wouldn't open. Only a lucky few were able to get inside.

"I've got to get my bag, or I'll miss my bus!" one girl was yelling.

"My dad's waiting outside," said a guy. "Who the hell did this? I've got a dental appointment!"

Buses sat idling in front of the school, and the line of cars and buses grew longer, snaking out into the street and far down the block. Horns were honking. The day had gone so well—been so funny—and now . . . It was too late for the wrestling team to take back their mascot, a blue monkey with long arms, dangling from one of the lockers near the end of the row.

The only guy I knew on the wrestling team was Brian Brewster, so I went looking for him. We'd had a great story for our last issue of *The Edge*, and I hated to see it ruined.

"Brian!" I yelled when I saw him far down the hall, and I knew he'd heard because he half turned, then ducked into a restroom with two other guys.

I could hear them talking when I got up to the doorway.

"They *know*, man!" Brian was saying.

"You said one good yank," another voice protested. "Shit! I yanked one myself and the thing wouldn't budge. We've got Beck out there, Gephardt, the security guys. . . ."

I walked in and they stared. Two guys at the urinals quickly repositioned themselves until they could get their jeans zipped.

"You're right," I said. "The whole school's waiting."

Brian stared at me. "I tried it with epoxy on a basement cupboard at home," he explained. "Four good yanks and it opened. I don't know why these handles are so different."

"Whatever. Senior Prank Day is riding on this," I said. "Somebody needs to make a statement."

To his credit, Brian went out first, and the others followed.

Beck and Gephardt were furious, and so were a bunch of parents, car keys in hand.

"It wasn't supposed to be like this," Brian apologized. "We thought a good hard yank would do it. We really messed up."

"Yes, you really did!" one father yelled. "My son has a trombone in there and a lesson in ten minutes. Suppose you work on number 209. Chew it open if you have to, dammit."

Brian and another guy headed for that locker, but neither could get the handle to budge.

The maintenance supervisor came on the scene with a small can of acetone and a rag. He poured some on the rag and applied it to the door handle, trying to jiggle it up and down until at last the handle began to move. Finally the door opened. He handed the can and the rag to Brian. "Only a few hundred more to go," he said. "Come on down to the maintenance room and get some more acetone."

"None of you leaves until every locker is open," Mr. Beck told the wrestling team. "Then I want to see Brian in my office."

Why are there always a few, it seems, to ruin something for the many? It had been such a great day—probably the best Senior Prank Day in the history of the school. But epoxy had practically been poured down all the sophomore locker handles sometime that afternoon, Phil told me when he called that night, and it had taken until almost seven o'clock before they all had been unglued. Music lessons had been missed, jackets left behind, homework gone undone, car keys not retrieved. . . . Nobody was injured because of it, and nothing had been irreparably damaged—except, that is, the reputation of the wrestling team and the goodwill of the parents.

"So how do we write this up when we don't know the outcome?" I asked Phil. "Prank Day was going to make such a great story."

"Let's write two separate stories," he suggested. "We'll title the first story 'Best Senior Prank Day Ever'—you can write that one—and I'll do 'Except for This,' concentrating only on the wrestling team stunt."

Like all the other seniors, I took advantage of Senior Skip Day the next day, but I almost wished I'd gone to the beach, rain or not, because there was texting all day about Brian and the locker incident. One of the rumors was that he wouldn't get his diploma. And though Brian has never been one of my favorite people, he was still part of our "family"—and we didn't want to see that happen.

Some people, I know, self-destruct. They get just so far, so high, so popular, so famous that they eventually light the fuse that blows them up. Maybe Brian was one of those people. Maybe he would always test the limits. Go one step further than he knew he should. We'd thought the car accident he'd been in last year might change him, but it didn't look as though it had.

But Friday night I got the news. Phil called. "It's over," he said. "We can print an end to our story."

"What happened?"

"Brian and every member of the wrestling team showed up

this morning in Beck's office. They asked if they could work the whole day helping out in maintenance, whatever needed doing around the building, to help make up for the epoxy incident."

"None of those seniors skipped?" I asked, incredulous. "I'd heard the whole team was going to Ocean City for Memorial Day weekend."

"They were, but they didn't. They stuck together to help out their captain and didn't leave for the beach till a little while ago. Beck took them up on their offer, the maintenance supervisor put them to work, and six hunks working eight hours got a lot of stuff done, I heard. On Tuesday, after we all get back, the sophomores will find a letter of apology in their lockers from the wrestling team, and Brian's cleared for takeoff."

30

ANYTHING COULD HAPPEN

It was Dad who found the printout on the coffee table.

"Al?" he said. "What *is* this?"

It was four days until graduation, and I had just looked out the window to see if anyone was hiding in the bushes.

Dad read a paragraph out loud: "'No killing during school hours. No killing on school days within a block radius of school. To and from grad parties you *can* be killed, but not at your own. . . .'"

"Relax already," I said, laughing. "It's a game. The seniors are playing Assassins. We only use foam darts, and it's a blast."

I don't know who thought this up. Other schools have played it, I know, but 156 of our seniors signed up for it on Facebook, and Drew Tolman was appointed record keeper.

Over Memorial Day each of us had put five dollars in the pot, and Drew divided us up into thirteen teams of twelve each. He was the only one who knew who was on what team and what names were on each other's hit lists. Each of us bought our own NERF dart gun, and as soon as you "killed" someone, you had to text Drew with a cryptic message, like: *Jane Doe shot Charlie Smith @ 7:32 p.m.*

When Dad was convinced that nobody was going to get hurt and that everything took place out of school hours, he said he'd leave it to my own common sense. But we had our own rules:

No killing @ work—going to and from OK.
No killing @ church, synagogue, or any other religious-affiliated event.
No killing at school-related events, practices, or games. Going to and from is OK.
No killing inside someone's house unless invited in by a family member.
No shields. If you are hit anywhere once, you are dead.
DO NOT bring your gun inside school. This is not affiliated with school.
DO NOT shoot at point-blank range and hurt someone.

The rules went on and on. The thing was, you had to keep your hit list secret. Most of my friends had signed up, and none of us had any idea which person or team had our names on their list. You could offer someone a ride home, and the minute he got in your car, he could shoot you. Once you left the one-block radius outside of school, you were fair game.

If you wanted to freak yourself out, you remembered that

someone was always out to get you. It could be your closest friend. A neighbor or a person you hardly knew. The school population came from all over Silver Spring and Kensington. The only people on my list that I knew well were Pamela, Phil, and Sam, and I figured Pamela would be the easiest to shoot. But I couldn't give myself away.

Dad said I could use his car for the rest of the week so I could get to school early and park in the student lot. A block away, and I'd be a target for the assassins. Teachers had lived through this before, evidently, and put up with our furtively checking our cell phones to see if anyone else had been zapped. The team that scored the most hits got to divide the pot—sixty-five bucks for each of the twelve players.

We broke into laughter when we got to history and the teacher started class by pulling out a NERF gun and shooting a dart at the clock. Then he announced that we could spend the whole class time talking about current events. How did we feel about gun control, for example? Who should be allowed to buy assault rifles? How was it that anyone could buy a gun at gun shows? And for the next forty minutes, we forgot we were assassins and concentrated on something with a little more depth.

Gwen hadn't signed up for the game and thought we were out of our minds to spend so much time at it, with all we had to do. Jill and Justin hadn't signed up either. They walked the halls with their arms around each other, and I think Jill was a little annoyed that they weren't the chief topic of conversation any longer.

As soon as school was out on Tuesday, I got in the car. People were ducking behind walls, aiming at friends who were running toward their cars farther down the street. I went straight home, then sat in the car, scrutinizing the territory before I made a mad dash for the house.

That night Liz called and asked if she could come over for a minute. Immediately, I was suspicious.

"What for?" I asked.

"I want to show you something," she said.

"Uh . . . no," I answered. "Show me at school tomorrow."

"What's the matter with *you*?" she demanded.

"I know what you're up to," I said, laughing.

"You're not on my list! Honestly!" she protested.

"Yeah, that's what an assassin would say," I told her.

"It's a picture of the haircut I want for summer," she said. "I want your opinion."

"Tomorrow," I said. "It can wait."

"You're no fun," said Liz, and hung up.

Things were getting really wild at school. The longer it took an assassin to find me, the more nervous I got. I'd had to get to school even earlier Wednesday to find a space at all, but Pamela hadn't been so lucky. I was just pulling out of the student lot at the end of the day when I saw her running down the street toward her dad's car at the corner. Someone was chasing her.

I pulled alongside.

"Pamela!" I called. "Hurry! Get in!"

She gave a little shriek as the gunman fired but missed, and as he reloaded, she made a dash for my car and collapsed in the seat beside me, locking the door.

"Saved!" she screamed happily to the guy who rushed the car and tried to get in, then walked away. But when Pamela turned to thank me, she was looking at my NERF gun pointed at her leg.

"You dog!" she screamed, trying to grab it from me, but I got her, and we were both yelping with laughter, even though she claimed she was crippled forever.

"What are friends for?" I said, and pulled slowly into traffic.

When Gwen picked me up later to go to her house—I wanted to see the bag she'd bought for the cruise ship, the bag with the zillion pockets—I sat on the floor of the backseat and didn't get out till the car was in her garage. I even wondered if someone had bribed her so they could assassinate me at her place, but I'd been desperate to get out for a while.

"Wouldn't it be easier just to die and get it over with? Then we could talk about packing," she said.

"Hey, I got through the first two days. I like living dangerously," I told her.

I shouldn't have stayed so long at Gwen's, though, because when I got home and looked at the stuff yet to sort, I was more conscious than ever of how little time I had left to pack. We'd be leaving for the Bay at noon.

I'd been listening to music while I decided what underwear to take and how much when Sylvia called from below. "Alice, Ryan's here to see you."

Ryan? I thought we were over. I thought he knew it. I stood there with a bra in one hand, pants in another. Was it possible he hadn't seen me at the prom with Patrick? And suddenly I realized that Ryan was playing Assassins too.

"Can he come up?" Sylvia called, waiting.

"Don't let him in!" I screeched, wondering where I'd left my NERF gun. But he wasn't on my hit list, so even if I shot him, he wasn't officially dead.

"What?" cried Sylvia.

I heard Ryan laughing. "Sorry about this," he said, and I realized he already *was* in. And then I heard rapid footsteps on the stairs. I screamed and ran into Dad and Sylvia's bedroom, their walk-in closet.

Dad and Sylvia were laughing too down on the landing as Ryan went slowly from room to room saying, "Might as well give up, Alice! I know you're here!" like a stalker in an old Hitchcock movie. My heart was pounding anyway.

When I heard him walking around in Lester's old room next door, I sprang for the bathroom and managed to lock the door just as his hand grabbed the knob.

"Too late!" I yelled. "So, so sorry!"

He was laughing then. "There's always tomorrow!" he said.

"Need any help up there, Al?" Dad called.

"I'm not coming out till he's gone and the front door's locked behind him," I said.

"I know when I'm licked," Ryan said. "And . . . by the way, Alice, you looked great at the prom."

"So did you," I told him, "but I'm still not coming out."

When he was gone at last and Sylvia assured me I was safe, I opened the door and collapsed on the pile of underwear on my bed, which I suppose Ryan had seen.

"How am I going to get through school tomorrow?" I said, still breathless. "I'm a marked woman!"

Sylvia sighed. "I'm so glad I don't teach high school," she said.

I'd only made one hit, and that was Pamela. I knew now that Ryan was gunning for me, but there would be others, too. I felt quite sure I wouldn't make it through the day without getting zapped, but I wanted at least one more notch in my belt before the game was over.

So on Thursday, I got up at five thirty, ate a piece of toast, and drove to Phil's house in Kensington. We'd been there once for a newspaper party, and I parked on a side street. Phil's house was on a cul-de-sac, only one way in and out.

It was six twenty-five, and I doubted he'd be leaving for school before seven. I dropped the car key in my jacket pocket, made sure my dart gun was loaded, then walked stealthily from tree to tree until Phil's house came into view.

I stopped and reconnoitered. There was a large lilac bush on one side of the front steps but not the other. To hide behind it, I would have to come in from the other direction. I would have to follow a neighbor's hedge to the backyard, then cut over into Phil's and come around from the other side. There was no garage and two cars were parked in the driveway, so I felt quite sure that this was the door Phil would use.

Checking to see if there was any activity in the neighbor's house, I entered their yard, hurried along their side of the hedge, head down, until I reached an open space in the backyard.

I ducked behind the toolshed in the neighbor's yard, behind the toolshed in Phil's, stood for a while behind the trunk of a large poplar at one side of the yard, then zipped around to the other side of the house, finally edging up to the lilac bush by the front steps, my heart beating wildly.

At any moment I expected a window to open and someone to call out. But nothing happened. A car went by on the street, and the driver didn't even look my way. Far off in the distance, a dog barked, then stopped. I waited, NERF gun in hand.

It's harder to hide behind a lilac bush than you might think. It's not thick, like a hedge, and the branches go every which way. The ground was wet from an overnight shower, and my shoes sank down a little in the bare earth.

What if I had miscalculated and Phil had gone to school early? It was Thursday, the day we usually distributed the newspaper, but this week it was coming out one day late to get in all the news. Still . . . What if he was cleaning out old files, getting ready for the new staff that would take over in the fall? It was hard to think of someone else putting out the newspaper, someone else being in on all the news and gossip, a new set of bylines showing up weekly.

I looked at my watch. I'd been standing there in the semi-mud for eleven minutes and it seemed like half an hour. I wondered if anyone was looking out a window overhead. A blue jay scolded me from a Japanese maple in the front yard. I was probably standing too close to its nest.

"Sorry. I'm not moving," I said under my breath.

Six fifty-eight. Phil had to come out soon if he had any hope of making first period, but then, probably half the seniors were sleeping in today. Tomorrow was graduation. We had it made.

Suddenly a voice behind me said, "Die, scum!" and I felt a little thump on my back. I wheeled around, and Phil was standing there grinning at me, his NERF gun in hand, a foam rubber dart on the ground beside me.

"Awwwwwk!" I screamed as I heard neighbors laughing from the porch next door, and Phil took out his cell phone: "Alice McKinley killed by Phil Adler at six fifty-nine a.m." he said aloud as his thumbs texted the message.

"I can't believe this!" I cried. "How did you know I was here? I was so careful."

"Neighborhood Watch Program," he joked. "Two different neighbors called and said there was a suspicious-looking girl lurking around my house, gun in hand. They relayed your every move."

"So I was on your hit list and you were on mine?"

"Looks that way," he said.

As it turned out, another team got the most hits, and each of those members got sixty-five dollars each, but I had more than my five bucks' worth of fun.

"Do you think we'll have this much fun in college?" Liz asked as we skipped one of our afternoon classes to wander around the school, saying good-bye to favorite teachers, our counselors, the security guys, even Mr. Beck and Mr. Gephardt. We were about to be has-beens, and we weren't too sure how we felt about it.

"We're going to try," I said.

And then . . . it was graduation. Each senior had been given four tickets, and I was astonished when my cousin Carol arrived at our house a few hours before we left for Constitution Hall.

"Carol!" I screamed. "Omigod! I had no idea! You came all the way from Chicago to see me graduate?"

"How could I possibly miss it?" She laughed, both of us knowing that even our closest, dearest family members had mixed feelings about sitting through a two- or three-hour ceremony. Then she told us that when her husband found out he had to be in Washington for a hotel conference, she called Dad and asked if there was any chance she could come to my graduation. "And a ticket miraculously appeared! So I get to sit with Les," she said.

I think Carol will go on looking glamorous well into her nineties. With Dad in his best suit and tie, Sylvia in a blue silk two-piece dress, Carol in a coral polka-dot top and black skirt, and my hunk of a brother in a brown shirt and yellow tie, I felt as though I were descended from royalty as I spotted my clan when I walked in during the processional, cap jauntily placed on one side of my head, the tassel flicking against my cheek.

All of us clapped like crazy when Gwen gave the valedictory. She thanked our parents for all they had done for us and said that graduation was a fork in the road in many ways, but we would be choosing the best parts of our parents to take along with us on life's journey, leaving the rest behind, as each generation must do. And it was this fork in the road, this choosing, these choices, that would, hopefully, make the world a better place.

And then, after the speeches and honors, the music and tributes, after all the names had been read and we'd received our diplomas, we tossed our caps wildly in the air.

Some had taped words on the top of their caps; some had special symbols to help their relatives spot them in the crowd. I don't think I believe in heaven, but I believe in eternal love. I had taped I MADE IT, MOM on the top of my cap, and I threw it as hard and as high as I possibly could, so that if Mom, wherever her spirit was, could see or sense it, she'd know I'd gotten this far. Then we marched back out into the June sunshine, holding whoever's cap we had managed to catch, and . . . it was over. We were leaving the nest.

Some of us would stick around our families all summer. Others would travel. Many would begin a summer job, and some, like Gwen and Liz and Pamela and me, would be combining work and travel. Ten weeks of dawn-to-dusk work on the Chesapeake Bay.

"Do we really want to do this?" Pamela murmured as we posed for pictures after the ceremony.

"Take pictures?" I asked.

"Clean people's toilets for ten weeks?" she said. "Wait on tables? Change linens? Get up at five every morning?"

"Well, don't we want to sit out on the deck and let the breeze blow our hair?" I answered.

"Don't we want to visit all the little towns and shops on the eastern shore?" said Gwen.

"Don't we want to meet *guys*?" said Liz.

"Smile, everybody. Say 'guys,'" said Les.

"Guys!" we all cried together, and summer, for us, had begun.

How it would end, I didn't know. As we were all so fond of saying, anything could happen.

Alice on Board

For Grace and Tess Meis,
who love books

* * *

With special thanks to Drew Godfrey
for his help and nautical knowledge

Contents

1

THE *SEASCAPE* AND THE *SPELLBOUND*

The ship was beautiful.

Of course, since none of us had been on one before, almost any ship would do. But this one, three stories of white against the blue of a Baltimore sky, practically had our names on it. And since it would be our home for the next ten weeks, we stood mesmerized for a moment before we walked on down toward the gangway, duffel bags over our shoulders. The early June breeze tossed our hair and fluttered the flags on the boats that dotted the waterfront.

This might possibly be our last summer together, but no one said that aloud. We were so excited, we almost sizzled. Like if we put out a finger and touched each other, we'd spark. We needed this calm before college, this adventure at sea.

Pamela had received a half-scholarship to a theater school in New York; Liz was officially accepted at Bennington; Yolanda was undecided; and Gwen and I would be going to Maryland. But right now the only future we were thinking about was that wide span of open water ahead of us.

"Which deck do you suppose we'll be on?" asked Liz in her whites. She looked like a sailor already.

"Ha!" said Gwen, the only one of us whose feet remotely touched the ground. "Dream on. I don't think we'll even have portholes. We're probably down next to the engine room."

"What?" exclaimed Yolanda, coming to a dead stop.

"Relax," Gwen said, giving her arm a tug. "We're not paying customers, remember. Besides, the only thing you do in crew quarters is sleep. The rest of the time you're working or hanging out with the gang."

"With *guys*!" said Pamela, and that got Yolanda moving again.

It's a wonder we were still breathing. Five hours earlier, four of us had been marching down an aisle at Constitutional Hall for graduation. And when picture-taking was over afterward, we had stripped off our slinky dresses and heels and caps and gowns, pulled on our shorts and T-shirts, and piled into Yolanda's uncle's minivan, which had been prepacked that morning for the mad dash to Baltimore Harbor. The deadline for sign-in was three o'clock. Yolanda had graduated the day before from a different school, so she was in charge of logistics.

It wasn't a new ship. *Completely refurbished*, our printout had read. But it was a new cruise line with two ships—the *Seascape* and the *Spellbound*, though the *Spellbound* wouldn't be ready till fall. The line sailed from Baltimore to Norfolk, with ports in between. The only reason all five of us were hired, we figured, was that we got our applications in early. That, and the fact that when we compared the pay to other small cruise lines along the East Coast, this line offered absolutely the lowest of the low. But, hey! Ten weeks on a cruise ship—a pretty glamorous end to our high school years!

A guy in a white uniform was standing with legs apart on the pier, twirling a pen in the fingers of his left hand. A clipboard rested on the folding chair beside him. The frames of his sunglasses curled around his head so that it was impossible to see either his eyes or eyebrows, but he smiled when he saw us coming.

"Heeeeey!" he called.

Pamela gave him a smart salute, clicking her heels together, and he laughed. "Pamela Jones reporting for duty, sir," she said as we neared the water. Flirting already.

"I'm just one of the deckhands," he told us, and checked off our names on his clipboard. JOSH, his name tag read. "Where you guys from?"

We told him.

"Silver Springs?"

"Singular. There was only one," Gwen corrected.

He scanned our luggage. "Alcohol? Drugs? Inflammables? Explosives?"

"No . . . no . . . no . . . and no," I told him.

"No smoking on board for crew. They tell you that?"

"Got it," said Liz, then glanced at Yolanda. We're never quite sure of anything with Yolanda.

"Okay. Take the port—that's left—side stairs down to crew quarters, then meet in the dining room for a late lunch. Follow the signs. You'll get a tour of the ship later."

We went up the gangplank, and even that was a thrill—looking down at the gray-green water in the space between ship and dock. Now I could *really* believe it was happening.

On the wall inside, past the mahogany cabinet with the ornate drawer knobs, was a large diagram of the ship, naming the major locations—pilothouse, purser's office, dining room, lounge—as well as each of the four decks: observation deck, at the very top; then Chesapeake deck; lounge deck below that, and main deck, where we were now. Crew quarters weren't even on the map.

A heavyset guy in a T-shirt and faded jeans, carrying a stack of chairs, called to us from a connecting hallway, "Crew? Take the stairs over here," and disappeared.

"How do you know what's port side if the ship's not moving?" I asked, confused already.

Nobody bothered to answer because we'd reached the metal stairway, and we hustled our bags on down.

Gwen was right; we had no porthole.

There were five bunk beds in the large cabin—large by shipboard standards, they told us. Ten berths in all, and other girls had already taken three of the lower berths. We claimed the remaining two bunk beds, top and bottom, and Gwen volunteered to sleep in the empty top bunk of an unknown companion.

"Ah! The graduates!" said a tall girl with freckles covering her face and arms and legs. She looked like a speckled egg—a pretty egg, actually. "I'm Emily." She nodded toward her companions. "Rachel and Shannon," she said, and we introduced ourselves.

"First cruise?" Rachel asked us. She was a small, elflike person, but strong for her size—the way she tossed her bags around—and was probably older than the rest of us, mid-twenties, maybe.

"We're green as they come," Liz answered.

"Same here," said Shannon. "I'm here because I'm a smoker."

We stared. "I thought there was a rule . . . ," Pamela began.

"There is. I know. I'm trying to kick the habit. Compulsory detox. I figure it will either cure me or kill me."

"Or drive the rest of us mad," said Rachel. And to us, "She's a dragon when she doesn't have a cig." She looked at Shannon. "Just don't let Quinton catch you if you backslide."

"Who's Quinton?" I asked.

"The Man. The Boss. You'll see him at lunch"—Emily checked her watch—"in about three minutes. I worked under him on another cruise line a couple of years back, so I know some of the people on this one."

"What's he like?" asked Gwen.

"Pretty nice. He's fair, anyway."

The last two girls arrived. The younger, Natalie, had almost white-blond hair, which she wore in a French braid halfway down her back, and then there was Lauren, with the body of an athlete—well-toned arms and legs. Only three of the girls had worked as stewards before—Rachel, Emily, and Lauren. And out of the ten of us, Lauren and Rachel seemed to know the most. Rachel, in fact, was a wellspring of information, the kind of stuff you never find in the rule books. Like Quinton's favorite drink when he was onshore—bourbon on the rocks—and how to keep your hair from frizzing up when you were at sea. She chattered all the while we put our stuff away, cramming our clothes in the three dressers provided. We'd been warned about lack of space, and I'd managed to bring only my duffel, my cloth bag, and the new laptop I got for graduation.

So here we were—ten women in a single room with a couch, a TV, and a communal bathroom next door. The walls were bare except for notices about safety regulations, fire equipment, the dress code, and various prohibitions: no smoking aboard the ship; no food or alcohol in crew quarters; no pets of any kind; no cell phones when on duty; no men in the women's cabin and vice versa. . . .

Welcome aboard.

The first thing we did was eat—on crew schedule, as I'd come to learn—and we were starved. I guess they figured that "stews," as we were called, would pay more attention in training later if we were fed. There were thirty of us in the dining room, counting the chef and his assistant—ten female stewards, ten male stewards, and eight male deckhands. We sat down to platters of hamburgers, potato salad, fries, and every other fattening food you could think of.

"Don't worry," Rachel told us. "You'll work it off. That's a promise."

But we weren't doing calorie counts as much as we were working out the male-to-female ratio. All the ice cream we could eat, guaranteed not to settle on our thighs, and two guys to every girl? Was this the ideal summer job or what, lowest salary on the Chesapeake be damned!

The guys, who had come in first, were grouped at neighboring tables, and we could tell from their conversation that most of the deckhands were seasoned sailors, older than the rest, who had worked for other cruise lines in the past. They were undoubtedly paid a lot more than we were. A couple wore wedding bands.

"I just decided to ditch my theatrical career and devote the rest of my life to the sea," Pamela breathed, after a muscular guy in a blue T-shirt grinned our way.

"Yeah, and what will you do in the winter months when the ship's in dry dock?" Lauren asked her.

Pamela returned the guy's smile. "Three guesses," she said.

I tried to imagine what this dining room would be like in two days' time when passengers came on board. The large windows spanning both sides would be the same, of course, but I'd seen pictures on the cruise line's website of white-clothed tables with sparkling glassware and candles. It must have been a special photo shoot, because this ship hadn't sailed before—not as the *Seascape*, anyway. Still, I bet it would be grand.

Quinton came in just as the tub of peanut butter ice cream was going around for the second time. We'd met Dianne, his wife, when we'd picked up our name tags. She did double duty as purser and housemother, Rachel told us, but it was Quinton who called the shots.

He looked like a former basketball player—so tall that his head just cleared the doorways. Angular face, with deep lines on either side of his mouth—the sort of person who always played Abraham Lincoln in grade school on Presidents' Day. Dianne was as short as Quinton was tall, and it was hard not to think of her—with her curly hair and the bouncy way she carried herself—as his puppy.

"Welcome, everyone!" Quinton said. He had a deep, pleasant voice and the look of a team player, standing there with his shirtsleeves rolled up to the elbows. "Glad to have all the new men and women on board as well as you old salts who have worked with Dianne and me on other cruises."

He gave a thumbs-up to two more guys who'd just come in, still in their paint clothes.

"This will be a first for all of us, though, as the Chesapeake Bay *Seascape* takes her maiden voyage," Quinton continued, "the first, we hope, of a long and successful run on the bay. This fall her sister ship, the *Spellbound*, will be launched. Dianne and I are from Maine, but we've both worked and played on the Chesapeake and are familiar with all that the bay and the eastern shore have to offer. . . ."

There were lots of handouts—work schedules and tour itineraries, names of officers and crew. There were lists of nautical terms—*abaft, bridge, gangway, starboard;* another list of emergency procedures—*fire, man overboard, abandon ship;* and Quinton and Dianne took turns doing the rundown.

"There are no days off, no vacations," Dianne reminded us, "though you'll get two or three hours of downtime in the afternoons and occasionally an evening out at one of our ports of call. You are going to be asked to work harder, perhaps, than you have ever worked before; you will have more rules regarding your appearance and behavior than you've ever had to follow. . . ."

I thought of all the requirements posted on the wall of women's quarters—*earrings no larger than the earlobe; clear polish on the nails; hair worn back away from the face, especially for servers at mealtime.*

"And for every minute you are in the public eye," Dianne continued, "you are required to be friendly and professional, even though, at times, you may be faced with the appalling conduct of a guest."

We gave each other rueful smiles.

Quinton did the closing remarks: "Remember that you are in a unique situation. You'll be living in close quarters, eating and sleeping on odd schedules, and working ridiculous hours at low wages." General laughter. "But you'll make some good friends here, have some fun, and will, I hope, look back on this summer with pride and say, 'I signed on for the maiden voyage of the *Seascape*.' And now let's get to work."

* * *

The stewards were divided into three groups. The first group went off for a tour of the ship with the first mate, a toothy, good-natured young man named Ken McCoy. The second group was to go with Dianne for a demonstration of cleaning the state-rooms, as the passenger accommodations were called. The third group consisted of the stewards who'd worked on other ships before, and these went with Quinton to tour the galley.

To begin, all the inexperienced people were appointed housecleaners in the mornings, dishwashers and busboys at night. After we proved we were reliable and could get along well with the passengers, we would be able to wait tables at breakfast and lunch, pass out the next day's programs, and turn down beds at night. And after the third or fourth week, we could take turns on the most coveted shift—sleeping in a little in the mornings, going on laundry detail, and serving the evening meal. But even then, Dianne told us, no one would work more than a week at a time in the galley, because with setup before meals and cleanup afterward, it was exhausting.

The staterooms were about the size of small bedrooms—a dormitory room, maybe: twin beds, with a narrow aisle between them; a dresser with four drawers; a small desk and chair; a closet; a picture window; and a bathroom the size of two phone booths. To bathe, a passenger stood in the small space between sink and toilet, pulled the waterproof curtain in front of the closed bathroom door, and turned on the shower—over himself, the sink, the toilet, the works. That was why the toilet paper was in its own closed container.

"Wow!" said Natalie. "I hope this isn't the luxury suite."

We laughed, Dianne included.

"Actually," Dianne said, "all the staterooms are alike on this ship. The *Spellbound* is a larger ship with eight suites, but the Chesapeake line is trying to keep costs down to stay competitive."

Getting down to the nitty-gritty, we learned about cleaning products. How you always wore latex gloves and never used the same cloth or brush on the sink that you'd used on the toilet. You cleaned all the corners. You vacuumed under the beds. And you never, ever, opened a drawer or a bag or the medicine cupboard. Theft called for immediate dismissal. You'd be dropped off at the next port of call. Find your own way home.

We were each assigned a few cabins in a row of staterooms on the lounge deck, where the rooms opened onto a narrow outer walkway that went around the whole of the ship, as it did on the deck above. Only the main deck, where the dining room was located, had cabins with doors that opened onto an inner hallway—no wraparound walkway down there. Dianne went from room to room watching us work, making suggestions, giving her critique.

I knew how to clean a bathroom. You don't grow up in a motherless house with a dad and older brother and not learn how to help with everything there is to do. Even after Dad married again, he and Sylvia and I managed to keep the place clean ourselves, but I had heard Sylvia tell Dad that after I left for college, she was hiring a weekly cleaning service. Fair enough, he said, because she was working full-time too, just like him.

Dianne's only complaint about my work was that I was too slow.

"You'll have fifteen rooms to clean in about five hours, Alice," she said. "You can't take a half hour per room, but your work is excellent."

Great, I thought. If I never get hired as a school counselor, I can always clean the building. I wiped one arm across my sweaty face.

A sandy-haired guy named Mitch was cleaning the room next to mine and gave me a sympathetic look. "It's even slower when the passengers get here, they tell me. Then you've got shoes and bags and shaving stuff in your way." He was making hospital corners on the sheet he'd placed over the bed. No fitted sheets on the Chesapeake line. The flat sheets had to do double duty.

"How you making out?" I asked Pamela as we passed on the deck. She gave a soft moan. There was no time to pause and observe the Baltimore skyline or the two guitarists performing on a sidewalk of the Inner Harbor. If any part of my job in housekeeping was supposed to be fun, I hadn't hit upon it yet. But we were so incredibly lucky to have this job—that all five of us had gotten hired together.

We cleaned up the last remnants of dust and lint and grout that builders and decorators had left behind, and each stateroom would be inspected carefully, possibly cleaned again, when we were through. As the afternoon wore on, we began to find shortcuts, better ways of doing things. Dianne applauded each completed room and gave us a breather when she went to get more towels.

Shannon and I rubbed each other's backs as we leaned over the rail. She was a round-faced girl with blue eyes who reminded me of my friend Molly.

"Tell me I don't need a cigarette," she said as I massaged her shoulders.

"You'd like one, but you don't need it," I said. "How's that?"

"I don't know. I think this might have been a mistake—signing on here. Some people can quit cold turkey, but that's not me."

"Ever tried it before?"

"No."

"Then hold on," I said.

It was around six by the time our group finished the few trial rooms we'd been assigned. We knew that the rest of the cabins had to be cleaned the following day—because passengers arrived on Sunday and the *Seascape* sailed out that evening—but we didn't see how that was possible. We were already sore, muscles stretched from squeezing ourselves into tight places and from twisting to clean behind the toilets. Somehow the promised tour of the ship didn't seem as wonderful as it had before. All we wanted to do was to sit down.

But when we exchanged places with the first group and went back down to the dining room for fruit and cheese and crackers, we found ourselves ready to go ten minutes later. We followed Ken McCoy back to crew quarters on the lowest level and checked out the engine room, storeroom, laundry hold, machine shop. No daylight down there.

Then it was back up to the main deck and a tour of the galley.

The lounge deck, next flight up, where we'd been working, had a lounge at one end—a huge room with a wraparound couch at the bow, game tables, a bar, and a library along one side.

The Chesapeake deck above that was all staterooms, including the pilothouse and the captain's quarters. A row of mops and brushes outside the rooms marked where the first group was now learning the fine art of housekeeping.

But our favorite level was the observation deck at the very top of the ship, with deck chairs, a few exercise bikes, and a shaded area for quiet reading. I stood at the rail listening to the sound of the ship's flag flapping, and as I watched the gulls circling and calling, I thought of Patrick and wished he were here.

Why couldn't we ever do something really fun together—I mean, for more than a day? More than an evening? Why couldn't he have taken the summer off from his studies—just one lousy summer—and spent it with me?

We could sit up here after dark and watch the sky as the ship silently plowed the water; visit the ports of call when we had the chance, our arms around each other, my head on his shoulder. I knew I'd probably watch some of the others pair off—the usual summer romances—before the ten weeks were over. But I'd be alone.

In one more week Patrick would be on his way to Barcelona to help one of his professors finish a book. And he'd be there for the next four quarters, getting in his year of study abroad now instead of later. "After that, I'll be back to stay," he'd told me.

But "back" was the University of Chicago, not Maryland. Meanwhile, he'd be seeing the sights of Barcelona alone. Or not. It wouldn't be me at his side, in any case. We wouldn't be watching a sunset together or walking along a beach or taking day trips into the Spanish countryside.

I was overcome suddenly by a wave of . . . homesickness? . . . that immobilized me momentarily—the same kind of sadness or panic you get when you're on a sleepover for the first time or that sinking stomach-twisting anxiety you feel as a kid when you've wandered away from your parents in a department store.

It lasted only six or seven seconds, then receded, but it left me feeling vulnerable. *What was that all about?* I wondered. Patrick as parent? As home? Security? My breath was coming back, and I inhaled slowly. Gradually I tuned in to the conversation around me, as other stews were pointing out the aquarium, the baseball stadium, and Federal Hill onshore.

I gripped the railing and looked straight up, squinting into the late afternoon brightness, watching one solitary gull fly a huge oval above the ship, its wings barely moving, and wondered if it was enjoying its solitude or missing a mate.

2
PUSHING OFF

It didn't take the five of us long to realize that this wasn't anything like summer camp. As I lay on my bunk that night, my thighs and shoulders aching, the summer we had been assistant counselors at Camp Overlook seemed like kindergarten compared to this.

How could we possibly have thought we'd be staying up half the night, joking around with the guys? That somebody would pull out a guitar or even a banjo, and we'd sing and horse around? Two of the guys had appeared half dead when we took a dinner break at eight, and the rest of us lasted till eleven, with the full knowledge that for some of us, alarm clocks would go off at five thirty the next morning—the next morning and the one after that. Were we insane?

It was Shannon who actually said it: "I was *insane* to think I could go ten weeks without a cigarette. I'm practically clawing at my skin already."

"The first twenty-four hours are the hardest," Emily told her in the dark. "Hang in there."

I was already floating in and out of consciousness. I think I heard Liz say "good night." I think I heard one of the other girls humming along with her iPod. I definitely heard someone tell Shannon to shut up about cigarettes.

And then it was morning. Or the middle of the night. I couldn't tell, because there was no sunlight. Only the sound of our door opening, the glare of the fluorescent light in the hall, and Dianne's cheerful voice: "Everybody up. We've got a lot to do today." And we all wanted to kill her.

"Once you get into the routine, it's easier. Really," Dianne assured us as we took turns in the communal bathroom and pulled on our clothes. We tied our hair back, washed the sleep from our eyes, brushed our teeth, ran some ChapStick over our lips, and sat down with the guys for breakfast.

Dianne insisted we eat a big one. "You start work on a near-empty stomach, and halfway through the morning, you'll eat coffee grounds, you'll be so hungry," she told us.

Liz and I studied the steaming platter of scrambled eggs and sausage that was making the rounds, wanting to opt for half a roll and some orange juice instead. We each took a small spoonful of eggs to make Dianne happy, but she was right: By ten fifteen, I was ravenous. I'd cleaned three more rooms, polished the chrome, brought a load of towels up from the laundry hold, and scraped off a bit of paint that had dried on one of the floors. When Rachel told us there were doughnuts and coffee in the galley if we wanted a break, I felt I needed a doughnut as much as I needed air and headed for the stairs.

"My God, my hair!" Lauren said as we passed the mirrored wall on the lounge deck and stared at our early-morning selves—no makeup, no mousse. . . .

"We look like inmates of a women's prison," Pamela wailed.

Our only consolation was that we all smelled alike, I told her.

When we had our two-hour break that afternoon, we were tempted to go back to bed. Shannon, in fact, did—mostly to take her mind off smoking. But the rest of us showered and washed our hair, applied some blush and mascara, and just that little luxury restored our energy. Then we went up on the top deck, where the guys were gathered in the shade area—all but Barry, who loved the sun. Dianne had left a tall pitcher of iced tea for us, and we sprawled on the vinyl lounge chairs, welcoming the late-afternoon breeze.

It was the first time since we'd come on board that we had a chance to really hang out with the guys, and I found myself studying them one by one. The quiet, broad-shouldered guy who smiled mostly with his eyes was Mitch; the talkative one, Flavian, with his dark good looks, could have been an extra on a movie set; all of us liked Barry, who lay bare-chested, his feet pointed outward, on a chaise longue; Josh, probably a few years older than the others, who had sailed before with Quinton and Dianne and also knew the engineer; and Curtis, who wore a wedding band. They looked great in their black T-shirts and sweat-soaked bandanas, but I couldn't be sure who were deckhands and who were stewards.

We sat around discovering a few connections: One of Lauren's friends was Flavian's ex-girlfriend; Natalie and one of the deckhands had gone to the same high school and had had some of the same teachers. . . . Each connection brought out memories and wisecracks, and we were beginning to feel more relaxed. There's something about letting guys see you at your worst, as we were at breakfast, that makes you feel you can let it all out; you can tell each other anything.

Barry, in fact, was so relaxed—eyes closed, hands folded over his stomach—that he didn't see the gulls that were circling overhead. And when one dropped a load on his chest, a wide splatter of white, he thought one of us had pelted him, and he opened his eyes, frowning around the circle. We broke into laughter.

"What?" Barry kept saying. "*What?*" His hand went automatically to his chest. Then, "Shit!" as he held his hand out in front of him.

"Exactly," said Flavian, and we laughed some more.

Barry's feet came down on either side of the chaise longue, and he grabbed Flavian's shirt from the arm of a chair. With one quick swipe and a satisfied grin, he wiped his chest clean.

"Hey!" Flavian cried. "You moron!"

But Josh was laughing. "You gotta watch that guy. We only did one cruise together, and he was goofing off the whole time."

"Yeah? Who had your back when you went AWOL that time in Savannah?" Barry said, tossing the shirt over to Flavian. "Who got the number of that girl in Martha's Vineyard for you?"

"My buddy!" Josh said. "What would I do without you?"

I wiggled my bare feet and thought how much this reminded me of the banter between Patrick and Mark and Brian back in Silver Spring. Around Mark's swimming pool in the summertime. Back when Mark was still alive.

Josh turned to Mitch. "How early did you sign up for this job, Mitch?"

"Would you believe March?" Mitch said, stretching his long legs out in front of him. "Surprised they were still hiring, but they told me I'd be either a deckhand or a stew, whichever they needed most. Just call me 'Whichever.'"

That got a laugh.

"Man, I applied last November," said Barry.

"Yeah, he heard that Steph was going to be cruise director," Josh told us.

"Stephanie? Stephanie Bowers?" said Rachel. "I heard she got fired from that cruise line down in Jacksonville a couple of years ago."

Josh shrugged. "Just goes to show . . ."

Gwen and Yolanda, Liz and Pam and I sat smiling, just

listening, though we didn't really feel left out. *Must be nice to be part of the "in crowd,"* I thought. Maybe sometime, on some future cruise, Josh and Barry would sit around talking about us. Favorably, of course.

We worked like dogs the rest of the day. Frank, the middle-aged engineer, was aboard now, checking things out. Those of us who had spent all our time cleaning cabins were given a crash course in working the galley—scraping the plates and stacking the dishwasher. And for those assigned to clean tables, Dianne demonstrated carrying a fully loaded tray of dishes, including a pot of coffee, on the flat of her hand, one edge resting on her shoulder.

"I couldn't do that in a million years," I said to Rachel. "I'd drop it on a passenger, first thing."

"Here's a hint," she told us. "If that ever happens, sink to the floor and hold your ankle."

"What?" said Pamela.

"Moan a little, and all the sympathy will be on you," she told us. As I said, Rachel knew the most amazing stuff.

Before we turned in that evening, each of us was given two long-sleeved white dress shirts and black bow ties to wear when serving meals, to go with the black pants we'd been required to bring with us; two short-sleeved white shirts for serving breakfast or lunch; and two black T-shirts with SEASCAPE printed on them that we were to wear with shorts when we cleaned the rooms.

And once again, we fell into bed without any midnight party, almost too tired to dream.

I woke to an earsplitting alarm and sat up, startled, confused, my heart pounding, desperately trying to remember the instructions for what to do in an emergency.

"What the heck?" Pamela was saying, as murmurs filled the room.

"What time is it?" asked someone else.

I grabbed whatever clothes were handy, making sure to put on shoes. That much I remembered.

When we emerged on the lounge deck, sleep-befuddled and disheveled, dragging our life jackets behind us, the first vermilion of a sunrise appeared in the sky, and my watch said four fifty-five. I would discover, as the summer wore on, that the Chesapeake had some fantastic sunrises and sets.

Quinton was there timing us, and he frowned at those who forgot their life jackets and had to go back. We sucked in the fresh, cool air of early morning and swayed slightly as we stood in a row and finished waking up.

Ken McCoy and Dianne were also up and dressed, as though their morning had started hours before.

"This is the only emergency drill you'll get, other than the routine muster we do at the start of each new cruise," Ken explained. "So if the alarm rings again at an ungodly hour, you'll know it's the *real* McCoy."

He gave step-by-step instructions for putting on the life

jackets, and Dianne and Quinton went up and down the row, making sure each strap was secure. Dianne made me take mine off and put it on again before I passed inspection.

Next we were each assigned a specific spot on the ship where we were to report. Both Gwen and I got the lounge deck, starboard aft, or "LSA." In case of fire, report and listen for further instructions. If we heard the "Man overboard!" alert, we were to race to our designated places, scan the water for the missing person, and, if spotted, keep pointing to the spot, never taking our eyes off him, while the ship turned around and the passenger or crew member was rescued. If the order was given to abandon ship, we were given the specific staterooms that were in our care during a muster. Our job was to see that all passengers were safely out of their staterooms and had put on their life jackets correctly.

Various possibilities played out in my mind. What if a passenger was in the shower? On the toilet? Were we to go in and drag him out?

"Don't worry," Ken added at the end of his little speech. "One of us—Quinton, Dianne, or I—will be on each deck helping out." And then, before the session was over, we had to take partners, each of us removing our vest and putting it on again, checked by our partner.

This was a different kind of morning. It may have been Sunday in Baltimore—I heard a church bell ringing at seven—but at six thirty the deckhands were pushing carts across the dock and up to the hold of the ship, carts loaded with crates of Florida citrus, boxes of New York cheesecake, grapes from California, pasta and wine and flour and coffee. . . .

Quinton checked off each shipment, each crate, and as the morning wore on, all the activity brought locals and tourists down to the waterfront to watch. I began to feel we were onstage.

Once we had cleaned ourselves up and eaten breakfast, Quinton assigned us a place to stand when passengers began arriving that afternoon. A florist's truck pulled up with a huge bouquet of exotic flowers for the cabinet just inside the entrance on the main deck, and Dianne helped Ken set up a folding table for refreshments in the lounge.

"You'd think we were expecting the queen," I said to Emily as we passed each other in the hall.

"We're waiting for the captain," she said. "That's even more important."

I wondered if there would be sailors flanking the gangway when the captain arrived. Rachel and I were arranging napkins by the punch bowl, and the engineer was tinkering with an air-conditioning unit beneath one of the built-in couches that lined the wall at the bow. Frank had just stood up and slipped his tools in his belt when we saw a taxi unload a passenger on the street and watched the man in the white uniform pay the driver.

Frank walked over to the window and peered down. "What the bloody hell?" he murmured.

* * *

Whatever that was about, we didn't have time to debate. All we got from Josh, who knew Frank from other trips, was that it wasn't the captain we'd been expecting. Meanwhile, the crew was told to eat an early lunch; passengers would start boarding at one.

I put on my short-sleeved dress shirt and took my place just inside the entrance on the main deck. Already I could hear Ken greeting guests who were wheeling their luggage up to the gang-plank, welcoming them to the *Seascape*. My job was to check their boarding passes and direct them to their staterooms. There was no elevator, so folks who found stairs difficult had taken rooms on this level, where the dining room was located.

Most of the passengers came aboard smiling broadly, eager for the adventure, and that made the crew even more enthusiastic. It was sort of like being in a school play, the way the audience's reaction can energize a cast.

"This is so exciting!" a woman said to me, clutching her purse tightly under her arm as she came through the gangway. "It's my first cruise."

"Mine too!" I told her. And, checking her name tag, I said, "You're up the stairs and to your left, Mrs. Schield."

"I've never been on a maiden voyage before," a chubby man said, coming up next. "Every woman here a maiden?" And he winked.

Oh, brother! I thought. "Welcome aboard, Mr. Knott," I said cheerfully. "You're on the Chesapeake deck, two flights up, and your bags will be delivered shortly."

This was the day the deckhands dreaded, I could tell.

Though they wore their crisp white shirts and shorts, they were already wet with perspiration. They sprinted through the hallways, a bag in each hand, sometimes two, or another beneath an arm. They were running partly to deliver luggage in a hurry and partly to escape the passengers who stood in their doorways, calling that they were still missing a bag or that they'd been given the wrong luggage.

"Don't worry, we'll sort things out," I assured the man who had come back out of his room at the end of the hall. "We take good care of the bags."

The strap of his camera seemed to pull his neck forward, and he studied me a moment. "There better not be any smoking," he said. "My wife's allergic. They promised us there's no smoking in the dining room."

"That's right, Mr. Jergens," I told him. "She'll be fine."

Slowly the noise level rose as more and more people arrived, and the cartloads of bags coming down from the Renaissance Hotel were higher still. The deckhands worked relentlessly, while passengers were already exploring the ship, peeking in each other's rooms, standing in doorways to chat, and impeding the deckhands' progress.

"Would you like to go up to the lounge?" I kept suggesting. "There are refreshments in the lounge. . . . Would you like to meet the other passengers in the lounge? . . . Perhaps you could continue your conversation in the lounge over refreshments. . . ."

Josh looked at me gratefully as I got a boisterous group of four to head for the stairs.

There weren't any children, and we were glad of that. No pool equals no kids, someone said. And when I heard big-band music wafting from the sound system, I realized we had a shipload of retirees—empty nesters, anyway. Flavian appeared in the hallway, a monstrous duffel bag in one hand, two smaller bags in the other. His forehead glistened. He grinned as he passed, but I'll bet we were both thinking the same thing: ten one-week cruises, ten embarkings, ten disembarkings, bags up, bags down. . . . Emily had told us that the turnarounds were the worst—the weekends these passengers got off and a new crowd got on—no time at all to ourselves.

Everyone seemed in a friendly, festive mood, though—until, that is, a man in a cowboy hat came down the stairs and faced me: "The letter I got said there would be lunch, and all we can find up there is cheese and crackers," he said.

My mind raced through the day's program. No one was assigned to the dining room until dinnertime. Only Rachel and Barry, the afternoon's lounge attendants, were keeping the refreshment table replenished. Surely the man was mistaken.

"Lunch?" I said. "Oh, I don't think so. But—"

"It says *lunch*!" he insisted, reaching inside his jacket pocket for a piece of paper. He unfolded it and thrust it under my nose.

I took the letter and skimmed the lines: *Welcome aboard the Seascape . . . a thoroughly modern cruise ship . . . Passengers are invited to board from one o'clock on . . . a light lunch will be available in the lounge.*

"I believe there's also fruit and coffee . . . ," I began.

"That's not a lunch," he said. "Where's all that gourmet food they brag about? We got on a plane at eight this morning, and all we've had to eat is one damn bag of pretzels. We were expecting lunch, like the letter says."

"Let me go find out," I said, keeping the letter, and off I went to find Dianne.

I ran into Quinton instead.

"I hate to bother you," I said, "but the man over there says they were promised lunch." And I gave him the letter, signed by the company's president. I could see Quinton's jaw stiffen as he read it.

"I never okayed this," he said. "Never even saw it. You don't say 'lunch' when it's finger food, you say 'refreshments.'" He handed the letter back. "I'll have the chef send sandwiches to his room," he told me.

Everything was different with passengers on board. No slouching through the halls lugging a bucket, no sinking down in a deck chair to catch my breath, no letting my hair fly around my face or simply pulling it back without combing it first.

I was continually aware of my appearance, my posture. Was my shirt tucked in? Were my nails clean? Passengers continued arriving all afternoon. I had barely directed the last couple toward their stateroom when the obligatory muster took place.

A memo to each passenger announced that an emergency drill would be held before dinner, so when the alarm sounded, I raced to crew quarters, grabbed my life jacket, and went up to my assigned emergency post on the lounge deck. Passengers were coming out of their staterooms, orange life jackets dangling awkwardly from their hands. They joked with each other about manning the lifeboats or jumping over the rail.

I saw our cruise director for the first time—a thirty-something woman, forty, maybe. "Please listen carefully to our instructions and remain outside your staterooms, wearing your life jackets, until one of our crew checks you out," Stephanie Bowers said. People paid attention not only because of the megaphone she was using, but also because she was gorgeous. Her brown hair was shoulder length and streaked with gold, her eyebrows delicately arched, her shirt showed just the right amount of cleavage, and she wore a skirt that hugged her hips. "Place the life jacket over your shoulders, like so," she said, demonstrating with her own, "the opening in front. Now thread the black strap through the ring on your left side. . . ."

"Whatever you say, baby," I heard a man murmur.

I walked slowly along the line of passengers, Gwen coming at me from the other direction, assisting where we could. I couldn't begin to fit the puffy orange jacket around the body of an enormous woman who was already embarrassed by the effort, and I congratulated myself that I got the strap through the ring at all, laughing with her when she tried out the attached whistle for distraction.

The men, I discovered, did not want any help but seemed to have more trouble getting the straps right than the women. I was glad when Ken McCoy appeared on the scene and I could bypass the frustrated man with straps all going the wrong way.

Ken gave a two-minute talk on ship safety, then Stephanie took the megaphone again and said she would be making some announcements after dinner regarding the excursion schedule. And finally, when the all-clear signal was given, people gave relieved sighs, yanking off their life jackets and going back inside to stow them under their beds. I was happy too.

"Glad *that's* over," said Gwen, who somehow managed to look as elegantly put together as she had at the beginning of the afternoon. She and Yolanda had done each other's hair in elaborate coils before we'd started the trip, threading beads into them on either side of their faces.

Passengers were gathering at the rail now, and Gwen and I joined them. A crowd had collected on the dock below to watch the gangplank being lifted and swung onto the bow of the ship. Already we could feel the vibration of the engines.

Now two deckhands on the pier were unwinding the lines that held us to pilings—one at the bow of the ship, another at the stern. Looping the lines around their arms like a lasso, they tossed them into the hands of two sailors on deck, then made the leap from shore to ship. The engine noise grew louder still as the bow thrusters in the depths of the ship moved us slowly away from the dock.

People we didn't know waved at us, and we waved back. The wind in our faces grew stronger, the space between us and the dock grew wider. Then I heard Dianne saying, "Girls—galley duty, pronto," and we remembered we were part of the crew.

We headed downstairs to change into T-shirts and shorts, to spend the evening scraping plates and filling the dishwasher—course after course after course.

Pamela and Natalie had it easy that night—shadowing some of the more experienced stews to learn how to turn down the beds when the guests were at dinner; put a chocolate imprinted with an *S* on each pillow and a program of tomorrow's events, plus the weather forecast, beside it. Pull the blinds, turn on the bedside lamp. . . .

But Gwen and Liz and I were in the galley till ten thirty. I was glad I wouldn't be there every evening—the dishes and all that cleaning up of the dining room afterward. You'd be surprised at how much grown people can spill on the floor. I was wiped.

When we got off at last, smelling of grease and detergent, Gwen opted for a shower and sleep, but Liz and I needed to unwind, so we decided to go up to the top deck for twenty minutes to cool off.

We were climbing the narrow staircase from the Chesapeake deck to the observation deck when we heard Dianne's voice just above us. ". . . too big a hurry," she was saying. "That letter was just an example—people expecting lunch. *We're* the ones who take it on the chin! And not a word to us about what happened to Captain Sawyer. Not even Ken knew about the switch."

"We've put up with worse than this." Quinton's voice.

Liz and I should have left, but we didn't. We just stood there, frozen, on the stairs, our heads below floor level.

"One of the reasons we agreed to take this on was that we got to sail with Sawyer," Dianne persisted.

"Well, it's not in the contract, Dianne. We're here, the ship has sailed, we've got a captain, we *make* it work, that's all. Nothing says we have to sign up for their fall cruises."

Liz and I were already backing down the stairs when the conversation stopped. I don't know if they'd realized someone was listening or not.

3
MITCH

When we woke the next morning, we were already docked in Norfolk, with its huge shipping port and naval base. It was weird to go out on deck and find a completely different landscape from the one you saw the day before.

Another cruise ship, slightly larger than ours, was just leaving port, and a few early risers were already at the rail, watching it move away from the dock. It reminded me that we weren't the only cruise line on the bay. Most of the others, though, added New England and Nova Scotia or the Bahamas to their itineraries. But the *Seascape* and the *Spellbound*, according to Josh, wanted to be Chesapeake Bay exclusives, sailing spring, summer, and fall, and eventually getting the lion's share of the market.

I didn't have to be told to eat a good breakfast, and afterward I reported to the linen hold for clean sheets and towels, then set off for my block of fifteen staterooms. It was hard not to get distracted by the planes flying in now and then and by the submarine one of the guys detected, trolling the water a ways out.

I'd been instructed not to start cleaning until the bell rang for breakfast. Since passengers could go anytime between seven and nine, this meant keeping an eye out to see when people left for the dining room, so we could rush into those staterooms and clean them.

You learn a lot about people when you clean up after them. Some left their quarters immaculate—clothes hung up, toiletries neatly assembled in one place, towels folded, even though we'd replace them with fresh ones. Other people left their towels on the floor, slippers askew, bottles and tubes and jars scattered around the sink, and dirty laundry dumped in a corner.

Those of us who cleaned staterooms would have two hours or so off in the afternoon before beginning our evening stint clearing tables during the dinner hour and scraping dishes in the galley.

"Anybody want to tour a battleship?" Barry asked when Gwen and I returned our buckets later and were heading for the showers. He and Mitch were coming up from crew quarters, obviously ready to leave.

"A battleship's about the last thing on my wish list," Gwen said, "but go for it."

"Actually, it's a submarine," said Mitch, waving a printout from Stephanie.

"Some other time," I told them as we went on by. "There are nine more Norfolks to go. See you guys later."

It was when we were rummaging through the dresser for clean clothes that Gwen dropped the bombshell: "Just thought I ought to mention that Austin and I aren't a couple any longer."

The bra I'd picked up fell out of my hands, and I turned to stare at her. Austin—the big, thoughtful guy we'd met at a soup kitchen one summer when we volunteered, the person we'd all felt was so right for Gwen, maybe on and on into the future—was out?

"You broke up?" I couldn't believe it. "When did *that* happen?"

Gwen knew how we felt about Austin, about them as a couple, and that's probably why she didn't look at me when she answered. "I simply thought we should. I've got a lot of school ahead of me. You know that."

Liz came in just then, all gung ho to go see Norfolk in the little time we had. She reacted the same way I did to the news.

"*Why?*"

"You want us to get engaged? Is that it?" Gwen was beginning to lose patience with us both. She flung a clean shirt over her arm. "Liz, I'm not the same person I was eight years ago when I was going out with Legs. I may not be the same person in eight years that I am now."

Liz looked at her wide-eyed. "Who would you *be*?"

"Who knows? Maybe I'll go through six years of med school

and then decide to dump it all and raise chickens! Maybe I'll want to make up for lost time and see the world. How can I ask someone to wait for me when I don't even know what I'll want?"

We picked up our towels and followed her to the showers.

"So . . . breaking up was your idea?" I asked.

"I suggested it, yes, and finally he agreed. I said I couldn't stand the thought of him waiting for me all those years—didn't want that hanging over my head, going through an internship and residency."

We went in the shower room and put the OCCUPIED sign on the door.

"Well, it wouldn't be like he was just cooling his heels," I reminded her. "He has plans for his life, too."

"Yeah, but before he waits that long for me, or is insane enough to think we could get married when I'm up to my ears in books, he'd better be sure." Gwen took one of the showers, her voice rising above the sound of the spray. "We need to go out with other people, Alice. How else will we ever know?"

I guess I didn't want to hear that because I was thinking of Patrick and me.

When I was dressed, I looked around for Pamela to see if she wanted to go ashore with us. Josh said he'd seen her on the observation deck, so I went up there. She'd finished cleaning before we had, so she was probably ready.

I found her sitting on the side of a lounge chair, arms resting on her knees, holding her cell phone.

"What are you *doing*?" I said. "I thought you wanted to walk into town with us."

She sighed but didn't move. "I do."

I walked over to stand in her line of vision. "Problems?"

"Only one. My mother. What else?"

"I thought things had been going okay for her, Pamela. What's wrong?"

"Her love life."

"That really nice management guy from Nordstrom—the one you liked?"

"Yeah. I thought maybe that was going somewhere, and so did she. But he's pulling back. He's not as serious as she'd hoped."

"And she's dumping on you?" I sat down across from her but leaned forward to show that time was short, we needed to leave. What was this, anyway? Breakup Summer?

"Actually, she's told me very little about that, but she fell recently at her apartment," Pamela said.

"Oh no. Was she hurt?"

"Nothing major—her ankle. But you know what this probably means—she's drinking again." Pamela covered her face with both hands.

"You think so?"

"As sure as I can be without a blood test," she said through her fingers.

"What does she expect you to do? She knows you're on a ship all summer. Why is she telling you this?"

Pamela dropped her hands and gave me a resigned look. "Because I made the mistake of returning her calls. Besides, who else has she got to tell? They're all little asides, actually. She talks about her apartment and the shoes she's trying to find and how things are going at work, and then a sort of P.S., that George hasn't come around much lately, and did she mention she'd somehow missed a step leaving her complex, and even if she'd found the shoes, she couldn't try them on now because her ankle's so swollen? 'Nothing serious,' she adds."

I stood up and gave her shoulder a little tug. "Well, if she says it's nothing serious, then take her at her word and don't worry too much about it," I said. "If you have to worry, concentrate on Gwen. She broke up with Austin."

"What?"

"She doesn't want him to spend eight years waiting for her since she might change her mind by then."

Pamela's reaction was not what I'd expected. "Well, better now than later," she said. "Let's go see Norfolk."

The Captain's Dinner was held that night, beginning with a reception in the lounge. This and the farewell dinner at the end of each cruise were the two occasions when passengers dressed up.

The captain, Joseph Haggerty, and Ken McCoy, in their dress whites, stood at the entrance to the lounge. Frank, the engineer, stood next to Ken, then Quinton and Dianne and Stephanie. Guests came through the door and were greeted by

Stephanie first, who introduced them to the next person as the passengers moved up the line toward the captain. The rest of us, in our starched white dress shirts and bow ties, hustled back and forth, seeing that champagne glasses were returned to the galley.

When the miniature crab cakes and quiches were almost gone, we were instructed to fill the gaps with cherry tomatoes and stuffed mushrooms. When we ran out of these, we took the trays off the table and brought out the celery and carrots. I quickly learned that all the effort went into first presentations, and after that, we filled in with cheaper fare. But after the champagne, few of the guests seemed to notice.

Dianne was in a royal blue cocktail dress with a neckline that plunged just enough to be daring, while Stephanie wore a short black sheath that showed off her tanned arms and legs.

"Wow!" I murmured to Rachel. "The *Seascape* must have been lucky to get her for the cruise."

"It's the other way around," Rachel whispered back. "She comes with a history. Had an affair with a customer on another line and has been out of work for the past two years. All us career sailors know about it."

Hmmm, I thought. This maiden voyage was starting out with both a second-choice captain and cruise director? No wonder Quinton and Dianne were a little upset. I gave Captain Haggerty a good look. It was the first time I'd seen him up close. He was about five foot ten or so, late forties, had a somewhat cocky manner, and looked as neatly pressed himself—perhaps more so—as his uniform. His smile never left his face—just stretched and retracted a little with each handshake.

Ken McCoy made up for it with his toothy grin and infectious laugh, and his eyes searched each name tag as he introduced the guests to the Captain. Frank, bald and bespectacled, did his part patiently, fixing his eyes on each guest and welcoming them to the *Seascape* without overdoing it. Stephanie was too effusive by half, but Quinton and Dianne, a bit more reserved, were a nice counterpart to the others, their faces relaxed and friendly.

If there was any tension among the officers and crew, it didn't show. But those of us helping out at the reception didn't miss the fact that when the last of the guests had passed through the receiving line, the VIPs didn't stand around chatting with each other. Quinton and Dianne moved off immediately to mingle with passengers on the port side of the lounge, and Frank disappeared entirely. Only Ken and Stephanie stood with the captain making small talk until Ken, realizing they were alone in the doorway, touched Haggerty's elbow lightly and guided him over toward the champagne.

When Dianne gave the signal for us to head to the dining room ahead of the guests, we worked our way to the exit and went down a flight.

The menu for dinner each day was placed in the glass case next to the dining room. When I read the menu for that evening, I wished I'd eaten something before I'd reported for work: shrimp bisque with tomato and goat cheese crostini; rack of lamb with fingerling potatoes and asparagus; sea bass with truffles; chocolate lava cake with fresh raspberry sauce.

The bell chimed for dinner. I smiled at a bejeweled woman who was being escorted to her table by a slender man with a thin mustache, and I folded my arms over my stomach to stop the rumblings.

After the main course had been served and eaten and the dishes taken away, Captain Haggerty took the microphone and gave a brief welcome: "Good evening, ladies and gentlemen," he said. "I want to extend an especially warm welcome to all you wonderful people aboard the maiden voyage of the *Spellbound*." I paused at the galley door with a tray full of dishes as a low murmur ran through the crowd, and then the captain added hurriedly, "Well, *that* got your attention!" and he laughed a little. "The *Seascape*, of course."

"Doesn't know his ass from his elbow," Barry whispered as he came in after me, carrying a pot of coffee.

We could still hear the captain through the sound system in the galley: "I'm jumping the gun because the *Spellbound*, too, will be taking her maiden voyage in September, and I'll be piloting that ship as well, so you know how eager I am to get her in the water. But I have the privilege of taking this fine ship out on the bay this summer, and I know we are going to have a terrific cruise."

He went on to introduce the others, who had been standing in the receiving line with him before dinner, and then, on signal, all of the crew—servers, deckhands, and chefs, all in our dress uniforms—came filing in, smiling, to introduce ourselves and tell where we were from. From all over, I discovered—mostly Maryland and Virginia, but New York was represented as well as Delaware, Pennsylvania, and even Hawaii—and after receiving an ovation from the passengers, who were eager for their dessert, we disbanded and went back to our assigned jobs.

This was finals week at the University of Chicago, I knew. Between his tests and my schedule, there was little time for Patrick and me to talk with each other. We couldn't have cell phones with us when we were on duty. No cell phones in our cleaning buckets, in our jeans, no walking along the deck holding cell phones to our ears. We could only use them during our breaks and after we'd finished for the day, but even then, it was sometimes hard—almost impossible—to get a connection down in crew quarters, and no matter where I was calling from, there was no guarantee I'd reach him.

This time, though, late at night with only a few people milling around the observation deck, I tried my luck and Patrick answered.

"You're there!" I said. "Hope you weren't studying."

"Hey! Nope. One more exam tomorrow and I'm done. Just finished a bruiser on international policy and global change."

"Arggghhh! Now, that's a winner," I said. "How are things going?"

"Totally hectic," he said. "Between exams, I'm trying to pack. Figure out what I can leave behind. We fly out on Friday, and I've got to send everything else home."

"Must be crazy."

"It is. But I'm pretty psyched."

"I don't know whether I'm more happy for you or sorry you're leaving," I said honestly.

"Be happy. We waste too much time when we're sad," he told me.

"I know, but Gwen told us this afternoon that she and Austin broke up. I still can't believe it." I realized that Patrick hardly knew the guy. "They just seemed so right for each other."

"She upset?" Patrick asked.

"It was her idea."

"Oh. Any idea why?"

"She's got eight years of medical school ahead of her, and she didn't want him just waiting around for her."

"Maybe he wouldn't."

"She may have worried about that, too," I said.

There were several seconds of silence. I did *not* want this to start a conversation about us and was relieved when Patrick said, "So where are you calling from?"

"I'm sitting here on the top deck, and there's a great breeze. Reception's good up here too, by the way. I can see the lights of a ship way out on the water."

"But where is the ship?"

"Norfolk. We just finished the Captain's Dinner. A lot of sailors here. Some are down on the dock right now, talking to the crew."

"Yeah? And how are the guys on the *Seascape*?"

"Big, bronzed, brawny," I teased.

"Should I worry?"

"Didn't you just say we should be happy?"

"Yeah, but not necessarily about that," said Patrick.

We were docked at Yorktown the following morning for our Yorktown/Williamsburg port of call. I had mixed feelings about going ashore. I remembered my visit to the College of William & Mary in the spring and wondered if I would always think of Williamsburg as the place that turned me down.

A lot of the stewards had been on class visits to Williamsburg back in middle school, but my class had never gone, so I decided to at least take the trolley around Yorktown. But after the Captain's Dinner the night before, passengers had been invited to the lounge for a slide show on Colonial Williamsburg and the Jamestown Settlement. And now a few of those passengers, having stayed up too late or drunk too much at the reception, hadn't come out of their staterooms yet, and those of us on housekeeping detail couldn't go off duty until all of the rooms were done.

"Darn!" said Natalie. "I've never seen Williamsburg or Yorktown or Jamestown, and if it always follows the Captain's Dinner and people sleep in, I'll never get there."

Gwen saved the day. "I went to Williamsburg back in sixth grade, so tell me the room numbers and I'll clean your staterooms for you."

"Really?" said Natalie. "We'll owe you one."

"Big time too!" said Gwen. "But go now while you have the chance."

Natalie, Liz, and I studied the little map of the town and set out along Water Street, looking for an ATM machine and, after that, Ben & Jerry's Green Mountain Coffee Café. When we recognized Mitch sauntering along solo, hands in his pockets, we invited him to come along.

"It's all so different from Silver Spring," Liz said, the York River on one side of us, side streets full of history on the other.

Mitch, with one of those Greek sailor caps perched on his head to shield his eyes, looked down a tree-lined side street and said, "Well, the streets are about as narrow as where I live, and almost as quiet."

"Where's that?" asked Natalie.

"Vienna, Maryland," he said. "You never heard of it. No one ever has. Over in Dorchester County, eastern shore."

"Then this is practically home to you," I said.

He grinned this time. "Well, we've got a couple of historic houses, but not like this."

Mitch was twenty or so, I figured. Large calloused hands. One of those blonds who tans easily. Looked pretty cute the other night in his white dress shirt and black pants, but seemed far more natural now in a T-shirt and khaki shorts.

We found the café and each ordered a different flavor of ice cream so we could share—a spoonful of Chunky Monkey for Cake Batter, a spoonful of Chubby Hubby for Dublin Mudslide. Sitting at a little table for four, we studied the printout we got on the ship. I pointed to the Watermen's Museum. "'The lore, legends, and equipment used by crabbers and oystermen over the past century,'" I read.

"I was there earlier," Mitch told us. "Wanted to see if they had anything about muskrat trapping, but they didn't."

"People trap muskrats? For what?" I asked.

"Their pelts. Women's coats," Mitch said.

"Are you a trapper?" Liz asked.

"Me and my dad and brothers. We trap and do oysters in winter, crab in the summer."

"How come you're not crabbing now?" asked Natalie.

"Just wanted something different for a change. I've watched the cruise ships going around the bay and heard there was a new line looking for deckhands. Dad said he figured he could spare me for a couple of months—at least it would be sure money. Can't count on much of anything from crabbing these days."

"You like it? Working on a ship?" Liz asked.

"Well, I applied for deckhand, but sometimes I'm a steward, too. I like the deckhand part. Hardly got my feet wet so far," Mitch said.

"But isn't it hard, jumping from deck to dock when we're coming in or going out?" I asked.

"Only the experienced guys do that," Mitch said. "Suppose I'll catch on to it before the summer's over." He stretched his legs out alongside the table. The hair on his thighs looked almost white in the sunlight.

"Yeah, but what would happen if a guy fell in that space between ship and dock when we're tying up? He'd be crushed," said Liz.

He shrugged. "So life's risky. You can die trapping muskrats too. My uncle died last year—drowned in the marsh."

"My God!" I said. "I'm sorry. That's awful."

"Yeah. We were all sorry to lose him. I think that's what made my dad say he could spare me this summer, though. Give me a chance to try something else."

We talked a little about families then, but Liz looked at her watch and saw we had only an hour before we had to be back on the ship.

Natalie grabbed the printout again, her fingers following along a street on the map, her French braid dangling over one shoulder.

"Reenergized!" she declared. "I'm off to look for earrings. I'm going to buy a pair in each port of call—mementos of my cruising summer."

"I'll go with you," said Liz.

But I wanted to see more of Yorktown while I had a chance, and so did Mitch, so we located a trolley stop on the printout and went outside to wait.

Emily, Yolanda, and Barry were on the trolley when it came, and we all sat together in the back. As we passed the old Custom House, the church, and an archeological dig, I wondered what it was like to live in a tiny place like this, where most of the people you met each day were tourists. How different it must seem to Mitch, who worked in the marshes with trappers. I was mentally composing an e-mail to Patrick—telling him I was a seeing a little more of life too, even if it wouldn't compare with Barcelona.

When we got off, we caught up with Liz and Natalie and all sauntered back together, not eager to spend the evening scraping plates and stacking the monstrous dishwasher—over and over and over again. As we approached the *Seascape*, I noticed a couple up on the lounge deck, and as we got closer, I saw that it was Flavian and Gwen. He had her cornered, his hands resting on the rail on either side of her, their faces a few inches apart. And Gwen was definitely smiling.

4

SINBAD

The Crisfield port of call, where passengers took a ferry to Tangier Island, was probably the one I wanted to visit most. The island sounded faraway and mysterious. Captain John Smith had once been there, our ship's pamphlet read, and residents still had traces of the Elizabethan accents of their ancestors.

But I didn't get to go, and neither did Liz, because this time Gwen had passengers who decided to sleep in instead of going ashore. One, in fact, was sick and needed not only the rug in his room shampooed and dried, but the blankets and bedspread washed as well. But fair was fair, so Liz and I loyally told Gwen we'd do the rooms she had left, and she headed for the ferry without a trace of guilt.

"That was quick," Liz said, peering over the rail as Gwen left the ship with Flavian.

"She's having fun," I said. "She deserves it."

I was glad in a way that I didn't take the tour, because it was a steamy, sticky day, and the only way to get around Tangier Island, Stephanie had told us, was on foot, unless you rented one of the few golf carts available. Consequently, passengers returned to the ship that afternoon tired and hot, and not too interested in evening entertainment. Out in the middle of the bay, or in remote places like Crisfield, we had little or no cell phone service either, though there was wireless Internet access throughout the ship that made us all the more eager to get moving.

When dinner was over, the dining room cleared sooner than it usually did, and after the crew had eaten and the galley was cleaned, some of the stewards started a poker game in air-conditioned comfort, and others sat around to watch. But I opted to go up on the observation deck with Emily and Liz, even though the air was humid and still.

Frank and some of the guys were already up there—Mitch and Josh, Barry and Flavian—all sitting around a big pitcher of iced coffee. We sat off to one side, faces tilted toward the night sky, letting their conversation float our way. We soon learned that the *Seascape* was perhaps not all it was cracked up to be.

"*Sinbad?*" Barry was saying. "This was the old *Sinbad*?"

"You're kidding!" I heard Flavian say.

In the half-light of the moon, I saw Frank wipe one hand

across his face as though to erase his smile. "You didn't hear it from me," he said.

"What was *Sinbad*?" Mitch asked.

Josh looked over at him. "Ever heard of those fantasy cruises? One time it's a pirate ship. Next it's the Wild West or Arabian Nights or something?"

"And?" said Mitch.

"And *Sinbad* had more things wrong with it than you could count," said Josh. "Like it was jinxed." He looked at Frank to see if he should go on, and when the engineer said nothing, Josh continued: "Anything that could break, broke. Anything that could leak, leaked."

"But now it's been refurbished!" said Barry.

Frank smiled and straightened up in his chair. "Yeah," he said. "So they tell us."

Barry propped his feet on the chair next to him. "So that's why Sawyer backed out? He knows something we don't know?"

"Sawyer wouldn't do that without a reason," said Frank. "Maybe he just didn't quite swallow the 'refurbished' bit. The only thing I know about Haggerty is that he hasn't sailed the Chesapeake, but he was available. But the fact they that had to take whatever captain they could get at the last minute—that can't be good."

"But, heck. *You* must feel confident enough to take this ship out," said Flavian.

Frank gave a small shrug and looked over the water once

more, rubbing one shoulder. "Sawyer's going on sixty, got a house on the Severn—he could retire anytime he wants. I haven't got the choice."

"So what is he—some sort of prima donna?" Emily cut in. Her freckles were hardly visible in the moonlight. "A ship's got to be brand-new or he doesn't sail it?"

"No. Prima donna he's not. He just wants a ship without problems," Frank told her.

"Then what would be his objection to the *Seascape*? He suspects we've got a leak?" asked Mitch.

"A leak we might be able to handle," Frank said, laughing a little. And then realizing, perhaps, that we'd all been listening, he reached for his glass. "Well, who's to say we won't have the best season ever?"

"At least we're not out on the ocean," Liz said when we were sacking up.

"I sort of like the idea of *Sinbad*," said Rachel when we told the others what we'd heard. "The curse of *Sinbad*. *Sinbad* strikes again!"

"Gotta have a little excitement," said Yolanda.

"Well, one of us seems to be feeling a little excitement of her own," I said, glancing over at Gwen, who was slipping a T-shirt over her head. "Getting pretty chummy with Flavian, Gwen?"

She grinned mischievously and pulled on her sleep shorts. "He's a fun guy."

"I still liked Austin," Liz said, as though that would change anything.

Lauren glanced over at Gwen as she crawled up into her bunk. "You got somebody back home?"

"I've been going with a guy named Austin," Gwen said. "But our future's up for grabs. I've got eight years of school ahead of me."

"Ouch!" said Shannon. "I couldn't wait to get out of school. What, you haven't had enough of it?"

"Gwen's going to be a doc-tor!" Yolanda warbled.

"What kind of doctor?" Natalie wanted to know.

"Male anatomy," Liz teased, and we laughed.

"I haven't decided," Gwen said. "Obstetrics, maybe. Pediatrics."

"I'd want to start a family before then," said Natalie. "I love kids. I've already decided that if I don't find the right guy by the time I'm thirty-two, I'm looking for a sperm donor."

"No way!" Shannon declared. "Go through all the work of pregnancy and labor and none of the fun? If I ever decided to use a donor, I'd pick him live and conceive the old-fashioned way."

"And if it didn't take the first time?" I asked.

Shannon grinned. "If at first you don't succeed . . . God, there was a guy in my tenth-grade civics class who would have made the most gorgeous kids!"

"*Listen* to her," said Emily. "Don't you people know it's past midnight? Somebody get the light."

We were becoming accustomed to little sleep, I discovered.

After a few days of getting up at five thirty or six, that groggy feeling in mid-afternoon was familiar.But still I lay awake a while longer because I was thinking about Patrick. Had I ever thought of what our children would look like if we married? Had we ever even talked about having children? We liked to watch them on a playground, and we'd laugh at the way babies would stare at us without the least bit of self-consciousness. But had we actually said we wanted to have babies together? No, because we'd never even discussed getting married. We'd been going together longer than most of our friends, but . . .

I was just drifting off to sleep when I heard *scritch, scratch, scratch.* I lay still, listening more intently. Nothing. Then, *scritch, scratch* . . .

I lifted my head from the pillow. "I hear a mouse," I said.

Instantly the room was filled with rustlings and mattress squeaks.

"What? What?" voices cried.

Feet thumped on the floor, the light came on, and Pamela dived back into bed, legs pulled up after her.

"I won't sleep for a minute with a mouse in the room," Liz declared. "Did you know they can climb up walls? That commercial where they're running across the drapes?"

"You don't have mice on a ship, you have rats," said Shannon. "I need a cigarette."

"Listen!" I cautioned as the scratching noise came again.

We all turned toward the smaller of the two dressers that stood in one corner, its bottom drawer opened an inch.

"It's coming from there," said Lauren. "Behind the dresser."

"Or in it," said Emily. "Get the plunger."

"The what?" I said.

"The toilet plunger. Don't we have a plunger? We can trap it under that and—"

"Get one of the guys," said Shannon.

"No! Wait!" Natalie sprang off her bunk and gave us a sheepish look. "Promise you won't tell?" And without waiting for an answer, she padded over to the dresser in her panda-print shorts, opened the bottom drawer, and lifted out a shoe box with a turtle in it, five inches across.

We stared.

"It's a Maryland terrapin," Natalie said proudly as she lifted it by its shell. "A kid was selling it in Crisfield this afternoon, and I bought it for my brother's birthday on Sunday. He'll be ten."

"Natalie!" we said, practically in unison.

"I wanted something really special, and Kevin will love it!"

"It's against regulations," Liz reminded her. "No pets of any kind."

"Just until we get to Baltimore. They're meeting me on the dock."

"That's four days off!" I said.

"Dianne checks our quarters once a day! You know that," Rachel said. "And she's a stickler for cleanliness, especially when it comes to transmitting diseases to the passengers."

We eyed the greenish-brown creature dangling from Natalie's

fingers, its legs flailing. I was only familiar with the small box turtles you find in pet stores. Natalie's turtle had extended its scrawny neck full length, and it slowly turned its head from side to side, as though taking us all in.

"What does it eat?" asked Shannon. "Do you even know?"

"The boy said to feed it chicken, fruit, and worms," Natalie said, stroking the terrapin's head with one finger.

"It needs water," said Liz. "Salt water or fresh?"

Natalie looked helplessly around. "Look. All I want to do is get him to Baltimore Sunday. I'll figure out the rest tomorrow."

"Okay, but keep him quiet," said Emily.

Natalie grabbed a handful of dirty laundry from a heap in the corner and lined the shoe box with underwear and socks. Then she put the terrapin back.

"Death by asphyxiation," Rachel said when the scratching stopped.

I met Captain Haggerty the next morning when I was coming up from the linen hold. We'd docked at Oxford, and when I reached the main deck, he was standing at the entrance to the dining room, drinking coffee and talking with Quinton. There must have been an awkward gap in their conversation, because they both turned and focused on me.

"Alice, I wonder if you've met the captain," Quinton said. The stewards had been introduced to him en masse, but not one by one.

Quinton, as always, was in his short-sleeved shirt and black pants, his head nearly reaching the door frame. Haggerty, a foot shorter, was in a T-shirt, but he still wore his captain's hat. He moved his body in a kind of swagger that said he could handle any ship, at any time.

"Hello," I said, and walked over, shifting the stack of towels into my left arm so I could shake hands. "I'm Alice McKinley."

He had a firm handshake, but he held it only a second. "How's it going?" he asked pleasantly.

"I guess you'd have to ask Quinton," I said. "But I think I'm doing all right. There's a lot to learn."

"First time at sea?"

"Yeah."

"This guy treating you okay?" he joked, nodding toward Quinton.

"A regular slave driver," I said, laughing. "But we're getting used to it."

"Well, if he gives you any trouble, let me know," the captain said, and took another sip of coffee from the black ceramic mug with a captain's insignia on it.

It was all in fun, of course, but there was something about the remark, something cocky, that sounded like showing his rank. Putting Quinton in his place by even *suggesting* that I go over his head and report something.

I shifted the towels again. "Well, nice to meet you," I said. "I'd better get back to work." And I quickly took the stairs two flights up to the Chesapeake deck. Maybe he was just one of those people, like me, who lets things slip out, sometimes the very thing you *don't* mean to say.

My first room for the morning was empty. The Colliers were early risers, and when I was ready for the second stateroom, the Anselminos were just leaving.

"Good morning, Alice," they said, holding the door for me. "You're looking perky today."

"And you look like you're setting off on a new adventure," I said.

"We signed up for the walking tour of Oxford," Mrs. Anselmino told me. She was short and round, with a wreath of dark curls around her face. "I hope you'll get a chance to see the town. Make sure you visit the Robert Morris Inn. We celebrated our thirty-fifth anniversary there."

"I'll put it on my list," I told her. "Have a good time."

I wished all the passengers were like the Anselminos. They wiped down the sink before I even had a chance to get at it, and picked up everything off the floor to make vacuuming easier. They'd only been aboard two days when the dining room servers had figured out that Mr. Anselmino had a great sense of humor, someone they could kid around with.

I finished their stateroom in record time and was about to head to the third when I heard a loud voice out on the walkway saying, "If you don't search her immediately, you won't find it."

I stayed out of sight in the doorway and listened.

"It was there when we went to breakfast—right there on the nightstand," a woman's voice was saying. "I remember it distinctly, and now it's gone. I *thought* she had a strange look on her face when I passed her on the deck a few minutes ago."

"Omigod!" I whispered to myself. Were they talking about me?

"Mrs. Collier, I want to find that watch as much as you do, but let's not jump to conclusions." Dianne's voice.

"What else *can* I think?" the woman continued. "No, you can't want to find it as much as I do, because that diamond watch belonged to my mother-in-law, and Gordon gave it to me when we married."

I set my bucket on the deck, locked the Anselminos' door behind me, and started down the walkway just as Dianne turned in my direction.

"Oh, Alice," she called. "Could you stop here, please?"

"She could have hidden it anywhere by now," came Mrs. Collier's voice from inside her room. When I reached her doorway, Mrs. Collier was sitting on the edge of one of the twin beds. Her cold gray eyes settled fiercely on me as I crossed the threshold, and Dianne closed the door behind us.

"You cleaned the Colliers' stateroom this morning, didn't you?" Dianne asked.

"Yes. It was my first one for the day," I said, and tried to keep my voice neutral, but I was furious inside.

"Well, my watch was—," Mrs. Collier began, but Dianne interrupted.

"Mrs. Collier's watch is missing, and she remembers leaving it there on the nightstand. Did you see it?"

I tried desperately to single out that particular nightstand in my memory. Every two rooms are exactly alike, the bathrooms placed side by side, except that they are mirror images of each other. Lamps are the same, bedspreads the same, even the pictures on the walls, nautical scenes of the Chesapeake Bay.

"No, I don't remember seeing a watch," I answered. "I saw a pair of glasses on a bedside table, but they may have been in the room next door."

The thin brunette sitting on the bed gave an exasperated sigh and turned her face away. She was wearing a sailor top with a wide blue and white collar over her white slacks, and one foot bounced up and down impatiently. "Talk is useless," she said.

My anger was getting the best of me, and I held my arms out at my sides. "Would you like to search me, Mrs. Collier?" I asked.

She startled, a little flustered. "That's not my job, but the watch could be anywhere by now. We need to search crew quarters."

"That won't be necessary, Alice," Dianne said. "Why don't the three of us check the room over again to see if perhaps it's in a drawer or—"

"I *know* what I *know*!" Mrs. Collier said emphatically. "The watch was here on the nightstand when I went to breakfast, and now it's gone."

"If you see or hear anything at all about a watch, Alice, I'm sure you'll let us know," Dianne said. And then, to Mrs. Collier, "I know you must be terribly upset, but I need to remind you that there is a safe in the purser's office, and we encourage people to keep their valuables in it."

"So I have to put my watch in the safe every evening and get it out again each morning?" Mrs. Collier said.

"We encourage that," Dianne repeated, and nodded me toward the door to show I was dismissed. As I went out, Mrs. Collier's voice trailed after me:

"That means you must expect thefts to happen. My husband is going to be extremely angry over this, I can tell you."

I had run out of miniature soap bars, so I went on down to the linen hold but ducked into crew quarters for a few minutes to calm myself. I'd barely sat down on my bunk when Gwen followed.

"I heard some commotion down on your deck. What happened?" she asked, and I told her.

"Mrs. Collier wanted Dianne to search my stuff, but Dianne said no. I'm sure that's not the last of it, though. It's my word against hers," I added. "I'll probably get fired."

"On what grounds?" Gwen asked.

But we knew the answer to that, and Gwen realized it too. The application form we'd signed said that we understood we were being hired "at will" for no definite period and that our employment could be terminated with or without cause at the option of the company.

"How can I go for nine more weeks knowing that Dianne will always wonder about me?" I said. "And if any of the other passengers misplace anything at all, I'll be the first suspect. You should have seen the look on Mrs. Collier's face when I left her room, Gwen. It was as though she were saying, 'You know and I know you're a thief and a liar.'"

Scritch, scratch, scratch came from the bottom dresser drawer.

"Well, if Dianne does search the room, she'll find that," Gwen said, and grabbed my arm. "Come on. Let's finish up our rooms and go see the Robert Morris Inn everyone's talking about. If you sit down here and worry, you'll fry your brain."

We finished our rooms, then showered and changed, but when we started up the stairs to the main deck, we met Dianne coming down.

"Alice, I saw Mrs. Collier in the library, and that little problem is resolved," she said. "Her husband had the watch in his pocket. I was just coming to tell you."

I came to a dead stop. I wasn't sure which I felt more: relief or anger. "Why didn't *she* tell me that?"

"She knew I'd let you know. Evidently, her husband left the breakfast table early for a walk but stopped in their stateroom first and saw the watch on the nightstand. Said he put it in his pocket for safekeeping, then forgot about it till his wife told him it was missing. So that's the end of it."

Not quite, I thought.

"Isn't she going to apologize?" I asked.

"I'm sure she feels embarrassed by the whole thing," Dianne said, and there was a hint of discomfort in her voice. "You girls have a good time in Oxford now. It's a very picturesque town." She turned and went back up the stairs. Gwen and I looked at each other.

"Wait here," I said, and went up to the library on the lounge deck.

Mrs. Collier was sitting at a little table checking things off on a brochure and drinking a Bloody Mary. A diamond watch on a black band glistened on her left wrist. I walked over.

"Hello, Mrs. Collier. Oh, you found your watch!" I said cheerfully. "What good news!"

She looked up and gave a little laugh. "Yes, my husband had it in his pocket, exactly where he should have put it. He took a walk right after breakfast, but I didn't know he'd stopped by our room first."

"Yes, I heard," I said. "I'm so relieved. As you can imagine, I was pretty upset with the accusation, so I thought you'd want the pleasure of telling me the good news yourself."

I was asking for trouble, I knew, but I had to get it out. And I was so sickeningly cheerful and smiley that I couldn't quite see her complaining to Quinton about it. "Well . . . of course," she said. "I didn't mean to imply that anyone here was dishonest, but . . . I was just . . . naturally . . . very worried."

"I accept your apology," I said. "Have a nice afternoon in Oxford."

"Oh, yes, I will, I will," Mrs. Collier said, and lifted her drink again.

I went triumphantly back down to the main deck where Gwen was waiting, through the gangway, and we set off to see the town.

5

A FORGETTABLE FRIDAY

We all wanted shore leave at St. Michaels. I woke Friday morning determined to clean my staterooms faster than ever before. Quinton had told us of a bed-and-breakfast that rented bikes, and I decided that's how I wanted to spend my afternoon, especially when I got up on deck and discovered a beautiful day. The temperature had gone from the low nineties to the mid-eighties, the humidity had dropped, and the passengers in my cabins were all going ashore.

I was ready by 1:30—showered and changed—and left the ship with Lauren, Pamela, and Shannon. Natalie, however, had finished even before us and was walking swiftly toward a grassy area, her large canvas bag slung over one shoulder, and we all knew what was in it. She'd been devoting all her break time for the last two days to that terrapin, her only goal being to keep it alive and kicking till Sunday.

"So what if I miss doing something now? I'll do it later," she'd said, and that became the mantra for all of us: We'd have nine more chances to do everything.

"Do you think things will grow old by the time the ten weeks are over?" Yolanda had asked yesterday.

"*I'll* grow old," Pamela said. "I've never worked so hard in my life."

"It's the hours," Emily told her. "It's the fact that we have so little time to ourselves. You'll toughen up. That's a promise."

Mitch and Barry were already at the bike place when we got there, and they waited till we'd rented ours. Then we all set out together. It wasn't long before Josh caught up with us, riding the last bike they had left—it didn't even have gears. But he didn't need them. The roads were flat, the scenery fantastic.

"Wow! This is the life, huh?" I said as we rode in and out of shade. "We're actually getting paid for this?"

"We're actually not," said Barry. "We're so low on the pay scale, we're practically paying *them* room and board."

We'd left in such a hurry that I'd brought only a comb, lip gloss, and money, so my hands were completely free. How long had it been since I'd ridden a bike?

Off to our right we could see the *Seascape*'s tour group entering the gate of the Maritime Museum—eighteen acres with exhibits, a working boatyard, and a lighthouse. Stephanie was following along behind the group, looking svelte in black pants and a black halter top. I saw Josh and Barry exchange knowing grins.

"Yeah?" I said, questioning.

"There goes trouble," Josh said.

"Who? Stephanie?" Pamela asked, following their gaze.

Lauren overheard and let her bike coast till we caught up with her. "Oh, c'mon, Josh. It takes two. He was as much at fault as she was."

"Hey, he was a passenger. You're not supposed to hit on passengers," said Josh.

"Give her a break. She lost a job over it, and she's probably sorry it happened."

Barry chuckled. "She look sorry to you? Looks like bait to me, not that I'm complaining."

"And they think *girls* are catty!" said Pamela. "Hey, careful, Barry. You almost ran into me."

I looked around to see if Mitch was still with us and saw him riding along with his arms folded over his chest. His bike began to wobble slightly when he saw me watching.

"Wow!" I said. "We've got a stuntman here."

He laughed.

"I can do that!" said Josh, folding his arms across his chest, and immediately his bike lurched and he almost went over. We hooted at him.

Josh made up for it by being our unofficial guide. Nice to have someone along who had been on a Chesapeake Bay tour with another line.

"Ladies and gentlemen," he said, "you are now touring the historic town that fooled the British. In the dark morning hours of August something or other . . ."

"Uh-oh. A dark-and-stormy-night story," said Barry.

"No, no, this is true. Some British barges planned to attack St. Michaels, and the people found out about it. They hoisted lanterns to the tops of trees, and when the British fired, they overshot."

"Cle-ver!" said Pamela.

"And," Josh continued, "if you now look to your left, you'll see the Cannonball House."

It really did begin to feel like we were back in colonial days. Even the names on mailboxes—like Haddaway and Hambleton—sounded historical. When did I ever meet anybody named Haddaway?

The trees opened up once to a particularly beautiful stretch—just water and boats, branches framing the picture. The way the sun glinted on the edge of each ripple, the deep blue of the sky—I couldn't help smiling. Mitch noticed and smiled back, and we didn't have to say anything, just knew we were enjoying the day, the moment, the crew.

We had about an hour and a half left before we had to be back on board, so we returned the bikes and went to the Maritime Museum. Lauren and Pamela and I headed for the lighthouse, but Shannon didn't want to come. When we looked down, we saw her over by the gate, smoking.

"Don't," she said, when we caught up with her later.

"Didn't say a word," I told her.

"You were going to, and I don't want to hear it," she said.

Lauren shrugged but asked anyway. "This your first since the cruise started?"

"No, and it won't be my last. I've decided I'm a smoker and that's that. I like myself better when I'm not so grumpy and nervous."

We couldn't argue much with that.

The boatyard sounded like you'd expect it to—the rasp of a saw, the thud of a padded hammer, the clinks and clunks—all laced with the scent of sawdust, glue, and varnish. We found the guys watching a white-haired man carving a wood canoe. His glasses rested on the end of his nose, and he reminded me of Geppetto, working in his shop in *Pinocchio*.

Leaving the museum, we ran into Gwen and Flavian and two of the deckhands. They were sitting at a table outside a small seafood place, so we grabbed another table, pulled some chairs over, and ordered po'boy sandwiches with fried oysters.

What interested me far more than the oysters, however, was the fact that Flavian, I noticed, was sitting with one arm over the back of Gwen's chair. She was wearing a yellow T-shirt and an intricate long necklace, each loop carved of wood. Flavian was examining the necklace.

"Plastic," he said.

Gwen elbowed him and laughed. "It is not! It's wood. My aunt bought it in Jamaica."

Flavian pretended to read some fine print on the back of one loop. "Made . . . in . . . China," he said.

Gwen smacked his hand, but he fed her the last remaining oyster from his paper plate, and she snapped at his fingers as though she might bite them. And laughed. And then they kissed.

She was out-and-out, full-speed-ahead making out with this gorgeous, olive-skinned, lightly stubbled guy she'd known for only a week. I guess Austin really was history. She and Flavian were looking into each other's eyes and smiling.

As we all headed back to the ship, Shannon lagged behind, smoking one cigarette after another, like she was making up for all the cigarettes she'd missed this week and all the ones she couldn't have till she was off the ship again.

Mitch noticed too.

"She's been trying to quit," I told him.

"Well, the stuff's addictive," he said as some of the smoke drifted our way. "I know, 'cause I was hooked for a while."

"Yeah?"

We were trailing the others, and as a group of passengers merged onto the sidewalk ahead of us, separating us even more from the crew, we were in no hurry to leave St. Michaels.

"Dip," Mitch said. When I looked puzzled, he added, "Dipping tobacco. You know, pinch." He motioned to a spot behind his lower lip.

"Oh. Like baseball players."

"Yeah. One little pleasure while you slog through the marsh in the winter."

I realized I knew not one thing about muskrat trapping. "Do you do this slogging on foot?"

"Yeah, once we get to the marsh by motorboat, usually solo. The dip keeps us company."

I couldn't be sure if Mitch was enjoying telling me about trapping or if he was doing it out of politeness. I'd asked out of politeness, but now I was curious. He was a lot taller than I am—taller than Patrick, even, a lot more solid. Wearing a faded gray T-shirt with a SMITHWICK'S ALE label on it. I was also curious about him.

I tried to picture what he was telling me. "How do you know where the muskrats are if you're in water?"

He walked on, hands in his pockets. "The marsh is a maze of muskrat tunnels, see, and you have to know where they run. You climb out of the boat in your hip boots, sack over your shoulder, and step from one clump of grass to another, checking the spring traps between."

I didn't look at him when I asked the next question: "How did your uncle die, Mitch?"

He was quiet for a moment, and I started to worry that I'd gotten too personal.

"We don't know for sure," he said. "You can be knee-deep in mud before you know it. Maybe he went under and couldn't right himself. Maybe he was so far in that he couldn't get out. He was sixty-eight. Or maybe he froze to death. Hard to think about, but it happens."

We walked on a little farther without speaking. Finally I said, "So trapping's in your family, huh?"

"My dad, my uncles, my grandfather . . . We do a little bit of everything, I guess, but all of it's in the water."

"And now you're *on* the water."

Mitch smiled this time. "Yeah. Imagine that. Nice for a change. Don't know I'd want to do it full-time, though."

Up ahead, we saw some more of the *Seascape*'s tour group coming along the path from the museum and merging with the line of people heading for the dock. Stephanie was walking with one of the male passengers and laughing at something he'd said. He was looking at her appreciatively.

"Careful, buddy," Mitch joked.

It was getting close to five by then, and . . . And suddenly I thought my heart was in seizure. *Patrick!* I glanced down at my watch and automatically reached for my bag before I realized I hadn't brought it. It was Friday afternoon. Late afternoon. Patrick's plane was leaving at . . . ? Was it five or six?

Think! Think! I told myself, fumbling for the cell phone that wasn't there. *Wake up! Wake up! This can't be happening.* It felt as though my whole head was heating up, hot pain behind my eyes, my forehead. I'd wanted to tell him good-bye! He may have been trying to call me!

I guess I'd stopped there on the sidewalk, saliva collecting in my mouth because I couldn't swallow. Mitch was looking at me strangely.

"Something wrong?" he asked.

"Oh my God!" I gasped. "I've got to make a phone call! I'll see you," I said, and began to run.

I was only fifty yards from the ship, but the tour group was already there, ambling one at a time up the gangplank. Dianne was checking off names on her clipboard as they passed, and women were chatting with her and with each other while my head was screaming, *Let me by! Let me by!*

I felt physically ill. How could I have forgotten? *How?* I'd thought about it several times yesterday, about calling Patrick before he left, thinking about the best time to do it. I hadn't wanted to interrupt him while he was packing; didn't want to bother him when he was trying to get a cab. What time was his flight? I couldn't remember his departure time! How could I not remember?

There was a break in the line. A man had gone up the gangplank, and the woman behind him had turned to talk to the person behind her. I edged around her saying, "Oh, sorry! Late for work. Excuse me."

Dianne frowned, but I zipped on ahead and bounded through the gangway, then clattered down the stairs to crew quarters. Grabbing my cell phone from my bag, I checked for messages, but there weren't any. I ran back up to the main deck. Mitch was standing in line on the dock and looked up at me quizzically, but I didn't stop. On up to the lounge deck, then the Chesapeake deck, to the observation deck at the top.

A small group of passengers was standing at the stern, drinks in hand, another in the shade area. I turned toward the shady side of the ship's funnel and punched in Patrick's number, my chest aching. It was 4:57, by my watch, 3:57, central time. I still had time, didn't I? Or were they an hour ahead? *Think!*

Answer, Patrick! Oh, please, please, answer! Eight rings. Nine. And then the voice message: "The party you are trying to reach is not available. Please leave a message . . ."

I pressed END, my mouth dry. If I left a message, I would sound breathless, hurried, anxious, hysterical, even. Did I want Patrick to remember me that way?

Okay, I told myself. *You have time to think. You can leave a message anytime. It doesn't have to be right this minute.* He could be in a taxi on his way to the airport. He could be going through security. *Slow down and breathe normally.*

I let out my breath and took several steps one way, then another, keeping in the shade of the huge exhaust funnel that rose like a giant shark's fin at the top of the ship. *Think!* I ordered myself. Why couldn't I remember his departure time?

Five o'clock kept coming to mind. No . . . six something or other. But I wouldn't have gone off without my cell phone if I thought I'd miss him, would I? Six o'clock Chicago time was seven o'clock here, so maybe he *hadn't* left yet. Or was I supposed to have remembered five o'clock *central* time? All I knew for sure was his flight number, 6739, so I needed to call the airline and find out when that flight was scheduled to leave. I began to feel better.

I dragged one of the deck chairs over and sat down. The plastic was warm beneath my bare thighs. I didn't know the airline's number, so I had to ask for the directory. When I got the number and was connected, I had to listen to the menu.

"Welcome!" said a friendly voice. "This is Susan. I'm an automated clerk, and I can help you. Tell me what you want to do. If you want to make a reservation, press or say, 'one.' If you want to check arrival or departure times, press or say, 'two.' . . ."

"Two," I said loudly.

"Great! You may speak to me in a normal voice. If you want to hear an arrival time, press or say, 'one.' If you want a departure time, press or say, 'two.' . . ."

"Two, damn it!" I said.

"I'm sorry," said the voice. "I believe you said, 'two.' Is this correct?"

"Yes!" I said pleadingly.

"Great!" the voice said again. "Do you have the flight number?"

"Yes!"

"Please tell me the flight number. Say each number distinctly. For example, one . . . two . . . three . . . four . . ."

I gave her the four-digit number.

"Thank you. I believe you said, 'six . . . seven . . . three . . . nine.' Is this correct?"

"Yes!" I said, almost sobbing with exasperation. The people at the end of the deck looked in my direction, then turned away again. It was now three minutes past five.

The automated woman was on again. "Flight six . . . seven . . . three . . . nine departed O'Hare International Airport on time at four . . . oh . . . two. . . ."

I dropped the cell phone in my lap, covered my face with both hands, and cried.

How could this have happened? What was the matter with me? I had gone trotting off to St. Michaels without even checking Patrick's departure time! My mind was still stuck on the number five—that his departure time was five something. That's six o'clock eastern time, so I must have thought I'd still have an hour to reach him after I'd returned to the ship. That he'd be sitting in the boarding area and his cell phone would go off and he'd smile when he saw it was from me.

I leaned my head against the base of the funnel and silently sobbed, my chest heaving. Patrick would be gone for a year, and I hadn't said a real good-bye.

It was only when a sob escaped that I realized someone was watching me. Through my tears, I saw Mitch standing over by the rail, looking at me, concerned.

I wiped one hand over my cheeks and blinked my eyes, but I kept my head down. Then I saw his feet standing beside my chair.

"What's wrong, Alice?" he asked.

I stifled another sob and glanced toward the little cluster of passengers who were looking at me again. Mitch pulled another chair into the shade, his back to the passengers, and sat down beside me.

"I just . . ." I began, "I missed telling my boyfriend good-bye before his plane left for Europe. I don't know *how* I let this happen. . . . I thought it was leaving later . . . and he—he'll be g-g-gone for a whole year!"

"Oh, jeez." I could see Mitch shaking his head. "Rotten luck."

"It's not luck, it's stupidity!" I wept. "How c-c-could I remember the flight number but not the departure time? Sane people don't do that!"

I needed a tissue. Mitch got up, went over to a small table next to the passengers, and returned with a cocktail napkin.

"Was he expecting you to call at a certain time?" he asked, handing it to me.

"Not exactly." I blew my nose. "I didn't tell him I'd call, but we haven't talked for a few days because he's had exams and he's packing—but he'd naturally think I'd want to say good-bye."

I was through crying now, and my hands went limp in my lap.

"Why . . . why didn't he call *you*?" Mitch asked.

"Well, I thought he might have, but there weren't any messages waiting. He knows I can't have a cell phone with me when I'm on duty, so I usually call him in the afternoon on my break when I can reach him. But I *didn't* this time, and I can't understand myself."

"You can't call him now?"

I looked over at Mitch. "You can't use a cell phone on a plane."

"Oh," said Mitch. "I didn't know that." He smiled a little. "Never been on a plane."

"I've only flown a couple of times." I could feel tears rising again, but I checked them. "It's just like . . . like I'm losing my mind. I mean, I've been so upset about his going away for a year, you'd think I'd make *sure* I didn't forget this. I even rehearsed what I was going to say. And then I didn't even check the departure time."

"Well," Mitch said, "you could always text him now, and he'll have a nice surprise waiting for him when he gets to wherever he's going. Where *is* he going, by the way?"

"Spain."

"Oh. Well, since you didn't get a message from him, it probably means he was rushing around like crazy right up to flight time. And if you *had* been able to reach him, you wouldn't have had a decent conversation anyway."

That was amazingly comforting. I smiled a little and blew my nose one last time. "Thanks," I told him. "I didn't mean to bother anyone else with this."

"No bother." He straightened up, hoisting his shoulders back, the T-shirt expanding across his chest. "The one thing I learned when my uncle died was to talk about it. It really helps."

I kept smiling at him a second or two longer, then suddenly looked at my watch.

"I'm late!" I said. "Galley duty."

"They'll survive," he said, and gave me a final once-over. "You okay now?"

"I think so," I said. "Thanks, Mitch."

6

CONNECTIONS

I went through the motions of work in the galley that night. Thankfully, I wasn't assigned to clear tables. I was one of the two "galley slaves" who slide uneaten food off the plates into the trash bags, spray the gunk off the plates, and load them in the huge dishwasher.

Natalie was the other slave on duty, and when I saw her dumping all but one grape off a salad plate and setting it aside, I remembered that the terrapin was still a passenger.

"Where is it?" I whispered as we shared the sink. "I didn't hear it last night."

"The engine room," she told me. "Frank won't say anything if I have it off the ship by Sunday."

"Is it doing okay?"

"I've added grass and water. Gwen donated a little worm this morning, but it's still there. Terrapins can go a week or more without eating, I read. I just hope the noise of the engine room doesn't do him in."

"It's a he?"

"Haven't the faintest idea. But Kevin will love it."

I wondered if there's always the urge to get something really special for a brother. Never having had a sister, I wouldn't know if that's even more special, but I had to smile as I remembered the angst I went through thinking up gifts for Lester over the years: the beer cookbook, the Mickey Mouse boxers, the two half-pound bars of Hershey's chocolate, and—omigod—his twenty-first birthday present!

"What are you smiling about?" Natalie asked curiously.

"A present that Pam and Liz and I cooked up for my own brother's birthday a few years ago," I told her. "They'd had a crush on Lester for as long as I could remember, and they wanted to be in on a surprise. I'd found out from Les that his girlfriend had promised him a surf-and-turf dinner, served by her in the outfit of his choice, which was a leopard-skin bikini and knee-high boots."

"Wow! Now, that's creative!" Natalie said.

"So Pam and Liz and I decided to serve him a surprise breakfast in bed in the outfits of *our* choice."

Natalie was grinning already. "And?"

"Liz was in a long high-necked dress, I was in my bathing suit with a sweatshirt over it because I was cold, and Pamela was in a skintight cat costume with black net stockings she'd worn at a dance recital. I think we blew his mind."

Thinking about Les almost pulled me out of my blue funk, but then I was back to figuring out how long it took to fly from Chicago to Spain. Hadn't Patrick said something about changing planes in New York? If so, this meant he could check his cell phone in New York, and there still wouldn't be a good-bye message from me. I watched an anchovy slide off a plate onto a half-eaten roll, and my stomach turned. But then I realized that Patrick could try *me* from New York, and I might still find a message waiting when I got off work.

I was holding the spray nozzle too close to a plate, and water splattered on my face. I wiped my cheek on my sleeve, set the plate on the rack, and went back to figuring out what time he'd reach Spain.

How many time zones would he cross? Was time going backward or forward? Did I even know that? Seven hours came to mind, but where did that come from? The flight number? I was really losing it. I thought of the way I'd been crying up on the top deck and the way Mitch brought me a napkin to blow my nose. And then I remembered what he'd asked—why hadn't Patrick called me?

And suddenly I thought of all the excuses I'd made for him: He had exams; he was packing; he knew I couldn't have my cell phone with me while I worked. . . . He could have texted me, couldn't he? He could have left a message.

"Alice!" the chef, Carlo, called. "Incoming."

I set to work removing plates and silverware from the trays, but my mind wasn't functioning. Was I just borrowing the seven from the flight number?

The thought that Patrick could have called but didn't bothered me even more, and I felt tears rising in my eyes again, but I checked them. There's a moment or two when you feel you can make tears subside without doing a thing. And, just as quickly, you can lose your chance, and water collects beneath your lower lids and won't go away. Newsflash: They do not evaporate. Either wipe your eyes or wait and wipe your cheeks. I dodged the bullet this time and found myself excusing him once again.

Okay, Patrick's flying across the Atlantic, so he's going east. Time gets later and later, so he's losing time. If it takes seven hours, and he crosses—what? Five, six, seven time zones . . . No. When Dad flew to England to visit Sylvia before they were married, it was a five-hour difference, wasn't it? It doesn't mean that Patrick will get there any later in real time, it just means that it will be later in Spain than it is here. Right?

The fish and garlic smells accumulating in the garbage can as the meal went on were like noxious fumes, and I had to turn my face away when I dumped a plate of food on top of the mess.

Why was I *doing* this? Patrick was the one who was leaving, not me! Why shouldn't *he* be calling *me* to say good-bye? Why was I putting myself through all the agony of "should have, would have," as though the whole relationship depended on me doing the thoughtful thing? What was I so afraid would happen if Patrick didn't get the right kind of farewell?

I didn't like the thought of separation, I knew. From anyone. Anything. I'd been fighting it all year, just thinking about leaving home for college. Maybe when you lose someone close—your mom, in particular—you go your whole life wanting things not to change. Wanting everyone you love to stay right where they are. But what kind of a life was that to wish on Patrick? On myself?

I almost dropped a water goblet that slipped from my soapy gloves. My thoughts seesawed back and forth. If it was a seven-hour flight, then I had seven hours to get a text message to Patrick before he landed and could turn on his cell phone. There was still time. . . .

Carlo came over to check out the uneaten food waiting to be dumped.

"Oyster mousse didn't go over so well, I see," he said.

"You win some, you lose some," his assistant said, and Carlo went back to the broiler, where the Cornish hens were spitting fat.

What would I say to Patrick if I texted? My first thought was to let it all hang out—tell him how much I'd fantasized about sending the perfect good-bye message, how mixed up I'd been about his departure time, and how I'd rushed up the gangplank to get to my cell phone and cried when the automated Susan told me the plane had taken off. Did I want him to think of me like that or as a woman of mystery, excitement, surprises, who lived an interesting life with or without him?

But . . . if two people really truly cared about each other—if you were "soul mates"—why *couldn't* you tell each other all your little troubles as well as your big ones? Talk about your feelings? Wasn't I interested in his? The thing was, I always seemed to be the one with the problems, who worried about everything little thing. Patrick, world traveler, the sophisticate, just knew how to navigate through life without hitting any sandbars.

I reeked when I finished work about ten. Despite the waterproof aprons we wore on galley duty, there were splotches of putrid water on my clothes. I could smell cooking oil on my arms—in my hair, even. But the minute I was off duty, I got my cell phone and sat down at a port-side window. The only other person in the dining room was Curtis, one of the deckhands, the married one, who was vacuuming the floor. How often did he call his wife? I wondered. I propped my feet on the chair beside me to keep out of his way.

> *Patrick—I don't know when or where you're reading this, but I hope you had a great flight.*

Great? Does anybody have even a *good* flight anymore? I changed it to *uneventful*, but that was too cold, so I settled for *good*, then continued:

> *It's been an insane day, and I missed telling you good-bye, but maybe this will be the first message you read when*

you get off the plane. If it is, I'm glad it's from me. Tell me everything!

Short and breezy. Interested in him. Fond but not fawning. I pressed SEND.

I sat at the table a long time, staring out over the dark water, not seeing much because of the reflections on the glass. If this had been a letter, I would have signed it, *Hugs, Alice* or something.

Is this the way it would be for the next year—worrying and waiting and wondering, revising my messages and e-mails over and over, working to get things just right, not wanting to depress him or annoy him? To show concern but not cling? If we were a couple, didn't he have a responsibility too? What I really wanted to say in that text message was *Why in hell didn't you call to say good-bye or leave me a message?* Weren't *my* feelings important? Didn't *I* matter?

The thing was, were we really a couple? We hadn't broken up, like Gwen and Austin, but it was understood from the time Patrick went away to college that there were no strings attached—we could, if we wanted, go out with other people.

Patrick and I had said "I love you" only once—the night of the prom in the limo, after our wild ride to the Bay Bridge and back. But I didn't want us to say it again unless we were sure of it. And even if we were sure, I didn't want us to keep on saying it like a mantra at specific times—signing off a phone conversation, for example, or walking to the store to buy fruit. Like if we didn't say it, we didn't love each other, and one of us would get run over by a dump truck.

We'd been careful up to this point to say we were special to each other, and we meant it. But we were thousands of miles apart. Was this even natural? To like—love?—someone for so long and yet so tenuously? Was it a mistake not to have slept together? Not to have that to remember?

I could hear Curtis closing up the galley. A thud, a click, a clank. And then it really was quiet. There was relief in knowing that my message was on Patrick's cell phone, however. I wasn't asking for promises or commitments or maybes. I was just here for him. Interested in him. And living my own life. Just what he wanted me to do.

Still, I longed to connect with *somebody* other than my crewmates. It was probably too late to call home—Dad and Sylvia would be in bed. So I punched in Lester's number and waited.

"Yeah?" came my brother's voice. "Al?"

"Hi, Les. I just wanted to see how things were going back home," I said.

"Not bad. How are you? Where are you right now?" He didn't sound eager to get rid of me, so I guessed he was alone, with time to kill.

"We're docked at St. Michaels, headed for Annapolis in the morning," I told him. "It's been a wild week, but I think I'm getting the hang of it."

"Good for you; build some muscles. Having any fun?"

"Yes. Some. I'm making friends. Have you rented your extra room yet?"

Lester lives with another Maryland graduate on the top floor of an elderly man's house in Takoma Park. They've been trying to find a tenant for the third bedroom since a friend of theirs got married and moved out.

"No, we'll wait till later in the summer to advertise it. Get a grad student."

"Are *you* having any fun, Les?" I asked. Meaning, did he have a new girlfriend? Lester used to have so many girls clinging to him, he practically had to swat them off. Now that he's "matured," you might say, with a steady job, I tease him that he's becoming an old stick-in-the-mud.

"Of course I am," said Les. "But don't expect all the details."

Neither of us said anything for a few moments. I knew I had to say something quick or he'd ask what I really wanted to talk about.

"Les," I said, "I forgot to call Patrick before he left. I mean, I didn't tell him good-bye."

"So why are you telling me? Call him up."

"He was already on the plane, so I sent a text message."

"And? What's the big deal?"

"Did you ever screw up big-time over something you should have remembered?"

"Oh, man. Did I ever!"

"What? Tell me."

"I sent flowers with a Happy Birthday note to a girl when it wasn't her birthday."

"That's not so bad," I said. "The fact that you gave her flowers should have made up for getting the date wrong."

"It was another girl's birthday, and they knew each other," said Les.

"Oh!" That was definitely worse than my forgetting Patrick's departure time.

"And . . . what happened?" I asked.

"They both married someone else," said Les.

I laughed in spite of myself. Marilyn and Crystal, I'll bet. "I feel better already," I told him.

When I woke the next morning, I realized I'd slept all night with my cell phone beside me. I pulled on shorts and a tee, my flip-flops, and ran up four flights of stairs to the sun deck where I could read a text message if there was one. There was:

Got your message. Here at baggage pickup. So far, all I've seen of Barcelona so far are the backsides of fellow passengers waiting for their luggage.
More later. Patrick

It was enough. The "more later" sustained me. Patrick was going to be busier than he'd ever been, trying to help his professor finish his book before fall classes began. It was like a huge load had lifted. We'd set the standard for text messages—for now, anyway. Short, breezy, informative, interesting, funny . . . He'd tell me about Spain, I'd tell him about the bay. Deal.

When I got back to crew quarters, there was a drama going on.

Natalie was standing in the middle of the floor, her long braid undone and dangling carelessly down the front of her T-shirt. Her sneakers had no laces, and her wrinkled shorts advertised the fact that she'd pulled on the first thing she grabbed.

"It's gone," she was saying as the other girls, in various stages of dress, paused, clothes in hand. "The box in the engine room is empty."

7
AWARDS NIGHT

"Did you check around?" Shannon said, reaching for a cigarette, then slowly slipping it back in the pack. "How far can a turtle get, after all?"

"I looked everywhere I could. There are a lot of places I can't get to in there, and the noise in that room is deafening. What will I do? Kevin's birthday's tomorrow, and they'll all be waiting for me on the dock."

"Have you asked Frank?" I put in.

"He's not there." Natalie sank down on one of the bottom bunks, then jumped up again. "The showers! I didn't check the shower room!" She bolted for the door.

We weren't that optimistic and resumed dressing. I changed from one T-shirt to another. "Anything could have happened to that turtle if Frank was the only one who knew about it," I said. "She said she put it in a bigger box with a lid. Someone could have piled stuff on top of it, then mistaken the whole heap for trash."

The door opened and Dianne peered in. "Who else is on galley duty for breakfast?" she asked. "Carlo needs some help up there. A busy day coming up."

"Coming!" said Emily, and followed Dianne into the hallway.

When Dianne had gone, Lauren said, "Natalie can't be *that* attached to a terrapin."

"She's attached to her brother and wanted to give him something really special," I said.

Natalie, of course, came back from the shower room empty-handed.

"Come shopping with me in Annapolis this afternoon," Lauren said. "There are some great shops—"

"I'm going to stay right here and search every inch of this ship," Natalie declared. "I've already told Kevin I've got a surprise for him, and he's so excited."

"Well, at least braid your hair," said Shannon, but she ended up doing it for her.

I don't know how we managed it, but Pamela, Gwen, Liz, and I all got to go visit the Naval Academy together that afternoon. Annapolis was our last port of call on the cruise, and the farewell dinner was that evening, before the whole thing started up all over again with a new set of passengers on Sunday. We had to be back at the ship by four, not five, but there we were, arms linked, walking four abreast around the grounds ("the Yard," they call it) of the Naval Academy.

There's something about all those men in white—well, women, too, but we weren't paying much attention to them. We watched the short video in the Visitor Center, but we missed the noon ceremony we'd heard about, when the Brigade of Midshipmen form for uniform inspection.

We didn't have reservations for a tour, either, so we did our own walking tour, watching the "middies" in racing canoes out on the water, instructors giving orders through a bullhorn from a neighboring canoe.

Another crew was just coming in off the Severn. We watched the way their bodies moved in unison as they rowed, each man falling into the rhythm of his own particular job as they reached the shore, an exercise practiced to perfection.

"I'll take the second guy from the bow," Liz told us, one hand shielding her eyes from the sun's glare on the water.

"I'll settle for number four or five," I said. "Four in particular. Woo! Look at that chest!"

"Yeah. That's the first thing guys notice on us," said Gwen.

When we left the river at last, we ambled through the Yard, around huge buildings with uniformed cadets murmuring a polite "Good afternoon" as they passed.

"Did that guy wink at us?" Pamela said, turning as a copper-haired midshipman passed by.

"He might have. I wasn't watching his face," Gwen said.

We entered a vast courtyard with buildings on all four sides—more like a town square. A place where Caesar might be crowned or something. We felt oddly conspicuous standing there by ourselves, no other visitors around, and suddenly from one of the doorways, a fiftyish man with stripes on his sleeve came walking briskly toward us. There was no "Good afternoon" from him.

"This is a restricted area," he said, and pointed us in the direction we'd come. "Please respect the signs."

All four of us began apologizing at once. He made no reply but stood with his hands on his hips until we were at least ten feet in retreat. Then he strode back out of sight, arms swinging. Sure enough, we'd passed a small sign that told us the courtyard was off-limits, but we were so busy checking out the middies that we'd walked right past it.

We were still giggling about it when we met up with more of our crew, all heading back to the shuttle the ship had provided. Some of our guys were bronze already from the sun, just a week into our season, and looked every bit as good as the midshipman who had winked. When Gwen sat down on Flavian's lap at the back of the bus, Mitch slid onto the seat beside me. Unlike the caps the midshipmen wore, Mitch was wearing an Orioles cap backward.

"Impressed?" he asked me, eyes twinkling. "All those sailors?"

"Aren't you?" I said. "But I don't know how they stand it—all those rules and regulations. I thought we had it bad on the *Seascape*."

"Yeah, I'm just contrary enough that if they said right foot, I'd lead with my left," said Mitch.

I laughed. "Me too." And then, thinking of Patrick, I added, "They see a lot of the world, though."

"But where do you stop?" Mitch seemed thoughtful. "I mean, it's not like you've seen one country, you've seen 'em all. There's always some other place you haven't been."

"But that's no excuse not to see any!"

He folded his large hands over his stomach. "No, it's not. How about you?"

"I guess I'd like to see some of the world, but . . . I don't know." I shrugged.

"Thing is, I like where I live now. The marsh, the bay, the rivers, the ocean. Just like being here, that's all," Mitch said.

"Nothing wrong with that. But . . . if you've never been anywhere else, how do you know you wouldn't like somewhere else better?" Who was I trying to convince? I wondered.

"Well, that's like what I'm saying—maybe I would. But then, how do I know that once I'd moved there, I'd want to try some place after that?"

I laughed out loud. "Mitch, you're hopeless."

"Suppose I am," he said, and smiled. "But then so was my dad and my uncle and my grandpa and his dad before him. We've been crabbers and trappers 'bout as long as anyone knows. But you give me the choice of waking up to geese calling overhead or some officer blowing his whistle in my ear, I'll take the geese any day."

"How do you stand the wake-up call on the *Seascape*, then?" I asked him as we neared the dock and the ship came into view.

"When you know it's temporary, you can take most anything," Mitch said. "The Canada geese and the autumn sky are still going to be here come September."

Natalie was on edge, not only because she now had no great surprise for her kid brother, but because wherever the terrapin turned up, somebody would have some explaining to do.

"I looked everywhere I could think of on this level, and all Frank can offer is that it's probably crawled in some unreachable crevice and won't be discovered till it's decomposed. Oh, man . . . I'd better tell all you guys good-bye now, especially if it's in an air vent."

"Quit worrying, Nat," Emily told her. "And check your nails. Dianne wants top performance tonight."

Pamela was supposed to work with me busing tables for the big farewell dinner—with filet mignon and lobster, baked Alaska and cherries jubilee—but she was nowhere in sight when dinner began.

"Has anyone seen Pamela?" Quinton asked me as I carefully maneuvered a tray of salad plates back to the galley.

"She was getting changed a half hour ago," I said.

Quinton took the tray from my shoulder and balanced it on one hand. "Would you go look for her, Alice? Tell her to get up here double time."

I took the stairs down to crew quarters and checked the

showers, the stalls. When I didn't see her in our cabin, either, I had a hunch she'd be on the top deck, since everybody else was at dinner. And as I emerged from the Chesapeake deck, I saw her perched on the edge of a chair, screaming into her cell phone.

"There's nothing I can *do*!" she was saying. "You've got to figure this out for yourself, Mom! Get a taxi if you have to!"

She saw me motioning to her, and I could read the exasperation in her eyes. "You have *friends*! *Somebody* can go with you! Mom, I'm supposed to be on duty this very minute. They're waiting for me. . . . I know . . . I know . . . I'll call later. Bye."

She stood up and dropped the phone in the pocket of her apron, her cheeks red, the way they get when she's really mad.

I took the cell phone from her pocket. "I'll put it down in our cabin," I said. "You can't have her ringing you during dinner, and you couldn't answer if she did. Quinton's asking for you. You'd better get down there fast."

"Thanks," Pamela said, and ran on ahead of me. But as she descended the stairs, she suddenly stopped, threw back her head, and wailed, "Damn it! Damn it all! I'm *sick* of this, Alice! Sick, sick, sick!"

She scooted on into the galley when we reached the main deck, and I went on down to our cabin. As I put the cell phone on her bunk, it rang again. I put a pillow over it and went back upstairs.

* * *

The farewell dinner went off without a hitch. There were champagne toasts among the passengers, to one another and to future cruises, and the captain told them—as he'd tell all the ones to come—that they were the best passengers he'd ever had on board. They clapped like they believed him.

It was late when the crew finally got their dinner. Thankfully, the passengers didn't linger after they'd eaten their cherries jubilee because all bags had to be sitting outside staterooms by six in the morning, all passengers out of their rooms by nine. Most people packed up that night.

We did get a good meal, though, in preparation for all the work we'd do on Sunday. Quinton stopped by briefly to thank us for a successful week and to remind the housekeeping crew that we had only a few hours between the departing and the incoming guests tomorrow to get the staterooms in order.

After he left, Josh got up ceremoniously and announced that in celebration of a successful first cruise, the deckhands wanted to present some awards.

"Hear, hear!" somebody said.

"This is tough work," Josh continued, putting on a sober face. "Blood, sweat, toil, and tears. Neither cold nor rain nor dark of night shall—"

"Cut the bull and get on with it," Flavian shouted, and the other deckhands clapped.

"O-kay!" Josh continued. "To the deckhand who snores the loudest, Barry Morris!"

Huge guffaws from the guys. Josh reached into an old

shopping bag and lifted out a harmonica. "We're going to tape it to your mouth, Barry, so at least you'll make sweet music when you snore," he said. More clapping and cheering.

Josh turned back again as the coffeepot went around the tables a second time.

"To the deckhand with the largest bladder." Louder laughter than the first time. "A man who has been known to stay at his post seventeen hours without once unzipping his pants." Josh reached into the bag once more and produced a latex glove that we housekeepers use when cleaning the bathrooms. This one was filled with water. "For you, Curtis Isacoff. In case you ever find yourself in a situation you can't handle, use this as a receptacle and let fly."

Curtis laughed and reached out to accept the artificial bladder, mindful of the leak that had started around the twist tie.

"And our last award," Josh said. "To the deckhand who eats the most and never met a food he didn't like, Mitch Stefans."

Mitch grinned, then looked nonplussed as the door to the galley opened and Carlo came out holding a chafing dish. When he reached Mitch, he leaned down to present it, lifting the silver lid with a flourish, and there lay Natalie's terrapin on its back, legs flailing wildly.

Natalie shrieked and leaped to her feet, not knowing whether to be grateful or furious. "You *guys*!" she sputtered, lifting it gently from Mitch's hands and turning it upright. "I looked *everywhere*!"

She was cradling it in her lap when Dianne stepped into the

room to see what all the laughter was about. When she heard that Josh was giving out deckhand awards, she laughed and said, “Keep it short, guys, because the more bags you can bring down tonight, the less you’ll have to do tomorrow.”

We had managed to survive the first week of ten, and no one got fired. Yet.

8
STORM

We felt like seasoned employees when we started the second cruise.

All the staterooms were cleaned before the next group got on, and when we'd finished, then showered and put on fresh shirts, we presented the same enthusiastic smiles to the world as we had a week ago, welcoming the newcomers aboard.

Josh and Curtis carted luggage down from the Renaissance Hotel to the ship, and Flavian, Mitch, and Barry ran up and down the three flights of stairs carrying bags as though the ship would sail any minute. This time I was assigned to sit with Stephanie at the activities desk and be her girl Friday, escorting passengers around the ship as she directed.

I started counting the number of times we were asked, "When do we sign up for excursions?"

"I'll be giving a short talk after dinner and passing around sign-up sheets then," Stephanie had answered cheerfully.

"Does this ever get old?" I asked her after the seventh consecutive question.

"Not at all," she said. "Every face is a surprise package—somebody else to know."

It was sort of awkward having a conversation with her, knowing what I did, what I'd heard about her, anyway: three broken marriages to her credit—the first one her own; the second that of a deckhand, a friend of Curtis's, whose wife and kids left him after his affair; and the third, that of the passenger on the Dutch line, which fired her as assistant cruise director when the news got out.

I could see why men were attracted to her, though. Along with her shapely legs and high cheekbones, she had expressive eyes that fastened themselves on every person who stopped by. But her skin seemed older than the rest of her—heavily made-up, with many small lines, like a ceramic plate with finely cracked glaze. Curtis was especially teed off with her because of his friend, as though the deckhand weren't responsible too. But I think for the rest of us, Stephanie was like our job insurance. If they hired someone with her reputation, then our jobs were probably safe.

"I've heard that the big cruise ships are like floating cities," I said, trying to make conversation with her, then desperately wishing I'd kept my mouth shut. I wondered if she thought I was referring to the one that fired her, if she suspected we'd been talking about her.

She knew. When my eyes met her steely look, I tried to change the subject: "Did you always want to be a cruise director?" I chirped. *Arrrggghhhh!*

She gave me a patronizing smile. "I always wanted to work with people," she said, and turned to the woman approaching our desk. "Yes, may we help you? Oh, what a gorgeous necklace!"

"I'm looking for your gift shop," the necklace woman said. "I do my Christmas shopping all year long, and I'd like first pick of whatever you have."

"Actually," Stephanie said, as though divulging a secret and leaving me out, "it's in the alcove behind this desk, but we're only open at certain hours. The thing to remember is that we put out something new every day, so you'll want to check it often." Stephanie was *good.*

The woman scrunched up her face to mimic a disappointed child. "Can't I just peek?"

Stephanie playfully returned the scrunch. "No," she whispered, "but if you tell me your stateroom number, I'll slip a preview list of items under your door."

The necklace woman went off pleased with the deal. Stephanie assembled some price lists and a photo or two, and sent me up to the Chesapeake deck to deliver them. "Then see if you can help out in the lounge," she said, and I knew I had been dismissed for the afternoon.

***

I was scheduled for one more week of housekeeping in the morning and busing tables at night before I'd be assigned to breakfast and lunch waitressing in the dining room. But by Sunday evening, I wondered if I'd even make it through the dinner hour, and I groaned as I climbed into my bunk afterward and sprawled out on the mattress.

"Even my blisters have blisters," Yolanda complained. "Why was this Sunday even harder than the first one?"

"Because then we were high on adrenaline," Lauren told her.

"Yeah, but you and Emily and Rachel have worked on cruise ships before," Natalie said.

"New cruise, new boss, whole new experience," Emily said.

It was a whole new experience, all right, because this time the ship didn't sail till later that evening. Something to do with a misunderstanding about a food delivery, or a change in the forecast, or a storm in the Midwest that had delayed the flights of six of our passengers . . . maybe all of these.

In any case, when we got up the next morning, whitecaps were forming on the water. Captain Haggerty announced that we'd arrive in Norfolk later than scheduled, and we might be in for a little rough weather on the way. But, he added cheerfully, it was all part of the adventure, and he was looking forward to seeing us at the Captain's Dinner that night. He suggested we stay inside, but there were already passengers at the railings on the decks above, practically welcoming the storm to come, as we departed the dock.

As the morning wore on, the wind grew stronger, and it rained heavily. At lunchtime Stephanie announced that there would be a game of Trivial Pursuit in the lounge, men versus women, and—just in case—guests could request seasick pills at the activities desk, but she doubted anyone would need them.

"Oh, she goofed there," whispered Lauren. "You never want to use the word 'seasick' on a ship. The power of suggestion, you know."

"This is June, after all," Stephanie continued, "and most of our summer cruises are calm and placid. But we're going to heat things up here with a battle between the sexes, so we invite everyone up to the lounge at two o'clock and let's see how you do."

It sounded like an interesting diversion, but the passengers were more interested in "storm at sea." They talked excitedly among themselves as to whether it was better to be high or low on a rocking ship and how high the waves might get on the Chesapeake.

When I went up to the observation deck to help Mitch and Barry secure the deck chairs—a long line over the row, tied down tightly at the other end—passengers were roaming about, head scarves and jackets flapping in the wind, taking pictures. Waves sloshed against the side of the ship, and the dark clouds moved even faster overhead.

I'll admit, I liked it too—liked listening to the thud as each wave slapped against the hull, sending spray several feet into the air.

The sky itself was like a sea, dark masses of roiling clouds racing above, the wind gusts so strong that passengers staggered backward, grasping the rail for support. Occasionally a wave was so high that the spray reached the floor of the lounge deck, and Ken McCoy made the rounds, ushering passengers inside.

When I checked the lounge at two-thirty, the Trivial Pursuit game didn't have many takers. A few men stood at the bar, drinks in hand, debating a history question, but the small group of women on the opposite side of the lounge were discussing something else entirely, and I saw Stephanie discreetly slip the cue cards back in the box. She checked the library shelves, instead, for books about weather and storms and placed them strategically around the room. But most of the passengers, by now, were in their staterooms.

As I helped straighten up the lounge—plastic cups that had slid off coffee tables, magazines on the floor—I saw the horizon out the windows disappear as the bow of the ship rose in the air, and then suddenly there it was again, disappearing once more as the bow dipped. It was then I began to feel queasy.

I went out in the hall and heard someone vomiting in the men's restroom, and I felt my own jaws tighten. How were we supposed to put on a Captain's Dinner that night with all this? I braced one hand against the wall to steady myself as the ship dipped again.

"Hey," said Josh, coming up the stairs from the main deck. "You don't look so good."

"Why doesn't the captain just dock somewhere?" I asked. "Most of the other boats went in an hour ago. We're the only ship out here."

"You can't dock a big ship like this in a storm," Josh said. "You try that with waves this high, we'd probably bring down half the pier and knock a hole in the hull too. If we're going to get tossed around, you want it to be out here, where we're not going to hit anything. Even if we got the ship docked, it would be too dangerous to try to get anyone off."

I closed my eyes and felt the tightness in my throat again as the ship rocked, the pull at the corners of my mouth.

Josh took my arm. "If you want the sailor's cure, come with me," he said.

"I'm not putting anything in my stomach, Josh."

"Don't have to." He gently pulled me toward the big panoramic window at the bow and positioned me right in front of the glass. "Now," he said, "focus on the horizon. Nothing else. Just focus."

I studied the faint demarcation line between gray sky and gray water.

"Now, no matter what the ship does, keep your eyes on the horizon," Josh said.

Standing at the bow of the ship with the huge picture windows, I could follow the horizon whether it rose or fell. I don't know if I was especially suggestive or whether it really worked. But like a ballerina focusing on one particular spot as she twirled, I guess, keeping an eye on the horizontal line ahead seemed to settle my stomach.

It was even better when Emily invited me to share her mackinaw, and we opened the lounge door to the deck, almost getting blown over by the wind. We went around to stand in front of the windows, the rain lashing our faces, and watched the horizon together from there. She was about six inches taller than me, and only my eyes peeked out from the collar of the rain gear.

"Let's don't tell anyone we're out here," she said, as though they couldn't see us through the window.

"Yes! We'll just stand here like the figurehead of a ship," I said.

"Two Maidens in Mackinaw," said Emily.

The worst of the storm was over by four thirty. The rain grew softer, the waves less forceful against the side of the ship, and though the sun never came out, the tumbling black clouds had floated away, leaving a dull gray sky in their wake.

The dining crew set up the reception in the lounge, and Emily and I went down to change into our dress shirts and black bow ties. When I came back up with Gwen and Pamela, guests were tentatively emerging from their rooms in cocktail attire, with their own story to tell of just how queasy they had been or how expertly they had survived the rock and rolling.

We didn't have a full house, though. A dozen or so passengers didn't show up all evening, and Shannon spent the whole time in the crew bathroom, we found out later. I also learned that none of our summer cruises had sold out completely, a worry for the company, which depended on every stateroom being occupied in order to break even.

But I'd made it through without barfing and had a good story to tell Patrick if I had time to text him later.

There was an e-mail waiting from him that night when I checked my laptop—a long one. In the few days he'd been in Barcelona, he told me, he'd walked along the Rambla, had made paella with his professor out of mussels and squid. He kept rolling off the couch where he slept at night, but he was easily falling into everyday Spanish, trying to strike up conversations with strangers, just to practice.

In turn, I e-mailed him about the bike ride around St. Michaels and the storm on our way to Norfolk.

We didn't have a full day in Norfolk because the storm had put us a few hours behind schedule. So Liz and I walked into town on our break to pick up a few things we needed from a drugstore and do a little window shopping.

A small boutique was advertising a new fragrance called Passion Petal, and Liz was overcome.

"It's the most glorious scent I've ever smelled," she said, and the woman in the purple smock behind the counter offered to spray her neck and shoulders.

"You'll just have to wash it off when you get back to the ship," I reminded her. I prefer a musky scent myself, but one of the rules was no perfume at all.

Liz felt obligated then to buy something, so she purchased a belt, but when we were starting back to the ship, she saw some flip-flops she wanted in a sandal shop. She had turndown duty that evening, but I was busing dinner, so I said I'd see her back on board and set off by myself.

I felt like a flight attendant, walking up the gangplank—one of the crew, not having to show a boarding pass—getting a nod from Ken or Josh or whoever was on duty. I went down to crew quarters and put on my uniform, checked my makeup, combed my hair. . . .

The ship sailed in twenty-five minutes, and people had gathered on the dock to watch us pull away. Deckhands were moving things around to make room for the gangplank when it swung back, but mostly it was showtime—all of us just waiting around, smiling at the children who waved up at us, willing the ship to move, ready for the blast of the horn.

I had just sauntered the length of the walkway when Dianne came hurrying toward me.

"Alice?" she said, and had the harried look she often gets just before we sail. "Where's Elizabeth?"

9
PASSION PETAL

I stared at her blankly. "She's not back?"

"No. And Pamela said she'd gone off with you."

"She did. We were shopping. But she has the late shift, so I came back early. She should be along any minute. Liz is *always* on time."

"Well, today she's not. And crew was supposed to be on board ten minutes ago. We sail in fifteen."

And when Curtis came up the gangplank, asking if it was time to bring it in, Dianne said, "Curtis, get the motor scooter and take Alice to wherever it was she saw Liz last. But be back before we sail. I can't afford to lose all three of you."

I had wondered about the motor scooter. I'd seen it locked to a chain on the *Seascape*'s stern. As Curtis wheeled it down onto the dock, I tried to remember what streets I'd been on with Liz. I hadn't been paying attention to street names.

Curtis handed me a helmet that was too big, but I buckled it under my chin, and when he asked, "Which way?" I could only tell him it was a small shop next to a CVS and I thought it had a blue sign with sort of yellow bubbles on it. I felt like an idiot.

"Hold on," said Curtis after I'd climbed on behind him, and I circled his body with my arms as we sped across the dock and waited for a light at the corner.

"Can you remember the name of the shop?" he yelled over his shoulder.

"No. I think it had the word 'song' in it, but . . . I can't remember."

The motor scooter sprang forward as the light turned green, and I pressed my cheek against his back to keep the wind out of my face. Now I knew why motorcyclists wore goggles.

"Tell me if you see anything familiar," Curtis shouted at the next intersection. "I think the shops begin about here."

He turned down another street, and I frantically surveyed the storefronts on one side, then the other. A nail store, a hair salon . . .

What would Liz do if the ship left without her? It was so unlike her not to be back on time. It was usually Liz who looked at her watch and said, "Let's hurry."

I saw a paint store on a corner and remembered that it had a color wheel in the window. We'd stopped to find teal, because Liz said the color had more blue than green, and I said more green than blue.

"It's down that street, I think," I said. "We're getting close."

But even before we reached the corner, we saw the flashing lights of a rescue squad double-parked outside a CVS and a policeman keeping people from entering the store.

"The drugstore!" I cried, tugging at Curtis's shirt. "And there's the boutique. Let me off."

"We've got about seven minutes," Curtis said.

I jumped off the scooter and ran across the street, looking both ways for the sandal shop. When I spotted it, a woman was standing outside, arms hugging herself.

"My friend Elizabeth was just here," I said. "She was interested in those blue flip-flops with the silver streaks? Do you have any idea where she went next?"

The woman nodded toward the CVS and said, "She bought flip-flops and then went across the street to shop. But about fifteen minutes ago she came back here and said she was feeling sick. She wanted a place to sit down. I told her there were chairs at the pharmacy in the back of the CVS and walked her as far as the entrance to make sure she got in okay. . . . I'm here alone so I can't leave my shop. And five minutes ago the rescue team pulled up."

A little crowd had gathered, but the policeman still wouldn't let anyone enter the store. Inside I could see two men moving about, coming toward the entrance. And then the glass doors of the CVS swung open, and a man backed out, pulling a stretcher, while a second man guided it out the door.

"Liz!" I cried, recognizing the dark hair splayed against the pillow.

She barely moved her head.

"It's Liz!" I called to Curtis.

"You know this girl?" one of the rescue workers asked.

"Yes! We're part of the crew on the *Seascape*. We've been looking all over for her. What happened?"

"You'd better ride along," said the other worker.

The next few minutes were surreal. I walked alongside Liz, holding her hand as they wheeled her toward the truck. One cheek looked puffy and her lips too full—like they'd been enlarged—and I wondered if some shop was offering free samples of collagen.

"Liz?" I kept saying. "I'm here. You okay?" which was stupid, because she obviously wasn't. All I could figure was that she'd fallen on her face or something.

Then they were lifting the stretcher up and sliding it into an ambulance while Curtis was talking to one of the guys. When I tried to climb in after Liz, the other man told me to sit up front.

"You can't ride back here," he said, motioning around to the other door. I ran to the passenger side and had to climb to crawl in. Then the truck was moving forward, and the siren was going, and cars were moving out of our way.

It was a hard, bumpy ride that must have felt even worse to Liz, whatever had happened. And it was so noisy—the engine itself was so loud—that it was hard to hear much of anything. I squirmed around enough under my seat belt to see Liz. She had an oxygen mask over her nose, but I was shocked to see that the man bending over her had turned her on her side and was pulling her shorts down.

"Hey!" I cried. I mean, you read about things like this in the paper, rescue workers and unconscious patients and . . .

But the molester paid no attention; he had pulled on surgical gloves, and then I saw him jab some kind of needle device into her left buttock.

Liz yelped.

"Hey!" I said again, but the worker rolled her onto her other side, picked up another syringe, and injected the right buttock. She yelped again and tried to swat at him, and this time he must have been talking into a radio phone because I heard him say, "Okay, Doc, I've given her one cc of epinephrine and one of Benadryl IM."

The driver glanced at me. "Bee sting. She's having a bad reaction, and we had to get medication into her fast."

I turned forward again and closed my eyes momentarily. Okay, so I overreacted.

If I didn't stop hyperventilating, I'd be the next patient.

I expected Liz to be unconscious, but by the time they had wheeled her into a cubicle at a local hospital and I could stand beside her, she'd turned her face in my direction. She was staring strangely at my head. I realized I was still wearing the helmet and lifted it off.

But I didn't even get a chance to say anything, because a doctor and a woman with a clipboard crowded into the cubicle behind me, and I squeezed out of their way. They rolled her onto another stretcher and attached an IV to her arm. More monitors. More oxygen. I was terrified.

"Elizabeth, do you know where you are?" asked the young doctor in a white coat with the name badge DR. GRINLEY, on it. I couldn't tell if she nodded or not.

"Would you tell me your full name?"

I started to answer for her, but Dr. Grinley shook his head.

It was obviously taking Liz some effort. She rolled her tongue around in her mouth, and finally said, "E-li-a-beh An Pr-i . . ."

"Good enough," Dr. Grinley said, checking the clipboard. "Elizabeth Ann Price, right?"

She nodded.

"You've had an allergic reaction to a bee sting," the doctor told her. "We're going to keep a close watch on you, but I think the medications we've given you are starting to take effect, and you should be fine." He turned toward me. "And you are?"

"Alice McKinley, her friend. We're part of the crew on the *Seascape*, but I think they must have already sailed. . . ."

I don't know if you can call a doctor cute, but Dr. Grinley wore glasses with designer frames that looked really good on him. Maybe he was more than an intern if he could afford those. He had the greenest eyes I'd ever seen. Usually green-eyed people have hazel flecks, but his irises looked more like shamrocks.

"You, uh, work in the engine room or something?" he asked with a trace of a smile, and I realized he was looking at the helmet in my hand.

"We were out looking for Liz on the ship's motor scooter," I said.

Dr. Grinley was watching the monitors hooked up to Liz and began reading off numbers, which the woman with the clipboard wrote down. "Blood pressure, one twenty-six over seventy-seven," he said. "Pulse, eighty-five." Then he said to Liz, "Excuse me," and slipped his stethoscope up under her T-shirt and checked her heart, then asked her to roll over on her side so he could hold it to her back, and checked her lungs.

"Breathing's good, vital signs good," he said, and relaxed a little. "Where's the ship heading?" he asked me.

"Yorktown next," I said.

"Well, I'm glad it's not heading for the Bahamas or the Caribbean, because we've got to keep Elizabeth here for at least another hour to make sure the allergen is out of her system."

At that moment Dr. Grinley got a call over the PA system, and he pulled off his gloves. "The nurse will keep an eye on you, and I'll check you again before you leave," he told Liz. "Would you allow your friend here to find your wallet and give us some information about your insurance?"

She nodded, and whoosh—the doctor was gone. We were left with the woman with the clipboard, who handed me Elizabeth's bag. I fished around for her wallet, found the insurance card, and gave the clerk the information she needed. As soon as she was gone, a nurse came in bringing Liz a glass of Gatorade or something with a bent straw.

"I'll be back in a few minutes. Press this buzzer if you need anything at all," she said.

For the first time Liz and I were alone.

I stared down at her and made a face. She smiled a little but still looked strange.

"Man, when you make a scene, you make a *scene*!" I told her. "Dianne sent Curtis and me out on the motor scooter to see if we could find you. What happened?"

Haltingly, stopping occasionally to roll her tongue around like she was trying to get it back in place, Liz told me how she had bought the flip-flops, done some more window shopping, and then, about the time she decided to head back, she'd felt a sting on her cheek and swatted a bee away.

Now she reached up and gingerly touched her lips. "It flew off, but . . . I don't know . . . my lips felt funny and my cheek was . . . beginning to swell, and I had this sort of panicky feeling. I went back to the shoe store to ask if I could sit down, and the woman told me to go to the CVS . . . and . . . I'm not sure what happened after that. I think the pharmacist called 911. And then you were there with that thing on your head . . . I'm sure the ship's sailed by now, Alice. What are we going to do?"

I hadn't got that far yet, but suddenly I realized I had nothing with me but a helmet that wasn't even mine. No toothbrush, no ID . . .

Liz nodded toward her bag. "Check my messages?" she asked.

I picked up her bag again, set it on my lap, and began rummaging through it. "Can I use your lip gloss and comb if we have to sleep all night on the dock?" I asked.

"Do I have any tampons?" she asked.

I fished around some more. "One. Can I have half?"

"If I get the half with the string," she said, and we were laughing when the nurse came back.

"Well, well, that's a good sign," she said. "We're going to get you up and moving, Elizabeth. We won't release you till we're absolutely sure you're going to be okay, but right now I'd bet on it. We'll give you some epinephrine syringes and Benadryl capsules to take with you."

While Liz stood and walked and turned and sat and performed all the other obedience tricks the nurse asked of her, the IV stand rolling along beside, I checked her messages. There was one from Dianne:

Goodness gracious, Liz! The hospital called with news about your allergic reaction. We do hope you're okay and are glad you got immediate help. We'll be holding the ship for a little while to see if you can make it. Check in with the harbormaster when you get back.

"This is forty minutes old," I said.

Liz looked pleadingly at the nurse. "I really need to leave," she said. "Look! I can stand on one foot!" She tried and almost fell over.

"Or not," the nurse said. "Sorry, but we've got to keep you a while longer. Doctor's orders. We'll call a cab to get you to the dock."

"I've been stung before and this never happened," Liz told her.

"She never wore Passion Petal perfume before either," I commented, and the nurse smiled.

"Bees love anything that smells floral, but I wouldn't press my luck. Especially with you out on a cruise ship where you can't get immediate help. If you're ever alone when this happens again and have to give yourself an epinephrine injection—and this is only if you experience a breathing problem or facial swelling—you can use your thigh. If someone's there with you, they can either inject your buttocks or inject you like this." She squeezed the inside of Elizabeth's upper arm and made a lump. "Right there," she said.

"Then why . . . ?" Liz asked, and flushed slightly.

"Why did the ER guys use your fanny? Well, what other excitement would they have on a slow Tuesday?" the nurse said. "Joke! Joke! Seriously, that's the best place because there's lots of muscle back there, and it's less likely to bother you."

"Less likely than to have a guy she doesn't know holding her down with one hand and pulling her pants down with the other?" I said. "No telling what would have happened if I hadn't been watching. You owe me one, Liz."

I nudged her and we laughed.

"The ER guys are trained to do what they do, and we're glad

to have them," the nurse said. "But I'm going to give you some towels and cleanser to get all that perfume off before you leave here. And if I were you, I'd shampoo my hair as soon as I was back on the ship." She unhooked Liz from the IV and pointed the way to a restroom.

As we went down the hall, Liz said, "I hate needles. I can't stand the thought of injecting myself."

"Not to worry," I said. "We'll get one of the guys to help out."

When Liz was released at last, we sprang out of the hospital entrance like runners at the sound of the starting gun. I guess people who have to work in linoleum-floored places with antiseptic smells and hallways lined with stretchers concentrate on other things, like flowers in the gift shop and coffee machines and sunrooms and the banter of staff in the elevators.

But all we wanted to do was get back on board and forget that this ever happened. Liz had stuffed the syringes and capsules in her bag along with her new flip-flops, and at last the taxi pulled up to the docking area. Liz paid the driver and asked for a receipt, and then we bounded down to the waterfront to face . . . a big empty space.

There's nothing quite like staring far out over the Chesapeake Bay at your cruise ship, sailing slowly out of sight.

10

STATEROOM 303

If ever there was a sinking feeling, this was the sinkiest.

"A-lice!" Liz whimpered. "Should we just jump?"

But somebody was looking out for us. A guy in a cap that made him look official walked over and said, "You wouldn't happen to be Elizabeth and Alice, would you?"

We turned and just stared at him, like he was the angel Gabriel.

"I'm harbormaster here, and I'm supposed to get you to Yorktown, which isn't far as the crow flies but sure is a round-about way by land. And since the *Seascape* left only ten minutes ago, why don't you get in my boat and I'll take you out to your ship? I'll call and let them know we're coming."

And that's how we found ourselves skimming across the

water in a fancy speedboat with a cabin up front, our hair tossed by the wind in an early-evening sky, grins on our faces. The harbormaster invited us to ride in the cabin with him, but we wanted to experience the whole nine yards, and Liz said no bees would bother her at thirty knots or whatever speed we were moving.

We were met by a little welcoming committee of Quinton and Curtis and Ken McCoy. The captain had to drop anchor to get us aboard, but we were so grateful that we kissed the harbormaster and he said he was glad to oblige, we were welcome to miss the ship anytime.

Liz had to sit out her shift that night, but Dianne wanted to keep an eye on her, so she put her to work folding napkins from the laundry. By the time she had recounted her adventure several times over to everyone in the galley, both she and I were sick of hearing it, but it made good material to e-mail home.

The air was super fresh in Yorktown the next day. Since I'd toured Yorktown the last time we were here, I opted to take a towel and lie out on the beach with Natalie and Lauren and Pam in our bikinis, away from the immediate gaze of passengers, but not so far away that no one could find us. I was mentally composing another e-mail to Patrick.

I really do wish you were here, I would say. *Or that I was there with you.* But I would stop just short of saying *I miss you*, like, if I went any further, it would open a whole universe of yearning.

Later I'd tell him my big surprise: I was saving all I earned this summer so I could visit him in Spain at Christmastime.

The ship headed for Crisfield the following morning, and once again, it didn't look as though I was going to be able to make the ferry along with the passengers to visit Tangier Island. There were too many dawdlers, and when Dianne told me I'd need to clean four more staterooms on the main deck as well, I knew for certain I wouldn't make Tangier Island.

"Is one of the crew sick?" I asked, wiping my forehead with my arm.

She gave me a woeful, resigned look. "Not exactly. But Shannon's getting off at Crisfield," she said.

Crisfield? No one would get off at Crisfield to stay unless they were fired, I thought. Dianne didn't stick around to explain, so I kept my questions to myself. All of a sudden I didn't feel so secure. Shannon had been a good worker, I thought. She didn't love her job, exactly, but she was polite to the passengers and reasonably friendly with them. Unless she'd done something horrendous, how could I be sure that Dianne wouldn't tell me or one of my friends to just pack up and get off if we did something inexcusable in her eyes?

I moved to the next stateroom, determined to do everything by the book.

"Housekeeping," I called as I tapped on the door. I glanced at my watch. It was ten. Passengers who were going ashore had already gathered on the main deck near the gangway.

I picked up my bucket and tapped once more, then turned my key in the lock. "Housekeeping," I called again as I opened the door.

As I entered, a man of about forty stepped out of the tiny bathroom buck naked, wiping his armpits with a towel.

"Oh! Sorry!" I said, and backed out so quickly that my bucket clanged against the door frame and clattered onto the deck.

I closed the door after me and felt my face burning. Either I hadn't heard him tell me he was there or he hadn't heard my knock. Dianne would probably get a complaint before the day was over. I went quickly on to the next room, hoping that if I met that man face-to-face, we wouldn't recognize each other.

I did all my other rooms, then went back to number 303. The curtains on the little walkway window were still drawn. I knocked two times and called two times, then opened the door a crack. And when I turned on the light, the room was empty. Only one of two beds had been occupied, so I realized it was a single man traveling alone, probably had to pay extra to occupy the room. I cleaned it hastily and left.

Back in crew quarters that evening, as we changed for dinner, the chief topic of conversation was why Shannon had left. No one had seen her go. She'd just packed her bag and was out of there.

"Her smokes," said Emily. "I think she was fired."

"But she could smoke onshore all she wanted," I said, buttoning my shirt and smoothing out the pocket. We have to share a washing machine with the guys, and if someone finds your stuff in the dryer, they just take it out and drop it, and the wrinkles are up to you.

"I think she was smoking on the ship too, up on the top deck when she thought no one else was there," Emily told us.

"I can't believe they'd let her go over that," Gwen said.

Lauren came in from the bathroom and joined the conversation. "The way I heard it from Josh, Dianne noticed the smell on her breath and thought it pretty offensive. She told Shannon she had the choice of keeping her breath fresh or sticking with housekeeping the whole ten weeks, that she couldn't wait tables because several passengers had complained. And Shannon said, quote, 'Enough of this shit, I'm outta here,' so Dianne told her she was off at Crisfield. Curtis said he didn't think they'd replace her. Which means the rest of us have to work harder."

"But when we divide up the tips at the end of each week, it means we each get a little more," said Rachel.

"Yeah, but, man! That was quick," Yolanda said. "I mean, the work gets you down now and then. Anyone could say something they might be sorry for later. You're out of your summer job, just like that?"

"You are when your employer knows that they could replace any one of us overnight if they wanted to. Just put up a notice at Harborplace when we get back, and I'll bet someone would apply within ten minutes," Rachel told us. "Even at *our* wages."

"Great," I said. "I'll probably be the next to go." And I told them what had happened that morning in room 303. They thought it was hilarious.

"Of course he won't report it," Emily said. "You can bet he won't be anywhere in sight when housekeeping comes around tomorrow."

There was a light tap on the door. Gwen checked to see that we were all dressed, then opened it. Curtis was standing there holding a peach-colored bra in one hand. "Found this in the dryer along with my stuff," he said, handing it over.

"Anybody?" Gwen asked, holding it up.

"The dryer?" Natalie asked. "It was in the dryer? The way I'm eating, I can't afford any shrinkage."

"Bon appétit," said Curtis, and went back to men's quarters at the end of the hall.

I didn't really mind missing Oxford the next day, because that was no biggie on my list. But the addition of four extra rooms to clean was a lot. When I came to room 303, I started to knock, thought better of it, and did two more rooms before I returned. The drapes were still closed, as they had been the day before.

I knocked. Loudly.

"Housekeeping," I called.

No response.

I knocked again. "Housekeeping!"

I turned the key and opened the door a couple of inches, calling again.

When I got inside and turned on the light, the man was lying naked on the bed, hands behind his head, smiling at me strangely.

I went back out without a word and closed the door, my heart pounding, my cheeks flaming once again. Was he *trying* to get me fired? What was his *problem*? What was I supposed to do? But it was his face that bothered me the most. I wouldn't call it seductive or threatening or anything. More . . . tentative? Anxious, even.

I was perspiring all over, and I walked to the fantail at the stern to cool off.

"What's the matter?" Yolanda asked me as I passed. She put down her bucket and followed me back. "That guy again?"

I nodded and told her what happened.

"Was he, you know? Did he have a hard-on?"

"I'm not even sure. Believe it or not, I was looking at his face."

"You going back there? Want me to go with you?"

"No! I'll wait. Last time this happened, he was gone when I got back." I truly didn't know what to do. I hated to tell anyone there was something I couldn't deal with on my own. And, as I'd hoped, when I finally went back to his cabin that afternoon, he was gone. I cleaned it in record time and left. Except for the unmade bed, the room had been neat. There were no suggestive magazines lying around. No condoms. No underwear on the floor.

But the next morning in Annapolis, as I was finishing up on the lounge deck, Dianne asked if I could help her on the main deck. I still hadn't knocked on door 303. I decided to level with her, explaining why I had one more room yet to do.

She listened, her head cocked to one side, then held my arm as we went back to room 303.

"You call, I'll go in," she said.

I clanked my bucket. "Housekeeping!" I called.

No response. If he was dressed now and answered the door, would Dianne ever believe me? If a passenger decided to make trouble for you, he could. What if Mrs. Collier had never found her watch? Would Dianne always wonder if I had taken it? What if I reported this guy and then he denied it?

I knocked again and called louder.

Nothing.

Dianne put her key in the lock. "Wait here," she mouthed, and went inside.

I didn't see what she saw, but I heard her say, matter-of-factly, "Good morning, Mr. Jurgis. We'd appreciate it if you'd get dressed so we can clean your room. I'll be back in a few minutes." She came out, closing the door behind her, and we walked to the stern and waited where we could keep an eye on the door.

"Was he . . . ?"

"Naked as a jaybird," she said.

"Is he dangerous?" I asked.

"Probably not. He likes the shock on women's faces when he exposes himself. He looked embarrassed, frankly, but I doubt it will happen again. Not on this cruise."

"He's sailed with you before?"

"Not him, but there have been a few others." She looked at

me, bemused. "He's just part of the great human swarm, Alice. We all have our eccentricities."

We heard the door of room 303 open, and seconds later Mr. Jurgis left, walking briskly, heading for the stairs.

Later, when I passed him in the lounge, he walked right by me as though he'd never seen me before.

11
HOMEBOY

You don't see much of the captain on a cruise ship. Whenever we spent evenings docked, Captain Haggerty usually went ashore for dinner. Like most pilots, I suppose, he had friends here and there along his route. But he and Ken McCoy often had lunch together in the pilothouse, and they spelled each other when one of them needed a break.

For the lowly crew, though, one of our favorite times aboard the ship was dinner, which we ate only after the last passenger had left the dining room. We didn't have the same menu, of course—no rack of lamb for us. Dormitory stuff all the way, but it was well prepared, and Chef Carlo's fettuccini was to die for.

Conversation at dinner depended on who was there. If

Quinton or Dianne ate with us, we kept things polite and light. If it was crew only, there was more gossip, more noise.

One thing I noticed was that we didn't talk much about our plans beyond the summer. Once in a while someone would mention that he was staying over when the fall cruises began or would be working for another line. We kept to the present—how many staterooms we'd been assigned to clean, where we could cash our checks, which bar might serve without checking your ID. There were a lot of stories about the past—getting stuck on a roller coaster at Kings Dominion or deep-sea fishing off Ocean City. It was understood, I guess, that this was time-out for whatever we might face in the fall.

At the start of the third week, Pamela and I were among the groggy ones who rose at five thirty to set the tables for breakfast and welcome the passengers, who began arriving at seven.

Breakfast, we discovered, was the most difficult meal of the day. Not only did people wander in at odd times, but each had her own routine—four prunes, not three; half a Belgian waffle and one strip of bacon, not sausage. At lunch people settled for a club sandwich and a bowl of soup; and at dinner either baked or scalloped potatoes would usually do. But at breakfast our order pads were full of instructions—coffee, no cream; toast, no butter; sunny-side up, not scrambled.

In the galley on Tuesday, Mitch was swearing under his breath as he fished out seven raisins from a bowl of oatmeal.

"You'd think they were bugs," he said. "She couldn't do this herself?"

"Don't forget to smile," I teased. But no sooner had we closed the dining room doors and vacuumed the rug then it was time to set the tables for lunch.

It was after three before we got our break, too late for any excursion, but at least we had it fairly easy the rest of the day. We did the bed turndowns during dinner, distributed the program for the following day, followed the chocolate-on-every-pillow routine.

Pamela and I usually went up on the observation deck after we'd finished, provided no passengers were up there and we could have it to ourselves. We stretched out on the lounge chairs or propped our feet on the railing. Pamela looked a little less harried this week, I thought.

"Things settling down on the mom front?" I asked, keeping it general.

She slowly turned her head in my direction and gave me a sardonic smile. "No, not really."

"Okayyyy," I said. "But I haven't heard your cell phone ringing so much."

"Because I don't bring it with me on breaks, and I keep it turned off in crew quarters, that's why. If Mom has a real emergency, she can call the main office and they'd get in touch with the ship."

"True," I said, and leaned my head back, enjoying the last rays of the sun that warmed without roasting.

But I'd left the conversation open, and Pamela was in a pensive mood: "It's all about *her*, you know? I finally figured that out the other day. *Her* car! *Her* doctor's appointment! *Her* schedule! It's like nobody else ever has problems!"

I followed the trail of a plane so high, I could barely see it—just a blinking dot of light across the ocean of sky. "I thought your mom was doing better for a while. What do you think—that things not working out with that guy started her off again?"

"That and the fact that Meredith's still in the picture."

"She and your dad ever going to get married?"

"I don't know. I wouldn't be surprised if she moves in with Dad after I leave for college. Meredith's good for him in a lot of ways. If they do ever marry, Mom will be the last person they'll tell."

"Well, *you* seem to be taking all this remarkably well," I told her.

"I made a deal with myself," Pamela said. "I'll check my cell phone twice a day to make sure there's no emergency, and I'll text Mom once a week, just to keep in touch. But that's it."

"Sounds good to me," I said.

Finally I got to Tangier Island. Quinton told us that if there was an excursion along the cruise that we really wanted to take, we could go if we found someone who'd trade jobs with us. Emily said she'd take my tables at breakfast and lunch if I'd take her galley duty that evening. So on Wednesday morning I stood in line at Crisfield with the *Seascape* tour group to board the ferry to the island, and I was pleasantly surprised to find Mitch waiting too.

"I figured this was the last port of call you'd want," I said.

He smiled down at me, the bill of his cap facing forward now to shield his eyes from the sun. He wore a nondescript T-shirt of an indeterminate color—khaki, perhaps—and cargo shorts and old deck shoes without socks. And he was perfectly put together.

"Why'd you think that?" he asked.

I shrugged. "I don't know. Just imagined you'd probably been here before."

"Five or six years ago. Wanted to see if it's changed."

"Good! Then you can show me around."

"Glad to." The smile again.

Mitch was one of those people who made you happy just by being there. I'm not sure what it was. He gave off a feeling of quiet acceptance. Whatever or whoever you were was okay with him. No agenda.

Stephanie, a sailor cap perched jauntily on her head, was handing out touristy maps of the seahorse-shaped island—Cod Harbor, Whale Point, the tidal flats. . . . Except for a couple of the other male stewards, Mitch and I were the only crew members on the ferry.

We sat on the back bench in the little throng of passengers who were listening to Stephanie's introduction to the island. She was speaking at a higher pitch than normal, trying to be heard above the drumming of the engine as the ferry moved across the water.

"Tangier—the place where time stands still," she was saying, "the most unbelievable sunsets you'll ever see. No cars, no buses . . ."

I wasn't prepared, I guess, for how wide the bay was, now that I could really pay attention to it. Looking at it on a map, the bay looks like the trunk of a tree, with rivers forming its limbs, then creeks branching off into smaller and smaller streams beyond. You'd think you would see a shore—both shores, perhaps—wherever you were on the bay. But here we were in the widest part, and I couldn't see land ahead or behind us or on either side.

It was cool on the ferry when the sun went behind a cloud, and we were just far enough to one side of the boat's cabin that we got the wind from the bow. I wished I'd brought a jacket. Mitch noticed the way I was hugging myself and pointed wordlessly to the goose bumps on my arms, one eyebrow raised in a curious, bemused way.

"Feels good to be cold for a change," I lied, but I knew that the minute the boat stopped, we'd get the unrelenting heat of the summer sun.

Slowly, slowly, a few blurred objects came into view as I got my first glimpse of the island—the steeple of a church, a water tower. . . . The base of all the low buildings seemed to be level with the choppy gray water as we approached. There was scarcely a tree higher than the roof of a house. The ferryboat's engine noise dropped to a mutter as we entered a narrow channel, and a white egret, balancing on one leg, didn't even move as its yellow eye followed us over to the dock.

Islanders waited there for relatives returning from the mainland, with small wagons or shopping carts to haul purchases back to their homes. Already my ears picked up the remnants of Old English in their dialect. As we waited to disembark, I heard one woman ask another if she had been able to see all her grandchildren this trip, and the woman replied, "Ever' one of 'em, and theer mamas let them speak theer mooinds no matter what they say. But, Lor', live and let live. Day I cain't go across the sound to see 'em, I know I'll doie."

Mitch and I smiled at each other, and as we stepped off the ferry, he lifted the woman's heavy bundle for her and placed it in the waiting cart of a friend.

"Much obliged," the round-faced woman said.

"Good day for strollin'," the friend remarked, and probably saw us as a couple.

We followed the *Seascape*'s tour group through the line of crab shanties and boat sheds, stopping to let a golf cart pass, the island's method of transporting tourists around. But when we reached King Street, which served as the backbone of the island, Mitch put one hand on my shoulder and we set off in a different direction.

"Let's see it on our own," he said. "I'd like to mosey around the way I did six years ago when I was here."

"Okay, let's mosey," I said, liking the idea. "What were you here for then?"

"Came with my dad to see about a boat for sale. Didn't end up buying it, but I got to look around a bit."

There wasn't much of a breeze, strangely. You'd think that an island would always have one, and there wasn't much shade, either. But I liked the feeling that I was here on an island in the middle of the bay and that I couldn't see land in any direction.

We headed for the salt marsh, ambling over to where two young boys—maybe ten and twelve—sat in a rowboat untangling some fishing line, both of them barefoot.

"How ya doin'?" Mitch asked them.

They shielded their eyes against the sun and looked up, lips parted, showing adult teeth they hadn't quite grown into.

"Mornin'," one of them said while the other went back to work on the tangled line.

"Catch anything yet?" Mitch asked.

"Nary a one," said the first boy. His tousled blond hair hung loose almost to his shoulders, wind-blown and sun-bleached. He could have been Emily's cousin, he had so many freckles. But then he brightened. "This here's my boat," he said proudly. "I'll be savin' up for a motor, and then I can take her out beyond the flats!"

"Hey! Good for you!" Mitch said, and watched them some more. The two were working together now to untangle the line, so we moved on. I heard Mitch chuckle.

I looked up at him. "What?"

"That was the biggest day of my life so far, when I got my first boat," he said. "I know just what that kid's feeling."

"Sort of like getting your own car?"

"Exactly. There's no fence out there on the water. You can go wherever you like."

As we walked across a large piece of plywood the boys had constructed as a sort of bridge to get to the next little ridge, Mitch grabbed my hand to help me across, and when we stepped off the other end, we jauntily fell into step walking arm in arm as we started our tour of the island.

It really was a walk back in time—a decaying trawler beached on a spit of sand; a couple of leather-faced watermen mending their nets; and, as we made another turn, the weather-beaten clapboard houses, some with raised graves and headstones in the front yard to protect them from the sea.

A sun-bonneted woman on a bicycle rode by, taking her time, her bedroom-slippered feet pressing down on the pedals.

Miss Molly's Bed and Breakfast, Hilda Crockett's Chesapeake House, Shirley's Bay View Inn, Spanky's Ice Cream, Lorraine's Sandwich Shop . . . Everything, it seemed, was named for somebody. Some of the names—Pruitt, Crockett, Parks—appeared again and again, as though there were mainlanders, like me, and then there were the real settlers, who had watched sunsets from these houses forever.

"You hungry for a soft-shell crab sandwich?" Mitch asked me, reading a sign in a window.

"There is such a thing?"

"Yep."

"I'm game if you are," I said, and thought how much more

willing I was to try something new with him than I was with Ryan McGowan last spring—Ryan, who had tried to change me from the inside out.

I don't think we'd passed a single person who didn't say hello, and the same happened when Mitch opened the screen door and we went inside the shop.

"You Earl Park's youngest?" asked the sixtyish man at the deep fryer. The lenses of his glasses were spotted with grease and foggy with steam.

"No, sir, I'm up in Dorchester County," Mitch said.

"Oh. Murland, then," the man said, giving us a welcoming smile, and I remembered that Tangier belongs to Virginia. Strange, the invisible line that travels across bay waters.

"Yeah, I was here six years ago and just wanted to see if things had changed," Mitch said.

"Boot the same, but thar's less of it," the man said, wiping his hands on his thick apron and coming closer to the counter. "Ever' year the bay takes a bit more of the island. Some day, they say, it'll take a boite and swaller it down. What'll you folks have?"

We placed our order and sat down at one of the few small tables by the window. The spicy scent of seasonings filled the air and made me realize how hungry I was.

"Lucky we got a table. I expect some of the tour group will be in here after a while," I said.

"No, they've got reservations at Hilda Crockett's—that's part of the tour," Mitch said. "Walk in there, you come out two pounds heavier, your wallet a little lighter." He took off his cap and placed it on the empty chair beside us. "Hilda used to advertise, 'If you leave hungry, it will be your fault, not ours.' Probably still does."

I watched him settle back in his chair. "You look more contented here," I told him. "More relaxed."

"More contented than where?"

"Back on board."

"Expect I am. Always figured I could feel at home most anywhere, though, long as it was on the bay. You ever feel that way about Silver Spring?"

No one had ever asked me that before. I started to say, *It's a much bigger place,* then realized that—compared to the bay—it was a speck on a map.

"I know the major streets," I said, "and if you dropped me off someplace, I could get somewhere I recognized. But I wouldn't call that 'feeling at home.'"

"Well, that's what I mean by home," Mitch explained. "Bay's sort of like a big, spread-out family—the watermen part of it, anyway. I don't feel the same about Baltimore or Annapolis, but leave me on an island—Smith, Tangier—along the coast or in the marshes, it's pretty much home territory, whether I've been there before or not."

We sat smiling at each other, and I was about to ask about his family when the counterman appeared with a platter in each hand. He set one down in front of me—fries at one end, coleslaw at the other, and in the middle, two pieces of white bread with a crab in between, its spindly, golden-brown legs hanging out at each side.

"Ulp!" I said, looking from my sandwich to Mitch and back again.

"If you don't want it, I'll eat yours, too, and you can order something else," he said.

And that's all it took to make me try it. I imagined fried onion rings. I imagined crusty Popeye's chicken. I took a bite of bread and lettuce and mayonnaise and something crispy and delicious, and the second bite was even better.

As we finished lunch, I told him about going out with Ryan after the spring play and how he had introduced me to oysters on the half shell, as well as all the things he found wrong with me.

"I'm glad this time was different," Mitch said. "Having fun?"

"Yes. I'm glad you came along."

"Something new to tell the boyfriend," he said, and his eyes were laughing as he wiped his mouth.

"You going to tell your girlfriend?"

"I would if I had one."

"That's hard to believe—that there's no one to tell."

He kept his eyes on me as he took a long swallow of Coke, but he had the same amused expression on his face. "There are only three hundred people in Vienna, Maryland, where I live, and most of them are middle-aged."

"Where exactly is Vienna, by the way?"

Mitch put on his country-boy accent: "Wah, it's haafway 'tween the Nanticoke and the Chicamacomico Rivers," he said.

"And of the nine gals my age in town, two of them's my cousins."

I laughed. "Where do you go to meet people, then?"

"Salisbury. Quantico, if you want to watch a bunch of Marines get drunk. But every once in a while a friend knows a friend. . . . That's the best way."

"So now you're cruising a cruise ship?" I said, and watched his grin spread across his whole face.

"There are some nice girls on that ship," Mitch said. Then, checking his watch, "Want to see the rest of the island?"

"I do," I said, wiping the grease off my mouth and chin.

"What we *can't* do," Mitch said as he scooted away from the table, "is miss the ferry. Do that, and we'd have to hire one of the watermen to carry us back."

We set out again up King Street. We passed the town hall and the New Testament Church; passed a girl of maybe thirteen or fourteen, leaning against a gate, ankles crossed. She was toying with a locket around her neck, talking with a boy about the same age who straddled a motorbike. And we could tell by the look in their eyes as we passed that they'd be seeing each other again.

12
THE GUESTS

Sometimes we fell into the rhythm of ship life so completely that it was as though fall and college and classes and grades were off in the distant future, not just weeks away.

Gwen and I had long ago decided we'd be roommates when we entered the University of Maryland. Then she found out that pre-med students could room for half the cost at a big house near campus, donated by a wealthy alumnus, and it would be crazy for her not to stay there for her eight years. So I was in the market for a roommate.

I'd indicated on Facebook that I was looking for a roomie, but being at sea most of the summer, I didn't get a chance very often to check and see if there were any takers. Like many colleges, the U of Maryland assigns roommates for the first year, but if two people both request each other, the housing office usually okays it. I'd posted my cell phone number and e-mail address, though, and now and then I heard from girls wanting to know if I was going to pledge a sorority or if I was into sports. As I only had a short time each day to use my cell phone, and even less chance to check my e-mail, I answered some messages too late or not at all.

Then late one night in the dining room, when we were checking our e-mails, I got one from a Margaret Sanderson—"Meggie," she called herself—who said she was the niece of one of Dad's customers at the Melody Inn, and she'd heard all about me and was so excited that I was going to Maryland too. *I read on Facebook you were looking for a roommate, and so am I, she texted. My aunt loves your dad's store, and so do I. Haven't decided on a major yet, have you?*

The message was three days old, and I hadn't had a chance to answer yet, but Meggie seemed possible.

Right now I'm working on a cruise ship, I e-mailed back, *but let's introduce ourselves.*

Ten minutes later, she answered:

> *Great! I hope I don't sound like I'm bragging, but I've got a 3.98 GPA. I write novellas, but none have been published yet (who knows? you may be a character in one someday!!!), and I've had a crush on a guy who doesn't even know me for, like, forever. But I could write about myself all day, who couldn't? Why don't we each ask three friends to say what they like about us (or not!!!)? Here are mine.*

I stared at my screen. She was serious!

Hi. I'm Paige, probably Meggie's best friend. If Meggie has a fault, it's that she's totally honest. She tells you just what she thinks whether you want to hear it or not. But when my cat died, she stayed with me all night just to make sure I was all right.

The next paragraph read:

I've been Margaret's friend for two years. She's perfect in every way except she reads your mail. Oops! Meggie's trying to take the laptop out of my hands. . . .

"I don't believe this!" I said aloud.

"What?" asked Liz.

I scanned down to the third paragraph.

Okay, we're serious now. Meggie is one of the nicest girls I know. We went to camp together once and she gave every girl in our cabin a pedicure. We had a lot of fun together. She was into hypnotism at one point and claims she can hypnotize a chicken. Really. She can! She'll talk about almost anything, but she hates potatoes. Especially potato salad made with vinegar.

"Oh . . . my . . . God!" I said.

"Who's e-mailing you?" asked Lauren.

"You guys have got to help me!" I said in answer. "How am I going to get out of rooming with the niece of one of my dad's best customers? This girl would drive me crazy."

"Just tell her you found somebody else to room with," said Emily. "Simple."

"Just ten minutes ago I e-mailed her that I was interested!" I said.

Rachel stretched out on her bunk and examined the blister on one heel. "Well, then, in the last ten minutes you've found someone else," she said.

"But I'm still looking on Facebook! She'll know that. And I've got to find someone soon or the university will decide for me!"

"Let me see that," said Pamela, reaching for my laptop and reading the messages. Her face broke into a smile.

"O-kaay!" she cried. "Meggie wants the recommendations of three of *your* friends!"

"Now, wait, Pamela, it's got to sound real. I don't want to offend one of my dad's customers."

"Oh, we'll make it real, all right," said Pamela. She placed my laptop squarely in front of her, hit reply, and started typing.:

I've known Alice since sixth grade. I guess I'd call her a friend, but she humiliated me once onstage in a school play. . . .

"Pamela!" I laughed.

She's nice, but she's got this streak of jealousy. If you can put up with that, however, she's great.

Pamela J.

"Tell her Alice is a compulsive eater," said Rachel. "That she hides snacks all over the room."

"Let me have that," said Liz, and Pamela slid the laptop across the table. Liz began typing:

Alice will be your friend forever, but you need to know that she has to have a light on when she sleeps, with music playing. And she won't wear earbuds at night because she says they hurt her ears.

Liz

We clapped. Then Gwen took over.

I've been Alice's friend since eighth grade. She'll give you the shirt off her back, literally, but she'll also take yours without asking. She has the feeling that once you room together, all possessions are mutually owned. We were camp counselors together, and I can't tell you how many shirts of mine she ruined with grease stains and tomato sauce. If you can put up with this, Alice is your friend for life.

Not-Quite-a-Friend

I didn't hear from Margaret for almost a week. Then I got a short e-mail saying that she thought she had someone else lined up and hoped to see me around campus.

So I was still minus a roomie come September.

We were all changing for our evening jobs the following afternoon—some in dress shirts and bow ties, some in their rattiest clothes for galley duty—when Pamela rushed in, all excited.

"Guess what!" she said. "Dad and Meredith signed up for this cruise next week!"

"Whaaaat?" I said. "Here? With us?"

"Dad just said that Meredith had gone online to see what the *Seascape* looked like, and she saw an ad for this huge discount—five hundred dollars off per passenger for immediate booking the second week of July."

"Wow!" I said. "That should be interesting!" I glanced over at her as I pulled on my shoes. "Will you like having them here, watching your every move?"

"I think so," she said. "They're not like that, and I get along with Meredith okay. It will be fun to show them around—let them see what we do."

And would you believe, I really *did* feel a tinge of jealousy, thinking how much fun it would be if Dad and Sylvia came on one of our cruises. Or Les! But I rose to the challenge: "It's only a week off. I'll trade shifts with you if you ever want to go on an excursion with them or something," I said.

"Me too, Pam," said Gwen. "Perfect chance to get in good with your new stepmom if they ever get hitched."

There was enough excitement even without that announcement, because it was the Fourth of July, and Chef Carlo was hosting a happy hour on the observation deck. Crew members who stayed aboard that afternoon to decorate got to mingle with passengers and chase down the red, white, and blue napkins that the breeze blew off the tables. But since I was on galley duty that night, I only got to emerge long enough to whisk away another tray of dirty dishes and pick up the strains of some band playing "God Bless America." My mouth watered when I glimpsed the appetizers Barry had just delivered. Every shrimp had a red, white, or blue toothpick in it; every hors d'oeuvre was topped with either a cherry tomato, a pearl onion, or a blueberry. I wished I'd eaten something before I went on duty.

Mitch had it worse, though—he was rinsing plates and filling the dishwasher by himself.

Since it was a Wednesday, we were docked at Crisfield as usual, and a waterman from Tangier had been invited onboard. After giving a short talk about the generations of Pruitts who had lived on the island before him and how the crab industry supported the local economy, he demonstrated how you crack open a steamed crab—what you eat and what you throw away. I heard only bits and pieces, desperately hoping each time I went on deck that there would be nothing more to carry below, but there always was.

It *would* have to be a night I had galley duty, because Captain Haggerty appeared at dinner and invited all passengers back up to the observation deck at dusk. He would be piloting the ship around the islands—Tangier and Smith and Tilghman—and along the coast, so they could enjoy the small local fireworks going off here and there while we cruised.

Mitch and I heard the announcement as we dealt with the reeking piles of crab carcasses waiting for the garbage bins.

"See what we're missing?" I told him.

He only grinned. "I liked our tour better," he said.

We finished up around ten thirty and went to the top deck to eat with the rest of the crew. Quinton had set up a long table and folding chairs at one end, and we devoured the biggest, fattest burgers Carlo could make, plus some of the leftover hors d'oeuvres from the cocktail party.

There was still an occasional rocket going off now and then, and we could see the sparklers along shore where there were campers. Sometimes we caught a whiff of gunpowder on the breeze from a short-lived fireworks display.

The *Seascape* was turning again and heading south when suddenly there was a muffled whump, and the whole ship jarred and shook.

I slid sideways on my chair for a moment, and someone's drink tipped over the edge of the table.

"What the . . . ?" Curtis said.

For a moment it seemed as though the ship's engine had

stalled. Silence. Then the sound of running feet on the deck below. We heard profanity from the pilothouse that mistakenly came over the loudspeaker, and Curtis headed for the stairs.

We went to the rail.

"Look!" Mitch pointed.

The ship's searchlight was swooping back and forth on the port side of the ship—back and forth, straight ahead, then to the side again. Then the grinding noise of the bow thruster—a shudder—and finally the ship moved sideways and on up the bay. We looked at Josh.

"Sandbar," he said, and smiled a little. "Captain grazed a sandbar. That's mud on *his* face."

"Doesn't he know where they are?" Liz asked.

"Supposed to, but this first-time cowboy thought he could cruise around at night."

"Really? First time?" I said. "This is his first ship or what?"

"No. First time piloting on the Chesapeake Bay. Not that it means anything in particular. Until now, anyway."

What the captain should do, Rachel told us, was get on the PA system and reassure the passengers—some of them, in their nightclothes, had come up to ask us what was happening.

"Not to worry," Josh told them. "Just scraped a sandbar. No big deal."

Finally Ken McCoy's voice came out of the speakers on both sides of the deck: "Ladies and gentlemen, we hope you have enjoyed Fourth of July on the bay, the very first for the *Seascape* . . ."

"Yeah, in its present form," Barry murmured.

". . . and we hope you had a most pleasant evening. The noise you heard a little while ago was simply the bow thruster, pushing us away from a sandbar. From all the officers and crew on the *Seascape*, we wish you pleasant dreams."

"Talk about smooth!" Rachel said.

"'The noise you heard was the bow thruster,' ha!" said Barry. "Notice how the big man passed the buck?"

"Maybe it was Ken who was piloting," Liz suggested.

"That's true," said Josh. "But I doubt you'll see the captain's face at breakfast."

We were all waiting for Frank to come up from below, and a little before midnight, he slipped onto one of the deck chairs, coffee in hand. He started to say something, then rubbed his jaw instead and burrowed down a little farther in his chair.

Josh's smile was more a smirk. "We got any damage?"

"Don't think so. Can't really tell unless I suit up and go down there, but the pressure's holding steady. Wish that were my biggest problem."

"What else?" asked Barry.

"Nothing yet. But as far as I can tell, the only 'new' things about this ship are the paint and the name."

"You want to know something else?" Rachel said, and we all listened, because as a lounge attendant she was in a position to pick up a lot of gossip we'd never hear. "It wasn't weather that delayed the start of our second cruise. The way I heard it from Stephanie, our major food supplier was about to pull the plug on our credit 'cause they still hadn't been paid for the first week. The front office probably had to put the ship up for collateral before they'd deliver the next order."

"Whaaaat?" said Barry.

"Okay, I'm exaggerating, but a pound of flesh, anyway."

"Well," said Frank, lifting the coffee mug again to his lips, "we're moving now. That's what counts. Let's don't go borrowing trouble. I mean, any more than we've got."

We took down the Fourth of July decorations from the dining room on Thursday, and that evening all the girls sat around women's quarters, winding each of the streamers into a tight little roll, to be used again next summer. Emily, who had worked in a craft store once, knew how to make rose petal wreaths out of crepe paper, and we decided to make one for our cabin door. Barefoot on our bunks, legs crossed—we folded, tucked, and stretched the little rectangles of crepe paper, turning them into roses.

"Reminds me of camp," Gwen said.

"What kind of camp was that?" asked Natalie.

"Disadvantaged kids," Liz explained. "It was the summer before our sophomore year. The four of us were junior counselors—Gwen and Pam and Alice and me."

"The summer Gwen broke up with Leo . . ." Yolanda added.

"Legs," I corrected.

". . . and started hanging out with Joe Ortega," Liz said.

"And *you* were dating Ross," I reminded her.

Emily threaded a needle through the rose in her lap, held the needle out away from her body as she pushed the rose down the thread, and secured it in place. "How long have you guys known each other, anyway?"

"Forever," said Pamela. "Liz and I started kindergarten together, Alice came into the picture in sixth grade, and we met up with Gwen in eighth."

"I'm just a tagalong," said Yolanda.

"I had a tight-knit bunch of girlfriends in high school, but then we all scattered," said Emily. "I miss the long talks and the closeness . . . the drama, even."

I passed another handful of roses to her. "What do you suppose guys talk about when they're alone?" I wondered aloud. "Like right now, when we aren't around?"

"S-E-X," Natalie spelled out.

"They probably aren't talking at all—probably watching TV," said Gwen.

"Football . . . soccer . . . cars," Lauren guessed.

"They tell stories, that's what they do," I said, thinking of Mark and Brian and even Patrick. "All the crazy stuff they've ever done, trying to top each other."

"Feelings?" Natalie asked. "Do they ever discuss those?"

"Are you kidding?" Yolanda rolled her eyes. "Have you ever heard a guy talk to a buddy about feelings?"

"That's what women are for," said Emily. "To help men express their emotions."

"Urges, you mean," said Lauren.

"Feelings, too," said Liz. "But guys aren't the only ones who hold back."

We worked silently for a minute or two, just enjoying the rare chance to hang out together, all at the same time. Emily strung another flower on her thread, then held it up to estimate how many more we'd need.

"What I've discovered about life is that feelings can change," Liz said. "I mean, a complete turnaround. Well, sort of." She held another petal between her fingers and curled the edges over. And then she confided what I'd thought only her few closest friends would ever know about: "I was molested when I was seven . . . by a supposed friend of the family."

Natalie gasped, and everyone else looked up.

"My parents had known him for a long time," Liz continued, "and he used to take me on, quote, 'nature walks.' He was a scientist."

Gwen and Pamela and I watched her, admiring her courage.

"My God!" said Natalie, not moving a muscle.

"Yeah, 'our big secret,' you know," said Liz.

"Was he ever arrested?" asked Lauren.

"No. He died in a car accident, and even then I didn't tell my parents what had happened until . . ." Liz looked over at Pamela and me. "Until these friends of mine got on my case and made me. But for years I had nightmares about his coming to get me and take me away. About hiding in the house and hearing him coming closer."

Not even Pamela and I had known about that.

"Oh, Liz," Emily said sympathetically.

But Liz continued: "After that I got angry—not just at him, but at my parents for not guessing what had been going on. I'd fantasize about smashing him in the face and kicking him in the balls. Scratching his eyes out. How I'd like to hurt him."

"Naturally!" said Rachel.

"Yeah, no guilt there," said Liz. "But a few months ago . . . I can't quite explain it . . . instead of that fantasy, I imagined myself sitting down across from him and saying, 'Okay. Tell me why you did it. Tell me if you felt it was wrong. If you ever asked yourself how *I* was feeling.'"

The room was absolutely still.

"I discovered I was as curious as I was angry. I wanted to know the *why*—the makeup of that pervert. I'm not entirely sure what it means, if I'm really over it or not, or—" She stopped.

"Maybe you've just . . . moved beyond it," I offered.

"I sort of think so too. I guess once I started applying to colleges, I felt I was . . . Yeah, you're right. I felt I wasn't just moving away, I was moving on. Like I wasn't going to rent him room in my head anymore; he'd been there long enough."

Gwen and Pamela and I just sat there beaming at her, and then Gwen leaned way over and gave her a hug. "That's my girl," she said.

"The feel of freedom," said Liz. "That's what it is."

Maybe she was feeling some of what I'd felt at Tangier Island with Mitch: being someplace I'd never been before; being friends with a guy I'd known for only a few weeks; watching the gulls soaring free overhead, going wherever they wanted. Just a sudden surge of freedom from . . . What, exactly? Giving myself a push, I guess. Getting on with life.

As the current passengers departed on Sunday and we worked like crazy cleaning staterooms, Pamela found out where her dad and Meredith would be staying—room 218, lounge deck—and we made sure it was perfect.

Mitch appeared at the door with Barry, holding a work order. "This the room that requests a double?" he asked.

"Yes," said Pamela. "Quinton said there are some over-sized sheets and blankets in the linen hold."

Mitch and Barry pushed the twin beds together and tied the adjoining legs to anchor them, then placed a foam divider between the twins to convert them into a two-sleeper. The guys were smiling as they left, and I heard Barry say, "*Somebody's* gonna have a good time this week." We didn't tell them who was coming.

I was glad I was on dining room service that week—Pamela, too—though we rotated again the week after. Mr. Jones and Meredith would see us in our starched shirts and black bow ties, not our baggy shorts and dirty T-shirts, carrying buckets.

Liz and I had never been on more than polite terms with Pamela's dad. He and Pamela's mom had been an attractive couple back when Pam was in middle school—cool, I guess you'd say. But once Sherry ran off with her fitness instructor,

Mr. Jones became a lonely, bitter man for a while. We didn't much like him, especially when he told Pamela that if she ever brought African-American friends home, he wouldn't let them in the house. He slowly eased up on that after he met Gwen, though he never said more than a few words to her. But once he started going out with a nurse named Meredith, he seemed to mellow.

Quinton made a final check of the ship around noon before we unlatched the line across the gangplank. Passengers had been getting out of cabs and wheeling their bags down to the dock, and deckhands were going up to help with the larger stuff. A few passengers, believe it or not, even came with small trunks, a different outfit for every hour of the day, it seemed.

Pamela and I stood at the rail of the Chesapeake deck, scouring the crowd gathered below.

"There they are!" she cried, pointing them out.

A tall, slim man in a dark brown sport shirt and tan pants, canvas bag over one shoulder, was pulling a suitcase, and walking beside him was a woman not much shorter, dark glasses beneath her sun visor, denim skirt, and tee.

Pamela was waving wildly. "Dad! Hi, Dad!" she called. "Meredith! Up here!"

The mustached man shielded his eyes and looked around, smiling, then focused on us and waved back, grinning.

"Hey, Pamela!" Meredith called, smiling broadly.

Pamela scrambled on down to meet them while I zipped to crew quarters for my camera.

"I'll get a picture of the three of you when we have a chance," I told Pamela later when we met on the main deck. "How do they like their room?"

"They like it, I think. I know Meredith does. It's smaller than Dad expected, but he likes the view. Curtis just delivered their bags, so they're putting stuff away right now."

"It's nice that they came, Pamela," I told her. "I mean, that they're interested in where you're working this summer, sort of including you in their lives, you know?"

"That's what I was thinking. And Dad's looking really relaxed. I think she's good for him. I hope they do get married."

We were heading up the stairs to the lounge deck when Pamela suddenly grabbed my arm to hold me back, her eyes huge.

"What?" I said, looking at her pale face. *"What?"*

Pamela's lips moved, but no sound came out. Her nails dug into my arm.

"Mom . . . ," she said finally.

13

UNBELIEVABLE

It was definitely Mrs. Jones.

The petite woman in the white pants and silky aqua top, clunky bracelets along one arm, was having a lighthearted conversation with a portly man about ship terminology.

"Here's the way I remember," the gentleman was saying. "When you bow"—and he demonstrated—"you lean *forward*. Remember that, and you'll automatically remember that the stern is in the rear."

Mrs. Jones laughed her high, tinkly laugh and thanked him as she strolled on, straw bag slung over one shoulder, platform shoes encasing her red-painted toenails.

Pamela turned to me with an expression of complete helplessness. Her face had gone from pale to pink. "What is she *doing* here? What can she be *thinking*?"

"Do you figure she knew that your dad and Meredith had signed up for this cruise?" I asked her.

"Of *course* she knew. Why else would she have come and not told me? I can't *believe* this!"

"Wait a minute," I said, pulling Pamela back as she started forward. "It's a stretch, but isn't it possible that she looked up the cruise line on the Internet—just like Meredith did— to see the kind of ship you were working on and read about the big discount they were offering for July? That she jumped at the chance and signed up, just as they did?"

Pamela shook her head, eyes blazing now. "Not without telling me."

"You haven't been answering her calls. . . ."

"No, but I've been reading her texts and I text her back once a week. Alice, don't you remember how she embarrassed me back in tenth grade when she signed up as a chaperone on the class trip to New York? That's the real Mom, in all her glory, come to mess things up for Dad and Meredith."

"Girls?" Dianne frowned as she passed. "We have enough help up here. Would you go back to the gangway and direct passengers from there?"

"Sure," I said, and my hand still gripping Pamela's arm, I guided her back down the stairs.

Pamela's "welcome smile" was a little too fake, but boarding passengers were either so confused or so excited, they didn't seem to notice the artificiality. The first pause we had in the stream of guests, however, Pamela got a copy of the passenger list from the reception desk—the list that would appear in all the rooms that night so people could get acquainted—and we scanned it quickly for her mom's name. Common as the name "Jones" is, there was only one listing: *Bill Jones and Meredith Mercer, Silver Spring, Maryland.*

"Your mom's not listed!" I said. "What *is* she? A stowaway?"

Pamela started at the beginning again and slowly traced her finger down the page, stopping at *Sherry Conners, Silver Spring, Maryland.*

"Here she is—her maiden name," said Pamela. "What if they're on the same deck? Oh, my God, Alice, what am I going to do?"

"Why do you have to do anything, Pamela?" I asked her. "*You* aren't involved in the hostilities. *You* didn't sign them up. None of the other passengers know they used to be married to each other. What will be will be."

"Yeah, and it could be awful," said Pamela.

"That will be between them if it is."

"I just feel so sad for Dad and Meredith. This was supposed to be such a fun trip," Pamela said, and I saw her lips tremble.

I stayed close to her for the next hour. I didn't see Mrs. Jones again, but I saw Pamela's dad standing in the doorway of his stateroom as we escorted a passenger up to her room, and when he saw Pamela, he called, "Pamela, when you have a minute, would you step in here?"

I watched her go in his cabin, a sinking feeling in my chest.

* * *

I had only a few minutes to talk with Pamela when we went down to crew quarters to freshen up for dinner service. It was the first time some of us had waited tables at dinner, so Pamela and I were nervous enough as it was.

"What happened with your dad?" I asked.

"He said he'd seen Mom in the lounge and wanted to know what the hell was going on—whether I'd known she was coming, which of course I hadn't."

"He's blaming you?"

"Not really, but he's pissed, and he's got a right to be."

"How did your mom find out they'd signed up, do you suppose?"

Pamela unbuttoned her shirt, rubbed deodorant in her armpits, and buttoned up again. "She's got spies. One of her friends works in the same hospital as Meredith, and it isn't too hard to find out who's going where and when."

Gwen came in just then to put on her bow tie. She took one look at Pamela and me and said, "What's going on?"

"Mom's on board," Pamela told her.

Gwen looked confused for a moment, and then her eyes widened. "Your *mom*?"

"Yes. Under her maiden name, Sherry Conners. Dad just found out."

"You *saw* her here? Omigod!" Gwen gasped.

We heard the clattering of footsteps on the stairs down the hall, and Liz burst in, followed by Emily and Rachel. "Pamela, I just saw your mom!" Liz cried.

"I know." Pamela flopped down on the edge of her bunk. To Emily and Rachel she said, "My dad's on board with his long-time girlfriend, and somehow, for some reason, my mom's here too."

Emily could only stare. "They're . . . divorced?"

"Yes," Pamela said. "And just when things are starting to go well for Dad—after Mom left us a few years back . . ."

"I'm surprised he didn't leave the ship," I said, remembering some awful arguments they'd had in the past.

"Well, that was his first reaction, but Meredith talked him out of it. 'Are we going to let Sherry control our lives?' she asked him. She said they'd come on this cruise to relax and have fun, and that's what she intended to do. 'If Sherry wants to make a scene,' she said, 'she'll have to do it without any help from us.' And finally Dad simmered down." Pamela gritted her teeth. I could actually hear them grinding. "She is so darn, damned selfish!"

"Oh, man!" Emily said. "What a situation!"

"What a *mom*!" said Rachel. "And I don't even know her."

"Dining crew!" came Dianne's voice from the end of the hall.

"Coming!" I yelled.

"I just hope I don't get Mom's table," breathed Pamela. "I don't trust myself to keep my cool. But I can't pretend I don't know her."

When we reached the main deck, Dianne took Pamela and me aside and into her office across the hall.

"I have a feeling there's something I should know," she said. "And I'd like you to level with me before we leave port. You both look upset, and I'm going to need your full concentration in the dining room."

A horrible thought crossed my mind. Could we both get sacked because of Pamela's mother?

Pamela gave a little groan. "Well, my parents are divorced, and my dad and his girlfriend are on board, as you know . . ."

"Yes?" Dianne studied us.

". . . and so is my mom."

Dianne looked confused. "I don't remember another Jones on the passenger list."

"She's under her maiden name, Conners. They don't get along, to put it mildly, and I just don't know what will happen. No one knew she was coming."

Dianne got the picture. "What will happen as far as the staff goes, Pamela, is that we will treat all our guests with courtesy. If they have issues with each other, that's between them. If they're disruptive, Quinton will step in. Believe me, he's handled such things before. But you're not responsible for your parents' behavior. Do your job. That's all we ask of you."

Pamela was visibly relieved. I could tell just by the shift of her shoulders. "Thanks, Dianne," she said.

"What Quinton and I *will* do," Dianne continued, "is try to seat them far apart in the dining room whenever possible. For tonight, since some people have already arrived and others aren't wearing their name tags, we'll just hope for the best."

* * *

We stood at the side of the dining room looking pleasant, small towels draped over our arms, as guests filed in. There was open seating at all meals, but if a couple hesitated or a single person held back, Quinton or Dianne promptly suggested a table and escorted them to it.

I watched Dianne have a quick conversation with Quinton, saw him listen and nod. But my eyes kept drifting back to Pamela. What was it like to have a mom who acted so hurtfully? What mother in her right mind would get it in her head to follow her ex-husband onto a cruise ship, their daughter watching helplessly from the sidelines?

My other thought, the one that always followed this question like a shadow, was what was it like to have a mother at all? I'd certainly got the feel of it once Dad married Sylvia. We'd had some arguments, but we also had a few close conversations, and I really did love her. But because she'd come so late in my life, it wasn't the snuggle-up-sit-on-her-lap-stroke-my-hair kind of love, much as I wanted that, down deep. She treated me as she should have then, as a young teenage girl, and it took a while for me to realize that I couldn't recapture my five-year-old self and the mother I'd needed then. She was really more like an older sister than a mom—a tutor, a mentor, an aunt, definitely a friend—but not exactly a mom. Right now, though, looking at Pamela, I could tell she wished that Sherry was anything but.

Mr. Jones and Meredith entered the dining room, still wearing the same clothes they had on when they boarded, as were most of the passengers. The first night aboard ship was always casual—everyone getting unpacked and settled, finding their way around, introducing themselves to each other. I saw Dianne scan their name tags when they came in and direct them to a round table over by the window with three other couples already seated, which meant that Pamela's mom couldn't possibly sit with them this first night. Six more nights to go, plus breakfasts and lunches, too.

As the room filled up, the noise level grew louder and I began to wonder if Pamela's mom had already come in and I'd missed her. Then a small woman in black silk trousers and a red clingy top showing lots of cleavage appeared in the doorway, crystal globes at her ears, and she stood there poised, expectant.

Quinton bent slightly to read her name tag, greeted her with his usual trademark smile, and suggested a place on the opposite side of the room, where two couples were waiting for their table to fill. I heard Pamela exhale gratefully as she picked up a water pitcher and headed to one of her tables. I did the same. We were going to get through this meal okay, even if it was the first time we'd served at dinner.

"Good evening, and welcome to the *Seascape*," I said cheerfully as I filled the glasses. "I hope you're all feeling a little bit settled?"

"Getting there!" a red-faced man said jovially. "We'll let you know after dinner."

"As long as we don't get seasick," said his wife. "This is my first cruise, and I don't do very well on boats."

"I think you're going to find it smooth sailing," I said

reassuringly. "I'm Alice, and I have the pleasure of serving you tonight. Someone will be by shortly to take your wine order, and in the meantime, let me know if you'd prefer soup or salad."

Across the room I saw Mitch talking to Pamela's mom, taking her order.

"Oh, look!" someone said. "We're moving!"

Passengers on both sides of the dining room looked toward their windows as Baltimore's Inner Harbor passed slowly before our eyes and the scenery changed from shops and restaurants to trees and water. Still the ship went on turning, the bow thruster doing its job, and finally, as I took my order to the galley, all I could see out the port side of the ship was water and sky.

You'll never believe this, I e-mailed Patrick that night. *Pamela's dad and girlfriend are on this cruise, and guess who else turned up? Pamela's mom!*

It was like a time bomb, I'd told him. But, as Quinton keeps telling us, every day on a ship is a surprise.

I don't know where Pamela went after we cleaned the galley, but when she came up on the top deck around eleven, all the girls were waiting.

"Well, I confronted her," she said, pulling a chair over and sinking down in it, hands folded over her stomach. "It didn't take me long to learn what room she's in—311, Chesapeake deck. I wasn't going to go the whole trip pretending I didn't know her."

"What did she *say*?" Liz asked. "How did she explain herself?"

"She didn't, and I don't know what to think. I followed her to her stateroom and said, 'Mom, how could you *do* this?' and she said, 'Do what? Is it so awful I wanted to surprise you?'"

We all rolled our eyes.

"'You *know* Dad and Meredith are on this ship,' I told her, and she said, 'Then they must have seen the same advertisement I saw, for bargain rates.'"

Lauren shook her head. "No, that's not the reaction a normal person would have had. That was just too cool and premeditated. If she hadn't known, she'd be completely surprised."

We agreed. But Pamela looked torn. "Still . . . it's possible, I suppose. And I'd feel ashamed if she really did just want to surprise me and didn't know they were here. And instead of being happy, I'm treating her like a criminal."

"Well, then, take her at her word!" Emily said. "Treat her like all the other guests and assume she'll make new friends. At least they're not on the same deck. Maybe she and your dad will simply ignore each other the whole trip, and all this worry will be for nothing."

At Norfolk the next day, Mr. Jones and Meredith went off to see the shipyard, and Pamela's mom stretched out on the observation deck in shorts and a halter top, with a drink and a magazine.

When she came to the captain's reception that evening, she was the most mesmerizing of the guests, in a short sequined cocktail dress, shockingly tight around the bust, and silver stilettos that would have killed a man if she'd used them as a weapon.

"Oh . . . my . . . God!' gasped Natalie, who was replacing the steamed shrimp platter. She looked at Pamela. "Is that your mom?"

"Does it show?" Pamela said.

"I just meant . . . wow!" Natalie said.

Mrs. Jones—Sherry—didn't do anything out of line, exactly. She didn't strike a model's pose in the doorway, but she had timed her entrance so that she was one of the last to arrive and could linger a bit longer with the captain and first mate. People did take notice.

Lauren overheard her ask the captain if she would be able to see the pilothouse, and he responded that every cruise had a ship's tour sometime on the schedule, pilothouse included, and she could sign up with either Stephanie Bowers or Ken McCoy.

Once again, Quinton carefully seated Bill and Meredith many tables away from Sherry, and we were glad to see that Mr. Jones seemed to be enjoying a conversation with the men at his table while Meredith chatted with the woman next to her.

The subject of Pamela's mom had been confined so far to the girls, but it came up at the crew dinner later that night. We had taken our dinners up to the observation deck and were chowing down on Sloppy Joes and fries when Barry asked, "Anyone know when the tour of the ship will be? The broad in the Saran Wrap dress was asking, and I said I'd try to find out."

We girls frowned his way. "The *broad*?" said Gwen, reprimanding him. "That is *so* forties."

"Okay, the silver stiletto babe," Barry said, and then, realizing he'd done it again, "Sherry Conners."

"That happens to be Pamela's mom," said Emily.

Barry did a double take. "Whoa! Sorry! But . . . wow!"

"Yeah, that's what *I* said," Natalie told him. "Pamela comes from hot stock."

I didn't know if Pamela had wanted us to keep it secret or not, but once it was out, it seemed easier, even for her.

"We've got a problem here," Lauren said, and told the guys about how Pamela's dad and girlfriend were on this cruise and how, somehow, Pamela's mom had booked herself on the very same one; we were trying to see that Sherry Conners didn't ruin the trip for them.

"They should all have code names," said Curtis, the snake-and-flag tattoo on his left arm moving a little when he flexed a muscle. "I could get on my walkie-talkie and say, 'Decup three stern.'"

"Decup?" I said.

Curtis grinned as he bit into his sandwich and chewed a couple of times. "Bra size," he said. "Sherry approaching Chesapeake deck at the stern."

"Oh, God, you guys are so sexist," Yolanda said. "You want to be known by the size of your jock?"

"Ouch," said Curtis. "Okay, okay, you think of a code name, then."

I figured it was all in fun.

"Cougar?" I suggested.

"Too obvious," said Lauren.

"Drama Queen?" said Liz.

"Too long."

It was Pamela who suggested it: "Flotsam, because we never quite know what will turn up."

"Flotsam it is," said Barry. "As long as she has a label, we probably don't need one for the others."

The talk drifted to what we might do in Baltimore the coming week if we had time to go out, but when a light rain began to fall, we decided to call it a night. I hung around a little longer to see if Patrick had sent me a text message on my cell. He hadn't, but I sent him one about how the evening had gone. Then I started down the back stairway.

What if it really *had* been a coincidence that Pamela's mom took this cruise? I wondered as I passed the Chesapeake deck and kept going. What if she needed a vacation as much as anyone else, and we were treating her as a joke, a threat to everyone's happiness? She might be trying just as hard to avoid Bill and Meredith, once she found them on board, as we were to keep them apart.

But as I reached the lounge deck and made the turn, I saw her, drink in hand, standing at the railing outside Bill and Meredith's stateroom. It was no coincidence.

14
GHOST STORY

It was awkward, but the next day went fairly smoothly. I didn't know what to call Pamela's mom when I passed her on deck or in the dining room. I'd always called her "Mrs. Jones" before, so how could I say, "Hello, Ms. Conners" now? And I certainly wasn't about to call her "Sherry."

She'd just smile and say, "Hello, Alice. Nice day, isn't it?" or something innocuous, and I went on by. I'm sure she noticed that whenever I happened to see her, I was in a hurry.

Occasionally my walkie-talkie would buzz, and I'd hear a male voice saying, "Flotsam to four, Flotsam to four." If one of the crew was on the sundeck, and Bill and Meredith were also, that crew member would make sure there were no empty chairs near the couple. If Pamela's mom was having a drink in the lounge, Rachel might go back in the supply closet, click on her walkie-talkie, and say, "Flotsam served on second."

To us, it was a game, but it wasn't to Pamela. The fact that her mom behaved herself, more or less, made Pamela feel all the more guilty for suspecting the worst, and I saw her wince once or twice when she heard the reference to "Flotsam." That didn't last long, though, because Quinton caught on and put a stop to it. But we couldn't help noticing that Pamela's mom was usually first at the bar when happy hour began, and her laughter got a little louder as she started her second or third drink.

Patrick's e-mails were full of the sights and sounds of Barcelona—one of the few places, it seemed, that his diplomat dad had never taken the family. They were more like essays, really. Sometimes he'd write something in Spanish and see if I could figure it out. *¿Cómo está pasando el crucero?*

He'd tell me about Gaudi's architectural wonders, "more like sand castles," he described them. Or he'd start his e-mail with *Greetings from the Iberian Peninsula* and tell me about the dark cavernous church off the Plaza del Rey, with its metal cages, lit by candlelight, and the plastic body parts that hung on the metal gates, asking a saint's help in healing an affliction.

My e-mails were mostly about people—about Pamela's parents on board and the beach in Yorktown, about the breeze up here on the top deck and the gulls that circled overhead.

As we set the tables for dinner that night, Barry said, "You girls want to do something this evening, late?"

"Other than sleep?" Emily said.

"Hey, you can always make up on sleep," said Flavian.

"What did you have in mind?" Gwen slowly lowered a tray of glass goblets from her shoulder to a rack.

"Ever see the York battlefield at night? Entirely different from how it looks in the daytime," Barry said.

"How do you know so much about Yorktown?" Liz asked.

"Eighth-grade civics class," said Barry. "Big field trip of the year."

"So how do we see anything at night?" I wanted to know.

"Full moon," said Flavian.

Gwen laughed. "You guys are so full of it! There was only a half-moon last night."

"Ah!" Flavian grabbed a steak knife off the table and held it like a foil in a fencing pose. "'The moon was a ghostly galleon tossed upon cloudy seas . . .'"

"Give me a break," said Pamela.

"What? You never had to memorize 'The Highwayman' back in junior high?"

"I just want to know how we're supposed to see a battlefield in the dark."

"Leave it to us," said Barry. "It's great weather for a change, and we can walk there from the ship."

"Okay, I'm in," I said.

"Me too," said Gwen and Pamela.

***

We got away around ten thirty, those of us who were going. Lauren and Emily opted out. Lauren said she'd seen enough of battlefields in the daytime, she didn't have to experience them at night, so it was just Gwen and Pamela, Yolanda and Natalie, Liz and me, along with Flavian and Barry.

I found myself disappointed that Mitch wasn't along, but Barry said that some of the deckhands had gone in search of a bar, so I guessed Mitch was with them.

We crossed the street from the dock, and Barry led us to a sort of grotto, where we could just make out a cave in the hillside with a closed metal gate across the entrance.

"And this is . . . ?" asked Gwen.

Barry put one finger to his lips. "The gate swings miraculously open at midnight, and all the tortured souls of British soldiers come out to walk the battlefield."

Natalie was trying to read a sign in the darkness. "Cornwallis' Cave?"

"That's it," said Barry. "The general who surrendered to George Washington. You're standing on hallowed ground."

"I'm so scared," Liz said.

"You can jump into our arms anytime," Barry said, but I noticed Gwen was already in Flavian's, and ghosts had nothing to do with it.

I had the feeling that the guys were taking the long way around to the battlefield, wherever it was, but I didn't care. It seemed as though we were the only ones in Yorktown. Once the tourists left for the day, the place was deserted.

We walked along the historic streets, Barry telling us how the battle was fought. And then, under a dim streetlight, he stopped and lowered his voice. "What I'm about to tell you is simply what people have reported, but there have been too many of these stories for them to be coincidence." We started walking again. "There was this man whose ancestors fought with Washington here at Yorktown, and his great-great-great-uncle had come across this dying British soldier who begged him for water. So he put his own flask to the soldier's lips and let him drink. But the guy was hurt really bad, and he flopped back down again, moaning with pain, a gaping wound in his chest. So this great-great-great-uncle took out his revolver and shot him in the head."

"Barry, that's horrible," said Liz.

"It was the most humane thing he could do," Barry continued. "And a few years ago one of his descendants was here visiting the battlefield—it was almost dark—and he was here with his wife and his wife's sister. The women had gone on ahead, back toward the parking lot, and to his right, he saw this . . . well, orb of light, I guess you'd call it—sort of like the top half of a luminous circle—on the ground about twenty yards away, slowly rising higher, until it was a full circle, about shoulder height . . ."

We stopped walking again.

". . . and then he saw that it was a man's head, a man's face, coming toward him in the moonlight."

I could feel goose bumps on my arms, and Liz grabbed me, both of us grinning but wanting to hear the rest of the story. We were barely moving, we were crowded so close to Barry, who was walking backward, facing us. His expression was serious in the shadows.

"The man said he stopped and stood perfectly still while the apparition came closer," Barry continued. "He didn't speak, and the expression on the orb didn't change. He described it as mostly sad-looking. And then, for just a moment, the man said, the ghost's upper torso was visible too—the uniform scruffy and wrinkled and stained with either mud or blood, he couldn't tell. But the ghost's hand was holding a flask—holding it out, sort of, like it was offering it to him. And then . . . it faded out—the face, the torso, the flask, everything."

"Arrrgggh!" I said. "That's all? That's the end? What did the guy do?"

Barry shrugged. "I don't know. I've heard two different versions of the story. One said he nodded to the apparition before it faded away, like he understood. The other version was that he told his wife and sister-in-law what he'd seen and they didn't believe him."

"Anybody got a flask?" Flavian joked. "Let's go."

I think the guys were taking us in the back way, because the park closed at dusk. We steered clear of the caretaker's house and bypassed the parking lot. The moon was little more than half full, but now and then the clouds moved across it, and we had to follow Barry single file so we wouldn't stumble over something or fall in one of the trenches. From what I could see of them, they were only a few feet deep and the sides had eroded so they were more like gullies, but you still had to be careful.

Flavian and Gwen were bringing up the rear. Every so often when the moon came out from behind a cloud, we could see the blurred outline of a cannon. But mostly the battlefield was just that—a huge open space with a gentle breeze blowing through.

It felt almost irreverent to be out here on a lark, at a place where the whole course of history had been changed. Weird to think that right where I was standing, maybe, a British soldier could have been struggling for breath and begging for a drink of water.

Suddenly I heard Liz gasp, and Pamela stifle a shriek. Then Yolanda gave an electrifying scream. Straight ahead, maybe twenty yards away, we saw what appeared to be a . . . an illuminated head . . . a face . . . there on the ground. And just as Barry had described it, the orb—the head, the face—seemed to be rising slowly up . . . a foot high . . . now higher . . . chest high . . . And then it was as tall as we were, coming right toward us. When a second head appeared, we were all clutching at Barry, trying to run, and then Yolanda screamed again and a light came on in the caretaker's cottage.

"Quiet, you guys!" came a familiar voice, laughing. "Now they'll turn the bloodhounds on us."

"Josh!" I cried.

He was close enough that we could see the flashlight he was holding under his chin as he'd climbed out of one of the trenches, and I heard Mitch's laughter behind him. The next thing I knew, they were pulling us down in a trench and warning us not to make a sound.

I found myself half sitting on Mitch's lap, leaning awkwardly back in his arms, my legs over Pamela, who was lying on her side.

"You dog!" she whispered, pounding on Josh's back.

"Shhhhh," he cautioned.

We all waited for the sound of footsteps. Finally Flavian inched up and peered over the edge of the trench. "Caretaker's on the back step, looking around," he said, ducking down again. "Got a high-beam flashlight."

Nobody moved.

Flavian rose up again, his eyes even with the grass. "I think he went back inside."

"Yeah, but he'll call the park police," said Josh. "He's not going to let a scream like that go unreported."

"Yeah, Yolanda. Anyone ever hire you for sound effects?" Mitch asked.

"Let's go and at least get back on the road," said Barry.

We climbed noiselessly up out of the trench and moved in a single row toward the tree line, following Barry, our dark silhouettes bent double as we crossed the field. We breathed easier once we were back on the road, and we pummeled Josh and Mitch for scaring the daylights out of us, then turned on Barry and Flavian.

But we hadn't gone more than a hundred yards when we

saw a patrol car turn onto the road ahead of us, lights flashing.

We staggered in the blinding light and stopped.

"We're fried," said Flavian.

"But who did we hurt?" I asked.

"Don't sweat it," Josh said.

The patrol car came slowly toward us. We waited as it stopped and a park officer got out.

"Where you folks headed?" he asked, stopping a few yards away.

"Going back to the *Seascape*, sir," Josh said, politeness in every syllable. "It's the only time we get a break, so we decided to look around."

"If you're from a cruise ship, then you know the park closes at dusk," the park ranger said. I couldn't see his face in the shadows, but his voice didn't sound friendly.

"Well, we know it now," Josh said. "We're sort of history buffs, and this was our only chance to see the battlefield. We sail out in a few hours."

The ranger studied us a bit longer. "Caretaker reported some noise out on the field."

"Yeah," put in Barry. "That would be Yolanda's scream. We told her to look out for trenches, and she almost fell in. That's why we realized we wouldn't get far trying to see anything tonight."

"You wouldn't know where we could get a map of the battlefield, would you?" Josh was really laying it on, but the officer wasn't impressed.

"Talk to your cruise director," he said. Then motioned us back toward the port.

The patrol car followed us to within a block of the ship before it turned off. And a half block from the ship, we saw a taxi unload its passengers. When the cab took off, we recognized Curtis, with one of the stewards leaning heavily on his shoulder.

"Looks like they found a bar," said Flavian. "Had to go to Williamsburg, I'll bet."

"Hey!" Barry called. "Curtis. What's up?"

Curtis stopped and turned his head, but he couldn't turn his body because the stew was sinking to his knees, and Curtis was trying to hold him up. It was Todd, one of the younger, skinnier guys, and he was obviously wasted.

"Oh, man!" Mitch said.

"Yeah. Got a situation here," Curtis said. "And it's my ass too if Quinton finds out."

"How many beers did he have?" Flavian asked.

"A couple more than he should have. I've never seen him this drunk." Curtis pulled Todd to his feet, but he wobbled unsteadily for a moment and began sinking again, carrying on a conversation with himself.

"It's going to be either Ken or Quinton checking off names when we reach the dock," Josh said. "And you can't get very much past Quinton."

"McCoy will go by the book, though. They'll leave Todd behind when we sail tonight," Barry said. "Turn him over to the park police. And if they didn't replace Shannon, you know darn well they won't replace Todd. We'll be working our butts off."

"What'll we do?" asked Mitch.

"We can't sober him up out here—curfew's in fifteen minutes," Curtis said. He gave Todd a little shake, but he only laughed, limp as a wet rag.

"I'll see who's on duty," Barry said, and was gone only a minute or so before he came back. "It's McCoy," he told us.

Josh was helping hold up Todd now, and it was obvious there was no way he was going to walk up the gangplank on his own. We moved on a little farther, Todd's feet dragging until we could see the ship.

"Okay, here's the deal," Curtis said. "We're having a race, see? I'm going to carry Todd piggyback, and Josh carries Flavian."

"Wait a minute!" said Flavian, but Curtis went on:

"The rest of you guys go on ahead. Laugh it up like we're all kidding around. Tell Ken you've got a bet on who reaches the ship first, and we'll do a little whooping back here on our own. Then I'll come galloping up to the ship, Todd on my back, and run up the gangplank, as Josh and Flavian follow close behind. You guys stop and talk with Ken while I get Todd down to his bunk and under the sheets. It's the best we can do."

The rest of us went on ahead, kidding among ourselves, letting our voices rise—swatting at one another. Ken smiled when he saw us coming. He checked off our names one at a time on his clipboard.

"You guys have a good time?" he asked.

"Oh, yeah. Any time on land's a good time," said Barry. And then, turning, "Okay, here they come. Let's see who wins the race. I've got five bucks on Curtis."

"Who's still out?" asked Ken, looking down the dock, then checking his clipboard.

"Two crazies," I told him as the shouts in the distance grew louder.

"They're all idiots," said Gwen as Curtis, with Todd on his back, came barreling onto the landing. He raced across the dock, and with a loud "Whoeeee!" went pounding up the gangplank, with Josh and Flavian not far behind.

"Hey! Keep it down!" Ken chided as Flavian slid off Josh's back and gave another yell. "Quiet down, you guys, or Quinton will have our necks."

We hushed immediately.

Ken checked off the last name on the list. "Anybody still out?" he asked.

"You got 'em all," said Mitch.

We were in. I was impressed.

We found out later that Todd threw up on Curtis about the time they reached crew quarters, and the guys put him under the shower, clothes and all. The next morning Todd was subdued, but sober, and Quinton, from whom no things are hidden, said simply, "You lucked out that time, Todd, but it can't happen again. Same for you, Curtis."

***

It was obvious what Pamela's mom was trying to do: simply be the most alluring, attractive passenger on the ship. Certainly to put a damper on her ex-husband's love life, if she could. And definitely to make him wonder if he had made a mistake about not taking her back. That was the way we saw it, anyway.

She usually skipped breakfast and had a roll and coffee up on the sundeck in her short shorts and halter tops. She signed up for nearly every excursion and, Rachel heard from Stephanie, asked frequent questions of the guides, more for their attention, it seemed, than for the information.

Every dinner, Pamela's mom was stunningly dressed in clothes that were one degree shy of too sexy, and by the fourth night of the cruise, she seemed to have caught on that Quinton always seated her on the opposite side of the room from Bill and Meredith.

"Oh," she said, pausing. "I think I see a seat over there I'd prefer."

What could Quinton say but, "Of course," and follow her to the table next to Pamela's dad, pulling out the chair for her.

"Did you see that? Did you *see* that?" Pamela whispered to me from the door of the galley.

Unfortunately, both of those tables were mine that evening, and as dinner progressed and wineglasses were refilled, Sherry's laughter grew a little louder and more frequent, while Pamela's dad, at the adjoining table, remained stone-faced and seemed to be eating faster than usual. He and Meredith were the first to excuse themselves after dessert and coffee had been served as Sherry lingered at her table, telling an impossibly long story.

"Oh, I wish this cruise were over," Pamela lamented later, as we got ready for bed.

"Only a few more nights and we'll have a whole new set of passengers," said Lauren. "Hang in there. None of the other passengers know they're related."

"I can see the tension in Dad's face, though," Pamela said. "Now he'll never take her ba—" She stopped, her eyes wide. "I can't believe what I think I was about to say!"

"Sort of the universal desire, isn't it?" said Emily. "After my parents split, even though they fought like tigers, I wanted us all under one roof."

"Maybe so," said Pamela, wrapping her arms around her knees. "I guess what I long for, really, is the family I *wanted* us to be."

The following day we were docked at Oxford, and Pamela's mom had gone on a tour of the ship for those who didn't go ashore. Somehow she had wrangled an invitation from the captain to dine at his table that night, one of the few evenings he was eating on board this week.

"I can't watch," Pamela told me when she saw them together. "How did she manage *that*?"

"Maybe this is just what she needs," Yolanda said. "Attention. From a guy in uniform, preferably."

Sherry Conners had dressed for the occasion in a white silk

dress, butt-enhancingly tight, with a deep neckline. Her fingernails and toenails were painted pearl white, and she was easily the most attractive woman at the table. Captain Haggerty sat next to her, and Ken McCoy introduced her to the five other guests in their party.

What she didn't have, however, was the satisfaction of seeing her ex-husband watch her dine with the captain because, we found out from Pamela, he and Meredith had reservations that evening for the Robert Morris Inn. And as the dinner progressed, we could see her eyes scanning the dining room for someone who wasn't there.

It was difficult to focus on my assigned tables. I found my eyes darting to the captain's table all night, where Mitch was serving, and I could tell that things were going from awkward to unpleasant. At one point, when Dianne approached the table with a new bottle of wine, I saw the almost imperceptible shake of the captain's head, and Dianne and the wine immediately disappeared.

I was taking dessert orders at the table next to the captain's when I heard Sherry say, "I'd think you'd be seated on the other side of the dining room, Captain. All the action seems to be over there, by the dock."

I saw the raised eyebrows of the other guests. Haggerty kept his composure but didn't smile: "I'm sorry you find this table disappointing," he said.

"On the contrary," one of the men said quickly, "the pleasure is in the company."

Pamela had heard too, and her face turned a fiery red, beginning at the neck.

Instead of apologizing, Pamela's mom continued her now-raspy harping: "It doesn't seem as though there are as many people in the dining room tonight as usual. I'm surprised passengers dine off the ship; I'd think they'd want to enjoy what they paid for."

The captain smiled politely. "We hold no prisoners, Ms. Conners, I assure you. Oxford has many lovely restaurants, particularly the Robert Morris Inn, which is a landmark here, and many of our passengers book reservations well in advance."

You could almost see the light beginning to dawn on Sherry's face. Her big night with the captain, and her ex-husband and his girlfriend were living it up somewhere else. "Well, no one told *me* about it," she said, and weaved slightly in her chair. The wineglass in her hand tipped dangerously before the captain steadied it for her. "Maybe our dinner should have been held there."

The other guests at the table were too shocked to comment, but Haggerty had obviously had enough.

"Officer McCoy," he said, "I believe that Ms. Conners is having a rather unpleasant evening. Would you escort her to her stateroom, where I think she'll enjoy the quiet?"

Sherry Conners looked shocked. She began to protest, but then she collected herself enough to thank the captain for inviting her, said good night to the others, and, leaning on Ken's arm, walked slowly away from the table.

Pamela was in tears when we met in the galley. I gave her a hug, but she turned for a moment, swallowed a sob, then gamely picked up her coffeepot and headed for the dining room once more.

After dinner I stood at the bow of the ship in the darkness with Pamela and Gwen, waiting for Liz to finish galley duty. There was a big poker game going on in the dining room among the stewards and deckhands, but we wanted to talk among ourselves, just the four of us.

We watched Pamela's dad and Meredith strolling leisurely back from their dinner out. Bill had his arm around Meredith's waist, and they'd obviously had a good time.

"It was every bit as wonderful as they say," we heard Meredith tell Quinton as they boarded below. "It was a fantastic meal."

"So glad you enjoyed it. We're always happy to recommend the Robert Morris," Quinton said.

"Hey! I put some extra chocolates on your pillows," Pamela called down to them.

They looked up and waved.

"A perfect end to the evening," Meredith said. "There's always room for chocolate."

Liz came up at last with lemonade, and we went up to the top deck, sitting in a little circle near the bow, our bare toes touching on the end of Gwen's chaise longue. Some of the guys sprawled nearby, Curtis and Josh comparing the calluses on their hands. Bugs circled and buzzed around a dim deck lamp.

"Well, so the worst happened and you're still here, Pamela," Gwen said.

Pamela sighed. "Yeah. I sort of think Mom will behave now that she's made a total fool of herself. And she wasn't so drunk that she didn't realize it."

"Maybe it's good that it happened, then. Get the venom out of her system," Liz suggested.

"Just so Dad and Meredith have a good time," said Pamela. "I promised to go biking around St. Michaels with them tomorrow if they get up early enough. I think they'd like that. It'd be nice to do something with my dad for a change."

"Four more weeks!" I said. "And then . . . we start a whole new life."

I had just reached for my glass of lemonade on the deck beside me when suddenly the air was split with the shriek of the alarm, immediately followed by Captain Haggerty's voice over the PA system: "Man overboard, man overboard, this is NOT a drill."

15
MISSING

Curtis got up so fast, his chair tipped over.

The captain's voice continued: "Passenger over port side aft. Go immediately to stations."

We were all on our feet and running. Each of us had our own assignment, and Pamela was beside me, her face chalk white. Then I lost her.

The door to the pilothouse must have been open as I passed the Chesapeake deck on my way down because I heard loud squawks coming from a transmitter. Passengers were gathering port side, many in robes and pajamas, but I continued on to the lounge deck's fantail. Gwen got there momentarily.

"Anyone know who it was?" I asked Rachel, who was looking over the rail.

She didn't take her eyes off the water. "No. Quinton and Dianne are checking the staterooms."

We heard the microphone click on again, and then Haggerty's voice: "This is your captain. All passengers return to your staterooms to be counted. All passengers, to your staterooms."

Gwen and I focused on the water.

A few yards from the ship, a life preserver made a ring of bright orange, bobbing up and down on the dark water. The flashing beacon from a buoy bobbed next to it. They separated, came together again, then the space between them grew wider. And all the while, a searchlight scanned the surface.

By leaning out and looking down, I could see Frank on the main deck holding a Jacob's ladder. I'd seen it before—a plastic device that floats and looks like a ladder to assist someone getting back onto the ship. Curtis was beside him with a shepherd's hook. While the deckhands prepared for a rescue, the stewards' job was to locate the person in the water and never take our eyes off him or her. But the ominous thing was that we couldn't see anyone anywhere on the surface.

"At least we're still in port," Rachel said. "If the ship had been moving, we'd immediately have to stop and go into reverse, and we might lose sight of the passenger altogether."

Ken McCoy came up from below to talk with a man who stood barefoot, shirt unbuttoned. It looked as though he'd been undressing for bed.

"Are you the one who saw the passenger fall in?" Ken asked.

"Like I said," the man told him, "all I heard was this woman's scream. So I opened our cabin door, and some lady was running by saying somebody jumped and pointing out there." The passenger turned and pointed in the direction of the life preserver.

"I heard the scream too," another passenger said, coming over. "My wife thinks she heard the splash."

"The splash and then the scream?" Ken asked. And, into the walkie-talkie, "I'm talking with some passengers now. They all seem to agree it was port side aft."

"Uh . . . I guess it was the scream and then the splash," the second man said.

The beam of a searchlight swept the water again. On the dock a small crowd was gathering, despite the hour.

"Can you tell me who the woman was who told you someone had jumped?"

The barefoot man let out his breath. "Whew. Haven't a clue. I mean, you hear someone jumped overboard, you head for the rail, that's all."

A woman behind him spoke up: "I heard that all you could see were two arms going under. That's what the woman next to us said."

"Did she see it?"

"No, she was in bed like we were. That's what she heard."

"I heard someone pushed her!" another voice called.

Quinton's voice behind them all: "People, we have an emergency situation here, and we're checking the passenger list now. Please go back to your staterooms so we can tell who's missing."

Some began to leave, others lingered, then left. I heard the harbor police arriving on the deck below, and a minute later we saw Josh and Curtis out in a speedboat, slowly circling the life preserver in wider and wider arcs.

Someone edged in beside me at the railing. It was Pamela. I slipped my arm around her. None of us had to ask what she suspected. And when Dianne and Quinton had checked off every person on the passenger list, the only one missing was Pamela's mom.

In the water the speedboat circled again and again. The police boat joined the search. We took Pamela around and around the walkway, just to keep moving.

"What are they doing?" someone on dock called up to us.

And when we didn't answer, one of the passengers called back, "Rescue operation. A woman jumped."

"Recovery operation," someone murmured behind us.

I'm not sure how long we waited. Forty minutes, maybe. Pamela sat down on a bench, wrapped in Gwen's arms. Mr. Jones sat on the other side of them, arms on his knees, hands dangling. Meredith stood at the railing, looking down. There's a point at which you feel that not knowing is worse than knowing, even when the news is bad. That not knowing is a poison that makes you sick all over. You're physically ill, not just worried.

A sudden commotion below, and Mr. Jones stood up. He went down to the main deck, and it was a while before he came back. His face was gray and drawn.

"Did . . . they find her?" Pamela asked weakly.

He had something in his hands and sat down beside her. It was a scarf. "They found this floating on the water," he said. "Was it hers, do you know?"

Pamela broke into tears, nodding violently, and this time leaned against her father. He pulled her close. My own knees felt shaky. I crouched down where I was so I wouldn't fall, and grabbed Liz's hand.

Not another summer like last one! How could Pamela cope with this? How could we? We weren't even halfway over the shock of losing Mark Stedmeister last August.

And suddenly I heard Meredith say, "Sherry!"

I rose to my feet and stared as Pamela's mom came through the little crowd and looked around.

"What's going on?" she asked timidly.

There were stains on the front of her jacket, and her hair was disheveled, her face groggy.

"Mom!" Pamela cried, startled, but she didn't stand up. Bill Jones stared at his ex-wife in disbelief.

In moments Captain Haggerty and a police officer came up from below.

"She's here!" people told him. "Sherry Conners is here!"

Haggerty looked at her closely, relief and doubt on his face. "Ms. Conners, you've been reported missing," he said.

"Why . . . no! I just heard all the commotion and . . ." Sherry looked around.

"Can you tell us where you've been the last hour?" the policeman said.

"Well, I don't know . . . I was in the restroom downstairs for a while—"

"We checked there, several times," said Dianne.

The barefoot man worked his way through the crowd. "That's her!" he said. "That's the woman who told me someone had fallen in!"

"Ms. Conners, would you come down to the office please so we can clear things up and let our other guests go to bed?" Captain Haggerty said. "Our hotel manager needs to file an onboard incident report."

Ken called down on his walkie-talkie to bring the speedboat in, retract the buoy.

Pamela and her dad and Meredith stood with their arms around each other. No one, not even Pamela, had welcomed Sherry back.

It was after one when we finally got to bed, and even then, we sat around crew quarters, trying to put it together.

"Where do you suppose she was all that time? We checked everywhere!" Yolanda said. Six of us had crowded onto Pamela's bunk; the others sat on the beds across from us.

"She's small—she could hide anywhere," said Pamela. "Under a desk. Behind a sofa."

"But *why*?" Liz asked.

Pamela turned on her. "There doesn't have to be a why, Liz. It's Mom! It's the way she operates. Whatever brings the most attention."

"What do you think they'll do to her?" asked Natalie.

"Nothing," said Rachel. "She said she couldn't remember anything, and who could prove she couldn't? Haggerty's so relieved we didn't lose a passenger on his watch that he could have peed himself."

Pamela hugged her knees, her chin resting on top. "It's the first time in my life that I hope she was dead drunk. I can't stand the thought that she probably planned the whole thing—the scarf and all. One minute I'm so glad she didn't jump, and the next minute I . . ." Her voice wobbled. "I feel like I hate her guts."

"I think a lot of us are pretty mad at her," I said.

"Know what?" said Emily. "Tomorrow everyone will be touring St. Michaels and what happened tonight will be yesterday's news. Let's get some sleep."

I couldn't, though, for a long time. Inside I was seething at Pamela's mom and aching for Pamela. She must have been having trouble too, because some time later she crawled in my bunk with me, snuggled up against my back, and put one arm around me. I patted her hand to let her know it was okay, and when I felt her breathing more slowly, I fell asleep too.

When I came up on main deck early the next morning, I saw Pamela's mother wrapped in a yellow raincoat, wearing dark glasses and a scarf around her neck, sitting beside two suitcases near the gangway.

I knew Pamela had seen her too because she'd been watching from the lounge deck. I paused, wondering if I should say something to her. But a taxi pulled up in the parking lot, and Curtis removed the line across the gangway and carried the bags down.

Pamela's mom followed without looking back and climbed in the cab. I watched her leave without a wave, a hug, a good-bye to her daughter, even.

Pamela was going to spend some time in St. Michaels with her dad and Meredith, but I just wanted to stroll around and see more of the town—let myself unwind. Mitch and I decided to eat lunch somewhere onshore.

"Pamela okay?" he said as we left the dock to the flapping of sails on the boats anchored nearby.

"I think so. She's with her dad, anyway."

"Anyone know where her mom was while we were all looking for her?"

"Rachel said she was sitting in Stephanie's office in the dark, watching us search the ship. Dianne found her when she turned on the light." I sighed. "She was doing so well for a while. We thought she had turned a corner when she started working, got an apartment, and had a boyfriend. . . . And Pamela's supposed to leave for New York this fall. Got a partial scholarship to a theater school."

"Man, you hear of parents having trouble with their adult children, but sometimes it's the other way around."

We settled on the Crab Claw Restaurant and went inside.

"Let me treat this time," I said, remembering the last meal I'd enjoyed at his expense.

"Only if you insist," he said, smiling. "I heard paychecks are going to be late this time."

"Doesn't make a whole lot of difference, does it?"

"Well, some of the guys send their paychecks home. I know Curtis does. But if we're paid eventually, I won't complain too much," Mitch said. "I pay my folks room and board every month, but most of my salary goes in the bank."

"What are you saving for? A bigger boat?"

He folded his arms across his chest and grinned at me. "Naw, just want to fix up the one I have, put a cabin on her. All I've got now is a sunshade. Would sure appreciate a way to get in out of the weather when a storm hits on the bay."

I leaned my chin on my hand and studied him. "Where do you see yourself five years from now, Mitch? I love hearing about life plans."

"Life plans? You selling insurance on the side?"

I laughed. "No, it's interesting, that's all."

"Well, in five years I'd like to think I'd have an all-weather boat; like to have me a wife—a pretty one." His grin grew wider still. "Maybe even have the first of nine children."

"Nine!" I bolted back in my chair.

I loved the way he chuckled. "Okay, how about the first of three? That would make a nice number."

"So tell me about your phantom wife."

"My wife. Well now, let's see . . ." He stopped as a waitress came and took our order, then left again. "I think it would have to be a girl who had lived for a while in the city."

"Really? That's surprising."

"Why? I wouldn't want to marry a girl who was always dreaming of leaving the marshland and moving to Richmond or Baltimore or someplace. I'd want someone who really liked the waterman's life and the work that goes with it."

"You may have to extend your search a little beyond Vienna, Maryland," I said.

"Hey! I'm looking around, aren't I? Not working on the *Seascape* for nothing." Mitch tapped my ankle with the toe of his shoe. "Where do you see yourself in five years?"

"Well, graduated from college, hopefully with an MA in counseling. So I guess in five years I'll be looking around for a job, preferably in a high school or possibly a middle school."

"Any idea where?"

I gave a loud sigh. "That's the unknown. I'd like to be within an hour or so of my family—Dad and Sylvia and Les—but who knows where Lester will be then? He's got resumes out all over the place."

"And what about Patrick?"

I wasn't sure how to answer that. "He could be anywhere in the whole world by then, and . . . if we marry . . . I'll probably end up working wherever he is."

"Will you miss home?"

"Probably. But Patrick's worth it. I guess we always give up one thing to get another, don't we?"

"I don't know. It hasn't happened to me yet," Mitch said.

We walked all over St. Michaels after lunch. Once we sat

for a while, and I actually nodded off on a bench near the dock, I'd had so little sleep the night before. Mitch joked that I was boring company, so we went back to the ship and I slept for a half hour before Gwen woke me to change for dinner.

We had good weather the rest of the cruise. Pamela didn't mention her mom again, and Bill and Meredith seemed to enjoy themselves. By the time of the farewell dinner Saturday night, with the usual lobster and filet mignon, everyone seemed in a good mood, even Pamela. It was almost eleven the following morning, after the last passenger had disembarked, that the arguments started.

Quinton had assembled staff and crew in the dining room—minus the captain and first mate—and announced that our paychecks would be a week late. "If anyone has a critical situation and needs it immediately," he said, "see me afterward, and we'll work something out."

Obviously, no one was delighted with the news. The deckhands grumbled the loudest.

"It may not be a critical need, but I had plans for that paycheck," I heard Curtis say to Dianne.

"So did we all," Dianne told him.

You could see the difference in morale the following week, unless I only imagined it. Seemed as though people worked a little slower, a bit less cheerfully. Fewer smiles. We blamed it on a somewhat lackluster group of passengers this time, who weren't as enthused as the group before, but they probably picked up vibes from us.

Quinton had arranged for a local band to come aboard one evening and play dance music; a comedy team came another. There was one glorious afternoon when the wind was just right that we had a kite-flying contest on the top deck, and Stephanie was a surprisingly good cheerleader. Mitch and I flew one together, battling the yellow and orange kite that Gwen and Flavian had launched, until they tangled in midair and came spinning back down to the deck.

When the following Sunday arrived, however, and the passengers left, Quinton had to announce that, once again, there was a shortfall. But we would absolutely get our paychecks by the end of the month. This time there were open hostilities.

"I need mine now, Quinton," Frank said. "I've got bills to pay, and I've certainly been doing cruises longer than the captain. He getting a paycheck?" I could tell by the murmurs that went around that he spoke for all of us.

"Cruising's our profession, Frank," Quinton said. "We both know that part of this job is being able to roll with the punches. But I can guarantee that everyone here will get their paychecks before Dianne and I get ours."

But even Quinton couldn't have known what would happen next.

16

CHANGES

Up until now, summer on the bay, though hot, had days of respite, when the breeze picked up and the humidity went down. On these days passengers preferred being out on the decks, not in the air-conditioned lounge looking through travel magazines about what it was like every other place in the world. But now, as we started the last full week of July, the temperature shot up to the mid-nineties every day.

Whatever the weather in Barcelona, Patrick was obviously enjoying himself:

Students are just beginning to arrive for fall quarter. I'll be transferring to a dorm as soon as summer courses are over. Finished all the graphs for Professor Eagan's book.

Just proofreading yet to do, so I'm free for most of the day now. He sends me on errands and I explore the city. His girlfriend's coming to stay with him middle of August. She's teaching a course too. . . .

The *Seascape* wasn't completely booked for the next cruise either. In fact, I heard from Lauren that people were now offered discounts of $800 for immediately booking in August. Dianne even told us—jokingly, maybe—that if we had relatives who were considering a vacation at sea, they might be able to get it at half price.

What Frank told us one night, though—and he's practically lived his life on cruise ships—is that in the heat of summer, most people think about cruising the New England coast or the St. Lawrence Seaway, or they fly out to Vancouver and take the Inner Passage to Alaska.

Even the *Seascape* crew hunkered down in air-conditioning. The only time we wanted to sit on the top deck was when the ship was moving or after dark. Few of us opted to take excursions, even when we had the time. If we left the ship, it was to find a bar or a pizza place, to go bowling in air-conditioned comfort, or to take in a movie. Our paychecks finally came through, as Quinton promised, but he said we would be paid again in two weeks, not one.

When we did go out at night, for a couple hours after the day crew finished up, I began to notice a change in Gwen and Flavian's relationship. It had started out as a parody of love—lots of one-liners and laughs—then a sort of affectionate joking around. But now . . .

Liz and Pamela and I were watching as Yolanda replaited the cornrows that decorated Gwen's head. "Cornrow rehab," we called it.

"Do you think I'm leading Flavian on?" Gwen asked no one in particular, staring straight ahead since she couldn't move her head.

I was trying to cut my toenails with fingernail scissors, which didn't work, and realized I'd have to buy a pair the next time we were in a drugstore.

"Does he think so?" I asked. If you don't know the answer, ask a question.

"I'm not sure. He's been kind of moody. Haven't you noticed?" Gwen said.

"A little."

"He says I've changed. I said, 'For the better, I hope.' 'No,' he said, 'That's not what I meant.'"

"NMI," said Yolanda.

"What does that mean?" asked Gwen.

"Need more information."

"I told him he seemed quieter, more uptight lately. Asked him what was wrong. And he said it was me who had changed. Okay, we were kissing—serious kissing, I mean—and I guess I pulled away. I like it more playful, the way it started out with Flavian . . . and he doesn't. He wants to take things up a notch."

"You don't like Flavian?" I asked.

"Sure, I like him, but I didn't sign on for another relationship. I thought he knew that. I mean—look! I've got eight years of medical school ahead of me. I just wanted to really cut loose this summer and have fun."

"Maybe you each have a different definition of 'really,'" I suggested.

"I just don't want any baggage when I start school. I don't want long text messages from Flavian about when we'll see each other again. On the outside, Flavian looks like a fun-loving, risk-taking Romeo, right? On the inside, he's . . . I think he just needs a woman to validate him."

"How do you know it isn't just you? I mean that he never really fell for someone until he met you?" I asked.

Gwen was quiet for a moment, and then she said, "That scares the hell out of me."

"Why?"

"Because I can't be anyone's 'all' right now. Not even Austin's. I can't have anyone that dependent on me. This is my one time to cut loose and enjoy myself and not take on anyone else's needs."

And listening to Gwen, I wondered if this was how Patrick felt about me. If, once I started college, I'd feel the same. But I decided this was a conversation we could have when I visited him at Christmas.

It was the start of our eighth week, and the humid weather hung on. It had reached 101 degrees the week before and then went down to 93 where it settled in. We'd known the forecast before we left Baltimore this time, and Stephanie planned a lot of onboard activities that the passengers could enjoy in air-conditioned comfort if they declined the open-air trolley in Yorktown or the unshaded walk around Tangier Island or hiking on St. Michaels.

There's not a whole lot you can do on ship without a pool, an orchestra, or a theater, however. Still, Stephanie tried her best. We had a make-your-own-sundae afternoon and a bubble-blowing contest; a crazy hat day and short films on sea chanties and "The Disappearing Islands on the Chesapeake."

For the most part, though, passengers seemed listless and lethargic, and the subtle changes in the menu didn't help either. The stewards knew funds were low when the caviar appetizer disappeared from the Captain's Dinner. There was no Chilean sea bass, no duck pâté or heirloom tomatoes. Raspberry ice cream replaced the molten chocolate cake with fresh raspberry sauce that had been so popular on the other cruises.

Quinton had been asked to save money by substituting some clearly inferior wine at dinner, Rachel told us, but he chose to raise the price of premium liquors at cocktail hour instead. "Let's try to keep some shred of dignity," she heard him tell Carlo.

The third night, after we'd left Yorktown and were en route to Crisfield, we were getting ready for bed, listening to Emily's account of a guy she used to date who made his own beer, when the lights flickered a time or two.

I had just taken off my shorts when the lights went off completely.

"Awwk!" I said. "I can't find my sleep shirt."

"Listen," said Gwen.

"What?" We were quiet a moment.

"The air just went off too," Gwen said.

In fact, there was no noise at all. No hum of the fan, no drone of the engine. I felt around for my shorts and put them on again, then fished about with one foot for my sandals.

"I can't tell if we're still moving," said Emily.

"We're not," said Lauren.

"The passengers are probably freaking out," Pamela said. "I hope most of them are asleep."

"They won't be if the air doesn't come on pretty soon," said Lauren. "It was only down to eighty-six degrees outside at dinnertime."

"Shouldn't somebody be announcing something on the PA?" I asked.

"If the electricity's off, so is the PA. So is everything," Rachel said.

The only light we had was from the small, dim EXIT sign above our door, not much better than a tiny night-light.

"Let's go up top and see what's happened," said Pamela. "Does anyone know where we are?"

"In the widest part of the bay, that's where," said Rachel. "I'll bet we're fifteen miles from land on either side."

"Well, it's not like we're lost at sea," said Lauren.

Some of the guys were already out in the hallway too, and we collided with semi-bare bodies as we groped our way to the stairs. We could hear clunks and clanks coming from the engine room, Frank's and Ken's voices, but the last thing they needed was us getting in the way.

"Blindman's bluff," Barry called out behind us. "Oops, sorry, ma'am."

"Watch it, Barry," I heard Natalie say.

"What do you think is wrong?" I asked the guys over my shoulder.

"Powers out, that's all I know" came Mitch's voice.

"Generator," said Josh. "Gotta be the generator."

"Is that bad?" asked Liz.

"That's everything," Josh answered.

It was a little easier to see once we reached a door on the main deck. There was enough of a moon that we could make out sizes and shapes, even if we still had to guess at who they were.

"Are we sinking?" an elderly voice asked, and as we strained to see through the darkness, a small figure emerged from a doorway.

"No, ma'am," said Mitch. "Just a little problem with the power. Engineer is working on it now."

She was unconvinced. "We don't need our life jackets or anything?"

"No, you can go back to bed. If there was any danger, we'd let you know."

Since we didn't have a clue what to tell people, we felt our way over to the outside staircase, and when we got up to the lounge deck, we found Quinton and Dianne. She was holding a flashlight and Quinton was rummaging around in a metal box.

"I can't believe that's all they've got," Quinton was saying. "There aren't even enough for each member of the crew, much less the passengers." He handed a flashlight to Dianne and then, hearing us, called us over. "Each of you take a flashlight and patrol the decks. I want one person at the top and one at the bottom of each stairway. The generator stopped working, and until we get power again, we're all on duty."

"What are we supposed to tell people?" I asked.

"Try to keep them in their staterooms. Help them prop their doors open if they're too hot, open their windows for them. Those with inside cabins can go to the lounge if they like; we're opening doors and windows in there."

"I'm going to put pitchers of iced tea and lemonade on the bar," Dianne told us. "Rachel and Lauren, come help."

I took the bottom of the third staircase, Josh said he'd take the top. I heard Quinton talking to one of the passengers.

"It happens sometimes," he was saying. "This has been an exceptionally brutal summer, as we all know. The equipment's had to work nonstop at maximum capacity, and sometimes it does break down. But we've got an expert engineer on board who's spent half his life on ships, so we have every reason to hope for the best."

Mitch and Liz were heading for their assigned stairways.

"I'm supposed to serve at breakfast," Liz said, stopping a moment, the beam of her flashlight aimed at my chin. "But refrigeration is gone too, right?"

"Refrigeration and everything else that's run by electricity," Mitch said, "including the toilets."

"We can't flush the toilets?" Liz yelped. "I mean, not even once, not even at all?"

"They all operate on electricity," Mitch told her.

Trust Liz to worry about toilets.

In the dark hallway of the main deck, it was sort of like playing Marco Polo out of the water. Passengers were coming out of their stifling cabins, aware that all vent noise had stopped, and were bumping into each other.

"Has this ever happened before?" people asked us.

"How long before the air comes back on?"

"Do we get a refund?"

It was the toilets that bothered them most. It was hard to convince people that toilets at sea are not like the ones at home.

It was going on three o'clock, and some of the crew's flashlights that had been dim to begin with were going out. Quinton swore at himself for not checking on them at the start of the season, even though it fell under Ken McCoy's list of duties. Passengers were clamoring for flashlights for themselves.

As I was leading another group of passengers upstairs to the lounge, I heard Quinton ask Stephanie, "What have we got in the gift shop? Any flashlights at all?"

"Small pen-type things on an anchor key chain," she said.

"We're giving them away," Quinton told her.

"How many?"

"The whole stock. To anyone who asks."

Natalie took over my post at the stairs, and Stephanie and I walked the decks giving out pen-size flashlights and helping people move their bedding to their open doorways, where they might catch some semblance of a breeze. I was sweaty from the back of my neck to the soles of my feet. Perspiration trickled down my spine and between my breasts. Stephanie must have been miserable too, but you wouldn't hear it from her.

At about four o'clock, a few of us made our way toward crew quarters to use the bathrooms. We could hear Haggerty's muffled voice coming from below, and we squatted on the steps listening. Only scraps of conversation came from the engine room.

". . . only one more thing to try, and the chances are next to nothing." Frank.

"So try, damn it!" Haggerty. "Do what you have to do. The last thing I want is to tell the front office I can't even get this thing into port."

We turned around and headed back up, not wanting to be caught eavesdropping. We stood to one side at the top of the stairs as Haggerty and Quinton came up.

"Could I have some coffee up on the bridge?" the captain asked in irritation. Then, "Oh. Guess not. What are you doing about the passengers' breakfasts?"

"It will be a cold one, of course, but it's what we do after that that concerns me," Quinton said. "We can serve food for only a limited time after the refrigeration's off."

They went on up the next flight, and we ran down to use the restrooms while our flashlights still worked. Josh and Curtis were standing in the hallway. They shone their flashlights on our faces to see who we were and then went on talking.

"Doesn't look good, does it?" Barry asked.

"Worse than bad," Curtis replied. "That sorry thing isn't going to start again. Generator's shot and Frank knows it. He said it should have been replaced before the *Seascape* ever sailed."

"Are they going to send us a new one?" Liz asked.

We could barely see Curtis's face as he turned toward her.

"What? A helicopter drop or something?" he said, and we could tell he was laughing.

"I don't know. By ship, maybe," she said.

"This crate needs to be back at port. Takes at least a week to replace a generator," Curtis said.

"What the heck do we do?" asked Emily "People are going to wake up in a couple of hours if they haven't already."

"Be glad you're not the captain," said Josh. "He's the one who has to tell them they can't flush their toilets, can't turn on the lights, can't have coffee. That everything in the refrigerator is melting or defrosting. Some cruise, huh?"

I was embarrassed that one of my first thoughts was that I had something else exciting to tell Patrick.

17

UNDER A CLOUDLESS SKY

We'd been up all night—the whole crew—and looked it.

Any minute, we expected the captain to make an appearance and explain everything.

Wrong.

It was Quinton who faced the disheveled passengers at a breakfast of cold cereal, fruit juice, bananas, and yesterday's muffins, on paper plates. No toast, no eggs, no oatmeal, and—what caused the biggest uproar—no coffee.

"By now," he said, "you're all aware that the *Seascape* is experiencing a mechanical problem. Around midnight last night, our generator broke down, and when that happens, we are totally without power. This means no hot water, no toilets operating, no laundry, no cooking, no air-conditioning, fans, lights, or TV. We're doing everything we can to correct the situation and deeply regret the disappointment and inconvenience to our passengers. We do hope you'll understand that loss of electricity means that many accommodations have to be made."

That didn't satisfy anyone, and though some passengers joked ("Well, we wanted an adventure, didn't we?") and others took a stoical view and prepared to endure, most of them—by the looks on their faces—wanted more information *now*.

"We'll bring you updates at every meal," Quinton promised. "Sooner, if there are any new developments."

The stewards assigned to housekeeping were instructed to make beds without changing the linens and to ask passengers to please use their towels for one more day. And to keep the lids of their toilets closed.

Dianne told the stewards we could sleep in four-hour shifts, but it was stifling in crew quarters, so we strung ups sheets for shade among all the mechanical stuff on the "crew only" section of the main deck and piled blankets underneath to lie on. Some of us succeeded in a few hours' sleep until someone else came to take our place.

There was, of course, no excursion to Tangier Island, and lunch—served late—consisted of chef's salad, deli sandwiches, cookies, and soft ice cream. Quinton simply made an announcement that there was no word yet from the pilothouse, but he expected news of some kind by dinner. We would be eating at six o'clock, he told us, and choices were obviously limited.

"What's Haggerty waiting for?" we asked Josh after we'd seen him talking with Quinton.

"Wants to review his options," Josh said.

The restroom outside the dining room had a CLOSED sign on it. Understandably, passengers had been choosing to use that room rather than their own staterooms, since they couldn't flush.

We hated mingling with passengers. Sweltering, exhausted people were draped over chairs, over railings, like laundry, waiting for every little breeze. Every part of the body that touched a deck chair or railing soon grew too warm for comfort. Each time one of us crew members walked by, people called out to us, confronted us, asked how long we'd be here—stranded in the middle of the Chesapeake Bay—with no land in sight. They didn't believe us when we said we didn't know any more than they did. One woman asked if we were sure we hadn't drifted out into the Atlantic Ocean.

There was no cheerful steward walking through the ship ringing the dinner bell that evening. No welcoming scent of croissants fresh from the oven. Staff members were dressed in the same wrinkled shirts they'd worn the day before, even Quinton. There were no white cloths on the tables, no ice in the glasses, and the buffet was a repeat of what had been available at lunch, with applesauce and sliced beets added.

And there were few smiles. Voices were low, the mood grim. When the meal was over, both Quinton and Ken faced the passengers as promised, the rest of us standing at the back, listening. Quinton began:

"I know this has been a frustrating day for you, as it has for all of us. It's now evident to our engineer that the generator will have to be replaced, and that's not something we can do out here in the middle of the bay. While this is certainly a logistical problem for the company, our main concern is you, our passengers—your comfort and safety, as well as your expectations of a pleasant trip. The captain and first mate have been discussing our options, so I'll let Officer McCoy take it from here."

What was immediately evident was that First Mate McCoy would rather be anywhere else on the planet than here.

"Good evening, ladies and gentlemen," he said, and cleared his throat. "If I sound as if I haven't had any sleep, I haven't, but neither have most of you."

"Uh-uh, Kenny boy," I heard Curtis whisper behind me. "Don't whine."

Ken continued: "I guess it's pretty obvious that this ship is not going to make it back to Baltimore on its own, but that's our problem, not yours."

Curtis groaned again.

"All I can tell you at this point in time is that one of our options is to send our newly built sister ship, the *Spellbound*, down here and transfer you all to that—"

"Are they crazy?" Josh whispered, but the passengers perked up. The thought of a transfer at sea, a brand-new ship, air-conditioning, food . . .

"—but no decision has been made yet. And I want to assure you that we will remedy this situation as soon as possible. That's all I can tell you at this point in time, but if you have any questions . . ."

When did "this point in time" get so popular? I wondered. But yes, the passengers had questions.

"How is it you don't have the necessary parts with you?" a man called out.

"We have extra parts for many of the things we might need on the cruise, but a generator, unfortunately, is not one of them," Ken said. "Too big a job."

"I thought this was a 'completely refurbished ship,'" the man shot back. "Was that everything but the generator?"

"Bingo," Curtis murmured.

"I'm sure it was checked before we started our season, but there were some other malfunctions in connection with the generator," said Ken, and his face was slightly flushed.

"So we've got a whole damn engine room breaking down? Is that what you're saying?" the irate man shouted.

"No, sir. But sometimes, regardless, parts do give out, especially in the weather we've experienced," Ken said.

"How long can we go without fresh water?" asked a woman, clutching her half-filled glass.

"If we're careful to conserve what we have, there should be enough for drinking and brief washups at your sinks. Please, folks, no showers until the cruise starts up again."

"Can you give us any idea when that will be?" the man next to her asked. "We've already been sitting out here not going anywhere for eighteen hours."

"At this moment I cannot," Ken replied. And again, a murmur ran through the crowd. "But we're not in the middle of the ocean. The Coast Guard knows exactly where we are."

"What about food?" someone else called. But at that precise moment, Ken's walkie-talkie buzzed, and I even wondered if that was prearranged with Haggerty up in the pilothouse.

"If you'll excuse me, the captain needs me up on the bridge," Ken said. "I'm sure that Quinton can answer the rest of your questions."

For a brief moment I could see clear irritation on Quinton's face. He was already weary and looking more like Lincoln than Abe himself. But he stepped right up.

"Although we have plenty of food on board, we can't keep it refrigerated, so we've had to discard some," he said. "The food in the freezer will keep a few more days, but there's no way to cook it when it thaws. I don't think you will go hungry, but we have to conserve the ice that's left and will offer only those foods we know are safe. Remember, we're just fifteen miles from shore, so we can get a delivery if necessary, but first we need to know where we'll be tomorrow. As for sleeping, we will be glad to move mattresses to the upper deck for those of you who find your staterooms too uncomfortable. Right now we're going to feed our crew before it gets too dark to see. Then, if we can help you in any way, please speak to a crew member and we'll do our best."

The passengers began talking heatedly among themselves as they filed out of the dining room. We turned to one another.

"Is the captain insane?" asked Lauren. "They can't be serious about getting another ship. The *Spellbound* is up in Rhode Island."

Curtis found it funny. "The last I heard, they were three weeks behind in getting it furnished. Even if they just threw stuff together, stocked it, and brought it down, it would take a week. If we just want to transport one hundred and ten people fifteen miles, let's rent a ferry."

"Shoot," said Mitch, "I'll call my dad and tell him to hire some men in their oyster boats to carry us off. It's not all that complicated."

"Yeah, it is, actually," said Josh. "There's insurance, there's refunds, there's safety, there's all that luggage. The company is responsible for everything that happens to passengers until they disembark."

"It's even more than that," Lauren added. "It's saving face. If there's any rescuing to be done, the front office wants it done by the company—keep it all in the family, you know."

"How are they going to do that?" asked Barry. "There was already a WTOP helicopter circling this afternoon taking pictures. Probably covered on the evening news."

We had to patrol the lower decks from time to time to assist passengers who stayed in their rooms. The most we could see were the little pinheads of light from the tiny key chain flashlights we'd distributed earlier or an occasional beam from a crew flashlight. Some of the passengers had already holed up on the observation deck, using blankets and pillows to reserve the chaise longues. When I checked on them, I found only the slightest breeze fanning the humid air. We were too far from the mainland to see any lights. Not even a faint glow in the sky. All we had were stars and moon.

Mitch and I stood together at the railing.

"This will be the end of our summer jobs," he said.

"You think?"

"What else are we going to do? Say we get to Baltimore before this week is over. This particular cruise is kaput. So is the ninth cruise, because they'll be using that week to replace the generator. If we stick around for the last cruise of the season, who's going to put us up meanwhile? Our paychecks are already delayed."

"You could always go home and come back when the ship is ready," I said, considering.

"Don't think I haven't thought about it." He put an arm around my shoulder and gave me a playful hug. "You could come too. Sleep on the couch with the dog."

I laughed. "What's its name?"

"Rags."

"Rags?"

"Because when she was a pup, she tore everything to shreds. Grab hold of a shirt and you could pull it forever, she wouldn't let go. Springer spaniel."

"I'm sure your mom would appreciate having me there."

"Oh, she's used to it."

"Bringing girls home to sleep on the couch?"

"Bringing friends home—usually guys who are going out trapping with me the next day."

"What would you tell your mom about me?"

"I'd say, 'Mom, this is my friend Alice. She's sleeping with the dog,' and she'd say, 'Fine, she can set the table.' And you're in."

Why did I feel so comfortable around Mitch? I wondered. Why did I believe it would almost be that way if I took him up on it?

"We'll see what happens tomorrow," I said. "A mutiny might decide the whole thing."

The top deck was crowded with people now, like a beach on a summer day, except it was night and there were even a few mattresses. So Mitch and I and a few of the others took our pillows to the lounge deck fantail around one in the morning and crawled into the sleeping space the others had rigged up.

Sleepy as I was, I lay on my back and looked out between the gaps in the sheets strung over us, studying the stars. Every so often one seemed to wink at me, and I wondered how many light-years away it was and whether it even *was* any longer. I could hear Mitch's soft breathing on one side of me, Gwen's on the other. How special was it to be lying here between two friends, and when, if ever, had I had a male friend, other than my brother, whom I felt so close to and comfortable with, just staying friends? So far, at least.

* * *

I slept longer that I thought was allowed. No one woke me, anyway. I had to pee and desperately needed to stretch one leg, which was cramping. I managed to extricate myself from the tangle of bodies around me without nudging either Gwen or Mitch. I made my way down to crew quarters and could smell the toilets even before I got there. I took a deep breath, then zipped in and out.

No one else on the ship seemed to be up—not surprising since we were all exhausted, passengers and crew alike. But if there was a coolest part of the day, this was it—more breeze than we'd had for the last two days. I took the stairs to the Chesapeake deck, wanting to go around the walkway a few times to stretch my legs. When I turned at the bow, I saw a man leaning his arms on the rail, smoking, as dejected a figure as I'd ever seen.

The captain saw me, dropped his cigarette in the water, and turned his head away.

The breeze didn't last. When the sun rose, the shimmering orange ball seemed even more threatening than it had the day before, and its reflection on the water was like a warning arrow pointing directly at the ship. I rinsed my face in the crew washroom beside the others, brushed my teeth, tied my stringy, limp hair back away from my face, and went to the galley.

Quinton was there, dark circles under his eyes.

"Start filling trash bags," he was saying to Carlo and the assistant cook. "The sausage, the ham. If it wasn't frosted over when you took it out, it goes in the garbage. Eggs—out. Butter we'll use one more day. I'd rather have a hungry ship than a sick one."

"Any update from the front office?" Carlo asked.

"We're supposed to find out today if the *Spellbound*'s coming down. There was talk of giving the passengers a free cruise on it later in the fall."

"Makes no bloody sense to me," Carlo said. "If the ship's not ready for a September launch, it's not ready now."

"I don't know, Carlo. We're taking one step at a time. Check the milk to see if we can offer cereal for breakfast. Cereal, cheese, and fruit. That's it."

An occasional fishing boat passed that morning, the watermen staring up at us talking among themselves. When two men came out in a speedboat and cut the engine, one of them yelled, "You guys having problems?"

And one of the passengers yelled back, "We're being held prisoner because the generator went out. Send food!"

The men laughed and the passenger did too.

"Can you give us a tow?" someone else shouted.

"Good luck with that," one of the men called, and they sped off again.

When Dianne found that a couple had taken a Magic Marker and printed SOS in huge letters on a sheet and hung it from the railing, she took it down. Quinton went through the ship with the megaphone and announced that the captain would speak to us in the dining room at noon.

Not even Ken McCoy was smiling this time.

When Haggerty came into the room at twelve, walking swiftly, like the president holding a press conference, he used "I," we noticed, when he talked about action taken, "we," when action was delayed.

"To all you good people who are sweltering along with the crew, I can tell you that I've been in contact with the front office almost continually since we lost power," he said, pausing as if for applause, but he got only silent stares from the crowd.

"It's certainly unfortunate that you have had to endure a disabled ship in the middle of your cruise, and the weather only adds to your discomfort. We had originally discussed the possibility that our sister ship, the *Spellbound*, could be launched immediately to pick you up, but that turns out to be not only impractical, but impossible. So without wanting to delay you any further, I am negotiating with a salvage company to tow us in."

"You mean they're going to junk this ship?" a woman asked in dismay.

"Why not?" a man yelled. "That's what it is."

Haggerty looked uneasy. "No, ma'am, I should have been clearer. Salvage companies offer many services, and one of them is providing tugs to pull or push a disabled vessel into port."

"So what's to negotiate?" another man asked. "We want to get off. We're all baking out here."

"I will definitely get you all off this ship, as soon and as safely as possible," Haggerty said. "But the front office has the final say on what the cost will be and where we'll be towed. They should reach a decision by the end of the day."

Now everyone began talking at once. One man even leaped to his feet. "That probably means we won't get towed till tomorrow! We're down to crackers and prunes, and this is one hell of a way to treat paying passengers. Pay whatever they damn want and get us *off* here!"

"Amen!" yelled someone else.

Haggerty was getting testy: "One of the things I learned in the navy is to expect the unexpected. Good sailors know there will be ups and downs."

Even I knew he was treading on thin ice—that is, if we had any ice.

"Well, this ain't the navy," yelled a man who needed a razor. "I'm a retiree with six years of combat in 'Nam, and I didn't sign on for ups and downs on a cruise ship."

"I understand and applaud you, sir," Haggerty said. "And I would be glad to talk with you longer, ladies and gentlemen, but I'm expecting some calls. And the sooner this is settled the better."

"After we're towed back, then what?" someone called after him. "Will the company pay our hotel bill?"

But Haggerty was out the door, heading for the bridge.

18
END OF THE LINE

The temperature climbed even higher the next morning, both in the air and in misery. Angry passengers gathered in the lounge and dining areas, watching the doorways for any sight of the captain or first mate.

"Probably abandoned ship," somebody joked, "Check the lifeboats—see if they're all here."

Quinton made a brief announcement: A decision had been made that we would be towed, but the question was whether it would be back to Norfolk or to Baltimore. When noon came, then one o'clock, and we still sat idled, tempers reached the boiling point.

The WTOP helicopter flew over again, and people yelled and waved, fruitlessly calling up to the crew. Someone had printed

WANTED: KFC on the floor of the top deck, probably five Magic Markers' worth of ink, and we could see the photographer on the passenger side of the copter, taking a photo.

"Just got a text from my dad," I told the others. "He said it was on the news last night. Wants to know if we're okay."

"Tell him to send a care package," Gwen said.

Most passengers didn't even want us to come into their staterooms because they were such a mess. We gave out the last of the clean towels. And Stephanie organized another Trivial Pursuit game in the lounge, with items from the gift shop as prizes.

Funny the way you can change your mind about a person. In all the trouble we were going through on the *Seascape*, I hadn't heard Stephanie complain once. I hadn't heard her gripe when our paychecks were late. Hadn't heard her grumble that it was damn hard to entertain 110 people in 100-degree weather on a stinking ship that was going nowhere.

Her clothes were wrinkled and sweat-stained, the same as ours, and her hair needed washing, too. Yet she helped carry pillows and blankets to the observation deck, same as us; and she tied up the plastic bags of used paper plates and napkins, same as us; she was as bone-tired as everyone else, yet she managed to look more optimistic and encouraging than we did.

Maybe it was all a sham and maybe she had a few more marriages to wreck in her future, but didn't she deserve a second chance? She sure rose up a few notches in my esteem.

"Is anything happening at all?" we asked Frank when he

surfaced in mid-afternoon for the slim lunch pickings offered to the crew. "What's holding things up?"

Frank looked even older than his sixty-some years. "The deal is that headquarters is sitting on its haunches because it doesn't want to pay what the salvage company is charging. And, not surprisingly, salvage wants the pay up front. Damned if I'll ever work for this line again."

It was almost four when I heard a huge cheer from the lounge deck. I dropped the stack of paper cups I was placing on the buffet table for dinner and ran upstairs. Passengers were crowded along the rail, waving at a large tug coming our way.

"What a relief," Dianne said beside us. "And they're towing us to Baltimore, saints be praised. More expensive because Norfolk is closer, but then the cruise line would have to pay travel expenses for all the passengers to get from Norfolk to Baltimore."

You'd think the seven men aboard the *Samuel Dawes* were heroes, the way passengers cheered when they pulled alongside us. Ken McCoy opened the side door on the main deck to let their pilot come aboard. Barry and Mitch were studying the tug.

"Can she pull a ship this big?" Barry wondered aloud.

"You watch," Mitch said.

Nothing is ever as simple as you imagine, though. The *Samuel Dawes* had brought fourteen cases of bottled water for the passengers, and these had to be carried aboard. Then there were papers to sign and a discussion between the towboat crew and Captain Haggerty, an inspection of the bow, another discussion with Frank, and two news helicopters this time to take pictures of the hookup. But once the cable was attached and we actually began to move, we caught a whiff of a breeze—the first in several days—and felt energized once again.

We were traveling at only half the normal speed, so I had no idea how long it would take to get to Baltimore. But when we passed Tangier Island in the early evening, another cheer went up as we slowly saw land appearing on first one side of us, then the other. There were more fishing boats, and of course we were the big attraction.

The company had arranged for a hastily prepared fried chicken dinner to be brought out to the ship from a restaurant on Tangier Island, and we watched as the food was transferred to us at the stern without our having to stop the tow—large plastic cartons of potato salad and cole slaw hauled up in a net. Fishermen seemed as delighted to deliver the food as we were to get it, broad smiles on their red, weathered faces.

After our "last supper," as Emily called it, passengers began packing up their things, and most opted to sleep in their staterooms with the doors open, now that we were manufacturing our own breeze.

The rumor was that the crew would stick around Baltimore for a week while the generator was replaced, then do the last and final cruise of the season, but who knew?

We bedded down after midnight wherever we could. Some of us sat on the floor at the bow of the lounge deck, our half-closed eyes focused on the lights of the tug, the chug of the motor lulling us to sleep.

Gulls woke us at dawn.

I found myself slumped with my head on Mitch's shoulder, knowing that my breath must be awesomely awful. It was comforting to feel his arm around me. I liked the way our feet splayed out in front of us, the sneakers and deck shoes that were scattered among the legs; liked the naturalness of the heads tipped this way and that, arms limp, all of us roommates on this crazy ship.

Liz and I got up eventually and went down to the "stink hole," as we'd taken to calling the crew toilets, to brush our teeth. We were on housekeeping duty this week, so we didn't need to help at breakfast, what breakfast there was. But we stopped at the dining room and picked up some oranges for our sleep mates.

I sat crossed-legged on the deck facing Mitch, pulling back the thick peel of my navel orange, lifting a segment and putting it in his mouth, then one for me. I didn't know when anything had tasted so delicious as the freshness of that orange with a breeze on my face from a ship that was moving at last.

It took the rest of the day to reach Baltimore, and everyone gathered on deck as the harbor came into view. We were greeted by two smaller tugs that helped nudge us into a berth, plus a Coast Guard cutter, there to be sure we did it safely.

We stewards did our best to look spiffy and act professionally as we commiserated with passengers in the lineup to get off.

"Well, you've certainly had an experience" was about all we could offer.

Captain Haggerty had shown up after dinner the night before—when stomachs were full, of course—and thanked the passengers for their patience. He explained that refunds would be mailed to them from the front office but made no promise to pay for a hotel once they disembarked. He also thanked the crew for their help and determination, but there was no promise of a hotel for us, either, and certainly no tip envelopes to pass out.

The gangplank was lowered to much cheering, and several reporters and photographers stood by to interview passengers about being "kept at bay" or "stranded at sea," as various passengers put it. I saw Dianne wince as one woman, eager to be interviewed, lifted her arms in the air in a victory pose and shouted, "I survived the worst cruise ever!"

Ken bravely shook hands with each passenger who left the ship, and so did Quinton. But Haggerty seemed to have slipped away unnoticed by us all. Finally it was just the silent ship and us, and we set to work stripping any beds we hadn't done yet, bagging the last of the trash, exchanging our white shirts for comfortable tees.

Most of us had contacted home by now, and I called Dad at the Melody Inn to tell him I was off the ship but would finish all ten weeks if I could.

"What an adventure, huh?" he said, laughing. "I wasn't worried about you, honey, but I knew it must by darn uncomfortable. Where are they putting you up tonight?"

"I don't know. Quinton is going to talk to us in an hour or so, but I'll be fine," I told him.

Sure enough, Quinton gathered us all on deck shortly after I'd talked to Dad. "The home office said they'll be caught up on bills by tomorrow, including paychecks. Let me know if you want to pick yours up in person or have us send it on to your home address. Your last paycheck, for this past week, will go out in about ten days."

"What about the final cruise of the summer?" Gwen asked.

"We won't know till tomorrow if they're canceling or not," Quinton said. "It's asking a lot of you, I know, to hang around for a week. If you'd rather go home now and come back for the final cruise, we'd be happy to have you. And if you decide to end your job today, we understand. I'll be at the branch office on Charles Street tomorrow after ten with more information."

Some of the deckhands had already taken off. Lauren and Emily went to stay with a friend, but six of us girls—Natalie, Gwen, Pamela, Liz, Yolanda, and me—plus Barry, Mitch, Josh, and Flavian, stood on the deck considering our options.

"Where you guys going to crash?" Flavian asked us. We had no idea.

Barry knew someone he thought would put the guys up for the night, but all we girls wanted was to find a motel and take a shower.

We sat down on some benches outside an ice-cream place while Josh looked up motels on his BlackBerry. We wanted a place we could walk to, if possible.

"The Renaissance?" Josh asked.

"Are you kidding?" Gwen said, looking at the expensive

place many of our passengers had stayed before boarding the *Seascape*.

"Pier 5 Hotel?"

"Get real," Pamela told him.

We finally settled on the Silver Motor Lodge and told the guys we'd meet them back on the dock at seven. Then we piled into a taxi van.

It was a crummy motel, a one-story building that had seen better days, and two of the letters on its neon sign were missing. They made the six of us take two rooms, so we divided up, three to a room. But a shower had never, ever felt so delicious. I shampooed three times just to feel that wonderful tingle and finally, reluctantly, let someone else have a turn.

We felt almost human again when we met the guys, then went to the Hard Rock Cafe. Despite our protests, they said they were paying, and we sat at two adjoining tables trading food back and forth, enjoying the huge fried onion that looked like a wig. It was great to be in a noisy place, with loud music and people laughing and *air-conditioning*. I felt that someone could lock me in a refrigerator, and even after an hour, it would still feel good.

We walked around Harborplace afterward, stopping to watch a mime, who pretended he was trapped in a box; danced a little outside a bar. Around midnight, when our sleep-deprived nights caught up with us, we looked for a cab back to the Silver Motor Lodge.

After the guys had put us in it, however, and waved good-bye, we noticed that they'd climbed into the cab behind us and were following along.

"They got the same motel?" asked Liz.

"I thought they were staying with a friend of Barry's," said Gwen.

We started giggling, bursting into laughter each time our cab made a turn and theirs followed. The driver was also laughing, and it came as no surprise when we reached the motel parking lot that the guys got out there too.

"Yeah?" Pamela said as they looked sheepishly in our direction. "And where are you guys sleeping?"

"On the floor?" said Mitch.

"Are you kidding?" I told them. "The rooms are doll-size."

"We're out of money," said Josh. "We spent it all on dinner. Honestly."

"We *said* we'd pay!" Natalie reminded them.

"That's when we thought we could stay with Barry's friend. Turns out he's not home," said Flavian.

"Listen, you guys," said Gwen. "They wouldn't even let the six of us stay in one room. 'Six girls, two rooms,' the woman told us."

"*Two* rooms? You've got two rooms?" said Mitch. "Come on! You've got to let us have one."

"How are we going to get you in there?" I said.

But it wasn't hard, actually. Our two adjoining rooms were along one corridor that ended at a door to the parking lot. No one could get in from outside without a key card, but it was easy for one of us to open the door from inside.

So the six of us girls came in the front entrance and said good night to the manager at the desk. She was a pink-haired, middle-aged woman in a thin nylon blouse with a black bra beneath and a cross around her neck. She had a tattoo of a guitar on her bicep, and her cherry-red nail polish was chipped.

"You have a nice evening?" she asked, not even taking her eyes from the reality show she was watching on TV.

"Yeah, the best," said Pamela.

"Checkout time's eleven," the woman said, and we passed her desk, made the turn, and walked all the way to the end. Yolanda opened the outside door, and the guys silently filed in.

This was almost too easy.

"Got to be bedbugs or something," Natalie said after we'd closed the door behind them.

"Shhhh. If we don't wake them, they won't bite," said Mitch.

"Hey! Adjoining rooms," said Flavian.

"And the door locks," said Gwen, giving him a look, and we laughed.

"Party time!" said Josh. "Who's going with me to get the brew? We passed a place just down the road."

"I'll go," Mitch offered. A half hour later they were back, both carrying a six-pack in each hand. They tapped on our window, and Liz went down the hall to let them in. We gathered in the guys' room.

"Bottle opener?" Natalie said.

Flavian produced the ship's flashlight key chain, whose anchor, we discovered, was also a bottle opener.

"To us," said Mitch, raising his bottle.

"To the *Seascape*. May she rest in peace," said Flavian.

"Aw, come on, she'll be good as new," Barry said. "She's *refurbished*!" And that got a laugh from all of us.

"Shhhh," Liz warned.

Someone suggested playing beer pong, but we didn't have enough beer for that, even though Liz and I wanted only one bottle. We were sprawled—all ten of us—on the two double beds and the floor.

So Barry opted for a game he called Truth or Fabrication.

"Drunk or sober?" asked Yolanda.

"That's up to you," said Barry. He dumped Natalie off the chair where she had been sitting.

"Okay," he said. "One at a time we have to sit in that chair and tell the others the most embarrassing thing that ever happened to us."

"Yeah, right. Like we'll tell the truth," said Liz.

"That's where the rest of us come in. If we decide you just made it up, or it's not embarrassing enough, you have to do whatever embarrassing thing we think of."

"Oh, no," I said. "We'll spill our guts and you'll still humiliate us."

"No, we won't. It'll be democratic. We'll vote," said Barry, and opened another beer.

What would I choose when it was my turn? I could practically remember every year of my life by my most embarrassing moments. Eating crayons in kindergarten? Asking Donald

Sheavers to play Tarzan and kiss me? Dinner at Patrick's parents' country club and bringing the napkin home in my bag? Bleeding through my white skirt at the dentist's office? Reciting the wrong poem in seventh-grade English? Falling down the stairs my first day of high school and wetting my pants?

Fortunately, the game started with someone else. Liz told the hilarious story of putting her push-up bra in the dryer and starting a fire. I knew it was true because I'd run across the street to comfort her and was there when the fire chief came out and warned her about putting rubberized products in a dryer. We gave Liz a thumbs-up.

Flavian was next, and it was hard to imagine that the guy with the movie-star looks would be embarrassed about anything. But then he told us about going to this fabulous water park with his friends when he was nine, and out of seven boys, he was the only one who wasn't tall enough to go down the huge slide.

"Awww," the girls all said in unison.

Then it was my turn. I sat in the chair, my back to the door.

"I don't remember where I was," I began. "Georgetown, I think. It was summer, I was wearing a tank top and full skirt. I'd used the restroom somewhere and was going back down the street when three guys walked past me from behind, and one of them said, 'Nice butterflies.' Then I discovered that in pulling up my underpants, I'd accidently tucked the hem of my skirt in the waistband and was exposing my bottom."

"Encore! Encore!" Mitch said, laughing. And they decided I

was telling the truth because my cheeks had flushed. There was a loud knock at the door, and I literally leaped out of the chair. The room fell silent.

"Who is it?" whispered Pamela.

I leaned over and peered out the peephole. The woman with the pink hair was looking right back at me. I turned to the others and pointed to my hair and then my bicep.

"Uh-oh," said Gwen.

People were sliding off the two beds, some heading for the next room, some the bathroom, but suddenly a key turned in the lock, and there she stood, taking in the whole situation.

"Well," she said as we froze in our tracks. "I didn't think that even six girls could make quite so much noise. We've had a complaint about the noise down here, and I see the population has doubled. Do you know what time it is?"

We looked at the bedside clock. Two forty-five, and our game was just beginning.

"We'll keep it low," Barry promised.

"The rate just doubled, due immediately, and you knock it off or you can pack up now—no refunds," Pink-Haired Woman said. "I don't like sneaks."

Josh got out his credit card. "Okay, you've got a right to be pissed. The truth is, we just got off that ship—"

"This is a seaport, buddy. People get off ships all the time."

"Well, we've been stranded out on the bay for three days without food or water."

The woman's face softened a little. "That seasick ship? That's what the newspaper called it. The one where the toilets wouldn't flush and the air-conditioning went out?"

"Yeah. You wouldn't believe . . ."

We thought of joining in, but Josh was doing a good enough job on his own.

"No lights, no hot water, food spoiling, passengers yelling at us, babies wailing, and we didn't even get paid for three weeks."

"The weather's been so hot and humid," Tattoo Lady said.

"Right. No breeze, not even on the water. We had to stand up all night at each stairway with flashlights to escort people up and down. Took two days to tow us in, the generator is shot, the cruise line defunct, and we're out of a job. We just wanted to have one more night together before we say good-bye."

The woman looked us over warily. "How do I know this isn't a bunch of bull?"

Barry picked up the flashlight key chain with *Seascape* printed on the little metallic anchor and handed it to her.

The pink-haired, black-bra lady studied it, and her forehead lit up. "Part of history," she said. "Okay, if you quietly sack up now, I'll keep the registration to six and you can say your good-byes at breakfast tomorrow."

"Deal," said Josh. "Thanks a lot. We appreciate it." She put her finger to her lips as she went out and closed the door softly behind her. We looked admiringly at Josh and Barry.

"Truth!" we said. "You win."

And so to bed. We girls headed to the next room. We were so tired, I'm not sure who slept where. It wasn't until the next morning that we discovered that Gwen and Flavian had spent the night wrapped in a blanket on our floor.

We managed to be out of the hotel by eleven thirty and had breakfast at a pancake place. We could have slept for five more hours, but we were hungry, too, and when we'd finished eating our strawberry-pecan-banana-chocolate-chip concoctions, we took cabs to the cruise line's branch office on Charles Street. We found Quinton and Frank talking in a small reception room with posters of ships on the walls and one-page information sheets with photos of both the *Seascape* and the *Spellbound*.

We gathered around as Quinton passed out our paychecks.

"So what's the word?" Mitch asked. "They going to make that final cruise?"

Quinton shook his head. "Afraid not."

We looked at Frank. "The generator won't be replaced by then?" I asked.

"Oh, the generator could be replaced, but they couldn't get it on credit. Their credit rating right now is about zero. By the time they send out those last checks and give refunds for cruises eight and nine, they'll have dug a hole so deep they can't get out."

"Wow," I said, and fingered one of the color brochures there on the desk.

"Yep. A shame," said Frank. "Big dreams, little cash. A small company trying to get going too soon. Should have waited till both ships could go out at once. But they just didn't have the cash to wait. Figured the summer cruises on the *Seascape* would pay the bills for fixing up the *Spellbound*, but things didn't turn out that way."

"So what are *you* going to do?" Josh asked him.

"Oh, I'll hang around Baltimore a day or two, talk to more shipping companies. See what's available. Something will turn up. Always does."

We looked at Quinton. "Dianne and I have a sailboat up in Maine. We just might take the autumn off. Sail around. Visit friends. Line up something for January. Frank knows he's welcome anytime."

I went back outside with the rest of the crew, and we sat on the steps of an office building, delaying our good-byes.

Liz called her dad, and he said he'd pick us up that afternoon. After a forty-seven-second kiss, Flavian said good-bye to Gwen and took a cab to the Amtrak station, and Josh and Natalie joined him. The rest of us wandered down to the harbor. We stood on the dock and looked at the *Seascape*, just as we had done the first day we came here in June.

It wasn't in the same berth, but farther down in a more out-of-the-way place where the mechanics could get at it. No crowd of people gathered on the dock, no activity. What would become of it? I wondered. All the planning, remodeling, the buying and hiring. All those dreams flying off like the swoop of a gull overhead.

Barry saw a friend of his and wandered off, and then it was time to say good-bye to Mitch.

"How do we do this?" he asked, smiling down at me. "Should we shake hands?"

"Not a chance," I said, and threw my arms around his neck for a long hug and then a kiss on the cheek and then another hug for good measure.

"Say hello to Patrick for me," he teased. And then he walked away.

19

HOUSEKEEPING

Yolanda had an aunt in Baltimore and had decided to visit her for a few days, so it was just Gwen and Pamela and me riding home with Liz and her dad.

Mr. Price was a willing listener to all the stories about the ship and its passengers. We didn't mention Pamela's mom—there were enough tales to tell without that.

"Everyone's a sailor at heart," he said. "And if he doesn't have his own boat, he likes to hear about people who do."

"So what's been happening in Silver Spring?" Liz asked him, leaning over to run her hand across his cheek. "Not thinking of growing a beard, are you?"

From the back, their hair color looked remarkably the same, except that we could see a spot on her dad's head where the scalp was beginning to show through.

"Just bumming around this weekend," he said. "And it's one way to get Nathan to bed—threaten to rub my grizzly cheek against his, and he goes screeching up the stairs." Liz laughed. "He's lost his first tooth. He'll want to tell you all about it."

Because we reached my street before the others, Mr. Price offered to let me off first, so we could at least dislodge some of the luggage. "Your dad know you're coming?" he asked.

"He knows the ship got in, but I'd thought I might be staying on for the final cruise."

"Yeah, that was a shame," Mr. Price said. "Messed up a lot of plans, I imagine." He got out and went to the trunk for my bag, then took Pamela and Gwen on home. I said I'd call them later.

I went up the steps to the porch, letting my duffel bang against my leg, thinking how much thicker the foliage seemed on the trees than when I left.

It was good to be home. I was thinking about Mitch and how he would be feeling walking into his house in Vienna, Maryland. I didn't know what it looked like. Didn't know a lot about his family at all. But I knew how much he liked the idea of home—the trees, the marsh, the muskrats, his boat. I couldn't identify with some of that, except that it was his idea of home, and that's what made it special.

I opened the door, then stopped and sniffed the air. What was that odor? I wondered. Something familiar. Closing the door behind me, I set my bag down and heard a noise upstairs. Voices. I had just started up when Sylvia appeared in the hallway above, her hair piled on top of her head, a paintbrush in one hand.

She stared. "Alice!" she cried.

"Yeah," I laughed. "I live here. I think."

"You're back!" She turned. "Alice is back," she called over her shoulder and Dad appeared behind her.

"Well, well!" he said, smiling and wiping his forehead. "Thought you were staying on! Cat's out of the bag, I guess, and here we wanted to surprise you."

"What?"

"We're painting your room," said Sylvia. "You said that it was time to get rid of the jungle look and that if you had a choice now, you would go with ocean blue, so . . ."

I ran up the stairs. "You remembered?" Sylvia and I had been looking at colors for the powder room last spring, and I'd fallen in love with a color called ocean blue, though she'd picked something else.

"We're not done yet. We still have two walls to go," Dad said as I whipped pass him.

"Oh my God!" I gasped. "I love it." I turned and looked at them bewildered. "But . . . I'm leaving for college."

"Well, we thought maybe this would lure you home from time to time," Sylvia said. "A new bedspread and curtains go with it. Crate and Barrel has some wonderful stuff, but we'll let you pick them out."

I started to throw my arms around her, but she held me off. There were paint spots all over her, so I hugged Dad from behind.

"Listen, kiddo," Sylvia said with a laugh, "the immediate problem is where you're going to sleep tonight."

I assumed Lester's old room, then realized they had moved all my stuff in there: headboard, mattress, dresser. A lightbulb went on. "Easy," I said. "Lester's. He still hasn't rented that room in his apartment, right?"

Dad chuckled. "He'll be delighted," he said.

"Yeah. Right. I've got a ton of laundry to do, so I'll do it there. He owes me one anyway."

"For . . . ?" Dad asked.

"On general principles," I said.

Dad gave me his car keys and I was off.

I called Les on my cell to tell him I was coming, but he didn't pick up, and I just drove on. If he wasn't home, I'd stay at Gwen's.

I decided I loved my home too—Silver Spring, I mean. The shady streets—that was something I'd missed this summer. Trees. Tall trees. The closer you get to the shore, the shorter the trees. Could I ever live on Tangier Island, without any really tall trees? I didn't think so.

As I drove, Silver Spring became Takoma Park, and the trees were even taller, the houses older, larger—relics of big families and bygone days. I pulled up to the yellow Victorian house with its wide porch and brown trim, the staircase at the side leading up to Lester's apartment. Lester's car was there and so was Paul's. I took my bag out of the backseat, went up the staircase, and rang the bell.

"Well, look who's back!" Les said when he opened the door. He was wearing an old pair of shorts and a torn tee and had a Dr

Pepper in one hand. "Thought for a while we'd have to call the Coast Guard." I grinned and walked on by him.

"Guess who's going to be sleeping in your spare room for the next week," I said.

"Whoa, whose idea was that?" he cried, but I think he was still smiling.

"Dad and Sylvia are painting my bedroom. They thought they still had two more weeks. Surprise, surprise."

"Well darn, there goes the girlfriend," said Les.

"What girlfriend?"

"There isn't one yet. Naw, it's okay. We'll put you to work. How are you, anyway? You're looking good. Got some sun, I see."

"What you see are freckles," I told him. "It was an experience and I'm glad I went. Got any more to drink?"

"Help yourself," he said.

I went to the fridge and got a 7UP. "I really will help around the place, " I said. "I'm not just here to crash."

"That's good, because Paul and I have a little project: girl bait."

"Girl bait? I'm supposed to be girl bait?"

"Not you. Come out and see." He led me back outside. We went down to the backyard, and there on cinder blocks was a sailboat. And Paul.

I stared. "You're serious? You guys bought this thing to attract women?"

"Actually, it belongs to Paul, but I get sailing rights if I help fix it up. A Flying Scot."

Paul beamed. "A nineteen-footer," he added.

It was in need of . . . well, everything. They had scraped off the paint about ten inches down all the way around, and I couldn't tell if some things needed tightening or replacing altogether. My tactless remark didn't seem to dampen their enthusiasm any. Paul ran his hand fondly over a smooth area.

"Well," I said, backpedaling as best I could, "I guess it would attract me. I mean, I'd be curious about the kind of guys who would put all that work into maintaining a sailboat. Like, it shows commitment, and if there's anything a woman loves—"

"Wasn't exactly what we had in mind," Paul said. "But, hey, welcome back, Alice. Heard you had quite a trip. Grab a sander there and a scraper, and we'll let you tell us all about your fateful adventure."

What was there about boats, anyway? Or was this just the month for painting, for refurnishing, for getting ready? Then I thought that I could invite the girls over here to help sand and paint, so I picked up a scraper and began.

Patrick: *So how does it feel to be home?*

Me: *Super terrific, except I'm not at home. Dad and Sylvia are painting my bedroom, so I'm crashing with some guys for a week.*

Patrick: *Twenty questions or what?*

Me: *Ha. I'm staying at Lester's. They don't have a third roommate yet. Paul bought an old sailboat, and I'm helping fix it up. Says he'll take me out in it sometime as payment.*

Patrick: *You haven't had enough of the sea?*

Me: *Hey, he's tall, handsome, has his MA . . .*

Patrick: *Uh-oh. She goes for older men.*

Me: *So what are the female students like so far in Barcelona?*

Patrick: *All babes.*

Me: *Any in particular?*

Patrick: *All of them.*

Me: *I'll think of you when I'm out on the bay with Paul, the wind blowing my hair.*

Patrick: *Gotta go. The lovelies await.*

Monday at Lester's was maybe the most beautiful day of the summer. It wasn't supposed to be. We were only days away from August, and August in the nation's capital, anywhere *near* the capital, is usually beastly—meaning that everything living, except at the zoo, takes off for the beach or the mountains. But on this day the humidity dropped along with the temperature, and I decided to play housewife while Les and Paul were at work. I started with the refrigerator.

I'd hung around Chef Carlo enough when I'd been on galley duty to see how he came up with the wonderful soups and stews he made for the crew dinners. He made them from whatever extra food he'd cooked for the passengers that never made it into the dining room. From these, he extracted meat and veggies, rice and noodles, and created these amazing concoctions, different every night.

I pulled out every leftover I could find and set it on the table: an ear of corn, some Wendy's fries, a dab of Popeye's red beans and rice, a McDonald's burger minus the bun. . . . I chopped and shredded, added two cans of V8, a chicken bouillon cube, some sautéed onion, a little minced garlic . . . *Stop! Stop!* I told myself, when I found a breaded pork chop in the back of the fridge and discovered it wasn't breaded at all, just moldy.

When the guys got home that evening with fish and chips, I had the beds made, a load of laundry done, the bathroom scrubbed, the table set, and a pot of soup on the stove.

They were clearly pleased.

"Maybe we should be looking for a live-in chef and butler, not a grad student," Paul said, his glasses fogging as he leaned over the soup pot to savor the smell. He strolled through the living room and looked around. "The apartment straightened up and—what's this? Laundry? Folded, no less?"

"Except that I didn't know what was whose, so you'll have to sort the underwear," I told him. "And I'm missing a yellow sock of my own, so if you find it clinging to your boxers, let me know."

"So they taught you to be useful?" Les said, opening a beer as we sat down to dinner.

"I'll say. Cracking crabs, man overboard, *Seascape* gripper . . ."

"What's that?" asked Paul. "Fishing tackle?"

"No. It's the way you grip a passenger's arm and he grips yours when he's going up or down a step, getting into a lifeboat and stuff—gives you a steadier grip."

"And 'man overboard,' what's that all about?"

I told them about the incident with Pamela's mom.

"Wow." Les leaned back in his chair. "She's done things like this before?"

"Not in front of an audience."

"Hardly got the reaction she expected," Paul guessed.

"No. Pamela thinks she thought her dad would be frantically looking for her, joining the rescue—"

"And hugging her to him when he discovered she'd been hiding somewhere, watching the whole thing?" Les asked incredulously.

"That he'd be so glad she was alive that his true feelings would come out and he'd drop Meredith and remarry her—I don't know," I said.

"Where is she now?" Paul asked. "Pamela doesn't live with her, does she?"

"No, fortunately. Mrs. Jones has an apartment in Glenmont, and Pamela will be going to school in New York this fall." I ate the last fry on the platter. "Would it be okay with you guys if I had the girls over here one night this week? It'd be great to have one last get-together before we all scatter."

"Sure," said Les, and for the first time, he didn't make some remark like, *Just let me know so I can be out for the evening*, as he usually did when I mentioned Pamela. But he added, "They could even help with the boat, if they wanted."

"They might," I told him.

Les made some coffee, and we sat around talking about what needed to be done to the sailboat. I couldn't help studying Paul. I'd always been attracted to him in a weird sort of way. Slim, bespectacled, introverted, and shy, he was a geology major; and for a long time that's the way I thought of him, as an intellectual type whose most intimate relationships were with rocks—billion-year-old rocks. And then I found out he was a ballroom dance instructor and a bluegrass musician in his spare time. I mean, go figure.

You can play with a band, though, and you're still the only one playing your particular instrument. You can be a dance instructor and still hold your partner out away from your body. I wondered if he was using his hobbies as a front, to make him appear far more social than he was.

But suddenly, with the purchase of the boat, he was like a

little kid. How fast it would probably sail, how he'd signed up for lessons this fall . . .

"What are you going to name her?" I asked.

He had an embarrassed smile on his face as he lowered his coffee cup. *"Fancy Pants,"* he said.

Les and I broke into laughter.

"Fancy Pants?" I cried.

"You're serious?" said Les.

"That's her name," said Paul.

"Uh . . . somebody you know?" I asked.

"My grandmother."

"Your *grandmother*?"

"Get's better by the minute," said Les.

I wondered what Mitch would say about this. But Paul explained: "Whenever she got really dressed up to go somewhere, my grandfather called her 'Fancy Pants.' But it was Grandma who loved the water, the sea. When I bought this boat, I kept thinking how much she would have loved sailing in it, so why not name it after her? Somehow 'Fancy Pants' sounds better than 'Ursula Birgit.'"

Couldn't argue with that.

"And you can tell each of your respective girlfriends you named it after her," I said.

"Now, that's an idea," said Paul.

Les and Paul cleaned up the kitchen while I got the TV all to myself. As he passed the living room, Les asked, "Any calls for me today, Alice?"

"No. Were you expecting one?"

"Probably not. But I sent out a new batch of resumes last week, and I listed our landline as well as my cell. I'm applying for some really nice spots, so . . . Well, if someone calls, be professional."

"Why me? I'm not applying for a job."

"You know what I mean. It might be a woman. Don't give her the third degree."

"You think I'd do that?"

"I'm just saying. If you know I'm waiting for an important call, you'll be ready."

"Of course I will."

"Good. I'm especially interested in a job at the Basswood Conference Center in West Virginia."

"Are you expecting any calls, Paul?" I asked when he came in to watch a program.

"No, I think I'll stay working where I am for a while," he said. "Now that I've got a boat, I'd like to be fairly close to the bay."

"Can't leave old *Fancy Pants*," said Les.

I was on Lester's computer most of the next day. I'd already told my friends that my room was being painted and I was staying at Lester's for a week until it was ready. Now I was desperately trying to catch up with Facebook and e-mail messages from potential roommates, and I found that many had given up on me. I hadn't responded fast enough or told them enough, or they had opted for the "experience" of letting the university pick a roommate for them.

A girl named Rainey said she hoped I wouldn't be offended, but she was really looking for someone more into the arts. Briana said she was Irish and wanted to know my "heritage." I didn't even answer. Kayla said her mom wanted her to room with a Christian.

For God's sake, I thought, *we're not getting married!* If I couldn't have Gwen for a roommate, I just wanted someone compatible. I finally agreed to room with a girl from Ohio named Amber because we looked at each other's pictures on Facebook, and she said she loved my freckles and I said I loved her tattoos.

On Wednesday morning I was about to call Pamela with the news when she called me.

"How you doing?" I said, not daring to ask if she'd visited her mom yet. She and her mom hadn't communicated since that awful man-overboard night. And when Pamela didn't answer right away, I asked, "Have you heard from your mom?"

"She just called," Pamela said. "She's been in the hospital. Wants me to come take her home."

20
BEING PROFESSIONAL

"What can I possibly do?" I asked.

Pamela had pulled up in Meredith's Honda, and I slid in beside her.

"Just help me get her back to her apartment. Moral support, if nothing else. I don't especially want to be in a car alone with her, and I'm not sure what to say."

"That makes two of us. Things got pretty weird the night she reported herself missing."

I was surprised at Pamela's response. "She didn't report herself missing! I wish people would quit using that term."

I glanced over at her, wondering, then faced forward again. I didn't know what to say to *Pamela*!

She exhaled, and her hands went slack for a moment on

the steering wheel. "All we really know is that she thinks she saw someone fall overboard and got emotional about it, then holed up somewhere for a while. She may have been confused, it may have been deliberate, it may not have been her at all who reported that someone fell—or whatever . . . People shouldn't jump to conclusions!"

What was happening here? I wondered.

"Okay," I said. "Point taken. What's the latest? Why has she been in the hospital?"

The sharpness went out of Pamela's voice. "She just called and said she'd been in an accident with her car—nothing serious, I guess—and was kept in the hospital overnight for observation. They wouldn't release her today unless she had someone to drive her home—said she couldn't take a taxi."

"All right."

I settled back in the seat, my eyes fixed on the white crocheted cross that dangled from Meredith's rearview mirror—a symbol of her faith and her nursing profession, I guessed. There was a tiny tissue holder attached to the dashboard and a collection of odds and ends in a console tray—lipstick, change, parking ticket, comb. . . .

"I'm totally freaked out," Pamela said finally. "Everything's happened so fast."

"I know."

"I mean, the cruise, Dad and Meredith being there, Mom showing up, the generator breaking down, getting ready for New York, and now this."

"Everything coming at you at once," I said.

"How am I supposed to deal with it all?"

"Just like you're doing, Pamela. One thing at a time."

"Thanks for coming with me," she said, glancing over.

At Holy Cross we had to go through a parking gate, and Pamela finally found a place in the visitors' lot. I went inside with her. Pamela's mom was sitting in the lobby in a wheelchair, an attendant on the bench next to her.

Mrs. Jones, or Sherry Conners, or whatever she was calling herself now, gave us an impatient smile. "I've been sitting here for thirty-five minutes," she immediately complained to Pamela. "It's a simple ride home, and I could have taken a taxi if they'd let me."

"Hospital rules," the attendant said.

"I just came along for the ride," I said, hoping to make it easier on Pamela.

Mrs. Jones ignored me completely. "You should have pulled up here in front, Pamela. Now I have to wait even longer while you get the car," she said.

Pamela turned on her heels. "I'll be right back," she said flatly, and headed for the entrance.

I stood awkwardly off to the side, wondering what I was supposed to do. Pamela certainly didn't need help getting the car she had just parked, but staying here with her mom . . .

I had no choice. The attendant looked at me impassively, took out her cell phone, checked caller ID, and slipped it back into the pocket of her smock.

What should I say to Mrs. Jones? Had I ever felt this awkward in my life? I wondered. Yes, plenty of times. But not in the same way. Not with an adult who, by all rights, should be the one feeling awkward.

"She had to park at the very end of the lot," I said finally. "But it shouldn't be long."

Silence. Another attendant appeared, pushing a young woman in a wheelchair. The patient, her brown hair pulled back away from her face and fastened with a rubber band, was holding a baby wrapped in a pink checkered blanket. All we could see of it was a pink knit cap peeking out and one tiny fist. The mother was smiling proudly.

It made me smile too, and Mrs. Jones's attendant looked over and cooed.

"The happiest place in the hospital—the maternity ward," she said. And to the young mother, "Let's see that fine baby."

The second attendant wheeled her over, and the young mother held her baby up. A little red, scrunched-up face. The mother beamed at her, then at us.

"What's her name?" I asked, grateful for this brief interlude.

"Rebecca Ann, named after my great-aunt," the young woman said, then looked expectantly toward the door where a car was pulling up. Her husband leaped out, grinning at everyone as he came through the door, and assisted his wife outside.

"I remember when Pamela was born, and I carried her out like that," Mrs. Jones said pensively.

"Did she have any hair?" I asked, glad I thought of something to say.

"A little—like corn silk," Mrs. Jones said, and fell silent again.

The Honda pulled up at last.

"That yours?" the attendant asked me, and I nodded.

She wheeled Mrs. Jones outside, and I held the passenger door open. Pamela's mom got inside. The attendant helped fasten her seat belt, shut the door, and took the wheelchair back inside. I got in the backseat.

Wordlessly, Pamela drove to the gate, paid the parking fee, and exited the lot, heading once more for the beltway.

Mrs. Jones reached up and fingered the crocheted cross. "Whose car is this?"

"Meredith's," Pamela said.

"Bill wouldn't let you use his car?"

"He's at work, Mom."

When we reached the ramp for 495, Pamela studied her driver's side mirror and, when she saw an opening, merged onto the beltway and into the middle lane.

"I'm sorry to cause you all this trouble," Mrs. Jones said at last. "I must have nodded off before I drifted into a ditch last night and got this big bump on my head—you can't see it under my hair. The hospital kept me overnight for observation."

Nodded off, my ass. I was sure Pamela and I were thinking the same thing. Neither of us said a word.

Mrs. Jones continued: "I called my friend Dorothy first, but she's in Towson today. She'll go with me tomorrow to get my car, though. It's impounded on some lot."

"Well, I'm glad I could help," Pamela said.

More silence.

"I'm such a bother to everyone," Mrs. Jones said finally, her voice shaky. "When you live alone, with no one to see or care that you get home okay, it's scary."

"I'm sure it is, Mom," Pamela said.

We reached the Georgia Avenue exit and went north toward Glenmont. When we reached her apartment complex, Mrs. Jones got out.

Pamela said, "Are you going to be all right now, Mom? Do you want us to come in and fix you breakfast or something?"

"I didn't get a blessed wink of sleep the whole night," her mom said. "I'll just make myself some tea and go to bed."

"We could come in if you want," Pamela repeated.

Mrs. Jones glanced toward me in the backseat. "Another time." She closed the door, turned, and started up the walk to the entrance.

When she was safely inside, I got out and climbed in front beside Pamela, uninvited. Was this part of the reason Pamela wanted me along? I wondered. So she wouldn't be invited in?

The car moved forward, Pamela reached over and turned on the radio, and she drove me back to Lester's without saying much at all.

* * *

Some of the sultriness of summer returned, and I could feel my helpfulness around the apartment eke away. Dad said the only thing left to paint in my room was the trim, and the paint smell should dissipate in a few days. If Les could come over on Sunday, he said, and help move my furniture back in, I'd have some time to enjoy my room before I left for college.

On Thursday, I made the beds, put a load in the washing machine, and made some deviled eggs, but by eleven, the humidity overcame me. Mr. Watts's old house had air-conditioning units in the windows of most of the rooms, but they weren't strong enough on the second story to keep us sufficiently cool. I stretched out on the sofa in my shorts and a cutoff T-shirt and fanned myself with an old *Sports Illustrated*.

There was the sound of the refrigerator's hum in the kitchen, the rhythmic churning of the washer going off and on, a couple of crows cawing back and forth somewhere in the distance.

I was in and out of sleep . . . that state of stupor where your arms and legs feel deliciously numb and weightless. I seemed to be talking with Mitch, and we were getting ready to go somewhere—to see Patrick, I think! Maybe I was going to call him first, but then he must have called me because the phone was ringing. As the *Sports Illustrated* slid to the floor, I realized that the phone really was ringing, and I was in Lester's apartment and I was supposed to be professional and . . . "Hello," I said, "Lester McKinley's . . ."

There was a pause at the other end of the line. Then a

woman's voice said, "This is the Basswood Conference Center. Is Mr. McKinley in?"

Awk! Wake up! Wake up! I told myself, and knew my voice sounded husky. "I'm sorry. Mr. McKinley is out right now," I told her, sounding as though I had just wakened, because I *had*. Maybe she thought I was a girlfriend and we were lazily sleeping away the day together.

"And you are?" the woman asked.

"Uh . . . Mr. McKinley's secretary," I said. "May I take a message?"

"Please," she said. "Would you ask him to call Rita in Mr. Burns's office?"

"Just a moment," I said, and dived for a pencil and the back of an envelope, my mind racing, my mouth dry.

She gave me the number and said that Mr. Burns had some questions about Lester's resume. I assured her that Mr. McKinley would get back to her as soon as possible.

"Actually, I'm leaving the office now for the afternoon, so tomorrow will be fine," she said.

When I hung up, my hand left a sweaty imprint on the phone.

What had I done? What had I said? Was I even awake enough to hold a coherent conversation? Why did Rita what's-her-name have to call here, anyway? Why hadn't she called Les on his cell? What would I tell him? That he'd received perhaps the most important call of his life, affecting his very future, and I'd answered it half asleep and said I was his *secretary*?

By the time the guys came home that evening, I had made chicken salad out of the rotisserie chicken that Paul had brought home the night before. I'd walked over to a farmer's market on Wayne Avenue for fresh tomatoes and sweet corn and had also baked a batch of brownies.

"Heeey!" said Les, and gave me a really appreciative smile—the kind that indicates honest-to-God gratitude and affection.

Paul, burnished bronze now by the sun, put it more bluntly: "I swear, Alice, if you were ten years older and could pass my genetics test, I'd propose," he said.

With a guy like Paul, you can never tell when he's joking, because he's usually so serious.

"And if you were a few years younger and didn't walk around with a genetics test in your pocket, I'd accept," I said, and that got a laugh. "What's it for, anyway? You're not a white supremacist, are you?"

"Oh, God no!" he said. "It just makes sense to be sure we're not carriers of the same diseases. I'm a big believer in the power of recessive genes."

"Oh, boy, I'll bet pillow talk with you is really exciting," I said, and he blushed a little. I guess he's not sure when I'm joking either.

"Oh, I wouldn't bring it up right away," Paul said, taking a seat at the dinner table. "But there are certain hereditary diseases more common to Scandinavians or Middle Eastern women, for example, than to other nationalities. It's fascinating, but I'd never use it to fall in love."

"I should hope not," I said. And then, because I had everyone in a good mood, I said casually, "You got a call from the Basswood Conference Center, Les." I handed the envelope to him with my scribbles on it.

"Yeah? Yeah?" Les grabbed the envelope excitedly and read the message. "Rita Ornosky. Did she say what her job was?"

"No. She just said that Mr. Burns had a few questions about your resume and that she'd be away from the office this afternoon, and you should call tomorrow." I motioned him to the table, where Paul was already buttering his ear of corn.

"Damn! What was I doing that I didn't answer my cell?" Les wondered aloud.

"It's okay. She said tomorrow would be fine."

Les was still trying to figure it out. "What time did she call?"

"Uh . . . about eleven forty-five, I think. Just before lunch."

"Arrrgh!" said Les. "I was in the restroom and left my cell phone on my desk. Why does this always happen to me?"

"Because you don't want to be one of those guys you hear sitting in a stall laughing and talking to himself?" said Paul.

Les sat down finally. "So tell me everything this Rita person said." He was looking directly at me. "Were you professional? What did you say?"

"I said you weren't here at the moment but you would call back as soon as possible."

"And did she ask who you were? Why you were answering my phone? I hope she doesn't think I still live at home with my mother."

"Oh, she doesn't," I said quickly.

"How do you know?"

"I told her I was your secretary."

"My *secretary*?"

"Well, she asked who I was, and you told me to sound professional, so . . ."

"Holy shit! What are we here? A corporation?"

At least Lester was on the defensive now, not me.

"Okay," I said. "I'll call her back and say I'm not your secretary."

"No!"

"Come on, Les, don't sweat it," Paul said. "Call tomorrow and say you'd be glad to answer whatever questions Mr. Burns has."

Lester settled down. "You're right," he said.

"Unless you *want* to be a corporation," I put in. "The Lester McKinley Institute of Female Studies."

"Center for the Advancement of Philosophy Majors," said Paul.

"Enough, enough," said Les, and dug into his food in earnest.

When the phone rang halfway through dinner, though, he almost knocked over his chair to get the landline.

It wasn't Rita Ornosky, however. It was Mr. Watts. He told Les he'd distinctly detected the scent of brownies baking this afternoon and what did he have to do? Beg? Les told him we'd bring some down.

I smiled. "Actually, I was planning to take him a whole meal," I said. "Chicken salad, deviled eggs, corn, the works. I'll put it together." I dug my fork into the chewy chocolate of a brownie, swished it through the glob of melting cream on top, and let them pleasure my tongue. Was there anything as delectable as this? I wondered.

Later, after I'd come back from a long chat with Mr. Watts, I sat down in the spare bedroom to e-mail Patrick. The day had gone so well, considering. Then I found Patrick had already e-mailed me:

> *Heard from Mom yesterday. They're doing okay. Seem to like living in Wisconsin. Big news! They're going to visit me in Barcelona for a month over Christmas.*

21
BREAKING AWAY

I invited Gwen and Liz and Pamela to Lester's for a sailboat-scraping party on Saturday. It would probably be our last get-together before we left for college—two of us were leaving the second full week of August, two the week after that. There was *lots* of prep work to do.

When I told Les, he said he and Paul would bring us a kebab dinner and whatever else our hearts desired. *Deal!* I'd planned to just order pizza, but Greek food sounded a lot better.

The weather cooperated—it does that sometimes. You think you're a prisoner of summer, with the hygrometer stuck on "hot and soupy," and then a taste of fall rolls through. You wake up to drier air, something clean and crisp, and you go, *Yes!*

"I didn't think I ever wanted to see a ship again," Liz said when she got out of the car.

"You gals are looking good," Les said when I brought them around back, where he and Paul had already been at work for an hour. Sweat soaked through their tanks, glistening on their shoulders.

"So this is *Fancy Pants*," said Gwen, walking slowly around it. "How many does it hold?"

"Four, max," said Paul.

"Just right for us girls!" said Liz.

Les laughed. "Start scraping."

It was laborious, but it didn't seem so bad because we were part of a team, a crew—and the four of us knew a lot about crew work.

"I got an e-mail from Flavian," Gwen said. "He heard that the cruise line canceled the whole fall season for the *Spellbound*."

I stopped scraping. "Oh, man, sounds like they're going under."

"They're gone," said Gwen. "No backup, no reserves . . ."

"That's scary," said Les.

The four of us girls stopped working for a moment, like we were observing a moment of silence. "All those plans—the ads, the brochures, blueprints, and stuff—just, like, washed away. They took a big chance and didn't make it," I said.

"And you can't even go back to mama; you declare bankruptcy," said Liz.

I rubbed my hand over the place I'd just sanded. "It's bad

enough when it affects only you and your own bank account. What does it feel like to have a whole staff and crew go down with the ship?"

"Could we stop with the sinking ship analogy?" said Paul.

"Oops! Sorry, Paul," I said. "Don't worry, when you take *Fancy Pants* out for the first time, the rest of us will be safely watching from shore."

"You wonder, though, where the rest of the crew will go this fall, everyone drifting off—uh, sailing off, I mean—heading in different directions," Gwen said.

"Mitch will be trapping," I told them.

"Lauren was supposed to work the *Spellbound* cruises," Pamela said. "She told me she might move in with her boyfriend if that didn't happen. Curtis will probably get a job on a freighter."

"What about you, Les?" Gwen asked. "What's going on in your life these days?"

"I've got an interview at the Basswood Conference Center in West Virginia. Would be great if that came through."

"Doing what?" asked Pamela.

"Actually, as assistant director. Companies use the place for conferences and retreats, with a back-to-nature venue."

"Great!" said Liz. "And, Paul! What are you going to do with *Fancy Pants* when winter sets in? Don't people usually think about getting their boats ready in the spring?"

"That's why I got the boat so cheap," Paul said. "Nobody wanted to buy it and store it through the winter. Except me, maybe. After I complete my sailing course, I'd like to take a leave of absence and go cruising off the Florida coast."

"In *this*? With no cabin?" Liz asked.

"Well, I'd go solo to start."

"I can see the headlines now: 'Maryland Man Missing Among the Manatee,'" said Gwen.

"I'll become a modern-day Gauguin. Sail to some faraway island, marry a native or two, raise my own crew, and come back to see how the rest of you are doing."

Around seven, he and Les stopped to go get dinner laid out. When they called us in later, we found the table set, kebabs on a platter, rice in a bowl, pita bread, hummus, feta cheese, and olives.

"Paul, you've got it made," I told him. "First you take the woman of your dreams out for a sail on the *Fancy Pants*, then you bring her back for a Greek dinner, with candles, and to whatever you propose to do next, she'll say yes."

"Darn! Why didn't we think of this before?" said Les.

We couldn't believe that the breeze coming in the window actually made us chilly. For an end to a special evening, Les said he'd pull out the cast-iron grate he'd stored under the back steps since March and let us have an outdoor fire.

"Paul and I are going to clean up the kitchen, then some guys are coming over later for poker. The patio's yours for the evening, so enjoy!" he said.

Les set up the grate on a heavy wood table, where we propped our feet. Once the sun set, we watched the flames dance and spit, and the fire lit up our faces so that we could see each other in the dark.

I decided to get the bad news over with, so I said, flat out, “Patrick’s parents are going to spend a month with him in Barcelona over Christmas.”

“They’ll love it! ” said Gwen. “Their own personal guide to—” She stopped short. “Oh Alice! Weren’t you planning a surprise visit then?”

“Yeah. I was going to tell him, of course. I was waiting for my final paycheck to see if I could swing it. Then I got a text from him. . . .”

“That really sucks!” said Liz. “Did you tell him?”

I shook my head. “No, and I’m not going to. He didn’t know I was planning to come, and he’s excited about showing his folks around.”

“Maybe you could still go and . . . no, I guess not,” said Pamela.

I sighed. “The Longs will naturally want him all to themselves, and so would I. He’d be pulled in two different directions. Maybe I’ll go over spring break. We’ll see.”

We watched the shadows appear and disappear on our faces. All of us had a sort of reddish glow.

“That’s a bummer,” said Gwen. “And *I* get home from a cruise that’s been canceled to find the battery’s dead in the car I bought from my brother. But Austin gave it a jump start.”

“Austin’s back in the picture?” I asked.

She gave me a sheepish little smile. "Yeah, we went to a movie. I guess we just missed each other too much. Haven't heard yet what he was up to over the summer, though."

"Will you tell him about Flavian?" Liz asked.

"Sure. He has no worries there."

"No?" I was surprised. "You and Flavian were . . . well . . ."

"We were wrapped up in a blanket and that's all that happened," Gwen said. "I'm not crazy."

We were quiet awhile. Then Liz turned to me again. "Maybe you should just take that money you saved for Barcelona and do something else with it. Go spend Christmas with Mitch in the marsh."

We laughed.

Gwen bumped my foot with her own. "He'd like that."

"I may visit him sometime, we'll see," I said. "But it's also just really nice having a guy friend, you know? Right now I'm going to concentrate on settling in at Maryland and decorating my new bedroom at home. Les is coming by tomorrow to help move my furniture back in."

"Hey, I met my roommate at Bennington on Facebook," said Liz. "She seems nice. A music major."

"What does she play? The tuba?" Gwen kidded. "She'll practice in your room."

"Voice and piano," Liz said. "I'm so psyched to go and get started."

"All I know about Amber, besides her tattoos, is that she seems laid-back, casual," I told them. "Didn't send me a virtual questionnaire to fill out. After all the excitement of this past summer, I could do with a little take-life-as-it-comes."

Interesting how you never think of measuring your friends, but as we sat leaning back in our patio chairs, legs stretched out before us, I realized that Gwen had the shortest legs and Pamela had the longest. Liz's were about as long as Pamela's, mine were slightly longer than Gwen's. . . .

"When do you have to be in New York?" Gwen asked Pamela.

Pamela didn't answer right away, and I stopped measuring legs and looked over at her.

"I may not go," Pamela answered.

I jerked up so suddenly, my feet slid off the table.

"Pamela? Why?" I asked, just now realizing that she had been unusually quiet all day, that there hadn't been the back-and-forth banter with Les that usually went on between them.

"I think Mom needs me," she said, shrinking down into herself.

We couldn't believe what we were hearing and stared at each other, then back at Pamela.

"Pamela, what are you *thinking*?" said Gwen. "You haven't officially pulled out, have you?"

"Not yet."

"Then *talk to us*!" I pleaded.

Pamela wouldn't look any of us in the eye. She wrapped her arms more tightly around her body. "Mom's just . . . so vulnerable now."

I thought of the way her mom had criticized her when we

picked her up at the hospital the other day. *Vulnerable* is not the adjective I would have used.

"Pamela, you've got a scholarship! You may never have another chance like this!" Liz cried. "After all the grief your mom has put you through, I can't believe it!"

"I know." Pamela's voice was soft, like a kitten's mew. "There on the ship, the morning she disembarked, all wrapped up in her raincoat—I was watching from on deck. She just looked so pitiful and alone. Dad and Meredith have started a new life, and here I am—about to leave too—and . . . she has nobody."

"One of the first lessons of life is that we have to live with the consequences of our actions," Gwen said. "And when you consider all your mom has done—"

"I know, I know. She really hurt Dad and me when she left us that time, and she's behaved like a lunatic more than once. But still . . . she just doesn't have many friends, and I could take courses in theater arts here at Montgomery College. I could live with Mom, and . . . she got some brochures for me . . ."

We sat in stunned silence.

"It's your mom's idea, then," Gwen said finally.

"She wouldn't have suggested it if there wasn't a way I could get the same thing here."

It was as though Pam had been brainwashed. Where was our fiery, gutsy Pamela who had sat with her hands over her ears on the floor of her bedroom when her mom threw gravel at the window, the Pamela who refused to go down and open the door? Living at home with a manipulative mom and taking courses at Montgomery College was not the same as being on your own in New York City, studying theater arts.

"There's a side of her you don't even know," Pamela said to break the silence. "Remember how devastated I was when I found out I was pregnant? I didn't feel comfortable telling Meredith, and I certainly wasn't about to tell Dad. And remember how you insisted I tell Mom, Alice, and went with me to her apartment and she didn't jump all over me or anything?"

I remembered, and yes, I did give Mrs. Jones points for that.

"Well, what I didn't tell you is that later on, before I miscarried, when Mom discussed my options with me, she said whatever I decided was up to me. If I decided to have an abortion, she'd go with me and see that it was done right. If I wanted to have the baby and put it up for adoption, she'd help me through it. But she also said that I could move in with her, and she'd fix up the spare room for both me and the baby. She said she'd help me raise it so that I could still date and have a life and everything. . . . I mean, how many moms would willingly offer to do all that for their daughters? She even showed me the catalog of baby clothes and furniture, and she had them all picked out and a design of how to rearrange the room."

I was listening to Pamela, but different pictures were bobbing about in my head.

"Pamela," I said, "do you remember when she first moved back here from Colorado, after her boyfriend walked out on her? How she fixed up that spare bedroom then, without even telling you, and how you reacted to it then?"

Pamela gave me a quick glance and looked away again. "Yes . . ."

"Why didn't you do it?"

She looked a little startled. "Why didn't I move back in with her then?"

"Yes."

"Because she would've controlled my life! I already had a home and a room. But it's different, offering to take in a pregnant daughter and her baby. That's real sacrifice."

"Pamela, don't you see?" said Liz. "It's all about her! She's playing the sacrificial mother! The long-suffering woman who was going to sacrifice her life for her child and grandchild."

"And she's still the mom who was so concerned about you and her family's welfare that she rode off into the sunset with a guy she barely knew until it all fell apart," I said.

Pamela glared at us. "But now she needs me. She thinks she seriously hurt her shoulder when she ran her car off the road and said she can hardly lift a coffee cup. She needs someone to be there and—" Pamela stopped and closed her eyes. "I'm so damned mixed up."

So was I. There were so many layers here. Why would Mrs. Jones want to deny her daughter a chance to pursue her dreams in New York? Could she be envious? Was that part of it, along with her loneliness? Did she need someone to help her with her drinking problem?

"Pamela," I said, "if you really, truly want to help your mom, go to New York. If you don't, you're saying, 'I think you're too weak to handle things here on your own, Mom. You're so weak that your only child has to give up her career plans, her scholarship, and move in with you.'"

"But what if she really *has* hurt her shoulder?" Pamela said, facing me now. "She *does* need help."

"Yes, and before you leave, you'll find someone who can come by regularly to check up on her," I said. "You know her friends. You'll call them and tell them about her accident, and you'll get her to an AA program. You said she used to attend those meetings."

"Don't be an enabler, Pamela," said Gwen. "The sooner your mom knows that she can't go on disrupting other people's lives, the sooner she'll look for her own solutions. You'll do everything you can to help before you leave, but you'll still leave."

We sat for several minutes without speaking, watching the tongues of red and orange in the iron grate, listening to the occasional rise and fall of men's voices coming through the open windows above.

"It doesn't . . . seem selfish?" Pamela asked finally.

"What? For you to go to New York, the chance of a lifetime, or for your mom to ask you to give it up?" Gwen said.

Pamela already knew the answer, so she didn't respond right away. "Okay," she said. "I'll go."

Our collective sigh of relief was audible. I leaned back in my chair, limp.

"Pamela," Liz said, "how do we know that after all we've said here, you won't have another talk with your mom and let her change your mind?"

"Because," Pamela answered, "I'd already written a letter to New York, telling them I wasn't coming, and . . . just before I came over here this afternoon, I tore it up. I just . . . I needed additional reinforcements, that's all."

"The Enforcers, that's us," said Gwen, smiling at her.

"But do you *promise*?" Liz wanted to know.

"I promise," Pamela told her. "You can even come over tomorrow and help me pack."

Was it always this hard, I wondered—this breaking away? Always so painful to move from one place to the next? Always so exciting and wonderful and . . . yes, so scary to make a pact with life that no matter what it might throw your way, you would deal?

"Know what?" I said. "I think—right now—we ought to make plans to go to California together."

Three faces turned my way, staring.

"When we're through with college, I mean. Like we talked about once. After we graduate, we should take a couple of weeks and just *go*. Do everything we ever wanted to do."

"In a red convertible!" Pamela said.

"I'm serious," I told her.

"So am I," said Pamela, and I think she meant it.

Gwen looked from one of us to the next. "I'll be in med school, but if I can make it, I'd sure like to."

"Count me in," said Liz.

We grinned around the circle in the darkness. We actually had a plan. It was a time for taking chances.

"And I get to drive," said Pamela.

AND DON'T MISS THE VERY LAST **ALICE**,

NOW I'LL TELL YOU EVERYTHING.

THE U OF M

The day I left for college, Lester borrowed a pickup for all my stuff.

"Anything that can't fit in the back can't go, Al," he said.

"I've got to take my beanbag chair. That's a *must,*" I declared, jumping down off the back end and wiping my hands on my cutoffs.

"*Take* it! *Take* it!" Dad said. "Just promise you'll leave it there."

We joke that while some kids suck their thumbs all through childhood and others hang on to a blanket, I've kept my old beanbag chair as a sort of mother substitute, a lap to cuddle in when things get tough. Mom died when I was in kindergarten, and I've had that beanbag chair almost as long. I'm even too big for it now, but I could always use it as a hassock, I figured.

All morning Elizabeth and Pamela had been helping me carry things out to the truck. Gwen's brothers had helped her move the day before, and Liz would leave for Bennington the next day. I was taking some stuff to my dorm at the U of Maryland and was lucky Liz and Pam were still around to see me off. We were standing out on the driveway in our shorts and T-shirts, studying the mountain of junk in the pickup, trying to think of anything I might have forgotten.

"Ironing board?" said Elizabeth. She's the gorgeous one, with creamy skin, thick dark eyelashes, and long, almost black hair.

"*Nobody* uses an ironing board at college, Liz!" said Pamela. "You just fold up a towel on the floor and iron on that, if you iron at all."

A gnat blew directly in front of Pam's eyes, and she tried to smash it between her hands. Sweat dripped off her face and onto the shoulders of her purple tee. We were all perspiring like crazy.

"Toaster?" said Elizabeth. "What will you do if you crave a grilled cheese sandwich at midnight and everything's closed?"

"Are you kidding?" Pamela exclaimed. "All you need is your iron. You put cheese between two slices of bread, wrap it in foil, and press down on it with a hot iron." She lifted her blond hair off the nape of her neck, as though even talking about ironing made her miserable.

"Your ingenuity is amazing," I said. "Next you'll tell us an iron can broil a steak and bake a potato. Hand me that box, Liz, and let's see if we can't squeeze it in beside my suitcase."

I've known Elizabeth Price and Pamela Jones forever, it seems. Well, since sixth grade, anyway. Pamela, a natural blonde, slim and talented, is going to a theater arts school in New York and is letting her hair grow so she can play more parts. Elizabeth's been admitted to Bennington in Vermont, and I'm going to Lester's alma mater, which is only about a half hour from our house. Like, I'm the adventurous one. Gwen's going there too—premed.

I think Dad believes I've grown up so close to him and Lester that I'm afraid to get too far away. So he insisted I live on campus, which is fine with me. It's about time he and Sylvia had the house to themselves. They've only been married three years.

"Oh, God!" I said. "Sheets and towels! I didn't pack any at all!"

Pamela looked at the stuff we still had to squeeze in. "We made a mistake. We should have put clothes in your minifridge and wastebasket before we set them on the truck. There's all that empty space inside." We collapsed on the front steps and took a break.

"I can't believe I have to go through this all by myself tomorrow," Elizabeth said.

"What about *me*? My dorm room's half the size of yours, and I'll have to keep most of my stuff under my bed. I'm still not through sorting," Pamela groaned. She was already looking like an actress. She had plucked her eyebrows into thin crescents over her eyes and wore black mascara and eyeliner.

We gazed wearily out over the yard and across the street,

where Elizabeth's big white house sat handsomely on its manicured lot.

"I remember when you first moved here from Takoma Park," Elizabeth said. "Mom and I were sitting out on the porch watching you guys carry things in."

"And you were wearing matching skirts," I told her.

"Skirts!" She turned and looked at me. "We *were?* You *remember*?"

"You looked so perfect to me, and I was so envious. The perfect mother and daughter, sitting there reading a magazine together. . . ."

"Don't remind me," Elizabeth said quickly. *Perfect* is like poison in her vocabulary now, she's trying so hard not to be.

"We've been through a lot together," said Pamela, and sighed. Then she asked, "If you could look into the future and see what was happening, what age would you pick?"

"Thirty. I'd pick thirty," said Elizabeth. "I figure that whatever I'm doing then will more or less dictate how the rest of my life is going to turn out."

"I'd choose a year from now, to see if I was going back to New York," said Pamela. "If you don't have talent, they don't encourage you to return for a second year." Both Pamela and Elizabeth looked at me.

"I'm not sure I'd want to know," I told them.

"Why *not*?"

"Because I'd probably pick age sixty or something, to see if I'd still be alive. And what if I wasn't?"

"Don't be morbid," said Pamela, and then, looking for a brighter note, "What's the latest from Patrick?"

"He's finished work on that book for his professor and is starting his year of study abroad. Loves Barcelona. Says he'd love to live there someday," I told them. The way I said it made it sound as though Patrick was just any guy, not the boyfriend I'd had almost continuously since sixth grade.

"I don't know how you stand it, Alice," Liz said, putting into words what I wondered about too.

"I don't know either, but—as Patrick says—the sooner it's over, the sooner he'll be back in the States." It was oppressively humid, and I thrust my lower lip out and blew, trying to cool my face. But it didn't help.

The front door opened behind us, and my brother came back out. Les got his MA from Maryland last December and just found out he was hired as the assistant director of a conference center in West Virginia, where corporations hold retreats and sales conferences and couples come to get in touch with their inner selves. He starts September first. Dad always wondered what Les would do with a philosophy degree.

"I *told* you I was going to sit on a mountaintop so people could come to me and ask the meaning of life," he joked.

Now he was standing beside us in shorts and sandals and was staring at the pickup truck, which looked positively pregnant.

"Say, Al, you really travel light!" he said. "Sure you don't want to take the piano too?"

Elizabeth and Pamela gave him their most seductive smiles. Lester's unmarried, and they've had crushes on him since they were eleven. *All* of my friends love Lester.

"Aren't you just the teeniest bit sad to see your sister off?" Elizabeth asked.

"Been wanting to boot her out since the day she was born," Les said. "I'm getting rid of all three of you, come to think of it."

"When are you going to get married, Les?" Pamela asked. "Or are you going to stay a bachelor all your life?"

"Oh . . . maybe twenty, thirty years from now I'll think about it," he said. And then, "Sylvia's got lunch ready, Al. And then we'd better get going."

I sniffed under one arm. "Oh, gross. I've got to have a shower first."

"How about you, Liz? Pamela? Want some lunch?" Lester said.

"Can't. I'm getting a manicure in twenty minutes," said Pamela. "Liz is coming with me, and we need to clean up."

"Well, let's get a move on," Lester said, and went back inside.

Elizabeth, who was sitting between Pamela and me, put one arm around each of us. "Do you remember what we promised once? That we'd always get together like this, no matter how old we got, and share our secrets?"

Pamela was grinning. "You mean, tell each other when we lost our virginity. As if any of us could forget." One of the hundred silly things we'd said. Pamela had already lost hers, so the rest was up to Liz and me.

Elizabeth gave our shoulders an exasperated shake. "I just hope we're always like this. They say you make your closest friends in college, but I don't know how anyone could be closer than we are."

"There's always texting," Pamela said.

"It's not the same," said Elizabeth.

"So if we can't actually get together, we'll make it a conference call," I suggested, knowing I'd better get inside.

We jokingly sealed it by placing our hands on top of each other's, the way kids do in grade school.

"Till Thanksgiving, then," I said.

"Or Christmas," said Pamela.

"Or even spring break," I added.

"Sisters forever," said Elizabeth solemnly. And, you know, she was serious!

Sylvia had lunch ready when I went inside—chicken salad with pineapple and almonds, my favorite. Dad gave me a bear hug before we even sat down. He had the look of a bear too, sort of pudgy and cuddly, his head slightly balding on top.

"Well, honey, it may be a while before you're here at the table again," he said.

"Probably all of one week," said Lester. "Wait till she tastes the food at the U. She'll be home every weekend, I'll bet."

"College food is mostly carbohydrates, as I remember," said Sylvia. "Potatoes, pasta, beans, bread . . ." She was all in coral today—light sweater, pants, loafers. As always, my stepmom looked stunning. "Come home whenever you want a good pot roast."

"When will we see *you* again, Les?" Dad asked.

"Oh, I'll be back from time to time," Lester said. "But I'd think you two would enjoy some privacy for yourselves."

Dad put one hand on Sylvia's shoulder. "We manage," he said.

I had to put my sheets and towels on my seat in the pickup and sit on them. It was the only space left, and my head almost touched the ceiling. I already had a box of books under my feet.

"I'll bet Dad and Sylvia are secretly glad to see me go," I told Les as we backed down the drive and watched them waving to us from the porch. "Do you realize they've hardly been alone since they married?"

"Yep. He's never had the chance to chase her around the table naked," Les said.

I gave him my sardonic look. "Yeah? Is that what married people do?"

"How do I know? I've never been married."

"Do you remember when you were dating Marilyn Rawley, and for your birthday she said she'd cook your favorite meal in the costume of your choice?" We both started to smile.

"And I chose surf and turf, with Marilyn dressed in high leather boots and a leopard-skin bikini," Les said, and we laughed.

"Did *you* ever chase *her* around the table naked?" I asked.

"Hey! She had on a bikini, didn't she?"

As more and more of my neighborhood disappeared behind us, I wasn't sure if I was feeling nervousness or excitement. I guess I'd call it nervous excitement. But just when I thought I was being cool about heading for college, I heard myself say, "Sylvia says Dad's afraid I'll become 'sexually active' at the university."

"Good old Dad," said Les. "Well . . ." He paused. "You know what to do, don't you?"

"What's this? A facts-of-life-before-I-go-off-to-college talk?" I said.

"Hey, you brought it up."

"If I have any urgent questions, I'll call you," I joked. Then, "Everyone makes sex sound so dangerous."

"It's dangerous, all right. It's dynamite!" said Lester, and grinned. It's hard to have a serious conversation with my brother, but I had myself to blame.

"The voice of experience," I commented.

"Not nearly enough," he sighed.

The only way to describe my dorm room was "semi-hideous." The cinder block walls had a fresh coat of yellow paint, but the room seemed stark and cheerless, like a women's prison, maybe? The mattresses sagged a little, and the sea-green drapes were missing some hooks. That's why people bring so much stuff from home, I guess. You have to cover every square inch of space with your own things to make it seem remotely livable.

Amber Riley—a large, not fat girl—was my roommate. Before I'd met her, I'd already seen her tattoos in Facebook photos—the dove on her ankle, the angel on her thigh, and the butterfly on her midsection—and they were cool. But after I'd met her, I discovered pretty quickly what I didn't like about her: She seemed to migrate all over the place.

Her cosmetics and lotions were always crowding mine on the bathroom shelf; her books were strewn everywhere; and her clothes pushed mine into a corner of the closet, where they cowered, begging me to rescue them. When she kicked off her shoes (which she invariably wore without socks, so they smelled), they always seemed to land over by my bed, so I was forever stumbling over them. She was like an oil slick that kept taking over more and more of the surface space, and there was no way to contain her.

She wasn't all that careful about personal hygiene, either. She'd drop used tampons in the wastebasket without even wrapping them up; let sweat-soaked T-shirts hang in the closet for days on end without washing them, till I hated to even open the door to our room. And she showered only when she felt like it.

But the maddening thing was, her boyfriend was always hanging around, usually as sloppy as she was.

Tolerance, I told myself. *Different people have different priorities, that's all.* Hygiene wasn't high on Amber's list.

Gwen and I got together whenever we could. There was a large house off campus—a gift to the university—where premed students could live at half the usual rate, so Gwen, understandably, chose to stay there, but we would have been such good roommates.

"So how goes it?" she asked one Friday a few weeks into school, when we'd managed to meet for dinner at a Burmese restaurant in town.

"I'm miserable," I told her. "Amber's a slob! She *smells*! Our room stinks. I dread going in there at night."

"Huh! Mine's the exact opposite. She even wipes off the toilet seat after she uses it!" Gwen said.

"Amber doesn't even use toilet paper when she pees!" I complained. "And don't ask how I know that—she pees with the door open."

Gwen burst into laughter. "You only have to put up with her for a year. Next fall you can choose someone different. Of course, you could get someone worse."

"Impossible," I said. Through the window, I watched a guy in a corduroy jacket pay for an order at the cash register and take it out to a girl in a waiting Toyota. I concentrated on Gwen again. She'd recently had her eyebrows shaped, two beautiful black curves extending out toward her temples, against her milky brown skin.

"Your mistake was not saying something right away," she told me. "You've let it go this long, she probably figures you're okay with it. You've got to talk to her."

I sighed deeply. "I hate confrontation."

"Then you've got to decide which you hate more: talking to her about it or slob city."

“What are you going to specialize in, Doctor? Psychiatry?” I asked.

Gwen ate another bite of her lemongrass beef and pointed to the last piece of my roti pancake. When I shoved it in her direction, she ate that, too, still thoughtful. “I don’t know. Pediatrics, I think. Or maybe Ob/Gyn. Remember what they told us when we were hospital volunteers? That there’s only one happy ward in a hospital, and that’s the maternity ward? What do you hear from Patrick?”

“I’m trying to follow your train of thought here,” I said, and we laughed. “He’s having a ball. He e-mailed me about all the different people in his classes—a guy who’s climbed Mount Kilimanjaro twice; a girl who’s joining the Peace Corps; a guy who pays his way through college by fishing; an artist; a priest . . . *He* gets to meet all these fascinating people, and I get Amber.”

“So plan to visit him over spring break or something.”

“Don’t think I haven’t considered it,” I told her. “I’ve even priced airline tickets. But that’s months and months away. I’ll probably seem pretty boring compared to all his friends there.”

“He’s coming back to you, remember,” Gwen said.

“That’s one thing to be happy about,” I agreed.

When I got up the next morning, there was a wet towel on the bathroom floor, along with Amber’s underwear, and a washcloth in the sink. A bottle of shampoo was lying on its side on the shelf, and a thin puddle of slippery goo was oozing across the shelf, surrounding my makeup. *Arrrghhhh! Enough!*

I whirled around and marched over to Amber's bed. She had thrown off her covers and was engaged in a giant stretch. Her T-shirt was bunched up around her waist, and the butterfly tattoo on her midsection seemed to spread its wings as she moved.

"Amber, your stuff's taking over that whole shelf in the bathroom," I said. "I'd really appreciate it if you'd clean it up."

She opened her eyes and squinted at me. "Just push them to one side. I won't care."

"Well, *I* care. And it's also annoying to keep stumbling over your shoes and things."

"O-*kay*!" she said, yawning. "Don't have a spaz."

There! I told myself. *That wasn't so hard.* It *was* possible to assert myself without a shouting match.

When I got home from classes that day, the towel was back on the rack and Amber's underwear was gone, but the shampoo bottle was still on its side, and pink liquid was now dripping off the edge of the shelf. I capped it, cleaned up the mess, and wiped off my cosmetics.

Things were a little better after that. For a week, anyway. Then I noticed she was using my deodorant stick.

"Hey, Amber, that's mine," I said.

"Oh. Do you care?"

"Well . . . sure! I mean, it'll be used up twice as fast, and I'm paying for it."

"I'll buy the next stick," she said.

***

I think it was that night that I woke up around two or three to a rattling sound, and my first thought was that Amber had locked herself out and was trying to wake me up. I lifted my head and listened.

It was a steady, rhythmical, squeaking sound, and then I realized that Amber had her boyfriend in bed. I didn't know if I was more angry, surprised, or embarrassed.

"Oh, you're so good . . . you're so good," Jerry's voice kept murmuring.

Little breathy moans from Amber. Her bed frame rattled louder as it knocked against the wall.

I didn't turn on the light, but I got up and went to the bathroom, slamming the door behind me. I heard the guy swear.

After I'd flushed the toilet, I went back to bed. I could hear the two of them whispering in the darkness, so I put my pillow over one ear and went back to sleep.

In the morning Jerry was gone, but he'd left his socks behind. Amber came out of the bathroom, brushing her teeth. She had on a wrinkled sleep-shirt with SURF CITY written on the front. She wasn't smiling.

"Thanks for nothing, Alice. You could at least have waited," she said.

I was sitting on the edge of the bed and stared at her. "Ex*cuse* me?"

"Jerry was pretty pissed off at you. You were banging around at the critical moment, and he lost it."

I knew exactly what Jerry had lost, but I said, "If he's looking for his socks, they're under your bed."

"You know what I mean," Amber said. "Let's have a little consideration."

I couldn't believe it. "Are you *serious*? I'm wakened at three in the morning by *you* and Jerry, and *I'm* the inconsiderate one?"

She simply went back in the bathroom, and this time she closed the door.

I called home.

"I can't stand it, Dad!" I said. "I shouldn't have to put up with this!"

"Then don't. Talk to your resident adviser and see what the rules are. Are men allowed in women's rooms?"

"Huh?" I said. "This is the twenty-first century, Dad! Of course they are! But we're supposed to show consideration. Amber claims I didn't show her any when I interrupted *them*."

"Well, honey, I'm here if you need help with life-or-death decisions, but I think this falls in the solve-it-yourself category," Dad said.

One thing about Amber, she didn't hold a grudge. She went right on as though nothing had happened. I hid my shampoo and deodorant, and she even asked if I had any. I lied and said no, and she washed her hair with hand soap.

I was facing a huge assignment due on Monday and knew I had to work on it all weekend. On Saturday afternoon, though, Amber decided to do her laundry—the first time I'd actually seen her to do any at all. Jerry came by, and they started stripping down her side of the room—sheets, towels, shirts—stuffing everything in a pillowcase to take to the washing machines in the basement. I headed for the library with a stack of books.

I worked right through dinner, stopping only long enough to get a tuna wrap and a bag of chips, but by nine that night, I'd had it. My eyes could scarcely focus and my head throbbed. I knew I had a full day of writing ahead of me on Sunday and wanted only to go to bed and sleep.

When I got back to our room, Amber was sitting at her desk, painting her toenails, one foot propped on our wastebasket. We talked a little about exams and grade points, and then I undressed in the bathroom, pulled on my pajamas, and got into bed.

My pillow had a dirty-hair smell that wasn't mine, and I could almost bet that Amber had borrowed my pillow. I was too tired to start an argument, though, so I turned it over and stretched out.

My foot touched something between the sheets, however, and suddenly I sat up, threw off the covers, and saw a rolled-up condom at the foot of my bed, along with Amber's underwear.

I leaped out of bed.

"Look!" I shouted, pointing.

Amber turned. "Oh! Sorry!" she said. She stuck another wad of cotton between her toes and padded across the room to retrieve the condom.

"This is *my bed*!" I yelled. "What were you *thinking*?"

"Well, *my* sheets were in the wash, and Jerry doesn't like

to do it on a bare mattress," she said. She shrugged. "You were gone, so . . ."

"It's *my bed*!" I screamed again.

I think I went a little insane. I pulled off my sheets and flung them on the floor. Then I grabbed Amber's underwear and tossed it out the window. I picked up her shoes, which were on my side of the room, and threw them against the wall. I scooped up everything of Amber's that had migrated over to my section and dumped them on her bed.

Amber left and didn't come back that night, or the next or the next. Gwen heard she'd moved into Jerry's room. I wondered what *his* roommate thought of that! Every so often, she'd come back to get some more clothes or drop something off, but we didn't talk much. And that was fine with me.